THE UNIVERSITY OF VIRGINIA EDITION OF
THE WORKS OF STEPHEN CRANE

VOLUME IX

REPORTS OF WAR

Stephen Crane meeting a guest. Aug. 1899.

Crane greeting a friend at Brede, 1899 (Cora Crane's Scrapbook, with her
inscription, University of Virginia–Barrett)

STEPHEN CRANE

REPORTS OF WAR

WAR DISPATCHES
GREAT BATTLES OF THE WORLD

EDITED BY
FREDSON BOWERS
LINDEN KENT PROFESSOR OF ENGLISH AT
THE UNIVERSITY OF VIRGINIA

WITH AN INTRODUCTION BY
JAMES B. COLVERT
PROFESSOR OF ENGLISH AT THE
UNIVERSITY OF GEORGIA

THE UNIVERSITY PRESS OF VIRGINIA

CHARLOTTESVILLE

91606

Editorial expenses for this volume have been supported by grants from the National Endowment for
the Humanities administered through the Center
for Editions of American Authors of the Modern
Language Association.

To
Clifton Waller Barrett

FOREWORD

THIS volume brings together all of Crane's known newspaper war dispatches from Greece, Florida, Cuba, Puerto Rico, and England, and to these appends the series "Great Battles of the World" first printed in *Lippincott's Magazine* and posthumously published in collected book form.

The dispatches are presented in the chronological order of the events they report, not in the order of their datelines (which are sometimes untrustworthy), nor in the order of their newspaper publication, since the mixture of cabled and delayed mailed dispatches occasionally produces some anomalies. The order of *Great Battles* is that of composition as reflected in the magazine publication. The arrangement of the articles in the book collection, particularly as it differs between the American and English editions, can have no authority.

In an attempt to establish the text of the dispatches from a large number of examples, thirty-eight newspapers * have been searched for the period 1897 to 1900. Three previously unknown dispatches have been discovered (Nos. 27, 29, 65). Two dispatches found by Professor Bernice Slote (Nos. 4, 18) and one by Professor Matthew J. Bruccoli (No. 44), first reprinted in 1969, have had six more appearances established. In addition, of the dispatches earlier collected by Professor

* The following newspapers have been searched for the purposes of the present volume: the *Boston Globe, Buffalo Commercial, Buffalo Evening News, Buffalo Morning Express, Chicago Daily News, Chicago Record, Chicago Tribune, Chicago Times-Herald, Cincinnati Commercial Tribune, Cincinnati Enquirer, Dallas News, Denver Republican, Detroit Free Press, Galveston News, Kansas City Star, Louisville Courier-Journal, Minneapolis Tribune, Nebraska State Journal, New Orleans Picayune, New Orleans Times-Democrat, New York Herald, New York Journal,* New York *Sun,* New York *World, Omaha Bee, Philadelphia Inquirer,* Philadelphia *Press, Pittsburgh Leader,* Portland *Oregonian, Rochester Democrat and Chronicle,* Salt Lake City *Tribune, St. Louis Globe-Democrat, St. Louis Post-Dispatch, St. Paul Pioneer Press, San Francisco Chronicle,* San Francisco *Examiner, Savannah Morning News, Washington Post.*

Stallman or Professor Fryckstedt a total of ninety-one previously unrecorded syndicated publications have been observed, plus the addition to the record of two new typescripts (Nos. 66, 71) and a manuscript (No. 69). Of the seventy-two dispatches in the present collection, then, three newspaper reports have not previously been reprinted (Nos. 27, 29, 65) plus the brief manuscript fragment No. 70, two have previously been reprinted only in excerpted form (Nos. 14, 16 from manuscript), and three have been available only in journals (Nos. 4, 18, 44).

On the other hand, the search for new appearances has produced results of considerable textual importance. This search has not been confined to syndicated publication outside of New York, for research assistants have also regularly examined the texts in both the city and the out-of-town editions of the *New York Journal* and the New York *World* and from these editions have turned up textual variation or added material not previously known to exist in five of the major stories (Nos. 5, 10, 29, 39, 63). The examination has, also, indicated that in the remaining dispatches variation of this kind in the New York editions need not be anticipated.

However, syndication over the country of dispatches that had been cut in the New York versions—the New York newspapers being the only sources previously investigated—provided more text in five dispatches (Nos. 5, 17, 22, 41, 57), and the typescript of No. 71 revealed a large amount of unrecovered material. Hence several thousand words of additional text in familiar dispatches are reprinted here for the first time. The search for syndicated appearances gathered further benefits in that most of these proved to be independent witnesses, not mere reprints of the New York versions, and thus it has been possible in a number of dispatches to purify the New York text by the evidence of multiple publication elsewhere. The search has been sufficiently exhaustive to identify the newspapers that would commonly print syndicated Crane dispatches from the *Journal* or the *World*. Although it is not improbable that a few more subscribing newspapers may be found to provide fresh witnesses, or that oversights (particularly among the unavailable different editions of the newspapers already searched) may have occurred in the examination, nevertheless some confidence may be felt that the bulk of this journalistic material has been identified and that a great deal more will not be turned up in the future to modify the establishment of the text attempted here insofar as the recovered syndicated publication of the dispatches permits. The 'Imogene Carter' reports (published and unpublished) collected here have not been printed before in complete form as a group. Crane certainly had a hand in at least one of these, and perhaps more.

The textual problems posed by some of these dispatches are not to be taken lightly, and indeed for intricacy the problem of the copy for No. 5(I,II,III) and its transmission has no rival, perhaps, in the late nineteenth century. A distinction must first be made between those reports that were cabled and those that were received by mail in New York. We have no means of knowing how expertly Crane conformed to the money-saving conventions of 'cablese' but it is evident that any cable needed to be given editorial reworking by the rewrite or copy editor to put it into acceptable form for print. Little or nothing of Crane's 'accidentals,' or the texture of the copy that he filed in respect to spelling, punctuation, word-division, and so on, could be preserved; moreover, his syntax and phraseology might suffer a sea-change according to the invention of the copyreader. Early and late states of this reworking may sometimes be detected when copy was filed for wiring to other newspapers according to the earliest rewrite whereas further modifications were made by the editor (or inadvertently by the compositor) before the final form was printed in the New York version; and even then the two editions for the city area and for out of town might still differ in their texts. Whenever the evidence permits, therefore, an attempt is made to print here a critical text that is as close as possible to the ultimate authority, such as it is, of the cable and one that contains the smallest amount of editorial reworking.

On the other hand, although, on the evidence, editorial attention was also given to the reports received in manuscript by mail, the rewriting was considerably reduced and it is possible to recover from multiple witnesses something of the 'accidentals' texture of the holograph as well as the maximum of Crane's own words. Few cases exist either for cables or for mailed reports in which syndication has not led to evidence by which the standard New York text has been improved.

In ordinary circumstances the New York newspaper versions have been chosen as the copy-texts since they are, in the stages of transmission, one step closer to ultimate authority. But the classic theory of copy-text familiar in Sir Walter Greg's formulation needs important modification when texts, such as syndicated versions each printed from independent telegrams sent out by the New York newspaper office from the same basic copy, radiate from a common original. Something of a new editorial theory has been adopted in the present edition to deal with these unusual circumstances whenever conditions permit, with the result that a critical text has been contrived that is closer to Crane's own copy (whether cable or holograph) than is present in any single witness, particularly in the New York newspaper text.

In dealing with journalism of this nature some few conventions must necessarily be adopted. For instance, the headlines by which the stories are identified could never have originated with Crane, and thus the use, ordinarily, of the New York headline title, familiar from bibliographies, is a useful convenience—but a convenience only. No one newspaper headline has any more authority than another even in the few cases of McClure or Bacheller syndication when it is evident that the proof sent out as copy had standard headlines made up by the syndicate editor. When, as with No. 4, parts of this headline title can be recovered, it is adopted even if it differs from that of the copy-text; but usually it has been simpler to identify the stories by the headline given them in the copy-text. The sub-headings that occasionally sprinkle the dispatches have no relation to Crane, either, and since they are a distraction to the reader have been banished to follow the Historical Collation in separate lists. The copy-text dateline is usually reproduced but its typography has been standardized. The only other silent alteration of the texts is also in a purely typographical feature: newspapers then as now did not use italic type, but to assist in making up a reading text the editor has silently put into italics the names of all ships and of newspapers. These italics will never have appeared in any original newspaper text.

The shorthand conventions of notation in the apparatus are described in the headnote to the Editorial Emendations in the Copy-Text. Paragraphing alterations in the copy-text are recorded in this Emendations list; but the nature and usual transmission of the journalistic text has led to the decision to confine the Historical Collation more strictly than usual to the record of substantive variation, and in the cable dispatches (but not in the mailed reports) to exclude the listing of rejected paragraphing which in the volumes of Crane's creative writing has been noted when present in authoritative texts although not recorded from derived documents. In the Historical Collation for *Great Battles of the World,* however, the publication of which was under different circumstances, the usual procedures for noting paragraph variation have been retained.

In general each dispatch is treated as a self-contained unit with its own styling for the accidentals and no attempt has been made to normalize spelling or word-division and other conventions between dispatches except when the evidence for variation in some authority enables an editor to restore the common forms by recorded emendation. Thus if the authoritative texts for a dispatch invariably read *torpedo-boat,* that will be the form reprinted; on the other hand, if some authority for this dispatch reads *torpedo boat* (which holograph indicates was Crane's preferred form), normalization to the unhyphenated words will be made throughout that single dispatch in an attempt to bring the critical text a shade closer, on some concrete evidence, to the more authoritative division. However, for articles printed in England, American spelling has been substituted in the copy-text by recorded emendation even if no American version of the text exists.

The articles in *Great Battles of the World* have been edited in general conformity with the principles stated in "The Text of the Virginia Edition" prefixed to Volume I of the *Works,* BOWERY TALES (1969). Consequent upon the discovery that the text of the first American edition of *Great Battles* was set throughout from uncorrected proofs of the *Lippincott's Magazine* versions, and was never authoritatively revised, the editor has been enabled to purify the magazine copy-texts by the restoration of readings from the original printer's copy that had been editorially sophisticated by the *Lippincott's* editor. The bibliographical descriptions describe the color of the bindings according to the Tanselle recommendations (see the Foreword to Vol. IV of this edition).

The Introduction by Professor Colvert places the war dispatches in the literary context of Crane's development as a writer. The editor's The Text: History and Analysis details the physical forms of the texts, their authority, transmission, and what is known of their composition and publishing history, and examines specific problems concerned with the establishment of the text in its present critical form.

The expenses of the preparation of this volume with its textual history and apparatus have been subsidized by a grant from the National Endowment for the Humanities administered through the Modern Language Association of America and its Center for Editions of American Authors, but with generous support, as well, from the University of Virginia.

The editor is much in debt for assistance and various courtesies to Professor Robert Stallman of the University of Connecticut, Professors Matthew J. Bruccoli and Joseph Katz of the University of South Carolina, and his colleague Professor J. C. Levenson of the University of Virginia. Professor Bernice Slote of the University of Nebraska generously placed her discoveries of new material at the service of this edition and assisted in uncovering Pittsburgh and Nebraska printings of the dispatches. Miss Lillian B. Gilkes most kindly advised on the transcription of the 'Imogene Carter' manuscripts from her expert knowledge of Cora Crane's handwriting. Professor William Gibson of New York University, who examined this volume for the seal of the Center for Editions of American Authors, made several suggestions. Mr. Kenneth A. Lohf, Librarian of Rare Books and Manuscripts of the Columbia University Libraries, has been of unfailing and particular assistance. The editor is grateful to the librarians of Syracuse University, Dartmouth College, and Yale University for their courtesies in making available unpublished letters in their collections. The constant assistance of the custodians of the Barrett Collection at the University of Virginia has been invaluable, and Miss Helena Koiner, former head of Interlibrary Loans, has placed the editor deeply in her debt for her help with the borrowing of newspapers on microfilm over an extended period. Mrs. David Yalden-Thomson undertook the detailed task of administering and supervising the extensive search for material in general newspaper publication and of securing reproductions of the newly discovered texts. The expert and scrupulous supervision of the production of this volume and the collation of its texts by the editor's Chief Research Assistant, Miss Gillian G. M. Kyles, and the work of her assistants Mrs. Malcolm Craig and Mr. William Holleman have been essential and much appreciated, for in these days of relatively rapid editorial publication no single scholar can hope to assume more than the ultimate responsibility for the repeated checking for accuracy of collation, reproduction, and notation enforced by the standards for the CEAA editions. Mrs. Martin C. Battestin recovered in the British Museum most of Kate Lyon's sources for her notes on *Great Battles of the World,* information which materially aided the identification of a number of editorial alterations in the *Lippincott's* text. Miss Joan Crane kindly checked the bibliographical descriptions and furnished the color designations.

The editor's personal debt to Mr. Clifton Waller Barrett and his magnificent collection at the University of Virginia remains constant and can be expressed only by the dedication of this edition to him. The editor is indebted to the Columbia University Libraries and to the University of Virginia for permission to utilize their manuscripts and typescripts of material in this volume and to illustrate selected specimens, and to Alfred A. Knopf, Inc., which holds the Crane copyrights to unpublished material.

F. B.

Charlottesville, Va.
February 15, 1971

Athens Greece, April 17.

In this time of change and surprise, it is hard to find something that does not move with either tide, possessing a stability that enables badgered correspondents to remark upon it without being confused when their articles appear in print to find by that time that the situation has been reversed. This unchangeable element is the spirit of the Greek people.

There is a kind of government that can make every man a soldier but there is no government that can make every man desire to be a soldier. The population of Greece is for this time practically a population of soldiers. The arming of the nation has progressed steadily for weeks and it is now about complete. It may be that this consummation will be directly followed by a return to the farms and flocks and fishing-boats but the best informed here deem it improbable. Greece has made a bludgeon to be used on somebody's head and it is not likely that she will stir porridge with her own accord. Some of these confounded spectators who are so busy will have to stop a pretty row. The intention of Greece is war.

In view of this fact, the Place de la Constitution in front of the royal palace has been interesting at these times. At all hours of the day the victims who have come from everywhere to be robbed by the hotel-proprietors in the vicinity have been aroused by the blare of bugles, the great roaring cheers of recruits mingled with the loud approbation of the populace. There is one thing about a Greek crowd, it never howls. From descriptions of the modern Greek made by the correspondents of London Conservative journals one rather expects him to howl. But he dont howl; these crowds cheer in a deep-throated and meanful way that stirs the heart. They are serious; constantly the news comes from the frontier that the Greek soldiers are kept from fighting — pitching into the Turks — only by the expert control which the officers have over them. They are insane to get at their ancient foes. Their enthusiasm is of the kind that has the dignity in it. Ask any Greek in the street his opinion of the situation and he will say: "We must fight. There is nothing else to do."

"Well but the Powers?" you say to him.

"Ah, yes, the Powers! Well, we must, anyhow. Does it seem right to you that the Powers should bully Greece in this way? Look at the

Manuscript page (reduced) of No. 2, "The Spirit of the Greek People" (Columbia University)

Stephen Crane as a war correspondent, Greece, 1897 (University of Virginia–Barrett)

Cora as a war correspondent, Greece, 1897 (Cora Crane's Scrapbook, University of Virginia–Barrett)

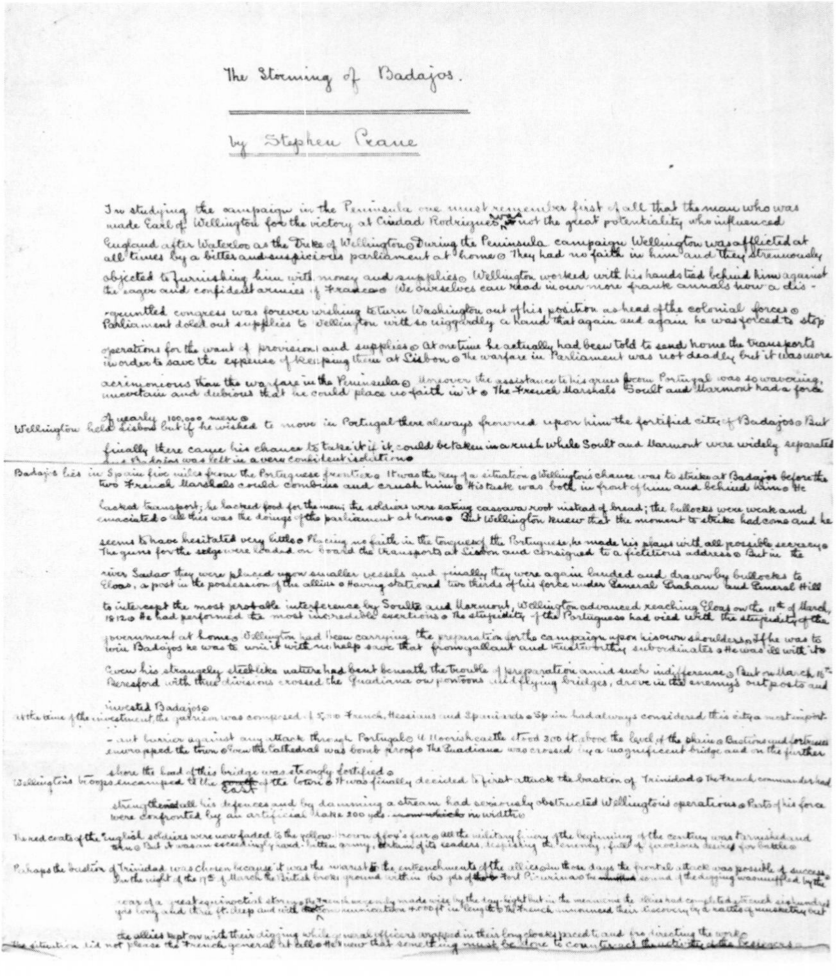

The Storming of Badajos.

by Stephen Crane

In studying the campaign in the Peninsula one must remember first of all that the man who was made Earl of Wellington for the victory at Ciudad Rodriguez was not the great potentiality who influenced England after Waterloo as the Duke of Wellington. During the Peninsula campaign Wellington was afflicted at all times by a bitter and suspicious parliament at home. They had no faith in him and they strenuously objected to furnishing him with money and supplies. Wellington worked with his hands tied behind him against the eager and confident armies of France. We ourselves can read in our more frank annals how a disgruntled congress was forever wishing to turn Washington out of his position as head of the colonial forces. Parliament doled out supplies to Wellington with so niggardly a hand that again and again he was forced to stop operations for the want of provisions and supplies. At one time he actually had been told to send home the transports in order to save the expense of keeping them at Lisbon. The warfare in Parliament was not deadly but it was more acrimonious than the warfare in the Peninsula. Moreover the assistance to his arms from Portugal was so wavering, uncertain and dubious that he could place no faith in it. The French Marshals Soult and Marmont had a force of nearly 100,000 men.

Wellington held Lisbon but if he wished to move in Portugal there always frowned upon him the fortified city of Badajos. But finally there came his chance to take it if it could be taken in a rush while Soult and Marmont were widely separated and Badajos was left in a very confident isolation.

Badajos lies in Spain five miles from the Portuguese frontier. It was the key of a situation. Wellington's chance was to strike at Badajos before the two French Marshals could combine and crush him. His task was both in front of him and behind him. He lacked transport; he lacked food for the men; the soldiers were eating cassava root instead of bread; the bullocks were weak and emaciated. All this was the doings of the parliament at home. But Wellington knew that the moment to strike had come and he seems to have hesitated very little. Placing no faith in the tongues of the Portuguese, he made his plans with all possible secrecy. The guns for the seige were loaded on board the transports at Lisbon and consigned to a fictitious address. But in the river Sadao they were placed upon smaller vessels and finally they were again landed and drawn by bullocks to Elvas, a post in the possession of the allies. Having stationed two thirds of his force under General Graham and General Hill to intercept the most probable interference by Soult and Marmont, Wellington advanced reaching Elvas on the 11th of March, 1812. He had performed the most incredible exertions. The stupidity of the Portuguese had vied with the stupidity of the government at home. Wellington had been carrying the preparation for the campaign upon his own shoulders. If he was to win Badajos he was to win it with no help save that from gallant and trustworthy subordinates. He was ill with it. Even his strangely steel-like nature had bent beneath the trouble of preparation amid such indifference. But on March 16th Beresford with three divisions crossed the Guadiana on pontoons and flying bridges, drove in the enemy's out posts and invested Badajos.

At the time of the investment, the garrison was composed of 5,000 French, Hessians and Spaniards. Spain had always considered this city a most important barrier against any attack through Portugal. A Moorish castle stood 300 ft. above the level of the plain. Bastions and fortresses enwrapped the town. Even the Cathedral was bomb proof. The Guadiana was crossed by a magnificent bridge and on the further shore the head of this bridge was strongly fortified.

Wellington's troops encamped to the ~~south~~ East of the town. It was finally decided to first attack the bastion of Trinidad. The French commander had strengthened all his defences and by damming a stream had seriously obstructed Wellington's operations. Parts of his force were confronted by an artificial lake 200 yds. ~~wide which~~ in width.

The red coats of the English soldiers were now faded to the yellow-brown of fox's fur. All the military finery of the beginning of the century was tarnished and thin. But it was an exceedingly hard-bitten army, certain of its leaders, despising the enemy, full of ferocious desires for battle.

Perhaps the bastion of Trinidad was chosen because it was the nearest to the entrenchments of the allies. In those days the frontal attack was possible of success. In the night of the 17th of March the British broke ground within 160 yds of ~~the~~ Fort Picurina. The ~~muffled~~ sound of the digging was muffled by the roar of a great equinoctial storm. The French only made wise by the day-light but in the meantime the allies had completed a trench six hundred yds long and three ft. deep and with communication 4000 ft in length. The French announced their discovery by a rattle of musketry but the allies kept on with their digging while general officers wrapped in their long cloaks paced to and fro directing the work.

The situation did not please the French general at all. He knew that something must be done to counteract the activities of the besiegers.

Page 1 of Edith Richie's manuscript (reduced) of "The Storming of Badajos" (University of Virginia–Barrett)

CONTENTS

INTRODUCTION

I T MAY seem regrettable, as John Berryman says, that
Crane drove himself at the expense of health and energy
to those "boring false wars, away from the passionate
private real war in his mind." [1] This is to say that thirty harrowing hours on the open sea in a ten-foot dinghy was a price too
high to pay for a confirming demonstration of that vision of
man's war against nature he first expressed in the Sullivan
County sketches of 1892. Or that the arduous journey which
led him to the spectacle of "insane, wicked" squadrons of
Turkish cavalry charging against intrenched Greeks at Velestino
was an unnecessary diversion from what his imagination had
already mastered. What impressed him at Velestino, he told
John Bass as he watched the first real battle he had ever seen,
was the mental attitude of the men, by which he meant, as
Crane's readers know, the mystery of man pitting himself
against inscrutable powers. The Turks, he said, "seem unreal.
They are shadows on the plain—vague figures in black, indications of a mysterious force." [2] But in *The Red Badge of Courage*,
long before, he had struck this theme, crucial to his vision:

. . . the youth saw that the landscape was streaked with two long,
thin, black columns which disappeared on the brow of a hill. . . .
They were like two serpents crawling from the cavern of the night.

As he told Joseph Conrad later, the war in Greece proved that
The Red Badge was "all right." [3]

Though his experience in Greece and Cuba added little of
radical importance to his resources, it was nevertheless a neces-

---

[1] Berryman, *Stephen Crane* (New York, 1950), p. 174.
[2] "How Novelist Crane Acts on the Battlefield," *New York Journal*, May 23,
1897, p. 37.
[3] Introduction, Thomas Beer, *Stephen Crane: A Study in American Letters*
(New York, 1923), p. 11.

sity, born in doubt of the absolute authority of his vision. *The Red Badge of Courage*, widely advertised by reviewers as an ingenious invention, brought this feeling of doubt and uncertainty to focus in the early months of 1896. He felt obliged to discount the novel as "a mere episode" and to reaffirm, defensively, his commitment to "truth" in literature. "I decided," he wrote in reference to the literary program he adopted in 1892, "that the nearer a writer gets to life, the greater he becomes as an artist." [4] He acceded reluctantly to editors' demands for more war stories, but so far as he was concerned they were mere exercises in "witty expedients." "I have invented the sum of my invention in regard to war," he wrote in 1895, "and this story ['The Little Regiment'] keeps me in internal despair." [5] "Positively," he said when he finally finished it, "my last thing dealing with battle." [6]

There is little reason thus to suppose (as our regret for his headlong pursuit of war implies we might) that Crane could have given us literature instead of war dispatches had he stayed home in pastoral Sullivan County, New York, to write about the "passionate private war in his mind." Having little confidence in the sufficiency of the unaided imagination, he was convinced that his subject could be mastered only through direct observation. He had to get close to life, as he said, and life for him was war of one kind or another—the war of life in the barbarous slums he studied in the early nineties, war on the lawless frontier contemplated in his tour of the West and Mexico in 1895, man's war against nature experienced on the open sea off the Florida coast in 1897. What he sought was the final revelation of the mystery of existence in violent event and ultimate crisis, and though actual experience of these things did little more than confirm what imagination alone had already grasped, he pursued them, nevertheless, out of radical conviction of their absolute necessity.

Yet for all his passionate advocacy of direct observation, it is

[4] *Stephen Crane: Letters*, ed. R. W. Stallman and Lillian Gilkes (New York, 1960), p. 78.

[5] Crane to Willis Brooks Hawkins, Hartwood, N.Y., [Nov. 12, 1895], *Letters*, p. 72.

[6] Crane to the editor of *The Critic*, Hartwood, N.Y., Feb. 15, [18]96, *Letters*, p. 117.

a curious (and instructive) fact that he seldom recorded what he saw and did as historical event. "The Open Boat," which he subtitled "A Tale Intended to be after the Fact," as indeed it may have been to him, seemed to Conrad—and to two generations of readers after him—"to illustrate the essentials of life itself, like a symbolic tale." [7] None of the pieces in this volume, many of which were hastily composed under difficult circumstances, approach the excellence of "The Open Boat," though a few, like the fine description of the Concert of Powers in the harbor at Crete, or that wry comedy of revolution, "The Man in the White Hat," and some of the Cuban dispatches, notably the rich description of the battle of San Juan, are developed compositions, comparable in their energetic elaboration of theme and image to the best descriptive writing in his fiction. Others, as might be expected, are routine journalistic reports, written more strictly within the limitations of the conventional form of the newspaper feature article. But even these, like the more elaborate pieces, are marked by Crane's style, by the sudden appearance of a characteristic metaphor or image, or by that "inspired audacity of epithet" which Conrad said was one of his greatest gifts.[8] However sporadically they may occur or however often left dangling in an inconsequential context of topical statement, they seem, read in the light thrown on them by the meanings given them in their fictional elaboration, to rise from the very depths of Crane's convictions about the nature of man and the world. Like "The Open Boat," these pieces render the observed event in language painstakingly invented for fiction, and the effect is to shift these events from the real world to the symbolic world of Crane's vision as an artist.

Crane's imagination was energized by an acute sense of the contradictory. He images the world as a complex of contrasts, a mystery of bewildering opposites impossible to reconcile. "But to get at the real thing!" he wrote in "War Memories." "It seems impossible." Is war "magnificent" or is it "squalid"? Neither, as the correspondent says. "It is simply life, and an expression of life can always evade us." [9] At Velestino, Crane reports, the

---

[7] Introduction, Beer, *Crane*, p. 13.
[8] *Ibid.*
[9] "War Memories," TALES OF WAR, *Works*, VI, 222.1–4.

musketry fire "was a beautiful sound; beautiful as had never been dreamed. . . . The crash of it was ideal." But then: "This is from one point of view. The other might be taken from the men who died there."[10] The retreating Turks leave the field "black with wounded and dead men and horses"; yet "From a distance it was like a game. No blood, no expressions of horror were to be seen; there were simply the movements of tiny doll tragedy."[11] And so in "The Open Boat" the desperate plight of the men in the dinghy might have been, "viewed from a balcony," merely "picturesque." A Spanish officer hopelessly besieged on San Juan Hill promenades in the lull of battle wearing "a summer-resort straw hat. He did a deal of sauntering in the coolest manner possible, walking out in the clear sunshine and gazing languidly in our direction. He seemed to be carrying a little cane."[12]

It is difficult to demonstrate at this level of detail the significance of such contrasts. They suggest a peculiar thrust of mind; but the full effect is in accumulation, in the expansion of such contraries in larger patterns of composition. A long strain of pastoral imagery—purling streams, shepherds, fair fields, sparkling skies—plays dramatically against a contrary strain of demonic imagery—monsters, sinister shadows, serpents of the night. Heroic reveries collapse under the iron weight of reality, and the exuberant, thoughtless gaiety of life opposes the horror of menace and death.

This ironic sense of the world's incongruities is symbolized with typical effect in the piece on Suda Bay, the harbor at Crete where Crane observed from the ship *Guadiana* the fleet of the Concert of Powers on station there to suppress war between the Greeks and Turks. The piece opens with a description of the landscape, rendered as it is typically in Crane in contrast to the activities of men. Over the motley crowd of ships representing the great nations of the world loom "exalted snow-draped mountains," a faint echo of those mystical, grand heights (the ever-recurring mountains and towering buildings of his fiction) as a mockery of the poignantly unattainable visions of mortal men. Below is the harbor, the world of men which slides into

---

[10] No. 5(II), p. 24.21–28.   [11] No. 5(II), p. 24.35–38.
[12] No. 39, p. 157.9–13.

view "like the scenes in a melodrama before the final tableau," a problematic contradiction of menacing power and comical vanity. A passage ordered in long perspective, a device Crane used often to throw odd and ambiguous light on commonplace events, sounds the first somber note of menace.

A scouting torpedo boat as small as a gnat crawling on an enormous decorated wall came from the obscurity of the shore. Apparently it looked us over and was satisfied, for in a few moments it was returned to the obscurity. Crete spread high and wide precisely like a painting from that absurd period when the painters each tried to reproduce the universe on one canvas. It merely lacked the boat with a triangular sail and a pie-faced crew occupying the attention in the foreground. It was lonely and desolate like a Land of Despair if it were not for the glory of the hills above all. Nothing lived there save the venomous torpedo boat, which, after all, had been little more than a shadow on the water. [5.24–6.4]

The desolate human world seems to harbor the malice of nature herself, the inscrutable scorpionlike boat that lives in the shadowy obscurity of the distant landscape. And yet there is the tantalizing mystery of "the glory of the hills above all." This is the master image of Crane's fiction; whatever he actually saw in the harbor at Crete is assimilated precisely in this passage to the symbolic system of his art.

The vision of the vicious scout boat merges into an image of human menace, the formidable fleet of the Powers—"this most terrible creature which the world has known." "As the *Guadiana* steamed forward, ship after ship became detached from the hedge and powerful ram-bows were drawn in formidable outline upon the water. . . . These great steel animals sat in a little bay menacing with their terrible glances." But still, as the correspondent sees it, there is in all this an aspect of hollow vanity. A comic note is sounded to counterpoint the sense of brooding violence, a characteristic modulation in Crane's descriptive style. "To one who did not care to feel that there was something in this affair which weighed as much as a planet, it would be a joke of a kind. But it was the Concert of Europe. Colossi never smile." In contrast is the vain irrepressibility of a swift little French launch which dashes around the bay in furious display of incompetent energy. "The French made the most uproar and they were the authors of whatever bungling was done. They were at the same time by far the proudest and most conscious. The eyes of the world were upon them surely, and they wanted to do everything with such heaven-born accuracy that they lost their minds at times." They are counterpointed in turn against the stolid, humorless Russians:

It was great then to see a French launch come flying down the harbor, turn to pass on the lee of the Russian launch and finally bat into her and scrape three yards of paint from her side. The Russian seamen looked at the Frenchmen and the Frenchmen laughed and nodded and chattered and apparently pointed out the incident as a bit of friendly wit. Whereupon the Russians smiled, faintly smiled. [8.21–28]

It may be instructive, as illustration of the way Crane adapted his literary style to the reporting of real-life observation, to compare the composition of this passage with that of a scene in "The Blue Hotel." In the story the obscure shadow concealing the torpedo boat becomes the sinister gloom which terrorizes the crazy Swede, and the heedless exuberance of the French seamen becomes the absurd and noisy chatter of old Scully, the bungling hotel-proprietor. Scully tries to distract the Swede's contemplation of "mysterious shadow" by showing him a photograph of his little girl:

he saw that the Swede was not contemplating the picture at all, but, instead, was keeping keen watch on the gloom in the rear.
"Look, man!" shouted Scully heartily. "That's the picter of my little gal that died. Her name was Carrie. And then here's the picter of my oldest boy, Michael. He's a lawyer in Lincoln an' doin' well. I gave that boy a grand eddycation, and I'm glad for it now. He's a fine boy. Look at 'im now. Ain't he bold as blazes, him there in Lincoln, an honored an' respicted gintleman. An honored an' respicted gintleman," concluded Scully with a flourish. And so saying, he smote the Swede jovially on the back.
The Swede faintly smiled.
[TALES OF ADVENTURE, *Works*, v, 150.35–151.7]

Old Scully's gratuitous commonplaces in the context of the Swede's profound terror and the violent energy of his joviality in contrast to the Swede's solemn immobility are instantly recognizable as typical elements of Crane's composition. Tenuous though the relation of the specifics is in the two passages, their dramatic arrangement was obviously inspired by the same imagination.

His eye for contraries and incongruities, particularly for those which seemed to confirm his sense of the absurd vanity of man driven to futile encounters in a problematic universe, was drawn to what must have seemed to editors improbable and irrelevant incidents. Certain details of image and metaphor, flickers of the irrepressible imagination, intrude into the most routine of reports. Describing the bay of Mariel from Admiral Sampson's flagship, he dutifully notes the fortifications, the armament, the military significance of the approach from sea, and then, unexpectedly, interrupts with an image of sinister abandonment, typically juxtaposed against a faint allusion to prospects of pastoral serenity: "but a more lifeless and desolate place could hardly be imagined. . . . The town beyond seemed like a cemetery around the large church. However, on the green palm-covered mountains to the left smoke raised in slanting lines" (106.5–11). Sampson's powerful fleet, like the navy of the Concert of Powers, was (for all Crane's admiration for the quiet competency of the modest Admiral himself, his model of the true hero in war) an emblem of vanity, ironically exposed by the serene indifference of men who peacefully cultivate the fruits of nature. "As the silent fleet passed Mariel in the earlier afternoon a man in a small boat was fishing in the harbor. He had his back to the squadron and did not turn his head." A signalman seems to be "holding talk with a faint gray thing far away," a phrase struck doubtless from his sense of the poignant impossibility of communication with the impalpable spirit that broods over the affairs of earth—a theme compulsively developed in the religious poems in *The Black Riders*. Ghosts and spirits, glaring sunsets, sinister shadows of evening, the crooning of unearthly melodies—images of his art—are also elements of real war.

Dusk calls out the crimson glare of the burning shops in the ruins of which stands the ghostly locomotive. The Cuban soldiers have occupied the houses of the village, and as they gather around their camp-fires some of them sing native melodies—weird, half-savage airs—accompanied by the booming of improvised drums. Night has come; a searchlight flashes pallidly over the foliage, throwing into gleaming relief the myriad leaves. [134.6–13]

Chapter VIII of *The Red Badge of Courage* opens with a descriptive passage that might have been the model for the scene:

> The trees began softly to sing a hymn of twilight. The sun sank until slanted bronze rays struck the forest. There was a lull in the noises of insects as if they had bowed their beaks and were making a devotional pause. There was silence save for the chanted chorus of the trees.

So also might have been a model the closing paragraph of a dispatch from Velestino:

> There were some mountaineer volunteers in great woolly grey shepherds' cloaks. They were curious figures in the evening light, perfectly romantic if it were not for the modernity of the rifles and the shining lines of cartridges. With the plain a sea of shadow below, and the vague blue troops of Greece about them in the trenches, these men sang softly the wild minor ballads of their hills. As the evening deepened many men curled in their blankets and slept, but these grey-cloaked mountaineers continued to sing. Ultimately the rays of the moon outlined their figures in silver light, and it was not infrequently that shells from the persistent Turco-German batteries threw a sudden red color on their curious garb and on the banner of their village which hung above them. They sang of war, and their songs were new to the sense, reflecting the centuries of their singing, and as the ultimate quiet of night came to the height this low chanting was the only sound. This ended one day at Velestino. [44.7–23]

Richard Harding Davis, dean of war correspondents and Crane's colleague in Greece and Cuba, wrote in 1899 that "the best correspondent is probably the man who by his energy and resource sees more of war, both afloat and ashore, than do his rivals, and who is able to make the public see what he saw." In Davis's view Crane "distinctly won first place," and he cited as models of descriptive reporting the pieces on Guantanamo and San Juan.[13] Although the New York *World* fired Crane just

---

[13] "Our War Correspondents in Cuba and Puerto Rico," *Harper's Monthly*, May, 1899, p. 941. Davis described or alluded to Crane's work in a number of his writings.

before the beginning of the Puerto Rico campaign in 1898, apparently in the mistaken belief that he was the author of an unsigned dispatch critical of the conduct of the Seventy-first New York Regiment, the newspaper later acknowledged that his dispatches were masterful descriptions of war.[14] Even so, it is not likely that either his editors or his colleagues in the field saw him as a true professional, master of the conventions and formalities of the newspaper war report. As readers of the *Journal*, the *World*, and the *Westminister Gazette* in 1897 and 1898 may have appreciated, he saw war, and often rendered it, as an artist rather than as a reporter.

A dramatic illustration of the difference is the brilliant sketch based on an event witnessed at the end of the war in Greece in 1897, a demonstration before the King's palace in Athens protesting the armistice as a betrayal of the Greek people. John Bass, Crane's superior as head of the *Journal* staff, also witnessed the incident and reported it in the following dispatch, which appeared in the *Journal* on April 30.

The popular feeling that the people have been betrayed by their leaders in the now famous stampede from Mati is, for the time, quieted. An incident showing the temper of the Greek people happened during the demonstration gotten up by Gennadius, who made a speech in which he called the King a traitor, and demanded that the royal family be driven from the country.

Then at the head of a numerous rabble, he marched to the palace, which was entirely unguarded. Alone he entered on violence bent, and demanded to see the King.

"His Majesty does not receive today," said the doorkeeper.

"I am sorry," replied Gennadius. Coming out he informed the rabble that His Majesty did not receive him. He then entered a carriage and drove away in triumph, followed by a crowd. The situation has many opera comique elements. The safety of the King lay in the shrewd removal of the palace guards through the advice of one of the Ministers.[15]

Crane's account (No. 13), one of a series of sketches published serially in the *Westminister Gazette* under the title "With

14 "Madcap Genius Stephen Crane," New York *World*, June 10, 1900, p. E3.
15 "Gallant Greeks Would Continue War," *New York Journal*, April 30, 1897, p. 1.

Greek and Turk," appeared six weeks later—a remarkable illustration of the enabling power of his literary imagination. Like those grim buildings, symbols of power and indifference in *Maggie* and the "Midnight Sketches," the palace of the King looms over the crowd, "its windows all heavily curtained as if it had closed its eyes purposely to this scene in the square below it." The crowd itself appears, as always in his fiction from the Sullivan County sketches on, as an emblem of mindless disorder and noisy gullibility. Energetic newsboys—presented in the imagery of violent motion of which Crane was a particular master—make the crowd their prey, just as the empty but fiery revolutionary makes it the dupe of his ambition.

Gennadius himself, "the hero of the minute," is drawn from a long gallery of vain and showy heroes that extends back through the fiction to that pompous orator and dogmatic moralist of Asbury Park, "Founder" Bradley, wickedly satirized in Crane's sketches to the New York *Tribune* in 1892. Like "Founder" Bradley, like the heroes of the Sullivan County sketches, *George's Mother*, and *The Red Badge of Courage*, he is an orator, with "the mobile mouth of a poet and the glance of surpassing vanity" (though obliged ironically to wait his turn while the wolfish newsboys "sated themselves upon the money of the crowd"). His demeanor and speech echo the "blood red dreams" of that "shining knight," Pete the bartender in *Maggie*. And in the background is the "mountain, rearing above the sallow dwelling of the King," that Henry Fleming dreamed of conquering in *The Red Badge*.

The deflation of "the hero of the minute," the inevitable fate of all those swaggerers against man and nature in Crane's stories, is depicted with telling irony. Rebuffed at the door of the palace by the old servant's cool declaration, "The King does not receive to-day," this man who wears the hat of "violence" and "terror," this "deputy of the Two-Miles-beyond-the-Extreme-Edge of the Radicals," can only stand in embarrassed frustration. " 'Oh—um,' said the statesman, at last. 'Well——' He went away." Yet another irony is his reception from the roaring crowd. "As he passed through the streets his trooping followers cheered and cheered the victor, and from time to time he modestly lifted in recognition his tall white hat."

To Bass, the professional reporter, this was rightly taken as "an incident showing the temper of the Greek people." To Crane, it was confirmation of his abiding vision of the vanity of man and the world, just as his wild ride in the open boat off the Florida coast was confirmation of his poignant sense of man's alienation from nature and God. The value—and fascination—of the war correspondence is that it confirms our understanding of that long metaphor of man in face of ultimate crisis which his fiction brilliantly elaborates.

J. B. C.

WAR DISPATCHES

GREECE

No. 1

AN IMPRESSION OF THE "CONCERT"

ON BOARD FRENCH STEAMER *Guadiana*—Leaving Marseilles, the passengers of this ship had no intention of anything more than a tedious voyage to Athens without pause, but circumstances furnished us with a mild digression. In the early morning of the fourth day a ponderous headland appeared to the north and we knew it to be the expected glimpse of Greece. Nevertheless, some hours later another ponderous headland appeared to the southward, and we could not arrange our geographical prejudices to suit this phenomenon until a man excitedly told everyone that we had changed our course, that we were not bound for the Pirée, but for the Bay of Suda in Crete. He told us of mail bags for the fleet of the Powers and pointed to the headland and called it Crete. All this increased our importance vastly.

This headland was rough and gaunt, a promontory that one would expect in Iceland. It was of a warm color, resembling rusted iron. It towered grandly until one found in the sky above it some faint crystalline markings which later turned into a range of exalted snow-draped mountains. The blue sea glimmered to the foot of the rusty cape and the sun shone full on the silver peaks. The English commercial traveler who was cock-sure by education decided that with these mountains for their final stand the Cretans could never be conquered.

A scouting torpedo boat as small as a gnat crawling on an enormous decorated wall came from the obscurity of the shore. Apparently it looked us over and was satisfied, for in a few moments it was returned to the obscurity. Crete spread high and wide precisely like a painting from that absurd period when the painters each tried to reproduce the universe on one canvas. It merely lacked the boat with a triangular sail and a pie-faced crew occupying the attention in the foreground. It was lonely and desolate like a Land of Despair if it were not for the glory of the hills above all. Nothing lived there save the venomous torpedo boat, which, after all, had been little more than a shadow on the water.

The *Guadiana* turned toward a faint indication among the hills, a little cleft. The passengers had become excited and were for the most part grouped forward. Some Greeks from the steerage were crooning, incomprehensibly, but in a way that we hoped supported war and glory and general uproar for the sake of one's country. Their small black and rather shifty eyes shone like buttons.

But this strange island presented nothing to their gaze. It still gave no hint of house, man nor cattle. It was like one of those half-named countries of the remote North. If this was the island upon which the attention of Europe was fixed it was certainly preserving an ulterior tranquillity at any rate. Surely a little decent excitement could be expected. Surely a few men in white kilts could have turned out and chased a few men in red fez up and down the hillsides. One wondered where the chanting Greeks in the bow got their impetus. This great high sun-burned island was simply as thrilling as a bit of good pasturage for goats.

Meanwhile the steamer churned through the shimmering sea, and at times from the cabin arose the thin wail of a baby that had objected without pause from Marseilles to the roll and heave of the ship.

A man with a glass discovered a tan-colored crease on one of the steep hillsides, and afterward it could be seen to be an earthwork. Below it, the hills had parted and exhibited a steel-colored water-way. The scene was always wide and fine with its great stretches of blue bay and the towering heights, silent in the sunshine. At last a genius found that the flag over the redoubt was the Turkish flag, and the passengers stared at the tiny blood-red banner.

Gradually the hills slid aside, and impressively like the scenes in a melodrama before the final tableau. The water-way widened to an inner bay. Then finally there were some faint etchings on the distances. They might have been like masts, but they were more like twigs. And before the steady ploughing advance of the steamer these twigs grew into the top-gear of warships, stacks of tan, of white, of black, and fighting masts and the blaze of signal flags.

It was the fleet of the Powers; the Concert—the Concert, mind you, this most terrible creature which the world has known, constructed out of the air and perhaps in a night. This fleet was the living arm and the mailed hand of the Concert. It was a limb of Europe displayed, actual, animate. The babe who disliked the motion of the steamer continued to cry in the cabin.

At first the vessels in the distance were blended into a sort of prickly hedge. It was very unlike the pictures in the illustrated papers which appear always to have been sketched from balloons. As the *Guadiana* steamed forward, ship after ship became detached from the hedge and powerful ram-bows were drawn in formidable outline upon the water. When the *Guadiana* had come into the middle of the company she paused, and her anchor chain roared.

Here they were, English, Russians, Germans, French, Italians, Turks and Austrians, all living peaceably in the same cage.

The attention of the *Guadiana* was immediately divided in twelve ways. The seamen found the great flagship of France, the *Admiral Charner,* and loved it with their eyes, while the English commercial traveler had a short bitter quarrel with a fellow-countryman as to the identity of a certain ship—whether she was the *Barfleur* or the *Camperdown.*

These great steel animals sat in a little bay menacing with their terrible glances a village of three rows of houses and a dock and vast stretches of hillsides whereon there was not even a tree to shoot at for fun. A group of vicious little torpedo boats also waited impatiently. To one who did not care to feel that there was something in this affair which weighed as much as a planet, it would be a joke of a kind. But it was the Concert of Europe. Colossi never smile.

It was hard to decide which of these national exhibits was the most interesting. The French flagship was imposing in the weird and solemn complexity of her appearance. Her deck and sides were a wilderness of dull grey appliances. She looked like a factory, this monster, whereas the *Camperdown* and more particularly the great *Revenge* were so well-proportioned and trim that one had to refer to a memory of their tonnage before they became as impressive. Italy's squadron, to the novice, looked as well as any of them. Her two battleships were large and powerful, and the *Etna* was obviously the best cruiser in the harbor. The Russian flagship lay near the French ships, while the Italians were rather close to the English. The *Kaiserin Augusta* was aloof and alone. On the other hand, the Austrian hesitated in the middle of the situation.

Launches and gigs innumerable played around the *Guadiana* and officers of all kinds came up the side. The play of the launches and gigs absorbed the attention of the passengers because a strong wind was blowing down the harbor and it made the management of the small craft enough of a trick. The French made the most uproar and they were the authors of whatever bungling was done. They were at the same time by far the proudest and most conscious. The eyes of the world were upon them surely, and they wanted to do everything with such heaven-born accuracy that they lost their minds at times.

Once, a launch from the Russian flagship lay on the water waiting for her officer who was on board the *Guadiana* to signal to come for him. Her crew lounged under the weather bulwark and she swung slowly and peacefully over the little waves. It was great then to see a French launch come flying down the harbor, turn to pass on the lee of the Russian launch and finally bat into her and scrape three yards of paint from her side. The Russian seamen looked at the Frenchmen and the Frenchmen laughed and nodded and chattered and apparently pointed out the incident as a bit of friendly wit. Whereupon the Russians smiled, faintly smiled.

Indeed, at any time when a Russian boat was near a French one, the Frenchmen smiled with bright friendliness. And the echoing amiability of these men of the Czar was faint, certainly, merely like a shadow passing softly across the face of a stone figure, and to the onlooker there was something grim and strange in it.

Whenever officers came aboard of the mail steamer, the passengers crowded about them and to the Frenchmen this was food and wine, apparently. They flourished and expanded and waxed taller under this nourishment. They were sublime. As for the Russians, they didn't care. The lieutenant who came for the British squadron's mail cared somewhat, because seventy-five people crowded to hear him stagger through the French language and it bored him. Down in the launch, however, there was a middy who was a joy. He was smaller than a sparrow, but—my soul—how bright and Napoleonic and forcible he was! He was as busy as a hive of bees. He had no time for poses and genuflections and other amusements. Once indeed he looked up from his business to the deck of the ship and this infant had a stern, quick glance, a man's eye. It was like hearing a canary bird swear to watch this tot put a speaking-tube to his mouth. He was so small that a life-sized portrait of him could be painted on a sovereign, this warrior.

She would be a fool of a mother who would trust him in a pantry where there were tarts, and his big sister can box his ears for some years to come, but of course there is no more fiery-hearted scoundrel in the fleet of the Powers than this babe. Of course he would drop to his knees and pray his admiral a hundred prayers if by this he could be at his station on the *Camperdown* and have her move into action immediately. Against what? Against anything. This is of the traditions that perforce are in the breast of the child. They could not be cut out of it under these circumstances. If another child of the *Camperdown* should steal this child's knife he might go to a corner and perhaps almost shed tears, but no hoary admiral can dream of the wild slaughter and Hades on the bosom of the sea that agitate this babe's breast. He is a damned villain. And yet may the God of Battle that sits above the smoke watch over this damned villain and all bright, bold, little damned villains like him!

The stout boats from the warships made ill navigation for the native craft that for various purposes thronged about the steamer. Some unconcerned gig's bow was forever bunting into a Cretan boat and causing the wildest panic, but pushing it aside and going ahead with gorgeous indifference. The native's nearest approach to redress was a jab in the eye with a boat-hook. It developed naturally that these natives had voices like fifes and those who have never heard a sacred concert in an insane asylum cannot appreciate the objections these men made to even the distant approach of a boat from a warship. They began to celebrate the terrors of a collision before there was a probability of it and if by chance there should happen to be a small crash, their cries were heart-rending. The twirling of their fingers as they waved their hands tragically over their heads at these times made a sight not to be seen in the West. This action seemed to stand out in their minds as being more likely to carry them safely through the crisis than a sudden and skillful application of the oars. But these oars, after all, looked to the Westerner to be as useful on the water as scythes. However, when the natives unfurled their sails and tacked for the shore, they were masters of their craft. All the boats then stood on their lee gunwales and the water behind them boiled. The men wore skirts and it was supposed to be axiomatic that none who wears skirts could sail a boat.

All the afternoon the passengers remained on deck and watched the fleet grouped on the bright bay. The launches were always speeding to and fro and from time to time a gig, wherein the many oarsmen caused it to resemble a water bug, walked over the water. The officers on the Italian cruiser *Etna* had pistol practice from the stern and the band on the Russian flagship played an uncanny melody. Late in the afternoon the English torpedo destroyer *Boxer,* a long grey wasp of a creature, came in from the sea. She did not join the collection of bottle-green scorpions on the Suda side of the harbor, but slid slowly over to an anchorage near the *Revenge.*

Then an Austrian torpedo boat—she was a bottle-green scorpion with a red and gold flag stuck in its back—moved listlessly about among the ships. French sailors from the flagship got a barge and their launch towed it down to the *Guadiana* after some freight which had been brought to them from Marseilles. The bringing of this barge alongside the *Guadiana* caused scenes of the wildest disorder. The language used was material for three riots in Dublin. All the same it was vastly exciting. These men were in earnest about it. They were going to bring that barge alongside the steamer, and one may be forgiven if one's temper gains an advantage during the stress of unusual excitement. Twice the peevish god of circumstance balked them and they were obliged to circle widely down the wind and return for other trys. At last a line was flung aboard and a sailor sprinted and caught it just as it was slipping over-side. Then the blue sailor bonnets with their red pom-poms jostled most surprisingly. There is one thing—a Frenchman can make a festival even of pulling on a rope. These tars had a perfectly delicious time at it. Perhaps the presence of an audience had something to do with the matter. Finally, when the barge was lined alongside, the French officer came aboard the steamer, his face beaming with a smile of victory.

In the meantime, against the darkening hills, strings of signal flags would suddenly burn out in splendid flashes and often the little voices of bugles called over the water. Smoke was drifting from the enormous funnels of some of the battleships.

Down the bay a fat tub of a thing appeared, puffing like an old woman and making trouble enough on the water for a Cunarder moving sideways. It took an infinite time for her to come up, but when at last she steamed laboriously past everybody went to the rail and grinned. It was the Turkish despatch boat arrived from her anchorage opposite the fort. She had come three miles. It was wonderful. How she could come three miles puzzled the ablest mariners. She was flimsy enough to have an effect like a pane of glass; one felt that one could see through her. There is nothing in the United States Revenue Marine to compare with her. There was a collection of red flags on the bridge and over her trailed the red banner.

The decks of the *Guadiana* had been glad all day with the blue and gilt of the naval officers, and now into our experience and into this assemblage—behold the Turks! Around the ship lay the power of Christian Europe, and now here was the other thing—here was the Turk. Here was the creature that had pulled Europe's nose, boxed its ears, kicked it downstairs and told it to go to the devil, all the time asking it to be quite patient, that the creature was really governed by the most amiable impulses and all would be right in time, making it finally furious enough for deadly assault and then ending by harnessing it and driving it off gaily. Surely the art of procrastination should be taught more if by it you can stab a man's children and then convince him that you are only feeding them with buns and that he owes you a sixpence for the buns.

Naturally, then, this Turk was interesting. He didn't care, however. He was rather tall and well made and had the face of a man, a man who could think, a man who could fight. He was fit for problems and he was fit for war, this fellow. The collar of his uniform was heavily flowered with gold and a sabre dangled to his spurred heels. He wore glasses, and about his eyes was the calm studious expression that one expects in professors at colleges. Unconsciously to us, perhaps, many of us have fashioned our idea of the Turk on this hang-dog photograph of the Sultan which has been reproduced everywhere. Probably this Turk was no nearer the controlling type, but then it was good to find him where one expected at least to find something fat and greasy.

In the array of genius that had boarded the ship there was even a little French officer of cavalry in a plum-colored coat and blue trousers, all heavily braided in black. He was rather acrobatic in his manner, and it seems that it was particularly necessary that he should do a great deal of flying about in the ensuing festivities. Then there were some consular officers and they also flew. But in the midst of all this palaver the Turk had the calmness of sense, the unconcern of a man who did not find it necessary to feel intimidated by the adjacent intellects. Once when he was free his glance remained reflectively for a time on these battleships, arrayed Europe.

The *Guadiana* at last hove anchor and departed from Suda Bay, and behind her the fleet again blended gradually into a hedge. For a long time the tall tan stacks of the *Camperdown* and the long grey hull of the *Kaiserin Augusta* remained distinct, but eventually in the twilight the fleet was only a great black thing, and afterward it was nothing. The hand of Europe was hidden by the hills lying in evening peace. The mother of the sick baby had come on deck and to the inquiries of some good-natured passengers she replied gratefully that it was rather better.

No. 2

THE SPIRIT OF THE GREEK PEOPLE

ATHENS, GREECE; April 17. In this time of change and surprise, it is good to find something that does not move with either tide, possessing a stability that enables badgered correspondents to remark upon it without being confused when their articles appear in print to find by that time that the situation has been reversed. This unchangeable element is the spirit of the Greek people.

There is a kind of government that can make every man a soldier but there is no government that can make every man desire to be a soldier. The population of Greece is for this time practically a population of soldiers. The arming of the nation has progressed steadily for weeks and it is now about complete. It may be that this consumation will be directly followed by a return to the farms and flocks and fishing-boats but the best informed here deem it improbable. Greece has made a bludgeon to be used on somebody's head and it is not likely that she will stir porridge with it of her accord. Some of these confounded spectators who are so busy will have to stop a pretty row. The intention of Greece is war.

In view of this fact, the Place de la Constitution in front of the royal palace has been interesting. At all hours of the day the victims who have come from everywhere to be robbed by the hotel-proprietors in the vicinity have been aroused by the blare of bugles, the great roaring cheers of recruits mingled with the loud approbation of the populace. There is one thing about a Greek crowd, it never howls. From descriptions of the modern Greek made by the correspondents of London Conservative journals one rather expects him to howl. But he don't howl; these crowds cheer in a deep-throated and meanful way that stirs the heart. They are serious; constantly the news comes from the frontier that the Greek soldiers are kept from fighting—pitching into the Turks—only by the superb control which the officers have over them. They are insane to get at their ancient foes. Their enthusiasm is of the kind that has the dignity in it. Ask any Greek on the street his opinion of the situation and he will say: "We must fight. There is nothing else to do."

"Well, but the Powers?" you say to him.

"Ah, yes, the Powers! Well, we must fight anyhow. Does it seem right to you that the Powers should bully Greece in this way? Look at the poor Cretans. Those men put their flesh against walls and capture a Turkish fort. Then as they stand panting after their victory, the fleet of the Powers shells them. Afterwards, perhaps, some Turkish troops assail a Cretan outpost and the ships sit idly on the water and watch it. They say they are there in the interests of peace but they do not stop the fighting, do they? No, they simply stop Cretan victories, it seems. I do not know what you may term it but to me it is infamous. Nevertheless you will see. The Cretans will not submit. It may be a spectacle of these islanders opposed to the force of Europe."

"And Greece?"

"We must fight. How can we do anything but fight? Can we submit to this series of impositions? The Powers have settled our affairs for us before, have they not? And always allowed Turkey to cheat us in the end. This time we shall fight. And it is better to be defeated than shamed."

This talk sounds like four glasses of cognac on the shady side-walk before a cafe but it is not that kind strictly. It may be said truly to represent the attitude of the Grecian people.

No. 3

STEPHEN CRANE SAYS GREEKS CANNOT BE CURBED

ATHENS, April 29.—I was with the Greek army in its campaign toward Janina, the principal town of Epirus, the southwestern province of Turkey, when I heard the first rumors of the hard fighting in Thessaly.

The journey from Arta overland to Thessaly requires a longer time than it does to go by the way of Athens, and so I have been fortunate enough to arrive in the capital in time to witness another popular outburst of the Athenians.

Crowds are in the streets, in the square before the King's palace and in every place of public congregation.

Practically every man in Athens is arming to go and fight the Turks. Every train into the city is loaded with other troops.

Yesterday crowds broke into the gun shops and took the practicable weapons. It was unanimous throughout all classes. To-day Greece is armed to fight for her life.

To-day I went to a shop and found no one there but a boy seated on a box.

"Where is the proprietor?" said I.

"He has gone to the war," said the boy.

This man had taken no time to arrange his affairs in careful detail. He might have been gone out to buy a cigar in another shop. The shelves were stripped and the counters were bare.

"The proprietor has nailed fast the lid of a great box in which are the things. I cannot sell you anything," the boy said hastily. "I am going to the front."

In my hotel here, which is usually very English and impressive, they are shy on waiters, porters and call boys. These men have gone to the war. There is a battalion now preparing that uses as uniforms the stable clothes of a squadron of cavalry already gone. In fact, this is not a king's war, not a parliament's war, but a people's war.

It is absurd to say that the Greeks undertook this contest because they believed they would take Constantinople in a fortnight. No nation ever had a truer sense of the odds. The concert of Europe had calmly informed them of possible consequences; there had been a general movement to impress Greece with her danger, but the Greeks said: "Well, we must fight anyhow."

There will be a great deal happen before these people of the mountains care to pause.

No. 4

GREEK WAR CORRESPONDENTS

ATHENS, GREECE, May 1.—The advantage of international complication is the fact that it develops war correspondents. There are now exactly one hundred and thirty-one correspondents sitting in Constantinople, Athens and on the frontier. They seriously interfere with the movements of the two armies. They cloud the air and officers have to sweep the sky with brooms before they can gain a chance for their field glasses. The only creature that has not been thrown off its natural balance by this invasion is the bold flea of Greece. Even this could not disturb the calm industry of the Grecian flea. These animals operate with drills which they work by foot treadles, and afterward one feels as if one had been attacked by a fleet of red-hot stove lids. The fleas were superior to the correspondent. They continued to lead their untroubled life of work and they reaped about all the vengeance which Greece was able to get as a nation.

The earl of Perth Amboy, N.J., arrived here lately to represent a New York newspaper. He discovered at once that the Parthenon is too little, that it is far smaller than the American Tract Society building in New York. Then he looked over the Eastern question and said that it was absurd and departed in a cloud of dust upon which a stereopticon threw fresh details of the increase in circulation of his journal. He left Athens dripping with perspiration and blind and dazed with amazement. The diplomatic corps was particularly prostrated. Upon being informed that he was likely to return, the citizens are considering a plan to set fire to the city and retreat to the hills.

But this American whirlwind is a bottle of beer and a plate of crackers to the English correspondent who understands the Eastern question. Of course, one can't throw a stick into any part of Athens without hitting three men who understand the Eastern question, but the English correspondent has an ironclad and immovable way of understanding a question which reminds one unmistakably of a god. He is perfectly simple and ingenuous about it. Apparently this ability to understand the Eastern question is given him because he is a British subject. He does not state this fact, but upon looking him over, one can see no other reason for his believing that he understands the Eastern question. He appropriates a knowledge of the Eastern question as blandly as his government appropriates an island or a tribe of negroes. The child-like air with which he recognizes his absolute infallibility is something very fascinating to those here who feel that the comprehension of the

Eastern question is a mouse that sleeps in the mind of the empire of Russia, and if there is a man who knows aught of that mystic thing, he is a man with no tongue.

A consular officer who has devoted a number of years to the study of the peoples of the East and the conditions here was obliged by an obligation of social amiability to listen to a prolonged elucidation of the problems of the East by a London correspondent. The consular officer was not greatly bored, because by this time consular officers are inured to those phenomena. Finally when the London correspondent arrived at some phase of the situation to which the official had devoted study and time, the official indifferently gave his opinion. There was silence for a moment while the correspondent looked proudly at the official. Then the correspondent said: "On that subject I talk with men whose opinions I respect." He turned his back on the official.

His allusion to men whose opinions he would respect caused considerable excitement here and the first report of it was not credited. It was believed to be a rumor set afloat by the extremists. Finally public opinion decided that he must talk in his sleep.

But if the London correspondent here has an iron-clad and immovable sense of the divinity of his intelligence there are also in Athens American correspondents of the type who write to their journals: "I am the only correspondent up to the present time who has been able to penetrate to the fastnesses of Larissa. During the terrible journey across the desert that surrounds this city I was three times prostrated by the heat and had five horses die under me. My dragoman, Murphy, had his ears frost-bitten."

Seriously, people in official circles who are posted in all matters of news say there has not been a report sent from Greece of this whoopetty-whoop description that is not terrifying in its assininity. The pity of it is that then the simple-minded people of Europe laugh at the poor correspondents instead of at the men who are really responsible for this sort of crime.

One expects foreigners to have a universal trust in the intelligence of the American people in the face of these splendid exhibitions.

There was a correspondent here who asked an interview of the king and because certain people took trouble for him he was granted it. He gave the interview to some of the Greek newspapers, also, and then by a singular juxtaposition of circumstances he left town. An aid-de-camp was sent to gather the editors of these newspapers and then an official spent a long time laboriously dictating the most sweeping denials. In delicate situations like an Eastern imbroglio an absurd interview is more than an annoyance. Later the correspondent cabled to his acquaintances in Athens to apply to the king for a decoration for him.

It would be deadly wrong not to speak now of the men who in affairs of this kind do their duty simply and faithfully and with no uproar. There is, for instance, an American correspondent here who has crossed Armenia in the midst of the troubles, who has lived in Crete with the insurgents and been in all the bombardments and fights there and who is now going to Arta in the hope of joining the wild band of volunteers who are about to raid into the troop-covered provinces of Turkey. In fact, he has as fine a record as a man can get out of such a situation. But, of course, no one knows him nor cares about it. He has no reputation at all relatively. His pay must naturally be in the same ratio.

To-day the king refused him an interview mainly because the wild ass of the desert who wanted a decoration had made the king wary of correspondents.

No. 5(1)

CRANE AT VELESTINO

ATHENS, May 10—(By Courier from Volo.)—When this war is done Velestino will be famed as its greatest battle.

The Greeks began with a reverse at Larissa, and the world expected the swiftest possible conclusion, but Velestino has proved that Greek soldiers when well led can cope successfully with Turks, even though outnumbered. This battle has proved them good fighters, long fighters, stayers. It must have surprised the world after Larissa.

I know all Greece rejoiced, and this battle's effect upon the Greek soldiers is like champagne. It made them perfectly happy. To be sure, the army retreated from Velestino, but it was no fault of this army. The commander bit his fingers and cursed when the order came to retreat. He knew that his army had victory within its grasp. For three days he had been holding the Turks beautifully in check, killing them as fast as they fell upon him. In the middle of intoxication of victory came the orders to fall back. Why? Reverses or something of the sort in other places may have been the reason, if there was a reason.

Smolenski knew, of course, that his retreat sacrificed Volo, and he raged like a soldier and a general. But, like a soldier and a general, he obeyed orders and the Turks occupied Velestino. And this after a three days' successful fight. The troops were jubilant, the commander confident—and then the Crown Prince ordered a retreat. My notion is that the Turks must have turned the far left of the Greeks. Probably by now New York knows more than Volo on this point. Anyhow, the Turks could never have turned the Greek right, and we who saw the worst of it feel doubts concerning the violence of the combat on the left.

The orders of retreat have crushed every man of this command. How the soldiers talked! Nobody wanted to fall back, save the few who would have fallen back anyhow. The Greeks understood the vastly superior number of the Turks, but they had whipped the vastly superior number of Turks three days and wanted to do it again.

Some other correspondents saw more of the battle than I did. I was rather laid up and had hurried on from Pharsala when I learned of the strong attack on Velestino. I knew that the taking of Velestino practically uncovered the base of the army at Volo, and so did not spare myself. But I only arrived at noon of the second day. I had seen skirmishes and small fights, but this was my first big battle.

The roll of musketry was tremendous. From a distance it was like tearing a cloth; nearer, it sounded like rain on a tin roof and close up it was just a long crash after crash. It was a beautiful sound—beautiful as I had never dreamed. It was more impressive than the roar of Niagara and finer than thunder or avalanche—because it had the wonder of human tragedy in it. It was the most beautiful sound of my experience, barring no symphony. The crash of it was ideal.

This is one point of view. Another might be taken from the men who died there.

The slaughter of the Turks was enormous. The fire of the Greeks was so fierce that the Turkish soldiers while charging shielded their eyes with their hands. Eight charges the Turks made on this day, and they were repulsed every time. The desperate Turkish cavalry even attacked their enemy on a steep, rocky hill. The insane, wicked squadrons were practically annihilated. Scattered fragments slid slowly back, leaving the plain black with wounded and dead men and horses. From a distance it was like a game. There was no blood, no expression, no horror to be seen.

All the assaults of the Turks this day resulted disastrously to them. The Greek troops fought with the steadiness of salaried bookkeepers, never tired, never complaining. It was a magnificent exhibition. The Greeks fought all the time with the artillery fire on them even in a musketry lull, but nobody minded anything. The Turks were in great numbers and fought according to the precepts of their religion. But the Greeks were never daunted and whipped them well. Sometimes it was fighting among gaunt hills, sometimes fighting on green plains; but always the Greeks held their position.

When night came shells burst infrequently, lighting the darkness. By the red flashes I saw the wounded taken to Volo. There was very little outcry among them. They were mostly silent.

In the gray early morning the musketry fire began again. It rattled from hill to hill, batteries awoke and soon the whole play was resumed.

The Turkish guns were superior to those of the Greeks, who had mostly mountain howitzers. The Turkish artillery consisted principally of regulation field pieces, and I learned to curse the German officers who directed their fire. I think these officers are the normal results of German civilization, which teaches that a man should first of all be a soldier; ultimately he becomes simply a soldier, not a man at all. I consider these German officers hired assassins. One has strong feelings under such circumstances as these.

I watched for a long time the blue-clad Greek infantry march into position across a small plain. War takes a long time. The swiftness of chronological order of battle is not correct. A man has time to get shaved, or to lunch or to take a bath often in battles the descriptions of which read like a whirlwind. While I watched the Turks changed their attack from the Greek right on the plain to the Greek left on the rocky hill. Then the fighting became obscured from view.

The Greeks lay in trenches, snugly flattened against the dirt, firing carefully, while the Turks loomed close before them. Every ridge was fringed with smoke. I saw soldiers in the trench ease off and take a drink from their canteens, twist their cartridge belts to put the empty links behind them, or turn around to say something to a comrade. Then they went at it again.

I noticed one lieutenant standing up in the rear of a trench rolling a cigarette, his legs wide apart. In this careless attitude a shot went through his neck. His servant came from the trench and knelt weeping over the body, regardless of the battle. The men had to drag him in by the legs.

The reserves coming up passed a wayside shrine. The men paused to cross themselves and pray. A shell struck the shrine and demolished it. The men in the rear of the column were obliged to pray to the spot where the shrine had been.

An officer of a battery sent a man to the rear after another pair of field glasses, the first pair having been smashed by a musket ball. The man brought a bottle of wine, having misunderstood. Meanwhile the Turks were forming on a little green hill 1,200 yards off. The officer was furious over the man's mistake, but he never let go of that bottle of wine.

A member of the Foreign Legion came from the left, wounded in the head. He was bandaged with magnificent clumsiness with about nine yards of linen. I noticed a little silk English flag embroidered on his sleeve. He was very sad and said the battle was over. Most wounded men conclude that the battle is over.

News came from the left that the Turks had tried to turn the flank and failed. I saw no correspondents and supposed them all to be in the thick of the fray.

The Turks formed on the right and moved slowly across the plain and the battery of howitzers opened on them. I saw troops moving to the rear to prevent a possible flank attack in the direction of Volo.

The fight on the plain to the right began. Masses of Turkish troops like shadows slowly moved toward the Greek trenches indicated by gray lines of smoke. Shots began to rake the trenches on the hill and to also rake the battery to the rear. I hoped the Greeks on the plain would hurry and drive the Turks from their position. They did it gallantly in a short, ferocious infantry fight. The bit of woods where the fight occurred seemed on fire. There was a great rattling and banging and then the Turks went out defeated. There was general rejoicing all along the Greek lines, the officers walked proudly, the men in the trenches grinned. Then, mind you, just at this time, late in the afternoon, after another successful day, came the order to retreat.

Smolenski had apparently received the brunt of the fighting. Yet the centre and left near Karadjah and at Pharsala had again retired. No one could explain it. We were not aware of the situation they faced, but it seemed an extraordinary order.

They say Smolenski wept.

I went down to see the retreat. A curious thing was that the Turks seemed to understand the order as quickly as we did. They moved up batteries with startling rapidity for the Turks. Your correspondent got well shelled on his way.

The retreat was not disorderly, but wrathful and sullen. A regiment of Ephzones, the kilted men, 2,000 strong, came down to cover the retreat and in the twilight, brightened by Turkish shells, the Greeks slowly withdrew. An order to advance and get whipped scares no soldiers, but an order to retreat scares a good many. No retreat can be as orderly as an advance. But this was distinctly a decent retreat. The troops moved at the usual time and kept well together.

A train came, the last Greek train to run on this road for a long time. It received a heavy fire. I wanted to see the engineer, but could not. There are few better men than this engineer even in the Greek army. A complication of a railroad accident and bombardment is a bad disease. All the way down on the train a man covered with bloody bandages talked to me in wild Greek.

I send this from Volo and before you print it the Turks will be here.

No. 5(II)

STEPHEN CRANE AT VELESTINO

BY COURIER FROM VOLO TO ATHENS, May 10.—Velestino will surely be famous as one of the greatest battles of this war. The Greek reverse began at Larissa, and the world expected a quick conclusion, but Velestino proved that Greek soldiers could, when well led, successfully cope with the overwhelming numbers of Turks. It proved them good fighters and long fighters and stayers. It must have been generally surprising after Larissa, and it occasioned general rejoicing throughout Greece, and its effect upon the Greek soldiers was great. It made them perfectly happy. To be sure, the army retreated from Velestino, but it was not the fault of this army. The commander bit his fingers and cursed when the order came to retreat. He was at that time perfectly confident of success. For three days he had been holding the Turks beautifully in check and inflicting heavy loss. Then came the orders to fall back, due to reverses or something else in other places.

General Smolenski knew, of course, that his retreat sacrificed Volo, and he raged and fumed, but orders must be obeyed, hence the occupation by the Turks of Velestino, and later the fall of Volo. This after a three days' successful fight.

The troops were jubilant, their commander confident. Then the Crown Prince ordered the retreat. I think the Turks must have turned the far left of the Greeks, near Pharsala, but probably now New York knows more than Volo on this point. Anyhow, the Turks could never have turned the Greek right at

Velestino, and we feel doubts concerning the violence of the combat on the left, which was under the immediate command of the Prince. The orders to retreat downcast every man under Smolenski's command. The talk goes among the soldiers that nobody wants to fall back save the few who would fall back anyhow. The Greeks understood that there was a vastly superior number of Turks, but they whipped this vastly superior number of Turks three days, and they wanted to do it again. This was the situation when the orders came.

Of the first two days' combat some other correspondents saw more than I did. I was rather laid up, and had hurried on from Pharsala when I learned of the strong attack on Velestino. I knew the taking of Velestino practically uncovered the base of supplies of the army at Volo, and so came immediately, but too late to see the whole three days' fight. I arrived at noon on the second day. I had been in skirmishes and small fights, but this was the first big battle.

The roll of musketry fire was tremendous. In the distance it sounded like the tearing of a cloth. Nearer it sounded like rain on a resonant roofing, and close by it was just long crash after crash. It was a beautiful sound; beautiful as had never been dreamed. It was more impressive than the roar of Niagara and finer than thunder or an avalanche, because it had the wonder of human tragedy in it. It was the most beautiful sound of my experience, barring no symphony. The crash of it was ideal.

This is from one point of view. The other might be taken from the men who died there. The slaughter of Turks was great, the fire of the Greeks fierce, the Turkish soldiers while charging often shielding their eyes with their hands. The Turks made eight charges this day and were repulsed each time. Desperate Turkish cavalry even attacked a steep rocky hill. The insane and almost wicked squadrons were practically annihilated, and their scattered fragments slid slowly back, leaving the plain black with wounded and dead men and horses.

From a distance it was like a game. No blood, no expressions of horror were to be seen; there were simply the movements of tiny doll tragedy.

All these assaults by the Turks on this day resulted disastrously for them. The Greek troops fought with the patience of salaried bookkeepers—never tired, never complaining; it was a fine exhibition. The artillery fire upon them was almost eternal; it continued even when the musketry lulled, but nobody minded anything. The Turks were in great numbers, and fought according to the precepts of their fatalistic religion, but the Greeks were perfectly undaunted and whipped them well. Sometimes they were fighting among the gaunt hills; sometimes they were fighting on the fine green plain, but always the Greeks held the position. When night came shells burst unfrequently, lighting the darkness with red flashes.

I saw the wounded taken to Volo. There was very little outcry, the sufferers being mostly silent.

In the gray early morning the musketry fire was resumed. It rattled from hill to hill. The batteries awoke. The whole affair was resumed. The Turkish guns were superior to those of the Greeks. The Greeks had mostly mountain howitzers. The Turkish guns were regulation field pieces.

I learned to curse the German officers who directed the fire of the Turkish batteries. I think they are a normal outgrowth of German civilization, which teaches that a man should be first of all a soldier. As a consequence, he ultimately becomes simply a soldier, and not a man at all. I consider these German officers hired assassins. One has strong feelings under the circumstances. I watched a long time the blue clothed infantry of the Greeks march into position across a small plain. War takes a long time. The swiftness in the chronology of battles is not correct in most books. Evidently one has time to get shaved or lunch or take a bath often in battles whose descriptions read like whirlwinds. The Turks changed their attack from the Greek right on the plain to the Greek left on the rocky hills. The fighting was then obscure to the view, only a detail being observable now and then. The men in the trenches were snugly flattened against the dirt and firing carefully. The Turks loomed close and the roar was great. Every ridge was fringed with smoke. Occasionally a soldier in the trench eased off, took a drink from his canteen, twisted his cartridge belt to put the empty links behind, said something to a comrade over his shoulder, and went at it again.

One lieutenant, standing up back of the trench, rolling a cigarette, his legs wide apart, and in a careless attitude, was shot through the neck. His servant came from the trench, kneeled over the body, regardless of the battle, and wept. Men had to drag him in by the legs.

Reserves coming up passed a wayside shrine. There the men paused to cross themselves and pray. A shell struck the shrine and demolished it. The men in the rear of the column were obliged to pray at the spot where the shrine had been.

An officer of a battery sent a man to the rear after another pair of field glasses. His first pair had been broken by a rifle shot. The man brought a bottle of wine. He had misunderstood. Meanwhile the Turks were forming on a little green hill twelve hundred yards away. The officer was wild and furious over the man's mistake, but he never let go of that bottle of wine.

A member of the foreign legion came in from the left wounded. His head was bandaged with magnificent clumsiness with about nine yards of linen. He had a little silk English flag embroidered on his sleeve. He was very sad, and said the battle was over. Most wounded conclude that a battle is over. I heard from the left that the Turks had tried to turn the flank and failed. I saw no correspondents, and supposed them all to be in the thickest of the fight.

The Turks formed on the right and moved slowly across the plain. New battalions on the right opened, and I saw other troops moving to the rear to prevent a possible flank attack in the direction of Volo. The fight on the plain to the right was begun. Masses of Turkish troops, like shadows, moved slowly across the plain. The Greek trenches were indicated by gray lines of smoke. Shots began to rake the trenches on the hill, also to rake a battery to the rear. I hoped the Greeks on the plain would hurry and drive the Turks from their position. They did this gallantly in a short, ferocious infantry fight in the woods. The bit of woods seemed to be on fire. After a great rattling and banging the Turks went out.

After this attack and defeat there was general rejoicing along the Greek lines and satisfaction over all. The officers walked proudly, the men in the trenches grinned.

Then, mind you, just at this time, late in the afternoon, after another successful day, came the orders to retreat.

General Smolenski had apparently received the brunt of the fighting, yet the centre and the left, near Kardetsa and at Pharsala, had again retired. No one could explain it. We were not aware of the situation they faced, but it seemed to be an extraordinary order. They say General Smolenski wept.

I went down then to see the retreat. It was a curious thing. The Turks seemed to understand our orders as quickly as we did. They moved up their batteries with startling rapidity for Turks. Your correspondent got well shelled on his way. The retreat was not disorderly, but wrathful and sullen. A regiment of Ephzones (the kilted men), two thousand strong, came down to cover the retreat. In the twilight, lighted by Turkish shells, the Greeks slowly withdrew.

An order to advance and get whipped scares no soldiers, but an order to retreat scares a good many. No retreat can be as orderly as an advance, but this was distinctly a decent retreat, the troops, in usual time, kept well together. A train came along. It was the last Greek train to run over this road for a long while. It got a heavy fire. I wanted to see the engineer, but was in somewhat of a hurry myself. Still I saw him. He was a daisy.

The complication of a railroad accident and a bombardment at the same time is a bad disease, and the engineer in bloody bandages talked to me in wild Greek. I cannot quote him. I send this from Volo and before you print it the Turks will be here.

No. 6

A FRAGMENT OF VELESTINO

THE sky was of a fair and quiet blue. In the radiantly bright atmosphere of the morning the distances among the hills were puzzling in the extreme. The Westerner could reflect that after all his eye was accustomed to using a tree as a standard of measure, but here there were no trees. The great bold hills were naked. The landscape was indeed one which we would understand as being Biblical. A tall lean shepherd was necessary to it. Furthermore, the rocks were grey, save when a reddishy tinge of lurking ores appeared on their rough surfaces.

There was a wide highway curving sinuously because of the grades. A trail for pack animals took less account of these grades, and cut a way over the ridge far straighter than the road. In the distance lay the town of Volo. It is in two parts. The port, with the business district, lies flat on the water's edge, while another portion is separated sufficiently to have another name, and is fastened to the side of an enormous mountain. Tiny house appears above tiny house, and streets can be seen from end to end. In fact, the mountain side is so steep that the entire town there is displayed as if one looked at a lithograph. One can only dream of the view of the blue gulf there to be obtained, and of the soft splendor of the fall of evening. Lights in the houses at night seem like stars to the people on the plain, and to those far out in ships. Many wealthy Athenians once preferred to spend there the summer months. The highroad was a broad, glaring yellow band in the Oriental sunshine, but no dust arose from it on this morning because there were no carts, no old crazy carriages. The trail was even bereft of donkeys. The road led to Velestino, and since the blue of early morning there had been curious sounds from there— the rolling boom of the guns, and the hot, dry crackle of the infantry fire, which grew more hot and more dry as the sunshine became stronger. On the quay at Volo, five miles away, one could see a vast concourse of people, fugitives mainly, but the harbor contained one little steamer.

On the lonely road from Velestino there appeared the figure of a man. He came slowly and with a certain patient steadiness. A great piece of white linen was wound around under his jaw, and finally tied at the top of his head in a great knot like the one grandma ties when she remedies her boy's toothache. The man had a staff in his hand, and he used it during his slow walk. He was in the uniform of the Greek infantry, and his clothes were very dusty—so dusty that the little regimental number on his shoulder could hardly be seen. Under other circumstances one could have sworn that the man had great smears of red paint on his face. It was blood. It had to be blood; but then it was weirdly not like blood. It was dry, but it had dried crimson and brilliant. In fact, this hue upon his face was so unexpected in its luridness that one first had to gaze at this poor fellow in astonishment. He had been shot in the head, and bandaged evidently according to the ability of the nearest comrade. Now, as he went slowly along two things smote the sense of the observer: first, the terrible red of the man's face, which was of the quality of flame as it appears in old pictures; and second, this same old ridiculous knot in the linen at the top of the head, which simply emphasized one's recollection of New England and the mumps. As he reached the top of the ridge Volo was under his vision. His calm, patient glance swept over it. To the things about him he paid no evident regard. He was hurt, and he had known enough of the hospital at Volo to have the thing become almost an instinct with him now. He was hurt, and he was going to Volo. Even as he plodded across the ridge a train loaded with other wounded rolled down the valley. It had started a long time after he had started, and it would be at Volo much sooner, but one can, perhaps, understand why he did not wait for it at Velestino. A rabbit when it is hurt does not wait for a train—it crawls away immediately into the bushes; and so this man had started for Volo.

Behind him was the noise of the battle, the roar and rumble of an enormous factory. This was the product. This was the product, not so well finished as some, but sufficient to express the plan of the machine. This wounded soldier explained the distant roar. He defined it. This—this and worse—was what was going on. This explained the meaning of all that racket. Gazing at this soldier with his awful face, one felt a new respect for the din.

Withal, one could muse upon the inexpressible and vast crime of by some chance addressing a flippant remark to this man. There was a dignity in his condition, a great and reaching dignity. It was of a kind that would have made marshals step aside for him at a king's levee. Five miles of hot road was still between him and Volo. He plodded steadily on, and became a dim and dimming figure.

The right flank of this wing of the Greek army was on a plain. In fact, this plain cut through the right flank and extended to the rear of the centre. Afterward it narrowed to a valley and passed on behind the left flank. The railroad came out from Volo toward Larissa across this plain, and a junction was formed at Velestino with the railroad that went to Pharsala, where lay the Crown Prince with the larger part of the Greek army. The Velestino portion of the army was primarily covering the railroad, because the railroad, besides being a railroad, and useful therefore in many military ways, was the connection between Volo, the base of supplies, and the troops at Pharsala. The part of the army at Velestino had its position on hills, when that was possible, but the railroad made a wide curve on the plain to turn toward Pharsala, and this wretched plain extended quite to Larissa, from which direction the Turks were pouring. So the Greek commander had not alone the task of battle with an enemy superior in force, but his great duty was to protect this important communication. Strategically, then, Velestino was the centre of the Greek position, although nominally it was the right flank, and strategically the railroad was an infernal nuisance.

Dust arose from the road on the plain where a cavalryman, his dark green uniform grey from the dust, his slanted carbine bobbing on his back, was galloping somewhere with orders. Long thick lines of troops were to be seen. They faced various ways, but mainly toward that part of the plain which extended in the direction of Larissa. There were trenches along the railroad track turned up in rich new earth. Many men in the blue of Greece lay in them. Some were asleep, sprawled out on their backs; some were eating hard-tack, cutting it with their knives with great difficulty, holding the bread and paring away as a cobbler does with a shoe. One strolled off with a great number of canteens. A large group was listening to someone's news from the fighting front. Most of the infantry officers had gone to chat with the officers of a mountain battery which was in the rear of the other line. The guns sat each in its own little tiara-shaped entrenchment. They were tilted, with an air of having been knocked under the chin and told to hold their heads up. The officer said something rather good perhaps, and the others all laughed appreciatively but carelessly, their legs wide apart, their caps set rakishly, like a lot of peacefully garrisoned hussars after evening parade. And yet from the hills on the left of their line the guns were roaring and the infantry fire was rattling and rattling, in spasms, light, heavy, heavy, light, describing all the moods of the battle that was raging there. People imagine battle to be one long muscular contortion with a mental condition corresponding to it. But just as it is impossible for a man to have convulsions eternally and without rest, so it is essential that when the other fellows are against the enemy the soldier should be superior to worrying too much about it. His turn will come; he will get all the worry that is due him. In the meantime let him gossip, with his legs wide apart, and pass around the cigarettes. One would not have thought these officers to be vitally interested in the outcome of this fight. Later, an order to move struck a lazy and indifferent battalion of infantry. Then the change was plain. The officers' faces became instantly hard, stern, military. The commands were so sharp as to sound almost impassioned. They had got their cause to worry. Meanwhile the officers of the battery continued to laugh and talk.

Apparently the Greek lines here lay in the form of two sides of a triangle, with the apex rather sharp. It was the result of the outstretching curve of the railroad, and the necessity for its defence, and this necessity adjusted to the topography of the country, as well as the gods would allow. The town of Velestino was in this apex. Velestino, before a friendly army sat down upon it, had been a most beautiful town. Even friendly armies can but destroy the more subtle effects of nature, although they substitute a wilder beauty of their own creation. Velestino has about it a great number of fine large trees, which in Greece is very unusual. Many of the houses were quite buried in foliage, and it was impossible to see the Turks toward Larissa owing to the many strips of forest on the plain. All the houses of any importance were tightly closed and barred, every door, every window. The huts of the peasants, made from stone-like cobbles, were not closed and barred, because they seemed never to have had doors, but the interiors were mere dark vacancies. It was a deserted village. One walked the streets wondering of the life that here had been, and if it would ever return—could it ever return. It is a human thing to think of a community that has been, and here was one with all its important loves, hates, friendships; all its games, spites, its wonderful complexity of relation and intercourse, suddenly smitten by the sledge of chance and rendered nothing—nothing but a few vacant staring houses. The chance-comer notes then that some villager had carefully repaired his front gate, and the chance-comer's sense of the futility of repairing that front gate causes him to know more of life for a moment than he had ever known before.

There was a mosque and minaret—evidences of a former Turkish occupation—near the foot of the hill. A little square faced the mosque, and there was a pool, a still and lovely pool. On its mirror-like surface it reflected part of the old dome of the mosque, and reproduced completely the round and pointed little minaret. Some cattle, deserted probably by their owner, came quietly down to the pool to drink. The sky was blue. A gentle wind rustled the foliage over a garden wall. To be sure, there was a soldier nursing a sore foot under the porch of the mosque, but even with him this scene in the angle formed by two lines of battle was eminently peace. And yet there was a curious sound in the square—spit—spit—spit; and with this sound a long tenor humming. Little clouds of dust flew from the roadway. Spit—spit. The little square, by baleful chance, had fallen under fire. Some Turks were firing at another thing, and consequently they were hitting this square. Spit—spit—spit. The cattle drank, gratefully rolling their fine and melancholy eyes. They were up to their knees in the cool water, and the pool reflected their stout dun-colored bodies. By strange chance they walked into the pool at a place which caused the mosque to be between them and the line of fire. They lazily swished their long tails, and as for this spitting and kicking of dust within ten yards of them, it was as if it were not happening.

A certain part of the Greek nature, or rather the nature of certain Greeks, can in action make it clear to the Anglo-Saxon that he has another way of doing things. There was a battery of howitzers on a hill above the mosque and the bullet-swept square. The captain of this battery walked out to his position at middle-rear. He addressed his men. His chest was well out, and his manner was gorgeous. If one could have judged by the tone, it was one of the finest speeches of the age. It was Demosthenes returned and in command of a battery of howitzers. There was in it a quality of the best kind of sentiment. One waited for the answering cheers of the men. The poor devils of men are always obliged to give answering cheers to the patriotic orations on the field. But what was the captain saying? He was merely ordering the gunners to elevate their pieces for a range of sixteen hundred metres.

From this hill one was enabled to see Turks. Down in the square the bullets might have been dropping from the clouds. Down in the square one ran a danger of being killed by some Turk who would not know that he did it, and who had never really intended, nor could he intend, to do that particular thing. It is a dreadful idea. But on this hill the Turks could be seen and the Turks could see the battery, and if a man was killed he could consider that there had been a certain election on the part of some Turk. It was very different down in the square.

The gunners having raised their pieces according to the captain's appeal, the guns were fired one by one. These little howitzers remind one somehow of children. When one exploded it threw itself backward in a wild paroxysm as does some angry and outraged child. And then the men ran to it and set it on its pins again, and straightened it out and soothed it. The men were very attentive and anxious. One of these howitzers would remain quiet then for a time, and all the trouble would be over. Then suddenly it would have another fit, and necessitate the scampering of a whole squad to set it right again. They were foolish little guns, peevish, intolerable as to their dispositions. It was a wonder the men would take so much trouble with them.

Out on the green plain there was a dark line, heavier than a shadow, and lighter than a hedge. Most of the plain was hidden from this hill by a higher hill forward and to the left, but this dark line afforded the essential interest. It was the Turks.

It is a great thing to survey the army of the enemy. Just where and how it takes hold upon the heart is difficult of description. Of course there is all the usual reflection concerning the chances of being killed, but there is another element, important and strong, and at the same time elusive to a degree. It has perhaps something to do with the enemy's persistent and palpable determination to kill you if possible. Here are a vast number of men convened evidently for this sole purpose. You can repeat to yourself, if you like, the various stated causes of the war, and mouth them over and try to apply them to the situation, but they will fail to answer your vague interrogation. The mind returns to the wonder of why so many people will put themselves to the most incredible labor and inconvenience and danger for the sake of this—this ending of a few lives like yours, or a little better or a little worse. This army on the plain was a majestic thing. It expressed power—power—power. The force one felt to be in those long dark lines was terrible. It could reach and pull down the clouds, this thing. It could let two seas meet, this thing. A soldier in the trenches suddenly screamed and clasped his hands to his eyes as if he had been struck blind. He rolled to the bottom of the trench, his body turning twice. A comrade, dazed, whistling through his teeth, reached in his pocket and drew out a hunk of bread and a handkerchief. It appeared that he was going to feed this corpse. But he took the handkerchief and pressed it on the wound and then looked about him helplessly. He still held the bread in his other hand, because he could not lay it down in the dirt of the trench. As for most of the men, they accepted this visitation in silence, merely turning their eyes to look at the body, and then perhaps shaking their heads mournfully while a strange wonder and wistful questioning of the future were in some glances. The crest of the hill had been a field of meagre but ripe grain. It had been trampled now until little of it appeared, although a yellow wisp or two might be trying to struggle out from under one of the ammunition boxes of the battery, all painted a light blue and scattered thickly over the field. To the rear lay a dead horse, and a number of blood-red poppies, miraculously preserved from the countless feet, bloomed near it. Continually there was in the air a noise as if someone had thrown an empty beer-bottle with marvellous speed at you. This hooting and whistling of some of the shells was like nothing if not like the flight of an empty beer-bottle. Then others just whined and sang in a sort of an arc of sound—an arc both in volume and in key. It was great to hear others go like immense birds flashing across the vision in their swift journey. The rapid flapping of their wings was perfectly obvious. Sometimes the blinding explosions of these shells dug holes on the hill among the trampled grain and the few poppies.

There was great trouble on the other hill in front and extending far to the left. Its summit was a long fringe of grey smoke floating backward. The volleys were rattling and crackling from one end of the hill to the other. Sometimes the pattering of individual firing swelled suddenly to one long beautiful crash that had something in it of the fall of a giant pine amid his brethren of the mountain side. It was the thunder of a monstrous breaker against the hard rocks. At times it was these things, and at times it was just the crack-crack-crackety-crack-crackle of burning timbers. Altogether the troops on the ridge were heavily engaged, and, as if by concert, the plain on the right became dotted with little puffs of smoke. The captain of the battery was furnished with a new and large number of targets. It was during the attendant excitement of this situation that he sent a man to the rear for another pair of field-glasses. His first pair had suffered a rifle-ball wound. The man misunderstood the order, and he came back with a bottle of wine. He stood until the captain should finish talking with a subaltern. There was a look of pious satisfaction on his face at having concluded his errand with wisdom and celerity. Suddenly the captain reached for his field-glasses and got instead a bottle of wine. Astonishment and incredulity mingled on his face. He looked sternly at the soldier and harangued him on the necessity of not being an idiot during battles. His gestures were wild and rapid. Nevertheless, he did not relinquish his fast grip on the bottle of wine. Presently he went along the lines giving an order, and sometimes he absent-mindedly waved the bottle toward the Turks. He looked down at last and saw that he still grasped the bottle. He went then and gave it into the care of the trusty corporal who commanded the horse and mule squad below the hill. When the actors are under fire, small dramas of this kind may be interesting to the spectator.

It was about this time, too, that a column of infantry marching to support the troops on the hill had its prayers interrupted. There was a small stone shrine at the side of the trail. It contained a little holy picture of a saint, a little chromo in red and green, with a frame of gilt paper. Under this picture was a little lamp, wherein oil was sometimes burned. It was the common wayside shrine of the Greek Church. The soldiers had been marched a long way. Their faces were warm with sweat. Their blanket-rolls lay heavily upon their shoulders. Their haversacks knocked awkwardly upon their tired hips. Their rifles and double rows of long Gras cartridges must have each appeared weighty enough to sink a yacht. Moreover, many of the men still wore their thick winter overcoats, as is rather a custom among Greek soldiers, no matter how warm may be the Oriental sunshine.

This weary column reached the little shrine, which was less than three hundred yards from the advanced firing line. The men at the front crossed themselves and prayed. As file after file passed, the men crossed themselves and prayed. Suddenly a great hooting shell struck the base of the shrine and lifted the structure in the air. It fell with a ringing smash, demolished. There was a spectacle of the nearest men scurrying in every direction to escape the flying stones, and as they ran the fingers of many of them were still at their chests as they had been when making the sign of the cross before the coming of the shell. The men in the rear of the column, finding no shrine, prayed quietly facing its ruins.

Naturally one wants now to be informed of the complexion of the battle. Who was winning? Was victory with the blue field and white cross of the Greeks? Or was it with the crimson banner of the Moslems? If a reader of a casual article of this kind wishes to know who was winning this battle, depend upon it there were men present upon the field who considered the question to be one of surpassing importance. But none knew. How could he know? The battlefield was spread over miles of ground. It had a multitude of phases. No one could judge

whether it was to be well or ill for Turk or Greek in the final
measure of the day. People would like to stand in front of the
mercury of war and see it rise or fall, and they think they ought
to demand it, more or less, in descriptions of battle; but it is an
absurd thing for a writer to do if he wishes to reflect in any
way the mental condition of the men in the ranks, and the
knowledge of a captain is very little better. Perhaps the general
ignorance extends to colonels, who in this army command from
two to five thousand men. A subordinate commander knows
this—he knows he was attacked and that he repulsed the
enemy or didn't repulse the enemy. He knows that he attacked,
and won or lost; whether or not this was vitally important to
the fortunes of the day he cares to learn, but probably he can't
find out. In the meantime, the men know this or less.

On this day in particular there was a rumor through the
army that the Turks were attacking in force. This is what
was known. The Turks were attacking in force.

Stragglers moving toward Volo told many tales. The Greeks
were on the edge of a great victory. The Greeks were on the
verge of a great defeat. The right flank had been driven back;
the right flank had advanced. The centre was crushed; the
centre was holding its own. The left flank was turned; the
left flank had taken a height in its front.

The column of infantry that had witnessed the destruction
of the shrine was composed of new troops. The men had
never been in battle. Indeed, three days previously they had
marched down the streets of Athens with flowers in their gun-
barrels and smiles on their faces, certain that war was but a
fête. Later they had learned that it was mainly hard work, and
now they were evidently going to be taught that it contained
certain elements of fighting. The summit of the ridge was still
a long grey fringe of smoke, and a tremendous banging came
from there. As the battalion reached the foot of the steep, stragglers were coming down. Some were in a great hurry. The new
men looked at them uneasily. "Well, how is it going?" they
asked. Some of the stragglers said "good," in assured tones,
but others shook their heads sadly and made little reply. As
the column slowly climbed the steep the men's countenances
became very thoughtful. There was a reason for this, too, out-

side of any perturbations of new men. The Greek army had been taught the horrors of panic. As for the Larissa panic, the tale of it was probably vastly exaggerated, but the tradition of the thing now has its influence in the army. The Greek soldier fighting on the defensive will probably stick to his trench as long as any man, but it will not do to shake a soldier's confidence from the rear. Even a war correspondent could find it in him to turn a wary eye occasionally in that direction, lest a retreat be suddenly ordered and tumultuously begun, and a journey with an army that has succeeded in routing itself is more instructive than pleasant. As has been said, the terrors of a rapid retreat were now a tradition in this army, and it was not good. Really, if orders to fall back are in the air, a man wants to be the first to note them afar, and he is apt to glance often over his shoulder to make sure he is not missing their arrival. It seems absolutely certain that this was all that was the matter with these new troops. To go in and help to whip the Turks— that was a fair proposition. That was why they had come. But what about a retreat, some kind of a weird and incomprehensible order to retreat that would get them cut up outrageously, practically have them destroyed? It is true that troops should not trouble themselves with a commander's business, but it is also true that a commander should remember that his men's brains are obliged to work, and he is careful, if he is a good soldier, of the kind of mental food with which he provides them. There had been, however, a conspiracy of general incompetency and stupidity to engrave the word retreat in the middle of the brain of the Greek soldier, and in his natural mental processes it occurs.

When the battalion came to the top of the ridge it found a great green plain spread out before it, and the plain was ruddy, almost brazen, in the light of the late afternoon sun. The distances here were magnificent. One could see even the long snowy summit of Mount Olympus in the far north, and as for the central plain of Thessaly, it was simply a great map. But these natural splendors did not occupy any serious part of the battalion's attention. The men had been projected into the middle of a good fight. Obliged to wait for a time, they peered cautiously over the crest of the ridge. Below and in front some yards there was a trench, and in this trench there were perhaps forty Greek soldiers. These soldiers had hollowed little places in the top of the trench, and had added the protection of stones. When a soldier had loaded his rifle, he rested it in this groove, and, taking aim at some tiny black figures on a knoll that arose from the plain half a mile away, he fired. The shiny Gras jumped a trifle with the explosion, and then the soldier rolled half on his back and drew his piece in to be again loaded. They were quite leisurely at this time. To the rear lay the body of a youth who had been killed by a ball through the chest. This youth had not been a regular soldier, evidently; he had been a volunteer. The only things military were the double cartridge belt, the haversack, and the rifle. As for the clothes, they were of black cloth with a subtle stripe or check in it, and they were cut after a common London style. Beside the body lay a black hat. It was what one would have to call a Derby, although from the short crown there was an inclination to apply the old name of dicer. There was a rather high straight collar and a little four-in-hand scarf of flowered green and a pin with a little pink stone in it.

This dead young Greek had nothing particularly noble in his face. There was expressed in this thing none of the higher thrills to incite, for instance, a company of romantic poets. The lad was of a common enough type. The whole episode was almost obvious. He was of people in comfortable circumstances; he bought his own equipment, of course. Then one morning news sped to the town that the Turks were beating. And then he came to the war on the smoke, so to speak, of the new fires of patriotism which had been immediately kindled in the village place, around the tables in front of the café. He had been perhaps a little inclined to misgiving, but withal anxious to see everything anyhow, and usually convinced of his ability to kill any number of Turks. He had come to this height, and fought with these swarthy, hard-muscled men in the trench, and, soon or late, got his ball through the chest. Then they had lifted the body and laid it to the rear in order to get it out of the way.

The fire from the ridge had been undergoing one of the merely crackling periods. Now, however, it blazed up again.

These wonderful little figures amid the green and brown fields of the plain had increased vastly in number. Little trickling streams of them began to flow slowly along the lines of the old hedges and ditches. In one place there was a great long heavy streak of them. It was more than human to see even the color of a fez from the height. As for a gesture, any expression at all, it could not be seen. And this quality provided the picture with its extraordinary mysticism. These little black things streaming from here and there on the plain, what were they? What moved them to this? The power and majesty of this approach was all in its mystery, its inexplicable mystery. What was this thing? And why was it? Of course Turks, Turks, Turks; but then that is a mere name used to describe these creatures who were really hobgoblins and endowed with hobgoblin motives. In the olden times one could have had a certain advantage of seeing an enemy's eyes. If one was anxious about the battle, one could have perhaps witnessed the anxiety of the enemy. Anything is better than a fight with an enemy that wears the black velvet mask of distance.

The trenches on the left part of the height became tumultuous with smoke and long thin rifle flashes. As the dark streams, rivulets, of the enemy poured along the plain, a large number of batteries opened, and great black shells, whirling and screaming, fled over the heads of the men in the trenches. There was going to be a good tight little fight.

The heads of the loose skirmishing columns of the enemy became hidden in rolling masses of smoke. The Turks were shooting low. Few bullets went over the trench. Many fell below it, and a certain number with great regularity went pum—pum—pump into the earthwork. The lieutenant in command of this trench walked slowly to and fro in the rear of his men. He was a fine-looking young chap with a bronzed skin and a clear eye, showing below the banded and peaked cap with its crown and arms. His dark coat fitted him bravely. There were two silver stars on the vivid scarlet facing at his throat. His light blue trousers were hidden below the knee by black walking boots. In fact, he looked like a soldier, and he wore his clothes as a soldier wears his clothes. He was trim, lithe, muscular, as a man to whom campaigning has begun to be easy work. As he walked to and fro under this strong fire he did not evince any fear, nor did he evince any strutting contempt. From time to time as he glanced up or to one side toward the particularly close path of some missile there was in his gaze more of a decent respect than of any other emotion—once he turned and rapidly called out to his men a new order concerning the range. The bullet that came there struck him in the throat— squarely in the throat. He fell like a flash—as if someone had knocked his heels from under him from behind. On the ground his arms made one long stiff and shivery gesture, and then he lay still. For a moment his men had a clear case of rattle, simply rattle. It was as when the captain is washed off the bridge at sea during a storm. There are two things lost—the captain, and what the captain knows about managing ships in storms. For a moment, these soldiers were wild-eyed. They screamed at each other. But then another trench with the rest of the company in it was very close. This trench was not a lone ship. The men settled down again to fighting.

All processes of battle are slower than accounts of them. There is plenty of time for everything if your side is holding its own. A big battle is not a whirlwind of many events, although many of the events may be of themselves whirlwinds. There are many pauses, many waits during a big battle, when apparently one would have time to lunch in great comfort. This statement can be accepted provisionally. This battle deals with the Turk. The Turk when he moves forward approaches with the celerity of a stone chariot going the other way. To be sure, he can carry a height with a wild rush and a roar, but first he has got to play around the question and fool with the enemy and lose some men.

The Turks were merely crawling across the plain toward the height. There was a Greek battery of the inevitable mountain howitzers, and its captain was inhaling more pure joy than had been his for many months. He had a raking fire on a dark slow column of Turkish infantry, and in the late afternoon atmosphere he could see the crimson outburst of shell after shell directly in the midst of it. The broad purple double-stripe on the captain's trousers flashed everywhere amid the men and guns of the battery. He had gone suddenly to his station at middle-rear, and paused there once, when there came to him a tall, pale young man in civilian garb. He was obviously English, and to this distinction was added a wild, wild eye. He carried a large bottle, loudly labelled "Poison," and a blanket.

He addressed the captain in rascally French. "Monsieur," he said, "I have come to take care of the wounded: can you tell me where they are?" The captain went away then and superintended the firing of the two guns of the first section. When he returned to middle-rear, he said in excellent English: "Sir, if you speak in English instead of French I may be able to understand you better." He went away and superintended the firing of the second section. When he returned to middle-rear the pale young man said to him: "Look here; you have insulted me, and I demand satisfaction." The captain went away and superintended the firing of the third section. When he returned he said: "I am sorry if I have offended you, and I can't give you satisfaction because I am very busy now, and so, if you will allow me, it gives me pleasure to apologize at once." He went away to re-fire the first section. The tall, pale youth wandered gloomily and vacantly down the hill, and as straggling soldiers saw him coming with his great bottle of poison clasped in his arms they sheered off.

And now began the infantry fight at the foot of the height. In this light of the concluding day both sides in the conflict were dim to the view. There was a vast amount of smoke, and bullets came and went from everywhere. The whole of this sharp, hard attack was incoherent, and the strength of the drama of it was in this incoherence. There was even no cheering to indicate the success of Turk or Greek. Only the roar of the guns and the terrific crashing of the musketry. It was one of eight attacks that the Turks had made that day, and perhaps the most formidable. The Turks did not come like a flood, nor did the Greeks stand like adamant. It was simply a shifting, changing, bitter, furious struggle, where one could not place odds nor know when to run.

A lot of Turks charged across a field, not in a line or anything approaching it, but in a sort of a herd, and they ran very slowly, very slowly, and with bowed heads. In this charge one could see this formidable precept: "If it is the will of God that I will be killed, why, I will be killed, but if not——" And they ran slowly with the idea of finding out. If they ran rapidly, and took an earthwork and so on, they could do a whole lot before they learned anything of the will of God. But no. They ran slowly, sometimes holding shielding arms up to their faces, and reflectively wondering of God's decision. Now, this is only as it appeared.

One can imagine that a slow charge of this kind over open ground does not stand every chance of success. The side of the ridge from the top almost to the bottom was a snarling, flaming thing. Twenty moments of uproar elapsed, and then there were no Turks in front save a great number of dead ones, and none of these lay close enough for one to see that the fez was red. There was no indication of posture, no expression, no human character—just some small dark blots on a green field. It was the same suggestion always—a battle with the un-defined, with phantoms.

The din did not abate in many other parts of the field, but here, on this height, there was a general pause. There were dead in the trenches, but the living were rejoicing. The new battalion had been placed in trenches, where it had had a fair shot at the charging Turks. It had probably done a great deal of high shooting, but then it was a fact never to be known. Turks had been killed, and everyone who fired a careful shot was in the credit of the repulse. Meanwhile the Turco-German artillery had not ceased its fire, and the quiet celebration in the Greek trenches was conducted with a certain amount of caution. When a shell fell among the rocks it flung dangerous frag-ments of stone in all directions.

A little to the rear, the captain of a mountain battery had called to a trusty corporal who commanded the horse and mule squad, and the corporal brought a bottle of wine. The captain and his subalterns perched on blue ammunition boxes and finished this wine with some bread and cheese from goats' milk. It was a cheerful party.

A venerable colonel of infantry sat on a rock and chaffed his line officers. They stood around him smiling. In the twilight on the height there was, in fact, a general satisfaction. Meanwhile one of a party of four privates who were carrying away the dead body of a Greek major stumbled in the dusk, and his three comrades rebuked him sharply and unreasonably.

There were some mountaineer volunteers in great woolly grey shepherds' cloaks. They were curious figures in the evening light, perfectly romantic if it were not for the modernity of the rifles and the shining lines of cartridges. With the plain a sea of shadow below, and the vague blue troops of Greece about them in the trenches, these men sang softly the wild minor ballads of their hills. As the evening deepened many men curled in their blankets and slept, but these grey-cloaked mountaineers continued to sing. Ultimately the rays of the moon outlined their figures in silver light, and it was not infrequently that shells from the persistent Turco-German batteries threw a sudden red color on their curious garb and on the banner of their village which hung above them. They sang of war, and their songs were new to the sense, reflecting the centuries of their singing, and as the ultimate quiet of night came to the height this low chanting was the only sound. This ended one day at Velestino.

No. 7

THE BLUE BADGE OF COWARDICE

ATHENS, May 11—(By Courier from Chalkis).—Back fell the Greek army, wrathful, sullen, fierce as any victorious army would be when commanded to retreat before the enemy it had defeated.

There was no "God Save the King" in the few cries that went up from Smolenski's men. They knew the grief and indignation of their brave general, and they knew he had to obey the order of Crown Prince Constantine. The men cursed the faint-heartedness of the Prince who will rule them, and the officers turned away because in their hearts was the same bitterness that doubled the weight of the soldiers' equipments.

So the army withdrew, and the Turks came on. The Greeks knew how disastrous this retreat must be. They knew Volo must be occupied by the enemy, and they guessed more might fall because of the incomprehensible order of the King's son.

The Turks are slow by God's requirement, so vast numbers of women and children got safely aboard ships in the harbor of Volo. There was no particular panic, because of the strong Greek fleet in the harbor and the foreign warships.

The foreign consuls all had their flags up and the consulates were crowded in anticipation of the coming of the Turk.

Volo is a beautiful town, a summer resort in time of peace for wealthy Greeks. The houses are gay with awnings and the situation high on the mountain side overlooking the harbor is charming.

Every available ship in the harbor was employed to transport fugitives—except one, the one which above all others should have been employed in the work. This was the English Red Cross ship, and its non-employment was due to a particular and splendid ass, the surgeon in charge. He had some rules—God knows what they were—and he was the kind of fool to whom a rule is a holy thing. This ship came away light when thousands of war victims suffered for the lack of just the aid she could have given. The blame is not on the English Red Cross, but on the accursed idiot who, by the devil's luck, was in charge. I promise myself the pleasure of writing about him later on.

Every Greek battleship was loaded with refugees. Fifteen hundred were on the *Hydra* alone. The condition of these people was pitiable in the extreme. Many of them were original refugees from Larissa and other northern points, who, flying before the march of the Turks, came to Volo as a place of certain harbor. Now they are obliged to flee even from there.

The foreign warships naturally refused to assist the people to safety, but it seems to me that had a United States vessel been there Americans would have regarded such a course as the reverse of natural. The pleasant hypothesis by which the foreigners squared their consciences was that there was no need of flight.

The London *Times* says the Turks are mild, woolly lambs. I saw at Epirus a Greek officer who had fallen wounded into Turkish hands. His body was headless when I saw it, and I do not consider the Turks as woolly lambs. I think the haste of the people rather natural.

Your correspondent left Volo when the advance guard of the Turks reached the hill-tops surrounding the town. The decks of every ship in the harbor except the English Red Cross ship were simply packed with women and children. Most of the men of these families were away fighting. Even the little sail boats and fishing smacks carried a heavy quota.

It was the great sudden evacuation of Volo which I had the luck to prophesy to you two weeks ago.

The Greek naval officers said they would not fire on the Turks because the town is Grecian, though it is expected the Turks will burn it. There will be a curious situation here when the Turks are in possession and the Greek warships lie four hundred yards away. I noticed the Greeks had their torpedo nets ready for lowering.

While the Turks came over the hills the right wing of the Greek army was falling back to Halmyros. Smolenski, I think, is sure to make such a stand there as he did at Velestino. But will it do any good? There is a feeling that should the main army retire from Domokos—and the Greek army is more afraid of such an order from the Crown Prince than it is of the Turks —Smolenski will get that same old order to retreat, regardless of a success at Halmyros.

While I write the glad news has come that the Crown Prince will not retreat further while the army lives. Everybody believes it. If it is true, the big ridge back of Domokos will be drenched with blood. There is where the hard fighting will be done— not at Domokos as the report goes. Domokos can be flanked, but the ridge is ideal for a defending army. It will be a sight worth seeing when the Turkish waves roll up against it.

But that fight is still in the future, and here at hand the scenes on the transports and merchant ships make one tired of war. Women and children are positively in heaps on the decks. They have no food, and they will be landed where they can.

I asked one of the officers how they expected to feed the people. He answered that they did not expect to feed them—that they could not feed them.

I went with a great crowd to Oreos. This town consists of six houses already crowded. The refugees came ashore carrying their household goods. They camped on the fields by great bonfires. These peasant women are patient, suffering in curious silence, while the babies wail on all sides.

This is war—but it is another picture from that we got at the front.

The Greek naval officers, with their eyes full of tears, swore to me the Turks would pay for all this misery. But the Turks probably will not; nobody pays for these things in war.

Eight thousand people at least fled from Volo. Their plight makes a man hate himself for being well fed and having some place to go. For instance, 700 fugitives landed at the village of six houses.

Who will feed them? There is no food. The mind of an American naturally turns to the wealth and charity of his own people. But such charity would be too late. Anyhow, organized American charity would likely proceed like the English Red Cross idiot. It is a case for the opening of skies, but no skies open. I wish I knew what is to become of these poor people. Warships are made to kill men, not to save men; otherwise the foreign warships at Volo would have assisted the stricken people. The Greek officers say the refugees landed at Oreos, Halmyros, and Chalkis will have to wait for provisions to be dispensed by the Government at Athens. My calculation, and I know the elements with which to figure, is that this relief will be six days in coming.

Rumor has it that the army at Domokos is very short of provisions. I do not see many chances for the people outside the war programme getting food.

I cannot guess what the immediate future holds in store for Greece. The Crown Prince's message that he will not fall back again has reinspired the troops. They are tired of falling back. The main body of troops would gladly give the Turks another battle. They accept their reverses with fine impassivity, and will fight well if provisions hold out and ammunition lasts.

The Turks move so sluggishly that no one can tell when they will get anywhere. They took almost three days to make the twenty miles from Velestino to Volo. Such marching gives the Greeks their opportunity.

I told some Greek officers to-day that in our country the Northern army fought for two years without winning a victory. They shrugged their shoulders and mildly said that fighting under such circumstances must be hard work.

Rumors are thick here. Every day a new one appears, generally referring to an intervention by the powers.

To-day we learn that the story has been told of a great panic at Volo. There was no panic; simply a most pitiable emigration.

No. 8

YALE MAN ARRESTED

ATHENS, May 13.—George Montgomery, an American graduate of Yale, '92, was arrested several days ago at the Greek outpost near Pharsala. He was in the company of Baron Bindter, an Austrian, and was arrested for prowling where he had no business.

Bindter is the correspondent of an Austrian newspaper, who was arrested once by officials of the insurgents in Crete for calmly breaking the rules of war.

At the time of their arrest the two men were wandering between the lines with no particular care where they were. Montgomery wore a Turkish fez and had a Turkish servant.

When they were brought to Athens the populace was inflamed at the sight of the two men, who appeared like Turkish spies. The people spat upon them.

The men have been released. Montgomery is correspondent of the London *Standard*.

No. 9

THE DOGS OF WAR

ON THE left of the pup, lines of Greek infantry lay on the high, bare hills, firing without intermission. Gray smoke went up and backward from all these lines. Sometimes wounded men came from there and passed the pup as he sat reflecting in the roadway. Directly in his front a mountain battery of the Greeks was roaring, and the horses and mules of the command were browsing the grass in a sheltered place not far from the pup. Some soldiers in blue overcoats lay in an upturned furrow of brown trenches.

If the pup had studied the vast green plain on his right he would have seen black lines and lines still fainter than black, and these lines were all Turks. Frequently a crescendo of hoots and hurtling noises was in the air above him and the shells crashed as they struck. Moreover, there was sometimes a curious singing of great insects. But for all these things the pup did not care.

He was a little pup, not larger than a kitten, but he was fat and fairly smothered in long white wool, marked here and there with black, and he had every indifference of a fat pup. Two soldiers came that way on their return to the front, and, seeing him, paused. One stooped and offered him gently a bit of hard biscuit, but he had been used to other food, and, with the insolence of babyhood, he scorned the generosity of these men who had stopped under fire to give him assistance. They laughed then, and stroked his long hair and went away to their business.

The pup's interest was always the thing directly under his nose. He was really in the battle of Velestino, but what he wanted to do was to waddle in his curious way among the stones of the roadway and smell at them and fall over them whenever he forgot that he was top heavy. Although he was not larger than a cake of soap, he had something elephantine in his movement. His little legs were still very weak, and he sprawled and spraddled over the road in a way that one would expect of a baby elephant. Once a cavalryman with orders galloped past him, and a hoof of the gray charger missed him by little, but he didn't care for that, either. He was busy with his geological survey.

The *Journal* correspondent came along from the firing line at that time and stopped when he saw the dog. The dog had been trying to scratch his near ear with his off hind leg, but he stopped when he saw the *Journal* correspondent. They looked at each other in reflective silence. The pup had a crafty eye, and he put his head on one side and surveyed the correspondent with much attention to detail. Another shell came close then, and your correspondent said: "Come on, pup." He took the pup in his arms.

The dog was naturally named Velestino at once. There was a thought in the correspondent's mind of calling him Loot. But then he was not really loot. He was simply a Greek pup deserted by his relatives and friends in a most trying hour, who had accepted the assistance of a correspondent of the *New York Journal*. His home had probably been in one of the stone huts that stood here and there along the road, now all lonely. His owners had probably scuttled out at word of the coming of the Turks. But he didn't care about this, either. He simply lolled on the correspondent's arm and blinked fatly at the passing landscape.

When the correspondent arrived at where his horses awaited him, he gave the pup Velestino into the hands of his Greek boy and stood and admonished him sternly for five minutes about the inadvisability of losing that pup. The boy grinned, and took Velestino in his arms.

Later the pup got under a particularly heavy artillery fire. While the correspondent's party were crossing a bit of plain, the Turks opened fire on a near-by house. One would have thought they had opened on the pup, because they came nearer to the pup than they did to the house. There was some excitement. The stragglers in the road scurried everywhere.

The correspondent had a bit of trouble with his horse, which had been hurt in the back by some kind of fragment, and when it was all over, he looked around for the pup, the two servants and the other horses, and there was none.

Late that night in Volo a knock came to the correspondent's door, and, as he called out, it opened and the Greek boy appeared, with a bow and a grin.

"Where is the pup?" said the correspondent, instantly.

The Greek boy had brought a great piece of shell, which he said had almost killed him, and he exhibited it proudly.

"Where is the pup?"

The boy said he was sure he was going to be killed when he heard the shell, and he now considered his escape to be a miracle. The correspondent arose impressively to his feet. "Where is the pup?"

Well—poor Velestino—poor correspondent—they were united only to be immediately parted. The boy said that he had brought the pup to Volo and had given it to a man to hold while he unsaddled his horse. The man ran away with Velestino.

There were dispatches to be sent, and the wires were muddled in a way that was simply scandalous. The correspondent left for Athens, reflecting from time to time upon the virtues of his lost pup.

Volo is, ordinarily, 300,000 miles from Athens. In time of war, it is the square of 300,000. Every route is impossible. All the steamers are on war business. All the carriages have vanished. There are no horses. It requires more energy to travel now in Greece than it does to do a three months' campaign. The correspondent struggled as far as Chalkis, with phenomenal good fortune. He was taking his breakfast in the restaurant there when he observed a peasant come in and walk toward the rear of the place. This man had a pup inside his shirt, and the little woolly head projected. The correspondent said to his dragoman: "That is my dog." The dragoman laughed. "There are a million dogs like that in Greece, sir."

"No, there ain't. I tell you that is my dog."

As the peasant with the pup disappeared through a door in the rear, the correspondent and the dragoman rushed after him. In a courtyard they found the peasant delivering the pup to another dragoman, the servant of an English correspondent. But the correspondent took the pup. "It is my dog."

"No, it isn't," said the dragoman of the English correspondent. "I got him at Volo."

"You got him at Volo, did you? Well, I got him at Velestino. He belongs to the *New York Journal* and it doesn't matter what you say, you can't have him."

"Well——"

"Shut up."

"Well, he has cost me two drachms for his food and care. Pay me that and it is all right."

Velestino thus rejoined the correspondent. His hotel bills were paid and he was invited to some bread and milk. The rounds he fought with this bread and milk were simply too exciting for words. He was not satisfied with putting all of his features in the plate. He waded up to his knees, and his subsequent cargo was altogether out of proportion to his displacement. His shape became suddenly like that of a toy balloon. But it filled him with a sort of glad satisfaction which was noticeable in his rollicking tipsy-sailor walk.

On his way to Athens the pup received constant ovations. The Greek boy was on the box, and he elaborated his own experiences, and incidentally the experiences of the pup. People gazed at Velestino with awe. He was such a wee thing that the correspondent was not sure whether he was going to grow to be a cow or a caterpillar, but the kilted mountaineers that studied him said that he was of the famous shephard dog breed of the Greeks and was destined to be a big dog.

"Wait until he grows," they said, "and then, if even a hundred bad men approach your house, you need not fear." Looking at Velestino, asleep in a fluffy ball in the carriage, the correspondent rather thought that the number of bad men was over the limit.

At Thebes, while the correspondent lunched, Velestino waddled, or, rather, fell around the floor of the cafe. The boys of the village congregated about him, and the Greek child, who thought he had been almost killed, dilated on the experiences of himself and the dog. All these popular honors the pup ac-

cepted with his usual sublime indifference. He interested himself in certain surprising physical eccentricities. For instance,
every time he tried to run he fell on his nose. When he tried
to catch his tail he fell on his shoulder. In fact, he was so much
of a pup that he could fall in almost any direction with equal
abandon. These manoeuvres were also conducted without regard to the interest and admiration of the populace.

People do not usually talk about dogs, and so, before he
reached Athens, he was easily the most famous dog in Greece.
In Athens itself he was put up at the best hotel, and the honors
he received befitted his social position.

At present he is with your correspondent. He has a personal
attendant engaged at a fabulous salary. He is well-known here
already, and his appearance on the street causes popular
demonstration. But he don't care.

No. 10

STEPHEN CRANE TELLS OF WAR'S HORRORS

ATHENS, May 22 (On Board the St. Marina, Which Left Chalkis,
Greece, May 18.)—We are carrying the wounded away from
Domokos. There are eight hundred bullet-torn men aboard,
some of them dead. This steamer was formerly used for trans-
porting sheep, but it was taken by the Government for ambulance purposes. It is not a nice place for a well man, but war
takes the finical quality out of its victims, and the soldiers do
not complain. The ship is not large enough for its dreadful
freight. But the men must be moved, and so 800 bleeding
soldiers are jammed together in an insufferably hot hole, the
light in which is so faint that we cannot distinguish the living
from the dead.

Above the vibration of the machinery and the churning of
the waves we have listened all night to the cries and groans
of those who stopped the Turkish bullets in the trenches.
Those who died, and there were not a few, could not be re-

moved, and the corpses lay among the living men, shot through arm, chest, leg or jaw. The soldiers endured it with composure, I thought. Their indifference will never cease to be a marvel to me.

Near the hatch where I can see them is a man shot through the mouth. The bullet passed through both cheeks. He is asleep with his head pillowed on the bosom of a dead comrade. He had been awake for days, doubtless, marching on bread and water, to be finally wounded at Domokos and taken aboard this steamer. He is too weary to mind either his wound or his awful pillow. There is a breeze on the gulf and the ship is rolling, heaving one wounded man against the other.

Some of the wounded were taken off at Chalkis; the others will be taken to Athens, because there is not room for them in the Chalkis hospitals. Already we have traveled a night and a day under these cheerful circumstances that war brings to some of those who engage in it.

When we with our suffering freight arrived at Piraeus they were selling the newspaper extra, and people were shouting "Hurrah, hurrah for war!" And while they shouted a seemingly endless procession of stretchers proceeded from the ship, the still figures upon them.

I have seen Greek officers watch without a murmur women and children flocking away from their homes, fearing the Turks. And I saw these turn away. I heard even an English doctor groan deep in his chest when his eyes surveyed the ship's cargo. Words are not adequate to describe it. Yet the wounded soldiers themselves retained that marvelous composure, indifference, or whatever else you choose to call it.

There is just enough moaning and wailing to make a distinct chorus above the creaking of the deck timbers over that low hole where the lamps are smoking.

This is Wednesday, I think. We are at Stylidia. All day there have been clouds of dust upon the highroad over which Smolenski's division is retreating toward Thermopylae. The movement completely uncovers this place, and the Turks are advancing from Halmyros.

What I saw at Volo is repeated here. Every one is terror-stricken. The *Journal's* dispatch boat, at Bay St. Marina, where the field hospital is located, was requested by the chief surgeon to go to Stylidia and save the last of the medicines of the field hospital. The dispatch boat took a schooner in tow and went to Stylidia, carrying an extra crew from the Greek warship. While the medicines were being put aboard I went ashore, where the last few women and children crowded the quay.

One long line of dust marked the road across the green plain where Smolenski marched away. And the people stared at this and then at the great mountains in back of the town, whence the Turks were coming. All the household goods of the city were piled on the pier. The town was completely empty, except for two battalions of Smolenski's rear guard, who slept in the streets, worn out, after a twenty hours' march. We loaded the steamer and schooner with women and children and household goods. The anchor was raised by two man-of-war's men, three fugitives and one Greek Red Cross nurse.

As we steamed away Smolenski's rear guard also left Stylidia. The beautiful little town, with its streets shaded by May trees and lemons and its ripening gardens, seemed to be putting on its best air, as to bid farewell to its citizens and to receive the Turks. The people on board are not looking at their city. They are asking if the Turks have reached Lamia and whether Thermopylae is safe.

With our departure Stylidia became as silent as a city of the dead. Its next inhabitants will be the Turkish soldiers. The steamer and schooner carried 183 people to safety, where the warships rode at anchor opposite Thermopylae. The women and children were drenched when we landed them in the small boats. There was a strong wind, and it was difficult, but our crew and the sailors from the warships worked like Trojans from the shore and back again. There were about thirty women with babies in their arms among the fugitives. The poor babies wailed and the mothers groaned. There were a lot of little girls, however, who sat quietly, not understanding what was the matter.

The refugees generally seemed dazed. The old women particularly. Uprooted from the spot they had lived so long, they kept their red eyes turned toward the shore as they sat on their rough bundles of clothes and blankets. Among the property we carried away was a goat and a calf, both protesting loudly. Our deck looked like an emigrant quarter of an Atlantic liner, except for the sick soldiers. The *Journal* steamer then went to St. Marina and landed the hospital stores.

Lieutenant-Colonel Caracolas came aboard there, much disturbed because some bread had been left at Stylidia. He was at the head of the commissary department of Smolenski's division. He asked us if we would try to get the bread. We agreed and found another schooner. We told the captain we were going to take him to Stylidia and he flatly refused to go. There was no time for argument; our extra bluejackets, seven in number, promptly stormed the schooner and took it by assault. I guess the captain of the schooner is talking of the outrage yet. The bluejackets got us a hawser, raised the anchor and we towed the protesting schooner back to Stylidia, with the captain on the bow, gesticulating violently throughout the voyage. Incidentally, we never found the bread.

Stylidia, now utterly deserted, was as dismal as a graveyard at midnight.

We steamed back to St. Marina and found Dr. Belline, chief surgeon of the Greek army. He was worried about the safety of the hospital at St. Marina, but no orders had been issued for its removal. The obvious thing to do was to get orders from Thermopylae headquarters, and we carried the doctor across the gulf. He got the orders promptly and we took him back to St. Marina and took aboard the wounded men and Red Cross nurses of the hospital. The last boat had left the shore when a soldier came and said something to the interpreter, who shook his head negatively. The soldier turned quietly away.

On board the steamer your correspondent idly asked the interpreter what the soldier had said, and he answered that the soldier had asked for transportation to Chalkis on the ground that he was sick. The interpreter thought the man too well to go on a boat containing wounded men.

We sent ashore and after some trouble found the soldier. He was ill with fever, was shot through the calf of the leg and his knees were raw from kneeling in the trenches. We added him to our list of wounded and then steamed away for Chalkis.

There is more of this sort of thing in war than glory and heroic death, flags, banners, shouting and victory.

No. 11

GREEKS WAITING AT THERMOPYLÆ

LAMIA, May 22, VIA ATHENS, May 23.—Still backward fall
the Greek soldiers. First it was Velestino, then Domokos, next
it will be Thermopylae. They have had a hard time of it. Their
fiercest fighting has been rewarded, not with victory, but with
orders to retreat. They have had a fierce, outnumbering enemy
before them and a rear fire from the vacillating Crown Prince.
They have had a campaign that has made officers cry like
hysterical women with weariness and disappointment; they
have marched uselessly day and night, have starved and suffered and lost, and yet they are stout-hearted and anxious for
another fight.

The main body of the army has already marched away for
the new position. Only the Thermopylae division, 15,000
strong, remains at Lamia. I have grown to know this division.
They are mainly Evzones. They are always last when the
Greek army retreats and first when it advances.

Here they are in their old position, the rest of the Greek
army miles away, and the Turks so near that their advance is
plainly visible from the top of the old Acropolis, about four
miles away. As they came closer I recognized them as Circassian
cavalry. There are the elements of a first-class scrap right
here in the range of my field glass.

There is a rumor all through the town and the army of an
armistice, but the Greeks have no thought that the war is over.
They all believe they will fight again soon and are glad of it.
There is no let-up of preparations for a stout resistance to the
Turks at the historic pass. Nine fresh battalions arrived here
late this evening from Athens, and they are eager for a chance.
I hope the armistice will be made to last long enough to give
the Greek infantry some rest. They need it.

Plans for truces are nice things, but I really don't know that
they are always possible of fulfilment. There is a strong prob-

ability that the next fight will be begun by Turkish irregulars. These are men from the wild mountains of Albania, who are in the war business exclusively. They don't know an armistice from a pie or a truce from a trilobite, and the shooting will surely go on with them in the game.

I hear the most dreadful tales of their cruelty, but have not been able to substantiate one. If the stories are true, the cruelties probably occur miles out on the flanks, where the Turkish irregulars raid villages.

I have been asking Greek soldiers if they were not tired of it; if they did not want the war stopped.

"No! we want to fight more," has been the invariable reply.

The officers, or many of them, on the other hand, seem to have had enough. Ask them the same question and they shrug their shoulders and say:

"What can we do? It is better to cease."

Maybe they appreciate the situation better than the men in the ranks; maybe the hasty orders to retreat that are always coming are more significant to them. Whatever the reason, they are willing to stop.

None of the soldiers admits the possibility of losing Thermopylae. Really, the new position is very strong. Although the pass has been widened and much changed since Leonidas' fight, it is still an ideal place to hold an enemy in check and here, if the war goes on according to the rules of the game and the supreme authority lets the Greek army do what is in it to do, the advance of the Turks may be dammed. I would like to write a dispatch telling of a full-blown Greek victory for a change.

No. 12

MY TALK WITH "SOLDIERS SIX"

ATHENS, June 1.—Since everybody has interviewed the King and the Crown Prince and Smolenski, it occurred to me that it might be well to interview the private soldier. There is more of him than there is of the King or of the Crown Prince or of Smolenski, and as he has had rather a hand in whatever has been done, it seemed fair to give him a chance to express his opinion. Here are some interviews with the Grecian soldier.

They may be this, they may be that, they may be anything, but they are reported with care and some conscience, and perhaps they contain a suggestion from time to time of a viewpoint which has not been particularly heeded.

One soldier sat by the roadside nursing a sore foot. I gave him a cigarette and he smiled. I said to him: "How many fights have you been in?"

"Three. One on the frontier and then at Pharsala and at Domokos."

"How did you feel in your first fight?"

"Well, when the first bullets came—just one, two, three—I didn't care. Afterward when they made more noise, I grew afraid, but yet afterward it was all right."

"How did you feel in your other battles?"

"I didn't think about it."

"Did you ever see a comrade that you knew intimately killed at your side?"

"No; that has not happened."

"Do you want to fight more?"

"Yes; certainly."

"Do all the other private soldiers want to fight more?"

"I think so."

"A great deal is said of the army wishing to stop the war. It does not, then?"

"The officers may want to stop."

"Are not the officers of your regiment good officers?"

"No."

"Why?"

"When an order comes to retreat they go first."

"But in action they stand up back of the trenches. That is not easy. And then see how many officers are killed."

"Well, this may be in other regiments."

"What effect have these consecutive orders to retreat had upon the soldiers?"

"Oh, it has broken their hearts."

"Whose was the fault?"

"The Crown Prince, I think."

"Is not he a good soldier?"

"No. He is forever turning pale and ordering us all to fall back."

"But you like the King?"

"No!"

"Why not?"

"He is not a good Greek. To be sure he was not born a Greek, but he is King, and a King of the Greeks ought to be more Greek than the Greeks."

"Do your comrades feel as you?"

"Yes."

"If your regiment is ordered to Athens after the war, what will it do? Will there be trouble?"

"I don't know. For my part, I want to go quietly home."

"How do your comrades feel about it?"

"Who knows what may happen?"

In Lamia there was an euzone, one of the kilted mountaineers, with a small rakishly piratical scarlet fez. He sat alone, because in the first place he was a man of the hills and in the second place because the other soldiers in the place were town-bred and knew him as we know a "hayseed." And in the third place he sat alone because he considered that the euzonoi had done the best of the fighting. He was a swarthy, flash-eyed chap, holding himself like a chief and paying no heed to the chatter about him. I said to him:

"Which is harder—marching or fighting?"

"Marching," he answered promptly.

"How many fights have you been in?"

"Oh, about ten."

"How did you feel in your first fight?"

"I am not sure. There were seventy of us holding in check a battalion of Turks. It was in a pass of the mountains. I think I was wondering how long we could hold them in check."

"How about the other fights?"

"Oh, perhaps they were the same. At Velestino I had fun.

We killed many Turks. Only when we covered that accursed retreat of ours were we hurt any."

"Do you want to fight more?"

"Certainly."

"Do all your comrades want to fight more?"

"Of course."

"Are the officers of your regiment good officers?"

"Yes."

"What effect have these successive orders to retreat had upon the soldiers?"

"We hate them. Often and often we are ordered to retreat, I tell you, when it is absurd. The euzonoi are usually ordered to cover these retreats, too. It is harder than any battle if the Turks come quickly."

"Whose was the fault?"

"Our leader."

"Whom do you mean?"

"Well, our regiment is under Smolenski. I don't mean him. He is a great chieftain. I mean the head of the whole army."

"Who?"

"The head of the whole army."

"Why is it his fault?"

"He orders all these retreats. He has taught us to retreat. The men of the hills did not know how."

"Well?"

"Well?"

"Um—after the war will you go home directly?"

"No. How can I go home if the war ends this way? I am disgraced. I am the shamed son of my father. I cannot go home."

"What do you wish to do?"

"I wish to fight the Turk until Greece is saved from dishonor. We are not beaten. At Larissa, at Velestino we were not beaten. Yet here we are at Lamia."

"But you must understand the importance of flank movements. Perhaps you were doing well on your part of the line, but how about the flanks? The Turks are many. We had in our army once a man named Sherman who used the same way of winning that the Turks use against you now. He made finally a great victory."

"I know nothing of the man you name, but I know we were not flanked at Velestino. We were not flanked at Domokos."

My third victim was a very young corporal in the infantry. He was of rather wealthy people in Athens. He had been educated in France, and was altogether a new type to find in any army, save this Greek army. Here you are likely to find anybody in the ranks. On second thought, it bears a resemblance in this way to our armies during the Civil War.

"Which is harder—marching or fighting?"

"Marching."

"What impressed you in your first battle?"

"I was much afraid of the shells."

"And in later battles?"

"I was still afraid of the shells."

"Did not the whistling of the bullets affect you more?"

"No."

"You have been under very heavy artillery fire?"

"Yes."

"Where?"

"At Domokos."

"Did you see anybody hurt by a shell?"

"Yes. A splinter laid open an officer's cheek."

"Was the infantry fire heavy in your front?"

"Not very heavy."

"What was the loss in your battalion from the Turkish infantry fire?"

"We lost twenty-eight men in killed and wounded."

"All from the infantry fire?"

"All but the officer who was struck by a splinter."

"It strikes me that you would be about twenty-seven times more afraid of the bullets than of the shells."

"Yes, but then the shells are very loud."

"Do you want to fight any more?"

"Yes."

"Why?"

"Because Greece has not had a fair chance. She has been betrayed."

"By whom?"

"I cannot say. We think it was somebody high in command."

"How high in command?"

"Well—very high."

"Do your comrades also wish to fight more?"

"Yes."

"Do they think Greece has been betrayed?"

"Yes."

"By whom?"

"They think as I think."

In front of the doors of a house that was being used as a field hospital many stretchers were crowded awaiting their turns, as carriages in front of a New York theatre around eight o'clock crowd and await their turns. The hospital was simply packed already and these stretchers remained a long time waiting. The prostrate figures of the wounded men were for the most part very still, quietly still, already like the dead. Their faces were yellow from suffering—seldom pallid, almost always yellow. Blankets usually covered them, but sometimes a blue trousers-leg with dark blood stains upon it projected from beneath the covering. The men were flat on their backs and looked at nothing. Through the door of the hospital could be seen a white-clothed surgeon, erect, serene, but swift-fingered. He was calm enough to be sinister and terrible in this scene of blood. He had every necessary casual mannerism of a surgeon facing his patients, but it was ghoulish anyhow. This thing was a banquet for him.

Sometimes a man came out with his arm in a sling or his head bandaged or his jaw tightly bound. They went off somewhere and sat down. Carriers would come out and get a stretcher and take it in to the surgeons. The business of the hospital went on in this way, smoothly, for hours and hours, fed regularly as a mill is fed by water, by the stream of wounded from the scene of the late battle. A hundred yards away there was some long grass and daisies and a peasant asleep in the shade of olive trees, while his donkey browsed near him.

Four men had brought an euzone on a stretcher and laid him on the outskirts of the crowd of stretchers thronged about the hospital door. This euzone had been shot through the leg just above the knee. He did not lay flat on his back like the others. He had turned his body and was reclining on one elbow. On one side of him was a man shot vitally, and the labored movement of his breathing caused the blanket over his chest to rise and fall. On the other side of the euzone was an officer shot through the head—worse than a corpse, because his eyes looked here, there, everywhere in slow sweeps.

The euzone was smoking a cigarette. He had drawn the blanket up to shield the fact evidently, as an ordinary precaution lest some surgeon detect it and upbraid him for a thing so utterly in opposition to the etiquette of his condition. But he was having a bully time with that cigarette. He was having more fun than a barrel of monkeys. Every puff was long and profound and comforting. Perhaps he had been far out in the front—these euzonoi are always in front—where there was no tobacco, and then he had been wounded and brought here— here he could crib a cigarette. The wound in his leg be blowed.

When the correspondent saw this euzone smoking a cigarette at this time and in this place it was to him a beautiful thing and he hoped the surgeon wouldn't catch him. He wanted to give the euzone another cigarette, or some tobacco and papers or a match—indeed anything to help on this crime—but he did not dare. The correspondent simply grinned at the euzone and the euzone grinned at the correspondent.

"Does your wound hurt you?"

"No."

"Is it a bad wound?"

"I think so."

"Well, then, perhaps it hurts you?"

"Perhaps it does."

"Are you satisfied? Are you going home?"

"No. I think I will be well soon. Then I will come back."

"Which is harder—marching or fighting?"

"Well, I have seen hard fighting, but I think long marches are worse than fights."

"What do you think of the Turkish artillery?"

"I don't understand why they don't kill everybody. But they

do not. The cannon always affect me a little, but I have never seen anyone hurt by them. Only a horse."

"Are all these orders to retreat good, do you think?"

"One of them."

"Which?"

"The order to retreat from Domokos. We were lost if we tried to hold Domokos. I know. My regiment was out on the left flank."

"Whom do you blame for the other retreats?"

"The royal family. They are cowards. They are not Greeks. They are foreigners."

"Did you ever kill a Turk?"

"Oh, many."

"Are you sure?"

"Oh, certainly."

"How do you know?"

"Well, I think I have killed many, but I am not sure. Anyhow, I know that I killed one, because it was in the mountains and my shot was the only shot fired from our side then, and I saw him tumble down the rocks."

"What is your business in time of peace?"

"I take care of a flock in the hills."

They came for the euzone then. It was his turn. They carried him toward this dreadful portal. It was the gates of Hades. As the bearers drew near it the euzone took one more puff at his cigarette and then tossed it away.

In Thurka Pass a member of the foreign legion was filling his canteen from a spring. He really held rank in one of the standing armies of Europe and had enlisted in this foreign legion in order to get some experience. The foreign legion in this war has provided its members with rather a deal of experience.

"Well, how do you like it?"

"The deuce! It is a great bore—all these retreats."

"Who do you blame?"

"I am inclined to think it is the Crown Prince."

"Is not he a good soldier?"

"He is a duffer."

"Do the Greek troops fight well?"

"When they are well led they fight as well as any troops."

"To your mind the difficulty is where, then?"

"General funk at headquarters. The retreat from Larissa was conducted in the most absurd fashion. Do you know, the staff was in such a hurry that they forgot the foreign legion entirely. Forgot to give us any orders whatever. We saw the whole army going back, and there we were without an order. Our captain said: 'Well, we will stay here until we see the Turks coming, anyhow.' We waited a decent time and no Turks came, and then we plodded off down to Velestino."

"Do you want to fight any more?"

"Yes, under certain circumstances. I haven't got enough fighting, but I have got enough of this kind of management."

"You are certain that it is the bad management of the Greek army and not altogether the good management of the Turkish army that causes these situations?"

"Yes."

Ten soldiers in Lamia were pounding on the closed and barred doors of a café. It was after the battle of Domokos, and Lamia was even then almost a deserted city.

The doors remained obdurate and the soldiers waxed enthusiastic in assault. One man brought a great stone and banged it against a door. The door broke and fell aside, disclosing inside doors of glass. Another soldier fetched a small wooden table from the plaza and hurled it through the glass doors. Then they reached in, unlocked the doors and entered the café.

The proprietor went wild and woolly mad. The soldiers said they wanted coffee. The proprietor swore by his gods that they could have no coffee in his shop. The soldiers said they wanted coffee. The proprietor called upon heaven to curse him and nine generations if he gave these men coffee. The soldiers said that they wanted coffee. The proprietor said that he had no coffee. The soldiers said that they wanted coffee.

Now there is a trick known to the Oriental. This is it. Suddenly the proprietor went to the charcoal furnaces and began to prepare the coffee, meanwhile chatting with the soldiers as amiably as a village priest. His rage was all forgotten—forgotten, mind you; not hidden, but forgotten. Nor did the soldiers for their part reproach him for his previous obstinacy. The incident was closed. It was now as if they had entered the coffee-house in the ordinary way and ordered coffee from the ordinary polite proprietor. This is the trick known to the Oriental. The correspondent entered the breach made by the ten soldiers and ordered coffee. There was a soldier there among the ten of a type I know. In the photograph galleries in Athens there are many portraits of bearded gentlemen in kilts festooned with five hundred yards of cartridge belt and gripping their Gras rifles ferociously. By the Athenians they are supposed to be away killing battalion after battalion of Turks. I know that type too, and I have never seen them do anything. Generally speaking, they are a pack of humpty-dumpties. But this brown-faced quiet lad, with his lamb-like eyes and gentle considerate ways, I know him too, and he will stick to a trench, and stick and stick and go without water and food and fight long and still stick until the usual orders come to fall back. Barring the genuine euzone, this gentle lad is the best man in Greece, even if he does wear the regulation uniform. When he gets up on his legs and retires he may get shot in the back by the close Turks, and if he be taken to a hospital some philanthropic doctor from London may, when observing his wound, think that he is a coward. But this is just in passing and wholly exceptional. The main point is that this lad is a soldier, and he has fought as a proportion of the French fought from Alsace back to Paris.

"Which is harder—marching or fighting?"

"Marching—as we have been marched."

"Are you tired of fighting?"

"Oh, no."

"How about these retreats? Who is to blame?"

"I cannot say exactly, but we all believe it is the fault of the Crown Prince."

"Do you remember the cries of 'À Berlin!' and that afterward the French people blamed the whole affair on the heads of the State, when as a matter of truth it was everybody's fault that they were well thrashed?"

"Yes, I remember. But even if it was everybody's fault in that case it is not consequently proven that it is everybody's fault in this case. We think not."

"It may be something of a general opinion throughout the world that your case in Greece parallels the previous case in France."

"If by the world you mean Europe, we have learned to expect injustice and stupidity from the Powers of Europe, and if that is their opinion, as you say, I am perfectly willing to recognize it as an exhibition of intellect."

"What do you think of the successive retreats?"

"The Crown Prince always thinks his army is beaten long before it is really beaten. Some men learn war in a day. These are the men who immediately plunge right in it up to their necks. There are others who never learn it because they always remain on the edge of battle merely. The Crown Prince is one of these last. He has never been further than the edge, and his immediate staff are known to be so careful of the person of His Highness that they seldom leave him to go closer to war themselves."

"You are severe."

"I am a soldier. I have been fortunate enough to have been wounded for Greece. I have lived on nothing practically for months, and marched many miles and fought a few battles. I have a right to name any man who I am sure has not done his duty by Greece, and I name the Crown Prince."

"Did not he say, or at least was he not reported to have said at Domokos that there he would stand or fall with his men?"

"Yes, such was the report. But where is Domokos now? It is in the hands of the Turks. As before, the Crown Prince thought that he was beaten when he was not beaten. These quotable sentiments are sometimes unfortunate. I know from experience."

"Why?"

"Well, when I left Athens there was a considerable celebration by my family and friends. Tears and flowers, added to a Spartan injunction from my mother. I believe I replied with a Spartan sentence, too. It is very difficult."

"When all these disappointed troops return to Athens what will they do?"

"I do not know."

"Will they wreak vengeance?"

"Perhaps."

"Upon whom?"

"Upon the King."

No. 13

THE MAN IN THE WHITE HAT

A GREAT crowd had gathered in the Place de la Constitution, in front of the royal palace, because it was understood that the editor of one of the Athenian journals was to come and address the populace from a position in front of a well-known café. Over the tops of some trees and above a stone terrace reared the quiet dwelling of the King, its windows all heavily curtained as if it had closed its eyes purposely to this scene in the square below it. The old building was sallow in the glare of the sun. A string of tramcars was forever tooling one way or the other way on the avenue which crossed on the terrace at the middle of the square, and dust from the travel blew white across the face of the palace. The crowd when they looked up the slant of the plaza could see a little sentry-box, and in it an euzone of the Royal Guard, framed as a mummy is framed in its case.

The editor was late. He was also a deputy, and as the Chamber was then in session he was supposed to be engaged there. The crowd did not display much impatience while awaiting him. For one thing, a swarm of newsboys suddenly came racing around the corner hoarsely shouting as charging savages might shout. They punged headlong into this concentration of their prey, dispensing papers and making change with rapidity, meanwhile yelling. This onslaught incited the crowd to bestow their interest elsewhere for a certain time, and it came to pass that when the hero of the minute finally appeared it took rather long for the news to reach the Athenians, who were standing calmly in their places and reading.

He had white hair. He was almost venerable. He had the mobile mouth of a poet and the glance of surpassing vanity. He wore a tall hat, grey in scheme, molded in a curious form. We usually lay the burden of responsibility for this shape upon the men of 1840, or of any date which lies far enough behind us. But it was an impressively-shaped hat. It was the hat of violence. It was the hat of insurrection. It proclaimed terror. In New York this hat would foreshadow the cessation of the cable-car, the disappearance of the postman, the subterranean concealment of the cook, the supreme elevation of the price of beer—all the horrors of municipal war. No one could wear this terrible and revolutionary hat unless he was a deputy of the Two-Miles-beyond-the-Extreme-Edge of the Radicals. Where this hat of anarchy and inhumanity appears there comes change. If you study the history of the famous revolutions you will be taught to tremble at this hat. In the black sea of men this floating hat glowed, glowed with threats.

There was at first a great deal of cheering by some twenty men who seemed to be the immediate escort of the white hat. Their enthusiasm was imparted gradually. After a time the welcome was general. A great cry rolled up from the square. It brought people swiftly to the windows of the hotels that fronted on the square.

The man in the white hat mounted a small iron café-table. It was like a pedestal. Suddenly the white hat shone high above the crowd. The journalist and deputy was about to begin his speech when there was a sudden new onslaught of newsboys, whose yells precluded any chance of his being heard. He was obliged to remain quietly on his little table until these wolves had sated themselves upon the money of the crowd. In the sentry-box near the palace steps, was still the immovable and indifferent figure of the euzone of the Royal Guard. In the clear air one could see plainly the fissures in the mountain afar off behind the palace and this mountain rearing above the sallow dwelling of the King, was beginning to turn faintly purple, a prophecy of evening.

Finally the man in the white hat was enabled to begin his

oration. He was interrupted by cheers from time to time. His incendiary hat bobbed from the ferocity of his gestures. Why was Greece shamed? Whose fault was it? He would go to the King—he would speak to the King—now—this instant—and ask him why was Greece shamed? What treacherous serpent had coiled in the path of Greece? And let the King answer!

A mighty roar came from the crowd or from a part of the crowd. Really, one could never tell how many people were seriously in the thing and how many were there only to see it. And amid these loud acclamations the hero of the minute was helped down from his table, and escorted by hundreds of his countrymen began a formidable march upon the palace of the King.

As the throng swarmed out upon the trodden place directly in front of the palace, the euzone on guard came out of his sentry-box and began to pace deliberately up and down in front of the steps. He did not look at the advancing crowd or heed it in any way.

The deputy left his myriad followers and went to the palace door. The euzone, a step above, walked thoughtfully to and fro before them.

A murmur arose at the back of the crowd. It was the audible machinery, the temper of the people, revolving and revolving toward turbulence. The throng was spread out like a wind-shaken lake to this one sentry who paced slowly before it.

Once the humming of voices in its crescendo almost reached the point of action. Then this kilted soldier, this simple child of the hills, darted a look at the crowd, and this look was so full of scorn, deep and moving scorn, that it must have been felt to the pits of their stomachs.

He stooped and picked from the ground a handful of pebbles. He raised his arm and, still profoundly deliberate and with supreme disdain, this solitary figure on the palace steps flung the handful of pebbles straight into the upturned faces of the Athenians.

Meanwhile the hero of the minute was met at the door by an old servitor. In a voice full of dignity and quiet strength the hero of the minute said: "I wish to see the King."

The old servitor replied to him tranquilly with this objection: "The King does not receive to-day."

There was a moment of silence while the peaceful old servitor stood with his hand on the door.

There are few statesmen that have been met on the threshold of an ambitious success by the cool words: "The King does not receive to-day." The hero of the minute stood irresolute. The servitor stood waiting. "Oh—um," said the statesman at last. "Well——" He went away.

When the white hat reappeared to the crowd they cheered clamorously. With the same quiet dignity which had marked his bearing throughout the more trying part of the incident the man of the white hat took his seat in a landau which his admirers had brought for him. As he passed through the streets his trooping followers cheered and cheered the victor, and from time to time he modestly lifted in recognition his tall white hat.

No. 14

A PORTRAIT OF SMOLENSKI

THERE are no illustrated papers in Greece but the war has developed a great and breathless movement in lithographs. They hang in every shop window and upon the day of some new issue there is always more or less popular excitement over the particular feat in art of the moment. As can be seen from the appended illustrations these pictures are strictly immense. Perhaps the greatest of all in breadth of treatment is the one called "The bombardment of Prevesa." It has breadth of treatment in a large degree because the scene of the festivities really extends over a goodly portion of the Turkish province of Epirus. Judging from an ordinary estimate of distance and of the stature of men the soldiers in this picture are about one mile high. Prevesa is denominated No. 1 and is that extraordinary collection of pink and white candy houses on the

left. Arta is thirty five miles from Prevesa under ordinary circumstances but it is plain that the Greek soldiers who are
crossing the pontoon can sprint down there in about two minutes.

The famous stone bridge at Arta which was the scene of so
many attacks by both Greek and Turk is numbered 9. The pontoon bridge is ten miles down the river from Arta and the
soldiers who are crossing there are chasing the horde of
Turks through the defile in the hills leading towards Janina.

Perhaps the anguish in red and green and blue which represents the fight at Velestino is not so notable for breadth of
treatment but at any rate it is a very bluggy creation. The figures in green uniforms represent the regular cavalry of the
Greek army. The equestrian heroic just below where the Greek
battery is shooting out of the sky is a noble portrait of Smolenski. If there is anything nobler in the picture it is probably
the bugler who is situated just above Smolenski's outstretched
sword. It is plain to even a casual observer that the Turks are
having rather a hard time of it. The Greek artists have a way
of killing Turks in these pictures which is almost monstrous.
The Turks don't get a show.

As a matter of truth the battle at Velestino which this picture celebrates was really the most bitter fight of the war. The
Turkish cavalry made a ferocious assault on a hill which was
held by the Greeks, and the Greeks whipped them with much
emphasis. Any body can see that the Greek soldiers behind the
trenches are having a lot of fun and that the Turks are not
having so much. By the Greek soldiers in the trenches I mean
the men who are located behind the three straw stacks in the
middle of the scene.

From time to time one will note that the soldiers of both
sides differ greatly in size, but this is because the perspective
in this work of art is not altogether correct. The ancient Greeks
evidently knew more about perspective than do these mod-
erns. If Phidias could see this picture he might not altogether
approve of it.

The little white men in kilts and red caps that are dashing
forward with the Greeks are Efzones. These Efzones have already become famous the world over. They are infantry troops

and are said to be the best in the Greek army. They are all mountaineers accustomed to clambering up and down these terribly steep hills and they are as muscular and tough and brown a set of men as anywhere exists. The palace guard at Athens is composed entirely of these men.

It can also be noted that the swordsmanship of the Greek cavalry is very beautiful. Also that the aim of the Greek artillery is nothing if not accurate.

The portrait of Smolenski with the figure of Fame futilely trying to fit a laurel wreath over his plumes is of a kind that has been flooded through Greece by the thousands. Smolenski is the hero of the people. He is the man who has reaped the popular glory of the war. Greece very nearly retrieved her military reputation at Velestino. It was there that Smolenski held off the Turks and inflicted heavy losses upon them, really beating them in a three days' battle and preserving the safety of Volo. The Crown Prince deemed it necessary to retreat from Pharsala and he also ordered Smolenski to retreat from Veles-tino. This I suppose had something to do wi⟨th⟩ the strategy of war and no doubt it was impossible for Smolenski to hold his position if the Crown Prince withdrew from Pharsala but everyone hears now that the order to retreat nearly broke Smolenski's heart. People say that he shed tears.

In fact through out this war as far as it's gone Smolenski is the man of whom a romantic people would make a natural idol. Everything that he has been in he has made a real fight. It is distinctly the opinion of the Grecian people that Smolenski has done almost all that has been well done, as far as the leaders go, in this war. In appearance he is a man of medium height and rather stout but his clothes fit him so well that he remains a military figure. He has a rather full face and a small black mustache. He is of the type of certain Frenchmen being not unlike some sort of popular impression of the ideal duellist. His manner is quick, sharp and at times imperious although like all bold, stern and very brave men he has a smile that at times softens and lights his face.

I was at the battle of Velestino but I did not s⟨ee⟩ Smolenski at all there, and I would not have cared to have seen him when the orders came to him to give up what he had earned after such long and stubborn fighting. Of course it is told often in the army that he is kept from almost supreme command of the armies of Greece only by the jealousies of other command-ers. I do not know if this be true but at any rate he seems to be the man who would naturally lead Greece. Many blame the Crown Prince for all the mistakes that have been so far made. He was at one time enormously unpopular throughout t⟨he country⟩ as well as in Athens but perhaps the soldiers and also the people are now beginning to understand that the blunders were the fault of everybody practically and cannot be laid with justice at the door of the poor Crown Prince. Nevertheless Smolenski stands out as a man who has made no blunders, as a general whose division has always done superb service and when this war is over the name that will be highest in the estimation of the Greek people will be that of Smolenski.

No. 15

THE EASTERN QUESTION

IF THERE is one man in Europe who is now more apparent than another it is the man who understands the Eastern question. He outnumbers the tinkers and the bakers and the butchers al-ready on the continent of Europe and in Great Britain alone his census dwarfs that of the people who like ale and roast beef. It is thought that someday he may go on strike in which case existence must necessarily cease. Half of the business of Europe would at once be paused.

The great advantage of understanding the Eastern question is that you can lecture other people about it and for obvious reasons make them wish that they understood it too. But it is essentially an accomplishment that benefits only the vocal organs and vanity. It is now a matter of record that when a man thinks he comprehends this puzzle well enough to risk his goods, his home, or his life on it he learns perhaps to his astonishment that it is still the most subtle and evasive creation that the Turk has yet achieved in long years of successful political legerdemain. In fact the Turk is nothing if not the Eastern question. He is the Eastern question. It is his profession. It has been his business for a long time to mystify and seduce and trick his neighbors and he does it with the skill that comes from perfect devotion to the game.

I have said that the limits of advantageous comprehension of the Eastern question lies in the vocal organs and that if a man risks his goods, his home, or his life on his knowledge he comes suddenly upon a great disaster. Greece understood the Eastern question and she has lost a vast amount even if she has not altogether lost her goods, her home and her life. But then the great powers understood the Eastern question and if they have not lost their self respect it is because it must have been fastened to them with a great many more tacks than is common. There has always been a calamity in store for the philosophy of statesmanship which believed itself to be competent to deal with the Turk at his own particular stunt. Anybody who has studied the negotiations between Turkey and the Powers over what the Sultan shall be paid in money, land and national advantages for the victories of his soldiers should see plainly that the Christian statesman of Europe is perfectly incompetent to play the game of diplomacy for one moment with the masters of the art at Constantinople.

The Turk invariably makes a monkey and a fool of any white man who deals with him in these matters. History does not show a purely diplomatic victory over the Turk. This is almost proof that diplomacy is composed too much of lies and procrastination to be the high art which Europeans love to name it.

Anyone who has been in the Orient can perceive in the manoeuverings of the Sultan's ministers during this great international crisis the very methods displayed which dumbfounded the traveler when he argued the price of a rug in the bazaar. And yet it puts to flight the brains of Europe. With every apparent advantage of force on their side, not to mention the great and important one of general harmony of purpose, the ambassadors of the Powers fail to bring the Turk to the point in less time than it would require to build a railroad from Pittsburgh to Philadelphia.

Long ago the Powers told the Turks to evacuate Thessaly. In reply, the Turk appoints civic officials to administer the government of the province as if it were a suburb of Constantinople. At the time of sweeping indignation he will reply that it is a shame to make him evacuate Thessaly when he has taken so much trouble to establish a good civil regime.

The ambassadors inform Tewfik Pasha that his government will be paid £4,000000 as indemnity.

Tewfik thinks that he will compromise on £4500000. In the bazaar you name your final price and the merchant thinks you are a liar. He promptly refuses to sell for that price. He must have a little, just a little, more. He squirms and squeaks and squeals over it until he is satisfied that you are serious— then he accepts with thrilling alacrity. Afterward you wonder if you can learn from the book of judgment how much you have over-paid this rascal.

So if the Porte says that four million pounds will not repay Turkey the cost of this war, the chances are fifty to one that the Porte lies. The other five hundred thousand pounds is simply the regular raise of the oriental vendor of fruits. In American poker terms it may be called a hike.

But it is in Crete particularly that Turkey has made a complete exhibition of Europe until the whole affair might perhaps be noted as resembling a Sunday inspection at an idiot asylum. It has not yet been disputed that if while Turkey was engaged with Greece, the Powers had kept their hands from Crete, that towering island in the Mediterranean would not now be free. The inhabitants are Christians in the proportion of five to one Mussulman and they are islanders as well as mountaineers, the two kinds of people who are most famous for fighting. Despite the talk of easy victories Turkey's hands were quite busy during the war with Greece and she would not have sent too many battalions to Crete. The Cretans would have conquered their own island. But by a number of roundabout and solemn maneuvres, Europe herself steps in between the Cretans and their liberty under the impression that a fight on this little island will, if the Cretans are supported by the Greeks, result in a general up-heaval of Europe. The contrary is proved to them by a war on the continent itself which involves only

Turkey and Greece and certain German sympathies and ends apparently at that point. But the Powers having grabbed this bear by the tail, find no precedent in diplomacy for relinquishing this grip and hang on heroically until Crete's opportunity is completely lost and hang on still more under the impression that having once hung on, it would be improper to let go.

Europe that has always pretended to find the Turk the one odious ingredient in the continental punch proceeds to defend the Turk at every point. She cleans his knives and washes his dishes for him. She shoots at the Christian in an outburst of indignation. She performs all other feats that are expected of a good Turk. The guns of the *Camperdown,* larger than any guns that have been in action in the past history of the world, make their initial appearance in an enthusiastic bombardment of the Christian as he attempts his freedom. The Turk is attacked and at once they devote a great deal of energy and practically all the naval forces in the Mediterranean to his protection.

Devious excuses occur. Since the war between Greece and Turkey took away any vestige of cause why the Powers should occupy Crete, the Powers advanced as their reason that if they withdrew their forces the Mohamedans would be massacred by their over-whelming Cretan foes. Is it massacres then that the Powers seek to prevent? If Crete is not to be vacated because there is a prospect of massacre, why was not Armenia occupied on the proof of massacre? Of course to occupy Armenia is a difficult military proposition but then we are speaking of the Powers who can do anything even to the adoption of a collective title which does not evidently belong to them. In fact it is further plain that the Powers have even no right to use the word massacre. With the prevention of massacres they have nothing to do. During the massacres in Armenia they called upon each other to recognize a sacred duty and then they contented themselves with this empty expression. As far as their sacred duty was concerned they let it be eaten by the dogs. It is proved that the Concert of Europe formed for the purpose of preventing bloodshed is an idle collation which continues to allow admirals [to exchange calls with] ⟨an⟩ unfailing regularity. When this farce is termed Peace or Humanity it is a crime. With these things it has nothing in common. It is a private establishment of sailors and ships combined under the influence of a mistake to enforce a certain expedient. And when the necessity for the expedient no longer exists, they raise semblances of it on the fighting-tops of the war-ships of the squadrons and proceed bravely in the same way. They refuse to define themselves because they cannot define themselves. They do not know. Questions as to their identity throw them into spasms of indignation. The whole affair dies down into a wearisome confusion of explanations on the part of governmental mouth-pieces in nearly every legislative chamber of Europe.

In the meantime the perplexed British citizen mumbles something about the work of the unseen hand of Russia while France cries out against German duplicity. Russia laments the strength of English influence at Constantinople and Germany blames the ambition of France.

But we who have never understood the Eastern question are at last able to see one thing clearly and that is the Turk seated coolly upon a pinnacle of success regarding with a singular smile the nations that have patronized him so long. This victory does not lie merely in the defeat of Greece; there is a far greater victory in the effect of this sudden disclosure, this coming from behind the glass, and appearing to astonished Europe as a gentleman in very fair health indeed. And from this vantage, he gaily waves the scalps of all the diplomats that have come against him.

They had called him the sick man of Europe but when he chose he showed them that at any rate he could knock together the heads of the nations. As far as the Concert was concerned, if its back was turned and if he felt in the humor, he quite often kicked it sharply and emphatically although perhaps not always in accordance with the law of pugilism.

One could hardly have the temerity to observe the emotions of this gigantic creature, the Concert, at this particular hour. It would be an intrusion too grievous. Nor would one dare to scan the colossal countenance, broken with surprise and pain. It no doubt feels itself to be an immense and hideous bit of nonsense. It went into a thing with a great deal of solemnity and with all sorts of kow-towing and salaaming on all sides and with a loud declaration to do its own will in a certain matter and there rose up from the dark East a little man in a red fez who took it by the hair and mopped the world with it.

No. 16

THE TURKISH ARMY

EUROPE is now naturally wondering just how formidable is the Turk. He had been out of all real measurements of the various forces that control Europe for a long time but now he is recognized invariably in them. Apart from his skilful diplomacy in which he always conquers, he is now known as a fighting man. It is doubtful if any of the men who have studied the East ever thought for a moment that the Turk wouldn't fight anything or everything at the drop of a hat but what is meant is that the great European publics all believed that the Turk could be blown over with a breath. But it is now apparent that if anyone is strolling around Europe looking for a fight he can get it from the Moslem whose late victories from inferior Greece have stirred not only his military spirit, but more than that have fired anew his religious zeal which now flames up to the sky. He had been called the sick man of Europe so long that he began to believe it himself. However he has discovered that he is quite well.

In Athens, or for that matter in London, before the war everyone understood that the Turkish army was about as disreputable and ragged an aggregation as could be assembled in any part of the world. The Greek Prime Minister informed the newspapers that the Turkish shells could not by any chance go off. They had no regular commissary department, their infantry ammunition was defective and scarce, and the men were in tatters and howling for the back pay which had been due to the army for several centuries.

It is now quite apparent that these statements are not true.

But the main point is that the Turks did not mind this condition at all. There is very little in this world that the Turks do mind if they are upon a business which can be presented to them as an excursion to advance the banners of their religion. As a matter of fact the shells of the Turks were not up to a modern standard. They often failed to explode and at other times simply broke against a house or on the ground with little more violence than a bursting can of tomatoes. As far as any investigations could be made of the deaths from battery fire in the Greek army it was found that they did not exist save in the most isolated and obscure form of legend. Moreover when one could get a view of a Turkish prisoner he was usually found to be in garments that an American tramp would not altogether appreciate. In Epirus, Colonel Manos'

FLORIDA

No. 17

JACKSONVILLE, FLA., Jan. 6.—It was the afternoon of New Year's. The *Commodore* lay at her dock in Jacksonville and negro stevedores processioned steadily toward her with box after box of ammunition and bundle after bundle of rifles. Her hatch, like the mouth of a monster, engulfed them. It might have been the feeding time of some legendary creature of the sea. It was in broad daylight and the crowd of gleeful Cubans on the pier did not forbear to sing the strange patriotic ballads of their island.

Everything was perfectly open. The *Commodore* was cleared with a cargo of arms and munitions for Cuba. There was none of that extreme modesty about the proceeding which had marked previous departures of the famous tug. She loaded up as placidly as if she were going to carry oranges to New York, instead of Remingtons to Cuba. Down the river, furthermore, the revenue cutter *Boutwell*, the old isosceles triangle that protects United States interests in the St. Johns, lay at anchor, with no sign of excitement aboard her.

On the decks of the *Commodore* there were exchanges of farewells in two languages. Many of the men who were to sail upon her had many intimates in the old Southern town, and we who had left our friends in the remote North received our first touch of melancholy on witnessing these strenuous and earnest good-bys.

It seems, however, that there was more difficulty at the custom house. The officers of the ship and the Cuban leaders were detained there until a mournful twilight settled upon the St. Johns, and through a heavy fog the lights of Jacksonville blinked dimly.

Then at last the *Commodore* swung clear of the dock, amid a tumult of good-bys. As she turned her bow toward the distant sea the Cubans ashore cheered and cheered. In response the *Commodore* gave three long blasts of her whistle, which even to this time impressed me with their sadness. Somehow they sounded as wails.

Then at last we began to feel like filibusters. I don't suppose that the most stolid brain could contrive to believe that there is not a mere trifle of danger in filibustering, and so as we watched the lights of Jacksonville swing past us and heard the regular thump, thump, thump of the engines we did considerable reflecting.

But I am sure that there was no hifalutin emotions visible upon any of the faces which fronted the speeding shore. In fact, from cook's boy to captain, we were all enveloped in a gentle satisfaction and cheerfulness.

But less than two miles from Jacksonville this atrocious fog caused the pilot to ram the bow of the *Commodore* hard upon the mud, and in this ignominious position we were compelled to stay until daybreak.

It was to all of us more than a physical calamity. We were now no longer filibusters. We were men on a ship stuck in the mud. A certain mental somersault was made once more necessary. But word had been sent to Jacksonville to the captain of the revenue cutter *Boutwell,* and Captain Kilgore turned out promptly and generously fired up his old triangle and came at full speed to our assistance. She dragged us out of the mud and again we headed for the mouth of the river. The revenue cutter pounded along a half mile astern of us, to make sure that we did not take on board at some place along the river men for the Cuban army.

This was the early morning of New Year's Day, and the fine golden Southern sunlight fell full upon the river. It flashed over the ancient *Boutwell* until her white sides gleamed like pearl and her rigging was spun into little threads of gold. Cheers greeted the old *Commodore* from passing ships and from the shore. It was a cheerful, almost merry, beginning to our voyage.

At Mayport, however, we changed our river pilot for a man who could take her to open sea, and again the *Commodore* was beached. The *Boutwell* was fussing around us in her vener-

able way, and, upon seeing our predicament, she came again
to assist us, but this time with engines reversed the *Commodore*
dragged herself away from the grip of the sand and again the
Commodore headed for the open sea.

The captain of the revenue cutter grew curious. He hailed
the *Commodore*: "Are you fellows going to sea to-day?"

Captain Murphy of the *Commodore* called back: "Yes, sir."
And then as the whistle of the *Commodore* saluted him Captain
Kilgore doffed his cap and said: "Well, gentlemen, I hope you
have a pleasant cruise," and this was our last words from shore.

When the *Commodore* came to the enormous rollers that
flee over the bar, a certain light-heartedness departed from the
throats of the ship's company. The *Commodore* began to turn
handsprings, and by the time she had gotten fairly to sea and
turned into the eye of the roaring breeze that was blowing
from the southeast there was an almost general opinion on
board the vessel that a life on the rolling wave was not the
finest thing in the world. On deck amidships lay five or six
Cubans, limp, forlorn and infinitely depressed. In the bunks
below lay more Cubans, also limp, forlorn and infinitely depressed. In the captain's quarters, back of the pilot house, the
Cuban leaders were stretched out in postures of complete con-
tentment to this terrestrial realm of their stomachs.

The *Commodore* was heavily laden and in this strong sea she
rolled like a rubber ball. She appeared to be a gallant sea boat
and bravely flung off the waves that swarmed over her bow.
At this time the first mate was at the wheel, and I remember
how proud he was of the ship as she dashed the white foaming
waters aside and arose to the swells like a duck.

"Ain't she a daisy?" said he. But she certainly did do a remarkable lot of pitching and presently even some American
seamen were made ill by the long wallowing motion of the
ship. A squall confronted us dead ahead and in the impressive
twilight of this New Year's Day the *Commodore* steamed
sturdily toward a darkened part of the horizon. The State of
Florida is very large when you look at it from an airship, but it
is as narrow as a sheet of paper when you look at it sideways.
The coast was merely a faint streak.

As darkness came upon the waters the *Commodore's* wake was

a broad, flaming path of blue and silver phosphorescence, and as her stout bow lunged at the great black waves she threw flashing, roaring cascades to either side. And all that was to be heard was the rhythmical and mighty pounding of the engines.

Being an inexperienced filibuster, the writer had undergone considerable mental excitement since the starting of the ship, and consequently he had not yet been to sleep, and so I went to the first mate's bunk to indulge myself in all the physical delights of holding one's self in bed. Every time the ship lurched I expected to be fired through a bulkhead, and it was neither amusing nor instructive to see in the dim light a certain accursed valise aiming itself at the top of my stomach with every lurch of the ship.

The cook was asleep on a bench in the galley. He was of a portly and noble exterior, and by means of a checker board he had himself wedged on this bench in such a manner that the motion of the ship would be unable to dislodge him. He awoke as I entered the galley, and, feeling moved, he delivered himself of some dolorous sentiments. "God," he said, in the course of his observations, "I don't feel right about this ship somehow. It strikes me that something is going to happen to us. I don't know what it is, but the old ship is going to get it in the neck, I think."

"Well, how about the men on board of her?" said I. "Are any of us going to get out, prophet?"

"Yes," said the cook, "sometimes I have these damned feelings come over me, and they are always right, and it seems to me somehow that you and I will both get out and meet again somewhere, down at Coney Island, perhaps, or some place like that."

Finding it impossible to sleep, I went back to the pilot house. An old seaman named Tom Smith, from Charleston, was then at the wheel. In the darkness I could not see Tom's face, except at those times when he leaned forward to scan the compass and the dim light from the box came upon his weather-beaten features.

"Well, Tom," said I, "how do you like filibustering?"

He said: "I think I am about through with it. I've been in a number of these expeditions, and the pay is good, but I think if I ever get back safe this time I will cut it."

I sat down in the corner of the pilot house and went almost to sleep. In the meantime the captain came on duty and he was standing near me when the chief engineer rushed up the stairs and cried hurriedly to the captain that there was something wrong in the engine room. He and the captain departed swiftly. I was drowsing there in my corner when the captain returned, and, going to the door of the little room directly back of the pilot house, cried to the Cuban leader:

"Say, can't you get those fellows to work? I can't talk their language and I can't get them started. Come on and get them going."

The Cuban leader turned to me then and said: "Go help in the fire-room. They are going to bail with buckets."

The engine room, by the way, represented a scene at this time taken from the middle kitchen of hades. In the first place, it was insufferably warm, and the lights burned faintly in a way to cause mystic and grewsome shadows. There was a quantity of soapish sea water swirling and sweeping and swishing among machinery that roared and banged and clattered and steamed, and in the second place, it was a devil of a ways down below.

Here I first came to know a certain young oiler named Billy Higgins. He was sloshing around this inferno filling buckets with water and passing them to a chain of men that extended up to the ship's side. Afterward we got orders to change our point of attack on the water and to operate through a little door on the windward side of the ship that led into the engine room.

During this time there was much talk of pumps out of order and many other statements of a mechanical kind, which I did not altogether comprehend, but understood to mean that there was a general and sudden ruin in the engine room.

There was no particular agitation at this time, and even later there was never a panic on board the *Commodore*. The party of men who worked with Higgins and me at this time were all Cubans, and we were under the direction of the Cuban leaders. Presently we were ordered again to the afterhold, and there was some hesitation about going into the abominable fire-room again, but Higgins dashed down the companionway with a bucket.

The heat and hard work in the fire-room affected me and I was obliged to come on deck again. Going forward I heard as I went talk of lowering the boats. Near the corner of the galley the mate was talking with a man.

"Why don't you send up a rocket?" said this unknown person. And the mate replied: "What the hell do we want to send up a rocket for? The ship is all right."

Returning with a little rubber and cloth overcoat, I saw the first boat about to be lowered. A certain man was the first person in this first boat, and they were handing him in a valise about as large as a hotel. I had not entirely recovered from my astonishment and pleasure in witnessing this noble deed, when I saw another valise go to him. This valise was not perhaps so large as a hotel, but it was a big valise anyhow. Afterward there went to him something which looked to me like an over-coat.

Seeing the chief engineer leaning out of his little window, I remarked to him: "What do you think of that blank, blank, blank?"

"Oh, he's a bird," said the old chief.

It was now that was heard the order to get away the life-boat, which was stowed on top of the deckhouse. The deck-house was a mighty slippery place, and with each roll of the ship the men there thought themselves likely to take headers into the deadly black sea. Higgins was on top of the deckhouse, and, with the first mate and two colored stokers, we wrestled with that boat, which I am willing to swear weighed as much as a Broadway cable car. She might have been spiked to the deck. We could have pushed a little brick schoolhouse along a corduroy road as easily as we could have moved this boat. But the first mate got a tackle to her from a leaward davit, and on the deck below the captain corralled enough men to make an impression upon the boat. We were ordered to cease hauling then, and in this lull the cook of the ship came to me and said: "What are you going to do?"

I told him of my plans, and he said: "Well, my God, that's what I am going to do."

Now the whistle of the *Commodore* had been turned loose, and if there ever was a voice of despair and death it was in the voice of this whistle. It had gained a new tone. It was as if its throat was already choked by the water, and this cry on the sea at night, with a wind blowing the spray over the ship, and the waves roaring over the bow, and swirling white along the decks, was to each of us probably a song of man's end.

It was now that the first mate showed a sign of losing his grip. To us who were trying in all stages of competence and experience to launch the lifeboat he raged in all terms of fiery satire and hammer-like abuse. But the boat moved at last and swung down toward the water.

Afterward when I went aft I saw the captain standing with his arm in a sling, holding on to a stay with his one good hand and directing the launching of the boat. He gave me a five-gallon jug of water to hold, and asked me what I was going to do. I told him what I thought was about the proper thing, and he told me then that the cook had the same idea, and ordered me to go forward and be ready to launch the ten-foot dingy. I remember very well that he turned then to swear at a colored stoker who was prowling around, done up in life preservers until he looked like a feather bed.

I went forward with my five-gallon jug of water, and when the captain came we launched the dingy, and they put me over the side to fend her off from the ship with an oar.

They handed me down the water jug, and then the cook came into the boat, and we sat there in the darkness, wondering why, by all our hopes of future happiness, the captain was so long in coming over the side and ordering us away from the doomed ship.

The captain was waiting for the other boat to go. Finally he hailed in the darkness: "Are you all right, Mr. Graines?"

The first mate answered: "All right, sir."

"Shove off then," cried the captain. The captain was just about to swing over the rail when a dark form came forward and a voice said: "Captain, I go with you."

The captain answered: "Yes, Billy; get in."

It was Billy Higgins, the oiler. Billy dropped into the boat and a moment later the captain followed, bringing with him an end of about forty yards of lead line. The other end was attached to the rail of the ship. As we swung back to leaward the captain said: "Boys, we will stay right near the ship till she goes down."

This cheerful information, of course, filled us all with glee. The line kept us headed properly into the wind and as we rode over the monstrous roarers we saw upon each rise the swaying lights of the dying *Commodore*.

When came the gray shade of dawn, the form of the *Commodore* grew slowly clear to us as our little ten-foot boat rose over each swell. She was floating with such an air of buoyancy that we laughed when we had time, and said: "What a guy it would be on those other fellows if she didn't sink at all."

But later we saw men aboard of her, and later still they began to hail us. I had forgotten to mention that previously we had loosened the end of the lead line and dropped much further to leaward. The men on board were a mystery to us, of course, as we had seen all the boats leave the ship. We rowed back to the ship, but did not approach too near, because we were four men in a ten-foot boat, and we knew that the touch of a hand on our gunwale would assuredly swamp us.

The first mate cried out from the ship that the third boat had foundered alongside. He cried that they had made rafts and wished us to tow them. The captain said: "All right."

Their rafts were floating astern.

"Jump in," cried the captain, but here was a singular and most harrowing hesitation. There were five white men and two negroes. This scene in the gray light of morning impressed one as would a view into some place where ghosts move slowly. These seven men on the stern of the sinking *Commodore* were silent. Save the words of the mate to the captain there was no talk. Here was death, but here also was a most singular and indefinable kind of fortitude.

Four men, I remember, clambered over the railing and stood there watching the cold, steely sheen of the sweeping waves.

"Jump," cried the captain again. The old chief engineer first obeyed the order. He landed on the outside raft and the captain told him how to grip the raft, and he obeyed as promptly and as docilely as a scholar in riding school.

A stoker followed him, and then the first mate threw his hands over his head and plunged into the sea. He had no life belt, and for my part, even when he did this horrible thing, I somehow felt that I could see in the expression of his hands, and in the very toss of his head, as he leaped thus to death, that it was rage, rage, rage unspeakable that was in his heart at the time.

And then I saw Tom Smith, the man who was going to quit filibustering after this expedition, jump to a raft and turn his face toward us. On board the *Commodore* three men strode, still in silence and with their faces turned toward us. One man had his arms folded and was leaning against the deckhouse. His feet were crossed, so that the toe of his left foot pointed downward. There they stood gazing at us, and neither from the deck nor from the rafts was a voice raised. Still was there this silence.

The colored stoker on the first raft threw us a line and we began to tow. Of course, we perfectly understood the absolute impossibility of any such thing; our dingy was within six inches of the water's edge, there was an enormous sea running, and I knew that under the circumstances a tugboat would have no light task in moving these rafts. But we tried it, and would have continued to try it indefinitely, but that something critical came to pass. I was at an oar and so faced the rafts. The cook controlled the line. Suddenly the boat began to go backward, and then we saw this negro on the first raft pulling on the line hand over hand and drawing us to him.

He had turned into a demon. He was wild, wild as a tiger. He was crouched on this raft and ready to spring. Every muscle of him seemed to be turned into an elastic spring. His eyes were almost white. His face was the face of a lost man reaching upward, and we knew that the weight of his hand on our gunwale doomed us. The cook let go of the line.

We rowed around to see if we could not get a line from the chief engineer, and all this time, mind you, there were no shrieks, no groans, but silence, silence and silence, and then the *Commodore* sank. She lurched to windward, then swung afar back, righted and dove into the sea, and the rafts were suddenly swallowed by this frightful maw of the ocean. And then by the men on the ten-foot dingy were words said that were still not words, something far beyond words.

The lighthouse of Mosquito Inlet stuck up above the horizon like the point of a pin. We turned our dingy toward the shore. The history of life in an open boat for thirty hours would no doubt be very instructive for the young, but none is to be told here now. For my part I would prefer to tell the story at once, because from it would shine the splendid manhood of Captain Edward Murphy and of William Higgins, the oiler, but let it suffice at this time to say that when we were swamped in the surf and making the best of our way toward the shore the captain gave orders amid the wildness of the breakers as clearly as if he had been on the quarterdeck of a battleship.

John Kitchell of Daytona came running down the beach, and as he ran the air was filled with clothes. If he had pulled a single lever and undressed, even as the fire horses harness, he could not to me seem to have stripped with more speed. He dashed into the water and grabbed the cook. Then he went after the captain, but the captain sent him to me, and then it was that we saw Billy Higgins lying with his forehead on sand that was clear of the water, and he was dead.

No. 18

THE FILIBUSTERING INDUSTRY

JACKSONVILLE, FLA.—Since this little Southern city has become the center of the filibustering industry in the United States there has been considerable excitement here of many different kinds. The town is really pro-Cuban in the most headlong fashion, and a rumor of an expedition can turn people out into the streets. If, for instance, the *Three Friends* happens to raise its long mournful whistle over the town at some sleepy midnight, it is cause for the most excited discussion whether the

Three Friends be bound for Cuba or bound for some stranded schooner.

When it is said in the South that the public is in favor of a certain cause, that statement counts for a great deal, because in the South there are many questions which are decided by the public will. In New York, for instance, it is of no importance to say that public opinion is in favor of a certain cause; in New York public opinion has nothing to do with affairs, unless, indeed, it should happen to really assert itself about once in ten years.

A Jacksonville attorney being in Washington held talk with a certain prominent government official.

"So you come from Florida, do you?" said the official. "Why, you fellows aren't in the United States at all down there, are you?"

"I never heard that, exactly," said the Jacksonville attorney, "but I have heard that you fellows up here are all Spaniards."

As this was during the last administration, the remark was not understood by the government official.

The first people to invade the South after the practice of filibustering became popular among a certain adventurous class were Pinkerton detectives. They came like lions roaring. They were going to devour the filibustering industry. Oh, they knew that sort of trick, they did, and it must stop. That is all there was about it; they were there to stop it and it must stop. Their chests were pushed out until they could not see their feet, and they expected people in their Sunday clothes to turn out upon their arrival, and opera glasses to go up to seven hundred dollars a pair.

But all this changed when they went away. They marched meekly and in silence, and Florida knew their glory no more. In the first place a detective went to the chief of police and, standing before him, made some mystic talk.

"Well," said the chief, "what is the matter with you?"

"Why, don't you know me?" said the man.

"No," replied the chief.

"Why, I am a Pink."

"A Pink?" said the chief.

"Yes, a Pink."

The chief surveyed him coldly and said: "You may be a daisy, but I don't see where you come in as a pink."

"Why, I mean a Pinkerton detective; don't you see?"

"Oh," said the chief, and after waiting a time he asked: "Well, what do you want?"

The Pinkerton man stated then what he wished done by the local police to assist Spain and incidentally of course to help the Pinkertons. He ended by asking for a permit to carry a revolver.

"What do you want of a revolver?" asked the chief. "Nobody's going to hurt you, is there? You don't want any revolver down here; if you don't get fresh nobody will bother you, and if anybody molests you unlawfully call an officer. That is why we have a police force down here."

The man departed. Later in their business of shadowing various citizens they were let in for a good deal of woe. The men of these parts objected to their shadows, and curious adventures were thereby the lot of some of the detectives. In one case two of them were arrested as vagrants and held over night in the city jail. This was when a detective was simply an emissary of Spain. Later the fair-minded administration at Washington found a way to circumvent the difficulties which confronted the detectives in Florida. In short, they made them United States marshals, and we then had a view of a wondrous creation—an Americo-Spanish two-priced political monstrosity. Of all the public works performed by the late administration, this will probably endure the longest.

Armed with the position of United States marshal, the paid spies of Spain were enabled to perform their wonders with some success and in safety. Some of the citizens of Jacksonville had resented the Pinkerton detective precisely as they would resent any other kind of insult, but a United States marshal was another matter.

The three vessels which have made themselves great names because of their services to the Cubans are the *Dauntless*, the *Three Friends* and the *Commodore*, which was lately foundered at sea. In fact, the reputation of these crafts is so enormous and world-wide that it seems that a sight of them almost invariably creates a grin. As a matter of truth, the *Three Friends* and the *Dauntless* are merely what would be called in the North sea-going tugs, and small ones at that. They are larger than the ordinary North river tug, but a New York sea-going tug like the *Sea King* is a monster to them. The *Commodore* was simply a fishing steamer, what is called in Northern waters a Menhaden pirate. And yet it is certainly true that they are as well or even better known than the battleships of the United States navy.

When it is reported here in Jacksonville that an expedition is about to start for Cuba on one of these vessels, it is an easy thing to pick up a crew. Men jump at the chance.

Filibustering is as near, perhaps, to the times celebrated by Charles Kingsley as we get in this day of other predominant ideals. The romance of it catches the heart of the lad. The same lad who longs to fight Indians and to be a pirate on his own account longs to embark secretly at midnight on one of these dangerous trips to the Cuban coast.

If there can only be muffled oars involved in some manner in the trip and perhaps some dark figure who hisses: "Silence" at the critical time, it is still more to the mind of the lad. Moreover, as far as the men who engage in it for commercial reasons are concerned, the pay is very good.

Of late filibustering from the coast of Florida has been oppressed with many more difficulties than usual. The revenue cutters have been reinforced by a formidable squadron of United States warships, and the officers of those vessels are most industrious and painstaking in their efforts to catch any breakers of the law. It is not believed that their hearts are in their business particularly, but they are firm in their intentions of obeying their instructions absolutely. If a man-of-war chases a filibustering craft there can be no doubt that more than half of the men on her wish to see the little boat escape, but that would not prevent them from firing away with a "long six" as busily as bees.

When the *Commodore* went down the river once, openly cleared for Cuba, she ran in the mud about two miles below Jacksonville. Word was sent to the captain of the revenue cutter *Boutwell* and the old craft came lumbering down the river, got a line to the *Commodore* and dragged her out of the mud. The

Boutwell then escorted the *Commodore* down the river and at the bar bid her a genial bon voyage, and the veteran captain of Uncle Sam's craft bowed from his quarterdeck and gave the men of the *Commodore* the last salute which many of them, by the way, ever heard. As the *Commodore* was openly cleared for Cuba under the decision of the supreme court, a loyal officer of the government could show in this way his true point of view. Ordinarily the captain of a United States revenue cutter would be scowling like a Turk, simply because it was his business to scowl like a Turk.

It is not to be supposed that the machinery of the filibustering business can be disclosed at this time. Of course, the natural question is: "How do they do it?" Nevertheless it is impossible that the public should know the interior of this thing now precisely as it is impossible that the public should know the inside of important diplomatic operations when they are in actual process. There is many a tale now held back by men who would like to talk for pride's sake, for they are proud of the cunning of the arrangements, proud of outwitting the force of a nation, of two nations. These men—simple American business men, for the most part—have stumped civilization. They insist on committing a political crime, and it would be absurd to say that they are any more than annoyed by the agencies pitted against them.

The filibusters began by letting the newspaper men into the secret of events to a large degree. Responsibility is so arranged upon the shoulders of the average correspondent that it is more cruel than kind to burden him with facts of vast political significance. As far as go personal or social facts, the average reporter knows enough to damn a continent, and these he keeps in silence for many reasons of sense and rule and still other reasons. But the reporter's business is to disclose, disclose, disclose. A newspaper article is purely a disclosure of certain facts concerning a certain association of persons to people who would never know otherwise or care, usually. The reporter is not to be presented with valued facts in the way that a man tells a friend certain affairs belonging strictly to himself. The friend can have no obligation, whereas the time perchance may arrive when the reporter is confronted by his obligation to his employer and although naturally as a man he then lets his obligation to his employer go to the eternal blazes, yet the confidential man has done him a wrong in forcing him into this position.

So the filibusters began by letting more or less newspaper men into the mystery of the process and they are more or less sorry for it. Some of the newspaper men have not let their obligations to their employers go to the eternal blazes. They have peached, that is the whole amount of it, they have peached. And peached in a way to deal havoc to parts of this delicious bit of outlawry in the evening of the nineteenth century. Correspondents who applied to the filibusters for passage to Cuba's insurgent camps and who were granted this privilege through friendly Cubans, and because it was the opinion that their pens would assist this cause, these men have been men beyond all others who have cursed many expeditions with the curse of an early telegraphic account. It is they beyond all others who aroused Madrid to bluffing a lambent American administration out of its very underwear, and to the point where it preferred to violate the constitution of the United States rather than be frightened still more by this terrible Madrid. They caused the Washington of that time to exhibit its willingness to smash every law of the land rather than have trouble with Spain. The administration of that time admitted it, not publicly, perhaps, but in a way that the Western Union telegraph company could preserve a record of it. The correspondents with their disclosures crowded that administration into a corner where it could not face the situation manfully. It weakened and crawled and departed finally in popular disgrace.

"Break a law to keep a law" is the precept which newspaper-dom unconsciously thrust down the throat of a national administration. And yet the Cuban cause gained its way to the popular heart through this very indulgence to the newspaper men.

Cuba

No. 19

THE TERRIBLE CAPTAIN OF THE CAPTURED PANAMA

KEY WEST FLA., April 27.—Propelled by the unmitigated efforts of some two hundred and fifty newspaper correspondents Key West furnishes a vast amount of news to the public. But if anything happens in another corner of the globe, Key West is the last place to hear of it. Under the present conditions of crowded cables, Key West is as remote and as silent as a lone reef until everything has finished vibrating, and then by reason of time-worn newspapers it achieves a separate and belated vibration of its own.

It was only lately that Key West had come to understand that when the Spanish steamship *Panama* left New York her officers and passengers had been very confident, very talkative, in their pride. Key West understands that the Spaniards boasted they were sure of doing certain things and they were also sure of doing certain other things. Key West understands they were full of taunts.

As everybody knows, the *Panama* was brought into harbor to-day, the prize of the *Mangrove* and the *Indiana;* and this article is to relate a change that has come over the spirit of the *Panama.*

She has lain all day in the sunshine of the bay with United States marines pacing her decks and with four armed jackies lounging under the awnings. Her crew, very dirty and a most remarkably diversified collection, crowded the rail with the passengers, and proved that to be captured in war is to cause a most extraordinary demand upon the linen supply. They also were still haggard from their uncertainty of mind during the first few hours after capture. They were a sleepy, pale, dead-gone crowd, with eyes that roamed suspiciously over the marines, approaching boats, everything. They did not know but what something might happen. The marines looked very grim. The jack tars looked more grim.

About 4 o'clock a Government tug came alongside, and, withdrawing the naval guard, deposited on board the crowded steamer a formidable array of three United States deputy marshals. The tug then steamed away, leaving the marshals and their charge far out and alone in the bay.

There was a discussion on the quarterdeck. All the passengers crowded aft to overhear it. There was a boy who kept first giggling and then almost weeping. There was a girl who had temporarily forgotten the feminine arts of preparation and pose. There were some ten officers in more or less soiled duck, smoking cigarettes with the air of men who found life intolerable.

The chief engineer, who spoke English like a tourist with an English passport, had been talking to the marshal in charge. It seems the captain wanted to go ashore to see the British Consul, but he was afraid. Afraid, mind you; this thundering, brass-bound captain was afraid. Then up spake the marshal, a collarless man but certain of himself.

"Well, I'll take him ashore," said he to the chief engineer, "and I'll guarantee he won't be hurt either."

When the captain and chief engineer, accompanied by the marshal, stepped down the side into *The World's* launch the remaining officers, the passengers and the crew thronged the rail, making a fringe of pallid faces from the stem to the stern of the *Panama*. The launch swung away for a moment and the waiting Spanish captain remained hanging to the brass rail of the gangway. He seemed about to fall. His face was yellow and lined like an ape's. If he had strutted in New York he was now a miserable man.

On the way to the dock nobody could help wondering what would happen when the inflammable populace saw two Spaniards in their streets.

The Spanish captain smoked hard. The Spanish chief engineer smoked hard, too; but that was all. In the meantime he talked coolly of the shipping in the harbor. He might have been Scotch.

The launch fastened alongside of a pile of palmetto logs. And it came to pass that these palmetto logs were absolutely the things to betray a man in terror. Their rounded surfaces made difficult footing at best, but a man with weak knees was bound to disclose it. And so the palmetto logs made a singular exhibition of the terrible captain of the *Panama*. One felt ashamed to scrutinize a creature who was the victim of such uncontrollable legs. He shambled, tottered, almost fell, caught himself, almost fell again and finally reached ground.

Nothing happened. Key West, enervated from too much excitement, slept in dust-thickened sunshine.

But the palmetto logs avenged New York.

No. 20

SAMPSON INSPECTS HARBOR AT MARIEL

ON BOARD UNITED STATES FLAGSHIP, *New York*, HAVANA, April 29, VIA KEY WEST, April 30. The flagship *New York* at daybreak this morning was at her station to the northeast of Havana. In her company were the *Newport* and the *Ericsson*. The flagship shaped a course to the westward, meeting and speaking off Havana the *Wilmington, Algonquin, Indiana, Iowa, Detroit* and *Mangrove*.

It was rumored on board that we were bound for Mariel to see if the Spaniards were erecting new batteries there. The *Newport* left us and the *Porter* came in from the horizon. Thereafter the torpedo boats *Ericsson* and *Porter* remained, one on each quarter. As Havana was passed the squadron presented rather an imposing appearance with five newspaper dispatch boats pounding along in the rear.

We were within long range, but the fortifications did not open fire. The enemy apparently has been perfecting his batteries to the eastward of Morro Castle.

The bay of Mariel, thirty-five miles to the west of Havana, was reached in the middle of the afternoon. An old Martello tower stands on the point to the left of the entrance and on a higher point to the right stands a blockhouse of the kind that sentinel the trocha. There is a big old-fashioned smooth bore battery near the blockhouse. These seemed to constitute the sole defenses.

The entrance to the bay is very narrow and faces due north. There is only fourteen feet of water on the bar. The flagship steamed up within easy rifle range of the shore, but a more lifeless and desolate place could hardly be imagined. At the great tobacco warehouses on the edge of the bay there was no movement. The town beyond seemed like a cemetery around the large church.

However, on the green palm-covered mountains to the left smoke raised in slanting lines. Two little gunboats and four schooners lay in the bay. The flagship could not get in very close, but was satisfied, perhaps, that the five smooth bores, the Martello tower and the blockhouse were not very worthy of attention by the flagship. The *New York* continued her way down the coast toward Cabanas, thirteen miles away.

On the route the little *Castine* swooped out of the northwest with a motionless white-clad lookout high on the head of her single mast. She was sent back toward Mariel.

The junior officers of the flagship were at supper in the steerage when about 6 o'clock the foggy voice of the boatswain could be heard roaring on the deck: "Man the port battery."

The boatswain of the *New York* has a voice like the watery snuffle of a swimming horse. It is delightfully terrible and no ballad singer could hope for such an ovation as he will have whenever he shouts "Man the port battery!"

Below decks was empty in a moment. The cruiser was off Cabanas and almost opposite the ruined hacienda of a tobacco plantation, from a point near which a troop of Spanish cavalry had dismounted and opened a musketry fire upon her.

The after port four-inch gun of the *New York,* taking a range of 3,700 yards, immediately sent a shell into that vicinity, and this shot was followed by six others from the after port guns.

When the flagship came about, Captain Chadwick himself aimed the after starboard four-inch gun. By this time the cavalry had decided that the engagement was over and were proceeding up a hill. The captain's shell dropped into the middle of their formation and they wildly scattered.

The flagship then placidly continued her way back toward

Mariel. The venture ended, leaving only one thoroughly dissatisfied man on board. Gunner's Mate Lentile, whose station is in the after turret, grumbled bitterly because those two eight-inch guns, "General Lee" and "Stonewall Jackson," were not called upon to disperse the Spanish soldiers.

Meanwhile the Spaniards are now probably gathered around some cognac bottles: "Ah, we fifty Spanish soldiers, we fought today a great battleship. Yes, we fifty men—a little band of fifty men—we fought a great ship. More cognac! Just think how easily we can thrash these Americans when fifty men can fight the flagship."

The signal officer on the after bridge states as the silent fleet passed Mariel in the earlier afternoon a man in a small boat was fishing in the harbor. He had his back to the squadron and did not turn his head. However, one of the gunboats had better eyesight and upon seeing the *New York* bolted so abruptly that she dragged half the mud in the bay loose with her anchor. Her men could be seen moving excitedly to and fro upon her decks. She was within an easy range of three miles, but in direct line with the town.

The coast from Havana to Cabanas is high and beautifully wooded, with lofty mountains in the background. This part of the island must be at all times more healthy than low-lying Florida and more suitable for military movements.

The flagship has returned to her station. The torpedo boats are evidently keeping Havana rather nervous tonight, for the searchlights have been frantically flashing on the horizon.

No. 21

INACTION DETERIORATES THE KEY WEST FLEET

ON BOARD THE *World's* DESPATCH BOAT *Triton*, OFF HAVANA, May 4—Key West, May 5.—The officers and men of the squadron are not happy. Beyond the eighteen-minute bombardment of the batteries at Matanzas and the shelling of some cavalry between Mariel and Cabanas they have not been allowed to make war.

Constant sea service gradually impairs the ability of the ships. The longer delay the more danger to the lives of each one of our men in the first fight. The increase in risk may be minute, but it is just as certain as it is unnecessary.

In the case of the torpedo boats the fact is peculiarly obvious. The little craft are now performing the very hardest kind of service, and in the mad waters of the Florida Strait they spin about like tops. In a seaway which does not move the larger ships from even keels they roll and pitch crazily. Their thin plate sides are regular burning glasses for this glaring sun, and under decks the temperature remains always close to 100.

All hands remain on deck where the watches are either twelve hours long or else there are no set watches, since the whole crew may remain on watch for sixty hours at a stretch.

No. 22

STEPHEN CRANE'S PEN PICTURE OF C. H. THRALL

KEY WEST, May 7.—Charles H. Thrall is a graduate of Yale and has for years represented extensive American manufacturing interests in Cuba. We had been hearing a good deal about Thrall for a long time. Everybody was aware of his immensely precarious situation, and everybody heaved a sigh of relief when he at last was known to be safe on board one of the American warships.

Dressed in the universal linen or duck and with a straw hat on the back of his head, Thrall differs little from a certain good type of young American manhood. The striking thing about him now is his eyes. The expression of them will doubtless change as he breathes more of the peace of the American side, but at present they are peculiarly wide open, as if strained with watching. They stare at you and do not seem to think, and at the corners the lids are wrinkled as if from long pain. This is the impress of his hazardous situation still upon him.

As for his own deeds, he talks as little and wants to talk as little as most intrepid men. Ask him of the situation in Havana, however, and he is eager at once. He says that the first day of the blockade brought tremendous confusion to Havana. Even in the batteries everything was pell-mell. In the city white-faced people thronged the streets crying: "Oh! they are going to open fire! they are going to open fire!"

On the second day the populace was calmed, mainly because they were sleepy. They had been up all the previous night. On the third day almost everybody who went upon the streets was rounded up and put to work upon the fortifications. They were paid $2 per day. As the days passed on and no bombardment ensued the spirit of the populace changed. They decided that the fleet was afraid. When Thrall left they were feeling very gay and content. It was also reported in Havana that the Spanish fleet had whaled the life out of Admiral Dewey's squadron in the East. Blanco is daily issuing proclamations about this thing and that thing. He issued one calling upon the insurgents to enlist in the Spanish army under the command of the traitor chieftain, Juan Parra. Thrall says that as far as he knows no aspirants for this distinction have appeared. As to the engagement of the *Marblehead* and *Eagle* with the defenses of Cienfuegos, the Spanish papers declare no shot reached within four miles of the town.

General Arolas, commanding at Havana, has embarked a stock of provisions for the reconcentrados sent in care of General Lee from the United States and turned it over to the commissary department of the army. Both silver and paper money have simply flunked, but in the way of provisions the Spaniards are good for two months, as everybody knows.

The 2d of May being a great patriotic fete day among all Spaniards, the people in Havana were certain that the American fleet would attack on that day and they were looking for it. They had a gambler's confidence in winning any game if it was played on their lucky day. Thrall's story of the American Major, W. D. Smith, who was arrested as a spy in Havana recently, will doubtless remain all that can be told of one of the melancholy and mysterious chapters of the war. The man must be dead by this time.

No. 23

WITH THE BLOCKADE ON CUBAN COAST

(ON BOARD *World* TUG *Three Friends,* OFF THE COAST OF CUBA, May 6, VIA TAMPA, May 8.)

A day on the Cuban blockade.

The coast of Cuba, a high, wooded bank, with ranges of hills in the background, lay ten miles to the south. The flagship *New York* lifted her huge slate-colored body moodily over the quiet waves, disclosing from time to time a bit of blood-red hull below the water-line. Some officers in various degrees of white duck were grouped on the quarterdeck and on the after bridge. The signal men were sending aloft a line of flags, holding talk with a faint gray thing far away, the only other ship on the sweeping expanse of sea.

To those who imagine the blockade of Cuba to be a close assembling of ships about the mouth of Havana harbor this would be confusing. It does not represent the popular idea of the blockade; but, nevertheless, on six days out of eight and twenty-two hours out of twenty-four this is the appearance of the Cuban blockade.

To the eastward another steamer lifted a vague shadow over the horizon and an officer instantly remarked that it was the torpedo boat *Porter,* although how he could identify this vacillating uncertain form is known only to seamen.

In a short time the *Porter,* rolling and tumbling in a sea that scarcely moved the *New York,* glided into the lee of the flagship. As she reeled from side to side her deck twirled as if it was spinning on an axle from bow to stern. Her crew, a sooty collection of men in the nondescript clothing of real torpedo boat service, turned their faces toward the flagship.

The commander, standing just behind the conning tower, lifted a megaphone to his lips. His voice rang clear to everybody aboard the flagship:

"I have to report, sir, that two of the enemy's torpedo gunboats tried to escape yesterday from Havana and were chased back by the *Iowa* and the *Wilmington*. One has since gotten out and gone to the eastward."

These sentences, spoken very deliberately, with a pause after every word, made everybody prick up his ears.

"Oh, ho!" said the junior officers; "this is not so bad, after all."

Below, officers just off the early morning watches were having a belated breakfast—two slices of toast, bacon and coffee. Other officers in bath robes departed toward the tubs.

Somebody was rattling away on the piano, the tones of which on this huge steel-bulwarked and compartmented mass penetrate only to the gun-deck through the medium of an open hatch. On the gun-deck the jack tars were asleep, writing or working, or in some cases grouped to discuss in angry despair the improbability of an immediate fight. One was sewing, scowling and with pursed lips, as attentive and serious over the task as a seamstress. Two paced nervously to and fro, explaining to each other their idea of a headlong assault on Havana. Others were thoughtfully polishing the guns.

The *New York* strolled westward on a line parallel with the coast. The *Wilmington* appeared close inshore to the east. The *Porter* loafed listlessly astern of the flagship, her keen bow and three slanted stacks lifting and falling with infinite grace over the choppy sea. See that yellow band on her forward funnel? Well, that is the easiest way to distinguish her from the *Dupont*.

The extremes of the coast line were misty, but an officer defined a certain depression in the hills as indicating the position of Havana.

The flagship steamed slowly inshore. Newspaper despatch boats, as if able to scent excitement or interest, loomed up to the north, a bunch of them, with every funnel streaming thick smoke, coming on furiously.

The details of Havana grew slowly out of the mist. Morro

Castle, low to the water, bared an outline which, strangely enough, was exactly like a preconception of it evolved from pictures. On the sides of the hills to its right were two long, straight yellow scars, modern batteries.

With immense dignity the *New York* steamed at a distance of six miles past the Havana fortifications. The deck forward was crowded with observant jacks and the quarterdeck was crowded with officers. The canvas surrounding the forward bridge allowed only the busts of officers to be seen, motionless heads in profile, crooked elbows with hands upholding glasses, which were all turned toward the grim capital. Far at sea were two faint, castellated, moving islands—the *Iowa* and the *Indiana*. Everybody thought the Spanish batteries would open on the flagship. Everybody on board the flagship hoped so. The newspaper boats pounded eagerly along in the rear. But Havana remained silent, enigmatical. The only fun was allowing the imagination to dwell upon the emotions, gestures, orations which were hidden behind the six miles which separated the ships from Havana.

Meanwhile the *Wilmington* had turned and headed off to sea. It was reported that she, at any rate, had been fired upon by the batteries, but no action was visible to the eye, other than the movement of innumerable waves and slow forging of the warships.

Presently the *Iowa* and *Indiana* disappeared. The *Wilmington* turned and resumed her beat to the eastward. The *Porter* sped away on some mission or to return to her station. And again the *New York* was alone, save for the two dim points on the horizon.

Over a brilliant sea she swung again to the northeast. The bugle for the regular call to quarters pealed through the ship, even when the houses of Havana could be counted, and as usual the marines and a division of blue jackets formed on the quarterdeck. After inspection they took their trot about the deck in perfect rhythm to the music of the band which played a rollicking, fascinating melody.

It was a peaceful scene. In fact it was more peaceful than peace, since one's sights were adjusted for war.

No. 24

SAYINGS OF THE TURRET JACKS IN
OUR BLOCKADING FLEETS

"WE'VE got a hot ship—hot ship. Yes, sir; lay her up against the *Pelayo* any old time. Well, I guess! We wouldn't do a thing to that there *Pelayo!*"

"Why, what ship are you on? The *Iowa?*"

"No; the *Vicksburg.*"

———

"Sail on the port bow, sir. A six-oared gallows with a man on it."

"We was going to take some people from our packet to the Red Cross ship in the la'nch, an' then we was goin' to go to the dock for a couple of our officers. We took the people to the Red Cross all right, an' we was a-headin' for the dock when one of the men says, 'There's the recall a-flyin' of the la'nch, Joe.' I looked, and, sure enough, our ship was a-flyin' the recall for the la'nch. So I took an' drove her back. As we came alongside I see ol' Sandwhiches, the officer of the deck, a-scowlin' over at me. He was mad as blazes. I didn't know what kind of a break I'd made, but I knew it was something serious, and Sand-whiches is a bad man to run against. As soon as he could he began to yell: 'What the hell are you doin' here? Think that la'nch is an excursion boat? What are you doin' here, anyhow?'

"Well, I was rattled, but I says,—'Thought I saw the recall, sir, a-flyin' for the la'nch.'

" 'Recall be——,' says the old boy; but just then he cocks his eye aloft, and there, sure enough, was the recall. 'Ahem,' he says. It turned out that there recall flag had been a-flyin' for three hours. It had been run up to bring back the la'nch from some other trip, an' old Sandwhiches had forgot to order it down.

" 'Ain't that the recall for the la'nch, sir?' I says up to him from the boat.

" 'Go on about your business!' he yells over the side."

———

"Oh, how sad I feel to be absent from those from whom I am absent!"

———

"Oh, yes, there was a woman aboard the prize. She was just coming out of the cabin as we came over the side. Was she scared? Well, I guess not. That girl was mad. She was mad as blazes. And she gave me a look that singed my hair. The lootenant he took off his cap and said 'Good morning!' to her, and maybe she didn't throw a knife glance clean through him. I had to laugh."

———

"That packet of yours—she ought to be fitted out as a Chinese laundry. That's all she's good for."

"That's all, is it? Just let us get astern of you some day, and if we don't overhaul that scrap-iron heap of yours in less'n no time, my name ain't what it is."

"That's right. Be proud of your ship. She's what's carryin' you through. But I'll just tell you—our captain says he wouldn't use her for no bathtub."

"Your captain? What the hell does he know about a ship? He ought to be on the board of directors of a milk route!"

"He had, had he? Well, for real sailorin' I'd like to see that ex-faro-dealer of yours get up against him once!"

"Yes? Maybe you think he could learn him something, hey? Why, our old man used to carry ships like yours around in his pockets when he was a kid!"

"Oh, say, when our captain ain't been shaved for two or three days he can take and shove his whiskers clean through that muslin packet of yours!"

———

"Sail on the starboard quarter, sir. Looks like a giraffe."

"Oh, that's the *Wilmington.*"

———

"I'm on the flagship. What ship are you on?"

"I'm on one of the tugs."

"Oh, Gawd!"

———

"Where's the *Vizcaya*? That's what I want to know. She came over here feelin' so brash, and had all them people in Havana cheerin' themselves to death. But where is she now? That's what I want to know."

No. 25

HAYTI AND SAN DOMINGO FAVOR THE UNITED STATES

PORTO PLATA, SAN DOMINGO, May 15.—Opinion and the direction of sympathy in the island of Hayti might at this time be of particular interest, since Hayti's proximity to both Cuba and Porto Rico has rendered a singular experience of the Spaniard and his ways.

The *World's* despatch boat, the *Three Friends*, was in Cape Haytien yesterday. Cape Haytien is the northern port of the republic of Hayti. It is situated at the side of a wide and deep roadstead, while splendid green mountains rise directly from its suburbs. It has the miscellaneous quality of all seaport towns. Among its population are negroes from every part of the West Indies. It is, in fact, a kind of eddy which has caught driftwood from every imaginable quarter of this vast collection of islands. Most of the people speak English, French and Spanish.

Everybody was found to be talking of nothing else but the war between America and Spain. The French cable company was issuing daily bulletins, very absurd, usually in detail and quite pro-Spanish, which were eagerly consumed by the people.

When inquiries were made as to their sympathies they were not backward in declaring their position. It was found that in the little but decidedly influential colony of foreign merchants the French and the Germans were all openly rooting for Spain. They liked Spain, they said; they did not like the United States and, anyhow, they were certain that the Spanish squadron would surely down Admiral Sampson's ships.

There was one venerable Frenchman, perhaps the doyen of the corps of foreign merchants, who positively refused to believe even then that Dewey had been victorious at Manila. We gently offered him such familiar information as we possessed, but he shook his old gray head in derision and scorn.

"All lies!" he said. "All lies by this—what you call?—damn telegraph."

It was another matter with the handful of Englishmen. They were completely American in feeling. One could not distinguish between them and the born Americans. As an addition, there was the captain of a Nova Scotian bark, who had nothing on his ship from a foretopsail to a drink that was not the property of any American that chose to ask for it.

The natives, drooning about the dirty, sun-smitten streets, would have no basis of information upon which to form an opinion if it were not for the comings, goings, all the changes which take place amid a semi-maritime population. Thus have they been brought into direct relations with the Spaniard. They hate him. A negro merchant said to me:

"The history of Spain is the history of cruelty."

This same merchant has many friends in Havana, and recently when a rumor was current there that the American fleet was off Cape Haytien, bound eastward, his friends cabled him for information. He answered deceptively. He explained yesterday that really it was not any of his business, but he could not bring himself to do anything which might even indirectly be of service to any part of the Spanish cause.

This is largely representative of the feeling of the people, but there is also a party who will look without satisfaction upon a complete success of the American arms. They say: "If Cuba and Porto Rico go it will probably be our turn after a while, eh?" They feel that the signal for the expansion of the giant republic is also a signal of certain danger to their integrity as an independent nation. This sentiment seemingly inspires the Haytien army, as much as that weirdly absurd institution can be inspired by anything. The negro soldiers think chiefly of

bread, bananas and rum, but they have somehow had it gim-
leted into their skulls that the Americans menace their country.
Yesterday one of *The World* correspondents casually was ex-
amining the gun-rack in the town's guard-room. The weapons
were old Remingtons of 1865, and the correspondent was interested in them mainly as antiques. He did not notice the
glowering soldiers, and turned presently to ask how many men
formed the garrison of Cape Haytien. The soldier to whom this
question was addressed stared angrily at the correspondent,
spat on the ground and, throwing his arm out in a defiant
gesture, said: "Plenty! plenty!" The correspondent was then
able to perceive that he had been taken for an American committee of investigation.

Here at Porto Plata, in the sister republic of San Domingo,
one finds the same condition of feeling, with a higher expo-
nent of intelligence. San Domingo is always the mental superior
of Hayti. Porto Plata has been largely under Spanish influence,
but little of it now remains beyond the language. As the *Three
Friends* steamed in to her anchorage this morning a crowd of
people gathered on the green headland that shields the little
cove and cheered the famous tug as if she were really the
Campania. Flags and handkerchiefs fluttered from every fist.
There is a considerable Cuban colony here, and only the requirements of journalism prevent us from being feted to-night
by an enthusiastic populace, with a band and a dinner and all
other modern excitements.

As in Cape Haytien, the group of French and German merchants is pro-Spanish. Moreover, the British Consul has a
Spanish wife, and this fact seems to prevent him from getting
facts into any kind of perspective. But the natives are for us.
They see in the destiny of the United States a destiny for themselves. They want to be let alone, but they want to follow the
great republic in the making of a western world which will
one day outshine the old civilization of the East. The citizen of
San Domingo is a good deal of a man. He has not too much of
the jealousy and suspicion that corrodes and perverts the
Haytien; he is able to grasp modernity and apply it. He has
distinctive ideas about sewage. There is not a town in a Spanish

colony so clean, bright, cheering in every way, as this Porto Plata. And, mark you, as soon as a tropical town becomes clean its intelligence can be rated as of superior excellence.

In short, then, we find the French and Germans invariably against us; the English and the natives almost invariably with us, and the more clean and modern the people the more they favor us.

No. 26

NARROW ESCAPE OF THE THREE FRIENDS

KEY WEST, May 20. Exceeding industry on the part of the naval commanders of the Cuban blockading fleet causes life in the service of newspapers to be full of interest.

More than one despatch boat flying the pennant of a newspaper has been held up at midnight by shells that had every serious intention, but it remained for *The World's* tug *Three Friends* to hold an interview last night with the United States gunboat *Machias* which probably climaxes the situation.

We were all greatly entertained over an immediate prospect of being either killed by rapid-fire guns, cut in half by the ram or merely drowned, but we do not now anticipate that a longing for diversion will cause us to seek the vicinity of the *Machias* on a dark night for some months.

We had sailed from Key West on a mission that had nothing to do with the coast of Cuba, and that night, steaming due east and some thirty-five miles from the coast, we did not think we were liable to an affair with any of the fierce American cruisers.

Suddenly a familiar signal of red and white lights flashed like a brooch of jewels on the pall that covered the sea. It was far away and tiny. Answering lanterns sprang at once to the masthead of the *Three Friends*. The warship's signals vanished and the sea presented nothing but a smoky black stretch, lit with the hissing white tops of the flying waves. A thin line of flame swept from a gun. Thereafter followed one of those silences which have become so peculiarly instructive to the blockade-runner. Somewhere in the darkness we knew that a slate-colored cruiser, red below the water-line and with a gold scroll on her bows, was flying over the waves toward us, and a time was approaching when our identity had to be bawled across the wind and made clear to the warship in a blamed sight less than seventeen parts of a second if we didn't care to be smashed instantly into smithereens.

The pause was long. Then a voice spoke from the sea through a megaphone. It was faint, but clear. "What ship is that?"

"The *World* tug *Three Friends*," thundered the first mate. No one hesitates over his answer in cases of this kind. Everybody was desirous of imparting the fullest information in the shortest possible time. We wished for one of the flaming electric signs of upper Broadway.

There was another pause. Then out of the darkness flew an American cruiser, silent as death, handled as ferociously as if the devil commanded her. Again the little voice hailed from the bridge: "What ship is that?" Evidently the reply to the first hail had been misunderstood or not heard. This time the voice rang with menace—menace of destruction—and the last word was intoned savagely and strangely, as one would explain that the cruiser was after either fools or the common enemy.

The yells in return did not stop her; she was hurling herself forward to ram us amidships, and the people on the little *Three Friends* looked at a tall, swooping bow, and it was keener than any knife that has ever been made. As the cruiser lunged every man imagined the gallant and famous *Three Friends* cut into two parts as neatly as if she had been cheese.

But of course there was a sheer, and a hard sheer, to starboard, and toward our quarter swung a monstrous thing, larger than any ship in the world—the U.S.S. *Machias*. She had a freeboard of about three hundred feet, and the top of her funnel was out of sight in the clouds. No living man has ever seen so big a ship as was the *Machias* last night. No living man has seen anything so sharp as her ram. And at a range of twenty paces every gun on her port side swept deliberately into perfect aim.

We all had an opportunity of looking several miles down the muzzles of this festive artillery before came the inevitable collision.

Then the *Machias* reeled her steel shoulder against the wooden side of the *Three Friends*, and up went a roar as if a vast shingle roof had fallen. The tug staggered, dipped as if she meant to pass under the warship, and finally righted, trembling from head to foot. The cries of the splintered timbers ceased. Men on the tug found time to say: "Well, I'll be —— ——." The *Machias* backed away into the darkness even as the *Three Friends* drew slowly ahead.

Later, from some hidden part of the sea, the bullish eye of a searchlight looked at us and the widened white rays bathed us in light.

Then there was another hail.

"Hello, *Three Friends!*"

"Aye, aye."

"Are you injured?"

"No, sir."

The incident was closed, but it had impressed us. The worst or the best of it was that when the *Three Friends* had met the *Machias* last before this terrific, bloodthirsty charge—it was late one afternoon off Cardenas—we had received this plaintive hail:

"Have you any onions, potatoes or eggs?" The gunboat had been on station for three weeks. Forthwith we had patriotically given up our last spud to the country's defenders. These, then, were the ungrateful people who came at us with such dangerous fury. We wanted to demand the return of our potatoes.

But, after all, this one thing is certain. If we had been a Spanish gunboat there would not have been enough left of us to patch a tooth. This is the satisfaction we gain from our short interview with that fiery, blood-curdling crowd on the United States gunboat *Machias*.

No. 27

HOW SAMPSON CLOSED HIS TRAP

KEY WEST, May 26.—*The World* tug left Key West last Friday night, dogging the heels of a massive battleship heading straight for Havana. In the morning when the pale hills of Cuba arose in the south the *New York* came sweeping at high speed over the seas. Now was in progress a huge game, with wide and lonely stretches of ocean as the board, and with great steel ships as counters. From the coast of Maine to wherever the battleship *Oregon* was swarming northward the play was going on almost in silence, with only the noise of the rumors, false or uncertain, rising from the sea as the smoky mist rises from the back of a fast-flying wave.

The Spaniard made the first move. He played his fleet plump into the middle of the board, and he watches eagerly to see if our next move is a blunder.

He wants it to be, of course, and then he will dodge north, and with the entire fighting strength of the American Navy clamoring behind him he will attempt one fine bold raid on the coast, bowling over en route some score of protected cruisers and auxiliaries that plant themselves desperately in his path. That is his idea. That is his little game. He is now brilliantly juggling with the ball to see if he can't induce our anxious rush line to leave him an opening.

He perfectly understands that he can successfully meet neither Schley nor Sampson, and he understands, too, that if one American squadron reinforces the other within striking distance of him his name is the equivalent of wet dust and Cadiz will see its ships no more.

So he is juggling his fleet here and there dexterously. Schley has gone somewhere at a pace and with enough coal to confuse and defeat a modest newspaper tug. Ostensibly he has gone to line up in the Yucatan Channel and send scouting cruisers to locate the enemy. He has probably found them by now, but off Havana here everything is peaceful save the sea, which is spinning the small fry as if they were tops.

The interest of Havana in our movements must be intense. Sometimes twenty sails are in sight of the shore batteries. Yesterday we steamed up within range and looked over the defenses. They are making a very nice collection of modern artillery in Havana and have it all arranged neatly behind earthworks. It makes a man sad to think they have accomplished all the formidable part of their system of defense since the beginning of the war.

Nobody cares about Morro Castle, which is about as important to Havana as Governor's Island is to New York, but it will be a bitter thing if we lose any gallant men from the fire of the batteries our strange policy allowed to be completed. A few shells judiciously applied from time to time would have prevented their completion.

Our scouts are out in the Windward Passage. It is possible that the enemy's fleet may escape Schley and instead of dashing far to the northward may attempt to run into Havana. If they do they will be gently but firmly received by a committee formed of Admiral Sampson's fleet. Meanwhile, with our cabin deep with threshing water and with the flying spray rusting the very top of our smokestack, we are pounding along after the flagship in the hope that something may happen.

All day Saturday and all day Sunday the *New York* lay off Havana palavering with this cruiser and that cruiser by wigwagging and otherwise. Then Monday morning the *New York* headed into the teeth of the eastern gale, and at her heels a fleet followed.

Heroically the infinitesimal newspaper tugs struggled on the trail. Slowly the fighting tops sank out of our sight over the horizon. But the newspaper contingent thrashed on. At noon on Tuesday we were rewarded. We sighted a regular pine forest of spars, and heading for it we raised one after another of the squadron from the deep. They were moving at a speed of about four knots toward the mouth of the Old Bahama Channel.

The *New York* of course led the van, followed by the castellated *Indiana*, which resembled the moving home of a Rhenish baron. After this fighting division came a swarm of impatient cruisers and gunboats led by a new member of the fleet, graceful and fine-bred as a cruiser could be.

If an artist wished to paint a picture of the battle of Mobile Bay he could in fact use as a model any of the *Newport* type of gunboats.

The *Mayflower* and the torpedo boats were lagging at the rear, and far to southward was a converted yacht, name unknown to us. All hands speculated in lively fashion as to the mission of the squadron. We felt, at any rate, that the flag was down and we were off.

Late in the afternoon another cruiser appeared from the direction of Key West steaming at full speed, with the blue pennant and white star of Commodore Watson flying at her masthead, which whirled in silence past the long line of warships. But everybody knew why she had come. It was to bring despatches to the Admiral.

About 4,500 pairs of eyes fastened eagerly on the flagship, but nothing came off. The sun fell amid marvellous tones of crimson, purple, orange, even blue and green, and on the lighted sea the grim ships raised their sombre shapes.

At twilight red battle lanterns flashed at the stern of each of these ominous slate-colored machines. Suddenly a blaze of signal lights appeared above the shadowy hull of the flagship. They changed, winked, vanished, reappeared, red, white, red, white, white, red, red, scintillant and beautiful as the jewels of a goddess. Then from the spaces of the dim blue sea before us appeared a sort of a bobble of entrancing lights. Every ship far and near was answering, calling, ordering, explaining, until the whole eastern horizon was dotted blood-red and white.

But finally, presto! the fleet was gone. The smoky blue darkness had swallowed them in a second. It was only when we had steamed forward several miles that we caught again the glimpse of the battle lanterns at the stern.

The whole thing had been an ideal subject for a capitalized "Night Before the Battle," and there were many who wondered if it were really so.

The dawn of Wednesday revealed the fleet headed in line to the westward again. Five miles to the northward a flying division of the fastest ships in the squadron had been formed under Commodore Watson. His flagship headed it, and then followed in line the others at perfectly preserved intervals.

No word came from either Key West or the speeding scouts ever guarding the Virgin, the Mona, and the Windward. No word from Schley. The fleet barely moved, but stayed always off Santa Maria Keys, on the Cuban coast.

The correspondents debated bitterly the question of why the Admiral clung so closely to this particular spot, but it was generally understood among the naval officers that Schley's raid into the waters of South Cuba had placed Sampson's fleet in position as the second line of defense, and that then the Strategy Board had probably ordered Sampson to assemble his ships at a point somewhere off Cayo France's light, or Cayo Santa Maria, because there was the junction of three vitally important channels—the Santaren, the Nicholas and the Old Bahama.

In case the scouts report the Spanish fleet is bottled in some southern harbor by Schley, or as coming toward some of the eastward passages, Sampson is already at the mouth of the Old Bahama Channel and has gained thirty-six hours from Key West for his heaviest ships. Then, in the remote possibility of some Spanish ships breaking around Cape Antonio and heading for Havana or if any happening demands the fleet's presence off Havana he has a short road by way of the Nicholas Channel.

No. 28

CHASED BY A BIG "SPANISH MAN-O'-WAR"

THE sea was like green satin, and at intervals the scud of the flying fish made bead-like traceries upon this oily, sheeny surface. Northward raised the tall blue mountains of eastern Cuba. The waters and the fair land composed one vast silence, and the seven correspondents under the awning at the stern of the newspaper despatch-boat spoke of their tobacco famine as if it were the central fact in the universe. The tropic sun smote outlying parts of the ship until they scarred the careless hand. Thank heaven, there was still ice and Apollinaris! The attire of the men was mainly pajamas, and sometimes it was less. Forward grimey and dripping stokers emerged frequently from a hatch and soused themselves with buckets of sea water. The bow of the boat steadily clove the flat sea and two curling waves wrinkled astern. It was about 1 o'clock in the afternoon.

The captain came aft and casually remarked, "Gentlemen, there is the smoke of a steamer close inshore." There was a general separation of correspondents from newspapers, novels and Apollinaris bottles. "Eh, what? A steamer? Where? Let's have a look. Lend me your glasses, Jim." Sure enough there floated against the deep-toned hills a trail of tawney smoke. "Yes, there he is. That's one of them little Spanish gunboats. How is he heading, skipper?"

"He's heading straight for us," said the skipper at last. Well, what was to be done? There was a remote chance that it was an American cruiser prowling to and fro before Santiago de Cuba, but—at any rate, let's wait until we see it.

The captain climbed with his glasses to the top of the wheel-house. "He's heading straight for us and he's smoking up to beat hell." The jocular-stage arrived.

"If he's a Spaniard, don't let a drop of whiskey fall into the enemy's hands."

"Wait until they get to stirring you up with a machete. Then you won't sleep so late in the mornings."

"Let's answer their hail in Chinese and say we are a junk loaded with tea."

Meanwhile the captain shinned down from the top of the pilot-house. "Two masts, two funnels and smoking up to beat hell!"

A busy stage succeeded the jocular stage. "Now, what American cruiser could that be? It isn't the *Marblehead* nor the *Montgomery*, because I know where they are."

"It isn't the *Nashville*, because her stacks are almost as high as her masts."

"It isn't the *Detroit* either. I know about where she is."

"It's a Spaniard!"

"It's a Spaniard!"

The stranger had lifted rapidly from behind the shoulder of the sea and disclosed her two masts and her two funnels even to the people on the deck of the despatch-boat. "Better hook her up, chief," said the captain. The boat turned her helm due south and the wake crumpled out into large and tumultuous waves.

A stern chase! Shades of Marryat and Cooper! And hail to the proverb asserting that the same is academically bound to endure a respectable prolongation.

"Got her hooked up, chief?"

"Hooked up! Well, I guess so! She's turning over about as fast as she ever did in her life."

Now, despite the fact that the despatch-boat was incapable under the circumstances of doing more than eleven knots, this chase was dramatic and fine. Over the great prairie of smooth water swept the little journalistic adventurer, and eight miles away sped her pursuer, with great clouds of dark smoke rolling from both funnels and tumbling in torn clouds close to the water and far astern. Spanish prisons and the practise of garotting! The absence of a British flag in the locker and the probability that the enemy would not believe it anyhow! A proclamation that newspaper men will be treated as spies and a boat going only eleven knots!

Seven idle men fixed their eyes astern and speculated rapidly, while in the stoke-room a devoted band, herculean for the time, at a bunker of coal—rampant, blind with the sweat that pours from the hair and the forehead into the eye cavities, cursing over a field that ranges from lichens to flying machines, bare to the belt, feet on hot iron plates, faces bloody with color from the glaring furnaces—they stoked, stoked themselves into the air, stoked themselves beneath the sea, stoked themselves into immortality, a fireless rest in a cool hereafter.

"Does she seem to be gaining?"

"Oh, yes, she's gaining."

"Can you hook her up any more, chief?"

"Hell! We are away over our limit now. We've got the safety valve weighted. If we do any more we'll blow up. We're carrying more pounds of steam than this packet ever saw before."

Well, give the boat a treat, man! Let her see more pounds of steam than she sees even now, when she sees more than she has ever seen before. Surprise and delight her with new wonders. Exhibit to her marvels. Blow her up, if need be, blow her up. Blow her into rat's-nest fragments. Blow her into a semblance of the output of a compound, eleven-story, triple-tooth coffee-grinder.

And Jamaica! Oh, happy isle, dream-haven, heart's ease, asylum, refuge, sanctuary, peace-place, resting spot, vast chamber of safety, paradise of the pursued, you are popular. Jamaica, however, was reported on the 29th of May to be 160 miles to the southward of a certain newspaper despatch-boat.

"He's smoking up to beat hell," said the captain.

"He's gaining," said one correspondent.

"No; he isn't," said another.

"He is," said another.

"I'll pass a cable under the ship and tie the valve with that," said the chief engineer.

"He's gaining," said everybody.

"___ ___ * * !!!" said the stoke-room.

The enemy was swelling out. He now exhibited a tremendous beam, and his spars could be counted without a glass. And still he grew. He was fairly flying. Billows of smoke were rolling out of his funnels, and a white shine at his forefoot told where his bow cut the sea.

Only four miles away! The game was up. He could fire and strike now whenever he liked. The despatch-boat fled still, but hope was gone. The warship simply ate the distance between them. The correspondents began mournful preparations for capture. How many dagoes did they have up in Atlanta? Were there enough to go around in case an exchange was arranged? Well! well! this was a queer end to the cruise.

On swept the pursuing steamer—inexorable, certain as a natural law. She had fired no gun. She was a terrible water sphinx in her silence. Presently her wheel swung her to starboard, and to the eyes of the speechless and immovable crowd on the despatch-boat was presented the whole beautiful length of the American auxiliary cruiser *St. Paul.*

No. 29

IN THE FIRST LAND FIGHT FOUR OF OUR MEN ARE KILLED

ON BOARD THE WORLD DESPATCH-BOAT *Triton,* OFF GUAN-TANAMO, VIA PORT ANTONIO, JAMAICA, June 12.—For thirteen hours the marines, under Lieut.-Col. Huntington, who landed from the *Panther* and raised Old Glory over the battered fortifications of the Spanish at the mouth of Guantanamo harbor, sustained an attack made by the Spaniards.

Four of our men were killed and one wounded. The killed are:
Assistant Surgeon JOHN BLAIR GIBBS, of Richmond, Va.
Sergt. CHARLES H. SMITH, of Smallwood.
Private WILLIAM DUNPHY, of Gloucester, Mass.
Private JAMES McCOLGAN, of Stoneham, Mass.

Corporal Glass was slightly wounded on the head.

The advance pickets under Lieuts. Neville and Shaw are thought to be prisoners.

The attack began at 3 o'clock Saturday afternoon. It lasted with almost continuous skirmishing until this morning.

It is not known how great was the Spanish loss. Their dead and wounded were carried off. It is thought from blood splashes found after the fighting that their loss was heavy.

The Spaniards advanced upon our outposts through thick tropical underbrush and began firing.

Sergt. Smith, who was at the extreme picket post relieving the guard, fell at the first fire.

The firing at first was desultory. The Spaniards drove in the outposts, a part of Capt. Spicer's company.

They fell back upon the camp, where the fighting was continued until 5 o'clock, when the Spaniards were repulsed.

Capt. McCalla landed reinforcements from the marines of

the *Marblehead* in the launch. Ensign Sullivan afterward went close to the shore in the launch trying to draw the enemy's fire, but failed to accomplish this.

The bodies of Privates McColgan and Dunphy were found in the brush. Both were shot in the head. The large cavities caused by the bullets, which inside a range of 500 yards have a rotary motion, indicate that they were killed at close range. Their bodies were stripped of shoes, hats and cartridges and horribly mutilated.

The marines received the attack upon the camp formed into three sides of a hollow square. The country about was craggy, cut with ravines and covered with a tropical thicket. The Spaniards up to midnight attacked from the cover of this undergrowth.

The afternoon was cloudy and the night windy. After sunset it grew very dark. At night the enemy was discoverable only by the flashes of their arms, save when occasionally the searchlights of the ships sweeping along the deep foliage discovered a party of the Spaniards.

Whenever this happened the guns of the marines lined along the camp and the machine gun of the launch of the *Marblehead* volleyed at the assailants.

The launch pushed up the bay along the shore firing upon the Spaniards with her gun. It is believed that her fire was deadly.

About midnight the Spaniards charged up the hill from the southwest upon the camp. Under repeated volleys of bullets they broke and retreated. So close did they come that revolvers were used.

Three Spaniards got to the edge of the camp, where Col. José Campina, the Cuban guide, fired upon them. They turned and ran helter-skelter down the hills.

It was during this assault that Assistant Surgeon Gibbs was killed. He was shot in the head in front of his own tent. He fell into the arms of Private Sullivan and both dropped. A second bullet threw dust in their faces. Surgeon Gibbs lived ten minutes, but did not regain consciousness.

Firing was kept up by small squads of Spaniards. The marines had lain upon their arms, and some of them, worn out with the fatigue of two days of labor and fighting almost without rest, had fallen asleep. At dawn all were aroused in anticipation of a second assault, but one was not made.

When daylight made it possible to use field guns three twelve-pounders opened upon the few Spaniards then visible, who fled.

Our men behaved well and are praised by their officers. The great majority of them had never before been under fire, and though a night attack is especially trying not one of them flinched.

They themselves give credit for courage to the Spaniards, whom they express a desire to meet again.

It is thought that most of the attacking party were guerillas.

It is not known how large the force of Spaniards were. They are said to be 3,000 strong in the vicinity of Guantanamo.

Three hundred Cubans were expected to occupy to-day the point opposite the camp.

————

Dr. John Blair Gibbs, who was killed at Guantanamo harbor, was known in New York.

His friends here say that he was highly courageous. He was forty years old, of medium height and strongly built. When war was imminent he was one of the first to offer his services to the Government. Two months ago he was ordered to the Surgeon-General of the Navy at Washington, and his friends understood he was appointed acting Assistant Surgeon. Later he was ordered to the transport *Panther*.

Dr. Gibbs had been practising in this city for four years. He was in partnership with Dr. Parker Syms, at No. 60 West Forty-seventh street. He had marked ability in his profession.

He came of two old Virginia families, the Blairs and the Gibbses. His father is dead, his mother is in Virginia, his brother lives at Altoona, Pa., and a cousin, Mrs. Roosevelt, in this city.

Dr. Gibbs was graduated from Rutgers College in 1878, and was a member of the University Club, the Southern Society and the Rutgers Alumni Association.

No. 30

ONLY MUTILATED BY BULLETS

CAMP MCCALLA, GUANTANAMO BAY, June 14, 6 P.M., VIA KINGS-TON.—The story of the mutilation of the bodies of the two young privates of Captain Spicer's company of marines, which was sent in on Saturday last, is now found to be entirely untrue. The officers and men of the party which recovered the bodies were misled by the frightful tearing effect of the Mauser bullets when deflected by anything like brushwood, or from close range.

The men had apparently been fired on by guerillas at a distance of fifteen feet. One body had eight bullet wounds, causing dreadful havoc. Surgeon Edgar states positively that the wounds were due to bullets only. Lieutenant Ingrate today took out a party to try and get the body of Sergeant Smith, killed on Saturday. The party was composed of twelve marines and ten Cubans. The body of Sergeant Smith had been lying within the enemy's lines nearly two days, and consequently any mutilating by the Spaniards could easily have been accomplished. The body, however, was found divested only of the rifle and accouterments. There was positively and distinctly no barbarity whatever. Lieutenant Ingrate's force reached the American lines in safety.

No. 31

CRANE TELLS THE STORY OF THE DISEMBARKMENT

DAQUIRI, June 22, 5.10 P.M.—Ten minutes ago the great crowd of soldiers working at the landing—the troops filing off through the scrub, the white-duck jack tars in the speeding launches and cutters, the ragged Cuban infantry—all burst into a great cheer that swelled and rolled against the green hills until your heart beat loudly with the thrill of it. The sea, thronged with transports and cruisers, was suddenly ringing with the noise of steam whistles from the deep sealion roar of the great steamers to the wild screams of the launches. For on a high plateau overlooking this hamlet was silhouetted a band of men and a flagstaff. One man was hauling upon some halyards, slowly raising to the eager eyes of thousands of men the Stars and Stripes, symbol that our foot is firmly and formidably planted.

Since this morning troops have been landing, boat after boat. About a hundred yards back from the beach the companies are formed and then marched off to the westward, disappearing amid the trees. A ceaseless groundswell makes the handling of the boats at the dock a difficult matter, but the blue-jackets from the warships work hard and patiently, to and fro, to and fro. The job seems endless. Sometimes boats get in the breakers and fill, then there is more labor for the jackies. But they say nothing. In fact, it is a day of universal back-breaking work, but on the plateau floats the flag. That is enough.

The Cubans—those who are not out on far out-post duty— stand looking, looking, looking. They stand in their tatters, brown bodies sticking out of a collection of rags, and survey what is to them an endless string of men. The Second Massachusetts is all ashore and moved out. The regulars come fast. To some unoccupied squads an insurgent points out many sacks of cocoanuts left by the Spaniards. Whoop! The way in which the regulars fall upon this loot is a marvel. Instantly every man in sight is eating pieces of white cocoanut. The insurgents chop the fruit with their machetes for their friends. An ambitious private desires two cocoanuts. He hauls out a handful of silver and begins to pantomime at a Cuban. The man shakes his head. He signifies that the American can have two cocoanuts—yes. But buy them—no.

In one of the cottages on the slope General Castillo has his headquarters, where men gallop every five minutes with reports from here, there and everywhere where the vigilant

Cubans are scouting. It is reported that the Spaniards have already retreated some miles. Not a shot has yet been fired. The men act as if they were still at Tampa; there is no excitement, no nerves. The regulars are businesslike and extremely placid. General Norton, tall and gray, has gone forward to arrange his lines. Meanwhile the flames from a burning blockhouse send gusts of intense heat down the slope. In the shops which the Spaniards had fired stands a Baldwin locomotive so gray with ashes that it seems like a ghost. Out into the cove sweeps a long, high iron dock for loading iron ore. It is American property and is untouched by American shells. The Spaniards were evidently in too much of a hurry to harm it. In the yard of one of the houses of the village lies an overturned bathtub. A Cuban officer has hastily explained that it must have belonged to one of the Americans when the company was operating. The Spaniards, he remarked, really have no use for bathtubs. They use powder, one layer over another.

The men from the ships are hungry for news from New York and Washington. They demand it of the correspondents, not knowing that most of us have been far longer without news from New York and Washington than any soldier of them all. Then they ask innumerable questions about the Spaniards. Are they hard fighters, do we think? Can they shoot straight? How long can Santiago hold out? Are the Spanish ships really in the harbor? Where is the *Vizcaya*? How about the marines at Guantanamo?

Bugles sound the assembly. Men hurry off to join their companies. Sergeants come looking for stragglers. And still the boatloads continue to come. A barge loaded with bags of something is being warped into the dock. The formidable craft is in command of a man with a rasping voice, who jaws away loudly and incessantly.

At last it has happened. A boat has been overturned. Men of the Tenth Cavalry, tied in blanket rolls and weighty cartridge belts, are in the water. It is horrible to think of them clasped in the arms of their heavy accoutrements. Wild excitement reigns on the pierhead; lines are flung; men try to reach down to the water; overboard from launches and cutters go bluejackets, gallant blue-jackets, while over all the hubbub tears the sound of that same rasping voice, screaming senselessly to do this and do that. * * * Well, two of them are gone—killed on the doorstep of Cuba, drowned a moment before they could set foot on that island which had been the subject of their soldierly dreams.

Dusk calls out the crimson glare of the burning shops in the ruins of which stands the ghostly locomotive. The Cuban soldiers have occupied the houses of the village, and as they gather around their camp-fires some of them sing native melodies—weird, half-savage airs—accompanied by the booming of improvised drums. Night has come; a searchlight flashes pallidly over the foliage, throwing into gleaming relief the myriad leaves.

No. 32

THE RED BADGE OF COURAGE WAS HIS WIG-WAG FLAG

GUANTANAMO CAMP, June 22.—It has become known that Captain Elliott's expedition against the guerillas was more successful than any one could imagine at the time. The enemy was badly routed, but we expected him to recover in a few days, perhaps, and come back to renew his night attacks. But the firing of a shot near the camp has been a wonderfully rare thing since our advance and attack.

Inasmuch as this affair was the first serious engagement of our troops on Cuban soil, a few details of it may be of interest.

It was known that this large guerilla band had its headquarters some five miles back from our camp, at a point near the seacoast, where was located the only well, according to the Cubans, within four or five leagues of our position. Captain Elliott asked permission to take 200 marines and some Cubans to drive the enemy from the well and destroy it. Colonel Huntington granted this request, and it was my good fortune to get leave to accompany it.

After breakfast one morning the companies of Captain Elliott and Captain Spicer were formed on the sandy path below the fortified camp, while the Cubans, fifty in number, were bustling noisily into some kind of shape. Most of the latter were dressed in the white duck clothes of the American jack-tar, which had been dealt out to them from the stores of the fleet. Some had shoes on their feet and some had shoes slung around their necks with a string, all according to taste. They were a hard-bitten, under-sized lot, most of them negroes, and with the stoop and curious gait of men who had at one time labored at the soil. They were, in short, peasants—hardy, tireless, uncomplaining peasants—and they viewed in utter calm these early morning preparations for battle.

And also they viewed with the same calm the attempts of their ambitious officers to make them bear some resemblance to soldiers at "order arms." The officers had an idea that their men must drill the same as marines, and they howled over it a good deal. The men had to be adjusted one by one at the expense of considerable physical effort, but when once in place they viewed their new position with unalterable stolidity. Order arms? Oh, very well. What does it matter?

Further on the two companies of marines were going through a short, sharp inspection. Their linen suits and black corded accoutrements made their strong figures very businesslike and soldierly. Contrary to the Cubans, the bronze faces of the Americans were not stolid at all. One could note the prevalence of a curious expression—something dreamy, the symbol of minds striving to tear aside the screen of the future and perhaps expose the ambush of death. It was not fear in the least. It was simply a moment in the lives of men who have staked themselves and have come to wonder which wins—red or black?

And glancing along that fine, silent rank at faces grown intimate through the association of four days and nights of almost constant fighting, it was impossible not to fall into deepest sympathy with this mood and wonder as to the dash and death there would presently be on the other side of those hills—those mysterious hills not far away, placidly in the sunlight veiling the scene of somebody's last gasp. And then the time. It was now 7 o'clock. What about 8 o'clock? Nine o'clock? Little absurd indications of time, redolent of coffee, steak, porridge, or what you like, emblems of the departure of trains for Yonkers, Newark, N.J., or anywhere—these indications of time now were sinister, sombre with the shadows of certain tragedy, not the tragedy of a street accident, but foreseen, inexorable, invincible tragedy.

Meanwhile the officers were thinking of business; their voices rang out.

The sailor-clad Cubans moved slowly off on a narrow path through the bushes, and presently the long brown line of marines followed them.

After the ascent of a chalky cliff, the camp on the hill, the ships in the harbor were all hidden by the bush we entered, a thick, tangled mass, penetrated by a winding path hardly wide enough for one man.

No word was spoken; one could only hear the dull trample of the men, mingling with the near and far drooning of insects raising their tiny voices under the blazing sky. From time to time in an hour's march we passed pickets of Cubans, poised with their rifles, scanning the woods with unchanging stares. They did not turn their heads as we passed them. They seemed like stone men.

The country at last grew clearer. We passed a stone house knocked to flinders by a Yankee gunboat some days previously, when it had been evacuated helter skelter by its little Spanish garrison. Tall, gaunt ridges covered with chaparral and cactus shouldered down to the sea, and on the spaces of bottom-land were palms and dry yellow grass. A halt was made to give the Cuban scouts more time; the Cuban colonel, revolver in one hand, machete in the other, waited their report before advancing.

Finally the word was given. The men arose from the grass and moved on around the foot of the ridges. Out at sea the *Dolphin* was steaming along slowly. Presently the word was passed that the enemy were over the next ridge. Lieutenant Lucas had meantime been sent with the first platoon of Company C to keep the hills as the main body moved around them, and we could now see his force and some Cubans crawling slowly up the last ridge.

The main body was moving over a lower part of this ridge when the firing broke out. It needs little practice to tell the difference in sound between the Lee and the Mauser. The Lee says "Prut!" It is a fine note, not very metallic. The Mauser says "Pop!"—plainly and frankly pop, like a soda-water bottle being opened close to the ear. We could hear both sounds now in great plenty. Prut—prut—pr-r-r-rut—pr-rut! Pop—pop—poppetty—pop!

It was very evident that our men had come upon the enemy and were slugging away for all they were worth, while the Spaniards were pegging away to the limit. To the tune of this furious shooting Captain Elliott with Lieutenant Bannon's platoon of C Company scrambled madly up the hill, tearing themselves on the cactus and fighting their way through the mesquite. To the left we could see that Captain Spicer's men had rapidly closed up and were racing us.

As we swung up to the crest we did not come upon Lucas and his men as we expected. He was on the next ridge, or rather this ridge was double-backed, being connected by a short transverse. But we came upon Mauser bullets in considerable numbers. They sang in the air until one thought that a good hand with a lacrosse stick could have bagged many.

Now the sound made by a bullet is a favorite subject for afternoon discussion, and it has been settled in many ways by many and eminent authorities. Some say bullets whistle. Bullets do not whistle, or rather the modern bullet does not whistle. The old-fashioned lead missile certainly did toot, and does toot, like a boy coming home from school; but the modern steel affair has nothing in common with it.

These Mauser projectiles sounded as if one string of a most delicate musical instrument had been touched by the wind into a long faint note, or that overhead some one had swiftly swung a long, thin-lashed whip. The men stooped as they ran to join Lucas.

Our fighting line was in plain view about one hundred yards away. The brown-clad marines and the white-clad Cubans were mingled in line on the crest. Some were flat, some were kneeling, some were erect. The marines were silent; the Cubans were cursing shrilly. There was no smoke; everything could be seen but the enemy, who was presumably below the hill in force.

It took only three minutes to reach the scene of activity, and, incidentally, the activity was considerable and fierce.

The sky was speckless; the sun blazed out of it as if it would melt the earth. Far away on one side were the white waters of Guantanamo Bay; on the other a vast expanse of blue sea was rippling in millions of wee waves. The surrounding country was nothing but miles upon miles of gaunt, brown ridges. It would have been a fine view if one had had time.

Then along the top of our particular hill, mingled with the cactus and chaparral, was a long, irregular line of men fighting the first part of the first action of the Spanish war. Toiling, sweating marines; shrill, jumping Cubans; officers shouting out the ranges, 200 Lee rifles crashing—these were the essentials. The razor-backed hill seemed to reel with it all.

And—mark you—a spruce young sergeant of marines, erect, his back to the showering bullets, solemnly and intently wig-wagging to the distant *Dolphin*!

It was necessary that this man should stand at the very top of the ridge in order that his flag might appear in relief against the sky, and the Spaniards must have concentrated a fire of at least twenty rifles upon him. His society was at that moment sought by none. We gave him a wide berth. Presently into the din came the boom of the *Dolphin's* guns.

The whole thing was an infernal din. One wanted to clap one's hands to one's ears and cry out in God's name for the noise to cease; it was past bearing. And—look—there fell a Cuban, a great hulking negro, shot just beneath the heart, the blood staining his soiled shirt. He seemed in no pain; it seemed as if he were senseless before he fell. He made no outcry; he simply toppled over, while a comrade made a semi-futile grab at him. Instantly one Cuban loaded the body upon the back of another and then took up the dying man's feet. The procession that moved off resembled a grotesque wheelbarrow. No one heeded it much. A marine remarked: "Well, there goes one of the Cubans."

Under a bush lay a D Company private shot through the ankle. Two comrades were ministering to him. He too did not seem then in pain. His expression was of a man weary, weary, weary.

Marines, drunk from the heat and the fumes of the powder, swung heavily with blazing faces out of the firing line and dropped panting two or three paces to the rear.

And still crashed the Lees and the Mausers, punctuated by the roar of the *Dolphin's* guns. Along our line the rifle locks were clicking incessantly, as if some giant loom was running wildly, and on the ground among the stones and weeds came dropping, dropping a rain of rolling brass shells. And what was two hundred yards down the hill? No grim array, no serried ranks. Two hundred yards down the hill there was a—a thicket, a thicket whose predominant bush wore large, oily, green leaves. It was about an acre in extent and on level ground, so that its whole expanse was plain from the hills. This thicket was alive with the loud popping of the Mausers. From end to end and from side to side it was alive. What mysterious underbrush! But —there—that was a bit of dirty, white jacket! That was a dodging head! P-r-r-rut!

This terrific exchange of fire lasted a year, or probably it was twenty minutes. Then a strange thing happened. Lieutenant Magill had been sent out with forty men from camp to reinforce us. He had come up on our left flank and taken a position there, covering us. The *Dolphin* swung a little further on and then suddenly turned loose with a fire that went clean over the Spaniards and straight as a die for Magill's position. Magill was immensely anxious to move out and intercept a possible Spanish retreat, but the *Dolphin's* guns not only held him in check, but made his men hunt cover with great celerity. It was no extraordinary blunder on the part of the *Dolphin*. It was improbable that the ship's commander should know of the presence of Magill's force, and he did know from our line of fire that the enemy was in the valley. But at any rate, in the heat and rage of this tight little fight there was a good deal of strong language used on the hill.

Suddenly some one shouted: "There they go! See 'em! See

'em!" Forty rifles rang out. A number of figures had been seen to break from the other side of the thicket. The Spaniards were running.

Now began one of the most extraordinary games ever played in war. The skirmish suddenly turned into something that was like a grim and frightful field sport. It did not appear so then —for many reasons—but when one reflects, it was trap-shooting. The thicket was the trap; the *Dolphin* marked the line for the marines to toe. Coveys of guerillas got up in bunches of five or six and flew frantically up the opposite hillside.

There were two open spaces which in their terror they did not attempt to avoid. One was 400 yards away, the other was 800. You could see the little figures, like pieces of white paper. At first the whole line of marines and Cubans let go at sight. Soon it was arranged on a system. The Cubans, who cannot hit even the wide, wide world, lapsed into temporary peace, and a line of a score of marines was formed into a firing squad. Sometimes we could see a whole covey vanish miraculously after the volley. It was impossible to tell whether they were all hit, or whether all or part had plunged headlong for cover. Everybody on our side stood up. It was vastly exciting. "There they go! See 'em! See 'em!"

Dr. Gibbs, Sergeant-Major Goode, shot at night by a hidden enemy; Dunphy and McColgan, the two lads ambushed and riddled with bullets at ten yards; Sergeant Smith, whose body had to be left temporarily with the enemy—all these men were being terrifically avenged. The marines—raw men who had been harassed and harassed day and night since the first foot struck Cuba—the marines had come out in broad day, met a superior force and in twenty minutes had them panic-stricken and on the gallop. The Spanish commander had had plenty of time to take any position that pleased him, for as we marched out we had heard his scouts heralding our approach with their wooddove-cooing from hilltop to hilltop. He had chosen the thicket; in twenty minutes the thicket was too hot for his men.

The firing-drill of the marines was splendid. The men reloaded and got up their guns like lightning, but afterward there was always a rock-like beautiful poise as the aim was taken. One noticed it the more on account of the Cubans, who used the Lee as if it were a squirt-gun. The entire function of the lieutenant who commanded them in action was to stand back of the line, frenziedly beat his machete through the air, and with incredible rapidity howl: "Fuego! fuego! fuego! fuego! fuego!" He could not possibly have taken time to breathe during the action. His men were meanwhile screaming the most horrible language in a babble.

As for daring, that is another matter. They paid no heed whatever to the Spaniards' volleys, but simply lashed themselves into a delirium that disdained everything. Looking at them then one could hardly imagine that they were the silent, stealthy woodsmen, the splendid scouts of the previous hours.

At last it was over. The dripping marines looked with despair at their empty canteens. The wounded were carried down to the beach on the rifles of their comrades. The heaven-born *Dolphin* sent many casks of water ashore. A squad destroyed the Spanish well and burned the commander's house; the heavy tiles rang down from the caving roof like the sound of a new volley. The Cubans to the number of twenty chased on for a mile after the Spaniards.

A party went out to count the Spanish dead; the daylight began to soften. Save for the low murmur of the men a peace fell upon all the brown wilderness of hills.

In the meantime a blue-jacket from the *Dolphin* appeared among the marines; he had a rifle and belt; he had escaped from a landing party in order to join in the fray. He grinned joyously.

Possible stragglers were called in. As the dusk deepened the men closed for the homeward march. The Cubans appeared with prisoners and a cheer went up. Then the brown lines began to wind slowly homeward. The tired men grew silent; not a sound was heard except where, ahead, to the rear, on the flank, could be heard the low trample of many careful feet.

As to execution done, none was certain. Some said sixty; some said one hundred and sixty; some laughingly said six. It turns out to be a certain fifty-eight—dead. Which is many.

As we neared camp we saw somebody in the darkness—a watchful figure, eager and anxious, perhaps uncertain of the serpent-like thing swishing softly through the bushes.

"Hello!" said a marine. "Who are you?"

A low voice came in reply: "Sergeant of the guard."

Sergeant of the guard! Saintly man! Protector of the weary! Coffee! Hard-tack! Beans! Rest! Sleep! Peace!

No. 33

STEPHEN CRANE AT THE FRONT FOR THE WORLD

SIBONEY, June 24.—And this is the end of the third day since the landing of the troops. Yesterday was a day of insurgent fighting and rumors of insurgent fighting. The Cubans were supposed to be fighting somewhere in the hills with the regiment of Santiago de Cuba, which had been quite cut off from its native city. No American soldiery were implicated in any way in the battle. But to-day is different. The mounted infantry—the First Volunteer Cavalry—Teddie's Terrors—Wood's Weary Walkers—have had their first engagement. It was a bitter hard first fight for new troops, but no man can ever question the gallantry of this regiment.

As we landed from a despatch boat we saw the last troop of the mounted infantry wending slowly over the top of a huge hill. Three of us promptly posted after them upon hearing the statement that they had gone out with the avowed intention of finding the Spaniards and mixing it up with them.

They were far ahead of us by the time we reached the top of the mountain, but we swung rapidly on the path through the dense Cuban thickets and in time met and passed the hospital corps, a vacant, unloaded hospital corps, going ahead on mules. Then there was another long lonely march through the dry woods, which seemed almost upon the point of crackling into a blaze under the rays of the furious Cuban sun. We met nothing but blankets, shelter-tents, coats and other impedimenta, which the panting Rough Riders had flung behind them on their swift march.

In time we came in touch with a few stragglers, men down

with heat, prone and breathing heavily, and then we struck the rear of the column. We were now about four miles out, with no troops nearer than that by the road.

I know nothing about war, of course, and pretend nothing, but I have been enabled from time to time to see brush fighting, and I want to say here plainly that the behavior of these Rough Riders while marching through the woods shook me with terror as I have never before been shaken.

It must now be perfectly understood throughout the length and breadth of the United States that the Spaniards have learned a great deal from the Cubans, and they are going to use against us the tactics which the Cubans have used so successfully against them. The marines at Guantanamo have learned it. The Indian-fighting regulars know it anyhow, but this regiment of volunteers knew nothing but their own superb courage. They wound along this narrow winding path, babbling joyously, arguing, recounting, laughing; making more noise than a train going through a tunnel.

Any one could tell from the conformation of the country when we were liable to strike the enemy's outposts, but the clatter of tongues did not then cease. Also, those of us who knew heard going from hillock to hillock the beautiful coo of the Cuban wood-dove—ah, the wood-dove! the Spanish-guerilla wood-dove which had presaged the death of gallant marines.

For my part, I declare that I was frightened almost into convulsions. Incidentally I mentioned the cooing of the doves to some of the men, but they said decisively that the Spaniards did not use this signal. I don't know how they knew.

Well, after we had advanced well into the zone of the enemy's fire—mark that—well into the zone of Spanish fire—a loud order came along the line: "There's a Spanish outpost just ahead and the men must stop talking."

"Stop talkin', can't ye, —— it," bawled a sergeant.

"Ah, say, can't ye stop talkin'?" howled another.

I was frightened before a shot was fired; frightened because I thought this silly brave force was wandering placidly into a great deal of trouble. They did. The firing began. Four little volleys were fired by members of a troop deployed to the right. Then the Mauser began to pop—the familiar Mauser pop.

A captain announced that this distinct Mauser sound was our own Krag-Jorgensen. O misery!

Then the woods became aglow with fighting. Our people advanced, deployed, reinforced, fought, fell—in the bushes, in the tall grass, under the lone palms—before a foe not even half seen. Mauser bullets came from three sides. Mauser bullets —not Krag-Jorgensen—although men began to cry that they were being fired into by their own people—whined in almost all directions. Three troops went forward in skirmish order and in five minutes they called for reinforcements. They were under a cruel fire; half of the men hardly knew whence it came; but their conduct, by any soldierly standard, was magnificent.

Most persons with a fancy for military things suspect the value of an announcedly picked regiment. Better gather a simple collection of clerks from anywhere. But in this case the usual view changes. This regiment is as fine a body of men as were ever accumulated for war.

There was nothing to be seen but men straggling through the underbrush and firing at some part of the landscape. This was the scenic effect. Of course men said that they saw five hundred, one thousand, three thousand, fifteen thousand Spaniards, but—poof—in bush country of this kind it is almost impossible for one to see more than fifty men at a time. According to my opinion there were never more than five hundred men in the Spanish firing line. There might have been aplenty in touch with their centre and flanks, but as to the firing there were never more than five hundred men engaged. This is certain.

The Rough Riders advanced steadily and confidently under the Mauser bullets. They spread across some open ground— tall grass and palms—and there they began to fall, smothering and threshing down in the grass, marking man-shaped places among those luxuriant blades. The action lasted about one-half hour. Then the Spaniards fled. They had never had men fight them in this manner and they fled. The business was too serious.

Then the heroic rumor arose, soared, screamed above the bush. Everybody was wounded. Everybody was dead. There was nobody. Gradually there was somebody. There was the wounded, the important wounded. And the dead.

Meanwhile a soldier passing near me said: "There's a correspondent up there all shot to hell."

He guided me to where Edward Marshall lay, shot through the body. The following conversation ensued:

"Hello, Crane!"

"Hello, Marshall! In hard luck, old man?"

"Yes, I'm done for."

"Nonsense! You're all right, old boy. What can I do for you?"

"Well, you might file my despatches. I don't mean file 'em ahead of your own, old man—but just file 'em if you find it handy."

I immediately decided that he was doomed. No man could be so sublime in detail concerning the trade of journalism and not die. There was the solemnity of a funeral song in these absurd and fine sentences about despatches. Six soldiers gathered him up on a tent and moved slowly off.

"Hello!" shouted a stern and menacing person, "who are you? And what are you doing here? Quick!"

"I am a correspondent, and we are merely carrying back another correspondent who we think is mortally wounded. Do you care?"

The Rough Rider, somewhat abashed, announced that he did not care.

And now the wounded soldiers began to crawl, walk and be carried back to where, in the middle of the path, the surgeons had established a little field hospital.

"Say, doctor, this ain't much of a wound. I reckon I can go now back to my troop," said Arizona.

"Thanks, awfully, doctor. Awfully kind of you. I dare say I shall be all right in a moment," said New York.

This hospital was a spectacle of heroism. The doctors, gentle and calm, moved among the men without the common-senseless bullying of the ordinary ward. It was a sort of fraternal game. They were all in it, and of it, helping each other.

In the meantime three troops of the Ninth Cavalry were swinging through the woods, and a mile behind them the Seventy-first New York was moving forward eagerly to the rescue. But the day was done. The Rough Riders had bitten it off and chewed it up—chewed it up splendidly.

No. 34

ROOSEVELT'S ROUGH RIDERS' LOSS DUE TO A GALLANT BLUNDER

PLAYA DEL ESTE, June 25.—Lieutenant-Colonel Roosevelt's Rough Riders, who were ambushed yesterday, advanced at daylight without any particular plan of action as to how to strike the enemy.

The men marched noisily through the narrow road in the woods, talking volubly, when suddenly they struck the Spanish lines.

Fierce fire was poured into their ranks and there began a great fight in the thickets.

Nothing of the enemy was visible to our men, who displayed much gallantry. In fact, their bearing was superb, and could not be finer.

They suffered a heavy loss, however, due to the remarkably wrong idea of how the Spaniards bushwhack.

It was simply a gallant blunder.

No. 35

HUNGER HAS MADE CUBANS FATALISTS

SIBONEY, June 27.—The day is hot and lazy; endless Cuban infantry straggling past the door of our shack send the yellow dust in clouds. The Thirty-third Michigan is landing in dribbles upon the beach.

Four Red Cross nurses, the first American women to set

foot on Cuban soil since the beginning of the war, came ashore from the *State of Texas* a few minutes ago, and the soldiers, dishevelled, dirty, bronzed, gazed at them with all their eyes. They were a revelation in their cool white dresses.

Life occasionally moves slowly at the seat of war. This makes two days of tranquillity. The Spaniards, when they fled from the conflict with Roosevelt's men and the First and Tenth Regular Cavalry, took occasion to flee a considerable distance; in fact, they went nearly into Santiago de Cuba.

No army can move ahead faster than its rations, and although here we picture the impatience of the bulletin board crowds who fancy that war is not a complication composed of heat, dust, rain, thirst, hunger and blood, yet it is impossible for the army to move faster than it does at present.

The attitude of the American soldier toward the insurgent is interesting. So also is the attitude of the insurgent toward the American soldier. One must not suppose that there was any cheering enthusiasm at the landing of our army here. The American soldiers looked with silent curiosity upon the ragged brown insurgents and the insurgents looked stolidly, almost indifferently, at the Americans.

The Cuban soldier, indeed, has turned into an absolutely emotionless character save when he is maddened by battle. He starves and he makes no complaint. We feed him and he expresses no joy. When you come to think of it, one follows the other naturally. If he had retained the emotional ability to make a fuss over nearly starving to death he would also have retained the emotional ability to faint with joy at sight of the festive canned beef, hard-tack and coffee. But he exists with the impenetrable indifference or ignorance of the greater part of the people in an ordinary slum.

Everybody knows that the kind of sympathetic charity which loves to be thanked is often grievously disappointed and wounded in tenement districts where people often accept gifts as if their own property had turned up after a short absence. The Cubans accept our stores in something of this way. If there are any thanks it is because of custom. Of course, I mean the rank and file. The officers are mannered both good and bad, true and dissembling, like ordinary people.

But there is no specious intercourse between the Cubans and the Americans. Each hold largely to their own people and go their own ways. The American does not regard his ally as a good man for the fighting line, and the Cuban is aware that his knowledge of the country makes his woodcraft superior to that of the American. He regards himself also as considerable of a veteran and there has not yet been enough fighting to let him know what immensely formidable persons are your Uncle Samuel's regulars.

When that fighting does come he will see, for marksmanship and steadiness, such a soldier as could never have come into his visions. The fighting of the Rough Riders, by the way, surprised him greatly. He is not educated in that kind of warfare. The way our troops kept going, going, never giving back a foot despite the losses, hanging on as if every battle was a life or death struggle—this seemed extraordinary to the Cuban.

The scene of the fight on the 24th is now far within our lines. The Spanish position was perfect. They must have been badly rattled to have so easily given it up at the attack of less than 2,000 men. Here now the vultures wheel slowly over the woods.

The gallantry of the First Regular Cavalry has not been particularly mentioned in connection with the first fight. There were five correspondents present under fire and we were all with the Rough Riders. We did not know until after the action that the First Regular Cavalry had been engaged over on the right flank. But when a second sergeant takes out a troop because its captain, lieutenant and first sergeant all go down in the first five minutes' firing there has been considerable trouble.

In fact, our admiration for our regulars is a peculiar bit of business. We appreciate them heartily but vaguely, without any other medium of expression than the term, "the regulars."

Thus when it comes down to action no one out of five correspondents thought it important to be with the First Regular Cavalry. And their performance was grand! Oh, but never mind —it was only the regulars. They fought gallantly of course. Why not? Have they ever been known to fail? That is the point. They have never been known to fail. Our confidence in them has come to be a habit. But, good heavens! it must be about time to change all that and heed them somewhat. Even if we have to make some of the volunteers wait a little.

Scovel and I swam two Jamaica horses ashore from the *Triton*, found some insurgents and took a journey into the hills. Colonel Cebreco's little force we found encamped under the palms in thatched huts with sapling uprights. The ragged semi-naked men lay about in dirty hammocks, but their rifles were Springfields, 1873, and their belts were full of cartridges. The tall guinea grass had been trodden flat by their bare feet.

We asked for a guide and the colonel gave us an escort of five men for our ride over the mountains. The first ridge we rode up was a simple illumination as to why the insurgents if they had food and ammunition could hold out for years. There is no getting men out of such hills if they choose to stay in them. The path, rocky as the bed of a stream, zig-zagged higher and higher until the American fleet blockading Santiago was merely a collection of tiny, shapeless shadows on the steel bosom of an immense sea. The woods, the beautiful woods, were alive around us with the raucous voices of birds, black like crows.

At the summit we looked upon a new series of ridges and peaks, near and far, all green. A strong breeze rustled the foliage. It was the kind of country in which commercial physicians love to establish sanitariums. Then down we went, down and down, sitting on the pommels of our saddles, with our stirrups near the ears of the horses. Then came a brawling, noisy brook like an Adirondack trout stream. Then another ascension to another Cuban camp, where just at dusk the pickets in bunches of three were coming in to report to the captain, lazily aswing. One barefooted negro private paused in his report from time to time to pluck various thistle and cactus spurs from his soles. Scovel asked him in Spanish: "Where are your shoes?"

The tattered soldier coolly replied in English: "I lose dem in de woods."

We cheered.

"Why, hello there! Where did you come from?" To our questions he answered: "In New York. I leve dere Mulberry street. One—t'ree year. My name Joe Riley."

There he stood, bearded, black, a perfect type of West India negro, speaking the soft, broad dialect of these islands and— harp of Ireland—his name was Riley. I have heard of a tall

Guatemalan savage who somehow accumulated the illustrious name of Duffy, but Riley——

As we swung and smoked in our hammocks, the Cuban soldiers crooned marvelous songs in the darkness while the firelight covered with crimson glare some naked limb or made tragic some dark patient face. The hills were softly limned against a sky strewn with big stars.

We were up in the cold of the dark just before dawn. With fifteen men as escort, we moved again up the hills. In time, we arrived on a path that curved around the top of a ridge. Here we found Cuban posts. They having no tools with which to dig trenches, naturally turn to the machete. They can't dig down, so they build up.

These Cuban posts were each fronted with a curious structure, a mere rack made of saplings, tied fast with sinewy vines and then filled with stones. They were about six feet high, one foot thick and long enough to accommodate from five to eight riflemen. These structures paralleled the path at strategic points.

Soon we came to a point where upon looking across a narrow but very deep valley we could see in the blue dawn the shine of Spanish camp-fires. They were within rifle range, but we slunk along unseen. Our horses had now been left behind.

Then came a dive into the dark, deep valley—into Spain. The hillside was the steepest thing in hillsides which could well be imagined. We slid practically from tree to tree, our escort moving noiselessly below and above us. By the time we reached the bottom of this hill the day had broken wide and clear. A stream was forded and then came a creep of five hundred yards through tall grass. There was a Spanish post upon either hand—100 men in one, 50 men in the other. The Cubans had no tongues and their feet made no sound.

To make a long story short, there were some nine miles of this sort of dodging and badgering and botheration—nine infernal miles, during which those Cubans did some of the best scouting and covering in the world. At last we were at the foot of a certain mountain. Olympus, what a mountain! Our weary minds argued that to this one the other hills were as the arched backs of kittens.

We ascended it—no matter how—it took us years. At the top we lay on the ground and breathed while the Cubans chopped a hole in the foliage with their machetes. Then we got up and peered through this hole and saw—what? Santiago de Cuba and the harbor, with Cervera's fleet in it and the whole show.

I had noticed that one of the men had carried with care something done up in a dirty towel and tied with creepers. When you see a man carrying with care something done up in a dirty towel and tied with creepers, what do you conclude he has? Why, a telescope, of course.

The hill was more difficult when going down than when coming up. We fell from tree to tree, from boulder to boulder.

The escort only behaved badly once. It seems they had had nothing to eat but mangoes for three weeks, barring a favorite mare which some stern patriot had sacrificed to the general appetite. We were within two miles of the insurgent lines and passing through a thick wood when the escort sighted a tree laden with mangoes and with luscious ripe ones crowding the ground. The captain raved in whispers and gestured sublimely, but it was of no benefit. That escort broke formation and scattered, flitting noiselessly and grabbing.

There was a time when a Cuban nursed a cartridge and there are some disadvantages to his having a-plenty. When we reached the open ground we were a little reckless, being homeward bound, and the insurgents on the ridge, not valuing ammunition as they once did, began to pot genially away at us.

In one of the camps we stopped to lunch upon one can of beef. It was a mango camp. Our mango escort was still with us. That orange-colored fruit seemed to look reproachfully at us from the stomach of every man present. They gathered sadly around to see us eat the beef. It was too much for us. We divided one pound of beef among about thirty men, including ourselves.

We told our fifteen men, loyal save for the incident of the laden mango tree, that as they had only done twenty-five miles over impossible mountains since daylight they had better come six more miles over more impossible mountains to our rendezvous with the *Three Friends* on the coast. Whereupon we would generously give them two good rations per man from the ship.

We mounted and rode away, while they padded along behind

us. As we breasted the last hillock near the coast we beheld the *Three Friends* standing out to sea, the black smoke rolling from her. We were about one half-hour late. There is nothing in any agony of an ordinary host which could measure our suffering. A faithful escort—thirty-one miles—mangoes—three weeks—*Three Friends*—promises—pledges—oh, horrors.

Scovel rode like mad through the guinea grass to the beach to make desperate signals. The escort ran headlong after us. I could hear the captain screaming to his men "Run! Run! Run! Run!"

"I can't run any more! I'm dying!" cried a hoarse and windless private.

"Run! Run! Run! Run!"

"If I take another step I will die of it," cried another hoarse and windless private.

"Ah," shrieked the captain wildly, "if you have to eat mangoes for another three weeks you'll wish you had run."

No. 36

PANDO HURRYING TO SANTIAGO

Playa del Este, Cuba, June 30.—General Pando is reported to be pushing from Manzanillo to Santiago with 8,400 men driving cattle along with his troops.

The Cubans deny the possibility of his reinforcing Santiago. They say the insurgent forces of General Rabi number enough even with General Garcia's men eastward of Santiago, to badly defeat General Pando.

However, anxiety is felt here as to the exact number of insurgents between General Pando and Santiago. They are said to be 7,500 strong.

No. 37

ARTILLERY DUEL WAS FIERCELY FOUGHT ON BOTH SIDES

PLAYA DEL ESTE, July 1.—After seven hours of hard fighting our troops are now moving up the green hills toward the outer defenses of Santiago City.

The artillery duel this morning between Grimes's battery and the Spanish battery which he engaged was of the fiercest character. It was his second engagement of the kind. His men threw their shrapnel directly into the Spanish trenches.

Grimes was reinforced by a reserve battery late in the morning. Guns are being dragged up the hill through the dense chaparral and cactus.

Most of our troops are hidden in the thick woods, and so are not aware of the splendid advance of our advance guard. On the faraway hills large forces of Spaniards are being held in reserve. The Spaniards can be plainly seen in the trenches firing without exposing themselves in the slightest, simply thrusting their gun barrels over the breastworks.

No. 38

NIGHT ATTACKS ON THE MARINES AND A BRAVE RESCUE

GUANTANAMO, July 4.—Once upon a time there was a great deal of fighting between the marines and the guerillas here, and during that space things occurred.

The night attacks were heart-breaking affairs, from which the men emerged in the morning exhausted to a final degree, like people who had been swimming for miles. From colonel to smallest trumpeter went a great thrill when the dawn broke slowly in the eastern sky, and the weary band quite cheerfully ate breakfast, that scandalous military breakfast which is worst when men have done their best, advanced far or fought long. Afterward the men slept, sunk upon the ground in an abandon that was almost a stupor.

Lieutenant Neville, with his picket of about twenty men, was entirely cut off from camp one night, and another night Neville's picket and the picket of Lieutenant Shaw were cut off, fighting hard in the thickets for their lives. At the break of day the beleaguered camp could hear still the rifles of their lost pickets.

The problem of rescue added anxiety to the already tremendous anxiety of the fine old colonel, a soldier every inch of him. The guerillas were still lurking in the near woods, and it was unsafe enough in camp without venturing into the bush.

Volunteers from Company C were called for, and these seventeen privates volunteered:

Boniface, Conway, Fitzgerald, Heilner, Harmson, Hemerie, Lewin, Mann, Mills, Monahan, Nolan, O'Donnell, Ryan, Riddle, Sinclair, Sullivan, W. A., and Smith, J. H.

They went out under Lieutenant Lucas. They arrived in Neville's vicinity just as he and his men, together with Shaw and his men, were being finally surrounded at close range. Lucas and his seventeen men broke through the guerillas and saved the pickets, and the whole body then fell back to Crest Hill. That is all there is to it.

No. 39

STEPHEN CRANE'S VIVID STORY OF THE BATTLE OF SAN JUAN

IN FRONT OF SANTIAGO, July 4, VIA OLD POINT COMFORT, VA., July 13.—The action at San Juan on July 1 was, particularly speaking, a soldiers' battle. It was like Inkerman, where the English fought half leaderless all day in a fog. Only the Cuban forest was worse than any fog.

No doubt when history begins to grind out her story we will find that many a thundering, fine, grand order was given for that day's work; but after all there will be no harm in contending that the fighting line, the men and their regimental officers, took the hill chiefly because they knew they could take it, some having no orders and others disobeying whatever orders they had.

In civil life the newspapers would have called it a grand, popular movement. It will never be forgotten as long as America has a military history.

A line of intrenched hills held by men armed with a weapon like the Mauser is not to be taken by a front attack of infantry unless the trenches have first been heavily shaken by artillery fire. Any theorist will say that it is impossible, and prove it to be impossible. But it was done, and we owe the success to the splendid gallantry of the American private soldier.

As near as one can learn headquarters expected little or no fighting on the 1st. Lawton's division was to go by the Caney road, chase the Spaniards out of that interesting village, and then, wheeling half to the left, march down to join the other divisions in some kind of attack on San Juan at daybreak on the 2d.

But somebody had been entirely misinformed as to the strength and disposition of the Spanish forces at Caney, and instead of taking Lawton six minutes to capture the town it took him nearly all day, as well it might.

The other divisions lying under fire, waiting for Lawton, grew annoyed at a delay which was, of course, not explained to them, and suddenly arose and took the formidable hills of San Juan. It was impatience suddenly · exalted to one of the sublime passions.

Lawton was well out toward Caney soon after daybreak, and by 7 o'clock we could hear the boom of Capron's guns in support of the infantry. The remaining divisions—Kent's and Wheeler's —were trudging slowly along the muddy trail through the forest.

When the first gun was fired a grim murmur passed along the lean column. "They're off!" somebody said.

The marching was of necessity very slow and even then the narrow road was often blocked. The men, weighted with their packs, cartridge belts and rifles, forded many streams, climbed hills, slid down banks and forced their way through thickets.

Suddenly there was a roar of guns just ahead and a little to the left. This was Grimes's battery going into action on the hill which is called El Paso. Then, all in a moment, the quiet column moving forward was opposed by men carrying terrible burdens. Wounded Cubans were being carried to the rear. Most of them were horribly mangled.

The second brigade of dismounted American cavalry had been in support of the battery, its position being directly to the rear. Some Cubans had joined there. The Spanish shrapnel fired at the battery was often cut too long, and passing over burst amid the supports and the Cubans.

The loss of the battery, the cavalry and the Cubans from this fire was forty men in killed and wounded, the First regular cavalry probably suffering most grievously. Presently there was a lull in the artillery fire, and down through spaces in the trees we could see the infantry still plodding with its packs steadily toward the front.

The artillerymen were greatly excited. Some showed with glee fragments of Spanish shells which had come dangerously near their heads. They had gone through their ordeal and were talking over it lightly.

In the meantime Lawton's division, some three miles away, was making plenty of noise. Caney is just at the base of a high willow-green, crinkled mountain, and Lawton was making his way over little knolls which might be termed foothills. We could see the great white clouds of smoke from Capron's guns and hear their roar punctuating the incessant drumming of the infantry. It was plain even then that Lawton was having considerably more of a fete than anybody had supposed previously.

At about 2,500 yards in front of Grimes's position on El Paso arose the gentle green hills of San Juan, dotted not too plentifully with trees—hills that resembled the sloping orchards of Orange County in summer. Here and there were houses built evidently as summer villas, but now loopholed and barricaded. They had heavy roofs of red tiles and were shaped much like Japanese, or, better, Javanese houses. Here and there, too, along the crests of these curving hillocks were ashen streaks, the rifle-pits of the Spaniards.

At the principal position of the enemy were a flag, a redoubt, a blockhouse and some sort of pagoda, in the shade of which Spanish officers were wont to promenade during lulls and negligently gossip about the battle. There was one man in a summer-resort straw hat. He did a deal of sauntering in the coolest manner possible, walking out in the clear sunshine and gazing languidly in our direction. He seemed to be carrying a little cane.

At 11.25 our artillery reopened on the central blockhouse and intrenchments. The Spanish fire had been remarkably fine, but it was our turn now. Grimes had his ranges to a nicety. After the great "shout of the gun" came the broad, windy, diminishing noise of the flung shell; then a fainter boom and a cloud of red debris out of the blockhouse or up from the ground near the trenches.

The Spanish infantry in the trenches fired a little volley immediately after every one of the American shells. It puzzled many to decide at what they could be firing, but it was finally resolved that they were firing just to show us that they were still there and were not afraid.

It must have been about 2 o'clock when the enemy's battery again retorted.

The cruel thing about this artillery duel was that our battery had nothing but old-fashioned powder, and its position was always as clearly defined as if it had been the Chicago fire. There is no secrecy about a battery that uses that kind of powder. The great billowy white smoke can be seen for miles. On the other hand, the Spaniards were using the best smokeless. There is no use groaning over what was to be, but——!

However, fate elected that the Spanish shooting should be very bad. Only two-thirds of their shells exploded in this second affair. They all whistled high, and those that exploded raked the ground long since evacuated by the supports and the timbers. No one was hurt.

From El Paso to San Juan there is a broad expanse of dense forest, spotted infrequently with vividly green fields. It is traversed by a single narrow road which leads straight between the two positions, fording two little streams. Along this road had gone our infantry and also the military balloon. Why it was ever taken to such a position nobody knows, but there it was —huge, fat, yellow, quivering—being dragged straight into a zone of fire that would surely ruin it.

There were two officers in the car for the greater part of the way, and there surely were never two men who valued their lives less. But they both escaped unhurt, while the balloon sank down, torn to death by the bullets that were volleyed at it by the nervous Spaniards, who suspected dynamite. It was never brought out of the woods where it recklessly met its fate.

In these woods, unknown to some, including the Spaniards, was formulated the gorgeous plan of taking an impregnable position.

One saw a thin line of black figures moving across a field. They disappeared in the forest. The enemy was keeping up a terrific fire. Then suddenly somebody yelled: "By God, there go our boys up the hill!"

There is many a good American who would give an arm to get the thrill of patriotic insanity that coursed through us when we heard that yell.

Yes, they were going up the hill, up the hill. It was the best moment of anybody's life. An officer said to me afterward: "If we had been in that position and the Spaniards had come at us, we would have piled them up so high the last man couldn't have climbed over." But up went the regiments with no music save that ceaseless, fierce crashing of rifles.

The foreign attachés were shocked. "It is very gallant, but very foolish," said one sternly.

"Why, they can't take it, you know. Never in the world," cried another, much agitated. "It is slaughter, absolute slaughter."

The little Japanese shrugged his shoulders. He was one who said nothing.

The road from El Paso to San Juan was now a terrible road. It should have a tragic fame like the sunken road at Waterloo.

Why we did not later hang some of the gentry who contributed from the trees to the terror of this road is not known.

The wounded were stringing back from the front, hundreds of them. Some walked unaided, an arm or a shoulder having been dressed at a field station. They stopped often enough to answer the universal hail "How is it going?" Others hobbled or clung to a friend's shoulders. Their slit trousers exposed red bandages. A few were shot horribly in the face and were led, bleeding and blind, by their mates.

And then there were the slow pacing stretcher-bearers with the dying or the insensible, the badly wounded, still figures with blood often drying brick color on their hot bandages.

Prostrate at the roadside were many others who had made their way thus far and were waiting for strength. Everywhere moved the sure-handed, invaluable Red Cross men.

Over this scene was a sort of haze of bullets. They were of two kinds. First, the Spanish lines were firing just a trifle high. Their bullets swept over our firing lines and poured into this devoted roadway, the single exit, even as it had been the single approach. The second fire was from guerillas concealed in the trees and in the thickets along the trail. They had come in under the very wings of our strong advance, taken good positions on either side of the road and were peppering our line of communication whenever they got a good target, no matter, apparently, what the target might be.

Red Cross men, wounded men, sick men, correspondents and attachés were all one to the guerilla. The move of sending an irregular force around the flanks of the enemy as he is making his front attack is so legitimate that some of us could not believe at first that the men hidden in the forest were really blazing away at the non-combatants or the wounded. Viewed simply as a bit of tactics, the scheme was admirable. But there is no doubt now that they intentionally fired at anybody they thought they could kill.

You can't mistake an ambulance driver when he is driving his ambulance. You can't mistake a wounded man when he is lying down and being bandaged. And when you see a field hospital you don't mistake it for a squadron of cavalry or a brigade of infantry.

After the guerillas had successfully rewounded some prostrate men in a hospital and killed an ambulance driver off his seat as he was taking his silent, suffering charges to the base, there were any number of humane and gentle hearted men in the army who were extremely anxious to see any guerillas that were caught hanged to the trees in which they were found. Our greatest punishment, after all, is to feed them until they are in danger of bursting.

As we went along the road we suddenly heard a cry behind us. "Oh, come quick! Come quick!" We turned and saw a young soldier spinning around frantically and grabbing at his leg. Evidently he had been going to the stream to fill his canteen, but a guerilla had barred him from that drink. Two Red Cross men rushed for him.

At the last ford, in the shelter of the muddy bank, lay a dismal band, forty men on their backs with doctors working at them and bullets singing in flocks over their heads. They rolled their eyes quietly at us. There was no groaning. They exhibited that profound patience which has been the marvel of every one.

After the ford was passed the woods cleared. The road passed through lines of barbed wire. There were, in fact, barbed wire fences running in almost every direction.

The mule train, galloping like a troop of cavalry, dashed up with a reinforcement of ammunition, every mule on the jump, the cowboys swinging their whips. They were under a fairly strong fire, but up they went.

One does not expect gallantry in a pack train, but incidentally it may be said that this charge, led by the bell mare, was one of the sights of the day.

At a place where the road cut through the crest of the ridge Borrowe and some of his men were working over his dynamite gun. After the fifth discharge something had got jammed. There was never such devotion to an inanimate thing as these men give to their dynamite gun. They will quarrel for her, starve for her, lose sleep for her and fight for her to the last ditch.

In the army there has always been two opinions of the dynamite gun. Some have said it was a most terrific engine of destruction, while others have called it a toy. With the bullets

winging their long flights not very high overhead, Borrowe
and his crowd at sight of us began their little hymn of praise,
the chief note of which was one of almost pathetic insistence.
If they ever get that gun into action again, they will make her
hum.

The discomfited Spaniards, recovering from their panic, opened from their second line a most furious fire. It was first
directed against one part of our line and then against another,
as if they were feeling for our weakest point, fumbling around
after the throat of the army.

Somebody on the left caught it for a time and then suddenly
the enemy apparently devoted their entire attention to the position occupied by the Rough Riders. Some shrapnel, with fuses
cut too long, passed over and burst from 100 to 200 yards to
the rear. They acted precisely like things with strings to them.
When the string was jerked, bang! went the hurtling explosive.
But the infantry fire was very heavy, albeit high.

The American reply was in measured volleys. Part of a regiment would remain on the firing line while the other companies
rested near by under the brow of the hill. Parties were sent
after the packs. The commands knew with what other organizations they were in touch on the two flanks. Otherwise they
knew nothing, save that they were going to hold their ground.
They said so.

From our line could be seen a long, gray Spanish intrenchment, from 400 to 1,000 yards away, according to what part of
our line one measured from. From it floated no smoke and no
men appeared there, but it was making a noise like a million
champagne corks.

Back of their intrenchments, perhaps another thousand
yards, was a long building of masonry tinted pink. It flew many
Red Cross flags and near it were other smaller structures also
flying Red Cross flags. In fact, the enemy's third line of defense
seemed to be composed of hospitals.

The city itself slanted down toward the bay, just a glimpse of
silver. In the clear, white sunshine the houses of the suburbs,
the hospitals and the long gray trenches were so vivid that
they seemed far closer than they were.

To the rear, over the ground that the army had taken, a

breeze was gently stirring the long grass and ruffling the surface of a pool that lay in a sort of meadow. The army took its glory calmly. Having nothing else to do, the army sat down and looked tranquilly at the scenery. There was not that exuberance of enthusiasm which surrounds the vicinity of a candidate for the Assembly.

The army was dusty, dishevelled, its hair matted to its forehead with sweat, its shirts glued to its back with the same, and indescribably dirty, thirsty, hungry, and a-weary from its bundles and its marches and its fights. It sat down on the conquered crest and felt satisfied.

"Well, hell! here we are."

News began to pass along the line. Lawton had taken Caney after a long fight and had lost heavily. The siege pieces were being unloaded at Siboney. Pando had succeeded in reinforcing Santiago that very morning with 8,400 men, 6,000 men, 4,500 men. Pando had not succeeded. And so on.

At dusk a comparative stillness settled upon the ridge. The shooting subsided to little nervous outbursts. In the trenches taken by our troops lay dead Spaniards.

The road to the rear increased its terrors in the darkness. The wounded men, stumbling along in the mud, a miasmic mist from the swampish ground filling their nostrils, heard often in the air the whiplash sound of a bullet that was meant for them by the lurking guerillas. A mile, two miles, two miles and a half to the rear, great populous hospitals had been formed.

The long lines of the hill began to intrench under cover of night, each regiment for itself, still, however, keeping in touch on the flanks. Each regiment dug in the ground that it had taken by its own valor. Some commands had two or three shovels, an axe or two, maybe a pick. Other regiments dug with their bayonets and shovelled out the dirt with their meat ration cans.

Darkness swallowed Santiago and the new intrenchments. The large tropic stars illumined the sky. On the safe side of the ridge our men had built some little red fires, no larger than hats, at which they cooked what food they possessed. There was no sound save to the rear, where throughout the night our pickets could be faintly heard exchanging shots with the guerillas.

On the very moment, it seemed, of the break of day, bang! the fight was on again. The firing broke out from one end of the prodigious V-shaped formation to the other. Our artillery took new advanced positions, but they were driven away by the swirling Mauser fire.

When the day was in full bloom Lawton's division, having marched all night, appeared in the road. The long, long column wound around the base of the ridge and disappeared among the woods and knolls on the right of Wheeler's line. The army was now concentrated in a splendid position.

It becomes necessary to speak of the men's opinion of the Cubans. To put it shortly, both officers and privates have the most lively contempt for the Cubans. They despise them. They came down here expecting to fight side by side with an ally, but this ally has done little but stay in the rear and eat army rations, manifesting an indifference to the cause of Cuban liberty which could not be exceeded by some one who had never heard of it.

In the great charge up the hills of San Juan the American soldiers who, for their part, sprinkled a thousand bodies in the grass, were not able to see a single Cuban assisting in what might easily turn out to be the decisive battle for Cuban freedom.

At Caney a company of Cubans came into action on the left flank of one of the American regiments just before the place was taken. Later they engaged a blockhouse at 2,000 yards and fired away all their ammunition. They sent back to the American commander for more, but they got only a snort of indignation.

As a matter of fact, the Cuban soldier, ignorant as only such isolation as has been his can make him, does not appreciate the ethics of the situation.

This great American army he views as he views the sky, the sea, the air; it is a natural and most happy phenomenon. He will go to sleep while this flood drowns the Spaniards.

The American soldier, however, thinks of himself often as a disinterested benefactor, and he would like the Cubans to play up to the ideal now and then. His attitude is mighty human. He does not really want to be thanked, and yet the total absence of anything like gratitude makes him furious. He is furious, too, because the Cubans apparently consider themselves under no obligation to take part in an engagement; because the Cubans will stay at the rear and collect haversacks, blankets, coats and shelter tents dropped by our troops.

The average Cuban here will not speak to an American unless to beg. He forgets his morning, afternoon or evening salutation unless he is reminded. If he takes a dislike to you he talks about you before your face, using a derisive undertone.

If he asks you a favor and you can't grant it his face grows sour in the expression of a man who has been deprived of an inalienable right. Then at all times he gibbers. Talk, talk, talk, talk. Heaven knows what it is all about; but certainly four Cubans can talk enough for four regiments.

The truth probably is that the food, raiment and security furnished by the Americans have completely demoralized the insurgents. When the force under Gomez came to Guantanamo to assist the marines they were a most efficient body of men. They guided the marines to the enemy and fought with them shoulder to shoulder, not very skilfully in the matter of shooting, but still with courage and determination.

After this action there ensued at Guantanamo a long peace. The Cubans built themselves a permanent camp and they began to eat, eat much, and to sleep long, day and night, until now, behold, there is no more useless body of men anywhere! A trifle less than half of them are on Dr. Edgar's sick list, and the others are practically insubordinate. So much food seems to act upon them like a drug.

Here with the army the demoralization has occurred on a big scale. It is dangerous, too, for the Cuban. If he stupidly, drowsily remains out of these fights, what weight is his voice to have later in the final adjustments? The officers and men of the army, if their feeling remains the same, will not be happy to see him have any at all. The situation needs a Gomez. It is more serious than these bestarred machete bearers know how to appreciate, and it is the worst thing for the cause of an independent Cuba that could possibly exist.

At San Juan the 2d of July was a smaller edition of the 1st. The men deepened their intrenchments, shot, slept and ate. On the 1st every man had been put into the fighting line. There was not a reserve as big as your hat. If the enemy broke through any part of the line there was nothing to stop them short of Siboney. On the 2d, however, some time after the arrival of Lawton, the Ninth Massachusetts and the Thirty-fourth Michigan came up.

Along the road from El Paso they had to pass some pretty grim sights. And there were some pretty grim odors, but the men were steady enough. "How far are they off?" they asked of a passing regular. "Oh, not far; but it's all right. We think they may run out of ammunition in the course of a week or ten days."

The volunteers laughed. But the pitiful thing about this advance was to see in the hands of the boys those terrible old rifles that smoke like brush fires and give the regimental line away to the enemy as plainly as an illuminated sign.

I remember that on the first day men of the Seventy-first who had lost their command would try to join one of the regular regiments, but the regulars would have none of them. "Get out of here with that d—— gun!" the regulars would say. During the battle just one shot from a Springfield would call a volley, for the Spaniards then knew just where to shoot. It was very hard on the Seventy-first New York and the Second Massachusetts.

At Caney about two hundred prisoners were taken. Two big squads of them were soldiers of the regular Spanish infantry in the usual blue-and-white pajamas. The others were the rummiest-looking set of men one could possibly imagine. They were native-born Cubans, reconcentrados, traitors, guerillas of the kind that bushwhacked us so unmercifully. Some were doddering old men, shaking with the palsy of their many years. Some were slim, dirty, bad-eyed boys. They were all of a lower class than one could find in any United States jail.

At first they had all expected to be butchered. In fact, to encourage them to fight, their officers had told them that if they gave in they need expect no mercy from the dreadful Americans.

Our great, good, motherly old country has nothing in her heart but mercy, and nothing in her pockets but beef, hard-tack and coffee for all of them—lemon-colored refugee from Santiago, wild-eyed prisoner from the trenches, Spanish guerilla from out the thickets, half-naked insurgent from the mountains—all of them.

In the church at Caney lie fifty-two Spanish wounded, attended by our surgeons. For a temporary affair, inaugurated in a moment, it is as good a hospital as ever raised its flag after a day of blood, and our surgeons and our Red Cross assistants were giving the best of their trained intelligence to the cure of the hurts of these men even while, on the road from San Juan to El Paso, the guerillas were shooting at our wounded.

No. 40

SPANISH DESERTERS AMONG THE REFUGEES AT EL CANEY

EL CANEY, July 5, VIA PORT ANTONIO, JAMAICA, July 7.—During to-day's lull in the hostilities a steady stream of refugees has poured into our lines from the beleaguered city of Santiago. Women, by far, have been in the majority. Men, strong and able-bodied, have been few indeed. Spain has urgent need of such, wherefore Santiago has given up few more than wrecked and helpless creatures, too far upon the road to death to aid in staying our advance.

Yet, as the truce advanced, it changed the number and the character of these refugees. More men flocked in, young men and strong men. Certainly among them were deserters. There was the air of the true Spaniard about them. They had cast aside their distinguishing uniforms, to be sure, but they could not so easily disguise the ways and bearing of the soldier. Undoubtedly they were renegades. But, then—what matter? They were permitted within the lines, the one place where they would find safety from the impending avalanche of death soon to roll down upon Santiago from the hillside.

One saw in this great, gaunt assemblage the true horror of war. The sick, the lame, the halt and the blind were there. Women and men, tottering upon the verge of death, plodded doggedly onward. Beyond were our lines and safety. But so long had this same horror of war been before them that no longer could they feel its horridness. Their air was stolid and indifferent. It was a forlorn hope at the best. If this was safety, well and good. If death, what difference how it came.

In sharp contrast to this, one saw, now and again, women radiant with joy. These were the kindred of the insurgents. Some had been separated from those stout hearts in the field for many weary weeks—yes, months, and even years. At the crest of that weary slope they knew whom they should find. Toiling upward and onward they pressed, and finally, with glad cries, in the great gathering of troops they came upon the ones they sought. This, indeed, was another side of war.

Again, in the throng toiling on to safety were men and women carried in chairs and litters, some even in cot-beds. Our ambulances went forth to meet them. Then when these stolid, hopeless, unimpassioned ones found the dreaded enemy receiving and aiding them with kindness they showed, for the first time, some trace of feeling. What! Should these mad, despised Americanos spend time aiding the weak and aged! This was a wonder, indeed.

But, though the Americans' hands were turned to doing gentleness, it was otherwise with those Spanish miserables, Spain's ignoble pride, the guerillas. They lurked along the roadsides, eager and ready for bloodshed, plunder and unnameable wickedness. To drive them back the American cavalry patrolled the road of the refugees, whereupon the guerillas withdrew.

At the church in Caney the American surgeons were laboring among the enemy's sorely wounded. Here fifty-two Spanish were under treatment. Their amazement was profound. In the centre of the church lies one of the Spanish commanders, sorely wounded. There never was a more astonished man than he. Like the others, he believed his position impregnable. How any mortal could cross the zone of fire and survive was a matter beyond his ken. By the saints, it was a miracle! Three thousand Mausers, he knew to his own knowledge, were trained down the one slope he guarded. Yet had the Americans plunged through the rain of death and driven all before them.

Almost as great was his amazement at our treatment of himself and his wounded men. Why should we waste time upon them, when so many of ours had been stricken? Why this kindness? They had expected to lie where they had fallen, waiting but to die. It was the fortune of war. Why should it not be?

Inside the limits of this town the foreign Consuls have made their headquarters. Here each one is ready to provide for the people of his flag. Also they are aiding in the care of the other refugees, so far as they are able. None of the refugees brought food—there was no food for them to bring. The Spaniards had planned to restock their commissary with the supplies they had arranged to capture from the Americans. It was a sad blow that the Americans declined to be captured.

Our course to all at Caney has been moderation. Sometimes we have been too kind. Everybody knows the story of the road from the battle-field—the guerillas hanging to the flanks of the long line of wounded going to the rear. Though these men of ours could fight no longer, though they were in sore distress, these fiends incarnate fired upon them. They picked off, where they were able, the ambulance men, the bearers of the Red Cross flag and the surgeons at their work. They bowled them over at every chance. Yet three of these miscreants, caught among the trees, wearing clothes stripped from our dead, have been set at work about headquarters.

No. 41

CAPTURED MAUSERS FOR VOLUNTEERS

GEN. SHAFTER'S HEADQUARTERS, July 7.—To men who have studied recent fighting in Cuba there is one point that occurs constantly and with increasing weight, and that point relates to the arms of the volunteers. The Springfield, 1873, was undoubtedly a good weapon in its time and certainly it is even now a very strong shooting rifle, but if we are conducting a modern war on modern lines we may just as well understand once for all that black powder will not do.

We cannot without cruel injustice send men using black powder into action against men who use a fair grade of smokeless. If any one wishes to learn more let him ask the Seventy-first New York or the Second Massachusetts or the Thirty-third Michigan.

The last-named regiment in particular has learned all the joys of being badly cut up by a force that they have never seen—whose positions they could not even suspect.

On July 1 the regiment was ordered to march on Aguadores and make an attack, which, it was hoped, would draw off a reinforcement from the Santiago trenches and make the work easier for Wheeler, Kent and Lawton. The men were marched up the railroad track, which is the only practicable road between Siboney and Aguadores. Dense thickets were upon either side.

The action was opened by a Spanish battery, which had been placed so as to rake the railway track. This battery used smokeless powder. A moment later Spanish infantry opened a heavy fire. The infantry, too, used smokeless powder. The Thirty-third Michigan became then involved in one of those battles with spectres which is so hard on the nerves of the oldest soldiers. What force was hidden in the chaparral they could not estimate. They could tell nothing save that they were losing men.

On the other hand, their position and everything that they did was always perfectly clear to the Spaniards. If they deployed a line of skirmishers to the left and opened fire the Spaniards were able not only to locate this line exactly but to estimate from the puffs of smoke how many men were engaged. In a word, the proceedings of the enemy were all shrouded in mystery, while the movements of the Amercians were always hopelessly palpable. So much for the Thirty-third Michigan and black powder.

The experiences of the Seventy-first at San Juan and of the Second Massachusetts at El Caney are better known. Every time they opened fire they called down a volley from every

Spanish rifle within range. It is a mistake to contend—as many of our men now do—that the Spaniards shoot well. The individual Spaniard rarely, if ever, shoots well. But two or three thousand Spaniards armed with Mausers and each man having from five hundred to a thousand cartridges at hand, are bound to hit at most everything when the enemy begins to cross open ground in their front.

It is destruction by volume of fire; not by individual accuracy. If the Americans do not cross open ground, but use black powder from the thickets, that is just as good for the Spaniards.

It is plain reasoning that we have not armed the volunteers with Krag-Jorgensens because we have not enough Krag-Jorgensens, and ordinarily there would be small use in scolding about it, but upon the fall of Santiago we should come into the possession of about ten or maybe fifteen thousand Mauser rifles in good condition and these should immediately go into the hands of our volunteers.

The Mauser is a more simple rifle than the Krag-Jorgensen and in a good many respects it is a better arm. The volunteers could learn its use easily and quickly, and in a trice their effectiveness would be increased fourfold.

At the battle of San Juan it was not unusual to see, when a regular fell, some volunteer throw away an old Springfield and possess himself of the regular's Krag-Jorgensen and ammunition. The men find out what is good for them quickly enough. They would welcome the Mausers, and it is to be hoped they will get them. If there turns out to be not enough Mauser ammunition to last them any great length of time let us set to work and make it. In war anything is justified save killing your own men through laziness or gross stupidity.

No. 42

REGULARS GET NO GLORY

SIBONEY, July 9.—Of course people all over the United States are dying to hear the names of the men who are conspicuous for bravery in Shafter's army. But as a matter of fact nobody with the army is particularly conspicuous for bravery. The bravery of an individual here is not a quality which causes him to be pointed out by his admiring fellows; he is, rather, submerged in the general mass. Now, cowardice—that would make a man conspicuous. He would then be pointed out often enough, but—mere bravery—that is no distinction in the Fifth Corps of the United States Army.

The main fact that has developed in this Santiago campaign is that the soldier of the regular army is the best man standing on two feet on God's green earth. This fact is put forth with no pretense whatever of interesting the American public in it. The public doesn't seem to care very much for the regular soldier.

The public wants to learn of the gallantry of Reginald Marmaduke Maurice Montmorenci Sturtevant, and for goodness sake how the poor old chappy endures that dreadful hard-tack and bacon. Whereas, the name of the regular soldier is probably Michael Nolan and his life-sized portrait was not in the papers in celebration of his enlistment.

Just plain Private Nolan, blast him—he is of no consequence. He will get his name in the paper—oh, yes, when he is "killed." Or when he is "wounded." Or when he is "missing." If some good Spaniard shoots him through he will achieve a temporary notoriety, figuring in the lists for one brief moment in which he will appear to the casual reader mainly as part of a total, a unit in the interesting sum of men slain.

In fact, the disposition to leave out entirely all lists of killed and wounded regulars is quite a rational one since nobody cares to read them, anyhow, and their omission would allow room for oil paintings of various really important persons, limned as they were in the very act of being at the front, proud young men riding upon horses, the horses being still in Tampa and the proud young men being at Santiago, but still proud young men riding upon horses.

The ungodly Nolan, the sweating, swearing, overloaded, hungry, thirsty, sleepless Nolan, tearing his breeches on the barbed wire entanglements, wallowing through the muddy fords, pursuing his way through the stiletto-pointed thickets, climbing the fire-crowned hill—Nolan gets shot. One Nolan of this regiment or that regiment, a private, great chums in time of peace with a man by the name of Hennessy, him that had a fight with Snyder. Nearest relative is a sister, chambermaid in a hotel in Omaha. Hennessy, old fool, is going around looking glum, buried in taciturn silence, a silence that lasts two hours and eight minutes; touching tribute to Nolan.

There is a half-bred fox terrier in barracks at Reno. Who the deuce gets the dog now? Must by rights go to Hennessy. Brief argument during which Corporal Jenkins interpolates the thoughtful remark that they haven't had anything to eat that day. End of Nolan.

The three shining points about the American regular are his illimitable patience under anything which he may be called upon to endure, his superlative marksmanship and his ability in action to go ahead and win without any example or leading or jawing or trumpeting whatsoever. He knows his business, he does.

He goes into battle as if he had been fighting every day for three hundred years. If there is heavy firing ahead he does not even ask a question about it. He doesn't even ask whether the Americans are winning or losing. He agitates himself over no extraneous points. He attends exclusively to himself. In the Turk or the Cossack this is a combination of fatalism and woodenheadedness. It need not be said that these qualities are lacking in the regular.

After the battle, at leisure—if he gets any—the regular's talk is likely to be a complete essay on practical field operations. He will be full of views about the management of such and such a brigade, the practice of this or that battery, and be admiring or scornful in regard to the operations on the right flank. He will be a tireless critic, bolstering his opinions with technical information procured heaven only knows where. In fact, he will alarm you. You may say: "This man gabbles too much for to be a soldier."

Then suddenly the regular becomes impenetrable, enigmatic. It is a question of Orders. When he hears the appointed voice raised in giving an Order, he is a changed being. When an Order comes he has no more to say; he simply displays as fine a form of unquestioning obedience as there is to be seen anywhere. It is his sacred thing, his fetish, his religion. Nothing now can stop him but a bullet.

In speaking of Reginald Marmaduke Maurice Montmorenci Sturtevant and his life-sized portraits, it must not be supposed that the unfortunate youth admires that sort of thing. He is a man and a soldier, although not so good either as man or soldier as Michael Nolan. But he is in this game honestly and sincerely; he is playing it gallantly; and, if from time to time he is made to look ridiculous, it is not his fault at all. It is the fault of the public.

We are as a people a great collection of the most arrant kids about anything that concerns war, and if we can get a chance to perform absurdly we usually seize it. It will probably take us three more months to learn that the society reporter, invaluable as he may be in times of peace, has no function during the blood and smoke of battle.

I know of one newspaper whose continual cabled instructions to its men in Cuba were composed of interrogations as to the doings and appearance of various unhappy society young men who were decently and quietly doing their duty along o' Nolan and the others. The correspondents of this paper, being already impregnated with soldierly feeling, finally arose and said they'd be blamed if they would stand it.

And shame, deep shame, on those who, because somebody once led a cotillon, can seem to forget Nolan—Private Nolan of the regulars—shot through, his half-bred terrier being masterless at Reno and his sister being chambermaid in a hotel in Omaha; Nolan, no longer sweating, swearing, overloaded, hungry, thirsty, sleepless, but merely a corpse, attired in about forty cents' worth of clothes. Here's three volleys and taps to one Nolan, of this regiment or that regiment, and maybe some day, in a fairer, squarer land, he'll get his picture in the paper, too.

No. 43

A SOLDIER'S BURIAL THAT MADE A NATIVE HOLIDAY

PONCE, PORTO RICO, Aug. 5—A company of regular infantry marched into the plaza at Ponce, halted, stacked arms and broke ranks. In the cool shade of the trees the men loafed carelessly while the natives, always intensely interested in the soldiers, gathered near and began their comic, good-natured pantomime. The lazy, still, tropic afternoon drifted slowly, hour by hour, with only the rumble of passing carriages to interrupt its profound serenity.

The captain of the regulars went down the street to where, before the door of a house, waited a hearse. There was a carriage containing two American women and on the pavement stood a little group of officers, with their battered old hats in their hands. The natives began to accumulate in a crowd, and from them arose a high-pitched babble of gossip concerning this funeral. They stretched their necks, pointed, dodged those who would interfere with their view. Amid the chatter the Americans displayed no signs of hearing it. They remained calm, stoical, superior, wearing the curious, grim dignity of people who are burying their dead.

The company of regulars swung down the street, drew up in front of the house, and presented arms with a clash. Six big, blue-shirted privates paced out with the coffin. The throng edged up suddenly, dodging and peering. The little band of Americans seemed like beings of another world, with their gently mournful, impassive faces, during this display of monkeyish interest.

The cortege moved off, preceded, accompanied, followed by the crowd of natives. Ponce, a large city, drowsed on peacefully in the sun, and the passing of the small procession brought no particular emotion to its mind. In the suburbs women hurried out to the porches of the little wooden houses, and naked babies, swollen with fruit, strutted out to see, sucking their thumbs. A man walking directly behind the hearse was hailed interrogatively from a distance. He answered loudly, waving his arm toward the graveyard.

A girl called greetings to some friends in the crowd. Suddenly, close to the road, a woman broke out in a raucous tirade at some of her children. The crowd still babbled. All these sounds beat like waves upon the hearse; noisy, idle, senseless waves beating upon the hearse, the invulnerable ship of the indifferent dead man. And the Americans, moving along behind it, were still calm, stoical, superior. The spray of the chatter whirled against them and they were bronze, bronze men going to bury their dead, and the humming and swishing and swashing were only as important as the rattling of so many pebbles in a tin box.

The graveyard was circled by a high wall which was surmounted by broken bottles sunk into the mortar. The interior presented the appearance of a misused potato patch were it not for the gaunt wooden crosses which upreared here and there. The crowd of natives ploughed through each other in order to reach the gate.

The troops marched forward and faced up sharply before an open grave. A chaplain appeared. The Americans, barring the infantry, stood bareheaded. The natives, noting this, took off their hats. There was a moment of intense expectancy.

"I am the resurrection and the life——" The chaplain's words were quite smothered in the ejaculations, inquiries, comments which came over the wall where many people were pushing toward the gate. An enterprising lot had climbed a bit of old wall which overlooked the cemetery wall and upon it they shrilled like parrots. The chaplain, beset, badgered, drowned out, went on imperturbably.

The first volley of the firing party created a great convulsion in the crowd outside, who could not see the proceedings and were taken by surprise. As the sound crashed toward the hills many jumped like frightened rabbits and then a moment later the whole mob, seeing the joke, burst into wild laughter.

A bugler stepped forward. Into a medley of sounds such as would come from a combined baseball game and clambake he sent the call of "taps," that extraordinary wail of mourning and song of rest and peace, the soldier's good-bye, his night, the fall of eternal darkness, the end.

The sad, sad, slow voice of the bugle called out over the grave, a soul appealing to the sky, a call of earthly anguish and heavenly tranquillity, a solemn heart-breaking song. But if this farewell of the soldier to the sky, the flowers, the bees and all life was heard by the natives their manner did not betray it.

No. 44

GRAND RAPIDS AND PONCE

PONCE, PORTO RICO, Aug. 7.—As one of the *Journal* dispatch boats circled slowly past the war ships and transports into the harbor of Ponce the correspondents, veterans of Santiago, and other campaigns, began to array themselves disreputably. They donned breeches of brown duck and shirts of the hues of almost every kind of vegetable, and their hats were slouch, dirty, twisty-wise and a discredit to them. The correspondents also armed themselves. In the end they somewhat resembled jail birds, which is the business of men good at the game of war.

The yacht dropped anchor and another correspondent came from the shore. He had arrived two days previously. Upon sighting the formidable group on the quarterdeck he burst into hoarse laughter. Later he explained the wonders of Ponce. It was no Daiquiri. It was no Siboney. It was no cable station at Guantanamo. Ponce, to be sure, was a city with hotels and shops and public hacks and barbers and ice and ales, wines, liquors and cigars. If a man lost all his lead pencils he could jaunt casually into the street and buy more. If there happened an unhappy soul with no tobacco, there was no period of intolerable anguish. In case of need, for instance, there could be found such a person as a dentist. And the correspondent went on to say that the generals and the newspaper men were in the habit of riding to the front—the terrible front—in carriages. The ferocity died out of the arriving war correspondents. In carriages? Name of heaven!

Viewed asho_e, Ponce, two miles from its little sea port, developed four striking things immediately—American buggies, naked babies, trees laden with flaming crimson blossoms, and the enigmatic smile of the Porto Rican. They were all burning in the sunshine and dimmed by the white dust of a tropic city. They were all guarded by the American soldier, a calm, bronze and blue man with a bayonet. And herein lay the supreme interest, the interest of the juxtaposition of Michigan and Porto Rico—Grand Rapids serenely sitting in judgment upon the affairs of Ponce. This made one marvel; this was the extraordinary situation that dazed the thoughtful American. It was as if a journal had announced: "A Rochester trolley car has collided with an ox cart in Buenos Ayres." You could not gauge the thing; you remained simply astounded.

Afterward there was the enigmatic smile of the Porto Rican. It was enigmatic at first because we thought of it too hard. We weighed it too much. We reflected upon it until it became simply confusion—a conciliatory, joyful, fearful, crafty, honest, lying smile. But at length emerged this fact—the Porto Rican, taking him as a symbolized figure, a type, was glad, glad that the Spaniards had gone, glad that the Americans had come. What the troops received at Ponce was a welcome. The cheering was led by the responsible men, the merchants, the land owners, the people with purses. When your man with a purse cheers he has got to mean it. Otherwise he would choke to death.

In the applause there is a stratum of deceit, but it is furnished mainly by the peasantry, who have been forcibly taught that the Spaniards are invincible and are sure to return. Meanwhile the American soldier expresses his opinion of this probability in a new word—Spinachers. The Jamaica negro cannot say Spaniard. His comic tongue makes him say Spuniard. The American soldier says Spinacher because when a thing becomes common he is nationally bound to extract from it whatever it may convey of our kind of irony.

Ponce, of course, bears the stamp of Spain, that stamp which shall remain forever upon Mexico and the States of Central America and South America, even as they are indelible in

Cuba. It is a thing which cannot be conquered even by such superb troops as United States regulars. You can shoot a man through the head, but you cannot remove from his brain a love for the bloody death of a bull. There is the inevitable little plaza in the centre of the city, shaded with beautiful trees and threaded with wide walks. In the Moorish band stand a Spanish band operated but yesterday. Sometimes now an American band plays there of an evening. In the plaza there is also the cathedral, a fine old Spanish sign, such as one sees even in California. From the plaza radiate such streets and such scenes as one can find in the City of Mexico, the only thing lacking being the persistent, harsh cries of the street vendors. The principal hotel is the usual, quaint place, with a courtyard in which men sit and have their cognac or coffee. The walls are decorated with lamentable pictures in oil—fat and shapeless lions, palm trees, absurd urns, white palaces, lakes. The tropic sun blisters the paint, and pieces of lion, tree, palace have fallen to the ground. Dilapidation is carefully prominent here as in all the city. Every door, every window is as high as aspiration and almost as dingy as fulfilment. The Spaniard, when he is once persuaded to polish, is a terrible person. He creates a newness a thousand times more ghastly than his ordinary dirtiness. A clean and newly painted house in a Spanish town is unreal and terrifying. And so the old city lies in the sun, dirty, romantic and patrolled by Wisconsin.

No. 45

THE PORTO RICAN "STRADDLE"

JUANA DIAZ, PORTO RICO, Aug. 10—The American soldier alludes often to the natives here as handshakers. It is his way of expressing a cynical suspicion regarding all the "viva Americanos" business that he hears and sees in this city of Ponce. One cannot define a type at once when the type has just been captured, and knows that it must be very, very good, although the same may be foreign to its ordinary manners. It is correct enough that the American soldier should be suspicious; there is more or less in the handshaking idea.

Johnson, one of the *Journal's* correspondents here, and myself had recently an opportunity to see the Porto Rican when he was right in the middle and couldn't tell which way to dodge. The incident was instructive.

Two companies of the Sixteenth Pennsylvania Infantry at that time formed the advance of the army along the main military road. They were encamped just beyond the town of Juana Diaz, which is nine miles from Ponce. We heard that General Ernst, the brigade commander, was going to reinforce these pickets with five more companies and then extend the American advance five more miles into the hills. When we reached Juana Diaz we could see the men slinging their kits, preparatory to marching, and in the little hotel facing the plaza and the old church the General and his staff were just finishing their luncheon. We thought it was only a question of minutes, so we passed them and went on along the road which the troops were to take. We were under the impression that an advance party had gone on ahead. However, it was not long before a peasant's answers convinced us that Johnson, mounted on a bicycle, was the sure-enough vanguard of the American army. His immediate support bestrode a long, low, rakish plug, with a maximum speed of seven knots. We had no desire to win fame by any two-handed attack on the Spanish army, so, on receiving the peasant's information, we slowed down to a pace that was little more than a concession to one man's opinion of the other.

The road, beautifully hard, wound through two thick lines of trees. We circled spurs of the mountains, the grass upon them being yellowish green in the afternoon sunlight. We crossed tumbling brooks. With the palm trees out, it was a scene such as can be found in Summer time in Southern New York. There was no man nor beast to be seen ahead on the road nor in the fields. We learned afterward that we were about two miles and a half ahead of the American scouts, the difficulties attending the work of the flanking parties causing the march to be extremely slow. Rounding a corner we came suddenly upon a country store. Chickens and pigs scouted in the road and in the yard of the house across the road. On the steps of the store, on a fence, on boxes and barrels, and leaning against trees were about thirty men dressed in civilian garb. As we appeared they turned their heads, and as we rode slowly up every eye swung to our pace. They preserved an absolute, stony silence. Now, here were men between the lines. The Americans were on one side and the Spaniards were on the other. They knew nothing of any American advance. They were, as far as they knew, on strictly independent ground, and could drop on either side of the fence. Americanism was here elective.

We drew up and looked at them. They looked at us. Not a word was said.

The native in the zone already ours is always quick to greet the American with a salute or with hat in hand. He cries out "Bueno!" at every opportunity, meaning, "I am glad you have come." When he is a crowd he is forever yelling "Viva Americanos!" When he is one he is forever nodding and smiling with absolute frankness and telling you that he prefers the Americans by all means. He is busy at it day and night.

But here was a contrast. This reception was new to our experience. These men were as tongue-tied and sullen as a lot of burglars met in the daytime. Not one of them could endure a straight glance, and if we turned suddenly we were likely to catch two of them whispering.

Time passed slowly, with no change in the situation. We remained in the road and grouped in front of the store was the crowd, with their strange foreign eyes moving in shifty glances. The situation got to be insupportable. It was no fun to stand there with an obligation of stoicism upon us and withstand this business of moving on a stage before an audience of thirty hostile dramatic critics. We finally developed a plan. We would concentrate our glance on one man and talk about him in English, ominously.

"Look at that brute on the barrel there. He certainly is glad to see us. Look at him, will you?"

"Ah, the whole crowd of 'em are Spanish—that's easy. Never mind. Let 'em wait. We'll know how it is later. Just size up the storekeeper. He'll be grinning, and charging the boys two prices to-morrow. But look at him, now. Never mind. We'll get even."

"Look at that Willie in the gray coat. See him stare back at us. Never mind. We'll fix him."

A half-hour passed as slowly as time in the sick room. Hardly a man in the crowd moved out of his place during this time. We called to the storekeeper for some cigarettes, and he came and handed them to us with a manner that was subtly offensive enough to be artistic. Some girls came out on the porch of the house and surveyed us impassively. A man talking with another glanced at us, and spat in a way that left a feeling in our minds that perhaps it was not altogether unlikely that he was referring insultingly to us.

We could not tell whether these people were all pro-Spanish Porto Ricans or whether a part of them were really pro-American but afraid yet to give themselves away to the others or whether they were all simply timid people who wanted to play both ends against the middle until they were absolutely sure who were to be supreme. At any rate, they were a sulky, shifty, bad lot, with the odds strongly in favor of Spanish leanings. They had nothing but distrust in their eyes, and nothing but dislike in their ways.

Up the cool, shady country road toward Juana Diaz appeared a figure. It was a quarter of a mile away, but no one could mistake the slouched service hat, the blue shirt, the wide cartridge belt, the blue trousers, the brown leggings, the rifle held lightly in the hollow of the left arm. It was the first American scout.

He stood for almost two minutes, looking in our direction. Then he moved on toward us. When he had come ten paces four more men, identical in appearance, showed behind him. The crowd around the front of the store could not see them. Their first information was when a young American sergeant galloped up on a native pony. Then two of them mounted their horses quietly and started off in the direction of the Spanish lines. The young sergeant cried to us:

"Well, say, I guess I won't have that. Those Indians riding off to give us away!"

He galloped hastily down the road and we piled after him, but the two Porto Ricans came back docilely enough.

The five soldiers on foot arrived opposite the store. They did not stop, paying little heed to any one. With their passing the

Porto Ricans began to brace up and smile. Then appeared the support of the scouts and flankers, forty men blocked in a solid wall of blue-black, up the road. The Porto Ricans looked cheerful. After the support had gone on there was a considerable pause. Then six companies of Pennsylvania infantry marched past, with a rattling of canteens and shuffling of feet. The Porto Ricans looked happy. By the time the general clattered forward with his staff they were happy, excessively polite, overwhelming every one with attentions and shyly confessing their everlasting devotion to the United States. The proprietor of the store dug up a new English and Spanish lexicon and proudly semaphored his desire to learn the new language of Porto Rico. There was not a scowl anywhere; all were suffused with joy. We told them they were a lot of honest men. And, after all, who knows?

No. 46

HAVANA'S HATE DYING, SAYS STEPHEN CRANE

HAVANA, Aug. 25.—Conditions in this interesting city are much better than anybody on our side has supposed. The people await the coming of the Commission with a rather brave steadiness when you come to remember that they will not concede for a moment that Havana itself was ever in the remotest danger of being captured by the Americans.

The new condition of tranquillity has been established by the city's newspapers, which are printing Spanish news from Santiago, Porto Rico and Manila, descriptive of the temperance and justice of the Americans, as well as of their courage and prowess.

When I first landed here it was difficult to withstand the scowls that one met everywhere, particularly from Spanish officers, who at that time were all exaggerating their gaits and generally improving and rearranging their "fronts."

That has now changed for the better, and one can now inhabit the hotels, cafes and streets without meeting any particularly offensive looks.

Even some good manners have been publicly exploited by the police. What might be called a correspondent's corral was established out in the harbor, and nine birds fluttered therein. On a certain night one escaped and was trying his wings in Havana when the police swooped down on him. It is said that the air of distinguished consideration which surrounded the incident was beyond words. Spectators informed me the next morning that at a late hour they had left the correspondent and four police officials drinking cognac with almost supernatural courtesy in the Cafe Inglaterra.

It becomes obvious that as time goes on many officials of many kinds here are arriving at the old Porto Rico proposition of playing both ends against the middle. This is a tremendous change for the Spanish officials.

The Spanish merchant, however, has a supreme admiration for the American as a customer. He will wait for him and give him a welcome in which Peninsula patriotism plays no part.

There are four gunboats in the harbor besides the emaciated cruiser *Alfonso XII.*, with no engines and no guns. The gunboats have been very useful in this war, but really they are boats which could have steamed out and destroyed the blockade at any time since our heavy ships have been away to Santiago. That is to say, they could have done so if their engines had been all right; but one can't tell whether it was a case of boilers or incompetence.

Their guns are all equivalent to six and twelve-pounders, and they could have wiped the ocean with ten or a dozen converted towboats if the Spaniard was only a sailor, and if the American was not such a fine sailor.

It is in the harbor where the war has marked Havana. The harbor is a soundless vacancy save for the gunboats. In the streets the change has not been so great. The cabmen charge fifty cents where once they charged thirty cents, and the commercial streets are dull, but it is on the water front where havoc has been wrought.

The prices for provisions have been about as known. The

staples never went to really killing prices, if you limit the staples to rice, beans and meat. The proprietor of the Hotel Pasaje tells me, however, that at one time he had to pay fifty cents for a piece of bread as large as your hand in order to provide his customers at the hotel table. The luxuries simply passed out of sight, but then, to deprive people of luxuries is not necessarily to enforce a good blockade.

The spirit of the people here has not been broken, and as usual they regard the prospective ending of the war as some new betrayal of ignorance of the Government at Madrid.

"Oh, yes, Santiago, I know. But Havana? Never!" Still, their opinions of the Americans have entirely changed, and names like Sampson, Schley, Shafter and McKinley are spoken now with a change of voice.

Nobody—popularly speaking—has ever heard of Dewey, mainly because the existence of the Philippines is not a particularly well established fact.

The Spaniards may hate us, or, at least many of them may hate us, but they will never again despise us.

The editors of the Havana papers have peculiarly difficult parts to play in this suspended crisis, and they are playing with splendid finesse and judgment.

Prominent citizens here do not see a convulsive future, the worst imagined being a time of festivities for the volunteers, when there is likely to be more or less ill-judged shooting. When that time comes certain prominent American journalists are likely to be seen writing their dispatches in the tops of tall trees.

No. 47

STEPHEN CRANE SEES FREE CUBA

HAVANA, Aug. 26, VIA KEY WEST, Aug. 27.—The feeling here grows stronger for annexation. Every day the Spaniards fear an onslaught from the Cuban troops, hungry for many things of which they have been long deprived. The Spaniards now respect the Americans, and probably will give hearty welcome to the American troops.

Reports from Santiago say the American soldiers have prevented any possible exuberance on the part of the insurgents, keeping them at the outskirts, and have made a great impression among the dominant mercantile classes. These regard the entrance of the Americans with tranquillity, and in many cases pleasure.

Four Havana thieves talking yesterday said: "We must steal as much as possible before the Americans come, for then we will get into great difficulty if we steal." They had been used to paying $5 immunity for each case caught. Their sentiments give a line on the prevailing idea regarding Americans.

There will be no trouble from the volunteers provided the United States protect everybody. Even in the unconquered city of Havana the American is conqueror, if we may be allowed to speak in that way.

Steamships loading or unloading here are delayed owing to the physical weakness of the stevedores, but the higher classes in every case have had plenty of food, the difference being in quality, never quantity.

Advices from Matanzas state that the condition of the poor people is simply horrible. Men, women and children lie in the street. The Consular authorities feel the Red Cross relief should come quickly. There is no such condition in Havana, where plenty of merchant ships are now coming.

The cane fields and sweet potato patches between here and Matanzas are well under way. The Spanish troops along the route look very hungry. No white flags are flying.

The better people of Matanzas also wish annexation. Along the route are temporary thatched villages for the reconcentrados. The armored cars still run on all trains, each car containing about thirty soldiers. Their rifles are in miserable condition, and the soldiers look as bad as reconcentrados. The garrison of Matanzas, amounting to 6,000, and a large force of insurgents under Betancourt are encamped within twelve miles.

No. 48

STEPHEN CRANE FEARS NO BLANCO

HAVANA, Aug. 28.—The change in the spirit of this city is something wonderful. It is signified by the increased use of a certain proverb. The proverb reads thus:

"It is better to be a lion's tail than a rat's head." If this doesn't edify any American who remembers the old rabid cries of the Havana populace, then all words have lost their significance.

Meantime everybody waits for the commission. Rumors both comic and serious fly in the streets. They do little more than indicate the desires of certain classes or parties. To-day it was said that the United States Government was going to buy for cash all the public buildings in Cuba, and that Spain was going to get the money to pay her troops.

An evening newspaper of yesterday printed an interview of over a column with Captain Stewart M. Brice, greatly to that young officer's astonishment. It seems that the interviewer breakfasted in Captain Brice's company, but as neither could speak the other's language none can tell why the interviewer thought he was interviewing anybody. Nevertheless, the article, apparently an outspoken statement by one of General Shafter's aides, set every tongue wagging. It was distinctly hostile in its estimate of the Cuban character, and Spaniards were much tickled.

All the newspapers comment on it solemnly this morning. Four Americans who were also at the breakfast say that Brice and his supposed interviewer did not exchange five words. They couldn't.

Many of the Cubans think as soon as the Americans come they are going to put the Spaniards out bag and baggage. They are happy over it. Columbus's bones are being dragged into the general misunderstanding to-day. Some high-priced dreamer got it into his head that the United States was going to seize the bones of the venerated discoverer. "These bones are ours, ours alone, and Spain cannot abandon them to the insults or indifference of an inimical race," he exclaims.

El Noticiero Universal this evening makes a laughable attempt to locate the future position of the Spaniards in Cuba. The article also indicates some of the popular misconceptions as to the intentions of the American Government. It begins with an expression of satisfaction that the American press has more or less changed its opinion of the Cubans, but sees very little on the horizon for the Spaniards, no matter which way the cat jumps.

"What are the Spaniards to do, facing this black future?" it asks. "Are we inclined to help the insurgents or are we inclined to favor the Yankees. The sentimentalism of blood and race alone calls us to the insurgents. If they rule we will have to leave this country in order not to become the victims of their hatred.

"The instinct of preservation calls us to the Yankees, because we are at least bound to confess without hypocrisy that they are a people of order. But sooner or later we will be driven out of the island by them, and we will never be able to forget that they are the people who ruined us. What, then, have we to do? This is our opinion.

"We must be only Spaniards; amalgamate, form a powerful colony detailed in every way to help the prestige of the fatherland. Leave the insurgents and the Yankees to settle their own disputes, and when they have solved the problem we will decide as to our future course, after having studied the pros and cons of our own interests."

For a reason unannounced the authorities have raked up an old law which declares that no prisoner shall wear chains, although chains have been in vogue here for twenty-five years. The convicts who work on the streets are no longer to wear leg chains. People believe that the authorities are now willing to let prisoners escape in order to avoid the expense of them.

An American who has been in Morro Castle, who has been mobbed in the streets of Havana, who has been pelted and hooted throughout the Province of Havana because he was an American, said to me to-day:

"Oh, to see the regulars come up Obispo street. We are all waiting for it." He had a memory for his wrongs, but we are all the same about one thing—we want to see the regulars march up Obispo street. There are few enough Americans here—maybe thirty, Red Cross members, tobacco buyers and correspondents.

"We are waiting to see our calm, steady, businesslike regulars swing up from the wharves to the Prado. It will be a great day in Havana."

To illustrate what I have previously said about the change of sentiment in Havana I must describe something which occurred this afternoon. With some friends I went to visit the graves of the dead sailors of the *Maine*. An old man conducted us to the pitifully bare little plot. As we were going he came to the side of the carriage and said:

"There are a great many people sitting by the gate, and as you go out would you mind looking back and bowing to me? I want to show them what great and fine people are my friends."

We grinned at each other in abashed fashion at the idea of our being called great and fine, but at the gate we turned our heads and bowed fraternally to the old man, thus allowing him to work the cold bluff on the populace that he is on intimate terms with all the Americans.

In fact the position of an American changes from day to day. At first scowls, then toleration, then courtesy. For my part I came into Havana without permission from anybody. I simply came in. I did not even have a passport. I was at a hotel while the Government was firmly imprisoning nine correspondents on a steamer in the harbor. But no one molested me.

I don't doubt I could have been insulted if I chose. I often suspected Spanish officers of leaving a foot or an elbow too far in order that I might strike it and become involved in an altercation, but I dodged them all easily, without seeming to pay any heed. All I had to do was to keep from forcing any official recognition upon the Government, in which case they would have been obliged to deport me or to take some other means of disposing of me.

At present the position of an American in Havana is one that many another here envies. There is one thing which we have forgotten in our intercourse with the Spanish-Americans. People of this class not only admire splendor, they reverence it. They mistake it for excellence and power.

One remembers the visit of the British deputation to the court of King Menelek. The men were decked out in all sorts of magnificence. They wore the shining uniforms of the Horse Guards, the Grenadier Guards and other lurid organizations. The sight smote the African soul of the monarch, and he promptly conceded more than he intended, even if that was not much.

The illustration is not perfect, but in dealing with a people of this kind we would find our path made much easier if we threw a few peacock feathers into our business.

I have said that the Spaniard here is going to make no trouble for the American. That is true; but there may be trouble. If so, it will be made by the man who is left behind—the Spaniard whose home and wealth is in Cuba and not in Spain. He is extremely likely to heave a few convenient rocks at the departing Spanish regiments.

No. 49

STEPHEN CRANE'S VIEWS OF HAVANA

HAVANA, Sept. 4, VIA KEY WEST, Sept. 6.—Two years ago the Spanish merchants of Havana, filled with patriotic ardor, began a collection for the purchase of a warship for the Spanish navy. A short time ago the money contributed had reached the comfortable sum of $800,000, which was given into the keeping of the Captain-General.

But now ensues one of the most strenuous and painful cases of bargain ruing the world has yet seen. The Spanish patriots want that money back, and they want it badly. They say with a deal of dry humor that they have discovered that a Spanish warship is not a good investment. But does the Captain-General loosen his grip? Oh, no! He declares that the money was donated to the Spanish navy, and it shall go to the Spanish navy. The Havana merchants now see themselves in the position of people who got over-patriotic at the wrong time. Their only solace now is to burst into tears.

An $800,000 joke is almost too expensive to incite laughter, especially in the man who pays, but the victims manage a feeble grin. They tried to withdraw the money in order to build with it a great Spanish clubhouse and in this way draw closer together the Spaniards who are to stay here and make them thus present a firmer front to the social and commercial attacks of the Cubans and the coming American. Even this fine idea did not catch the Captain-General.

About half a dozen unarmed men landed yesterday from the relief ship in the uniform of the United States regular army. They strolled around the streets, entered the cafes; did as they pleased. Of course, they attracted a great deal of attention. They were very tall men, giants to the people of Havana, and beside that they were American soldiers. I asked them how they had been treated and they answered: "Oh, we've been used all right. We mind our own business and nobody says anything to us." When all has been said and done, the recent war was a most curious war.

The newsboys went screaming through the streets yesterday selling a translation of the Constitution of the United States. They flew here and there with it excitedly, as if it were a war extra. So much so that two or three Americans were misled into buying it, expecting to read of the fall of New York.

The bones of Columbus still agitate a few minds. To-day the papers announce joyfully that the Duke of Veragua, lineal descendant of the discoverer, has decided that he and he alone shall have the bones.

The harbor is growing lively with shipping. The time to make 2,000 per cent on the sale of provisions in Havana has already past. Merchants who think otherwise are likely to incur serious loss. In three days the whole situation has changed. The wharves are now piled high, and there is even more still in the bay. When Blanco decided to refuse Red Cross relief it was pretty certain that Havana had plenty of food.

If the army is making any preparations for embarking for

Spain it is not apparent. Officially there is barely a mention of any such possibility. The great function of the soldier in Havana is to have nothing whatever to do. The Spanish officer has still less to do than the soldier. A brigade of volunteers is, however, aligned for inspection every morning in the Prado. It is a weird scene. However, the hotel fronts the Prado and when the band plays it is worth even the endurance of an inspection of volunteers.

The authorities, by the way, have always spoken highly of these volunteers and valued them, but in action they certainly would make a sorry exhibition. Doubtless the standard of bravery would be creditable but they don't know the business of soldiering at all. On drill they make a most unsoldierly appearance, and it is doubtful if one of them is sure whether he is carrying a gun or a handspike. But the Mauser is a fine weapon.

No. 50

THE GROCER BLOCKADE

THE Spaniard is evidently an epigrammatic person. He makes a serious attempt to reduce everything to a basis of one line. Sometimes he misses it, but more often he hits it. The people here are now saying, "We were not blockaded by the warships; we were blockaded by the grocers." It is quite true. Immediately the blockade was declared the grocers of Havana, stirred by a deep patriotism, arose to the occasion and proceeded to soak the life out of the people. It was a wonder that some sensible person did not go quietly about rearranging matters with an axe, but no one did so, and the grocers throughout the war continued to gracefully pillage the public pockets.

Blanco's order establishing a standard of reasonable prices had no effect upon them. Before war was declared they put into hiding a large amount of stock. War came, and soon they declared that they had nothing to sell. Their stores were all empty.

They had nothing; no, not so much as a pound of rice. The war had ruined them. Ah! those devils of Americans, thus to torment the honest grocers. In time, however, wealthy citizens might be seen wending their way with much gold to secret conferences with a grocer. Oh, no. Impossible! At no price! A pound of bread is worth more than a pound of gold. It is impossible. Well, if I sell some to you I would have to take it probably from the mouths of my own children, who are in danger of starving. A little, a very little; yes, perhaps.

Thereupon ensued the spectacle of a respectable citizen digging into his own bowels for gold to buy a little of the flour which the grocer had cleverly made to appear like pounded pumice stone.

Of course, in all wars there is invariably a class of patriots who seize their commercial opportunities to trade upon the preoccupation, the consequent vulnerability of the people who are deeply engaged with the palpable facts of the conflict. Doubtless during the civil war in America our particular breed of sutlers defended themselves in argument on the purest, most virtuous business lines. It was not until afterward that the people got their sense of proportion adjusted truly and saw that the system usually operated as a crime. And by that time the individual culprit was safely blurred in a sentimental resentment against a class. In the end, the affair was mainly a joke.

The grocers here were forced to play a bolder game. Upon the news of the raising of the blockade the market slumped from under them. The people simply refused to pay so much. They evidently felt capable of enduring until the supply ships came. The time of arrival of the supply ships was not known.

And now the grocers, as men with honest faces, were in a fair quandary. They would either have to give themselves away as cheats and lower prices and sell stocks as fast as possible, or —they would have to lose money.

What did they do? Did they lose money, like men who would care for an appearance of consistency, or did they give themselves away rather than lose a centavo?

In one day they lowered the price of rice 60 per cent. They lowered other staples proportionately. There had been no influx to the market. There had been simply a rumor that the blockade was about to be raised.

It was shameless. Our chill-blooded Northern race would have hung each grocer to his own signboard. These people, so fiery, so dangerous in temper, so volcanic, alive with p-p-passion, they did nothing. They perhaps expended themselves in talk —which is not impossible to their natures. They made an epigram: "We were not blockaded by the warships; we were blockaded by the grocers." At any rate, one must admit that it is a good epigram.

No. 51

AMERICANS AND BEGGARS IN CUBA

THE American commissions have had better care than any people who have yet invaded the island of Cuba. There has been more anxiety for their health and cuddling and precautions and general conference and discussions than is known in most sanitary philosophies. Five of them are dead.

In the meantime, there have been in Havana since about the 23ᵈ of August an unregenerate and abandoned collection of newspaper correspondents, cattle men, gamblers, speculators and drummers who have lived practically as they pleased, without care or restraint, going—most of them—wherever interest or whim led, with no regard for yellow fever or any other terror of the tropics. None of them are dead.

Probably it would be absurd to make any philosophic deductions from these certain facts but at least the facts remain interesting.

*   *   *   *   *

There was at one time in Spain a regular commercial concern whose business it was to import into Cuba maimed and haggard beggars. The latter worked on a commission. The same company is said to be still doing business but that is quite impossible to learn. An organization of the kind does not advertise. At any rate, the streets of Havana are now infested with hideous spectacles. Creatures of disease squat on prominent corners and thrust their terrors pitifully out for the eyes of the passers-by and bands of shrill children haunt the cafes. It is like Italy.

The American is for a long time a quite reckless person with this kind of thing. He doesn't care for coppers anyhow and by profligate distribution he soon succeeds in calling all the beggars for miles down upon his own unhappy head. The beggars of Havana pay small heed to the rest of the world if they once sight an American. They at once head to cross his bows and if he escapes it is not because a wild clamor of begging has not whirled around him. One can note already that a little of the kindness of the average American's heart has already been fretted and pestered out of him.

It is also notable that the beggars rarely approach a Spanish officer. They will storm any American position and they will heroically besiege the Cubans but they habitually shy away from a Spanish officer. This is either because the Spanish officers are never known to give anything away or because they have frightened an immunity out of the beggars. It is probably a combination of both.

An incident of another kind of begging occurred last Sunday at the camp of the Cuban general Cardenas.

No. 52

MEMOIRS OF A PRIVATE

As I understand it, the American public is now going about with a club crying: "Where is he? Where is he?" The American public is now about to chastise the one who can be proven responsible for the general incompetence and idiocy existing in several departments of the army during the last war.

I don't want to startle or anger the American public, but I feel impelled to point out to it that during the last few weeks it has caused a certain number of men in the regular army of the United States to laugh hoarsely and bitterly.

So you are looking for the responsible party, are you? You want to discover the culprit, do you? You want to visit dire punishment on him, do you?

Well, excuse the blunt language of a soldier, but you really strike me as being about the most comic spectacle that has yet crossed my thrilling journey toward a Soldiers' Home. Why, you are the culprit. You are responsible. Put up your searchlights and your bludgeons and merely ruminate quietly and see if you can't get something into your peculiarly ingenuous head.

Here is the first test. Go out into the street and ask any person to name the secretaries of war of the last five administrations. The citizen will tell he doesn't know. Try another citizen; he won't know. There you are! Nobody knows; nobody cares. That is exactly the case. Nobody cares who is Secretary of War. It has been accounted—since Lincoln's time—a highly honorable post which is the proper loot of some faithful partisan. It goes to this man or it goes to that man, and in any case nobody makes any row or conceives the event to be of importance save those gentlemen who wished the post for themselves.

Then suddenly there comes on a war, and—behold—you find the chair occupied by a doddering feckless old man who can't even defend himself by remaining silent. You talk about mismanagement! You talk about incompetence and gross criminality! Why, you are to blame! You are the criminals! You have for years persisted in raising monuments to your own incapacity for knowing anything about the army; for years you have conscientiously and steadfastly ignored every detail of it. What then, in the name of God, did you expect?

Every four years in our luxurious posts in Arizona or Wyoming we watched with feverish interest the appointment of the new Secretary of War. It was a solemn event always, for us. We cared who would be Secretary of War. But you never cared. You never gave three whoops in hades. In the first place you always proceeded on the stupid assumption that the country would never become involved in another conflict, and so you were constructively willing that any fool should be Secretary of War.

But the war came, my brothers, and found you dwelling in the midst of your blind idiocy. And now you are beating the tom-tom and screeching for somebody's blood. You know a real soldier always regards the civilian as an aimless, hapless, helpless blockhead, who tries to go three ways at once and say three things with one tongue, and the idea never strikes me with such force as when I contemplate the frantic revolutions your belated conscience is now making.

Why, we knew all this long ago, and we cried out to you, we begged you to heed us, and you were deaf; you would not listen, and now you have paid for it—paid with the blood of your best beloved; paid with your dead, God pity you!

No. 53

THE PRIVATE'S STORY

A HARD campaign, full of wants and lacks and absences, brings a man speedily back to an appreciation of things long disregarded or forgotten. In camp somewhere in the woods between Siboney and Santiago I happened to think of ice cream soda. I hadn't drunk anything but beer and whiskey for fifty moons, but I got to dreaming of ice cream soda and I came near dying of longing for it. I couldn't get it out of my mind, try as I would to concentrate my thoughts upon the land crabs and mud with which I was surrounded. All I could do was to swear to myself that if I reached the United States again I would immediately make the nearest soda water fountain look like Spanish fours. I decided upon the flavor. In a loud, firm voice I would say: "Orange, please." What with the work and everything, I suppose some of us got to be a little childish.

But here is the funny part of it. In due time, I with many other heroes was loaded upon a Chinese junk. We knew, however, that it was a United States transport because it was commanded by a fool who was all bluster and bad manners and fear of Spaniards. In rough weather we made a sort of a pool of all the sound legs and arms, and by dint of hanging hard to each other, we lived until the old trap reached Fortress Monroe.

As we slowed down opposite the main battery—known to the department as Chamberlain's—we witnessed something which informed us that with all our wounds and fevers and starvations we hadn't felt it all. We were flying the yellow flag, but a launch came and circled swiftly about us. There was a little woman in the launch and she kept looking and looking and looking. Our ship was so high that she could see only those who hung at the rail, but she kept looking and looking and looking. Presently there was a commotion among some black dough-boys who had seen her, and two of them ran aft to their colonel. The old man got up quickly and appeared at the rail, his arm in a sling. He cried: "Alice."

The little woman saw him, and instantly she covered her face with her hands as if blinded with a flash of white fire. She made no outcry; it was all in this simple, swift gesture, but we—we knew then. It told us. It told us the other part. And in a vision we all saw our own harbor lights. That is to say, those of us who had harbor lights.

My difficulty being of a minor description, I was one of the first ashore. A company of volunteers dug a way for us through a great crowd. The verandas of the two big hotels were thronged with women and officers in new uniforms. Everybody beheld us. It was very hard to face it out. Some of the boys had something which might be called stage fright. I knew we looked tough, but I didn't know how tough we looked until I saw all this splendid five-dollar-a-day crowd.

Some of the boys could walk, but naturally there were many who couldn't, and these last they loaded upon a big flat car and towed it behind a trolley car. When that load passed the hotel, there was a noise made by a crowd which brought me up trembling. Perhaps it was a moan, perhaps it was a sob—but, no, it was something far beyond either a moan or a sob. Anyhow, the sound of women weeping was in it, for I saw many of those fine ladies with wet cheeks when that gang of bandaged, dirty, ragged, emaciated, half starved cripples went by in review.

And let me tell you, it brought something to my eyes which I was ashamed to have seen, and my sabre arm went stiff and strong as steel and I swore that, despite legislation and the appointment of incompetent quartermasters, I would live and die a good soldier, a true, straight, unkicking American regular soldier.

Now here is a funny thing. Avoiding the hospital people who were herding us, I entered a drug store and marched up to the soda water counter. The boy looked at me and I said: "Orange, please."

No. 54

STEPHEN CRANE MAKES OBSERVATIONS IN CUBA'S CAPITAL

HAVANA, Sept. 20.—Well, it seems that the American regulars are not going to march up Obispo street for some time. War is long, and it makes no provision for impatient and exasperated patriots who refuse to attend strictly to their own affairs. Those of us who are waiting here to see the regulars march up Obispo street can wait and be damned. We thoroughly understand that part of it, and the present expression is intended more as a wail of anguish than as a plea to which anybody is likely to pay the slightest heed.

Still there are some things which might be said. In the first place, any intelligent person can see that the Spaniard is making a laudable effort to take every possible dollar out of Cuba before leaving it. His policy is necessarily a policy of delay. The longer he can stay the more Cuban millions will he take back to Spain. He is in no hurry; he doesn't want to talk to a commission; he wants to collect duties and taxes.

Of course, we are a very generous people, and we so want to be kind to our fallen enemy that we hesitate to interrupt him in his occupation of robbing the populace of Cuba. That is all very charming as a sentiment, but it is doubtful if Bismarck's stern, quick terms to a conquered France were not more truly merciful than this buttermilk policy of ours. The intellectual result so far has been to produce here, at least, a state of absolute stupefaction. It is impossible to halt the economy of a country while a number of duly accredited gentlemen exchange notes. Yet that is what we are performing with great success. The next three months are likely to be more disastrous for Cuba than were the months of the war. The war was a tangible condition, plain as your nose. The present situation is a blank mystery. Merchants grope blindly, afraid to advance a step in any direction. Business pauses, waits. Business is the name for a process of exchange by which people are enabled to procure those things which support and protect life.

If a man lacks a spine it is not of a surety his privilege to enter heaven without challenge as a just and charitable spirit. The lack of a spine is not mentioned by any available authority as the supreme virtue of mankind. What we mistake for generous feeling for our late enemy is more than half the time merely a certain governmental childishness, and it benefits the Spaniard no more than it benefits us, and as for the inhabitant of this island, he finds a grim and inexplicable fate fall from a sky which he thought was the sky of promise.

In our next war our first bit of strategy should be to have the army and the navy combine in an assault on Washington. If we could once take and sack Washington the rest of the conflict would be simple.

No. 55

HOW THEY LEAVE CUBA

THERE is one thing relating to the Spanish evacuation of Havana of which, surely, the less said the better, and yet the exquisite mournfulness of it comes to one here at all times. For instance:

A friend and myself went on board the *Alfonso XIII.* a few days ago as she was about to sail for Spain with an enormous passenger list of sick soldiers, officers, Spanish families, even some priests—all people who, by long odds, would never again set their eyes on the island of Cuba.

The steamer was ready to sail. We slid down the gangway and into our small boat. There were many small boats crowding about the big ship. Most contained people who waved handkerchiefs and shouted "Adios!" quite cheerfully in a way suggesting that they themselves were intending to take the next steamer, or the next again, for Spain. But from a boat near to ours we heard the sound of sobbing. Under the comic matting sun shelter was a woman, holding in her arms a boy about four years old. Her eyes were fastened upon the deck of the ship, where stood an officer in the uniform of a Spanish captain of infantry. He was making no sign. He simply stood immovable, staring at the boat. Sometimes men express great emotion by merely standing still for a long time. It seemed as if he was never again going to move a muscle.

The woman tried to get the child to look at its father, but the boy's eyes wandered over the bright bay with maddening serenity. He knew nothing; his mouth was open vacuously. The crisis in his life was lowering an eternal shadow upon him, and he only minded the scintillant water and the funny ships.

She was not a pretty woman and she was—old. If she had been beautiful, one could have developed the familiar and easy cynicism which, despite its barbarity, is some consolation at least. But this to her was the end, the end of successful love. The heart of a man to whom she at any rate was always a reminiscence of her girlish graces was probably her only chance of happiness, and the man was on the *Alfonso XIII.,* bound for Spain.

The woman's boatman had a face like a floor. Evidently he had thought of other fares. One couldn't spend the afternoon for three pesetas just because a woman yowled. He began to propel the boat toward the far landing. As the distance from the steamer widened and widened, the wail of the woman rang out louder.

Our boatman spat disdainfully into the water. "Serves her

right. Why didn't she take up with a man of her own people instead of with a Spaniard?" But that is of small consequence. The woman's heart was broken. That is the point.

And that is not yet the worst of it. There is going to be a lot of it; such a hideous lot of it! The attitude of the Cubans will be the attitude of our old boatman: "Serves them right; why didn't they take up with men of their own people instead of with Spaniards?" But, after all—and after all—and again after all, it is human agony and human agony is not pleasant.

No. 56

STEPHEN CRANE IN HAVANA

HAVANA, Oct. 3.—The citizen of Havana has an extraordinary lack of what might be called the sense of public navigation. It is a common lack on all shores of the Mediterranean, and the dearth of it even extends to Paris, where it is always clear that a kind of special deity continually has to protect from the pain of collision all drivers of fiacres.

But there is no special deity for the people here. They are children of pellucid chance, and if Havana was a tub and they were a lot of rubber balls prancing and bouncing within they could not be more joyously irresponsible and incompetent.

An opportunity to view this matter to good advantage is given every Thursday and Sunday evening, when a band plays in the square. A great crowd attends, and with the lights and the music and all it is not unlike the board walk at Asbury Park, without the boards and without the sea.

If two friends meet face to face on Broadway their greeting, if begun in the middle of the stream, is never finished there. They instantly move to the curb or in to the walls, to the slack water. They always do it, and there is nothing marvellous about it. But you should see two friends meet here when, for instance, the band is playing in the plaza and a great crowd is strolling.

Well, for their ceremony of greeting, they camp indefinitely right in the middle of everything. Of course, in Spanish countries it is customary to express joy and welcome by rushing forward and at once engaging the other man in a catchweight wrestling contest.

Suppose that there are two hundred people coming along on the same route. They are stopped, bothered, compelled to change their gait and their course. But they say not a word. They move around the impediment in silence and patience. It does not occur to them—they have no necessity for knowing—that traffic is blocked, as we say.

Nature is usually seeking to alleviate, to mend, but circumstance is always perverse, aggravating. The English are not a particularly amiable people; at least, they are not suave, and so circumstance provides them with a pattern of railway carriage which is the cruelest test of manners which life affords.

In Havana, where people do not comprehend public navigation, this perverse circumstance provides sidewalks from eighteen to forty inches wide, upon which only acrobats can make their way.

But, at any rate, a grand mystery of Spanish romance has been cleared for one mind, at any rate, by these Spanish sidewalks of Havana. In every one of those delightful tales there was a street scene in which a gallant cavalier going one way was met by a gallant cavalier going the other way. They stopped, then the first cavalier, twirling his mustache, said: "Senor, I take the wall."

But the second cavalier, laying his hand upon his sword, invariably replied: "You are mistaken, senor. I take the wall."

Whereat they drew and fell upon each other like brave gentlemen, giving and receiving wounds in the groin, lungs, liver and heart, until one was down and after he had said, "Oh, I am dead," the other sheathed his sword and went home—taking the wall.

This fighting for the inside track, for the privilege of passing next to the wall, was a mystery and an annoyance to my boyish mind. I wanted my hero to fight over the lady behind the lattice. Anything connected with that intrigue was good cause for the gore of cavaliers.

But to go out and fight with comparative strangers over the privilege of passing next to the wall, giving and receiving wounds in the groin, lungs, liver and heart, seemed a very pointless proceeding. But it is all plain at present. It was because the Spaniard had as much sense of public navigation as he has now, and because the sidewalks of Seville were only from eighteen to forty inches wide.

No. 57

HOW THEY COURT IN CUBA

HAVANA, Oct. 17.—Cuban courting is on a plan that is strange and wonderful to us. It is full of circumlocution and bulwarks and clever football interference and trouble and delay and protracted agony and duennas. There is no holding hands in it at all, you bet. It is all barbed wire entanglements.

In the higher orders of society young men and young women have conventional opportunities of meeting each other and becoming acquainted, but that is not the situation among the masses. In the latter case a young man almost invariably falls in love with a fair face seen through a grated window. He could not tell if the lady was deaf and dumb. As for her disposition, she might, for all he knows, be accustomed to dragging her mother up and down stairs by the hair and beating her father daily with the cooking instruments. She might even have a wooden leg successfully concealed by her reposeful attitude. But, anyhow, he takes this wild whirl into romance, and only the gods know his end.

The first thing to be done is to attract the attention of the lady. This he usually accomplishes by a process of heroic patrolling to and fro in front of her house. She sits in the window and observes this scene. If she glances at him he smiles, looks foolish and adoring, acts like an ass.

This stage may be long or short; that depends upon the man and the maid. But sooner or later there comes a time when he shys up to the window and fillips a letter behind the bars, and the girl conceals it hastily in all likelihood, although the supposition is that she takes it immediately to her mother. And this letter! It breathes a passion which could only grow from the young man's lack of knowledge of the object of his devotion. It sings a perfect adoration, which could emanate only from a young man who is not thoroughly familiar with his subject. From it arises a perfume of love which could be created only by a young man who had acted always as a spectator from without the bars.

Very well, then; this patrolling and grinning and this note have an effect, or else they don't have an effect. Let us suppose that the young man has not paced futilely to and fro, wearing out the pavements of a beneficent city government. In that case it is a race horse to a corn dodger that she will not write an answer to his note without communicating news of the solemnity of the crisis to her anxious parent. It then becomes the duty of the anxious parent to collar the young man at some good time and ask him what the devil are his intentions, anyhow. He replies, of course, that his intentions are quite beyond reproach, and he hopes—he hopes—if he is not too unworthy—he—he will be allowed to pay his suit.

A leathery and cynical old woman, having her cold fist down the middle of this kind of an affair, is bad at the best, but here they have arranged to be worse. Here they have a chill, calculating eye that would cut a cable. Their minds were born in suspicion and have advanced amid attacks from all sides. They are so wise in their one direction that they would madden an intelligent mind with their wide and deep ignorance.

But, at any rate, the young man's position and prospects are weighed, and if they are satisfactory he is admitted to call upon the young woman. The young woman's opinion in the case is a blooming small matter. The young man is put on the scales, and if he don't tip them properly he goes, and if the girl wants to cry her eyes out she cries them out without moving the disposition of the ironclad parents.

The young man being accepted, then begins the real courtship. A sort of schedule is established, and the young man runs on time. He turns up every evening—say—at 8 o'clock and goes away—say—at 10 o'clock. The moon and the transatlantic steamers and a good valet are all beaten in punctuality by this young man. The time table does not change for Sundays, nor for illness, nor for anything save mortal accident.

It is not so much the uninterrupted punctuality. It is the length of the siege. It endures for ages. It is common for this sort of thing to last as long as eight years. Five years, or perhaps three years, is the habit.

What the young man does is to come into a drawing room, sit down in a chair near the young lady, and talk in a subdued and downtrodden voice, half to the young woman and half to the implacable mother, who holds her position with a courage born of the noble cause. She is always something like the Western man who chewed tobacco, and yet, in certain poker games, acknowledged that he dared not turn his head long enough to perform a certain obligation of men who chew tobacco.

Imagine this state of affairs enduring for eight years, or even for three years! It has all the fiery excitement of being cashier in a shoe store.

This call becomes a function of the daily life of the family, precisely like the morning coffee or dinner. If he failed to appear for one evening, there would be a panic in the household, and the young woman would be heartbroken at this scandalous exhibition of infidelity. He would be obliged to make elaborate and fervid explanation.

Time moves at its allotted speed slowly over the years; nothing changes, routine is routine. And in the end, what? Who knows? Perhaps our fine young man sights a woman who rightly or wrongly blots out in four minutes the memory of the girl that he has arduously courted for three years. Then, again, perhaps not.

After all, there is small use of discussing any such matters. Men seek the women they love, and find them, and women wait for the men they love, and the men come, and all the circumlocution and bulwarks and clever football interference and trouble and delay and protracted agony and duennas count for nothing, count for nothing against the tides of human life, which are in Cuba or Omaha controlled by the same moon.

No. 58

STEPHEN CRANE ON HAVANA

HAVANA, Oct. 28.—When in other cities of the world the church bells peal out from their high towers, slowly and solemnly, with a dignity taken from the sky, from the grave, the hereafter, the Throne of Judgment—voices high in air calling, calling, calling, with the deliberation of fate, the sweetness of hope, the austerity of a profound mystic thing—they make the devout listen to each stroke, and they make the infidels feel all the height and width of a blue sky, a Sunday morning golden with sun drops. But—when at blear dawn you are sleeping a sleep of both the just and the unjust and a man climbs into an adjacent belfry and begins to hammer the everlasting, murdering Hades out of the bell with a club—your aroused mind seems to turn almost instinctively toward blasphemy. Religion commonly does not go off like an alarm clock, and, as symbolized by the bells, it does not usually sound like a brickbat riot in a tin store. However, this is the Havana method. I fancy they use no such term here as "bell ringer"; they probably use "bell fighter." But, such passion! Such fury! One can lie awake for hours and listen to the din of a conflict, which reminds one of nothing but a terrible combat between two hordes of gigantic blood-mad knights of the Middle Ages, whose armor had unfortunately been constructed from resonant metal. On feast days the clamor simply shakes out of one all faith in human intelligence. It is so endless, so inane, so like the din of monkeys with tin kettles. But the bells must be very good bells. Otherwise they could not stand these tremendous assaults. The bell fighters must be very good men. Otherwise they would soon succumb to the physical strain.

One apprehends that as soon as the tangled affairs of Cuba are arranged in some fashion there will be a considerable inflow of Americans looking for work. In a small way it has already begun. But there is no market for American labor in Cuba. Naturally, labor is the one thing that the island contains in ever-increasing abundance. There is the remnant of reconcentrados; there are the refugees returning from foreign ports; there will soon be a great mass of disbanded insurgents, and, last, there are many Spanish soldiers who intend to stay here. Labor will be for a long time almost as cheap as it is in China.

Such a thing as a clerkship will be grabbed by competent, well-educated, but financially reduced, Cubans for a wage that would not support an American. The island is not at all a Klondike, where a man might go with only his wits, a pick and a pan and yet win success.

The vanguard of a caravan of indigent Americans looking for fortune in this new country has already succumbed here, and one or two have even been shipped home by subscription of the newspaper men, cattlemen and others.

Cuba is the place for a wise investment of capital, but it offers no gold mine to the American who has none. Tobacco land, for instance, can be had very cheap, but before the appearance of the first crop a great deal of money—in proportion to acreage—has to be expended. Tobacco raising, indeed, is an expensive business, and, disclaiming all idea of speaking with authority, it is at least proper for me to warn all small capitalists to consider the question as something beyond small farming in the United States and to thoroughly look into the matter before embarking for Cuba.

One newly arrived American announced that he had come to open a law practice. His equipments for this venture were youth, a very recent diploma, some few dollars and a perfectly ingenuous ignorance of the Spanish tongue. The fortunes of men are in the wind, and the wind blows where it pleases. No one can say that this young man may not succeed, but at least it does seem that he is a little too soon.

However, his inexperience of American practice will not militate against him here. There is nothing in the American forms of procedure that resembles the Spanish forms of procedure. As near as one may learn, the function of a lawyer in Havana is mainly that of a go-between, who arranges a dicker between the honorable court and the client who has the most money. All that will be changed? Yes, but there are a great many things in Cuba which are not going to be changed in two minutes.

When the Earl of Malmesbury was Minister for Foreign Affairs, he in 1852 wrote to the British Ambassador at Berlin about a certain political complication in the following terms: "You will, I hope, use all your influence at Berlin to show the King that the Duke of Augustenberg only delays his assent to the indemnity from a foolish hope that a row may take place somewhere and somehow among the five powers, and that in the scuffle he may get something more. It would be very desirable for the King of Prussia to make him understand that by further delays the only chance he runs is that of losing the terms now offered him."

If it would do any good the fine thing would be to have this straightforward parable printed on cardboard convenient for pasting in the hats of Spaniards here and elsewhere. They are figuring precisely on the lines of that illustrious Duke of Augustenberg. Some political miracle, some tremendous war that will force the United States to engage herself tooth and nail in the defence of her own soil, will enable Spain to sail in again and hold or regain her precious islands. It is stupid, but —what would you? The ordinary Spaniard has little knowledge of how the nations conduct their relations with each other. He interprets the mere land-hungry policy of Germany to mean a formidable enmity to the United States. He thinks the Parisian journals mean what they have said, and, meaning what they have said, that they voice a menace to the greater Republic. He thinks even that our Southern States are only waiting for a supreme crisis to again disengage themselves from the Union. In fact, he dreams still of a miraculous rescue of his country from her sorry plight.

Furthermore, he drinks in every sound of the tumult in the United States over the management of our army in the Santiago campaign and over the distress and illness in the American camps at Chickamauga and other places. This uproar causes him to believe that if he had the whole thing to do over again he would have been victor. If he had known the plight of the American army at Santiago he would have done better; he would have held on; he would even have attacked. A thousand expedients occur to him now that he has all this information from inside the American lines, so to speak. And he gnashes his teeth over it.

No. 59
"YOU MUST!"—"WE CAN'T!"

HAVANA, Nov. 4.—The dull times in this city are in no way improved by the fact that an American commission and a Spanish commission are in a juxtaposition here which might be intended for the preservation of silence and inertia. For a long time everybody prayed for the coming of the American military commission. All would be arranged and improved immediately after the arrival of that distinguished body. The Cubans rather expected them to come with trumpeters and banners, escorted by both cavalry and infantry; field guns and warships would boom, and the Cuban populace and those Spaniards who have climbed hastily to the correct side of the fence were prepared to line Obispo street and cheer themselves black in the face. It was to be the grand emancipation, a magnificent ceremony of gold lace and cocked hats. Even the little American colony often said to itself: "Oh, just wait until the commission gets here."

The commission arrived ultimately, after we had been harrowed in proper fashion by a series of rumors and false starts. For my part, I was sitting in the Cafe Inglaterra one morning when some of the waiters suddenly crowded toward the door and stared into the plaza. Being interested in finding out what so attracted them, I looked also, and saw a young man in a white duck uniform of the American navy crossing the plaza. It was Lieutenant Marsh, of Admiral Sampson's staff.

This to the greater part of Havana was the arrival of the American commission. It was an event, of course, but never a spectacle. Havana opinion of the conquerors faded 50 per cent in a single day. The reconcentrados found to their intense amazement that on that night they were not merely as hungry as ever, but that they had now to struggle with an appetite whetted out of all proportion by a false and absurd anticipation. Really, in the strictest sense, nothing whatever had happened.

At present the two commissions are engaged in a sort of a polite and graceful deadlock. The Americans say: "You must!" The Spaniards reply: "We can't." The Spaniards will soon have to make the best of a bad business, but they hold on with the tenacity and hopeful innocence of children. It seems impossible to beat any truth into their heads save with a hatchet. Something will turn up, they think. It is impossible to many of these minds that such a calamity as this evacuation should come to pass. France, or Germany, or civil war in the United States, or Divine Providence, will make interposition in time.

Meanwhile, although the reconcentrados are gradually getting their voids partly occupied, the people who are the greatest sufferers are the Cuban insurgents, who are still in the field. Their mental condition approximates stupefaction. They don't know whether they are afoot or ahorseback. They ask the same questions of everybody who they think is entitled to know the slightest things. "Well, what is going to become of us, eh? Are we all Americans now? What are we, anyhow? When are the Spaniards to be put out? When? When? When?"

There is a certain eloquence in the speech of a hungry, half-clad, homeless man who has lived three years in the manigua and who is wondering if the sweetheart he left long ago in town could still distinguish between him and any other. They are marvellously patient about it—the men more than the officers. Just here it might be well to interpolate that the Havana province insurgents are very different from those patriots who so successfully did little or no fighting at Santiago.

This province has been loaded, always, with Spanish troops, and the revolutionary bands have been kept on the keen jump, with perhaps a fight every day. They had none of those lovely mountain sanitariums which at critical times formed the safe abode of the Santiago warrior.

It is only fair to say that the present situation does not seem to be at all the fault of the American Military Commission. I have an idea that they are mad clear through to the bone, although they are as reticent as so many Russian diplomats. They have bucked squarely into the Spanish Commission, and have been met with the usual reply of "We can't," and also with "Wait until we hear from Madrid," and "Wait for the decision of the Paris Commissions." The first Spanish intrenchment is "We can't;" the second is "Wait." And they fight it out on those lines with heroism.

Some day we will get over considering these people clever in some ways. As a matter of truth, they are shockingly stupid. They are of the Mediterranean, that accursed sea which in modern times bathes only the feet of liars and of men of delay. Catch any Spaniard in a lie—it may be a Havana cabman or it may be the redoubtable Weyler—and he fights you off with the unthinking desperation of a cat in a corner. He will never admit it—never—never. Confront him with proofs; show him a sworn statement signed by the flaming pen of the recording angel, but no—he looks at you with dull, senseless eyes and shakes his head eternally. "No, senor! No, senor! No, senor!" You can't move him. You can't even budge him an inch. There he sticks in his corner. You can only get a confession out of him by killing him and then journeying to hell to wrest it from his spirit.

This is about the measure of his intelligence. He has no knowledge of the tremendous and terrible art of half truth. He proceeds always on the basis of flat, wooden lying. A good many fine American tempers are doomed to be ruined in Cuba before the evacuation.

His other great principle of action is delay. Instead of opposing rational statement and argument, he will often meet the other side with seeming amiable acquiescence which is positively alluring and then he will proceed to organize a system for delaying the proceedings which can't be beaten anywhere in the world.

There are two elements at work in the Spanish mind at present. One is the dogged fatalism that Cuba will always belong to Spain. This arises simply from the fact that within everybody's recollection Cuba has always belonged to Spain. The other element arises from the opportunity, whatever betide, to pinch a few more millions out of Cuba. So naturally they have got their lies and their delays all up in harness, and are working them night and day. When our military commission returns to the United States, there won't be a sweet disposition left in it.

No. 60

MR. CRANE, OF HAVANA

HAVANA, Nov. 4.—One speaks of it with hesitation, but it is a fact sufficiently known among correspondents and other well-informed persons, that some of the regiments which have garrisoned the city of Santiago since the surrender have not behaved well or even decently toward the citizens of that town. They were not regiments which took part in the fights at El Caney or San Juan, but were commands that were sent in much later to relieve Shafter's troops. Particularly at fault were a certain regiment of immunes and a certain volunteer colored regiment. In these two corps there were many cases of drunken sentries, and the promiscuous shooting at night by these men in the streets made it unwise to be too confident about one's safety if one had to travel after dark. On a certain evening a shot from one of these enthusiastically intoxicated gentlemen entered a window of the Santiago Club, breaking up a most virtuous poker game which was in progress there, and all Western gentlemen will agree with me that such conduct on the part of the sentry was unworthy an American soldier and a gentleman.

The occupation of surrendered cities is the most delicate business of war. It is plain that this applies threefold to towns in which the populace is favorably disposed to the victors. Soldiering at its best is cruel, hard work, and when the enwearied but triumphant soldier gets at last among the houses, where the people and their wine shops and other luxuries are practically at his mercy, he should not relax and go to pieces like a child, but, on the other hand, he should consider that he owes a double duty to his flag.

Indisputably the less said about these Santiago affairs the better, since every one has confidence in the admirable, soldierly and just administration of General Wood and his ability to straighten out any of his force who get bumptious, but we must not forget that, in one sense, our men are now on exhibition alike before Spaniards and Cubans, and when two regiments who were not in at the taking of Santiago at all, but are there now simply as military police—when these two regiments endanger by their behavior the prestige which the Fifth Army Corps so gallantly won and preserved as long as it remained in Cuba, it is time for us to blush a little and wonder if we can't improve matters.

No doubt the men in these regiments are good fellows enough, generous, kind, brave, devoted to their country, but they have not played the part of thorough soldiers, and the only man who has any business to engage in war is the soldier. The irresponsible whooper should remain at home.

The war is over, but—mark you this—that does not mean that we have no enemies. In the first place, the Cubans of Santiago province will never forgive us the fact that they took no part in the battle of San Juan and a distinctly secondary, even inconsequent, part in the fight at El Caney. They know perfectly well that they had nothing practical to do with either of these victories. It was the Americans alone who stormed these positions, and it was American blood that was poured out in the green fields. That is the truth, and none know it so well as the Cubans of Santiago province. If they could not know it with their own senses our men certainly told them it with great force both during the battle and after it.

But far more seriously distressing is the fact that tales of the adventures of our soldiers in the streets of Santiago have gone broadcast through the island. Here in Havana, for instance, *La Lucha*—a newspaper which is against us as much as it dares—prints almost every day an account of the behavior of our troops in the city of the other end of the island. Of course, they are grossly and viciously exaggerated, according to the policy of a large body of Spaniards here; the articles are meant to establish a fear of American rapacity in the minds of the people of Cuba; their intention is thoroughly vindictive. But, nevertheless, there is not an American steamship agent, cattle man, provision speculator or correspondent who was in Santiago for any length of time after its fall who will not frankly tell you that such and such things happened there. The lamentable breaking up of the poker game heretofore described is merely used as an illustration of the quaint spirit of gayety which at times animates some of our men.

Now, Havana expects soon to be occupied with American troops. Havana listens with all her ears to these stretched-out yarns which *La Lucha* prints with such glee. To the citizen here they sound like truth. He wonders whether he will be let in for some game of the kind when the American troops occupy this city. His doubts are cheerfully encouraged by Spaniards of the *La Lucha* stamp. They laugh and say: "Oh, you will see! Your Americans so kind, so gentle, so just!" And yet anything in the way of ill-feeling or suspicion would never have occurred if a certain number of our soldiers could completely understand that whenever they wear the uniform of a United States soldier they carry upon their shoulders the weight of the honor and dignity of their country, and that their responsibility has increased a million fold.

For example, when four joyous privates enter a cafe in Santiago, order several drinks and then hilariously refuse to pay for them, they don't know that the story of it, enlarged and improved into a gigantic generalization, will go broadcast over Cuba, and that in countless minds they will have created a wrong opinion of every man who wears the blue, has worn it or ever will wear it. Tell one of these boys that to a million people he has dishonored the name of the United States army and he would probably drop dead. Tell him that he has insulted the flag and he would probably kill you. It all lies in the fact that he does not comprehend his new importance. He is not now just come to the tavern from a hard day in the fields, free of everything but a certain personal responsibility, free to be a regular wild ass of the desert if he so elects. He is part of the dignity, the justice, the even temper of the American Government.

It seems senseless that these silly little yarns from Santiago should stir so much apprehension, but it is no more senseless than any other natural law. It is what occurs in the lives of individuals, crowds, nations. A man spills some claret down his cuff and the report goes abroad that he has been drowned in a wine vat.

No. 61

SPANIARDS TWO

HAVANA, Nov. 5.—Then there is General Pando. He claims to have found out by personal inspection absolutely everything concerning the army at Tampa. He ridicules it; calls it, in fact, an army of duffers; says our officers were so many wooden men. That is all very fine, but what did Pando do with all this wonderful information of his? Apparently what he did with it was to wait until the war was over and then use it as material for boisterous and insulting talk in the American and English newspapers. It is plain that he did not use one of the invaluable facts to benefit his country during the war. He did not say to Toral: "Don't surrender; you are faced by a mere lot of incapable and illy provided people who will compass their own destruction if you give them a little time." In fact, what use did he make of his information, anyhow? None save in these uproarious and insolent interviews.

One does not expect a military spy to hold his own counsel until the war is over. Perhaps Pando did not do so. Perhaps he imparted his golden treasures to his comrades in arms. And what did they do with it? Where was this mine of information lost?

There is something wrong in this Pando game. Pando was undoubtedly a very genius of discovery and investigation, but he wandered into the woods somewhere and came out too late. In truth, Pando is but a soldier embittered because his side has been soundly whipped. After Waterloo, some of Napoleon's superb gray veterans wrote pamphlets proving that the English knew nothing of the art of war.

But Havana hears Pando. Pando was always known as the active fighting commander. Havana listens to his howl and grows more chagrined, more anxious to contend that Spain lost by a fluke, more angry.

The frenzy for not losing any single chance at a dollar displays itself in more wonderful ways than in a tax upon American ships bringing relief for the people of Cuba. Montoro, the chief of the treasury, has lately distinguished himself. Some Havana people projected a fair to be held at the Theatre Orajoa for the benefit of the hospitals which the Americans will establish for the sick among our troops. Although these hospitals are as remote and vague in point of time as the landing of a United States force here, yet these good people thought they would seize time by the hair and have a little fund all in readiness for the ailing boys in blue.

The response from the Cubans, from the Americans and from one or two straddling Spaniards was very hearty. Everything bloomed; it only remained for a committee to wait upon Montoro and gain his consent. But the gay Montoro at once announced to the committee when he saw it that they could hold the affair on condition that twenty-five per cent of the profits should go to the Government. Having recovered its composure with some difficulty the committee left him.

As far as goes the mere accident of birth Montoro is a Cuban, but even as the Tories of our Revolutionary War were usually too brutal for the stomachs of regular English troops, so this man is Cuba's most implacable and deadly foe. He and Fernando de Castro, the Civil Governor, another Cuban, will have to go to Spain when the change comes. They can't stay here. The

Cubans are going to be very law-abiding, but it would be too bad to stuff these two rascals down their throats.

No. 62

IN HAVANA AS IT IS TO-DAY

THE insurgent posts are not far from Havana on all sides, and such is the present condition here that the main trouble of visiting any of them exists in the fabulous sums charged by the livery people for any kind of transportation. However, three of us yesterday combined to expend our hopes of a pensioned old age and hired a trap to take us to the camp of General Rodriguez, insurgent commander-in-chief in Havana Province. The distance from Guanabacoa is twenty-six kilometres over one of the few good military roads in Cuba.

The ground in front of the Spanish lines is favorable to the deploying of large bodies of troops, and the cavalry would have had considerable work cut out for it. The dense thickets of the ground before Santiago here do not exist. The high main position is led up to by a series of rolling, grassy mounds probably four miles in extent. Primarily there would have been some handy picket fighting and skirmishing around and over these mounds.

One must not leave discussion of these Havana defences without mentioning the barbed wire entanglements. They exist in profusion. They are not mere fences. Fences of barbed wire are the easiest of such entanglements. But these are laid in horizontal webs and meshes about nine inches from the turf, and so form a most formidable china shop for any living bull. The men who cut them would be within forty yards of the intrenchments, and men in these times do not cut barbed wire entanglements that are within forty yards' range of a rifle pit.

We had not gone three hundred yards from a pair of indolent cavalry pickets when we came upon five men in linen, yellow from dirt, who grinned at us in a most friendly fashion and arrived in some curious way at the position of order arms. As soldiers they were laughable. Yes, laughable, for those who do not know. Their pretence of coming to attention and doing us honor thereby was purely comic, but the first man in the file happened to resemble an insurgent whom I had seen killed at Cusco—really the tightest, best fight of the war—and thus I was enabled to know in some way that all was not to be judged by appearances.

They were armed with Remington rifles, every one of which was in more or less bad condition. However, in the Spanish army one never sees a rifle in good condition. In fact, the rifles of the insurgents are usually in better shape. They came to this grotesque attention and surveyed us with wide smiles—smiles of ivory purity on their black faces.

We supposed that, having passed this rebel outpost, we had entered the zone of the insurgents. But it was not so. To our military astonishment we found that the outposts interlaced. First you came upon the Spanish sentries; then an insurgent outpost; then a block house occupied by the Spaniards; then more insurgents; then another block house. During the war this road had been vigorously defended, and about all the Cubans could do was to cross it whenever they liked, but now, under the flag of truce, or peace, or whatever it is, the road seems to have come upon a manner of joint ownership, in which both sides exist on it without friction.

One incident will display the situation. A man in the coach, a Cuban, had come out heavily loaded with cigarettes for the patriots. Once he sighted an outpost and asked of a soldier: "How many are you here?"

The soldier answered: "Twelve men and a corporal, sir."

Whereupon our friend dished out a commensurate number of cigarettes. The soldiers were very grateful, very grateful indeed. They were Spanish soldiers. Our patriot kicked himself for some miles, but to no purpose. The cigarettes were gone, and they were gone firmly into the mouths of sundry hated Spanish infantrymen.

This happened to be the last Spanish post. Thirty yards from it were three serene insurgent pickets. They were apparently keeping out of sight of the enemy because of a sense of the decencies of the situation, but plainly theirs was a lazy job. They smiled at us, too—the same cavernous, ivory smile.

The carriage rocked tremblingly over a mile of wood road. We came upon other sentries more formal and then at last we arrived at that most interesting thing called an insurgent camp.

Evidently that wide avenue of palms led to the relics of a plantation, but now this palm-lined avenue was only the main street of an insurgent camp.

Primarily, we had come to see an American, Lieutenant-Colonel Jones, on General Menocal's staff. Jones had been for three years on campaign. He had raised himself on his ability as an artilleryman. Artillerymen were almost as few as guns in the Cuban army, and every one was valuable. Jones, by his correct and intrepid handling of whatever guns went into action, was promoted steadily by Gomez until he has now reached a position second to no artillery officer in the Cuban service.

We had some money for Jones; we had some tobacco for Jones; we had some sandwiches and some rum for Jones. We expected a welcome. Did we get it? We did. We got one of those open-armed, splendid welcomes which are written for the coming of dukes. After all, we were of his kind. He had been three years in the woods and with others, but when he saw us he was almost childishly delighted. It mattered nothing who we were or what we were; it was only that we were of his kind, and the hours we sat with him were glad ones, because he was glad, glad to be chock-a-block once more with his own. We could see him breathe in the outright Americanism as if it were some perfume wafted from the folds of the flag and we were not too noble representatives, either.

When we first sighted him he was lying in his hammock. It is impossible to state how universal is this condition of lying in a hammock—especially at this time when there is no occasion for activity, no fighting. Once the insurgents in Havana Province had more high stepping and tall jumping to do than has come to the lot of any military force in the world, barring the Apaches for some occasions. This present complacence of nature startles them into a curious state of fretful rest which they account almost as a disease after their three years of jumping, flying, aerial life.

The furniture of Jones's hut consisted mainly of a hammock and a soap box. In the soap box were some newspapers—now become universal in every jungle—a tin cup, a bottle of ink, some writing paper. On a rafter of his rude dwelling hung his belt, with his machete and his revolver. Beside him lay his saddle, which looked as if dogs had chewed it. This was apparently and truly all he possessed. The house was wide to the air; there were no sides. Outside crouched two of those quick-eyed military servants which one can find in any Cuban camp. To their services they imparted a good-natured or, rather, a friendly quality, which was infinitely grateful to the senses. They dodged, swung, lifted, carried in a certain indescribable way which impressed one that the will was good, all true, all amiable, all kind.

Presently we went to visit General Menocal. General Rodriguez was commander of the forces in the province, but he had gone away somewhere on horseback, riding a good white horse, and, for a wonder, riding it well.

We found Menocal to be a young man—not more than thirty-five years. His coat was much in the manner of a duck coat of an American naval officer. It had the same wide, white braid, but on the collar shone two gold stars, the sign of a general of division.

He is a Cornell graduate of the class of '88. He talks English consequently, clean out of all courier and hotel runner latitudes. He is soon to be a major-general, and it is a promotion that strikes every one with its extraordinary correctness. Menocal is one of the men in the game. When Garcia was ploughing around the eastern end of Cuba Menocal was his chief of staff. Menocal had more to do with Garcia's success than we can talk about, and that is enough said. He will be one of the men who will comprehend the American point of view. He will know how honestly we mean in this affair.

The horseflesh to be seen was in bad condition, but no worse than the Spanish mounts. They were all odd, unmatched little beasts, with an infinite variety of accoutrement ranging from ragged and war-worn saddles with the padding leaking out to dazzling tan equipments from the best Havana saddlers, the latter being gifts of joyful friends since the pause in the conflict. In fact, the donations of Havana were everywhere plain. The officer of the day, for instance, wore a gorgeous crimson sash embroidered in white. The beloved, the sweetheart, has again entered the life of the lonely insurgent.

Food, if not exactly plentiful, was had in at least sufficient quantities for the troops. The pitiful sight was to see the last of the reconcentrados hanging about the camp, miserable women and babes, ragged, dirty, diseased, more than half famished. They are in desperate straits. Such, indeed, is the condition that a gift of a little bread sometimes brings the virtue of women to the feet of the philanthropist.

No. 63

OUR SAD NEED OF DIPLOMATS

HAVANA, Nov. 9.—One of the foreign consuls, a man who has been for many years and in many lands in the diplomatic service of his country, when asked his opinion of the American commissions here, answered at once that they are too big, too unwieldy: there are too many men. He gave it as his idea that the European governments found it far more satisfactory and expeditious to leave the most important negotiations in the hands of three or four men trained to the game, who would have only such subordinates as were needed for bare clerkly duties, and practically carry everything in their own heads. He confessed that in a considerable experience at the London, Berlin and Vienna embassies of his country he had never succeeded in espying any such noble diplomatic caravans.

This seems partly true. For instance, the Evacuation Commission or, rather, the Commission-Appointed-to-Negotiate-and-Superintend-an-Evacuation-Which-at-Some-Future-Date-Is-More-or-Less-Likely-to-Take-Place,-Although-It-Must-Be-Said-There-Is-No-Direct-Evidence-at-Present-to-Prove-That-Said-Gentlemen-Might-Not-with-More-Comfort-Have-Remained-at-Home-and-There-Drawn-the-Salaries-Duly-Provided—this commission lives in a hotel, an entire hotel, the best hotel. Of course, the private citizen is naturally aggrieved at having the best hotel and restaurant wrested from him, even by a commission. This is especially true in a town like Havana, where the best is not startling. But, after all, when the Standard Oil Company comes to town, it consists of a man with a valise. People like Senator Hanna walk about with an entire State in a waistcoat pocket, and plenty of men jingle counties and cities carelessly, like so many coins. Alone, Napoleon once settled a treaty by hurling a porcelain vase to the floor in fragments and declaring to the Austrian Ambassador that his country would look that way if he did not instantly submit to the imperial terms. The great things of the world are invariably done by machines which do not require as housing an entire hotel.

One harrowing local phase of it is the absolute impossibility of getting familiar with all the faces of the commissioners and their suites. One will become quite convinced that one is well versed in the official countenances, when suddenly into some public place will come a bewildering string of colonels, majors and captains, all utterly new, and yet all obviously as important as the very devil. It makes one's head ache.

If I may be allowed to say so, I have already pointed out in the *Journal* that one of the principal Spanish ideas of cleverness and craft is a policy of stone-faced delay. Heaven knows what they suppose it accomplishes, but at any rate they adopt it.

An American business man, many years the agent here of an important New York firm, remarked to me to-day: "When I came here first I tried to hurry these people. If I called on some firm and they kept me waiting an hour, I used to kick like blazes. I'd say: 'Look here, I'm in a hurry! My time is valuable! I can't wait here all day!' Then they would merely raise their shoulders in maddening indifference and say: 'Well, we are very sorry.'

"It took me a long time to find out that it was merely a ruse, a trick, because the fools worked it often enough when it was greatly to their advantage to bring off a deal with me."

For my part, I believe all this is a direct inheritance from ancient Moorish vendors of fruit, tobacco, rugs, water jars, brass trinkets. We are, in fact, dealing with a lot of pedlers.

Colonel Hecker's career here is highly amusing and instructive. "I want so-and-so. Have you got it? Yes? How much do you want for it? No—won't give it. Bang!—negotiations off!" While the pedler is just getting into shape to wheedle and dicker and snivel and bluff, Hecker is a mile away, dealing with another man. Hecker has greatly rumpled them up here. He charges them like a wild bull and won't stand for a minute their little Mediterranean tricks. For his dock and other works he has got nearly everything he wants in a short time, and—so business men tell me—he paid only the just price. The Spaniards think he is a marvel. They expected to have a pie.

Before the war, when the American colony was leaving Havana in haste, the Spanish pilot who was taking a steamer out of the harbor addressed one of the American passengers. "Well, good-by. I'll see you again soon."

"See me again soon?" said the American in surprise. "How will you see me again?"

"Oh, I'll soon be over there," answered the pilot grimly, pointing into the north. "I'm going on board one of our warships."

The American laughed then. "Why, your warships can't move. They haven't any coal."

"Yes; but," answered the Spaniard, "there is plenty of coal at Key West."

"How are you going to get it?"

"We will go and take it," said the pilot, with a shine in his eye and disclosing his teeth.

Well, the amount of coal captured by the Spaniards at Key West turned out to be not enough to carry them far, and at the end of the war the American returned to Havana. Luck had it that he was spoken of a great deal about the harbor as the probable American appointee as captain of the port. This turned the pilot quite woolly with fright, and his teeth have been chattering ever since in the expectation that when the Americans come his head will be among the first to fall.

There are plenty of people here who are sorry that they were

so mighty cocksure in the early days. The roots of their existence are fastened in Cuba even as that pilot's sole hold on the
world is his knowledge of the waters of Havana. Many of them
who gratuitously insulted Americans before the war and in the
early stages of the conflict now sometimes find that these individual Americans are likely to be their governmental masters.

A good many are trying to get in out of the wet, and although
revenge is usually foreign to an American character, the reversal of form is so pitifully bald and shameless that it goes
against the northern stomach.

An extraordinary number of people are inquiring the where-
abouts of Joseph A. Springer. He was consular agent here for
over thirty-five years. He was the wheel horse of American diplomacy. In short, he was the consulate. He departed with Lee
just previous to the war.

We, as a people, know as much about diplomacy as we do
about hatching fighting cocks by holding eggs over a gas jet,
but unconsciously and without any virtue of our own, we have
reared in certain places men who perfectly understand the
business which, by mandate of Government, they are required
to manipulate. These are invariably subordinate officers. The
great men, the high-steppers, they come for a time, lean heavily
upon the shoulders of the wheel horses and then retire to ob-
livion or Congress. The wheel horse puts some liniment upon
his shoulder and stands then ready to pull the next high-stepper
out of a mudhole.

Meanwhile, he never, by any chance, gets the slightest credit
for anything. The great man, the Ambassador, or the Minister,
may go home with his very boots full of laurels, but the wheel
horse in all probability gets flung into some adjacent abyss
without any one taking trouble to listen whether or no he hits
a projecting ledge.

One familiar with our European affairs could cite unnum-
bered cases of the kind, but the case of Springer is point enough.
On these commissions here is about everybody who ever officially sighted Cuba through a telescope. The young men who
were under Springer's consular tutelage before the war are

here, officially. Everybody is here but Springer. Springer has no influence. Heaven help Springer.

I often think of the fate of White, the first secretary of our Embassy in London. He has pulled Ambassadors through knotholes and up through cracks in the floor until he is prematurely gray, and at last he will be flung out somewhere to die—all same Springer.

No. 64

MR. STEPHEN CRANE ON THE NEW AMERICA

FEW men know as much of Cuba and the Cubans as Mr. Stephen Crane, who for the past three years has been in close touch with the people and leaders there. His late story, "The Open Boat," is a true account of an unenviable experience of his when on a filibustering expedition. His ship, the *Commodore,* was wrecked, and he himself with others given up as lost. He has a very interesting book made up of his own obituary notices which he greatly treasures. Mr. Crane's marked success as correspondent during the late war is well known, and, as far as United States battles on land are concerned, it can be truthfully said that he was the only man actually present at every engagement. He has, however, had to suffer for these experiences, and is only just recovering from a sharp attack of yellow fever contracted during his services with the United States army and the insurgents. A mutual friend, calling upon him at his English home, found Mr. Crane particularly communicative.

"That is a large question to ask a small man," he replied, in answer to this friend's inquiry as to the Future of Cuba. "The island has passed through practically thirteen years of continuous war. A very small war can destroy a very enormous commerce. Outside the American garrison the island now contains about one-fifth of a normal population. But its industries of tobacco, sugar, and ore are vast in possibility, and must exert an influence upon the shifting masses who are always searching for work.

"Under the evil Spanish Government, Cuba might as well have been a desert. No matter the wealth in the soil or in the rocks, it was kept there by thieving Spanish officials, unless it came forth with oppressive and almost murderous levy. I know this to be true. Everybody who knows the old life of Cuba knows that it was a life of officialdom, of corruption, ranging from petty bribes to grand gifts. This was true up to the very moment of the raising of the American flag on Morro Castle. I was present to see the wild fleeing of a multitude of little sharks. Parenthetically it might be said that Spain has been ruined mainly by men who in Cuba were engaged in babbling the loudest of their love for the Peninsula. It is easily then, my belief, that the new Government will be in the way of developing a Cuba of which the oldest Cubans could not dream. No one wants to speak of the Americans as an immaculate race; but I feel sure that my own people stand well in honesty with the rest of the world—else they would not accuse themselves so violently and continually.

"The Cubans will be given their independence—despite all cavilling and arguing—but they will be given it not until they have grown to manhood, so to speak."

Of influences to come Mr. Crane ventured to prophesy: "I think it can fairly be said that nations move without regard for either pledges or men; but the word that 'Cuba shall be free' has so freely been given through every city and village of the United States that I am confident it will be kept. I am sure that it has become almost a national creed that we shall do as we declared in the beginning. Governments break their word for the glory of nations, but peoples do so at their peril."

"And now comes the sore part," resumed Mr. Crane. "The Cubans have not behaved well in the most prominent cases. And this makes the common American soldier very angry. And the common soldier is the common American man. The Cuban says, 'We took San Juan Hill.' Any of us who were there know that there were no Cubans present within any other range than spent-shell range. The common American soldier, having died to some extent in Cuba, does not like these statements.

Moreover, when he was in a hurry, the Cuban back of the firing line stole his blanket-roll and his coat, and maybe his hat. Sixteen thousand United States soldiers returning home, wofully ill of their Cuban ally, and being themselves brought from every corner of the United States, impress the entire people. And the entire people immediately say, 'Well, if this is the real Cuban, we know much more than we did previously.' And consequently I can assure you that they are perfectly willing to deal with the Cuban on a new basis, if the Cuban thinks he cares to have it done."

"As for annexation and its results," continued Mr. Crane, "Cuba is too small to affect the United States to an appreciable extent. Its financial question will grow easier and easier. As for the other questions, it seems to me to be a matter of the effect of the United States upon Cuba—that is the main consideration. The United States preponderates, and weighs down upon Cuba. With all mankind's sluice gates opened—I mean, at least, some of the sluice gates—I am, of course, a Free-trader —it is certain that the warmth from this natural mother-country will heat the little Cuba to its proper temperature. When you come to think of it, the island is only ninety miles distant from the United States."

And then they fell to talking of "American Imperialism." Here also Mr. Crane was enlightening.

"The people of the United States," he said, "consider themselves as a future Imperial Power only vaguely and with much wonder. The idea would probably never have occurred to them had it not been for foreign statements and definitions. The taking of Cuba was what they intended, and the taking of Porto Rico and the Philippines was a military necessity incumbent upon one country when it is engaged in war with another. The Philippines—speaking of them as the only international intrusion—were taken quite in the way of the most ordinary naval attack, the usual supports came for the attacking party, and after a time the United States finds itself confronted with some people—liberators, patriots, and others—who believed themselves valuable enough to appear as nuggets for which the entire world is going to scramble. That is as far as the United States went in Imperialism. The forces of the nation are now engaged in trying to comfort these people and tell them that they are not going to suffer oppression. If these people don't happen to believe it, there will be fighting on some Eastern islands. As far as I see, there is no direct American sense of Imperialism. America stands on her land and she meets what she meets; she challenges whomsoever she challenges, and whosoever comes may find her weak, but will never find her unwilling. I say this because I believe it."

When the talk passed on to the Tsar's peace Rescript, Mr. Crane would formulate no personal opinion, but as to the opinion of the people in the United States he was more communicative. "I may say," he observed, "that in America I thought they took it in a fashion quite between the indifferent and the humorous. Outside of saying the ordinary thing, that nobody in America cares for what the Tsar of Russia says, it seems to me that they thought it quite unreal, the Tsar of Russia being notable to them as a man who obeyed his councillors, and otherwise being a man from whom nobody expected any heaven-sent statements. In reality, the United States has seldom been armed. An appeal of the sort from a completely military Power may properly strike them with a certain humor. The Powers of Europe have often plainly laughed at them as a great fat, unfortified mass. We can be military if we choose. The art of war is applied mechanics. It only needs one goading, two asides, and three insults. Thereupon we become a military people. If an apostle of peace does appear with true spirit and with true eloquence, he will not be the Tsar of Russia, nor will he be of the Russian General Staff. He will be some poor devil, and will probably be stoned to death for talking beyond his audience. And days will come and days will go before there appears a man who will stop the human race from 'Fighting like Hell for conciliation.' "

No. 65

HOW AMERICANS MAKE WAR

Sir,—The American news printed in the journals of London never fails to interest Americans in Europe, but if you will allow me to say so, it interests us principally as an expression of opinion. We commonly are obliged to sift everything through a net composed of our superior knowledge of our countrymen. This is no hardship; I cite it simply in the way of suggesting, if I can, that international correspondence is the most difficult work which falls to the lot of the men of the public Press.

The Philippine Islands are at present absorbing a great deal of attention, and it is fair to say that no correspondent could possibly make head or tail out of the wonderful nonsense which reaches Washington, and, after being still further confused, is officially announced to the world. Having a few scraps of information at my command, I beg leave to place them at your disposal.

In the first place, I would like to contend for a moment that General Otis himself is largely responsible for the present lamentable conditions in the Philippines. Scarcely had Otis set his foot squarely on shore when he announced to the Government of the United States, and in the public Press, that with 25,000 or 30,000 men he could put down the revolt in three weeks. Those of us who knew better were simply prostrated with dismay when we read this news. It defined an ignorance of the situation on the part of the American chief which would surely lead to all manner of fuss and trouble. We—the knowing ones—thought we could see why Otis had made the statement. He was a soldier of the old school, and he thought the natives were soldiers of the old school. He had a vision of taking out his 25,000 or 30,000 men and meeting the native army drawn up in form and hammering the life out of it in one satisfactory day's work. We groaned at this preposterous idea, and it is a sorry, sorry pleasure to find, soon enough, that we groaned for good reason.

When the Cubans were insurgent to Spain, the Spanish generals announced victories every day for three long years, and about once a month they declared that the spine of the insurrection was broken. The victories were victories in one way. The Spanish advanced—150 rounds per man; the insurgents retired—sometimes as many as ten rounds per man. The Spanish burned a camp of palm-bark huts which had been built in about twenty minutes. The Spanish returned to their garrison victorious; the insurrectos returned to the scene of the victory, and built another village in another twenty minutes. There was about one insurgent to every six Spanish soldiers in Cuba, and the insurgents never, never allowed the Spaniards to clinch with them until the odds were emphatically in favor of the men under the lone star flag. If they could raid suddenly down from the mountains in strong force upon some unfortunate isolated detachment and tear it to pieces, they did it. When the angry Spaniards afterward swarmed to the region and called upon their enemies to come out and fight fair, the only reply would be, probably, a shot from some Cuban scout who had found a chance to pot down at them from a position absolutely safe. This is not poetic war; but men do not go to war to be picturesque, I hope. They play to win. When fanatics rush blindly upon machine-guns and magazine rifles, it is all very grand and imposing, and attracts the admiration of brave enemies; but I cannot but think that the reason the Khalifa fought a campaign was that he wanted to win it.

The Spaniards had no foolish scruples against learning from the Cubans and then using their experience against the Americans in the Santiago campaign. Every informed person was struck by the fact that Americans were now playing a Spanish part, and the Spaniards were virtually Cubans. They bushwhacked us magnificently. After a serious skirmish, with a loss of some eighty men to us, I have heard soldiers say: "I didn't catch sight of a single Spaniard; not one." When war came, the regular United States regiments heaved a sigh of relief, and said: "Well, the (Red) Indians have been bush-whacking us all our lives, and we've been bush-whacking Indians; now, thank heaven, we've got an enemy that will come out and fight." But the Spaniards were no greater fools than the Red Indians or the Cuban insurgents, or—the Filipinos. On only one occasion did the Americans get what the men called a "square crack" at the enemy. A battalion of the 22nd United States Infantry was sent to a hill in the rear of El Caney, and when what was left of the garrison broke in the direction of Santiago this battalion found itself in a position to rake the retreat at fair ranges and in a good light. No man passed that way to Santiago. Most of them fell—in heaps—the others surrendered. The men of the 22nd, using a Red Indian phrase, called it "a big killing." But it was the only time the Americans got a "square crack" in open ground.

The policy of the Filipino, with his inferior army, is naturally and quite correctly one of elusion and concealment. It is the business of his "republic" to have a government which can be packed on a native pony. He should develop no philosophy against running away. These principles many men understood; one man conspicuously did not—General Otis, who naturally, then, is kept in command at Manila.

When Major-General Lawton arrived at Manila in a subordinate capacity, he is understood to have remarked that 100,-000 men would be a proper number for the occupation of the island. Lawton is one of the best soldiers in the American Army. There is some mystery about Lawton being sent to Manila. Manila is usually understood to be a repository for obsolete ideas in the minds of very respectable old gentlemen.

In the meantime, a ray of light has shone through this humiliating fog. We have developed some very gratifying volunteers—and at one time this seemed impossible. The American volunteer was at one time the despair of every man who could distinguish between a good soldier and a mere brave high-minded youth.

In conclusion, I wish to suggest that the situation in the Philippines is the result of an obstinate effort on the part of General Otis to make his first silly and ignorant prophecy turn out to be true. With the mind of a politician who fears a popular outburst, he dares not admit that he was absurdly wrong. He would rather take towns and leave them again, and—censor the news dispatches.—Yours, &c.,

July 20.   STEPHEN CRANE.

ENGLAND

No. 66

THE LITTLE STILETTOS OF THE MODERN NAVY WHICH STAB IN THE DARK

IN THE past century the gallant aristocracy of London liked to travel down the south bank of the Thames to Greenwich Hospital, where venerable pensioners of the crown were ready to hire telescopes at a penny each, and with these telescopes the lords and ladies were able to view at a better advantage the dried and enchained corpses of pirates hanging from the gibbets on the Isle of Dogs. In those times the dismal marsh was inhabited solely by the clanking figures whose feet moved in the wind like rather poorly constructed weather cocks.

But even the Isle of Dogs could not escape the appetite of an expanding London. Thousands of souls now live on it and it has changed its character from that of a place of execution, with mists, wet with fever, coiling forever from the mire and wandering among the black gibbets, to that of an ordinary, squalid, nauseating slum of London, whose streets bear a faint resemblance to that part of Avenue A which lies directly above Sixtieth street in New York.

Down near the water front one finds a long brick building, three storied and signless, which shuts off all view of the river. The windows, as well as the bricks, are very dirty, and you see no sign of life, unless some smudged workman dodges in or out through a little door. The place might be a factory for the making of lamps or stair rods or any ordinary commercial thing. As a matter of fact the building fronts the ship yard of Yarrow, the builder of torpedo boats, the maker of knives for the nations, the man who provides everybody with a certain kind of efficient weapon. One then remembers that if Russia fights England, Yarrow meets Yarrow; if Germany fights France, Yarrow meets Yarrow; if Chili fights Argentina, Yarrow meets Yarrow.

Besides the above-mentioned countries, Yarrow has built torpedo boats for Italy, Austria, Holland, Japan, China, Ecuador, Brazil, Costa Rica and Spain. There is a keeper of a great shop in London who is known as the Universal Provider; if a general conflagration of war should break out in the world, Yarrow would be known as one of the Universal Warriors, for it would practically be a battle between Yarrow, Armstrong, Krupp and a few other firms. This is what makes interesting the dinginess of the cantonment on the Isle of Dogs.

The great Yarrow forte is to build speedy steamers of a tonnage of not more than 240 tons. This practically includes only yachts, launches, tugs, torpedo boat destroyers, torpedo boats, and of late shallow-draught gunboats for service on the Nile, Congo and Niger. Some of the gunboats that are now shelling dervishes from the banks of the Nile below Khartoum were built by Yarrow. Yarrow is always in action somewhere. Even if the firm's boats do not appear in every coming sea-combat, the ideas of the firm will, for many nations, notably France and Germany, have bought specimens of the best models of Yarrow construction in order to reduplicate and reduplicate them in their own yards.

When the great fever to possess torpedo boats came upon the powers of Europe, England was at first left far in the rear. Either Germany or France to-day has in her fleet more torpedo boats than has England. The British tar is a hard man to oust out of a habit. He had a habit of thinking that his battle ships and cruisers were the final thing in naval construction. He scoffed at the advent of the torpedo boat. He did not scoff intelligently, but because, mainly, he hated to be forced to change his ways.

You will usually find an Englishman balking and kicking at an innovation up to the last moment. It takes him some years to get an idea into his head, and when finally it is inserted he not only respects it, he reveres it. The Londoners have a fire brigade which would interest the ghost of a Babylonian as an example of how much the method of extinguishing fires could degenerate in two thousand years. And in 1897, when a terrible fire devastated a part of the city, some voices were raised challenging the efficiency of the brigade. But that part of the London County Council which corresponds to our fire commissioners laid their hands upon their hearts and solemnly assured the public that they had investigated the matter and had found the London fire brigade to be as good as any in the world. There were some isolated cases of dissent, but the great English public as a whole placidly accepted these assurances concerning the activity of the honored corps.

For a long time England blundered in the same way over the matter of torpedo boats. They were authoritatively informed that there was nothing in all the talk about torpedo boats. Then came a great popular uproar, in which people tumbled over each other to get to the doors of the Admiralty and howl about torpedo boats. It was an awakening as unreasonable as had been the previous indifference and contempt. Then England began to build. She has never overtaken France or Germany in the number of torpedo boats, but she now heads the world with her collection of that marvel of marine architecture —the torpedo boat destroyer. She has about sixty-five of these vessels now in commission, and has about as many more in process of building.

People ordinarily have a fasle idea of the appearance of a destroyer. The common type is longer than an ordinary gunboat— a long, low, graceful thing, flying through the water at fabulous speed, with a great curve of water some yards back of the bow and smoke flying horizontally from the three or four stacks.

Rushing this way and that way, circling, dodging, turning, they are like demons.

The best kind of modern destroyer has a length of 220 feet, with a beam of 26½ feet. The horse power is about 6,500, driving the boat at a speed of thirty-one knots or more. The engines are triple expansion, with water tube boilers. They carry from seventy to a hundred tons of coal, and at a speed of eight or nine knots can keep the sea for a week; so they are independent of coaling in a voyage of between 1,300 and 1,500 miles. They carry a crew of three or four officers and about forty men.

They are armed, usually, with one twelve-pounder gun and from three to five six-pounder guns, besides their equipment of torpedoes. Their hulls and top hamper are painted olive, buff, or, preferably, slate, in order to make them hard to find with the eye at sea.

Their principal functions, theoretically, are to discover and kill the enemy's torpedo boats, guard and scout for the main squadron, and perform messenger service. However, they are also torpedo boats of a most formidable kind, and in action will be found carrying out the torpedo boat idea in an expanded form. The four destroyers of this type now building at the Yarrow yards are for Japan.

The modern European ideal of a torpedo boat is a craft 152 feet long with a beam of 15¼ feet. When the boat is fully loaded a speed of 24 knots is derived from her 2,000-horse-power engines. The destroyers are all twin screw, whereas the torpedo boats are commonly propelled by a single screw. The speed of 24 knots is for a run of three hours. These boats are not designed to keep at sea for any great length of time, and cannot raid toward a distant coast without the constant attendance of a cruiser to keep them in coal and provisions. Primarily they are for defence. Even with destroyers, England, in lately reinforcing her foreign stations, has seen fit to send cruisers in order to provide help for them in stormy weather.

Some years ago it was thought the proper thing to equip torpedo craft with rudders, which would enable them to turn in their own length when running at full speed. Yarrow found this to result in too much broken steering gear, and the firm's boats now have smaller rudders, which enable them to turn in a larger circle.

At one time a torpedo boat steaming at her best gait always carried a great bone in her teeth. During manoeuvres the watch on the deck of a battle ship often discovered the approach of the little enemy by the great white wave which the boat rolled up at her bows during her headlong rush. This was mainly because the old-fashioned boats carried two torpedo tubes set in the bows, and the bows were consequently bluff.

The modern boat carries the greater part of her armament amidships and astern on swivels and her bow is like a dagger. With no more bow-waves and with these phantom colors of buff, olive, bottle-green or slate, the principal foe to a safe attack at night is bad firing in the stoke-room, which might cause flames to leap out of the stacks.

A captain of an English battle ship recently remarked: "See those five destroyers lying there? Well, if they should attack me I would sink four of them, but the fifth one would sink me."

This was repeated to Yarrow's manager, who said: "He wouldn't sink four of them if the attack were at night and the boats were shrewdly and courageously handled." Anyhow, the captain's remark goes to show the wholesome respect which the great battle ship has for these little fliers.

The Yarrow people say there is no sense in a torpedo flotilla attack on anything save vessels. A modern fortification is never built near enough to the water for a torpedo explosion to injure it, and, although some old stone flush-with-the-water castle might be badly crumpled, it would harm nobody in particular even if the assault were wholly successful.

Of course, if a torpedo boat could get a chance at piers and dock gates they would make a disturbance, but the chance is extremely remote if the defenders have ordinary vigilance and some rapid fire guns. In harbor defence the searchlight would naturally play a most important part, whereas at sea experts are beginning to doubt its use as an auxiliary to the rapid fire guns against torpedo boats. About half the time it does little more than betray the position of the ship. On the other hand, a port cannot conceal its position anyhow, and searchlights would be invaluable for sweeping the narrow channels.

There could be only one direction from which the assault could come, and all the odds would be in favor of the guns on shore. A torpedo boat commander knows this perfectly. What he wants is a ship off at sea with a nervous crew staring into the encircling darkness from any point in which the terror might be coming.

Hi, then, for a grand, bold, silent rush and the assassin-like stab!

In stormy weather life on board a torpedo boat is not amusing. They tumble about like bucking bronchos, especially if they are going at anything like speed. Everything is battened down as if it were soldered, and the watch below feel that they are living in a football, which is being kicked every way at once.

And finally, while Yarrow and other great builders can make torpedo craft which are wonders of speed and manoeuvring power, they cannot make that high spirit of daring and hardihood which is essential to a success.

That must exist in the mind of some young lieutenant who, knowing well that if he is detected, a shot or so from a rapid fire gun will cripple him if it does not sink him absolutely, nevertheless goes creeping off to sea to find a huge antagonist and perform stealthily in the darkness an act which is more peculiarly murderous than most things in war.

If a torpedo boat is caught within range in daylight, the fighting is all over before it begins. Any common little gunboat can dispose of it in a moment if the gunnery is not too Chinese.

No. 67

SOME CURIOUS LESSONS FROM THE TRANSVAAL

THE war in the Transvaal is developing curious facts in regard to the reporting of battle news, and in some quarters it is even said that this generation will see the last of the war correspondent. The generals don't want him at all, and the public, even with its keen interest, does not want him if a dreadful censor is to sit perpetually on his chest. It all arrives at the question whether if an army loses an engagement the country and the world should know it. Military men seem to think that it is nobody's business whether or no an army has been whipped.

But when all is said and done, a strict censorship is an absolutely essential military thing, and it can also be said with confidence that the Spartan or the Stoic censor will not do in these days. He must be strict, but he must also have a feeling for the people at home, who for some centuries have understood that they pay for wars. They will not sew their sons up in black bags and hand them over to a government for a mysterious period of indefinite length. The military authorities of the more educated nations must learn that they must study the popular opinion at home as carefully as they study the enemy's ammunition supply.

The censorship at the Cape is apparently working to perfection. All the papers in London have been printing accounts of victories thus: "A strong column under General Blank advanced at daybreak this morning and gallantly drove the enemy for miles, inflicting enormous losses. At nightfall the column safely returned to its original position." It sounds like Mr. Dooley, but it is just as true in fact as the sage is true in point of view. Even a stupid public, a public so stupid that they can chuckle over the advantage gained, will not endure such conditions for long. It will come to them in time that there is something wrong. Then the censor must go. But he won't. Because of the swiftness of modern means of communication a modern war may not be conducted without the employment of a censor of news.

Then the war correspondent must go.

He must.

He must go because ocean beds are laid with cables, because range and plain are strung with the telegraph, because fast trains and fast steamers are plentiful. His spark of information flies too quickly around the world and into the enemy's camp. This is why London has been reading news carefully selected for Boer appetites.

There are now many people in England who would like to find the man who before the war constantly named the Boer reputation for valor and military ability as "the biggest unpricked bubble in the world." It had been for some years a favorite phrase to the minds of leader writers. I may say that it is now what might be termed a disengaged simile. No one is using it at present.

Also, several famous poets must be rather nervously considering the advisability of making a general overhaul of some of their proudest verse.

Nevertheless, the country remains very steady in its determination to fight everything out to a finish. Within a few days the Englishman has had to read of Gatacre's incomprehensible defeat, of Methuen's desperate attack and withdrawal and of Buller's reverse. It would be idle to say that British pride has not sunk down into the tips of the national toes. But it would be just as idle to withhold admiration for the quick general decision made on all sides and by all parties that the painful business must be grimly and silently endured and the struggle in South Africa carried to a successful British conclusion. Writing under this date, the direct future is mysterious and filled full of shadows, but I conclude that one tangible thing is the resolution of the British people.

The bewildering thing to the British mind has been the mauling received at the hands of bewhiskered farmers by many regiments which were such favorites, whose records so blazed with glory that they were popularly accounted invincible. For instance, "The Black Watch" (Royal Highlanders), a regiment composed of the old Forty-second Foot and the old Seventy-third Foot, has traditions which are superior to that of any regiment in the world, perhaps. Very well—an unimposing body of men who don't wash very often batter this regiment out of shape.

However, it might be said that of late years the "Gordon Highlanders," a regiment composed of the old Ninety-second and the old Seventy-fifth, have had more campaigns and have achieved a name second to none. In the last campaign against frontier tribes of Northwest India the Seventy-fifth made the famous charge at Darghai. Very well—the Ninety-second is with Sir George White and the Seventy-fifth is with Lord Methuen. Both battalions are at this writing mere skeletons, having been so hammered and pounded by the "unpricked bubbles" that they would do well in a representation of the famous picture "Roll Call After Quatre Bras."

It is not necessary to say much of the hammering received by the brigade of Foot Guards. The Foot Guards are a beautiful body of troops, but it has always been understood—notably by the line regiments, who envy them their swagger—that when the guards should meet hard-muscled, hard-shooting, tenacious foes there might be a great surprise. At this writing the brigade of Foot Guards is cut off with Lord Methuen, having already suffered severely.

In every report of an action in South Africa there has appeared a statement of the terrible execution done by the British guns. This may be accounted for by the fact that the observer posted near the position of the gun is not at all able to tell the amount of execution done by that gun's fire. These artillery duels have been fought at ranges which sometimes are as long as 7,000 yards. At a much lesser range than that the spectator is almost certain to conclude that every shell is bursting in the enemy's position.

However, there is one thing which guns may always do. If they are directed against the enemy's guns and handled in a superior fashion they are fairly sure to so involve him with flying showers of dirt and stones from his own earthworks that he is glad to run away for a time. It happened at Matanzas, when the *New York*, the *Puritan* and the *Cincinnati* made beautiful practice, and yet the Spanish loss was probably the famous mule. It happened often enough before Santiago harbor, and it is happening every day in South Africa.

No. 68

STEPHEN CRANE SAYS: WATSON'S CRITICISMS OF ENGLAND'S WAR ARE NOT UNPATRIOTIC

MR. WILLIAM WATSON was recently challenged in the London *Daily News* with being out of sympathy with his country in her conflict in South Africa. Mr. Watson has made a reply to the *Daily News*, and, without knowing how much of this reply has been already dispatched to the United States, the present writer feels that everything can safely be repeated.

Mr. Watson begins: "Forgive me if I venture to say that, in a very deep and abiding sense, I am far from being 'out of sympathy' with my country. I have never in my life been able to divest myself of those unreasoning primitive instincts which predispose every man to sympathize with his own race or tribe, to lean toward them and wish them well, be they in the right or in the wrong."

This splendid Stone Age and twentieth century truth is confessed by Mr. Watson with a candor which for the moment takes absolutely no account of high ethics, but deals clearly with what he no doubt regards as a fundamental fact of humanity. It seems to me that we should be grateful to him. In this second sentence he formulates in a somewhat cruel manner a truth with which perhaps we Americans have more or less unconsciously dealt for many weeks. One does not hail the sentiment as something unprecedented, newly worded; one simply remarks that here is formulated, expeditiously and in time, a feeling which at this day occupies a large number of minds in the United States and Great Britain.

And now let us quote Mr. Watson's third sentence: "But it is possible to be patriotic and yet to draw a clear distinction between one's country and certain of her actions—between one's country and those passing impulses and moods of hers which, perhaps, conceal as often as they reveal her nobler nature."

This is disaproval; but this is not a Bostonese disapproval. No one will mistake it for a Great Movement. It is the quiet assumption of a certain man that he is in the right. It will get no extra British soldiers killed in the Transvaal. From Boston one could work back, I should think, mathematically, to a number of dead American soldiers in the Philippines. But it is inferred that Mr. Watson did not care to have any British soldiers killed in South Africa because he in England was able to trumpet encouragement to the Boers. He pays in his little objection like a man and waits to hear who heeds him. He doesn't start out at once to overturn the Governmental omnibus. The overturning of the Governmental omnibus might be no calamity, but at any rate he understands that experiments are untimely.

In the end, one seems to find in Mr. William Watson's letter an expression of decent, equitable patriotism which might be worth perusal. First, he says he loves his country because he can't help it. Second, he says he disapproves of some of his country's acts because he can't help it.

There is no screaming, no demand for this thing and that thing. Instead of being the letter of a fiery agitator, it is the letter of a saddened man.

It all plainly resolves itself to a nationalistic basis. One hardly knows how to state it. One has the burning wish for the quick success of the American arms in the Philippines. At the same time, one has a still more burning wish that the Filipinos shall see us as just men, willing, anxious to deal fairly, govern with studious equity; depart, if need be, with honor.

However, Mr. Watson failed to express that comic vanity which leads one to long that the enemy should know that one is an honorable man. It could not possibly be admitted as necessary, but still Mr. Watson does not send any statement to the Boers assuring them that the English are honorable men. The feeling is certain to have been in Mr. Watson's bosom, but he said nothing. In these immense things one may have to watch the revolving of ponderous wheels with respect. A socialist cannot be sure what is best for the world at the moment as a paregoric, as a sleeping powder or as a disinfectant.

No. 69

STEPHEN CRANE SAYS: THE BRITISH SOLDIERS ARE
NOT FAMILIAR WITH THE "BUSINESS END"
OF MODERN RIFLES

THE white flag has caused mutual accusations in South Africa. Each side has claimed that the other has fired wantonly upon the emblem of succor to the helpless. Such questions are not to be decided here or anywhere. They always remain as discussions in which the more ignorant of each people play the part of virulent gossips. One reads in an English newspaper a letter from a lancer written to his relations at home. "They cried for mercy but we gave them none because we knew they had fired upon the Red Cross." The words of this terrible lancer are only worth repeating because they indicate one of the kinds of lies which private soldiers commonly write home in all sincerity. Here this soldier is seen protesting that he took part in a bloody massacre of men who cried aloud for mercy. The letters of the private soldiers which teem in the London papers often tell such tales of merciless slaughter. Wise people do not regard them but, when perusing them, we are able to reason back to the question of white flags.

As a matter of fact, the proud British soldier has never known the range of the modern rifle—not when it was pointed at him. He knew how to shoot with it but he did not know the business end. But he thought he did. He said he did and everybody listened eagerly to his words upon war.

But he forgot the business end.

After the Spanish-American war, an American came to England and one evening before the Transvaal war when he was seated in his club he said arrogantly to a circle of English acquaintances: "Why, you have no knowledge of modern fire-arms at all. What do you know of the rapid-fire gun and the magazine rifle?"

The derisive laugh almost lifted the ceiling. "Why, my boy," said an Englishman, "we have been familiar with these weapons ever since they were invented."

"Familiar with which end?" asked the American. Then he laboriously tried to say that one could not be really familiar with the modern rifle until one was familiar with both ends. One had to know both things. It was not enough to pot savages armed with rapid-fire clubs and magazine-spears. This was inadequate. The experience of facing this modern fire was also a part of the knowledge. Whereupon they proved that the hill tribes on the north-west frontier of India were always amply provided with large numbers of gold-mounted, diamond-inlaid repeating rifles.

Well, very good. They go to South Africa and are shown first of all that they don't know anything about fire-arms. Buller, White, Gatacre, all of them get badly scorched in the London press. That does not matter very much. They take the usual medicine of defeated generals.

Then the question of knowledge of modern rifle fire appears in the campaign. A man arises to remark that a British field-hospital has been fired upon. Could he really mean merely that a British field-hospital was under fire? Does he remember the range of the Mauser and does he remember that any field-hospital, to be effective, would have to be within that range? In these days, a field-hospital is almost certain to be under fire—not necessarily fired at.

In the meantime, the latest British reverse is characteristically chronicled in a leading London newspaper. "We have again shown the Boers what it is to face the steady valor of British troops." Yes; that's all right; but it would be less inexpensive to the teachers if the Boers could be shown the steady valor of the British troops by means of a cinematograph.

No. 70

MANUSCRIPT FRAGMENT

THE New York correspondent of the London *Times* candidly admits that English criticism has greatly assisted the judgment of American officers operating in the Philippines. This gratuitous contribution to contemporary inanity leaves one free to make several remarks on the judgment of English officers in South Africa who have not benefited by American criticism. One had thought to receive in courteous silence the news of constant bungling in Natal

No. 71

THE GREAT BOER TREK

WHEN, in 1806, Cape Colony finally passed into the hands of the British government it might well have seemed possible for the white inhabitants to dwell harmoniously together. The Dutch burghers were in race much the same men who had peopled

England and Scotland. There was none of that strong racial and religious antipathy which seems to make forever impossible any lasting understanding between Ireland and her dominating partner.

The Boers were more devoid of Celtic fervors and fluctuations of temperament than the English themselves; in religion Protestant, by nature hard-working, thrifty, independent, they would naturally, it seems, have called for the good-will and respect of their conquerors. But the two peoples seemed to be keenly aware of each other's failings from the first. To the Boers the English seemed prejudiced and arrogant beyond mortal privilege; the English told countless tales of the Boers' trickery, their dullness, their boasting, their indolence, their bigotry. The burghers had transplanted the careful habits of their home in the Netherlands to a different climate and new conditions. In South Africa they were still industrious and thrifty, and their somewhat gloomy religion was more strongly rooted than ever. Although they lived nomadic lives on the frontier, yet they had made themselves substantial dwellings within the towns; the streets were blossoming bowers of trees and shrubs; their flocks and herds increased, their fields produced mightily. In the courts of law they had shown conspicuous ability whilst acting as heemraden; they had made good elders and deacons in their churches, and good commandants and field-cornets in war—the ever recurring conflicts with the fierce Kaffirs.

Many observers have noted the strong similarity of thought and character between the Dutchmen and the Scotchmen. There is the same thrift which is often extreme parsimony, combined with great hospitality, the same dogged obstinacy and the same delight in over-reaching in matters of business and bargain-driving. Moreover, the Dutch Reformed Church and the Presbyterian Church are practically the same. In his character as a colonist the Boer certainly showed magnificent qualities; he could work and endure and fight, but in spite of his dour sanctimoniousness, he was not a perfect person, any more than his brother Briton. The English missionaries objected to his treatment of the natives, but there was never any of the terrible cruelty practised that the Spaniards used

toward the natives during their colonization of Mexico—
nor that of various French, English and Portuguese adventurers
in Africa during the seventeenth century. But the fact remains
that the entire race of Hottentots has been modified through
the Dutch occupation; it is said that no pure-blooded Hottentot
remains. This amalgamation was treated by the Boers as a
common-place thing. That habit of theirs of producing scrip-
tural authority for all their acts must have begun with their
settlement in Cape Colony.

The "bastards," as they were openly called, were well-treated,
brought up as Christians and to lead a tolerably civilized life.
The English missionaries were filled with disgust at this state
of things, and the Boers were denounced from missionary plat-
forms throughout England. Undoubtedly the missionaries were
right, but the Boers, alas, are not the only white race who have
taken this patriarchal attitude toward the natives of the country they were engaged in colonizing. The missionaries in their
other charges were fanatical and ridiculous; they described the
Boers as cruel barbarians because they would not allow the
vermin-haunted Hottentots to join them at family prayers in
their "best rooms." The sting of the matter lay in the fact that
the Colonial Office acted on these representations, and refused
to listen to any complaints of the Boers. As they numbered less
than ten thousand, and English emigrants were constantly
pouring into the colony, the Boers were considered of little
importance to the Government; it was not imagined that they
could do anything effectual in the way of resistance. In short,
they, who had been the ruling race in the colony for over a century, were now a subject race; they were hampered and re-
stricted on every side.

The first intolerable grievance of the Boers was the attitude
of the English missionaries. Some of these were men of really
high religious ideals, but most of them were politicians. Mr.
Vanderkemp and Mr. Read, missionaires of the London society
who had taken black wives, and announced themselves cham-
pions of the black race against the white, had sent to England
reports of a number of murders and outrages said to have been
committed upon Hottentots by the Dutch colonists. By order
of the British government fifty-eight white men and women

were put upon their trial for these crimes, in 1812, and over a thousand witnesses, black and white, were called to give evidence. Several cases of assault were proved, and punished, but none of the serious charges were substantiated. In 1814 a farmer, Frederik Bezuidenhout, quarreled with his native servant, and refused to appear at a court of justice to answer the charge of ill treatment. A company of Hottentots was sent to arrest him; he fired on them and they shot him dead. A company of about fifty joined an insurrection under the leadership of Bezuidenhout's brother Jan. But a strong force of Boers aided the government in putting down this rebellion; all surrendered but Jan who was shot down and killed, while his wife and little son stood by.

Lord Charles Somerset, who drew a salary of ten thousand pounds a year, with four residences, was Governor at the time. He was arbitrary as a prince, and afterward suppressed a liberal newspaper and forbade public meetings. The prisoners taken were tried—they were thirty-nine in number—and six were sentenced to death, while the others all received some form of punishment. Somerset was entreated to annul the death sentence but would only do so in one instance. The remaining five were executed in the presence of their friends, and the scaffold broke with their weight; they were all unconscious and were resuscitated. When they had been brought to consciousness their friends vehemently besought Somerset to reprieve them, but he was firm in his refusal and they were hung again.

This event caused a lasting bitterness among the Boers; the place of execution is known as Slachter's Nek to this day.

In 1828 the Dutch courts of justice were abolished with their "landdrosts" and "heemraden." In their place English courts were established, with magistrates, civil commissioners and justices of the peace. The burgher senate was abolished, also, and—what must have seemed a last touch of insolence—notices were sent to the old colonists that all documents addressed to the Government must be written in English—otherwise they would be returned. Shortly after this a case was to be tried at the circuit court at Worcester, and one of the judges removed it to Cape Town because there were not a sufficient number of

English-speaking men to form a jury, though the prisoner and the witnesses could speak Dutch only, and whatever they said had to be translated in court. The judges were divided in their opinion as to whether it were necessary for every juryman to speak English; in 1831 an ordinance was issued defining the qualifications of jurymen and a knowledge of English was not one of them. But in the meantime the Boers had been greatly embittered by their exclusion from the jury box. They would not write memorials about it to the government, because they refused to write English.

During the years of English occupation the frontier aggressions of the Kaffirs were of frequent occurrence. The document called "An Earnest Representation and Historical Reminder to H. M. Queen Victoria, In view of the Present Crisis, by P. J. Joubert," published a few months ago, contains this reference to the frontier wars: "Natives molested them [the Boers]; they were murdered, robbed of their cattle, their homes were laid waste. Unspeakable horrors were inflicted on their wives and daughters. The Boers were called out for commando service at their own expense, under command and control of the British, to fight the Kaffirs. While on commando, their cattle were stolen by Kaffirs. After, they were made to wait until troops re-took the cattle, which were afterward publicly sold as lost in the presence of their owners, the Boers being informed that they should receive compensation—not in money or goods, neither in rest or peace, but instead, indignities and abuse were heaped on them. They were told that they should be satisfied at not being punished as the instigators of the disturbance."

As far back as 1809 Hottentots were prohibited from wandering about the country without passes, and from 1812 Hottentot children who had been maintained for eight years by the employers of their parents, were bound as apprentices for ten years longer. The missionaries were dissatisfied with these restrictions; both of them were removed by an ordinance passed July, 1828, when vagrant Hottentots began to wander over the country at will. Farming became almost impossible; the farm-laborers became vagabonds and petty thefts took place constantly.

Early in 1834 Sir Benjamin D'Urban, called "the Good," was appointed Governor. A legislative council was then granted the colony, but its powers were not great. Sir George Napier who was afterward Governor, remarked to a member who was arguing a point with him: "You may spare your breath in this matter. Everything of importance is settled before it comes here."

During the early years of the colony, when it was under the Dutch East India Company, slaves had been imported in small numbers, but during the first English occupation—from 1795 to 1803—a great many more had been sent in, as it was a profitable trade. The Batavian government, which lasted only from 1803 to 1806, was against slavery, and would have gradually abolished it. Since 1806 only five hundred slaves had been imported.

The Boers had never been greatly in favor (many opposed it strongly) of slavery, but they had yielded to the general custom and over three million pounds was invested in slaves throughout the colony. In 1834 Sir Benjamin D'Urban proclaimed the emancipation of the slaves, who had been set free throughout the British Empire in August, 1833. This freeing was to take effect in Cape Colony 1st December, 1834.

These slaves had been well treated and their work had been light, but since 1816 laws had been passed reducing the power of the masters. These had been of so irritating a nature that the colonists had resolved that if the English government would stop this legislation—which rendered the slaves insubordinate —they themselves would arrange a plan whereby all female children should be free at birth, so that slavery should gradually die out. But in 1830 an Order in Council was issued prescribing the quantity and quality of food to be given to slaves, the clothing that should be provided for them *etc*. In 1831 another Order was so definite in its restrictions as to hours of labor and other matters that there was great and angry excitement throughout the colony. The high-handed Governor, Lord Charles Somerset, prohibited public meetings and threatened to banish disturbers of the peace. When the excitement subsided, a meeting of two thousand slaveholders was held, who sent a messenger to the Governor to the effect that they would never obey the Orders in Council.

The news of the emancipation was felt to be a relief, but the terms on which it was conducted were productive of unending trouble. The slave owners of Cape Colony were awarded less than a million and a quarter for their slaves—and the imperial government refused to send the money to South Africa; each claim was to be proved before commissioners in London, when the amount would be paid in stock. To make a journey of one hundred days to cross to London was of course impossible to the farmers; they were at the mercy of agents who made their way down to the colony and purchased the claims, so that the colonist received sometimes a fifth, sometimes a sixth, or less, of the value of his slaves. The colonists had hoped that a Vagrant Act would have been passed by the Council when the slaves were freed, to keep them from being still further over-run by this large released black population, but this was not done.

In 1834 the first band of emigrants left the colony—forty-five men under a leader named Louis Triechard, from the division of Albany. He was a violent tempered man, and so loudly opposed to the Government that Colonel Harry Smith offered a reward of five hundred cattle for his apprehension. He left then, at once, being of the class of Boers on the frontier, who lived in their wagons, as though they were ships at sea, and had no settled habitation. His party was joined before it left the colonial border by Johannes Rensburg. Together they had thirty wagons. They traveled northward; all but two of Rensburg's party were killed and those of Triechard's party who escaped the savages reached Delagoa Bay in 1838 after terrible hardships, where they received great kindness from the Portuguese. But their sufferings had been so great that only twenty-six lived to be shipped to Natal. But before the emigration reached its height another Kaffir war came on. There was a tremendous invasion of savages, between twelve and twenty thousand warriors, who swept along the frontier, killing, plundering and burning. Under Colonel Harry Smith a large force was raised; they marched into Kaffirland, and defeated and dispersed the invaders, who were compelled to sue for peace. As a security for the future, Sir Benjamin D'Urban, who was also at the front, issued a proclamation, declaring British sovereignty to be extended over the territory of the defeated tribes as far as the Kei River. But while the people were still suffering from the effects of the invasion, an order came from Lord Glenelg—who became Secretary of State for the Colonies in April, 1835—peremptorily ordering that the new territory must be immediately given up, on the ground that it had been unjustly acquired.

The Boers now felt that no security existed for life or property on the frontier; all the support of the British government was given—with a fanatical philanthropy stimulated by the missionaries—to the black races against themselves. The feeling had now become general among them that they must escape British rule at any cost. They left their houses and cultivated fields and gardens—the homes of over a century's growth—and started into the wilds. Purchasers were not frequent; a house sometimes was sold for an ox; many of them were simply left, with no sale having been made. All over the frontier districts the great wagons set out, loaded with household goods, provisions and ammunition, to seek new homes further north. Each party had its commandant and was generally made up of families related to each other. When the pasturage was good, the caravans would sometimes rest for weeks together, while the cows and oxen, horses and sheep and goats grazed. General Joubert declares that they were followed as far as the Orange River by British emissaries who wanted to be sure that they took no arms nor ammunition with them. However, he adds, the Boers were able to *conceal* their weapons—a fact that seems a very modern instance indeed.

North of the Orange River the colonists regarded themselves as quite free, for Great Britain had declared officially that she would not enlarge her South African possessions.

The emigrants were ridiculed for leaving their homes for the wilderness—"for freedom and grass," and were called professional squatters. One English writer said: "The frontier Boer looks with pity on the busy hives of humanity in cities, or even in villages; and regarding with disdain the grand, but to him unintelligible, results of combined industry, the beauty and excellence of which he cannot know, because they are intellectually discerned, he tosses up his head like a wild horse, utters a neigh of exultation, and plunges into the wilderness."

The number of "trekkers" has been estimated at from five thousand to ten thousand. The tide of emigration (they went generally in small bands) flowed across the Orange River and then followed a course for some distance parallel with the Quathlamba Mountains. By this route the warlike Kaffirs were evaded, the only native tribes passed through being the disorganized bodies known as the Barolongs, Basutos, Mantatees, Korannas, Bergeners and Bushmen, occupying what is now the Orange Free State. Near the Vaal River, however, were the powerful Matabele nation, under the famous Moselekatse, a warrior of Zulu birth, who had established himself there and brought into complete subjection all the neighboring tribes.

One band of emigrants under the Commandant Hendrik Potgieter, a man of considerable ability, arrived at the banks of the Vet River, a tributary of the Vaal. Here he found a native chief who lived in constant dread of Moselekatse, who sold to Potgieter the land between the Vet and the Vaal Rivers, for a number of cattle, Potgieter guaranteeing him protection from Moselekatse. After a while, Commandant Potgieter with eleven others went to explore the country, and traveled north to the Zoutpansberg, where the fertility of the soil seemed encouraging. They also believed that communication with the outer world could be opened through Delagoa Bay, so that the country seemed to offer every advantage for settlement. In high spirits they came back to rejoin their families, but a hideous surprise awaited them; they found only mutilated corpses. Expecting an immediate return of the Matabele who had massacred his people Potgieter made a strong laager on a hill, by lashing fifty wagons together in a circle, and filling all the open spaces, except a narrow entrance, with thorn trees. Presently the Matabele returned and with great shouts and yells stormed the camp, rushing up to the wagon wheels and throwing assegais. But the Boers with their powerful "roers" or elephant guns kept such a rapid and skilful fire, while the women kept the spare guns reloaded, that the Matabele were forced to retire, but they drove with them all the cattle of the party. They left one hundred and fifty-five dead, and one thousand one hundred of their spears were afterward picked up.

The emigrants in the laager were left without the means of

transportation, and very little food, while they had lost forty-six of their people. But fortunately they were near the third band of emigrants under the Commandant Gerrit Maritz who encamped near the mission station at Thaba Ntshu, and now sent oxen to carry away Potgieter and the others. Also a native chief Marroco, brought them milk and Kaffir corn, and pack oxen to help them away. It was resolved to revenge the massacre, to follow up Moselekatse and punish him. One hundred and seven Boers mustered for this service, besides forty half-breeds and a few blacks to take care of the horses. A deserter from the Matabele army acted as guide. The commando surprised Mosega, one of the principal military towns, and killed four hundred. Then setting fire to the kraal, they drove seven thousand head of cattle back to Thaba Ntshu. Potgieter's party then formed a camp on the Vet (they called it Winburg) which was joined by many families from the colony. Another band soon reached Thaba Ntshu, under Pieter Retief, a man of great intelligence. June 6th, 1837, a general assembly of Boers was held at Winburg, when a provisional constitution, consisting of nine articles, was adopted. The supreme legislative power was entrusted to a single elective chamber, termed the Volksraad, the fundamental law was declared to be the Dutch, a court of landdrost and heemraden was created, and the chief executive authority was given to Retief with the title of Commandant-General. One article provided that all who joined the community must take an oath to have no connection with the London Missionary Society.

New bands of emigrants were constantly arriving and some of them wished to go into Natal, although the condition of the camp at Winburg was very satisfactory. Pieter Uys, one of their leaders, had visited Natal before, and had been impressed with its beauty and fertility. Retief finally decided to go and see for himself if Dingaan the Zulu chief would dispose of some land below the mountain.

While he was gone, a second expedition against the Matabele set out, consisting of one hundred and thirty-five farmers, under Potgieter and Pieter Uys. They found Moselekatse with twelve thousand warriors, brave and finely trained, but at the end of nine days' warfare, Moselekatse fled to the north, after a loss of something like one thousand men. Commandant Potgieter now issued a proclamation declaring that the whole of the territory overrun by the Matabele and now abandoned by them was forfeited to the Boers. It included the greater part of the present South African Republic, fully half of the present Orange Free State, and the whole of Southern Bechuanaland to the Kalahari desert, except that part occupied by the Batlapin. This immense tract of land was then almost uninhabited, and must have remained so if the Matabele had not been driven out.

Much has been written of the beauties of Natal, with its shores washed by the Indian Ocean, its rich soil, luxuriant vegetation and noble forests. When Pieter Retief first saw it from the Drakensberg Mountains, it was under the despotic rule of the Zulu chief Dingaan, who had succeeded Tshaka, the "Napoleon of Africa," the slayer of a million human beings. A few Englishmen who were allowed to live at the port gladly welcomed the emigrants, and took them to Dingaan's capital, called Umkungunhlovu, acting as guides and interpreters. There was an English missionary clergyman living there called Owen. Dingaan received them graciously and supplied them with chunks of beef from his own eating mat, and huge calabashes of millet beer. But when Retief spoke about Natal, the despot set him a task, such as one reads of in folk-lore legends. Retief might have Natal for his countrymen to live in, if he would recover a herd of seven hundred cattle that had been stolen from him by Sikonyela, a Mantatee chief. Retief accepted the condition, and actually made Sikonyela restore the cattle, which he drove back to Dingaan. The Boers at Winburg felt distrustful of Dingaan, and dreaded to have Pieter Retief trust himself again in the tyrant's hands. But in February, 1838, Retief started with seventy persons, armed and mounted, with thirty attendants. Again Dingaan received them hospitably, and empowered the missionary Owen to draw up a document granting to Retief the country between the Tugela and the Umzimvubu. But just as the emigrants were ready to leave, they were invited into a cattle kraal to see a war dance, and requested to leave their arms outside the door. While sitting down they were overpowered and massacred, the horror-stricken Owen being a witness of the sight.

Immediately after the massacre, Dingaan sent out his forces against all the emigrants on the eastern side of the Drakensberg. Before daylight they attacked the encampments at Blaauwkrans River and the Bushman River—ten miles apart. It was a complete surprise and a terrible slaughter of the Boers, although a brave defence was made. The township which has since arisen near the scene of the conflict still bears the name of "Weenen"—the place of wailing.

As soon as the emigrants on the west of the Drakensberg heard of the disasters, they formed a band of about eight hundred men to punish Dingaan for his treachery. But they were led into an ambush, and finally defeated by the Zulus, and forced to retreat after a tremendous loss of life. The condition of the emigrants was now one of terrible distress and privation. They had many widows and orphans to provide for. The Governor of Cape Colony sent word to them to return, and there were many who felt willing to go but it was the women of the party who sternly refused to go back; they preferred liberty, although that liberty had cost them so dear. In November, 1838, Andries Pretorius arrived in Natal from Graaff Reinet and was at once elected Commandant-General. He organized a force of four hundred and sixty-four men and marched toward Umkungunhlovu. He took with him a sufficient number of wagons to form a laager; wherever the camp was pitched it was surrounded by fifty-seven wagons; all the cattle were brought within the enclosure, the whole force joining in prayers and singing of psalms. The army made a vow that if victorious they would build a church and set apart a Thanksgiving day each year to commemorate it. The church in Pietermaritzburg and the annual celebration of Dingaan's defeat bear witness that they kept their pledge. They were not fighting for revenge. On three occasions the scouts brought in some captured Zulus, and Pretorius sent them back to Dingaan to say that if he would restore the land he had granted Retief he would enter into negotiations for peace.

Dingaan's reply came in the form of an army ten thousand or twelve thousand strong, which attacked the camp December 16th, 1838. For two hours the Zulus tried to force their way into the laager, while the Boer guns and the small artillery made dreadful havoc in their ranks. When at length they broke and fled over three thousand Zulu corpses lay on the ground and a stream that flowed through the battlefield was crimson. It has been known ever since as the Blood River.

Pretorius marched on to Umkungunhlovu as soon as possible but Dingaan had fled and set the place on fire.

Dingaan, with the remainder of his forces, retired further into Zululand. There, soon after, his brother Panda revolted, and fled with a large following into Natal, where he sought the protection of the Boers. Another and final expedition was made against Dingaan in January, 1840, the farmers having Panda with four thousand of his best warriors as an ally. By February 10th, Dingaan was a fugitive in the country of a hostile tribe who soon killed him, and the emigrant farmers were the conquerors of Zululand. On that day Panda was appointed and declared to be "King of the Zulus" in the name and behalf of the Volksraad at Pietermaritzburg, where the Boers established their seat of government as "The South African Society of Natal."

Four days afterward, a proclamation was issued at the same camp, signed by Pretorius and four commandants under him, declaring all the territory between the Black Umfolosi and the Umzimvubu Rivers to belong to the emigrant farmers. "The national flag was hoisted," says a chronicler, "a salute of twenty-one guns fired, and a general 'hurrah' given throughout the whole army, while all the men as with one voice called out: 'Thanks to the Great God who by his grace has given us the victory!' "

Now that the "trekkers" had freed South Africa from the destructive Zulu power and had driven the Matabele away, they wished to settle in Natal, and rest from the nomadic existence that had so long been theirs. But the British now came forward to hunt them on again. The Governor of Cape Colony, Sir George Napier, proclaimed that "the occupation of Natal by the emigrants was unwarrantable," and directed that "all arms and ammunition should be taken from them, and the port closed against trade."

What followed—the British bombardment of the port, the Dutch surrender, are well known facts of recent history. May

12th, 1843, Natal was proclaimed a British colony, and the emigrants again took to their wagons.

Pieter Retief's Proclamation giving his reasons for emigration.

(1) We despair of saving the colony from those evils which threaten it by the turbulent and dishonest conduct of vagrants, who are allowed to infest the country in every part; nor do we see any prospect of peace or happiness for our children in a country thus distracted by internal commotions.

(2) We complain of the severe losses which we have been forced to sustain by the emancipation of our slaves, and the vexatious laws which have been enacted respecting them.

(3) We complain of the continual system of plunder which we have for years endured from the Kaffirs and other classes and particularly by the last invasion of the colony, which has desolated the frontier and ruined most of the inhabitants.

(4) We complain of the unjustifiable odium which has been cast upon us by interested and dishonest persons, under the name of Religion, whose testimony is believed in England to the exclusion of all evidence in our favor; and we can foresee, as the result of this prejudice, nothing but the total ruin of the country.

(5) We are resolved, wherever we go, that we will uphold the just principles of liberty; but whilst we will take care that no one is brought by us into a condition of slavery, we will establish such regulations as may suppress crime and preserve proper relations between master and servant.

(6) We solemnly declare that we leave this colony with a desire to enjoy a quieter life than we have hitherto led. We will not molest any people, nor deprive them of the smallest property; but if attacked, we shall consider ourselves fully justified in defending our persons and effects, to the utmost of our ability against every enemy.

(7) We make known that when we shall have framed a code of laws for our guidance, copies shall be forwarded to this colony for general information, but we take the opportunity of stating

that it is our firm resolve to make provisions for summary punishment, even with death, of all traitors, without exception, who may be found amongst us.

(8) We propose, in the course of our journey and on arrival at the country in which we shall permanently reside, to make known to the native tribes our intentions and our desires to live in peace and friendly intercourse with them.

(9) We quit this colony under the full assurance that the English government has nothing more to require of us and will allow us to govern ourselves without its interference in future.

(10) We are now leaving the fruitful land of our birth in which we have suffered enormous losses and continual vexation, and are about to enter a strange and dangerous territory; but we go with a firm reliance on an all-seeing, just and merciful God, whom we shall always fear and humbly endeavor to obey.

In the name of all who leave this colony with me.

P. Retief.

No. 72

THE TALK OF LONDON

PEOPLE who contended that neither France nor Russia would make a colonial move while the greatest colonist of them all was more busy in South Africa than ever she had been since the time of Napoleon may study with interest the move of Russia on Persia and the Persian Gulf. At present it is a financial move rather than a military one, but nevertheless it has made Great Britain very uneasy, for no country knows better than she what kind of a move usually precedes a military occupation.

In the meantime France has quietly sent to her possessions in the Barbary States four times as many men as were required to subjugate those savage countries in the first campaign. Where the posts on the frontier usually required a small garrison of a few companies, brigades are now stationed. In fact

France has in northern Africa a large army ready to take advantage of a political opportunity. She must be rather certain that her opportunity is approaching, for ministries do not send brigades so far for nothing.

The Emperor of Germany devotes himself at this time to declaring to his people that the plight of England is an object lesson which teaches that the German Empire should have a largely increased navy. This, apparently, is the only advantage he sees or is willing to take, although the excitement among his people against the English is greater even than it is in France. For some years his ambitions have been strongly colonial, and he required an efficient navy, moderate in size, to further his far-reaching plans. However, there was from the beginning a vehement opposition by many political parties of the Empire. His Ministry now sees in the popular feeling against England and her war in the Transvaal a chance to get a large bill through the Reichstag.

Italy lifts her lazy head and begins to feel that she should properly occupy Egypt in the place of England, but she is not yet prepared to make many remarks upon the subject.

One can conclude with a statement of the belief that an early and brilliant British victory in the Transvaal would smite many political ambitions in Europe. Russia's clever and sly agents, France's waiting brigades in Algeria, would be very likely to stand in their tracks for some time to come.

A strong battle ship division of the Toulon squadron of the French navy has been for some weeks in a Morocco harbor which has been famous in the diplomatic relations between England, France and Spain.

Throughout the war debates in the last session of the House of Commons the Irish Nationalists have occupied themselves mainly in having fun with the opposition. All went well until one time some speech of an Irish member stirred Colonel Saunderson, member for Armagh, North. He lost his temper to such a degree that he allowed himself to make some of the most offensive observations that were ever made in the House. "So that was the plan of campaign?" said he. "Not only were the British soldiers to be attacked in front, they were liable to be attacked in the rear, for the Nationalists never attack in front."

Whereupon the Irish benches were in an uproar. Mr. T. M. Healy and Mr. Dillon and Mr. Redmond all pointed out the insult, and also the fact that they were in no humor to stand things of that sort. Through the din the Speaker's voice could be heard giving Colonel Saunderson a rather feeble support, declaring that he had not been out of order in his remarks.

Colonel Saunderson finally arose to make an explanation. This explanation was really a perfect bit of impudence. He said that he would withdraw the expression. When it came to his lips he had not meant to insult the honorable gentlemen opposite. He continued: "I am as proud of Irish valor as they are, and when I used the expression I was simply thinking of the historical records of Ireland and thought I was justified in saying what I did. I wish to withdraw it."

Again there was a great beating of tomtoms and hammering of war-posts among the Irish benches. Mr. Dillon shouted: "That is making the observation twice as bad. Withdraw it like a gentleman." Mr. A. J. Balfour then arose to cover the retreat of his party friend, who was suffering the heaviest kind of a fire. In his suavest manner the leader of the House begged the gentlemen on both sides to forget an expression which was not intended to be offensive. The clamor from the Irish benches arose again. And Mr. MacNeill, looking at Colonel Saunderson, remarked: "Send him to the House of Peers. We've had enough of him."

But Mr. Balfour persevered in his attempt to help Saunderson, and really got him out of a great deal of trouble. Ultimately Colonel Saunderson withdrew his expression without attaching to it any acrimonious phrases. It was not an important scene in the House of Commons, but it will be celebrated as one of the most noisy.

IMOGENE CARTER

No. 1

WAR SEEN THROUGH A WOMAN'S EYES

ATHENS, April 26.—To a woman, war is a thing that hits at the heart and at the places around the table. It does not always exist to her mind as a stirring panorama, or at least when it does she is not thinking of battles save in our past tense historic way, which eliminates the sufferings. One cannot, however, be in any part of Greece at this time without coming close to the meaning of war, war in the present tense, war in complete definition. I have seen the volunteers start amid flowers and tears and seen afterward the tears when the flowers were forgotten. I have seen the crowds rave before the palace of the King, appealing to him for permission to sacrifice, as if death was a wine. I have seen the wounded come in hastily and clumsily bandaged, unwashed and wan, with rolling eyes that expressed that vague desire of the human mind in pain for an impossible meadow wherein rest and sleep and peace come suddenly when one lies in the grass. In Athens this is war—the tears of mothers, the cheers of the throng and later the rolling eyes of the wounded. In Athens one can get an idea of war which satisfies, it is true, the correspondents of many London newspapers, but surely this is not the whole of war. War here is tears and flowers and blood and oratory. Surely there must be other things. I am going to try and find out at the front.

It is an encouraging prospect. People point to the hospital corps and say: "Look! Do you see the cartridge belts around the waists of these men who wear the Red Cross, the emblem of mercy? Do you see that they carry rifles? Do you know what it means? No? It means that a Turk fires on a hospital as quickly as he fires on charging infantry. Do you know what they do to prisoners? Do you know what they do to an enemy's wounded on the field? Do you know what becomes of the

women they capture? No? Well, no license of words can describe the horrors of this last thing. The most common Turkish
outrages are the ones that don't get into print. We assure you
this on the word of every one who knows. The facts simply
can't be printed. This American journalism is very strange to
our minds. Why don't they send a man?"

"They have sent many men," I reply, "but now they want to
know what a woman thinks of a battle." The Greeks then
solemnly shake their heads. All this is very enfeebling. Nevertheless one cannot remain in this atmosphere long without
gaining something from the resolution and fortitude of this
Greek people.

No. 2

WOMAN CORRESPONDENT AT THE FRONT

ATHENS, April 29.—I start to-day for the front of the Greek
army to see how the men fight. I learn that even the English
nurses have returned from the hospitals of the army because
the Turks fire on the Red Cross flag with the same enthusiasm
with which they fire on the lines of battle.

From this and from other rumors I am quite sure that the
Journal will have the only woman correspondent within even
the sound of the guns.

Acquaintances among the foreign residents here all strongly
advise me not to go. At first I was flatly refused letters of introduction to people at the front in an effort to make my going
impossible, but, as a matter of fact, I do not believe altogether
in the point of view of the women of Athens, and, at any rate, I
am going.

No. 3

IMOGENE CARTER'S ADVENTURE AT PHARSALA

[Crane's hand]

PHARSALA, May—. My first adventure of importance is just now over and I am glad, exuberantly glad, that it is over. I hope the Graeco-Turkish war holds no worse situations for me. And yet it is no worse than sleeping on a pool table under disadvantages. It was midnight when the diligence rolled into Pharsala and I could see nothing in the unlighted street but a row of stores barred and bolted and sealed by their owners who were evidently fled from the town. Sometimes a shadowy patrol passed in the darkness and once a horse loomed at the side of the carriage. The dragoman in an awe-struck whisper mentioned the name of one who was apparently a Greek officer high in rank but the name sounded only like a term in chemistry to me and I have never been able to do better with it. The officer would have been no more than a dark shadow if it were not for the gleam of his gold braid. After him came ten dim and silent carbineers.

At last the diligence paused in front of a dismal coffee-house. The dragoman then began one of his celebrated struggles with an adverse fate. But it was of no use. There was simply nothing in town. Finally a brilliant idea struck me. We would charter the coffee-house. It was the principal coffee-house in Pharsala but we tried this plan on the proprietor and it worked. So the soldiers were put out. They wouldn't budge at all until they understood the circumstances and then they went quietly off. The dragoman took possession in the name of myself and my Greek girl.

It was a wretched old place. The walls were high and dingy

[Cora's hand]

At one A.M. the diligence stopped in front of a dismal coffee-house called "The New World." My dragoman suggested we go at once to headquarters and get permission to sleep in some deserted house but I decided it was too late and persuaded the proprietor of the coffee-house to let us sleep in his place. He consented and turned out a few straggling soldiers. Imagine a barnlike room that had evidently once been whitewashed, as I could see faint traces of it yet left on the walls, a bare and very dirty floor, in one corner a tiny counter from whence Turkish coffee and native cognac and mastika were dispensed. To the right, was an ancient pool table. A few old benches against the walls and many little tables and chairs were all the furniture. It was dimly lighted by two oil lamps. At first I intended rolling up in my rugs and sleeping on the floor but it was too dirty. The benches were in almost as filthy a condition and at last I decided on climbing on the pool table. My maid who had grumbled constantly at everything and who had cried over our dinner of black bread (which is very sweet and good) and cheese, now flatly rebelled—and I paid her and sent her to the diligence by which she returned to Lamia—and so I was alone, the only woman in Pharsala or within many miles of it. The old proprietor of the coffee-house seemed to have the general Greek admiration for Americans, and fixed my rugs for me on the pool table. He then got his rifle and patrolled around it while I slept. Every few moments a knock would come at the door, some late soldier wanting a drink. He had locked the door by piling a table and a few chairs in front of it. Several times these were pushed away and the soldiers would enter to receive nothing but the information that an American woman was sleeping on the pool table and that he wanted them to get out. Finally he secured the door firmly in some way. When other knocks came, he would mutter in Greek and shake his fist at the door, then look towards me and if he caught me peeking out from a corner of my blanket would lay his head on his hand, and then pat his rifle, trying to tell me to go to sleep, he would protect me. Toward day I fell asleep. It did not seem but an instant when a loud knocking awakened me to the fact it was daylight. A voice demanding to be admitted and the scuffling of many feet on the stone porch, again had caused the landlord to shake his fist and mutter. Finally some one said "The Gendarmes command you to open." He looked towards me, shrugged his shoulders, and opened the door. At once the place was filled with officers who loudly called for coffee. I laid quiet for a quarter of an hour—then sat up, put on my hat and climbed on a chair and to the floor. It was embarrassing but I tried to look as if it was my usual manner of sleeping and awakening. I must here express my admiration for the manners of these Greek officers. They also tried to appear unconscious—and when one did look at me it was in a respectful manner. As new officers entered and saw a woman, they would for an instant gaze in astonishment, and then pass on. At Head-quarters the Crown Prince sleeps late and so I had to wait until nine or ten o'clock before I could find a place to go. At last, a deserted house, one of the best in the village, was given me. It was high on the hills and the view from the balcony was superb. The entire plain of Pharsala—where Caesar defeated Pompey in 48 B.C.—lay before me, covered with waving grain. On each side of the road which crossed it towards Velestino troops were camped. They were far out and looked like the tin soldiers children play with. I could see them moving about in long lines and in squads of about fifty, and some on tiny horses. Occasionally a cavalryman with orders perhaps would gallop up the road towards Pharsala and grow larger and larger as he approached. Infantry soldiers were also constantly coming and going on this road, increasing or diminishing in size as they came and went. On the opposite mountain, a flash attracted my attention. It was messages being sent by the mirror system of field telegraphing. This kept up for half an hour. Just below me to the left was the jail queerly constructed, with the roof covered with storks' nests. The storks were flying about making queer noises and flapping their wings. The only inhabitants of Pharsala who were not afraid of the coming Turk and who did not desert the home nest. To the right down a narrow winding rough road was the head quarters of the Crown Prince, a good sized low building which had evidently been a Hotel recently built for the benefit of the tourists who visit the historic battle field of Pharsala.

No. 4

IMOGENE CARTER'S PEN PICTURE OF THE FIGHTING AT VELESTINO

ATHENS, May 9.—By Courier from the Front.—I returned to Volo to-night (Thursday) from Velestino after witnessing a hard fight there. I spent most of the time with the Second Battery of mountain howitzers.

The reinforced Turks, under Osman Pasha, made a heavy attack upon the Greek right and left wings.

I was among the last of the correspondents to leave the field. Shells screamed about me as I went toward the station, and I had one narrow squeak.

The soldiers were amazed at the presence of a woman during the fighting.

Our train was shelled on the way to Volo. We expected a panic here last night, despite the presence of English, French and Italian men-of-war.

The arrival of the Turks is looked for at any moment.

No. 5

MANUSCRIPT NOTES

LEFT Athens 30th April 1897—steamer to Stylis—Left 9. P.M.—stopped noon next day Chalkis—Got left—Dispatch boat, with new minister war on board, took us* on board—cought up—our steamer & were transfered—Arrived Stylis six P.M.—went ashore sail boat—Got carriages—drove to Lamia, which was reached midnight—Bunked on Floor wierd Hotel—Cafe—Soldiers—Drove

---

* us] *following 'us' is deleted* 'bo'

to Domokos—started 7 A.M.—Arrived 5 P.M.—Shepperds & goat-
herds driving flocks along route—Entire population of villiages
fleeing away to[b] the frontier & the coming Turk—moving hous-
hold goods on Cammels, in carts, some modern Greek and some
old turkish with huge wooden disks for wheels—Children piled
on top—Constantly meeting volunteers—with Guns on shoulder
& cartridge belt—ect   stopped to lunch by spring.

Domokos situated on top of mountain—grim old tumbled down
place—cobbled, narrow streets very turkish—figures on top
houses—guns saved from Larrisa—old fortifications top mountain
—crowds curious people—Greek officer—Left Domokos about 7
P.M. drove to Pharsala—more fleeing villiagers, flocks ect in great
numbers—some camped along route. Halted by outposts—Fallen
soldier—slept billiard table coffee house—miserable morning—
Room overlooking plain—curious officers—Bass desertion—Davis
gave deserted house—article—pictures on wall—Left morning
picked up by carriage—what troops eat—how cooked—R. W.
carriage—met French officer from Guadiana[c]—breakfasted with
us Volo—Old[d] mosque at Pharsala—storks—mouse ill—8 P.M.
word has just come the Greeks have killed 2000 Turks Cavelery-
men—Volo sea port. Surounded by mountains. Mosque war
ships. Greek fleet—one English—one French—lumpy looking
mountains with patches brown, red-Brown, yellow different
greens black rocks & shaddows—House, shops closed

[in ink] Got horses—rode to Valestimo—warned to turn back—
but kept on. went on mountain Battery no 2—   Under actual
fire. shells over head—got to Station for train shell over my head
five feet—just cought train. which Turks shelled—Panic Volo—
people leaving in boats—which are pilled High household goods
—Hotel staff[e] sent away—Dog—[in pencil, new leaf] < > turkish shell—Dog lost—remained til every boat gone—Got permission flag ship Greek to come on man of war as far [Areos?]—2
thousand women children, priests. Turks expected enter Volo
tonight. Peasants rejoice at saving their lives—hardly having
time yet to regret home—

[b] to] *added in ink after deleted* 'from'
[c] Guadiana] *just possibly spelled* 'Guardiana'
[d] Old] *preceded by deleted* 'Volo'
[e] staff] *just possibly* 'stuff'

GREAT BATTLES
OF THE WORLD

THE BRIEF CAMPAIGN AGAINST
NEW ORLEANS
DECEMBER 14, 1814—JANUARY 8, 1815

THE Mississippi, broad, rapid, and sinister, ceaselessly flogging its enwearied banks, was the last great legend of the dreaming times when the Old World's information of the arisen continents was roseate but inaccurate. England, at war with the United States, heard stories of golden sands, bejewelled temples, fabulous silks, the splendor of a majestic barbarian civilization, and even if these tales were fantastic they stood well enough as symbols of the spinal importance of the grim Father of Waters.

The English put together a great expedition. It was the most formidable that ever had been directed against the Americans. It assembled in a Jamaican harbor, and at Pensacola, then a Spanish port, and technically neutral. The troops numbered about fourteen thousand men, and included some of the best regiments in the British army, fresh from service in the Peninsula under Wellington. They were certainly not men who had formed a habit of being beaten. Included in the expedition was a full set of civilian officials for the government of New Orleans after its capture.

A hundred and ten miles from the mouth of the Mississippi, New Orleans lay trembling. She had no forts or intrenchments; she would be at the mercy of the powerful British force. The people believed that the city would be sacked and burned. They were not altogether a race full of vigor. The peril of the situation bewildered them; it did not stir them to action.

But the spirit of energy itself arrived in the person of Andrew Jackson. Since the Creek War, the nation had had much confidence in Jackson, and New Orleans welcomed him with a great sigh of relief. The sallow, gnarled, crusty man came ill to his great work; he should have been in bed. But the amount of vim he worked into a rather flabby community in a short time looked like a miracle. The militia of Louisiana were called out; the free negroes were armed and drilled; convicts whose terms had nearly expired were enlisted; and down from Tennessee tramped the type of man that one always pictures as winning the battle—the long, lank woodsman, brown as leather, hard as nails, inseparable from his rifle, in his head the eye of a hawk.

The Lafitte brothers, famous pirates whose stronghold was not a thousand miles from the city, threw in their lot with the Americans. The British bid for their services, but either the British committed the indiscretion of not bidding enough or the buccaneers were men of sentiment. At any rate they accepted the American pledge of immunity and came with their men to the American side, where they rendered great service. Afterward the English, their offer of treasure repulsed, somewhat severely reproved us for allowing these men to serve in our ranks.

Martial law was proclaimed and Jackson kept up an exciting quarrel with the city authorities at the same time that he was working his strange army night and day in the trenches. Captain John Coffee with two thousand men joined from Mobile.

The British war-ships first attempted to cross the sand bars at the mouth of the river, and ascend the stream, but the swift Mississippi came to meet them, and it was as if this monster, immeasurable in power, knew that he must defend himself. The well-handled war-ships could not dodge this simple strength; even the wind refused its help. The river won the first action.

But if the British could not ascend the stream, they could destroy the small American gun-boats on the lakes below the city, and this they did on December 14 with a rather painful thoroughness. The British were then free to land their troops on the shores of these lakes and attempt to approach the city through miles of dismal and sweating swamps. The decisive word seems to have rested with Major-General Keane. Sir George Pakenham, the commander-in-chief, had not yet arrived. One of Wellington's proud veterans was not likely to endure any

nonsensical delay over such a business as this campaign against
a simple people who had not had the art of war hammered
into their heads by a Napoleon. Moreover the army was impatient. Some of the troops had been with Lord Ross in the
taking of Washington, and they predicted something easier
than that very easy campaign. Everybody was completely cock-
sure.

On the afternoon of December 23 Major-General Gabrielle
Villeré, one of the gaudy Creole soldiers, came to see Jackson
at head-quarters and announced that about two thousand British had landed on the Villeré plantation, nine miles below the
city. Jackson was still feeble, but this news warmed the old
passion in him. He pounded the table with his fist. "By the
eternal!" he cried. "They shall not sleep on our soil!" All well-
regulated authorities make Jackson use this phrase—"By the
eternal"—and any reference to him hardly would be intelligible
unless one quoted the familiar line. I suppose we should not
haggle over the matter; historically one oath is as good as another.

Marching orders were issued to the troops and the armed
schooner *Carolina* was ordered to drop down the river and open
fire upon the British at 7.30 in the evening. In the meantime,
Jackson reviewed his troops as they took the road. He was not
a good-natured man; indeed, he is one of the most irascible
figures in history. But he knew how to speak straight as a stick
to the common man. Each corps received some special word of
advice and encouragement.

This review was quaint. Some of the Creole officers were very
gorgeous, but perhaps they only served to emphasize the wildly
unmilitary aspect of the procession generally. But the woodsmen were there with their rifles, and if the British had beaten
Napoleon's marshals, the woodsmen had conquered the forests
and the mountains, and they too did not understand that they
could be whipped.

The first detachment of British troops had come by boat
through Lake Borgne, and then made a wretched march through
the swamps. Both officers and men were in sorry plight. They
had been exposed for days to the fury of tropical rains and
for nights to bitter frosts without gaining even an opportunity

to dry their clothes. But December 23 was a clear day, lit by a mildly warm sun. Arriving at Villeré's plantation on the river bank, the troops built huge fires and then raided the country as far as they dared, gathering a great treasure of "fowls and hams and wine." The feast was merry. The veteran soldier of that day had a grand stomach, and he made a deep inroad into Louisiana's store of "fowls and hams and wine."

As they lay comfortably about their fires in the evening some sharp eye detected by the faint light of the moon a moving, shadowy vessel on the river. She was approaching. An officer mounted the levee and hailed her. There was no answer. He hailed again. The silent vessel calmly furled her sails and swung her broadside parallel. Then a voice shouted and a whistling shower of grape-shot tore the air. It was the little *Carolina*.

The British force flattened themselves in the shelter of the levee and listened to the grape-shot go ploughing over their heads. But they had not been long in this awkward position when there was a yell and a blare of flame in the darkness. Some of Jackson's troops had come.

Then ensued a strange conflict. The moon, tender lady of the night, hid while around the dying fires two forces of enfuriated men shot, stabbed, and cut. One remembers grimly Jackson's sentence—"They shall not sleep on our soil." No; they were kept awake this night at least.

There was no concerted action on either side. An officer gathered a handful of men, and by his voice led them through the darkness at the enemy. If such valor and ferocity had been introduced into the insipid campaigns of the north the introduction would have made overwhelming victory for one people or the other. Dawn displayed the terrors of the fighting in the night. In some cases, an American and an English soldier lay dead each with his bayonet sheathed in the other's body. Bayonets were rare in the American ranks, but many men carried long hunting knives.

As a matter of fact the two forces had been locked in a blind and desperate embrace. The British reported a loss of forty-six killed, one hundred and sixty-seven wounded, and sixty-four missing. In this engagement the Americans suffered more severely than in any other action of the short campaign.

On the morning of December 24, Sir George Pakenham arrived with a strong reinforcement of men and guns. Pakenham was a brother-in-law of Wellington. He had served in the Peninsula and was accounted a fine leader. The American schooners *Carolina* and *Louisiana* lay at anchor in the river, firing continually upon the British camp. Pakenham caused a battery to be planted which quickly made short work of these vessels.

During the days following the two armies met in several encounters which were fiery but indecisive. One of these meetings is called the Battle of the Bales and Hogsheads.

Jackson employed cotton-bales in strengthening a position, and one night the British advanced and built a redoubt chiefly of hogsheads containing sugar and molasses. The cotton suffered considerably from the British artillery, often igniting and capable of being easily rolled out of place, but the sugar and molasses behaved very badly. The hogsheads were easily penetrated, and they soon began to distribute sugar and molasses over the luckless warriors in the redoubt, so that British soldiers died while mingling their blood with molasses, and with sugar sprinkling down upon their wounds.

Although neither side had gained a particular advantage the British were obliged to retire. They had been the first disciplined troops to engage molasses, and they were glad to emerge from the redoubt, this bedraggled, sticky, and astonished body of men.

On the opposite bank of the river a battery to rake the British encampment had been placed by Commander Patterson. This battery caused Pakenham much annoyance, and he engaged it severely with his guns, but at the end of an hour he had to cease firing with a loss of seventy men, and his emplacements almost in ruins. The damage to the American works was slight, but they had lost thirty-six in killed and disabled.

Both sides now came to a period of fateful thought. In the beginning, the British had spoken of a feeble people who at first would offer a resistance of pretence, but soon subside before the victorious colors of the British regiments. Now they knew that they were face to face with determined and skilful fighters who would dauntlessly front any British regiment whose colors had ever hung in glory in a cathedral of old England. The Americans had thought to sweep the British into the Gulf of Mexico. But now they knew that although their foes floundered and blundered, although they displayed that curious stern-lipped stupidity which is the puzzle of many nations, they were still the veterans of the Peninsula, the stout undismayed troops of Wellington.

Jackson moved his line fifty yards back from his cotton-bale position. Here he built a defensive work on the northern brink of an old saw-mill race known as the Rodriguez Canal. The line of defence was a mile in length. It began on the river bank and ended in a swamp, where during the battle the Americans stood knee-deep in mud or on floating planks and logs moored to the trees. The main defences of the position were built of earth, logs and fence-rails. In some places it was twenty feet thick. It barred the way to New Orleans.

The Americans were prepared for the critical engagement some days before Pakenham had completed his arrangements. The Americans spent the interval in making grape-shot out of bar-lead, and in mending whatever points in their line needed care and work.

Pakenham's final plan was surprisingly simple, and perhaps it was surprisingly bad. He decided to send a heavy force across the river to attack Patterson's annoying battery simultaneously with the deliverance of the main attack against Jackson's position along the line of the Rodriguez Canal. Why Pakenham decided to make the two attacks simultaneous is not quite clear at this day. Patterson's force, divided by the brutally swift river from the main body of the Americans, might have been considered with much reason a detached body of troops and Pakenham might have eaten them at his leisure, while at the same time keeping up a great show in front of Jackson, so that the latter would consider that something serious was imminent at the main position.

However, Pakenham elected to make the two attacks at the same hour, and posterity does not perform a graceful office when it re-generals the battles of the past.

Boats were brought from the fleet, and with immense labor

a canal was dug from Lake Borgne to the Mississippi. For use in fording the ditch in front of Jackson, the troops made fascines by binding together sheaves of sugar-cane, and for the breast-work on the far-side of the ditch they made scaling ladders.

On January 7, 1815, Jackson stood on the top of the tallest building within his lines and watched the British at work. At the same time Pakenham was in the top of a pine-tree regarding the American trenches. For the moment, and indefinitely, it was a question of eyesight. Jackson studied much of the force that was to assail him; Pakenham studied the position which he had decided to attack. Pakenham's eyesight may not have been very good.

Colonel Thornton was in command of the troops which were to attack Patterson's battery across the river, and a rocket was to be sent up to tell him when to begin his part of the general onslaught.

Pakenham advanced serenely against the Rodriguez Canal, the breast-work and the American troops. One wishes to use here a phrase inimical to military phraseology. One wishes to make a distinction between disinterested troops and troops who are interested. The Americans were interested troops. They faced the enemy at the main gate of the United States. Behind them crouched frightened thousands. In reality they were defending a continent.

As the British advanced to the attack, they made a gallant martial picture. The motley army of American planters, woodsmen, free negroes, ex-convicts, and pirates watched them in silence. Here tossed the bonnets of a fierce battalion of Highlanders; here marched a bottle-green regiment, the officers wearing furred cloaks and crimson sashes; here was a steady line of blazing red coats. Everywhere rode the general officers in their cocked hats, their short red coats with golden epaulettes and embroideries, their skin-tight white breeches, their high black boots. The ranks were kept locked in the manner of that day. It was like a grand review.

But the grandeur was extremely brief. The force was well within range of the American guns when Pakenham made the terrible discovery that his orders had been neglected; there was neither fascine nor ladder on the field. In a storm of rage and grief the British general turned to the guilty officer and bade him take his men back and fetch them. When, however, the ladders and fascines had been brought into the field a hot infantry engagement had begun and the bearers becoming wildly rattled, scattered them on the ground.

It was now that Sir George Pakenham displayed that quality of his nation which in another place I have called stern-lipped stupidity. It was an absolute certainty that Jackson's position could not be carried without the help of fascines and ladders; it was doubtful if it could be carried in any case.

But Sir George Pakenham ordered a general charge. His troops responded desperately. They flung themselves forward in the face of a storm of bullets aimed usually with deadly precision. Back of their rampart the Americans, at once furious and cool, shot with the quickness of aim and yet with the finished accuracy of life-long hunters. The British army was being mauled and mangled out of all resemblance to the force that had landed in December.

Sir George Pakenham, proud, heart-broken, frenzied man, rode full-tilt at the head of rush after rush. And his men followed him to their death. On the right, a major and a lieutenant succeeded in crossing the ditch. The two officers mounted the breast-work but the major fell immediately. The lieutenant imperiously demanded the swords of the American officers present. But they said: "Look behind you." He looked behind him and saw that the men whom he had supposed were at his back had all vanished as if the earth had yawned for them.

The lieutenant was taken prisoner and so he does not count, but the dead body of the major as it fell and rolled within the American breast-work established the high-water-mark of the British advance upon New Orleans.

Sir George Pakenham seemed to be asking for death and presently it came to him. His body was carried from the field. General Gibbs was mortally wounded. General Keane was seriously wounded. Left without leaders, the British troops began a retreat. This retreat was soon a mad runaway, but General Lambert with a strong reserve stepped between the beaten battalions and their foes. The battle had lasted twenty-five minutes.

Jackson's force, armed and unarmed, was four thousand two hundred and sixty-four. During the whole campaign he lost three hundred and thirty-three. In the final action he lost four killed, thirteen wounded. The British force in action was about eight thousand men. The British lost some nine hundred killed, fourteen hundred wounded and five hundred prisoners.

Thornton finally succeeded in reaching and capturing the battery on the other side of the river, but he was too late. Some of the British war-ships finally succeeded in crossing the bars, but they were too late. General Lambert, now in command, decided to withdraw and the expedition sailed away.

Peace had been signed at Ghent on December 24, 1814. The real battle of New Orleans was fought on January 8, 1815.

THE STORMING OF BADAJOZ

I N STUDYING the campaign in the Peninsula one must remember first of all that the man who was made Earl of Wellington for the victory at Ciudad Rodrigo was not the great potentiality who influenced England after Waterloo as the Duke of Wellington. During the Peninsula campaign Wellington was afflicted at all times by a bitter and suspicious Parliament at home. They had no faith in him and they strenuously objected to furnishing him with money and supplies. Wellington worked with his hands tied behind him against the eager and confident armies of France. We ourselves can read in our more frank annals how a disgruntled Congress was forever wishing to turn Washington out of his position as head of the colonial forces. Parliament doled supplies to Wellington with so niggardly a hand that again and again he was forced to stop operations for the want of provisions and supplies. At one time he actually had been told to send home the transports in order to save the expense of keeping them at Lisbon. The warfare in Parliament was not deadly but it was more acrimonious than the warfare in the Peninsula. Moreover the assistance to his arms from Portugal was so wavering, uncertain and dubious that he could place no faith in it. The French Marshals Soult and Marmont had a force of nearly one hundred thousand men.

Wellington held Lisbon but if he wished to move in Portugal there always frowned upon him the fortified city of Badajoz. But finally there came his chance to take it if it could be taken in a rush while Soult and Marmont were widely separated and Badajoz was left in a very confident isolation.

Badajoz lies in Spain five miles from the Portuguese frontier. It was the key of a situation. Wellington's chance was to strike at Badajoz before the two French Marshals could com-

bine and crush him. His task was both in front of him and behind him. He lacked transport; he lacked food for the men;
the soldiers were eating cassava root instead of bread; the
bullocks were weak and emaciated. All this was the doings of
the Parliament at home. But Wellington knew that the moment
to strike had come and he seems to have hesitated very little.
Placing no faith in the tongues of the Portuguese, he made his
plans with all possible secrecy. The guns for the siege were
loaded on board the transports at Lisbon and consigned to a
fictitious address. But in the river Sadao they were placed upon
smaller vessels and finally they were again landed and drawn
by bullocks to Elvas, a post in the possession of the allies. Having stationed two-thirds of his force under General Graham
and General Hill to prevent a most probable interference by
Soult and Marmont, Wellington advanced, reaching Elvas on the
11th of March, 1812. He had made the most incredible exertions.
The stupidity of the Portuguese had vied with the stupidity of
the government at home. Wellington had been carrying the
preparation for the campaign upon his own shoulders. If he
was to win Badajoz he was to win it with no help save that
from gallant and trustworthy subordinates. He was ill with it.
Even his strangely steel-like nature had bent beneath the
trouble of preparation amid such indifference. But on March
16th Beresford with three divisions crossed the Guadiana on
pontoons and flying bridges, drove in the enemy's outposts
and invested Badajoz.

At the time of the investment, the garrison was composed
of five thousand French, Hessians and Spaniards. Spain had
always considered this city a most important barrier against
any attack through Portugal. A Moorish castle stood three
hundred feet above the level of the plain. Bastions and fortresses enwrapped the town. Even the Cathedral was bomb-
proof. The Guadiana was crossed by a magnificent bridge and
on the further shore the head of this bridge was strongly fortified.

Wellington's troops encamped to the east of the town. It
was finally decided to first attack the bastion of Trinidad. The
French commander had strengthened all his defences and by
damming a stream had seriously obstructed Wellington's opera-

tions. Parts of his force were confronted by an artificial lake two hundred yards in width.

The red coats of the English soldiers were now faded to the yellow-brown of fox's fur. All the military finery of the beginning of the century was tarnished and torn. But it was an exceedingly hard-bitten army, certain of its leaders, despising the enemy, full of ferocious desire for battle.

Perhaps the bastion of Trinidad was chosen because it was the nearest to the entrenchments of the allies. In those days the frontal attack was possible of success. On the night of the 17th of March the British broke ground within one hundred and sixty yards of Fort Picurina. The sound of the digging was muffled by the roar of a great equinoctial storm. The French were only made wise by the day-light but in the meantime the allies had completed a trench six hundred yards long and three feet deep and with a communication four thousand feet in length. The French announced their discovery by a rattle of musketry but the allies kept on with their digging while general officers wrapped in their long cloaks paced to and fro directing the work.

The situation did not please the French general at all. He knew that something must be done to counter-act the activity of the besiegers. He was in command of a very spirited garrison. On the night of the 19th, a sortie was made from the Talavera Gate by both cavalry and infantry. The infantry began to demolish the trench of the allies. The cavalry divided itself into two parts and went through a form of sham fight which in the darkness was deceptive. When challenged by the pickets they answered in Portuguese and thus succeeded in galloping a long way behind the trenches where they cut down a number of men before their identity was discovered and they were beaten back. General Phillipon, the French commander, had offered a reward for every captured intrenching tool. Thus the French infantry of the sortie devoted itself largely to making a collection of picks and spades. Men must have risked themselves with great audacity for this reward since they left three hundred dead on the field but succeeded in carrying off a great number of the intrenching tools.

Great rain storms now began to complicate the work of the

besiegers. The trenches became mere ditches half full of discolored water. This condition was partly improved by throwing in bags of sand. On the French side a curious device had been employed as a means of communication between the gate of the Trinidad bastion and Fort San Roque. The French soldiers had begun to dig but had grown tired so they finished by hanging up a brown cloth. This to the besiegers' eye was precisely like the fresh earth of a parallel and behind it the French soldiers passed in safety.

Storm followed storm. The Guadiana, swollen past all tradition by these furious down-pours, swept away the flying bridges, sinking twelve pontoons. For several days the army of the allies was entirely without food, but they stuck doggedly to their trenches and when communication was at last restored it was never again broken. The weather cleared and the army turned grimly with renewed resolution to the business of taking Badajoz. This was in the days of the forlorn hope. There was no question of anything but a desperate and deadly frontal attack. The command of the assault on Fort Picurina was given to General Kempt. He had five hundred men including engineers, sappers and miners and fifty men who carried axes. At nine o'clock they marched. The night was very dark. The fort remained silent until the assailants were close. Then a great fire blared out at them. For a time it was impossible for the men to make any progress. The palisades seemed insurmountable and the determined soldiers of England were falling on all sides. In the meantime there suddenly sounded the loud wild notes of the alarm bells in the besieged city and the guns of Badajoz awakened and gave back thunder for thunder to the batteries of the allies. The confusion was worse than in the mad nights on the heath in *King Lear* but amid the thundering and the death, Kempt's fifty men with axes walked deliberately around Fort Picurina until they found the entrance gate. They beat it down and rushed in. The infantry with their bayonets followed closely. Lieutenant Nixon of the Fifty-second Foot (now the Second Battalion of the Oxfordshire Light Infantry) fell almost on the threshold but his men ran on. The interior of the fort became the scene of a terrible hand to hand fight. All of the English did not come in through the gate.

Some of Kempt's men now succeeded in establishing ladders against the rampart and swarmed over to the help of their comrades. The struggle did not cease until more than half of the little garrison were killed. Then the commandant, Gaspar Thiery, surrendered a little remnant of eighty-six men. Others who had not been killed by the British had rushed out and been drowned in the waters of that inundation which had so troubled Wellington and so pleased the French general. Phillipon had estimated that the Picurina would endure for five days but it had been taken in an hour, albeit one of the bloodiest hours in the annals of a modern army.

Wellington was greatly pleased. He was now able to advance his earth-works close to the eastern part of the town while his batteries played continually on the front of Fort San Roque and the two northern bastions, Trinidad and Santa Maria.

But at the last of the month, Wellington was confronted by his chief fear. News came to him that Marshal Soult was advancing rapidly from Cordova. It was now a simple question of pushing the siege with every ounce of energy contained in his army. Forty-eight guns were made to fire incessantly and although the French reply was destructive, the English guns were gradually wearing away the three great defences. By the 2nd of April, Trinidad was seriously damaged and one flank of Santa Maria was so far gone that Phillipon set his men at work on an inner defence to cut the last-named bastion off from the city. On the night of the 2nd an attack was made on the dam of the inundation. Two British officers and some sappers succeeded in gagging and binding the sentinel guarding the dam and having piled barrels of gun-powder against it they lighted a slow match and made off. But before the spark could reach the powder the French arrived under the shelter of the comic brown cloth communication. The explosion did not occur and the inundation still remained to hinder Wellington's progress. On the 6th it was thought that three breaches were practicable for assault and the resolute English general ordered the attack to be made at once. To Picton, destined to attach his name to the imperishable fame of Waterloo, was given an arduous task. He was to attack on the right and scale the walls of the castle of Badajoz which were from eighteen to twenty-four feet high. On the left General Walker marching to the south was to make a false attack on Fort Pardaleras but a real one on San Vincente, a bastion on the extreme west of the town. In the centre the Fourth Division and Wellington's favorite Light Division were to march against the breaches. The Fourth was to move against Trinidad and the Light Division against Santa Maria. The columns were divided into storming and firing parties. The former were to enter the ditch while the latter fired over them at the enemy. Just before the assault was to be sounded a French deserter brought the intelligence that there was but one communication from the castle to the town and Wellington decided to send against it an entire division. Brigadier-General Power with his semi-useless Portuguese brigade was directed to attack the head of the bridge and the other works on the right of the Guadiana.

The army had now waited only for the night. When it had come, thick mists from the river increased the darkness. At ten o'clock Major Wilson of the Forty-eighth Foot (now the First Battalion of the Northamptonshire Regiment) led a party against Fort San Roque so suddenly and so tempestuously that the work capitulated almost immediately. At the castle, General Picton's men had placed their ladders and swarmed up them in the face of showers of heavy stones, logs of wood and crashing bullets while at the same time they were under a heavy fire from the left flank. The foremost were bayoneted when they reached the top and the besieged Frenchmen grasped the ladders and tumbled them over with their load of men. The air was full of wild screams as the English fell toward the stones below. Presently every ladder was thrown back and for the moment the assailants had to run for shelter against a rain of flying missiles.

In this moment of uncertainty one man, Lieutenant Ridge, rushed out rallying his company. Seizing one of the abandoned ladders, he planted it where the wall was lower. His ladder was followed by other ladders and the troops scrambled with revived courage after this new and intrepid leader. The British gained a strong foot-hold on the ramparts of the castle and every moment added to their strength as Picton's men came swarming. They drove the French through the castle and out at the gates. They met a heavy reinforcement of the French and after a severe engagement they were finally and triumphantly in possession of the castle. Lieutenant Ridge had been killed.

But at about the same time the men of the Fourth Division and of the Light Division had played a great and tragic part in the storming of Badajoz. They moved against the great breach in stealthy silence. All was dark and quiet as they reached the glacis. They hurled bags full of hay in the ditch, placed their ladders, and the storming parties of the Light Division, five hundred men in all, hurried to this desperate attack.

But the French general had perfectly understood that the main attacks would be made at his three breaches and he had made the great breach the most impregnable part of his line. The English troops, certain that they had surprised the enemy, were suddenly made plain by dozens of brilliant lights. Above them they could see the ramparts crowded with the French. These fire-balls made such a vivid picture that the besieged and besiegers could gaze upon each other's faces at distances which amounted to nothing. There was a moment of this brilliance and then a terrific explosion shattered the air. Hundreds of shells and powder-barrels went off together and the English already in the ditch were literally blown to pieces. Still their comrades crowded after them with no definite hesitation. The French commander had taken the precaution to fill part of the ditch with water from the inundation and in it one hundred fusiliers, men of Albuera, were drowned.

The Fourth Division and the Light Division continued the attack upon the breach. Across the top of the breach were a row of sword-blades fitted into ponderous planks and these planks chained together were let deep into the ground. In front of them the slope was covered with loose planks studded with sharp iron points. The English stepping on them, rolled howling backward and the French yelled and fired unceasingly.

It was too late for the English to become aware of the hopeless quality of their undertaking. Column after column hurled themselves forward. Young Colonel Macleod of the Forty-third Foot (now the First Battalion of the Oxfordshire Light Infantry), a mere delicate boy, gathered his men again and again, and led them at the breach. A falling soldier behind him plunged a bayonet in his back but still he kept on till he was shot dead within a yard of the line of sword-blades.

For two hours the besiegers were tirelessly striving to achieve the impossible while the French taunted them from the ramparts.

"Why do you not come into Badajoz?"

Meanwhile, Captain Nicholas of the Engineers with Lieutenant Shaw and about one hundred men of the Forty-third Foot actually had passed through the breach of the Santa Maria bastion but, once inside, they were met with such a fire that nearly every man dropped dead. Shaw returned almost alone.

Wellington who had listened to these desperate assaults and watched them as well as he was able from a position on a small knoll gave orders at mid-night for the troops to retire and re-form. Two thousand men had been slain. Dead and mangled bodies were piled in heaps at the entrance to the great breach and the stench of burning flesh and hair was said to be insupportable.

And still in the meantime, General Walker's brigade had made a feint against Pardaleras and passed on to the bastion of San Vincente. Here for a time everything went wrong. The fire of the French was frightfully accurate and concentrated. General Walker himself simply dripped blood; he was a mass of wounds. His ladders were found to be all too short. The walls of the fortress were thirty feet in height. However through some lack of staying power in the French, success at last crowned the attack. One man clambered somehow to the top of a wall and pulled up others until about half of the Fourth Foot (now the King's Own Royal Lancaster Regiment) were fairly into the town. Walker's men took three bastions. General Picton, severely wounded, had not dared to risk losing the castle, but now hearing the tumult of Walker's success, he sent his men forth and thousands went swarming through the town. Phillipon saw that all was lost and retreated with a few hundred men to San Christoval. He surrendered next morning to Lord Fitzroy Somerset.

The English now occupied the town. With their comrades lying stark or perhaps in frightful torment in the fields beyond the walls of Badajoz, these soldiers who had so heroically won this immortal victory became the most abandoned, drunken wretches and maniacs. Crazed privates stood at the corners of streets and shot everyone in sight. Everywhere were soldiers dressed in the garb of monks, of gentlemen at court, or mayhap wound about with gorgeous ribbons and laces. Jewels and plate, silks and satins, all suffered a wanton destruction. Napier writes of "shameless rapacity, brutal intemperance, savage lust, cruelty and murder, shrieks and piteous lamentations——."

He further says that the horrible tumult was never quelled. It subsided through the weariness of the soldiers. One wishes to enquire why the man who was ultimately called the Iron Duke did not try to stop this shocking business. But one remembers that Wellington was a wise man and he did not try to stop this shocking business because he knew that his soldiers were out of control and that if he tried, he would fail.

THE SIEGE OF PLEVNA

WHEN the Russian army swarmed through the Shipka Pass of the Balkans, there was really nothing before it but a man and an opportunity. Osman Pasha suddenly and with great dexterity took his force into Plevna, a small Bulgarian town near the Russian line of march.

The military importance of Plevna lay in the fact that this mere village of seventeen hundred people was the junction of the roads from Widdin, Sophia, Biela, Zimnitza, Nikopolis, and the Shipka Pass. Osman's move was almost entirely on his own initiative. He had no great reputation, and, like Wellington in the early part of the Peninsula campaign, he was obliged to do everything with the strength of his own shoulders. The stupidity of his superiors amounted almost to an oppression.

The Russians recognized the strategic importance of Plevna a moment too late. On July 18, 1877, General Krüdener at Nikopolis received orders to occupy Plevna at once. He seems to have moved promptly, but long before he could arrive Osman's tired but dogged battalions were already in the position.

The Turkish regular of that day must have resembled very closely his fellow of the present. Von Moltke, who knew the Turks well and whose remarkable mind clearly outlined and prophesied the result of several more recent Balkan campaigns, said: "An impetuous attack may be expected from the Turks, but not an obstinate and lasting defence." Historically, the opinion of the great German Field-Marshal seems very curious. Even in the late war between Greece and Turkey the attacks of the Turkish troops were usually anything but impetuous. They were fearless, but very leisurely. In regard to the lasting and obstinate defence, one has only to regard the siege of

Plevna to understand that Von Moltke was for the moment writing carelessly.

After Plevna, the word went forth that the most valuable weapon of the Turk was his shovel. When Osman arrived, the defences of Plevna consisted of an ordinary block-house, but he at once set his troops at work digging intrenchments and throwing up redoubts which were located with great skill. Soon the vicinity of the town was one great fortress. Osman coolly was attempting to stem the Russian invasion with a force of these strange Turkish troops, patient, enduring, sweet-tempered, and ignorant, dressed in slovenly overcoats and sheep-skin sandals, living on a diet of black bread and cucumbers.

Receiving the order from the Grand Duke Nicolas, General Krüdener at Nikopolis despatched at dawn of the next day six thousand five hundred men with about seven batteries to Plevna. No effective scouting had been done. The Russian General, Schilder-Schuldner, riding comfortably in his carriage in the customary way of Russian commanders of the time, had absolutely no information that a strong Turkish force had occupied the position. His column had been allowed to distribute itself over a distance of seventeen miles. On the morning of the 20th an attack was made with great confidence by the troops which had come up. Two Russian regiments even marched victoriously through the streets of Plevna, throwing down their heavy packs and singing for joy of the easy capture. But suddenly a frightful fusillade began from all sides. The elated regiments melted in the streets. Infuriated by religious ardor, despising the value of a Christian's life, the Turks poured out from their concealed places, and there occurred a great butchery. The Russian Nineteenth Regiment of the line was cut down to a few fragments. Much artillery ammunition was captured. The Russians lost two thousand seven hundred men. The knives of the Circassians and Bashi-Bazouks had been busy in the streets.

After this victory Osman might have whipped Krüdener, but the Russian leaders had been suddenly aroused to the importance of taking Plevna, and Krüdener was almost immediately re-enforced with three divisions. Within the circle of defence, the Turk was using his shovel. Osman gave the garrison no rest. If a man was not shooting, he was digging. The well-known Grivitza Redoubt was greatly strengthened, and some defences on the east side of the town were completed. Osman's situation was desperate, but his duty to his country was vividly defined. If he could hold this strong Turkish force on the flank of the Russians, their advance on Constantinople would hardly be possible. The Russian leaders now thoroughly understood this fact, and they tried to make the army investing Plevna more than a containing force.

The Grand Duke Nicolas had decided to order an assault on the 30th of July. Krüdener telegraphed—the Grand Duke was eighty miles from Plevna—that he hesitated in his views of prospective success. The Grand Duke replied sharply, ordering that the assault be made. It seems that Krüdener went into the field in the full expectation of being beaten.

Now appears in the history of the siege a figure at once sinister and foolish. Subordinate in command to Krüdener was Lieutenant-General Prince Schakofskoy, who had an acute sense of his own intelligence and in most cases dared to act independently of the orders of his chief. But to offset him, there suddenly galloped into his camp a brilliant young Russian commander, a man who has set his name upon Plevna even as the word underlies the towering reputation of Osman Pasha. General Skobeleff had come from the Grand Duke Nicolas with an order directing Prince Schakofskoy to place the young man in command of a certain brigade of Caucasian Cossacks. The Prince grew stormy with outraged pride, and practically told Skobeleff to take the Cossacks and go to the devil with them.

The Russians began a heavy bombardment, to which Osman's guns replied with spirit. The key of the position was the Grivitza Redoubt. Krüdener himself attacked it with eighteen battalions of infantry and ten batteries. And at the same time Prince Schakofskoy thundered away on his side. The latter at last became furious at Krüdener's lack of success, and resolved to take matters into his own hands. In the afternoon he advanced with three brigades in the face of a devastating Turkish fire, took a hill, and forced the Turks to vacate their first line of intrenchments. His men were completely spent with weariness, and it is supposed that he should have waited on the hill for support from Krüdener. But he urged on his tired troops and carried a second position. The Turkish batteries now concentrated themselves upon his line and, really, the Turkish infantry whipped him soundly.

The Russians did not give up the dearly bought gain of ground without desperate fighting. Again and again they furiously charged, but only to meet failure. When night fell, the stealthy-footed irregulars of the Turkish forces crept through the darkness to prey upon the route of the Russian retreat. The utter annihilation of Prince Schakofskoy's force was prevented by Skobeleff and the brigade of Cossacks with which the Prince had sent him to the devil. Skobeleff's part in this assault was really a matter of clever manœuvring.

Krüdener had failed with gallantry and intelligence. Schakofskoy had failed through pigheadedness and self-confidence.

After this attempt to carry Plevna, the important Russian generals occupied themselves in mutual recriminations. Krüdener bitterly blamed Schakofskoy for not obeying his orders, and Schakofskoy acidulously begged to know why Krüdener had not supported him. At the same time they both claimed that the Grand Duke Nicolas, eighty miles away, should never have given an order for an assault on a position of which he had never had a view.

But even if Russian clothing and arms and trinkets were being sold for a pittance in the bazaars of Plevna, the mosques were jammed with wounded Turks, and such was the suffering that the dead in the streets and in the fields were being gnawed by the pervasive Turkish dog.

A few days later Osman Pasha received the first proper recognition from Constantinople. A small troop of cavalry had wormed its way into Plevna. It was headed by an aide-de-camp of the Sultan. In gorgeous uniform the aide appeared to Osman and presented him with the First Order of the Osmanli, the highest Turkish military decoration. And with this order came a sword the hilt of which flamed with diamonds. Osman Pasha may have preferred a bushel of cucumbers, but at any rate he knew that the Sultan and Turkey at last understood the value of a good soldier. To the speech of the aide, Osman replied with another little speech, and the soldiers in their intrenchments cheered the Sultan.

On August 31st the Turkish General made his one offensive move. He threw part of his force against a Russian redoubt and was obliged to retire with a loss of nearly three thousand men. Afterwards he devoted his troops mainly to the business of improving the defences. He wasted no more in attempts to break out of Plevna.

At this late day of the siege, Prince Charles of Roumania was appointed to the chief command of the whole Russo-Roumanian army. But naturally this office was nominal. General Zotoff had the real disposition of affairs, but he did not hold it for very long. General Levitsky, the assistant chief of the Russian general staff, arrived to advise General Zotoff under direct orders from the Grand Duke Nicolas. But this siege was to be very well-generalled.

The Grand Duke Nicolas himself came to Plevna. One would think that the Grand Duke would have ended this kaleidoscopic row of superseding generals. But the Great White Czar himself appeared. Osman Pasha, shut up in Plevna, certainly was honored with a great deal of distinguished interest.

However, Alexander II. did his best to give no orders. He had no illusions concerning his military knowledge. With a spirit profoundly kind and gentle, he simply prayed that no more lives would be lost. It is difficult to think what he had to say to his multitudinous generals, each of whom was the genius of the only true plan for capturing Plevna.

At daylight on the 7th of September the Turks saw that the entire army of the enemy had closed in upon them. Amid fields of ripening grain shone the smart red jackets of the hussars. The Turks saw the Bulgarians in sheepskin caps and with their broad scarlet sashes stuck full of knives and pistols. They saw the queer round oilskin shakoes of the Cossacks and the greatcoats of thick gray blanketing. They saw the uniforms of the Russian infantry, the green tunics, striped with red. For five days the smoke lay heavy over Plevna.

The 11th was the fête day of the Emperor, and the general assault on that day was arranged as if it had been part of a fête.

The cannonade was to begin at daybreak along the whole line and stop at eight o'clock in the morning. The artillery was to play again from eleven o'clock until one o'clock. Then it was to play again from two-thirty to three.

Directly afterwards the Roumanian allies of the Russians moved in three columns against the Grivitza Redoubt. At first all three were repulsed, but with the stimulus of Russian re-enforcements they rallied, and after a long time of almost hand-to-hand fighting the evening closed with them in possession of what was called the key of the Plevna position. They had lost four thousand men. The victory was fruitless, as anticipating the attack on Grivitza, Osman had caused the building of an inner redoubt. After all their ferocious charging, the Russians were really no nearer to success.

At three o'clock of that afternoon, Redoubt Number Ten had been assailed by General Schnidnikoff. The firing had been very terrible, but the Russians had charged to the very walls of the redoubt. The Turks not only beat them off, but pursued with great spirit. Two of the scampering Russian battalions were then faced about to beat off the chase. They lay down at a distance of only two hundred yards of the redoubt, and sent the Turks pell-mell back into their fortifications.

At about the same time Skobeleff, wearing a white coat and mounted on a white charger, was leading his men over the "green hills" towards the Krishin Redoubt. There was a dense fog. Skobeleff's troops crossed two ridges and waded a stream. They began the ascent of a steep slope. Suddenly the fog cleared; the sun shone out brilliantly. The closely massed Russian force was exposed at short range to line after line of Turkish intrenchments. They retired once but rallied splendidly, and before five o'clock Skobeleff found himself in possession of Redoubt Number Eleven and Redoubt Number Twelve.

His battalions were thrust like a wedge into the Turkish lines, but the Turkish commander appreciated the situation more clearly than any Russian save Skobeleff. The latter's men suffered a frightful fire. Re-enforcements were refused. All during the night the faithful troops of the Czar fought in darkness and without hope. They even built little ramparts of dead men. But on the morning of September 12th Skobeleff was compelled to give up all he had gained. The retreat over the "green hills" was little more than a running massacre.

After his return, Skobeleff was in a state of excitement and fury. His uniform was covered with blood and mud. His cross of St. George was twisted around over his shoulder. His face was black with powder. His eyes were bloodshot. He said: "My regiments no longer exist."

The Russian assaults had failed at all points. They had begun this last battle with eighty thousand infantry, twelve thousand cavalry, and four hundred and forty guns, and they lost over eighteen thousand men. The multitude of generals again took counsel. There were fervid animosities, and there might have been open rupture if it were not for the presence of the Czar himself, whose gentleness and good-nature prevented many scenes.

It was decided that the Turks must be starved out. The Russians sent for more troops as well as for heavy supplies of clothing, ammunition, and food. The Czar also sent for General Todleben, who had shown great skill at Sebastopol, and the direction of the siege was put in his hands.

The Turks had been accustomed to reprovision Plevna by the skilful use of devious trails. Todleben took swift steps to put a stop to it, but he did not succeed before a huge convoy had been sent into the town through the adroit management of Chefket Pasha. But the Russian horse soon chased Chefket away and the trails were all closed.

For the most part, the September weather was fine, but this plenitude of sun made the Turkish positions about Plevna almost unbearable. Actual thousands of unburied dead lay scattered over the ridges. At one time the Russian head-quarters made a polite request to be allowed to send some men to enter Grivitza and bury their own dead. But this polite request met with polite refusal.

On October 19th the Roumanians, who for weeks had been sapping their way up to the Grivitza Redoubt, made a final and desperate attack on it. They were repulsed.

In order to complete the investment, Todleben found it necessary to dislodge the Turks from four villages near Plevna.

The weeks moved by slowly with a stolid and stubborn Turk

besieged by a stubborn and stolid Russian. There was occasional firing from the Russian batteries, to which the Turks did not always take occasion to reply. In Plevna there was nothing to eat but meat, and the Turkish soldiers moved about with the hoods of their dirty brown cloaks pulled over their heads. Outside Plevna there were plenty of furs and good coats, but the diet had become so plain that the sugar-loving Russian soldiers would give gold for a pot of jam.

On the cold, cloudy morning of December 11th, when snow lay thickly on all the country, a sudden great booming of guns was heard, and the news flew swiftly that Osman had come out of Plevna at last and was trying to break through the cordon his foes had spread about him. During the night he had abandoned all his defences, and by daybreak he had taken the greater part of his army across the river Vid. Advancing along the Sophia road, he charged the Russian intrenchments with such energy that the Siberian Regiment stationed at that point was almost annihilated. A desperate fight went on for four hours, with the Russians coming up battalion after battalion. Some time after noon all firing ceased, and later the Turks sent up a white flag. Cheer after cheer swelled over the dreary plain. Osman had surrendered.

The siege had lasted one hundred and forty-two days. The Russians had lost forty thousand men. The Turks had lost thirty thousand men.

The advance on Constantinople had been checked. Skobeleff said: "Osman the Victorious he will remain, in spite of his surrender."

THE BATTLE OF BUNKER HILL

O N THE 12th of June, 1775, Captain Harris, afterwards
Lord Harris, wrote home from the town of Boston, then
occupied by British troops:

"I wish the Americans may be brought to a sense of their duty.
One good drubbing, which I long to give them, by way of retaliation,
might have a good effect towards it. At present they are so elated by
the petty advantage they gained the 19th of April, that they despise
the powers of Britain. We shall soon take the field on the other side
of the Neck."

This very fairly expressed the irritation in the British camp.
The troops had been sent to Massachusetts to subdue it, but as
yet nothing had been done in that direction.

The ignominious flight of the British regulars from Lex-
ington and Concord was still unavenged. More than that, they
had been kept close in Boston ever since by the provincial
militia.

"What!" cried General Burgoyne, when on his arrival in May
he was told this news. "What! Ten thousand peasants keep
five thousand King's troops shut up? Let *us* get in, and we'll
soon find elbow-room!" "Elbow-room" was the army's name for
Burgoyne after that.

A little later General Gage remarked to General Timothy Ruggles, "It is impossible for the rebels to withstand our arms a
moment."

Ruggles replied: "Sir, you do not know with whom you have
to contend. These are the very men who conquered Canada.
I fought with them side by side; I know them well; they will
fight bravely. My God, sir, your folly has ruined your cause."

Besides Burgoyne the *Cerberus* brought over Generals Clinton and Howe and large re-enforcements, so that the forces under General Gage, the commander-in-chief, were over ten thousand. By June 12th the army in Boston was actually unable to procure fresh provisions, and Gage proclaimed martial law, designating those who were in arms as rebels and traitors.

The *Essex Gazette* of June 8th says: "We have the pleasure to inform the public that the Grand American Army is nearly completed." This Grand American Army was spread around Boston, its head-quarters at Cambridge, under command of General Artemas Ward, who had fought under Abercrombie. The Grand American Army was an army of allies. Ward, its supposed chief, was authorized to command only the Massachusetts and New Hampshire forces, and when the Connecticut and Rhode Island men obeyed him it was purely through courtesy. Each colony supplied its own troops with provisions and ammunition; each had its own officers, appointed by the Committee of Safety.

To this committee, June 13th, came the tidings that Gage proposed to occupy Bunker Hill, in Charlestown, on the 18th, and a council of war was held, which included the savagely bluff, warm-hearted patriot, General Israel Putnam, of the Connecticut troops; General Seth Pomeroy, Colonel William Prescott, the hardy, independent Stark, and Captain Gridley, the engineer—all of whom were veterans of the French and Indian War.

As a result of the meeting, a detachment of nine hundred men of the Massachusetts regiments, under Colonels Prescott, Frye, and Bridge, with two hundred men from Connecticut and Captain Gridley's artillery company of forty-nine men and two field-pieces, were ordered to parade at six o'clock P.M., the 16th, on Cambridge Common. There they appeared with weapons, packs, blankets, and intrenching tools. President Langdon, of Harvard College, made an impressive prayer, and by nine o'clock they had marched, the entire force being under the command of Colonel Prescott.

A uniform of blue turned back with red was worn by some of the men, but for the most part they wore their "Sunday suits" of homespun. Their guns were of all sorts and sizes, and many carried old-fashioned powder-horns and pouches. Prescott walked at their head, with two sergeants carrying dark lanterns, until they reached the Neck.

The Neck was the strip of land leading to the peninsula opposite Boston, where lay the small town of Charlestown. The peninsula is only one mile in length, its greatest breadth but half a mile. The Charles River separates it from Boston on the south, and to the north and east is the Mystic River. Bunker Hill begins at the isthmus and rises gradually to a height of one hundred and ten feet, forming a smooth, round hill.

At Cambridge Common, the night the troops started for Bunker Hill, Israel Putnam had made this eloquent address: "Men, there are enough of you on the Common this evening to fill hell so full of the red-coats to-morrow that the devils will break their shins over them."

At Bunker Hill the expedition halted, and a long discussion ensued between Prescott, Gridley, Major Brooks, and Putnam as to whether it would be better to follow Ward's orders literally and fortify Bunker Hill itself, or to go on to the lesser elevation southeast of it, which is now known as Breed's Hill, but had then no special name. They agreed upon Breed's Hill.

They began to intrench at midnight.

Prescott was consumed with anxiety lest his men should be attacked before some screen could be raised to shelter them. However enthusiastic they might be, he did not think it possible for his raw troops to meet to any advantage a disciplined soldiery in the open field.

So the pickaxe and the spade were busy throughout the night. It was silent work, for the foe was near. In Boston Harbor lay the *Lively*, the *Somerset*, the *Cerberus*, the *Glasgow*, the *Falcon*, and the *Symmetry*, besides the floating batteries. On the Boston shore the sentinels were pacing outside the British encampment. At intervals through the night Prescott and Brooks stole down to the shore of Charles River and listened till the call of "All's well!" rang over the water from the ships and told them that their scheme was still undiscovered.

At dawn the intrenchments were six feet high, and there was a great burst of fire at them from the *Lively*, which was joined in a few moments by the other men-of-war and the batteries on Copp's Hill, on the Boston shore.

The strange thunder of the cannonade brought forth every man, woman, and child in Boston. Out of their prim houses they rushed under the trellises heavy with damask roses and honeysuckle, and soon every belfry and tower, house-top and hill-top, was crowded with them. There the most of them stayed till the thrilling play in which they had so vital an interest was enacted.

Meanwhile Prescott, to inspire his raw men with confidence, mounted the parapet of the redoubt they had raised and deliberately sauntered around it, making jocular speeches, until the men cheered each cannon-ball as it came.

Gage, looking through his field-glasses from the other shore, marked the tall figure with the three-cornered hat, and the banyan—a linen blouse—buckled about the waist, and asked of Councillor Willard, who stood near him:

"Who is the person who appears to command?"

"That is my brother-in-law, Colonel Prescott."

"Will he fight?"

"Yes, sir; he is an old soldier, and will fight as long as a drop of blood remains in his veins."

"The works must be carried," said Gage.

Gage was strongly advised by his generals to land a force at the Neck and attack the Americans in the rear. It was also suggested that they might be bombarded by the fleet from the Mystic and the Charles, and, indeed, might be starved out without any fighting at all. But none of this suited the warlike British temper; the whole army longed to fight—to chase the impudent enemy out of those intrenchments he had so insolently reared. The challenge was a bold one; it must be accepted. The British had the weight in all ways, but they also had the preposterous arrogance of the British army, which always deems itself invincible because it remembers its traditions, and traditions are dubious and improper weapons to fire at a foe.

At noon the watchers on the house-tops saw the lines of smart grenadiers and light infantry embark in barges under command of General Howe, who had with him Brigadier-General Pigot and some of the most distinguished officers in

Boston. They landed at the southwestern point of the peninsula.

When the intelligence that the British troops had landed reached Cambridge it caused great excitement. A letter of Captain Chester reads:

"Just after dinner on the 17th ult. I was walking out from my lodgings, quite calm and composed, and all at once the drums beat to arms, and bells rang, and a great noise in Cambridge. Captain Putnam came by on full gallop. 'What is the matter?' says I. 'Have you not heard?' 'No.' 'Why, the regulars are landing at Charlestown,' says he, 'and father says you must all meet and march immediately to Bunker Hill to oppose the enemy.' I waited not, but ran and got my arms and ammunition, and hastened to my company (who were in the church for barracks), and found them nearly ready to march. We soon marched, with our frocks and trousers on over our other clothes (for our company is in uniform wholly blue, turned up with red), for we were loath to expose ourselves by our dress; and down we marched."

After a reconnoissance, Howe sent back to Gage for re-enforcements, and remained passive until they came.

Meanwhile, there were bitter murmurings among the troops on Breed's Hill. They had watched the brilliant pageant—the crossing over of their adversaries, scarlet-clad, with glittering equipments, with formidable guns in their train—and were conscious of being themselves exhausted from the night's labor and the hot morning sun. It was two o'clock, and they had had practically nothing to eat that day. Among themselves they accused their officers of treachery. It seemed incredible that after doing all the hard work they should be expected to do the fighting as well. Loud huzzas arose from their lips, however—these cross and hungry Yankees—when Doctor—or General—Joseph Warren appeared among them with Seth Pomeroy.

Few men had risen to a higher degree of universal love and confidence in the hearts of the Massachusetts people than Warren. He had been active in every patriotic movement. The councils through which the machinery of the Revolution was put in motion owed much to him. He was president of the Committee of Safety, and probably had been one of the Indians of the Boston Tea Party. But a few days before he had been appointed major-general. In recognition of this, Israel Putnam, who was keeping a squad of men working at intrenchments on Bunker Hill, had offered to take orders from him. But Warren refused, and asked where he might go to be of the greatest service. "Where will the onset be most furious?" he asked, and Putnam sent him to the redoubt. There Prescott also offered him the chief command, but Warren replied, "I come as a volunteer with my musket to serve under you, and shall be happy to learn from a soldier of your experience."

At three o'clock the redoubt was in good working order. About eight yards square, its strongest side, the front, faced the settled part of Charlestown and protected the south side of the hill. The east side commanded a field; the north side had an open passage-way; to the left extended a breast-work for about two hundred yards.

By three o'clock some re-enforcements for General Howe had arrived, so that he now had over three thousand men. Just before action he addressed the officers around him as follows:

"Gentlemen, I am very happy in having the honor of commanding so fine a body of men. I do not in the least doubt that you will behave like Englishmen and as becomes good soldiers. If the enemy will not come out from their intrenchments, we must drive them out at all events; otherwise the town of Boston will be set on fire by them. I shall not desire one of you to go a step farther than where I go myself at your head. Remember, gentlemen, we have no recourse to any resources if we lose Boston but to go on board our ships, which will be very disagreeable to us all."

From the movements of the British, they seemed intending to turn the American left and surround the redoubt. To prevent this, Prescott sent down the artillery with two field-pieces—he had only four altogether—and the Connecticut troops under Captain Knowlton. Putnam met them, as they neared the Mystic, shouting:

"Man the rail fence, for the enemy is flanking of us fast!"

This rail fence—half of which was stone—reached from

the shore of the Mystic to within two hundred yards of the breast-works. It was not high, but Putnam had said:

"If you can shield a Yankee's shins he's not afraid of anything. His head he does not think of."

Captain Knowlton, joined by Colonels Stark and Reid and their regiments, made another parallel fence a short distance in front of this, filling in the space between them with new-mown hay from the fields.

A great cannonade was thundering from ships and batteries to cover Howe's advance. His troops, now increased to three thousand, came on in two divisions, the left wing under Pigot, towards the breast-work and redoubt; the right, led by Howe, to storm the rail fence. The artillery moved heavily through the miry, low ground and the embarrassing discovery was made that there were only twelve-pound balls for six-pounders. Howe decided to load them with grape. The troops were hindered by a number of fences, as well as the thick, tall grass. Their knapsacks were extraordinarily heavy, and they felt the power of the scorching sun.

Inside the redoubt the Americans waited for them, Prescott assuring his men that the red-coats would never reach the redoubt if they obeyed him and reserved their fire until he gave the word. As the assaulting force drew temptingly near, the American officers only restrained their men from firing by mounting the parapet and kicking up their guns.

But at last the word was given—the stream of fire broke out all along the line. They were wonderful marksmen. The magnificent regulars were staggered, but they returned the fire. They could make no headway against the murderous volleys flashed in quick succession at them. The dead and wounded fell thickly. General Pigot ordered a retreat, while great shouts of triumph arose from the Americans.

At the rail fence Putnam gave his last directions when Howe was nearing him:

"Fire low: aim at the waistbands! Wait until you see the whites of their eyes! Aim at the handsome coats! Pick off the commanders!"

The men rested their guns on the rail fence to fire. The officers were used as targets—many of the handsome coats were laid low. So hot was the reception they met that in a few moments Howe's men were obliged to fall back. One of them said afterwards, "It was the strongest post that was ever occupied by any set of men."

There was wild exultation within the American lines, congratulation and praises, for just fifteen minutes; and then Pigot and Howe led the attack again. But the second repulse was so much fiercer than the first that the British broke ranks and ran down hill, some of them getting into the boats.

"The dead," said Stark, "lay in front of us as thick as sheep in a fold."

Meantime Charlestown had been set on fire by Howe's orders, and the spectacle was splendidly terrible to the watchers in Boston. The wooden buildings made a superb blaze, and through the smoke could be seen the British officers striking and pricking their men with their swords in the vain hope of rallying them, while cannon, musketry, crashes of falling houses, and the yells of the victors filled up the measure of excitement to the spectators.

Twice, now, the Americans had met the foe and proved that he was not invincible. The women in Boston thought the last defeat final—that their men-folk had gained the day. But Prescott knew better; he was sure that they would come again, and sure that he could not withstand a third attack.

If at this juncture strong re-enforcements and supplies of ammunition had reached him, he might well have held his own. But such companies as had been sent on would come no farther than Bunker Hill, in spite of Israel Putnam's threats and entreaties. There they straggled about under hay-cocks and apple-trees, demoralized by the sights and sounds of battle, with no authorized leader who could force them to the front.

As for their commander-in-chief, Ward, he would not stir from his house all day, and kept the main body of his forces at Cambridge.

When General Clinton saw the rout of his countrymen from the Boston shore, he rowed over in great haste. With his assistance, and the fine discipline which prevailed, the troops were re-formed within half an hour. Clinton also proposed a new plan of assault. Accordingly, instead of diffusing their forces across the whole American front, the chief attack was directed on the redoubt. The artillery bombarded the breast-work, and only a small number moved against the rail fence.

"Fight! conquer or die!" was the watchword that passed from mouth to mouth as the tall, commanding figure of Howe led on the third assault. To his soldiers it was a desperate venture —they felt that they were going to certain death. But inside the redoubt few of the men had more than one round of am-munition left, though they shouted bravely:

"We are ready for the red-coats again!"

Again their first fire was furious and destructive, but al-though many of the enemy fell, the rest bounded forward without returning it. In a few minutes the columns of Pigot and Clinton had surrounded the redoubt on three sides. The defenders of the breast-work had been driven by the artillery fire into the redoubt, and balls came whistling through the open passage.

The first rank of red-coats who climbed the parapet was shot down. Major Pitcairn met his death at this time while cheering on his men. But the Americans had come to the end of their ammunition, and they had not fifty bayonets among them, though these were made to do good service as the enemy came swarming over the walls.

Pigot got up by the aid of a tree, and hundreds followed his lead. The Americans made stout resistance in the hand-to-hand struggle that followed, but there could be only one end-ing to it, and Prescott ordered a retreat. He was almost the last to leave, and only got away by skilfully parrying with his sword the bayonet-thrusts of the foe. His banyan was pierced in many places, but he escaped unhurt.

The men at the rail fence kept firm until they saw the forces leaving the redoubt; they fell back then, but in good order.

A great volley was fired after the Americans. It was then that Warren fell, as he lingered in the rear—a loss that was passionately mourned throughout New England.

During their disordered flight over the little peninsula the Americans lost more men than at any other time of the day, though their list of killed and wounded only amounted to four hundred and forty-nine. The heavy loss of the enemy—ten hundred and fifty-four men—had the effect of checking the eagerness of their pursuit; the Americans passed the Neck without further molestation.

General Howe had maintained his reputation for solid courage, and his long white-silk stockings were soaked in blood.

The speech of Count Vergennes, that "if it won two more such victories as Bunker Hill, there would be no more British Army in America," echoed the general sentiment in England and America as well as France. So impressed were the British leaders with the indomitable resolution shown by the Provincials in fortifying and defending so desperate a position as Breed's Hill, that they made no attempt to follow up their victory. General Gage admitted that the people of New England were not the despicable rabble they had sometimes been represented.

Among the Grand Army itself many recriminations and court-martials followed the contest. But Washington soon drilled it into order.

The most important thing to be remembered of Bunker Hill is its effect upon the colonies. The troubles with the mother country had been brewing a long time, but this was the first decisive struggle for supremacy. There was no doubt of the tough soldierly qualities displayed by the Colonials; the thrill of pride that went through the country at the success of their arms welded together the scattered colonies and made a nation of them. The Revolution was an accomplished fact. "England," said Franklin, "has lost her colonies forever."

"VITTORIA"

THE campaign of 1812, which included the storming of Ciudad Rodrigo and Badajoz and the overwhelming victory of Salamanca, had apparently done so much towards destroying the Napoleonic sway in the Peninsula that the defeat of the Allies at Burgos, in October, 1812, came as an embittering disappointment to England; and when Wellington, after his disastrous retreat to Ciudad Rodrigo, reported his losses as amounting to nine thousand, the usual tempest of condemnation against him was raised, and the members of the Cabinet, who were always so free with their oracular advice and so close with the nation's money, wagged their heads despairingly.

But as the whole aspect of affairs was revealed, and as Wellington coolly stated his plans for a new campaign, public opinion changed.

It was a critical juncture: Napoleon had arranged an armistice with Russia, Prussia, and Austria, which was to last until August 16, 1813, and it became known that this armistice might end in peace. Peace on the Continent would mean that Napoleon's unemployed troops might be poured into Spain in such enormous numbers as to overwhelm the Allies. So, to insure Wellington's striking a decisive blow before this could happen, both the English Ministry and the Opposition united in supporting him, and for the first time during the war he felt sure of receiving the supplies for which he had asked.

The winter and spring were spent by Wellington in preparing for his campaign: his troops needed severe discipline after the disorder into which they had fallen during the retreat from Burgos, and the great chief entered into the matter of their equipment with most painstaking attention to detail, removing unnecessary weight from them, and supplying each infantry soldier with three extra pairs of shoes, besides heels and soles for repairs. He drew large re-enforcements from England, and all were drilled to a high state of efficiency.

It is well to quote here from the letter published by Wellington on the 28th of December, 1812. It was addressed to the commanders of divisions and brigades. It created a very pretty storm, as one may readily see. I quote at length, since surely no document could be more illuminative of Wellington's character, and it seems certain that this fearless letter saved the army from the happy-go-lucky feeling, very common in British field forces, that a man is a thorough soldier so long as he is willing at all times to go into action and charge, if ordered, at even the brass gates of Inferno. But Wellington knew that this was not enough. He wrote as follows:

"GENTLEMEN: I have ordered the army into cantonments, in which I hope that circumstances will enable me to keep them for some time, during which the troops will receive their clothing, necessaries, etc., which are already in progress, by different lines of communication to the several divisions and brigades.

"But besides these objects, I must draw your attention in a very particular manner to the state of discipline of the troops. The discipline of every army, after a long and active campaign, becomes in some degree relaxed, and requires the utmost attention on the part of general and other officers to bring it back to the state in which it ought to be for service; but I am concerned to have to observe, that the army under my command has fallen off in this respect in the late campaign to a greater degree than any army with which I have ever served, or of which I have ever read.

.   .   .   .

"It must be obvious, however, to every officer, that from the moment the troops commenced their retreat from the neighborhood of Burgos on the one hand, and from Madrid on the other, the officers lost all command over their men.

.   .   .   .

"I have no hesitation in attributing these evils to the habitual inattention of the officers of the regiments to their duty as prescribed by the standing regulations of the service and by the orders of this army.

"I am far from questioning the zeal, still less the gallantry and spirit, of the officers of the army; I am quite certain that if their minds can be convinced of the necessity of minute and constant attention to understand, recollect, and carry into execution the orders which have been issued for the performance of their duty, and that the strict performance of this duty is necessary to enable the army to serve the country as it ought to be served, they will in future give their attention to these points.

"Unfortunately, the experience of the officers of the army has induced many to consider that the period during which an army is on service is one of relaxation from all rule, instead of being, as it is, the period during which of all others every rule for the regulation and control of the conduct of the soldier, for the inspection and care of his arms, ammunition, accoutrements, necessaries, and field equipments, and his horse and horse appointments, for the receipt and issue and care of his provisions, and the regulation of all that belongs to his food and the forage for his horse, must be most strictly attended to by the officer of his company or troop, if it is intended that an army —a British army in particular—shall be brought into the field of battle in a state of efficiency to meet the enemy on the day of trial.

"These are points, then, to which I most earnestly entreat you to turn your attention, and the attention of the officers of the regiments under your command, Portuguese as well as English, during the period in which it may be in my power to leave the troops in their cantonments.

.   .   .   .

"In regard to the food of the soldier, I have frequently observed and lamented in the late campaign the facility and celerity with which the French soldiers cooked in comparison with those of our army.

"The cause of this disadvantage is the same with that of every other description, the want of attention of the officers to the orders of the army and the conduct of their men, and the consequent want of authority over their conduct.

.   .   .   .

"But I repeat that the great object of the attention of the general and field officers must be to get the captains and subalterns of the regiments to understand and perform the duties required from them, as the only mode by which the discipline and efficiency of the army can be restored and maintained during the next campaign."

The British general never refrained from speaking his mind, even if his ideas were certain to be contrary to the spirit of the army. I will quote from "Victories of the British Armies" as follows:

"Colborne marched with the infantry on the right—Head, with the Thirteenth Light Dragoons and two squadrons of Portuguese on the left—and the heavy cavalry formed a reserve. Perceiving that their battering train was endangered, the French cavalry, as the ground over which they were retiring was favorable for the movement, charged the Thirteenth. But they were vigorously repulsed; and, failing in breaking the British, the whole, consisting of four regiments, drew up in front, forming an imposing line. The Thirteenth instantly formed and galloped forward—and nothing could have been more splendid than their charge. They rode fairly through the French, overtook and cut down many of the gunners, and at last entirely headed the line of march, keeping up a fierce and straggling encounter with the broken horsemen of the enemy, until some of the English dragoons actually reached the gates of Badajoz."

And now I quote from Wellington's comment to Colborne:

"I wish you would call together the officers of the dragoons and point out to them the mischiefs which must result from the disorder of the troops in action. The undisciplined ardor of the Thirteenth Dragoons and First Regiment of Portuguese cavalry is not of the description of the determined bravery and steadiness of soldiers confident in their discipline and in their officers. Their conduct was that of a rabble, galloping as fast as their horses could carry them over a plain, after an enemy to whom they could do no mischief when they were broken and the pursuit had continued for a limited distance, and sacrificing substantial advantages and all the objects of your operation by their want of discipline. To this description of their conduct I add my entire conviction, that if the enemy could have thrown out of Badajoz only one hundred men regularly formed, they would have driven back these two regiments in equal haste and disorder, and would probably have taken many whose horses would have been knocked up. If the Thirteenth Dragoons are again guilty of this conduct I shall take their horses from them, and send the officers and men to do duty at Lisbon."

The incident of the dragoons' charge happened early in 1811, but it shows how Wellington dealt with the firebrands in the army. However, imagine the feelings of the Thirteenth Dragoons!

As for the Allies, they were for a long time considered quite hopeless by British officers; the Portuguese were commonly known in the ranks as the "Vamosses," from *vamos*, "let us be off," which they shouted before they ran away. (The American slang "vamoose" may have had its origin in the Mexican War.)

The Spanish and Portuguese hated each other so cordially that it was with the greatest difficulty that they could be induced to coöperate: they were continually plotting to betray each other, and, incidentally, the English. Wellington had a sufficiently hard task in keeping his English army in order and directing the civil administration of Portugal— which would otherwise have tumbled to pieces from the corruption of its government—but hardest of all was the military training of the Spanish and Portuguese. He was now in supreme command of the Spanish army, concerning which he had written:

"There is not in the whole Kingdom of Spain a depot of provisions for the support of a single battalion in operation for one day. Not a shilling of money in any military chest. To move them forward at any point now would be to insure their certain destruction."

After that was written, however, he had been able to equip them with some degree of effectiveness, and had worked them up to a certain standard of discipline: they were brave and patient, and susceptible to improvement under systematic training. Beresford had also accomplished wonders with the Portuguese, and Wellington's army now numbered seventy thousand men, of whom forty thousand were British.

Wellington, with his lean, sharp-featured face, and dry, cold manner, was not the typical Englishman at all. He was more like the genuine Yankee of New England. He made his successes by his resourcefulness, his inability to be overpowered by circumstances. As he said: "The French plan their campaigns just as you might make a splendid set of harness.

It answers very well until it gets broken, and then you are done for! Now I made my campaign of ropes; if anything went wrong I tied a knot and went on."

He was always ready, when anything broke or failed him, to "tie a knot and go on." That is the suppleness and adroitness of a great chieftain, whereas the typical English general was too magnificent for the little things; he liked to hurl his men boldly into the abyss—and then, if they perished, it had been magnificently done, at any rate. But Wellington was always practical and ready to take advantage of any opportunity that offered. He had no illusions about the grandeur of getting men killed for nothing.

There were still two hundred and thirty thousand French troops in Spain, but they were scattered across the Peninsula from Asturias to Valencia. To the extreme east was Marshal Suchet, with sixty-five thousand men, and an expedition under General Murray was sent against him, which kept him there. Clausel was prevented from leaving Biscay with his forty thousand men by the great guerilla warfare with which Wellington enveloped his forces. There remained, then, for Wellington to deal with the centre of the army under Joseph Bonaparte, whose jealous suspicions had been the means of driving from Spain Marshal Soult, a really fine and capable commander. The weak Joseph was now the head of an immense and magnificently equipped army of men and officers in the finest condition for fighting, but who were to prove of how little effect fine soldiers can be when they lack the right chief.

The army of Joseph lay in a curve from Toledo to Zamora, guarding the central valley of the Douro, and covering the great road from Madrid through Burgos and Vittoria to France. Wellington's plan was to move the left wing of his army across the Douro within the Portuguese frontier, to march it up the right bank of the Douro as far as Zamora, and then, crossing the Esla, unite it to the Galician forces; while the centre and right, advancing from Agueda by Salamanca, were to force the passage of the Tormes and drive the French entirely from the line of the Douro towards the Carrion.

By constantly threatening them on the flank with the left

wing, which was to be kept always in advance, he thus hoped to drive the French back by Burgos into Biscay. He himself expected to establish there a new basis for the war among the numerous and well-fortified seaports on the coast. In this way, forcing the enemy back to his frontier, he would at once better his own position and intercept the whole communications of the enemy. The plan had the obvious objection that in separating his army into two forces, with great mountain ranges and impassable rivers between them, each was exposed to the risk of an attack by the whole force of the enemy.

But Wellington had resolved to take this risk. Sir Thomas Graham, in spite of his sixty-eight years, had the vigor and clear-headedness of youth, and the very genius for the difficult command given him—that of leading the left wing through virgin forests, over rugged mountains, and across deep rivers.

The march of Wellington began May 22d, and an exalted spirit of enthusiasm pervaded the entire army. Even Wellington became expressive, and as he passed the stream that marks the frontier of Spain he rose in his stirrups and, waving his hand, exclaimed "Farewell, Portugal!"

Meanwhile Graham on May 16th, with forty thousand men, had crossed the Douro and pushed ahead, turning the French right and striking at their communications. Within ten days forty thousand men were transported through two hundred miles of the most broken and rugged country in the Peninsula, with all their artillery and baggage. Soon they were in possession of the whole crest of mountains between the Ebro and the sea. On the 31st Graham reached the Esla. The French were astounded when Graham appeared upon their flank; they abandoned their strong position on the Douro; then they abandoned Madrid; after that, they hurried out of Burgos and Valladolid.

Wellington had crossed the Douro at Miranda on May 25th, in advance of his troops, by means of a basket slung on a rope from precipice to precipice, at an immense height above the foaming torrent. The rivers were all swollen by floods.

Graham, with the left wing of the Allies, kept up his eager march. Many men were lost while fording the Esla on May

31st. The water was almost chin-deep and the bottom was covered with shifting stones. Graham hastened with fierce speed to the Ebro, eager to cross it before Joseph and break his communications with France. Joseph had wished to stop his retreat at Burgos and give battle there, but he had been told that incredible numbers of guerillas had joined the English forces, and so he pushed on, leaving the castle at Burgos heavily mined. It was calculated that the explosion would take place just as the English entered the town, but the fuses were too quick—three hundred French soldiers, the last to leave, were crushed by the falling ruins. The allied troops marched triumphantly through the scene of their earlier struggle and defeat.

On abandoning Burgos Joseph took the road to Vittoria and sent pressing orders to Clausel to join him there, but this junction of forces was not effected—Clausel was too late.

Wellington's strategy of turning the French right has been called "the most masterly movement made during the Peninsular War." Its chief merit was that it gave Wellington the advantage of victory with hardly any loss of life. It swept the French back to the Spanish frontier. And Joseph, whose train comprised an incredible number of chariots, carriages, and wagons, bearing a helpless multitude of people of both sexes from Madrid (including the civil functionaries and officers of his court), as well as enormous stores of spoil, began to perceive that this precipitate retreat was his ruin, and that he must risk the chance of a great battle to escape being driven in hopeless confusion through the passes of the Pyrenees.

The sweep of the Allies under Graham around the French right had taken them through the wildest and most enchantingly beautiful regions. At times a hundred men had been needed to drag up one piece of artillery. Again, the guns would be lowered down a precipice by ropes, or forced up the rugged goat-paths. At length, to quote Napier, "the scarlet uniforms were to be seen in every valley, and the stream of war, descending with impetuous force down all the clefts of the mountains, burst in a hundred foaming torrents into the basin of Vittoria."

So accurately had Graham done his work in accordance

with Wellington's plans, that he reached the valley just as Joseph's dejected troops were forming themselves in front of Vittoria.

The basin or valley of Vittoria, with the town in its eastern extremity, is a small plain about eight miles by six miles in extent, situated in an elevated plateau among the mountains and guarded on all sides by rugged hills.

The great road from Madrid enters the valley at the Puebla Pass, where too the river Zadora flows through a narrow mountain gorge. This road then runs up the left bank of the Zadora to Vittoria, and from there it goes on towards Bayonne and the Pyrenees. This road was Joseph's line of retreat.

King Joseph, burdened by his treasure, which included the plunder of five years of French occupation in the Peninsula, and consisted largely of priceless works of art, selected with most excellent taste by himself and other French connoisseurs, had despatched to France two great convoys, a small part of the whole treasure, along the Bayonne road. As these had to be heavily guarded against the Biscay guerillas, some thousands of troops had gone with them. Joseph's remaining forces were estimated at from sixty thousand to sixty-five thousand men.

The French were anxious above all things to keep the road open—the road to Bayonne; there are several rough mountain roads intersecting each other at Vittoria, particularly those to Pampeluna, Bilboa, and Galicia, but the great Bayonne road was the only one capable of receiving the huge train of lumbering carriages without which the army was not to move.

On the afternoon of the 20th Wellington, whose effective force was now sixty-five thousand men, surveyed the place and the enemy from the hill ranges and saw that they were making a stand. He decided then on his tactics. Instead of pushing on his combined forces to a frontal attack, he made up his mind to divide his troops; he would send Graham with the left wing, consisting of eighteen thousand men and twenty guns, around by the northern hills to the rear of the French army, there to seize the road to Bayonne. Sir Rowland Hill with twenty thousand men, including General Morillo with his Spaniards, was to move with the right wing, break through the Puebla Pass, and attack the French left.

The right centre under Wellington himself was to cross the ridges forming the southern boundary of the basin and then move straight forward to the Zadora River and attack the bridges, while the left centre was to move across the bridge of Mendoza in the direction of the town.

The French right, which Graham was to attack, occupied the heights in front of the Zadora River above the village of Abechuco, and covered Vittoria from approach by the Bilboa road; the centre extended along the left bank of the Zadora, commanding the bridges in front of it, and blocking up the great road from Madrid. The left occupied the space from Arinez to the ridges of Puebla de Arlauzon, and guarded the pass of Puebla, by which Hill was to enter the valley.

The early morning of June 21st was, according to one historian, "rainy and heavy with vapor," while an observer (Leith Hay) said: "The morning was extremely brilliant; a clearer or more beautiful atmosphere never favored the progress of a gigantic conflict."

The valley was a superb spectacle, occupied by the French army with the rich uniforms of their officers. Marshal Jourdan, the commander, could be seen riding slowly along the line of his troops. The positions they occupied rose in steps from the centre of the valley, so that all could be seen by the English from the crest of the Morillas as they stood ready for battle. In his "Events of Military Life" Henry says:

"The dark and formidable masses of the French were prepared at all points to repel the meditated attack—the infantry in column with loaded arms, or ambushed thickly in the low woods at the base of their position, the cavalry in lines with drawn swords, and the artillery frowning from the eminences with lighted matches; while on our side all was yet quietness and repose. The chiefs were making their observations and the men walking about in groups amidst the piled arms, chatting and laughing and gazing, and apparently not caring a pin for the fierce hostile array in their front."

At ten o'clock Hill reached the pass of Puebla, and forced

his way through with extraordinary swiftness. Morillo's Spaniards went swarming up the steep ridges to dislodge the French, but the enemy made a furious resistance, and re-enforcements kept coming to their aid. General Morillo was wounded, but would not be carried from the field. Hill then sent the Seventy-first to help the Spaniards, who were showing high courage, but being terribly mown down by the French musketry. Colonel Cadogan, who led the Seventy-first, had no sooner reached the summit of the height than he fell, mortally wounded. The French were driven from their position, but the loss of Cadogan was keenly felt. The story of his strange state of exaltation the night before the battle is well known—his rapture at the prospect of taking part in it. As he lay dying on the summit he would not be moved, although the dead lay thick about him, but watched the progress of his Highlanders until he could no longer see.

While this conflict was going on, Wellington, with the right centre, had commenced his attack on the bridges over the Zadora. A Spanish peasant brought word that the bridge of Tres Puentes was negligently guarded, and offered to guide the troops to it. Kempt's Brigade soon reached it; the Fifteenth Hussars galloped over, but a shot from a French battery killed the brave peasant who had guided them.

The forces that had crossed Tres Puentes now formed under the shelter of a hill. One of the officers wrote of this position: "Our post was most extraordinary, as we were isolated from the rest of the army and within one hundred yards of the enemy's advance. As I looked over the bank, I could see El Rey Joseph, surrounded by at least five thousand men, within five hundred yards of us."

It has always seemed an inconceivable thing that the French should not have destroyed the seven narrow bridges across the Zadora before the 21st had dawned. Whether it was from over-confidence or sheer mental confusion it is impossible to know.

The Third and Seventh Divisions were now moving rapidly down to the bridge of Mendoza, but the enemy's light troops and guns had opened a vigorous fire upon them, until the riflemen of the Light Division, who had crossed at Tres Puentes, charged the enemy's fire, and the bridge was carried.

Sir Thomas Picton was a picturesque figure in this part of the operations. Through some oversight he and his men, the "Fighting Third," were neglected. Orders came to other troops, bridges were being carried, but no word was sent to Picton. "D—— it!" he cried out to one of his officers, "Lord Wellington must have forgotten us!" He beat the mane of his horse with his stick in his impatience and anger. Finally, an aide-de-camp galloped up and inquired for Lord Dalhousie, who commanded the Seventh Division. In answer to Picton's inquiries he stated that he brought orders for Dalhousie to carry the bridge to the left, while the Fourth and Sixth Divisions were to support the attack. Picton rose in his stirrups, and shouted angrily to the amazed aide-de-camp:

"You may tell Lord Wellington from me, sir, that the *Third* Division, under my command, shall in less than ten minutes attack the bridge and carry it, and the Fourth and Sixth may support if they choose." Then, addressing his men with his customary blend of affection and profanity, he cried: "Come on, ye rascals! Come on, ye fighting villains!"

They carried the bridge with such fire and speed that the whole British line was animated by the sight.

Maxwell says: "The passage of the river, the movement of glittering masses from right to left as far as the eye could range, the deafening roar of cannon, the sustained fusillade of the artillery, made up a magnificent scene. The British cavalry, drawn up to support the columns, seemed a glittering line of golden helmets and sparkling swords in the keen sunshine which now shone upon the field of battle."

L'Estrange, who was with the Thirty-first, says that the men were marching through standing corn (I suppose some kind of grain that ripens early, certainly not maize) yellow for the sickle and between four and five feet high, and the cannon-balls, as they rent their way through the sea of golden grain, made long, hissing furrows in it.

The hill in front of Arinez was the key of the French line, and Wellington brought up several batteries and hurled Picton's division in a solid mass against it, while the heavy cavalry of the British came up at a gallop from the river to sustain the attack.

This hill had been made the scene of a great fight in the

wars of the Black Prince, where Sir William Felton, with two hundred archers and swordsmen, had been surrounded by six thousand Spaniards, and all perished, resisting doggedly. It is still called "the Englishmen's hill."

An obstinate fight now raged, for a brief space, on this spot. A long wall was held by several battalions of French infantry, whose fire was so deadly as to check the British for a time. They reached the wall, however, and for a few moments on either side of it was a seething mass of furious soldiers. "Any person," said Kincaid, who was present, "who chose to put his head over from either side, was sure of getting a sword or bayonet up his nostrils."

As the British broke over the wall, the French fell back, abandoning Arinez for the ridge in front of Gomecha, only to be forced back again.

It was the noise of Graham's guns, booming since mid-day at their rear, that took the heart out of the French soldiery.

Graham had struck the great blow on the left; at eleven he had reached the heights above the village and bridge of Gamara Major, which were strongly occupied by the French under Reille. General Oswald commenced the attack and drove the enemy from the heights; then Major-General Robinson, at the head of a brigade of the Fifth Division, formed his men and led them forward on the run to carry the bridge and village of Gamara. But the French fire was so strong that he was compelled to fall back. Again he rallied them and crossed the bridge, but the French drove them back once more. Fresh British troops came up and the bridge was carried again, and then for the third time it was lost under Reille's murderous fire.

But now the panic from the centre had reached Reille. It was known that the French centre was retreating; the Frenchmen had no longer the moral strength to resist Robinson's attacks, and so the bridge was won by the English and the Bayonne road was lost to the French.

In the centre the battle had become a sort of running fight for six miles; the enemy were at last all thrown back into the little plain in front of Vittoria, where from the crowded throng cries of despair could be heard.

"At six o'clock," Maxwell says, "the sun was setting, and his last rays fell upon a dreadful spectacle: red masses of infantry were advancing steadily across the plain; the horse artillery came at a gallop to the front to open its fire upon the fugitives; the Hussar Brigade was charging by the Camino Real."

Of the helpless encumbrances of the French army an eyewitness said: "Behind them was the plain in which the city stood, and beyond the city thousands of carriages and animals and non-combatants, men, women, and children, were crowding together in all the madness of terror, and as the English shot went booming overhead the vast crowd started and swerved with a convulsive movement, while a dull and horrid sound of distress arose."

Joseph now ordered the retreat to be conducted by the only road left open, that to Pampeluna, but it was impossible to take away his train of carriages. He, the King, only escaped capture by jumping out of one door of his carriage as his pursuers reached the other; he left his sword of state in it and the beautiful Correggio "Christ in the Garden," now at Apsley House in England.

Eighty pieces of cannon, jammed close together near Vittoria on the only remaining defensible ridge near the town, had kept up a desperate fire to the last, and Reille heroically had held his ground near the Zadora, but it was useless. The great road to Bayonne was lost, and finally that to Pampeluna was choked with broken-down carriages. The British dragoons were pursuing hotly, and the frantic French soldiers plunged into morasses, over fields and hills, in the wildest rout, leaving their artillery, ammunition-wagons, and the spoil of a kingdom.

The outskirts of Vittoria were strewn with the wreckage. Never before in modern times had such a quantity of spoil fallen into the hands of a victorious army. There were objects of interest from museums, convents, and royal palaces; there were jewels of royal worth and masterpieces of Titian, Raphael, and Correggio.

The Marshal's baton belonging to Jourdan had been left, with one hundred and fifty-one brass guns, four hundred and fifteen caissons of ammunition, one million three hundred thousand ball cartridges, fourteen thousand artillery rounds of ammunition, and forty thousand pounds of gunpowder.

Joseph's power was gone; he was only a wretched fugitive. Six thousand of his men had been killed and wounded and one thousand were prisoners.

It has not been possible to estimate the value of the private plunder, but five and one-half millions of dollars in the military chest of the army were taken and untold quantities of private wealth were also lost to their owners; it was all scattered—shining heaps of gold and silver—over the road, and the British soldiers reaped it. Wellington refused to make any effort to make his men give up the enormous sums they had absorbed: "They have earned it," he said. But he had reason to regret it. They fell into frightful orgies of intemperance that lasted for days. Wellington wrote Lord Bathurst, June 29th:

"We started with the army in the highest order, and up to the day of the battle nothing could get on better. But that event has, as usual, totally annihilated all order and discipline. The soldiers of the army have got among them about a million sterling in money, with the exception of about one hundred thousand dollars which were got in the military chest. I am convinced that we have now out of our ranks double the amount of our loss in the battle, and have lost more men in the pursuit than the enemy have." It was calculated that seven thousand five hundred men had straggled from the effects of the plunder.

The convoys sent ahead by Joseph had contained some of the choicest works of art; they reached France safely, and are displayed in the museums of Paris. In justice to the Duke of Wellington it must be said that he communicated with Ferdinand, offering to restore the paintings which had fallen into his hands, but Ferdinand desired him to keep them. The wives of the French officers were sent on to Pampeluna the next day by Wellington, who had treated them with great kindness.

As for the rest of the feminine army, the nuns, the actresses, and the superbly arrayed others, they made their escape with greater difficulties and hardships. Alison says: "Rich vestures of all sorts, velvet and silk brocades, gold and silver plate, noble pictures, jewels, laces, cases of claret and champagne, poodles, parrots, monkeys, and trinkets lay scattered about the fields in endless confusion, amidst weeping mothers, wailing infants, and all the unutterable miseries of warlike overthrow."

Napoleon was filled with fury at his brother for the result of Vittoria, but he instructed his ministers to say that "a somewhat brisk engagement with the English took place at Vittoria in which both sides lost equally. The French armies, however, carried out the movements in which they were engaged, but the enemy seized about one hundred guns which were left without teams at Vittoria, and it is these that the English are trying to pass off as artillery captured on the battle-field!"

One of the most important captures of the battle was a mass of documents from the archives of Madrid, including a great part of Napoleon's secret correspondence—an invaluable addition to history.

Napier's summing up of the results of the battle reads:

"Joseph's reign was over; the crown had fallen from his head. And, after years of toils and combats, which had been rather admired than understood, the English general, emerging from the chaos of the Peninsula struggle, stood on the summit of the Pyrenees a recognized conqueror. From these lofty pinnacles the clangor of his trumpets pealed clear and loud, and the splendor of his genius appeared as a flaming beacon to warring nations."

However, Napier always was inclined to be eloquent. Perhaps it was lucky for Wellington that the worthless make-trouble, Joseph Bonaparte, had been in the place of his tremendous brother.

A SWEDE'S CAMPAIGN IN GERMANY

I

LEIPZIG

AT THE opening of the seventeenth century the prospects of Sweden must have seemed to offer less hope than those of any nation of Europe.

Only a scanty population clung to the land, whose long winters paralyzed its industrial activities for many months of the year; and the deadly proximity of the insolent conqueror, Denmark, cut her off almost entirely from European commerce and made her complete subjugation seem but a question of time.

Then it was that the powerful Gustavus Vasa took charge of Sweden's destinies, delivering the country from Danish tyranny and establishing his new monarchy with the Lutheran Church for its foundation.

He was the first of a great race of kings. From the beginning of his reign, 1527, to the death of Charles XII., 1718, every monarch displayed some signal ability. But the finest flower of the line, the most original genius and hero, and one of the world's greatest conquerors, was Gustavus Adolphus, the "Northern Lion."

He was the grandson of the liberator, Gustavus Vasa, the first Protestant prince ever crowned, and the son of Charles IX., who came to the throne in his son's tenth year.

Gustavus Adolphus was born in 1594, his advent bringing great joy to the Swedes, as it shut out the possible accession of the Polish house of Vasa, who were Roman Catholics. From early childhood it was apparent that he had unusual qualities of mind, great steadfastness, and high ideals of duty, while his perceptions were swift and wonderfully luminous.

From the first he was inured to hardships—early rising, simple fare, indifference to heat and cold; much the same sort of discipline, I suppose, to which the boys of the house of Hohenzollern are now habituated. His father felt the necessity of securing the most distinguished men that were to be found for his son's education, both from Sweden and foreign lands. Count de la Gardie had charge of his military education; Helmer von Morner, of Brandenburg, was his teacher in science and languages, and John Skythe, a man of great learning, had general charge. So much severe military drill, combined with constant lessons perseveringly administered by intellectual martinets, has had the effect of crushing the spontaneity, the power of taking the initiative, out of many a callow princeling; but Gustavus was not of any ordinary princely metal. He took kindly to handling a musket and playing soldier, while at the same time he displayed a wonderful facility for learning anything that was presented to him.

Besides his mother tongue, he understood Greek, Latin, German, Dutch, Italian, Polish, and Russian, using Latin in daily speech with special fluency. His vigorous memory and brilliantly keen understanding were at the service of his natural desire to know, and all combined to make the work of teaching him a delight.

His father was proud of the promise he showed, and from his tenth year onward allowed him to take part in his councils and audiences, and sometimes even to give his answers in council. Records of reports of foreign ambassadors contain many praises of his intelligence and keen discernment in abstruse questions. When he visited Heidelberg in 1620 the Duke of Zweibrücken gave an extremely admiring account of him.

Mathematics came to him easily. His favorite subjects were the various branches of military science, and fortifications, their plans and erection, exercised his mind almost unceasingly. Grotius's treatise on the "Right of War and Peace" and Xenophon's "Anabasis" were among his favorite readings.

The family of Adolphus owed their position as the reigning power of the country to their espousal of Protestant principles, and it was therefore considered essential that the youth should be brought up to consider himself as the champion and defender of the Protestant faith.

But it seemed a part of his very being to feel sympathy with this belief only. He indeed seemed to have been born an ardent Protestant. The fine austerity of his temperament, the elevation and purity of his mind, made it impossible for him ever to relax his views. Protestantism, or Lutheranism, as the latest form of religion of which he was aware, excited his sincere devotion, which throughout his career only grew to greater heights of self-effacing enthusiasm.

Gustavus is described as being tall and slim in his early youth, with a long, thin, pale face, light hair, and pointed beard. But in after years he grew to great height and bulk, and is said to have been extremely slow and clumsy in his movements, and so heavy that no Swedish horse could carry him in armor.

It is a curious physical fact in connection with this indisputable one that his mind formed its lucid conclusions like lightning, and that much of his success as a soldier was due to the marvellous speed of his operations.

His portrait, taken at this later period by Van Dyke, shows the long face well rounded; the nose is of the prominent Roman type, while the pointed beard is still worn, also a mustache curved up at the ends. The eyes are large and beautifully shaped; they were steel-gray, and capable of fearful flashes of anger when the quick and often-repented temper of the monarch was aroused; but the brows are finely arched, and the whole face expresses justice and benevolence. Sternness is in it, but it is the face pre-eminently of a good man. One can read in it the courage of high principles and a great mind; it is absolutely unlike the portraits of the ferocious and dissolute warriors of the time.

His first campaign was undertaken when he was only in his seventeenth year. He stormed the city of Christianople, which then belonged to Denmark, and triumphantly entered the town, but afterwards, when attacking one of the Danish islands, the young leader came to grief; his horse broke through the thin ice over a morass, where he floundered for some time, surrounded by his enemies. He was finally rescued by young Baner.

In the same year Charles IX. died, and the queen-dowager, the step-mother of Gustavus, having made a full resignation of her claims to the regency, which under Swedish law she might have claimed until Gustavus had reached his twenty-fourth year, he succeeded to his father's title of "King Elect of the Swedes, Goths, and Vandals."

For a young man of eighteen it was a formidable undertaking to ascend the throne of Sweden, and he behaved with modesty and dignity at a session of the States Assembly convened to discuss the rights of succession. He spoke of his youth and inexperience, but added manfully, "Nevertheless, if the States persist in making me king, I will endeavor to acquit myself with honor and fidelity."

He was formally proclaimed king on December 31, 1611.

All the force of his character was now called into play. Among the nobility there was a great deal of jealousy; people of a certain rank felt that there was no reason why he should occupy the throne—each of them had quite as good a claim to it as this grandson of a former subject.

But here Gustavus's great personal force made itself apparent. The malcontents found it impossible to treat him otherwise than with the respect due to a sovereign. He was able to control his natural impetuosity in all matters of court usage; his nobles were first made to feel that they were kept at a distance and under the dominion of a powerful will, and then they seemed glad to serve him as he wished. His appointments of men to fill public posts, civil and military, showed remarkable acumen. For his principal counsellor he chose the famous Oxenstiern, distinguished at twenty-eight as the coldest, most practical of diplomats, and who has left a reputation as an unequalled statesman.

Two sets of questions now presented themselves to the King and the Senate; one related to the development of agriculture and mining in the country, the other to the critical condition of the kingdom, between Danes, Polanders, and Muscovites.

The King decided to continue the war with Denmark, but as King Christian got the better of him, he astutely receded,

and signed a treaty of peace in 1613. He then proceeded
against the Czar of Muscovy, and thereby augmented the
Swedish kingdom by several provinces of importance, one of
which included the ground on which St. Petersburg now stands.

In 1617 peace was concluded with Russia through the
mediation of James I. of England, who was always offering
himself as a peace-maker.

Gustavus now went through the ceremonies of a coronation
at Upsal. It is said that this brief time of festivity was the
only rest he ever enjoyed from the end of his childhood to the
abrupt close of his life. At this time of so-called rest, indeed,
he was concentrating all his mind on international affairs,
studying the laws of commerce, and trying to lift the burden
of taxation from his people as far as was possible.

He looked over his ships, which were in a wretched condition as a whole, and sent for the best mariners he could
obtain from Holland and the Hanse Towns, with the idea of
building up a good and sufficient navy.

His army also profited by his inventions in arms and artillery; indeed, he had at all times a watchful eye upon his soldiers, providing for their comfort and well-being. They had
fur-lined coats for cold weather and comfortable tents, and
they could take the field in the bitterest winter as well as in
summer.

Sweden was continually exporting steel for armor to Spain
and Italy, so it occurred to Gustavus to establish home manu-
factories of fire-arms and swords that should equal those of
any other country. Among his many useful improvements and
inventions the leather cannon was the most curious. These
pieces, being very light, were easily shifted on the battle-field
and rapidly hauled over rugged country. They were made of
thick layers of the hardest leather girt around with iron or
brass hoops. After a dozen discharges they would fall to pieces,
but they were made in camp in quantities, and could be replaced at once. Gustavus attributed many of his most brilliant
victories to them and used them till the day of his death.

At this time the King and Oxenstiern were staying for a time
at a castle which he had inherited from a cousin, when a fire
broke out in the night and raged up all the staircases. They

could only save themselves by jumping out of the windows and wading up to their shoulders through a filthy moat, but both escaped with nothing worse than bruises.

Schiller speaks admiringly of Gustavus for "a glorious triumph over himself by which he began a reign which was but one continued series of triumphs, and which was terminated by a victory."

This triumph of duty over inclination was Gustavus's yielding to the entreaties of his step-mother and other counsellors and giving up the beautiful Emma, Countess of Brahe. He was deeply in love with her—the chroniclers assure us that his intentions were honorable—and she had promised to be his wife, but it was represented to him that although the Countess of Brahe had all the necessary merits and virtues, marriage with a subject would seriously impair the power of his throne. So, to quote Schiller again, he "regained an absolute ascendancy over a heart which the tranquillity of a domestic life was far from being able to satisfy."

His marriage, however, although it was dictated by considerations of policy, seems to have been a successful one.

In the summer of 1620 Gustavus made a tour, incognito, of the principal towns of Germany, with the object of seeing for himself, in Berlin, the sister of the Elector. His suit prospered, and it is said that in defiance of the Elector's wishes the Princess Maria Eleonora, who was then in her twentieth year, accepted Gustavus and eloped with him to Sweden. They were married in Stockholm with great pomp. She was graceful and majestic, and we are assured that she made Gustavus a worthy and Christian queen.

The relations of Sweden with Poland were perpetually unsatisfactory. Sigismund, its Catholic king, disputed the throne with his cousin Gustavus, and a tedious eight years' war resulted.

But instead of exhausting Sweden, it had the effect of developing the consummate military genius of her King; of bringing his army, by its constant exercise, to an extraordinary degree of skill, and of making ready for the coming great struggle in Germany the new principles of military art introduced by Gustavus.

Not only was he a brilliant strategist, but the King looked after his army with paternal care; it was well fed, well clad, and promptly and well paid. Every detail was attended to by him. Religious services were held, morning and evening, by every regiment. No plunder, cruelty, intemperance, no low and slanderous talk or immorality, were allowed—his officers and soldiers alike were obliged to follow his example.

It is not to be wondered at that this army was led from one victory to another, or that the fame of its discipline and its successes should be noised all over Europe. The great Thirty Years' War, that stupendous struggle of Roman Catholicism to blot out the work of the Reformation in Germany, was now raging, and in the various Protestant countries, notably England and Holland, as well as the anti-Papist states of Germany, people were beginning to look towards Gustavus as the most likely champion to give them victory. There were no such generals on the Protestant side in Europe, and it was known that Gustavus was deeply and sincerely religious, leading an upright life—a man of honor, who might be relied upon to keep his word.

Ferdinand, the Catholic Emperor of Germany, laughed at the idea of the Swedish champion; the "Snow King," he said (this being one of the favorite names for Gustavus), would melt if he tried coming south.

As for Gustavus, he had longed for years to try conclusions with Tilly and the other Imperial generals, but more particularly since Ferdinand in 1629 had promulgated the Edict of Restitution, whereby at one stroke the Archbishoprics of Magdeburg and Bremen, the Bishoprics of Minden, Verden, Halberstadt, Lübeck, Ratzeberg, Misnia, Merseburg, Naumburg, Brandenburg, Havelberg, Lebus, and Camin, with one hundred and twenty smaller foundations, were taken away from the Protestant Church and restored to the Roman Catholic Church.

To restore these lands and dignities, which had been from fifty to eighty years in the possession of the Protestants, was of course impossible without the use of brute force. By using the armies of Tilly and Wallenstein to compel it, the Emperor Ferdinand proclaimed himself the author of a political and religious revolution, the success of which must depend entirely upon military despotism, and which was without any moral basis whatever.

There were many different motives prompting Gustavus to enter the lists against Ferdinand's forces. It was not only that there was great flattery in the appeal to help the oppressed—not only that war was his native element, wherein he felt sure of success; besides all this, he had bitter grievances to redress. In 1629 Ferdinand sent sixteen thousand Imperialist troops to take part against him in the war with Poland. To Gustavus's remonstrance Wallenstein had replied, "The Emperor has too many soldiers; he must assist his good friends with them." The envoys sent to represent Gustavus at the Congress of Lübeck were insolently turned away. Ferdinand also continued to support the claims of the Polish King, Sigismund, to the Swedish throne, refused the title of king to Gustavus Adolphus, insulted the Swedish flag, and intercepted the King's despatches.

However, Gustavus would enter the war only at his own time and on his own terms. He was far too prudent and wise, far too dutiful, to impoverish his own country or leave her exposed to the attacks of enemies. In 1624 England had approached him, wishing to know his terms for invading Germany, but would not accede to his rather high stipulations.

The King of Denmark then underbid Gustavus, made terms with England, and rushed into the German conflict with great confidence, but was ignominiously defeated, while Wallenstein (at that time Ferdinand's best general) established himself on the Baltic coast. This was getting dangerously near, as Gustavus felt.

In 1628 Gustavus Adolphus made an alliance with Christian of Denmark, his old enemy, but as a Protestant and a foe to Catholic rule in Germany his loyal friend—for the time. It was agreed between them that all foreign ships except the ships of the Dutch should be excluded from the Baltic. In the summer of the same year he sent two thousand men to defend Stralsund against Wallenstein.

In 1629, through the secret intervention of Cardinal Richelieu, a treaty of peace was signed with Poland at Stuhmsdorf. Again, in 1630, Cardinal Richelieu, the wily diplomatist who governed France for Louis XIII. and had a hand in all the affairs of Europe, sent Baron de Charnace to Gustavus at Stockholm and made the same proposals in the name of France that England had made in 1624. But the flippant manner of de Charnace disgusted the King, and the terms did not please him: he did not care to assume the rôle of a mercenary general paid by France and bound for a limited number of years, and so de Charnace returned home without having accomplished anything.

Richelieu, as the minister of a Catholic king and a prince himself of the Roman Catholic Church, of course did not dare to openly ally himself with Gustavus in the latter's character of defender of the Protestant faith. But in his desire to frustrate the ambitions of the House of Austria, against which he had schemed for years, he was quite willing to support any power that would directly or indirectly advance the supremacy of France.

Gustavus now felt comparatively free to leave Sweden and invade Germany. By his treaty with Denmark he was free to retreat through her territory.

After the unsuccessful attempt made by Christian of Denmark to oppose the Emperor by leading the forces of the Protestant Union, Gustavus remained the only prince in Europe to whom the Germans felt they could appeal—the only one strong enough to protect them, and upright enough to insure them religious liberty.

Pressing appeals came from all sides now to add to his own personal motives for embarking in the German war. He raised an army of forty-three thousand men in Sweden, but set out on his expedition with only thirteen thousand. On the occasion of taking his leave, Gustavus appeared before the Estates with his little daughter of four in his arms. This Princess was born so "dark and ugly," with such a "rough, loud voice," that the attendants had rushed to Gustavus with the news that a son was born to him. When this was found to be a mistake they were reluctant to tell him, as his joy at having an heir to his military greatness was so openly expressed. But finally his sister, the Princess Catherine, took the child to him and explained that it was a daughter. If he felt any disappointment he did not show it; tenderly kissing the child, he said: "Let us thank God, sister; I hope this girl will be as good as a boy; I am content, and pray God to preserve the child." Then, laughing, he added, "She is an arch wench, to put a trick upon us so soon."

In this manner did the celebrated Christina of Sweden enter the world. Her father was deeply fond of her, and enjoyed taking her to his reviews; there she showed great pleasure in hearing the salutes fired, clapping her little hands, so that the King would order the firing to be repeated for her, saying "She is a soldier's daughter."

There is a famous letter of Gustavus's still preserved in which he wrote to Oxenstiern: "I exhort and entreat you, for the love of Christ, that if all does not go on well, you will not lose courage. I conjure you to remember me and the welfare of my family, and to act towards me and mine as you would have God act towards you and yours, and as I will act to you and yours if it please God that I survive you, and that your family have need of me."

It is said that when Gustavus presented the little girl to the Estates as his heir, tears came to the eyes of those northern men, who had the name of being cold and stern, as they repeated their oath of allegiance to the young Princess.

"I know," the King said to them, "the perils, the fatigues, the difficulties of the undertaking, yet neither the wealth of the House of Austria dismays me nor her veteran forces. I hold my retreat secure under the worst alternative. And if it is the will of the Supreme Being that Gustavus should die in the defence of the faith, he pays the tribute with thankful acquiescence; for it is a King's duty and his religion to obey the great Sovereign of Kings without a murmur. For the prosperity of all my subjects I offer my warmest prayers to Heaven. I bid you all a sincere—it may be an eternal—farewell."

At this time he could hardly speak for emotion. He clasped his wife to him and said "God bless you!" and then, rushing forth, he mounted his horse and galloped down to the ship that was to take him away from Sweden.

Sweden was anything but rich, yet so inspired had the people become by the exalted spirit of their monarch, that they were eager to contribute whatever they could to the campaign.

On June 24, 1630, Gustavus was the first man of his expedition to land on the Island of Usedom, where he immediately seized a pickaxe and broke the soil for the first of his intrenchments. Then, retiring a little way from his officers, he fell upon his knees and prayed.

Observing a sneering expression upon the faces of some of his officers at this, he said to them: "A good Christian will never make a bad soldier. A man that has finished his prayers has at least completed one-half of his daily work."

A painting commemorating this event is said still to be in existence in a Swedish country-house belonging to the family of de la Gardie.

Hardly a month after the landing of Gustavus, Ferdinand deprived himself of his most able general; he removed Wallenstein—the Duke of Friedland—disbanding a large part of his army, and putting the rest under the command of Tilly, who, now being over seventy, was slow in getting his army ready for the field.

When Ferdinand heard of the Swedish King's arrival on German soil he had said lightly, "I have got another little enemy!" But by Christmas time Gustavus was established firmly on the banks of the Rhine, while ambassadors and princes surrounded him.

On reaching Stettin, in Pomerania, the King found his course opposed by Boguslas, the aged and infirm Duke of Pomerania, who feared to espouse the cause of the Protestant Prince. But Gustavus insisted upon entering Stettin and seeing the Duke. When the latter came to meet him, borne along the street on a sedan chair, he responded to Gustavus's hearty greetings by saying lugubriously, "I must necessarily submit to superior power and the will of Providence." At which Gustavus said with gracious pleasantry, that was no doubt trying to the timid old man: "Yonder fair defendants of your garrison" (the windows were crowded with ladies) "would not hold out three minutes against one company of Dalicarnian infantry; you should behave yourself with greater prowess in the married state" (the Duke was over seventy and had no children) "or else permit me to request you to adopt me for your son and successor." This was a jest in earnest, for on the death of the Duke the Swedes held possession of Pomerania, which was confirmed to them by subsequent treaty.

Germany was astounded at the orderly and moral behavior of the Swedish soldiers; nothing save "vinegar and salt" were they allowed to make any demand for outside the camp. In January a notable event occurred. Richelieu, having in view the effect that so favorable a diversion would have on the war then going on in Italy between France and the House of Austria, had at last arranged conditions that Gustavus could accept.

Richelieu, as Wakeman says, "had long fixed his eyes on Gustavus as one of the most formidable weapons capable of being used against the House of Austria, and he desired to put it in the armory of France."

In January, 1631, Gustavus signed the treaty of Barwalde, by which he undertook to maintain an army of thirty-six thousand men, to respect the Imperial Constitution, observe neutrality towards Bavaria and the Catholic League as they observed it towards him, and to leave the Catholic religion untouched in those districts where it was established. France was to supply the King with two hundred thousand dollars yearly for six years.

In March a great gathering of Protestants was held in Leipzig; they agreed to raise troops if they themselves were attacked, but they were willing to submit to the Emperor if he would but repeal the Edict of Restitution. There seems to have been some distrust of Gustavus among them; no doubt they began to fear already that he would prove too much of a conqueror.

There had been great sympathy in England with Gustavus in his character as a Protestant champion. Charles I. himself was quite indifferent, but his subjects, particularly his Scotch subjects, were anxious to be of service in the campaign.

In July of 1631 the Marquis of Hamilton had landed on the shores of the Baltic with six thousand troops, generously raised at his own expense. The Marquis was a magnificent fellow, who lived in the field like a prince, with gorgeous liveries, equipages, and table. The King received him affectionately, but although he commanded his own troops he never achieved the rank of general in the Swedish army.

It is said that the English soldiers were not of great service in the war, and that they were fearfully affected by the strange food. The German bread gave them terrible pangs (it must have been Pumpernickel); they over-fed themselves dreadfully with new honey, and the German beer played havoc with them. In this way the British contingent was soon reduced to but two regiments, finally to only one, and the Marquis of Hamilton was content to follow Gustavus as a simple volunteer.

An expostulating letter from Charles I. to Gustavus in relation to Hamilton is said to be almost unintelligible except for a postscript, which reads:

"I hope shortly you will be in a possibility to perform your promise concerning pictures and statues, therefore now in earnest do not forget it."

Gustavus Adolphus sent back to Scotland many well-trained commanders who had occasion afterwards to use their skill acquired under him. Some of these had a European reputation: Spence, of Warminster, created by Gustavus Count Orcholm; Alexander Leslie, afterwards Earl of Leven; Drummond, Governor of Pomerania; Lindsay, Earl of Crawford; Ramsay; Hepburn; Munro, and, most devoted and beloved of all the King's Scottish officers, Sir Patrick Ruthven.

Various squabbles have been recorded as taking place between the Scotchmen and the King. One relates to Colonel Seton, who was mortally offended at receiving a slap in the face from the King. He demanded instant dismissal from the Swedish service, and it was given him. He was riding off towards Denmark when the King overtook him.

"Seton," he said, "I see you are greatly offended with me, and I am sorry for what I did in haste. I have a high regard for you, and have followed you expressly to offer you all the satisfaction due to a brother officer. Here are two swords and two pistols; choose which weapon you please, and you shall avenge yourself against me."

This was too great an appeal to Seton's magnanimity; he broke out with renewed expressions of the utmost devotion to the King and his cause, and they rode back to camp together.

At one time Hepburn declared with fury to Gustavus that "he would never more unsheath his sword in the Swedish quarrel," but, nevertheless, he did so, and was made Governor of Munich. The truth was that Gustavus had a domineering spirit and a fiery temper, but meanness or injustice had no part in him, and his noble candor won the true and everlasting attachment of those who were near him.

At one time Douglas, a Scotchman who had enrolled himself in the Swedish army in 1623, behaved in so unpardonable a fashion in Munich as to cause his arrest. Sir Henry Vane, the British Ambassador to Sweden, who was greatly disliked there for his insolence and pig-headedness, approached Gustavus and demanded the release of Douglas.

"By Heaven!" replied the King, "if you speak another syllable on the subject of that man, I will order him to be hanged." Presently, however, he said: "I now release him on *your* parole, but will not be affronted a second time. By Heaven! the fellow is a rascal, and I do not choose to be served by such sort of animals."

"May it please your Majesty, I have always understood that the subjects of the King my master have rendered you the most excellent and faithful services."

"Yes, I acknowledge the people of your nation have served me well, and far better than any others, but this dog concerning whom we are talking has affronted me, and I am resolved to chastise him." Within a few moments he had grown calmer and said: "Sir, I request you not to take exception at what has dropped from me; it was the effect of a warm and hasty temper. I am now cool again, and beseech you to pardon me."

He once spoke of this temper to his generals, saying, "You must bear with my infirmities, as I have to bear with yours."

That Gustavus had so open a way before him this far in Germany, that he had been able to walk through Pomerania and Brandenburg without encountering any opposition that he could not easily overcome, was owing to Wallenstein's Imperial command having been taken from him.

One of the cleverest strokes Richelieu had ever made was the securing the dismissal of Wallenstein from the Imperial army. It seems a miraculous piece of craft, at the very moment when

Wallenstein's arms had brought glorious victory to the Emperor, and when Gustavus, absolute master of his military operations, was advancing on German soil, to deprive the Imperial armies of the only leader whose authority could stand against the great talents of Gustavus.

To be sure, there was great dissatisfaction with Wallenstein among the Catholic League on account of his personal pretensions, but this of itself would not have brought about his downfall. The only effectual voice to influence Ferdinand was the voice of a priest. His own confessor wrote of Ferdinand:

"Nothing upon earth was more sacred to him than a sacerdotal head. If it should happen, he often said, that he were to meet, at the same time and place, an angel and a priest, the priest would obtain the first and the angel the second act of obeisance."

So Richelieu introduced in his court a gentle Capuchin monk, Father Joseph, who lived but to scheme for his master the Cardinal. He told the Emperor, among other arguments, that "It would be prudent at this time to yield to the desire of the princes the more easily to gain their suffrages for his son in the election of the King of the Romans. The storm once passed by, Wallenstein might quickly enough resume his former station."

Ferdinand piously gave in to the gentle monk, although he afterwards discovered the trickery; Wallenstein was removed and Tilly was made commander-in-chief.

Johann Tzerklas, Count von Tilly, was born in South Brabant in 1559, of an ancient and illustrious Belgian family. It is thought that he was educated for the Jesuit priesthood, and in this way became fanatically attached to Rome. At twenty-one he gave up the priesthood to enter the army of the Duke of Alva. Adopting the Imperial service, he followed the Duke of Lorraine into Hungary, where in some campaigns against the Turks he rose rapidly from one step to another.

At the conclusion of this war Maximilian of Bavaria made him commander-in-chief of his army with an unlimited power. When the unfortunate Elector Palatine Frederick accepted the crown of Bohemia and defied the Emperor and his Catholic League, Maximilian took part with the Emperor against him, and was rewarded, at the successful termination of the war, by having the Palatine countries given to him. The defeat of Frederick's forces in 1620 was no doubt due to Tilly's generalship. Poor Frederick, who fled from Tilly in terror and abdicated his electorate when he had two armies ready to support him, explained his poltroonery by saying philosophically: "I know now where I am; there are virtues which only misfortune can teach us; and it is in adversity alone that princes learn to know themselves."

Tilly, like Wallenstein, paid his troops on "the simple plan, that they shall get who have the power, and they shall keep who can."

But Tilly was undoubtedly more disinterested in his character than Wallenstein, who worked for his own aggrandizement, and only pretended to be at one time Protestant, at another Catholic.

Tilly was a sincere bigot, of the sort of stuff that the infamous Duke of Alva, whom he was said to resemble personally, was made. "A strange and terrific aspect," says Schiller in describing Tilly, "corresponded with this disposition: of low stature, meagre, with hollow cheeks, a long nose, a wrinkled forehead, large whiskers, and a sharp chin. He generally appeared dressed in a Spanish doublet of light green satin with open sleeves, and a small but high-crowned hat upon his head, which was ornamented with an ostrich-feather that reached down to his back."

This horrible fanatic, with his ferocious thirst for the blood of Protestants, nevertheless appreciated his adversary's powers: "The King of Sweden," he said in the assembly of the electors at Ratisbon, "is an enemy as prudent as brave; he is inured to war and in the prime of life; his measures are excellent, his resources extensive, and the states of his kingdom have shown him the greatest devotion. His army, composed of Swedes, Germans, Livonians, Finlanders, Scotch, and English, seems to be animated by but one sentiment, that of blind obedience to his commands. He is a gamester from whom much is won even when nothing is lost."

Tilly had no fondness for parade, and appeared among his troops mounted on a wretched little palfrey. By a curious contradiction, this man, who allowed his men to perform unspeakable acts of cruelty and lust, was himself by nature both temperate and chaste.

Field Marshal Tilly was now an old man, but he could boast that he had never lost a battle. Yet he who had vanquished Mansfeld, Christian of Brunswick, the Margrave of Baden, and the King of Denmark was now to find the King of Sweden too much for him.

The progress of the "Snow King" in Pomerania and Brandenburg made the new commander-in-chief put forth all his powers to collect the military forces scattered through Germany, but it was midwinter before he appeared with twenty thousand men before Frankfort-on-the-Oder. Here he had news that Demmin and Colberg had both surrendered to the King of Sweden, and giving up his offensive plan of attack he retired towards the Elbe River to besiege Magdeburg.

On his way, however, he turned aside to New Brandenburg, which Gustavus had garrisoned with two thousand Swedes, Germans, and British, and, angered by their obstinate resistance, put every man of them to the sword. When Gustavus heard of this massacre he vowed that he would make Tilly behave more like a person of humanity than a savage Croatian.

Breaking up his camp at Schwedt, he marched against Frankfort-on-the-Oder, which was defended by eight thousand men —the same ferocious bands that had been devastating Pomerania and Brandenburg. The town was taken by storm after a three days' siege. Gustavus himself, helped by Hepburn and Lumsden, whom he asked to assist him with their "valiant Scots, and remember Brandenburg," placed a petard on a gate which sent it flying. The Swedish troops rushed through, and when the Imperial soldiers asked to be spared, they cried "Brandenburg quarter!" and cut them down. Thousands were killed or drowned in the river. The remainder, excepting a number of officers who were taken prisoners, fled to Silesia. All the artillery fell into the hands of the Swedes. For the first time the King was unable wholly to restrain his men—all the stores of ill-gotten Imperialist wealth in Frankfort were grabbed by his army.

Giving Leslie charge of Frankfort, and having sent one detachment into Silesia and another to assist Magdeburg, he then

—turning aside, incidentally, to carry Landsberg-on-the-Warth —proceeded towards Berlin with troops and artillery, sending couriers in advance to explain his mission, which was to demand help from his brother-in-law, the Elector.

The Elector invited the King to dine and sleep at Berlin under the protection of his own guard, and consented to the temporary occupation of the fortresses of Spandau and Kustrin by the King's men, a permission which was withdrawn within a few weeks. When remonstrated with for these concessions the next day, by one of his advisers, the Elector said: "Mais que faire? Ils ont des canons." It is a remark which seems to explain the lazy, inconsequent character of the Elector, who, however, was always ready to admit the logic of superior force.

Magdeburg, one of the richest towns of Germany, enjoyed a republican liberty under its wise magistrates. The rich archbishopric of which it was the capital had belonged for a long period to the Protestant princes of the House of Brandenburg, who had introduced their religion there. The Emperor Ferdinand had removed the Protestant administration and given the archbishopric to his own son, Leopold, but, nevertheless, the city of Magdeburg had found it possible to conclude an alliance with the King of Sweden, by which he promised to protect with all his powers its religious and civil liberties, while he obtained permission to recruit in its territory and was granted free passage through its gates.

He sent there Dietrich of Falkenberg, an experienced soldier, to direct their military operations, and the magistrates made him governor of the city during the war.

While Gustavus was hindered from coming to its relief, Magdeburg was invested by the forces of Tilly, with those of Count Pappenheim, who served under him. Having ordered the Elector of Saxony to comply with the Edict of Restitution and to order Magdeburg to surrender, and having received a firm refusal, Tilly proceeded, March 30, 1631, to conduct the siege personally with great vigor, and finally, after a long, heroic defence, his men carried it by storm May 20th. Falkenberg was one of the first to fall. Then began the storied horrors of Magdeburg, the slaughter of the soldiers, the citizens, the children, the out-

rages and murder of the women, many of whom killed themselves to escape the demons let loose by Tilly.

Many Germans felt pity for the wretched women delivered
into their hands, but the Walloons of Pappenheim's army were
monsters of brutal fury. The scenes of crime in Magdeburg were
unsurpassed in animal insanity by anything that has been recorded. When some officers of the League, sickened with these
sights, appealed to Tilly to stop them, he said, "The soldier must
have some reward for his danger and his labors."

The inhabitants themselves, it is said, set fire to the city in
twelve different places, preferring to be buried under the walls
to yielding, but some authorities say it was fired by Pappenheim.
Only the Cathedral and fifty houses were left from the conflagration; the rest had gone to ruin, soot, and ashes.

At last, on May 23d, Tilly walked through the ruined streets
of the city. More than six thousand bodies had been thrown into
the Elbe; a much greater number of living and dead had been
consumed in the flames—altogether thirty thousand were killed.

On the 24th a Te Deum was chanted in the Cathedral by
Tilly's orders, and he wrote to his Emperor that since the taking of Troy and the destruction of Jerusalem no such victory had
been seen. He then marched his men away through the Hartz
Mountains, avoiding a meeting with Gustavus.

Great and bitter complaints arose in all quarters now against
Gustavus for not succoring the city that depended upon him,
and he was obliged to publish a justification of himself. The
facts had been that the two Protestant Electors of Saxony and
Brandenburg insisted, in the most cowardly spirit, upon preserving their neutrality, and would not allow the King's army
to cross their territory. Had he done so in despite of them, his
retreat might have been cut off. While the siege was in progress, however, Gustavus finally came to Berlin, and said to the
pusillanimous Elector:

"I march towards Magdeburg not for my own advantage, but
for that of the Protestants. If no person will assist me, I will
immediately retreat, offer an accommodation to the Emperor,
and return to Stockholm. I am certain that Ferdinand will grant
me whatever peace I desire; but let Magdeburg fall, and the

Emperor will have nothing more to fear from me; then behold the fate that awaits you!" The Elector was frightened, but would not yield a free passage for the Swedes through his dominions, and insisted upon having Spandau given back to him, and while Gustavus was arguing the question with him the news came that Magdeburg had fallen.

The horrible fate of the city sent a shudder throughout Germany. On the strength of it Ferdinand began to make fresh exactions, clearing out more Protestant bishoprics and demanding more men and funds from the Electors; but all this had the effect of opening the eyes of the members of the Protestant Union to their own foolishness in not supporting Gustavus, "and the liberties of Germany arose out of the ashes of Magdeburg," says Schiller.

It was now realized that within eight months the "Snow King" had made himself master of four cities, forts, and castles, and had cleared the whole country behind him to the shores of the Baltic—a territory one hundred and forty miles wide. But while other princes were changing their attitude, the Elector of Brandenburg remained obstinately, stupidly resolved on his own idea—he must have Spandau back; at last Gustavus ordered his commander to evacuate the fortress, but he declared that from that day his brother-in-law should be treated as his enemy. To emphasize this, he brought his whole army before Berlin, and when the Elector sent ambassadors to his camp he said to them:

"I will not be worse treated than the Emperor's generals. Your master has received them in his states, has furnished them with all necessaries, surrendered every place which they desired, and, notwithstanding so much complaisance, he has not been able to prevail upon them to treat his people with more humanity. All that I require from him is security, a moderate sum of money, and bread for my troops; in return for which I promise to protect his states and to keep the war at a distance from him. I must, however, insist upon these points, and my brother the Elector must quickly decide whether he will accept me for his friend or his capital plunderer."

A report of this speech, together with pointing the cannon against the town, had the effect of clearing away the Elector's doubts and sweetening his fraternal relations with Gustavus.

Most amiably he concluded a treaty, in which he consented to pay thirty thousand dollars monthly to the King, to allow the fortress of Spandau to remain in his hands, and engaged to open Kustrin at all times to his troops.

This decisive union of the Elector of Brandenburg with the Swedes was soon followed by others. The Elector of Saxony, who had had two hundred of his villages burned by Tilly, now joined Gustavus eagerly. When Gustavus, in order to test the Saxon ruler, who had heretofore been so shifty, sent word that he would make no alliance with him unless he would deliver up the fortress of Wittenberg, surrender as a hostage his eldest son, give the Swedish troops three months' pay, and surrender up all the traitors in his ministry, the Elector replied:

"Not only Wittenberg, but Torgau, all Saxony, shall be open to him; I will surrender the whole of my family to him as hostages; and if that be insufficient, I will even yield up myself to him. Hasten back, and tell him that I am ready to deliver up all the traitors he will name, to pay his army the money he desires, and to venture my life and property for the good cause."

The King, convinced of his sincerity, withdrew his severe conditions. "The mistrust," said he, "which they showed me when I wished to go to the aid of Magdeburg awakened mine; the present confidence of the Elector merits an equal return from me. I am content if he will furnish my army with a month's whole pay, and I even hope to be able to indemnify him for this advance." The Landgrave of Hesse-Cassel also joined him. The Dukes of Mecklenburg and Pomerania were already his firm friends.

Shortly after these events the King summoned his allies to meet him at Torgau at a council of war, for Tilly had invested Leipzig with a large army, and was threatening it with the fate of Magdeburg. The council decided upon pursuing Tilly at once, the Saxon Elector saying this vehemently. Gustavus had had a short respite from warlike labors; he had visited Pomerania in June, where great rejoicings had been held on his behalf, and where he was joined by his queen, Maria Eleonora (just a year after he had landed), who had come from Sweden with re-enforcements of six thousand Swedes.

But, after all, war was the dominating thought always with

Gustavus; soon he was at head-quarters making active preparations for the next battle. Cust, in his "Lives of the Warriors of the Thirty Years' War," says: "The bridge of Wittenberg being in his hands, he had already issued orders to Horn and Baner to meet him at this place of rendezvous, about sixteen miles from thence; Colonel Hay had been directed to occupy Havelberg; while Banditzen was now directed to remain in charge of the camp at Werben. The King, however, with the delicacy of a man of honor and station, kept all his troops on the western bank of the Elbe, that he might leave the Saxon army encamped on the right bank until he obtained from the Elector his authority in writing to cross the bridge."

The united Saxon and Swedish armies joined their forces on September 7, 1631, and came within sight of Tilly's forces near Breitenfeld, a small town four miles from Leipzig. The King's governor of Leipzig had surrendered to Tilly two days before, but the "old corporal," as Gustavus called him, had inflicted no outrages upon the town.

Gustavus pushed his men forward rapidly, leaving tents and baggage behind him in his camp, thinking his men might well sleep in the fields at this season of the year. On the evening before the action Gustavus called his generals to him, explained the plan of battle to them, and told them that "they were about to fight to-morrow troops of a different stamp from Polanders or Cossacks, to whom they had hitherto been opposed."

"Fellow-soldiers," he said, "I will not dissemble the danger of the crisis. You will have a day's work that will be worthy of you. It is not my temper to diminish the merit of veteran troops like the Imperialists, but I know my own officers well, and scorn the thought of deceiving them. Our numbers are perhaps inferior, but God is just; and remember Magdeburg."

After riding about through the ranks with the sanguine, light-hearted manner that always inspired courage in his men, he retired for a few hours' sleep in his coach. And here, the chroniclers say, he dreamed that he had a pugilistic encounter with Tilly and floored him.

Tilly was waiting for them next morning on the slope of a hill, with large woods behind him and his artillery on an eminence. His men wore white ribbons in their hats and helmets, and the allies, or confederates, as they were called, sprigs of holly or oak. The Imperial army was stretched in a single line, having neither a second line nor a reserve.

Gustavus kept his own men well separated from his Saxon troops. The Saxons were upon and behind a hill with their guns while his own men were in separate bodies, each under its own commander, but capable of being shifted or massed according to the will of Gustavus in an incredibly short space of time. This manner of making his battle-field a chess-board, on which only his hand controlled the moves, was at that time unknown. It has been said by experts that Gustavus's tactics on the day of Leipzig added more to the art of war than any that had been invented since the days of Julius Cæsar.

A strong wind raged, blowing thick dust in the faces of the Swedes, and, as the battle proceeded, the smoke of the powder. As Gustavus moved his men to the attack in compact columns, in order to pass the Loderbach, Pappenheim, at the head of two thousand cuirassiers, plunged at them with violence. The King, clad in gray, with a green plume in his gray beaver hat, and mounted on his horse—of the sort called "flea-bitten"— made a dash forward at the head of his cavalry, anxious to get the wind in his favor and to get his left flank out of range of a battery. Pappenheim, whose advance had been made without orders, received a volley from the musketeers that made him reel, and Baner at the head of the reserve cavalry, and Gustavus himself with the right wing, came on him with such impetus as to drive him fairly from the field.

Meanwhile on Tilly's extreme right Fürstenberg threw himself on the Saxons; they had no such training as the King's old forces, and flew in a wild rout. The Elector of Saxony, who was in the rear, joining their flight with his body-guard, never stopped until he reached Eilenburg, where he consoled himself with deep draughts of beer, quite content to be out of the fray.

Gustavus witnessed the panic and flight of the Saxons—from whom he had not expected too much—and an officer he had summoned being shot dead in the saddle, the King took his place and cheered his men forward, crying "Vivat! vivat!"

The enemy fell back before the vigor of this attack. At the same time the King discovered from the thick clouds of dust about him that some large body of troops was near; he was told they were Swedes, but they were not there in accordance with his plan of battle, so he galloped up close to them, and coming back quickly organized his troops to receive an attack. "They are Imperialists," he said; "I see the Burgundian cross on their ensigns." It was here that the two Scottish regiments under Hepburn and Munro first practised firing by platoons. This was so amazing to the veteran Cronenberg and his fine Walloon infantry that they retired with all speed.

At four o'clock the King took charge of his right wing, wheeled it suddenly to the left, dashed up to the heights where the Imperial artillery was placed, and, capturing it, turned the fire of their own guns on the enemy. Gustavus now swooped down upon Tilly's rear.

Caught between this cavalry attack at the rear and Horn's infantry in front, the Imperialists made a tough struggle. When the sun went down only six hundred men were left to close around Tilly and carry him from the field. With that exception the army had been destroyed. Seven thousand lay dead on the field; five thousand prisoners remained to take service with the victors, as the custom was at that time.

The King threw himself on his knees among the dead and wounded to offer up thanksgivings. He had the alarm-bells set ringing in all the villages round about to apprise the country of his victory. He encamped with his army in the deserted camp of the enemy. Almost all the baggage of the Imperialists fell into the hands of the conquerors. Hardly a soldier among the killed and wounded had less than ten ducats in his pocket or concealed within his girdle or saddle. Now that the battle was over, the Elector of Saxony joined Gustavus in his camp at night. The King, who could be astutely diplomatic, gave him all the credit for having advised the battle and kept silent as to the Saxon troops. The Elector, transported with joy at the issue of the day, promised to Gustavus the Roman crown. Gustavus lost no time in dallying with the Roman crown, but made new plans for action. He left Leipzig to the Elector and set forward for Merseburg, which, with Halle, at once surrendered.

Here he gave his army a rest of ten days, and many Protestant princes joined him in council.

II

LÜTZEN

FROM the day of Leipzig, Tilly's fortunes left him; his past victories were forgotten and execrations were heaped upon him. Though he was wounded, he went to work with all his old energy to form a new army, but the Emperor expressly commanded that he should never again risk any decisive battle.

The glorious victory at Leipzig is said to have changed not only the world's opinion of Gustavus, but his own opinion of himself. He was now more confident; he took a bolder tone with his allies, a more imperious one with his enemies, and even more decision and greater speed marked his military movements, though nothing tyrannical or illiberal was seen in him.

The Emperor and the Catholic League were dumfounded at the annihilation of Tilly. Richelieu was beginning to think his auxiliary too powerful; Louis XIII. even was heard to mutter, "It is time to put a limit to the progress of this Goth."

"Alone, without a rival," Schiller says, "he found himself now in the midst of Germany; nothing could arrest his course. His adversaries, the princes of the Catholic League, divided among themselves, led by different and contrary interests, acted without concert, and consequently without energy. Both statesman and general were united in the person of Gustavus. He was the only source from which all authority flowed; he alone was the soul of his party, the creator and executor of his military plans. Aided by all these advantages, at the head of such an army, endowed with a genius to profit by all these resources, conducted besides by principles of the wisest policy, it is not surprising that Gustavus Adolphus was irresistible. In not much more time than it would have taken another to make a tour of pleasure, with the sword in one hand and pardon in the other he was seen traversing Germany from one end to the other, as a conqueror, lawgiver, and judge. As if he had been the legitimate sovereign, they brought him from all parts the keys of the towns and fortresses. No castle resisted him, no river stopped his victorious progress, and he often triumphed by the mere dread of his name."

Many of his advisers pressed Gustavus to attack Vienna, but after careful consideration he thought he would serve his cause best by marching straight into the heart of Germany on the Main and the Rhine.

Ten days after Leipzig the King reached Erfurt, and ordered Duke William of Saxe-Weimar to take possession of the city. Proceeding through the Thuringian Forest, he reached Königshofen Schweinfurt, which yielded to him, as did Wurzburg. Marienberg he was obliged to take by storm; a great store of treasure was here, as well as the money which the Elector of Bavaria had sent to Tilly for the purpose of replacing his shattered army.

Great quantities of provisions, corn, and wine fell into Swedish hands. A coffin filled with ducats was found, and as it was lifted the bottom gave way, and the soldiers began to help themselves to the coin in the presence of the King. "Oh, I see how it is," said he; "it is plain they must have it; let the rogues convert it to their own uses."

In truth, the character of the Swedish army was no longer beyond suspicion; the soldiers had become to some extent demoralized with their conquests; the cruelties and barbarities that they had suffered had forced upon them terrible reprisals, and the usage of looting was so universal that they could not be held back from it.

Tilly had by this time collected a new army out of the Palatinate and come back to Fulda, and here he tried to get the consent of Maximilian of Bavaria to engage Gustavus in battle again, but the Duke was fearful of having another army wiped out, now the only one the Catholic League possessed, and refused him.

The Swedish King now advanced rapidly towards the Rhine by way of the Main, reducing Aschaffenburg, Seligenstadt, and the whole territory on both sides of the river. The Count of

Hanau made but slight resistance when his citadel was captured, and gladly agreed to pay two thousand five hundred pounds a month for the support of the army and to recall his retainers from the Imperial service.

Nothing now kept Gustavus from marching on Frankfort-on-the-Main. The magistrates of the city begged the ambassador that he sent to entreat him to consider their legitimate oaths to the Emperor, and to leave them neutral, on account of their annual fairs, which were their chief commercial enterprise. The King was not moved by these touching business considerations; he was surprised, he replied, that while the liberties of Germany were at stake and the Protestant religion in jeopardy, they should convey to his ear such an odious sentiment as neutrality, and that the citizens of Frankfort should talk of annual fairs, as if they regarded all things merely as tradesmen and merchants, rather than as men of the world with a Christian conscience. More sternly he went on to say that he had found the keys to many a town and fortress from the Isle of Rugen on the Baltic to the banks of the Main, and knew well where to find a key for Frankfort.

The magistrates were filled with alarm at this, and asked for time to consult the Elector of Mayence, their ecclesiastic sovereign, but the King replied that he was master of Aschaffenburg; he was Elector of Mayence; he would give them plenary absolution.

"The inhabitants," he said, "might desire to stretch out only their little finger to him, but he would be content with nothing but the whole hand, that he might have sufficient to grasp."

He then moved his army on to Saxenhausen, a beautiful suburb of the city, and here the magistrates met him, and after taking the oath of fidelity opened the gates of the city to him. The King made a solemn public entrance into the city, leading his troops with uncovered head, as a mark of respect, and bringing in fifty-six pieces of artillery. He was welcomed by the magistracy to a great banquet in the coronation hall of the Imperial palace of Braunfels. Maria Eleonora, his queen, now joined him in Frankfort, and when she met him was so overcome with joy that, throwing her arms around him, she cried, "Now is Gustavus the Great become my prisoner!"

The next event of importance in this victorious progress was the carrying of Mayence, which after a short siege capitulated on December 13th. On the 14th the King celebrated his thirty-seventh birthday by entering Mayence with great pomp, and took up his residence in the palace of the Elector, ordering a service of thanksgiving for his success to be held in the Roman Catholic Cathedral. Provisions, artillery, and money fell into the hands of the army. The King seized as his personal share the library of the Elector, and gave it to Oxenstiern for one of the Swedish universities, but, alas! it was lost in the Baltic.

The exhausted Swedish soldiers were now allowed a space of rest to recuperate their energies. On January 10th the Queen arrived in Mayence and shared with Gustavus for a short time the ceremonial splendors of a regal court, where five German princes and many foreign ambassadors had come to confer with the King and transact important negotiations with him. Among these was the Marquis de Breze, an ambassador from the French court; by his conversation Gustavus detected something of the truth, that Richelieu now feared him and was trying to undermine his power.

Accordingly, he sent word to Louis XIII. that he wished to speak with him personally. The French ambassador tried to persuade Gustavus that an interview with Richelieu would do as well, but he replied haughtily:

"All kings are equal. My predecessors have never given place to the Kings of France. If your master thinks fit to despatch the Cardinal half way, I will send some of my people to treat with him, but I will admit of no superiority."

When the King and Queen left Mayence, in mid February, Gustavus had had a new citadel built at the confluence of the Rhine and Main, which was called at first "Gustavusburg," but in after days lapsed into "Pfaffenraube" (Priest-plunder). A lion of marble on a high marble pillar is near Mayence, holding a naked sword in his paw and wearing a helmet on his head, to mark the spot where the "Lion of the North" crossed the great river of Germany.

During February Kreutznach in the Palatinate, one of the strongest castles in Germany, and the town of Ulm surrendered to the King.

Leaving Oxenstiern, his Minister and friend, to protect his conquests on the Rhine and Main, Gustavus began his advance against the enemy March 4, 1632, with an army—including his allies' forces—of one hundred thousand infantry and forty thousand cavalry under arms. The Catholic League had been extremely active during the months since the defeat of Tilly at Breitenfeld and Leipzig, and had raised even larger forces.

By the capture of Donauwörth it was evident to Tilly that Gustavus's next move was to be towards Bavaria, for he was now master of the right bank of the Danube. Accordingly, after destroying all the bridges in the vicinity, Tilly intrenched himself in a strong position on the other side of the River Lech. Numerous garrisons defended the river as far as Augsburg. The Bavarian Elector shut himself up in Tilly's camp, feeling that the issue of the coming battle must decide everything for him.

The Lech, in the month of March, is swollen to a great torrent by the melting snows from the Tyrol, and dashes furiously between high, steep banks. The officers of Gustavus considered it impossible to effect a crossing and urged him not to try it. But he exclaimed to Horn:

"What! Have we crossed the Baltic and so many great rivers of Germany, and shall we now for this Lech, this rivulet, abandon our enterprise!"

He had made the discovery that his side of the river was higher by eleven feet than the opposite bank, which would greatly favor his cannon. He immediately took advantage of this by having three batteries erected on the spot where the left bank of the Lech forms an angle opposite its right. Here seventy-two pieces kept up a constant cannonade on the enemy.

He had now to invent a bridge that would cross the torrent, and also think of means to distract the enemy from noticing its construction. He made a strong set of trestles of various heights and with unequal feet, so that they would stand upright on the uneven bed of the river; these were secured in their places by strong piles driven into the river-bed. Planks were then nailed to the trestles. While this went on, the cannonade drowned the noise of the hammers and hatchets; one thousand musketeers lined the Swedish bank and kept the Imperialist soldiers from coming near enough to discover the work, while a thick smoke, made by burning wood and wet straw, hid the workmen for the most part.

Before daybreak the bridge was finished and an army of engineers and soldiers selected by the King soon crossed it and threw up a substantial breastwork.

Tilly saw his foes intrenched on his own side of the river and, under the tremendous firing of the guns from the higher bank, was utterly powerless to keep them from coming. For thirty-six hours the cannonade went on, the King standing most of the time at the foot of the bridge and sometimes acting as gunner himself to encourage his men. The Imperialists made a desperate effort to seize the bridge, but a large number were cut down in the attempt.

Finally, Tilly, whose courage was heroic throughout the day, fell with a shattered thigh, and had to be borne away. Maximilian, the Bavarian Duke, now precipitately abandoned his impregnable position and moved the army quietly away to Ingolstadt.

When Gustavus next day found the camp vacant his astonishment was great:

"Had I been the sovereign of Bavaria," he cried, "never, though a cannon-ball had taken away my beard and chin— never would I have quitted a post like this and laid my states open to the enemy."

Bavaria, indeed, lay open to the conqueror; before occupying it, however, he rescued the Protestant town of Augsburg from the Bavarian yoke, Augsburg being in his eyes a special object of veneration on account of the famous "Confession"— the place "from whence the law first proceeded from Sion." Augsburg, indeed, at first resisted him, but when he saw the dread devastation that his guns began to make on its beautiful buildings he stopped them and insisted on an interview with the Governor, who, seeing the hopelessness of resistance, yielded.

Tilly died in Ingolstadt, the Elector of Bavaria sitting by his bedside. He adjured Maximilian to keep Ingolstadt with all his powers against Gustavus, and to seize Ratisbon at once; begged him never to break his alliance with the Emperor; and besought him to appoint General Gratz in his place. "He will conduct your troops with reputation, and, as he knows Wallenstein, will traverse the designs of that insolent man. Oh," he sighed, "would that I had expired at Leipzig and not survived my fame!"

So died Tilly, bigoted, merciless, cruel, but nevertheless faithful and zealous to his last breath in defence of his religion and the League.

Ingolstadt was a fortress considered impregnable; it had never been conquered. Gustavus had determined to take it, and made a partial investment only, for on one side of it was the whole Bavarian army under Maximilian.

While riding about the walls one day, and going very near to take observations, on account of his short sight, a twenty-four pounder killed his horse—the favorite "flea-bitten" steed—under him; he rose tranquilly and, mounting another horse, continued his reconnoitring. In camp in the evening his generals in a body protested against his risking so valuable a life in this way; but he replied that he had a foolish sort of a fancy that always tempted him to imagine that he could see better for himself than others could, and that his sense of God's providence gave him the firm assurance that he had other assistance in store for so just a cause than the precarious existence of one Gustavus Adolphus.

Within a few days news came that the Bavarian troops had taken the Imperial town of Ratisbon, and this caused a change in the King's plans; he had spent eight days on Ingolstadt, but he now suddenly abandoned it, because it would have been of no special advantage to him without Ratisbon in his scheme of cutting off Maximilian from Bohemia.

Munich was his next objective point, and he now proceeded into the interior of Bavaria, where Mosburg, Landshut, all the Bishopric of Freysingen, surrendered to him. But the Bavarians looked upon Protestants as children of hell. Soldiers who did not believe in the Pope were to them accursed monsters. When they succeeded in capturing a Swedish straggler they put him to death with tortures the most refined and prolonged. When the Swedish army came upon mutilated bodies of their comrades they took vengeance into their own hands, but never by consent of Gustavus.

His approach to Munich threw the capital into an agony of terror. It had no defenders, and they feared that the treatment his soldiers had met at the hands of the country-people might lead him to use his power cruelly. Some Germans in his army begged to be allowed to repeat here the sacking of Magdeburg, but such a low revenge was impossible to the King. When the magistracy sent to implore his clemency, he answered that if they submitted readily and with good grace, care should be taken that no man should suffer with respect to life, liberty, or religion. Only one act of questionable taste accompanied his public entry, and that was the presence of a monkey in the procession—a monkey with a shaven crown and in a Capuchin's dress, with a rosary in his paw. One hopes that the King was not responsible for this.

He found an abandoned palace; the Elector's treasures had been removed. There were left, though, many fine canvases by Flemish and Italian masters. His officers urged the King to plunder or destroy these, but he said: "Let us not imitate our ancestors, the Goths and Vandals, who destroyed everything belonging to the fine arts, which has left our nation a proverb and a byword of contempt with posterity for acts of this wanton barbarity." He had evidently forgotten the earnest request of Charles I. for "pictures and statues."

The construction of the palace—a magnificent building—caused the King to express great admiration; he asked the steward the name of the architect. "He is no other than the Elector himself," was the reply. "I should like to have this architect," replied the King, "to send him to Stockholm." "That," said the steward, "he will take care to avoid."

The guns in the arsenal had been buried so carefully, that they would not have been discovered if it had not been for a treacherous insider, who told the secret. "Arise from the dead," cried the King, "and come to judgment!" and one hundred and forty pieces of artillery were dug up, a large sum of gold being found in one of them.

Appointing the Scotchman Hepburn to the post of Governor of Munich, Gustavus soon started forth with his army.

Meanwhile Maximilian, although besought by his Bavarians to come and deliver them from the Swedes, could not resolve to risk a battle. The wonderful victories of Gustavus had indeed a paralyzing effect upon the country. As yet no one had been found capable of resisting him. Richelieu himself was horror-stricken at the power he had helped to raise. It was expected in France that an invasion of Swedes would be the natural continuation of the Rhine conquests; it was said that Gustavus would not rest until he had made Protestantism compulsory throughout Europe. Nothing less than the command of the German Empire was supposed to be his ultimate aim.

There is no doubt that his ambitions steadily enlarged themselves, but there is nothing to prove that he contemplated supplanting Ferdinand. His enemies were disheartened. Ferdinand was now brought to the pass of abjectly begging Wallenstein to resume his command, and Wallenstein was assuming airs of indifference and allowing himself to be persuaded only with great pressure.

This extraordinary man was the son of a Moravian baron of the ancient race of Waldstein. As a youth he was notably proud and stubborn, ambitious and conceited, often saying, "If I am not a prince, I may become one." He fell from a very high window whilst at the University of Goldben and was quite unhurt, which is said to have been the beginning of his certainty of future greatness. He was grossly superstitious always and entirely an egotist. At twenty-three he married a wealthy widow, who in a fit of jealousy gave him a "love philter" in his wine, from which he narrowly escaped death. Dying in 1614, she left him a large property, and later he married a Countess Isabelle von Haggard of immense fortune and of much "beauty, piety, and virtue."

Wallenstein now began to invest his great wealth in the purchase of confiscated properties, and it was said that through his knowledge of metallurgy he adulterated the coin which he paid. At all events, his wealth assumed fabulous dimensions, and through his wife's relations he mingled with the highest nobles of the Empire. He always spoke with affection of his wife, but did not live with her nor write to her for long years at a time.

In person Wallenstein was very tall and thin, with a yellow complexion, short red hair, and small, twinkling eyes. His cold, malignant gaze frightened his great troop of servants, who nevertheless stayed with him because they were unusually well paid. His military career had begun in his youth, when he served in Hungary. Afterwards he raised a body of horse at his own expense for a war against the Venetians. On the breaking out of the war in Bohemia, in 1618, he was offered the post of general to the Bohemian forces, but adopted the side of the sovereign in whose family he had been brought up.

After putting down the Bohemian rebellion, in which Tilly had served Maximilian, the Emperor decided that it was necessary for him to have a powerful army under his own orders. Wallenstein offered to raise an army, clothe, feed, and arm it at his own expense if he should be made a field general, an offer which the Emperor accepted and which Wallenstein carried out.

His military activities from this time on are historical, as well as the details of his cold, pompous nature. He lived like a king, with great state, had no principles whatever about the way he acquired wealth, and spent it with magnificent lavishness.

At the time Ferdinand deprived him of his command, just as Gustavus was entering Germany, Wallenstein had become Duke of Friedland, Sagan, Glogau, and Mecklenburg, and was more insolent than if he had had royal blood in his veins. He spent an income of three million of florins yearly, for his armies had plundered the land for years with great effect. He was able to control his rage at his sudden downfall because his Italian astrologer, Seni, who ruled him completely, assured him that the stars showed that a brilliant future awaited him, exalted beyond anything he had yet known. And so he was led on to close his career by plots against his Emperor and to meet death by the hand of assassins.

All of Gustavus's successes were the source of deep satisfaction to Wallenstein; they brought nearer his inevitable recall.

Now when Tilly was dead, and the Emperor was beseeching him to again take command of the Imperial troops, Wallenstein sent an envoy to convey the congratulations of the Duke of Friedland to the King of Sweden, and to invite his Majesty to a close alliance with him. He undertook, in concert with Gustavus, to conquer Bohemia and Moravia and drive the Emperor out of Germany.

Gustavus felt that help would be very welcome, and he seriously considered the offer, but he could not bring himself to believe in a success promised by such an unscrupulous adventurer, who so willingly offered to become a traitor. He courteously refused, and Wallenstein accepted the Emperor's offer of chief command with a salary amounting to the value of one hundred and eight thousand pounds per annum. He demanded that he should have uncontrolled command of the German armies of Austria and Spain, with unlimited powers to reward and punish. Neither the King of Hungary (to whom the Emperor had wished to give the highest command) nor the Emperor himself was ever to appear in his army or exercise the slightest authority in it. No commission or pension was to be granted without Wallenstein's approval. An Imperial hereditary estate in Austria was to be assigned to him. As the reward of success in the field he should be made Lord Paramount over the conquered countries, and all conquests and confiscations should be placed entirely at his disposal. All means and moneys for carrying on the war must be solely at his command.

The ambassador to whom he made these terms suggested that the Emperor must have some control over his armies, and that the young King of Hungary should at least be allowed to study the art of war with Wallenstein, but the reply was: "Never will I submit to any colleague in my office, no, not even if it were God Himself with whom I should have to share my command," and in his extremity the Emperor accepted these conditions, April 15, 1632.

Although an avowed Jesuit, Wallenstein had no religious scruples whatever, and the Catholics feared and hated him as much as the Protestants. The gorgeous luxury of his surroundings was apparently only designed to impress the world; he was not a sensualist, but seems to have been actuated only by an insane love of power. Soldiers flocked to his standard and worshipped the mighty warrior who rewarded them with ceaseless plunder, but the princes, nobles, and peasantry of the countries through which he passed were left with a blight upon them. He seemed to be unable to see in a country any reasons for industrial prosperity or for conserving wholesome conditions of any sort; he was a brave, fearless leader—after that, a robber, and nothing else.

He distributed enormous sums among his favorites, and the amount he spent in corrupting the members of the Imperial Court was still greater. The height to which he raised the Imperial authority astonished even the Emperor; but his design unquestionably was, that his sovereign should stand in fear of no one in all Germany besides himself, the source and engine of his despotic power. He cared nothing, however, himself, for popularity from his equals, and less for the detestation of the people or the complaints of the sovereigns, but was ready to bid a general defiance to all consequences.

Wallenstein raised his army. From Italy, Scotland, Ireland, as well as from every part of Germany, men flocked to him in thousands, who cared little for country or religion, but were attracted by the prospects of plunder and of distinction under the renowned soldier who had made himself a dictator.

In May, 1632, his organization was complete. He began by driving Gustavus's Saxon allies out of Bohemia, while Pappenheim scourged the Rhine country. Then he directed his forces upon rich Protestant Nuremberg.

Gustavus, before he could get there, threw himself into Nuremberg and fortified it, and then, gathering his army together, prepared to give battle to Wallenstein. But the latter had made up his mind to starve out Gustavus. With his own light cavalry, superior in number to that of the Swedes, he could more readily obtain supplies than they.

Forming a huge camp on an eminence overlooking Nuremberg, he prepared stolidly to wait until the King should be forced to go. At the end of June the camp was finished, and Gustavus held out until September.

His men were starving and dying, discipline had become relaxed, even his generals becoming cruel and rapacious. On September 3d he had led his men against Wallenstein's intrenchments, but was forced to retire. A few days later he left Nuremberg, providing it with a garrison, although he had lost through battle, disease, and starvation nearly twenty thousand men. Wallenstein's loss in the same time was thirty-six thousand. No attempt at pursuit was made by Wallenstein. Turning north into Saxony, he proceeded to choose a position between the Elbe and the Saale, where he might intrench himself for

the winter and carry on what to him was one of the most necessary features of a campaign—the sending of bands of maraud-
ers and requisitioners through the country.

He also had in mind detaching the Saxon Elector from his
alliance with Gustavus, this vacillating Prince having shown
symptoms of yielding to the great furore caused by Wallenstein's
resumption of power.

Gustavus determined that he should not lose Saxony by want
of decision. Summoning Oxenstiern and Bernhard of Saxe-
Weimar to his aid, he forced his army with all speed through
Thuringia, and before Wallenstein could recover from his astonishment he seized both Erfurt and Naumburg. At Erfurt
he said farewell to his Queen, who never saw his face again
until he was in his coffin at Weissenfels.

The weather had become so bitterly cold that Wallenstein
had expected no further advances from Gustavus during the
winter. He was preparing to intrench himself between Merseburg and Torgau. He had sent Pappenheim again to the Rhine-
land. Gustavus took advantage of this division and resolved to
fight before Pappenheim could return to re-enforce his adversary. Wallenstein sent messenger after messenger to bring back
Pappenheim, and hastily throwing up intrenchments, he
awaited the onslaught of the Swedish King at the village of
Lützen, November 6th.

On the southern side of the large highway leading from Lützen to Leipzig lay the Swedes; to the north, the Imperialists.
Two ditches ran by the sides of this road, and some old willow-
trees bordered it. The deep, rich mould of the soil is heavy for
horse and foot. On Wallenstein's right was a hill where a group
of windmills waved their arms.

On the evening of the 5th the Duke of Friedland had ordered
his men to deepen and widen the ditches, and he planted two
large batteries on the windmill hill. Gustavus had passed the
night in his coach with the Duke of Saxe-Weimar, for he owned
no tent nor field equipage. He had ordered his army to be ready
two hours before daylight, but there was so solid a fog that the
darkness was intense, and not a step could be taken. Gustavus
had his chaplain perform divine service while waiting. He never
forgot, it was said, either the time to pray or the time to pay—

never leaving his men's wages in arrears. He would take no breakfast and declined to put on his steel breastplate, as a wound he had received made it uncomfortable. He was clad in a new plain cloth doublet and an elk-skin surtout.

Riding along the ranks, he encouraged each regiment, addressing Swedes and Germans in their respective tongues, and urging all to valor and steadfastness. "God with us!" was the rallying-cry of the Swedes. "Jesu Maria!" was the shout of the Imperialists.

The morning wore on, as the soldiers waited still in impenetrable darkness. At one time Gustavus threw himself on his knees and began a hymn, the military band accompanying him. His terrible weeks at Nuremberg and the hardships of the late toilsome march had seemed to bring out more strongly than ever the fervent piety of his nature. When, on his arrival a few days before at Naumburg, the people had rushed from all the country round to see him, and had prayed on their knees for the favor of touching the hem of his garment or his sword in its scabbard, he was touched by this innocent worship, but he was moved to say to those with him: "Does it not seem as if this people would deify me? Our affairs go on well without doubt, but I much fear that Divine vengeance will punish me for this rash mockery, and soon convince the foolish multitude of my weak mortality."

Towards eleven o'clock the fog began to lighten and the enemies could see each other, while the Swedes beheld the flames of Lützen, set on fire by Wallenstein that he might not be flanked on that side.

Gustavus now mounted his horse and drew his sword for action, placing himself at the head of the right wing. Wallenstein opened the attack with a tremendous fire of musketry and artillery, with which Gustavus's leather guns found it hard to cope. The ditches of the road made a formidable obstacle to the Swedish cavalry, being lined with musketeers. But at length the Swedish musketeers cleared the others away. The horsemen, however, under the heavy firing, now seemed to find the ditches impassable; they hesitated before them, whereupon Gustavus dashed forward to lead them across.

"If," said he sternly, "after having passed so many rivers,

scaled so many walls, and fought so many battles, your old courage fails you, stand still but for a moment and see your master die in the manner we all ought to be ready to do."

He leaped the ditch, and they were after him like the wind, urging him to spare his invaluable life and promising to do everything. On the other side of the road and ditches he observed three dark masses of Imperial cuirassiers clad in iron, and turning to a colonel said:

"Charge me those black fellows, for they are men that will undo us—as for the Croats, I mind them not."

The royal order was at once executed, but the Croats suddenly swept down upon the Swedish baggage and actually reached the King's coach, which, however, they failed to capture.

Both sides fought desperately; it had to be decided whether it was Gustavus's genius that had won at the battle of the Lech and at Leipzig, or if Tilly's want of skill had been the only cause. On this day Wallenstein, Duke of Friedland, had to justify the Emperor's confidence and the enormous demands he had made upon it. Each soldier of each side seemed to feel that the honor and success of his chieftain depended solely on his individual efforts.

The Swedes advanced with such velocity and force that the first, second, and third Imperial brigades were forced to fly; but Wallenstein stopped the fugitives. Supported by three ranks of cavalry, the beaten brigades formed a new front to the Swedes and struck furiously into their ranks. A murderous series of combats then began; there was no space for even loading muskets—they fought wildly with sword and pike. At last the Swedes, exhausted, withdrew to the other side of the ditches, abandoning a battery they had gained.

In the meantime the King, at the head of his right wing, had attacked the enemy's left. His splendidly powerful cuirassiers of Finland had easily routed all the Croats and Poles covering this wing, and their flight spread confusion among the rest of the cavalry. But he then received the news that his infantry had retired, and that his left wing, under the heavy fire of the windmill hill, was about to yield.

Ordering Horn to pursue the wing which he had just defeated, he turned to fly to the assistance of his own men. His horse carried him so swiftly that no one kept up with him but the Duke of Lauenburg.

He galloped straight to the place where his men were being assailed with the greatest fury, and his nearsightedness led him too near. An Imperialist corporal noticed that all gave way before him with great respect, and shouted to a musketeer:

"Fire at him! That must be a man of distinction!" and the King's left arm was shattered.

He begged Lauenburg to help him to a place of safety, but the next moment he was shot in the back. Turning to Lauenburg he said:

"Brother, I have enough; seek only to save your own life."

As he spoke he fell to the ground, where a volley of other shots pierced him.

A desperate struggle still took place over him. A German page, refusing to tell the royal rank of his master, was mortally shot. But Gustavus still had life enough to say:

"I am the King of Sweden, and seal with my blood the Protestant religion and the liberties of Germany." Then he murmured: "My God! Alas! my poor Queen!"

For a long time the Duke of Lauenburg was accused of assassinating the King, and there is a great deal to be said in support of such a charge. Among the Spanish archives were found papers showing that there was a plot in progress to kill Gustavus. Still, it is conceivable that his death was caused by the ordinary chances of war.

It was the King's charger, galloping into the Swedish lines covered with blood, that brought the news of the King's death. The Swedish cavalry came with furious speed to the place to rescue the precious remains of their King. A great conflict raged around his dead body until it was heaped with the slain. The dreadful news, spreading through the Swedish army, inflamed their courage to desperation. Neither life nor death mattered to them now; the Yellow Guard of the King was nearly cut to pieces.

Bernhard, Duke of Weimar, a warrior of great skill and courage, took command of the army. The Swedish regiments under General Horn completely defeated the enemy's left wing, took possession of the windmill hill, and turned Wallenstein's cannon against him. The Swedish centre advanced and carried the battery again, and while the enemy's resistance grew more feeble, their powder-wagons blew up with fearful roars. Their courage seemed to give way and victory was assured to the Swedes.

Then Pappenheim arrived at the head of his cuirassiers and dragoons, and there was a new battle to fight. This unexpected re-enforcement renewed and fired the courage of the Imperialists; Wallenstein seized the favorable moment to form his lines again. Again he drove the Swedes back and recaptured his battery. Every man of the whole Yellow Regiment, which had most distinguished itself on the side of the Swedish infantry, lay dead in the order in which they had fought.

The Blue Regiment had also been blotted out by a terrific charge of the Austrian horse under Count Piccolomini, who had, during the charge, seven horses shot under him, and was hit in six places.

While the worst of the conflict was going on, Wallenstein rode through it with cold intrepidity; men and horses fell thick around him and his mantle was full of bullet holes, but he escaped unhurt.

Pappenheim was wounded in the thigh, and the next moment a musket-ball tore his chest. He felt that he had got his death-blow, but was able to speak cheerfully to his men, who carried him away in his coach to Leipzig. He was replaced by Holk.

Duke Bernhard re-formed his men and the fight went on with a stubborn fury that nothing could assuage. Neither side would be beaten. Again and again the Swedes were forced back; again and again they rallied and drove back their antagonists.

Ten leaders on each side had fallen. The Imperial side finally weakened with the loss of its generals. At nightfall the Swedes formed all their broken regiments into one dense mass, made their final movement across the ditches, captured the battery, and turned its guns on the enemy.

Confused as the Imperialists had become, they still fought.

The bloody struggle went on until it was too dark to see anything; both armies then left the field, each claiming the victory. Pappenheim's army left their guns, being without a general and having no orders. It was said that after Pappenheim was borne away Wallenstein betook himself to a sedan chair and did not again expose himself to the enemy. He was reproached for this afterwards by his army, who also said that he retired from the field before it was necessary. Proceeding to Leipzig, he witnessed the death of Pappenheim. Piccolomini was the last of his side in the field.

The Duke of Friedland insisted on having the Te Deum sung in honor of a victory in the churches, but this deceived no one. It was no victory, but a defeat from which he never recovered. While at Leipzig he accused his officers of cowardice, and after a court-martial had several of the bravest of them disgraced or shot. But neither this nor a few inconsequent successes were sufficient to restore the prestige that Wallenstein had lost at Lützen.

Nearly one hundred thousand corpses remained unburied on the field, and the plain all around was covered with wounded and dying.

It was not until the next day that the Swedes were able to find the body of their King; it was almost unrecognizable with blood and wounds, trampled by horses' hoofs, and naked. A huge stone was rolled by the soldiers as near as they could get to the place where the royal corpse was found; it still rests where they left it, and is known as "The Stone of the Swede."

The Imperialists had stripped the body in their eagerness to preserve relics of the great Gustavus. Piccolomini sent his buff waistcoat to the Emperor. His rings, spurs, and gold chain are still in possession of various families. A famous turquoise is supposed to have passed into the hands of a Roman Catholic bishop who desired a trophy of "Anti-Christ," as Gustavus was called by the Catholics.

The body was carried from the field in solemn state amid a procession of the whole army. It was taken to Weissenfels, and from thence to Sweden. There the whole nation mourned, knowing well that they should not have another monarch like Gustavus Adolphus.

Nothing has ever transpired to change the world's opinion of him as one of the world's greatest and best. Although the Thirty Years' War was not concluded for several years after his death, yet he was, nevertheless, the cause of its cessation. Through his agency alone the cause of the Protestant belief triumphed, and the effects of the great upheaval of the Reformation were not allowed to be obliterated in Germany.

Professor Smyth said of him: "It is fortunate when the high courage and activity of which the human character is capable are tempered with a sense of justice, wisdom, and benevolence; when he who leads thousands to the field has sensibility enough to feel the responsibility of his awful trust, and wisdom enough to take care that he directs against its proper objects alone the afflicting storm of human devastation. It is not always that the great and high endowments of courage and sagacity are so united with other high qualities as to present to the historian at once a Christian, a soldier, and a statesman. Yet such was Gustavus Adolphus, a hero deserving of the name, perfectly distinguishable from those who have assumed the honors that belong to it—the mere military executioners with whom every age has been infested."

Cust says: "Gustavus Adolphus is thought to have been the first sovereign who set the example of a standing army. The feudal association of barons with their retainers had given way in the previous century to a set of military adventurers, who made war a profession to gratify their license and their acquisitiveness, and who were commissioned by kings and leaders to collect together the assassins of Europe.

"These constituted at the very time of the Thirty Years' War the unprincipled and insatiate legions who harried Germany, who, without much discipline, were continually dissipated by the first disaster and collected together again, as it were from the four winds of heaven, to cover the face of the land again and again with terror, devastation, and confusion.

"Gustavus, who had witnessed this from afar, or experienced it in his Polish wars, had in him that spirit of organization and order which signally distinguished him above every great leader who preceded him. He saw that a well-disciplined force of men to be commanded by a superior class of officers of high honor and intelligence, and who should constitute an armed body that might obtain the dignity of a profession of arms, would be more efficient and a cheaper defence of nations than the hap-hazard assembling of mere bloodhounds, and he first executed the project of having a force of eighty thousand men, part in activity and part in reserve, who should be constantly maintained well-armed, well-clothed, well-fed, and well-disciplined."

THE BATTLE OF SOLFERINO

"ITALY," said Prince Metternich, "is merely a geographical expression."

The sneer was justified; the storied peninsula was cut up into little principalities for little princes of the houses of Hapsburg and Bourbon. The millions who spoke a common tongue and cherished common traditions of a glorious past were ruled as cynically as if they were so many cattle.

The map of Italy for 1859 is a crazy-quilt of many patches. How has it come about, then, that the map of Italy for 1863 is of one uniform color from the Alps to the "toe of the boot," including Sardinia and Sicily? We must except the Papal States, of course, still separate till 1870, and Venetia, Austrian until 1866, when the "Bride of the Sea" became finally one with the rest of Italy.

This was the last miracle that Europe had looked for. Unity in Italy! "Since the fall of the Roman Empire (if ever before it)," said an Englishman, "there has never been a time when Italy could be called a nation any more than a stack of timber can be called a ship." This was true even in the days of the mediæval magnificence of the city-States—Venice and Genoa, Milan and Florence, Pisa and Rome. But in modern times Italy had become only a field for intriguing dynasties and the wars of jealous nations.

During the latter half of the eighteenth century Italy was strangely tranquil; was she content at last with her slavery? Never that; the people had simply grown apathetic. Their spasmodic insurrections had always ended in a worse bondage than ever: their very religion was used to fasten their chains. Perhaps nothing could have served so well to awaken them from this torpor of despair as the iron tread of the first

Napoleon. The "Corsican tyrant" proved a beneficent counter-irritant, a wholesome, cleansing force throughout the land. It was good for Italy to be rid, if only for a little while, of Hapsburgs and Bourbons; to have the political divisions of the country reduced to three; to be amazed at the sight of justice administered fairly and taxation made equitable.

But the most significant effect of the Napoleonic occupation was this, that the hearts of the Italians were stirred with a new consciousness: they had been shown the possibility of becoming a united race—of owning a nation which should not be a "mere geographical expression."

And although 1815 brought the bad days of the Restoration, and the stupid, corrupt, or cruel princes climbed back again on their little thrones, and the map was made into pretty much the same old crazy-quilt, still it was not the same old Italy: all the diplomats at Vienna could not make things as they had been before. The new spirit of freedom came to life in the north, in the Kingdom of Sardinia, that had made itself the most independent section of the country. In the beginning it was only Savoy, and the Dukes of Savoy, "owing," as the Prince de Ligne said, "to their geographical position, which did not permit them to behave like honest men," had swallowed, first, Piedmont; then, Sardinia; and then as many of the towns of Lombardy as they could. The Restoration enriched the kingdom by the gift of Genoa—where, in 1806, Joseph Mazzini was born.

Mazzini, Garibaldi, Cavour—those names will be always thought of as one with the liberation of Italy.

Though frequently in open antagonism, yet the work of each of the three was necessary to the cause, and to each it was a holy cause, for which he was ready to make any sacrifice:

"Italia! when thy name was but a name,
When to desire thee was a vain desire,
When to achieve thee was impossible,
When to love thee was madness, when to live
For thee was the extravagance of fools,
When to die for thee was to fling away

Life for a shadow—in those darkest days
Were some who never swerved, who lived, and strove,
And suffered for thee, and attained their end."

Of these devoted ones, Mazzini was the prophet; his ideal-
ism undoubtedly made too great demands upon the human beings he worked for, but let us bear in mind that it needed a
conception of absolute good to rouse the sluggish Italian mind
from its "materialism and Machiavellism." Mazzini wore black
when a youth, as "mourning for his country," and when his
university course was at an end he took up the profession of
political agitator and joined the Carbonari.

But the greatest service he ever did his cause was the organization of a new society—on a much higher plane than the
Carbonari and its like. The movement was called "Young Italy,"
famous for the spirit it raised from end to end of the peninsula. Among those attracted by Mazzini's exalted utterances
was the young Garibaldi, who, taking part in Mazzini's rising
of 1834, was condemned to death, and made his escape to
South America. In constant service in the wars between the
quarrelsome States, he gained his masterly skill in guerilla
warfare which was afterwards to play so great a part in the
liberation of his country. He did not return until it seemed as
though the hour of Italy's deliverance was at hand, in 1848,
which only proved to be the "quite undress rehearsal" for the
great events of 1859.

Garibaldi has been called "not a soldier but a saint." Most
great heroes, alas! have outlived their heroism, and their wor-
shippers have outlived their worship, but Garibaldi has never
been anything but the unselfish patriot who wanted everything for his country but nothing for himself. He has been
described, on his return to Italy from South America, as "beautiful as a statue and riding like a centaur." "He was quite a
show," said the sculptor Gibson, "everyone stopping to look at
him." "Probably," said another Englishman, "a human face
so like a lion, and still retaining the humanity nearest the
image of its Maker, was never seen."

The third of the immortal Italian trio, Count Camillo di
Cavour, was, like Mazzini and Garibaldi, a subject of the

Sardinian Kingdom. There was no prouder aristocracy in Europe than that of Piedmont, but Camillo seems to have drawn his social theories from the all-pervading unrest that the great Revolution and Bonaparte had left in the air, rather than the assumed sources of heredity. In his tenth year he entered the Military Academy at Turin, and at the same time was appointed page to the Prince of Carignan, afterwards Charles Albert, father of Victor Emmanuel. This was esteemed a high honor, but it did not appeal to him in this light. When asked what was the costume of the pages, he replied, in a tone of disgust: "Parbleu! how would you have us dressed, except as lackeys, which we were? It made me blush with shame."

His attitude of contempt for the place occasioned a prompt dismissal. At the Academy he was so successful with mathematics that he left it at sixteen, having become sub-lieutenant in the engineers, although twenty years was the earliest age for this grade. He then joined the garrison at Genoa, but the military career had no allurements for him. Taking kindly to liberal ideas, he expressed himself so freely that the authorities transferred him to the little fortress of Bard, till, in 1831, he resigned his commission.

Having by nature a "diabolical activity" that demanded the widest scope for itself, he now took charge of a family estate at Leri, and went in for scientific farming.

"At the first blush," he wrote, "agriculture has little attraction. The habitué of the salon feels a certain repugnance for works which begin by the analysis of dunghills and end in the middle of cattle-sheds. However, he will soon discover a growing interest, and that which most repelled him will not be long in having for him a charm which he never so much as expected."

Although he began by not knowing a turnip from a potato, his invincible energy soon made him a capital farmer; his experiments were so daring that "the simple neighbors who came trembling to ask his advice stood aghast; he, always smiling, gay, affable, having for each a clear, concise counsel, an encouragement enveloped in a pleasantry."

Besides agriculture, his interests extended to banks, railway companies, a manufactory for chemical fertilizers, steam mills for grinding corn, and a line of packets on the Lago Maggiore. During this time he visited England, and was to be seen night after night in the Strangers' Gallery of the House of Commons, making himself the master of the methods of parliamentary tactics, that were to be of such value to Italy in later years.

In 1847 Cavour started the "Risorgimento," a journal whose programme was simply this: "Independence of Italy, union between the princes and peoples, progress in the path of reform, and a league between the Italian States." As for Italian unity, "Let us," Cavour would say, "do one thing at a time; let us get rid of the Austrians, and then—we shall see." After returning from England in 1843, he wrote: "You may well talk to me of hell, for since I left you I live in a kind of intellectual hell, where intelligence and science are reputed infernal by him who has the goodness to govern us."

The King, Charles Albert, had called him the most dangerous man in the kingdom, and he certainly was the most dangerous to the old systems of religious and political bigotry; but his work was educational; gradually he was enlightening the minds of the masses, and preventing a possible reign of terror. In 1848 he wrote: "What is it which has always wrecked the finest and justest of revolutions? The mania for revolutionary means; the men who have attempted to emancipate themselves from ordinary laws. Revolutionary means, producing the Directory, the Consulate, and the Empire; Napoleon, bending all to his caprice, imagining that one can with a like facility conquer at the Bridge of Lodi and wipe out a law of nature. Wait but a little longer, and you will see the last consequence of your revolutionary means—Louis Napoleon on the throne!"

Charles Albert, the King, who, as Prince Carignan, had been one of the Carbonari, and secretly hated Austria, has been accused of treachery and double dealing (he explained that he was "always between the dagger of the Carbonari and the chocolate of the Jesuits"); but the time came when he nobly redeemed his past. In 1845 he assured d'Azeglio that when Sardinia was ready to free herself from Austria, his life, his sons' lives, his arms, his treasure, should all be freely spent in the Italian cause.

In February, 1848, he granted his people a Constitution;

a Parliament was formed, Cavour becoming member for Turin.

In this month the revolution broke out in Paris and penetrated to the heart of Vienna. Metternich was forced to flee his country; the Austrians left Milan; Venice threw off the yoke—all Italy revolted. The Pope, it is said, behaved badly, and left Rome free for Garibaldi to enter, with Mazzini enrolled as a volunteer.

Even the abominable Ferdinand of Sicily and the Grand Duke of Tuscany had been obliged to grant Constitutions; all the northern States had hastened to unite themselves to Sardinia by universal plebiscite. At the very beginning, Charles Albert fulfilled his pledge: he placed himself at the head of his army and defied Austria.

But it was too soon: Austria was too strong. On the 23d of March, 1849, Charles Albert was crushingly defeated by Radetsky at Novara. There, when night fell, he called his generals to him and in their presence abdicated in favor of his son, Victor Emmanuel, who knelt weeping before him. The pathos of despair was in his words: "Since I have not succeeded in finding death," he said, "I must accomplish one last sacrifice for my country."

He left the battle-field and his country without even visiting his home; six months later he was dead. "The magnanimous King," his people call him.

The young Victor Emmanuel began his reign in a kingly fashion; pointing his sword towards the Austrian camp, he exclaimed: "Per Dio! d'Italia sarà." It seemed at the time a mere empty boast—his little country was brought so close to the verge of ruin. The terms of peace imposed an Austrian occupation until the war indemnity of eighty million francs should be paid. Yet Cavour was heard to say that all their sacrifices were not too dear a price for the Italian tricolor in exchange for the flag of Savoy. It was not until July that Rome fell—Rome, where Garibaldi had established a republic and Mazzini was a Triumvir!

At the invitation of the Pope, Louis Napoleon, then President of the French Republic, seeing the opportunity for conciliating the religious powers, poured his troops into Rome, and Garibaldi fled, with Anita at his side. The brave wife with her unborn child would not leave her hero, but death took her from him. In a peasant's hut, a few days later, she died, his arms around her. As for Mazzini, the fall of Rome nearly broke his heart. For days he wandered dazed about the Eternal City, miraculously escaping capture, till his friends got him away.

It was not until April, 1850, that Pius IX. dared to come back to Rome, where a body of French troops long remained, to show how really religious a nation was France. From his accession there had been a Papal party in Italy, who, because of the good manners of the gentle ecclesiastic, had wrought themselves up to believe that Italy could be united under *him*. But as early as 1847 d'Azeglio wrote from Rome: "The magic of Pio Nono will not last; he is an angel, but he is surrounded by demons."

After the events of the 1848 rising, and his appeal (twenty-five Pontiffs had made the same appeal before him!) to the foreigner against his own people, the dream of a patriotic Pope melted into thin air.

And so Austria came back into Italy, and seemed again complete master there. It would be interesting to be able to analyze the sensibilities of these prince-puppets who were jerked back to their thrones by their master at Vienna. Plenty of Austrian troops came to take care of them. As for the bitter reprisals Italians had to bear, it is almost impossible to read of them. In certain provinces everyone found with a weapon was put to death. A man found with a rusty nail was promptly shot. At Brescia a little hunchback was slowly burnt alive. Women, stripped half-naked, were flogged in the market-place, with Austrian officers looking on. It was after his visit to Naples in the winter of 1850 that Gladstone wrote, "This is the negation of God erected into a system of government."

But Italy had now a new champion. When Victor Emmanuel signed his name to the first census in his reign, he jestingly gave his occupation as "Rè Galantuomo," and this name stuck to him forever after. A brave monarch Victor Emmanuel proved, whose courage and honesty were tried in many fires.

When arranging negotiations with Radetsky after Novara, he was given to understand that the conditions of peace would be much more favorable if he would abandon the Constitution granted by Charles Albert.

"Marshal," he said, "sooner than subscribe to such conditions, I would lose a hundred crowns. What my father has sworn I will maintain. If you wish a war to the death, be it so! My house knows the road of exile, but not of dishonor."

The Princes of Piedmont had been always renowned for physical courage and dominating minds. Effeminacy and mendacity were not their foibles. It is hinted by the Countess of Cesaresco, in her "Liberation of Italy," that sainthood was esteemed the privilege strictly of the women of the family, but then sainthood is not absolutely necessary to a monarch. The Piedmont line had always understood the business of kings, but none so thoroughly as Victor Emmanuel.

He was unpopular at first; the Mazzinists cried, "Better Italy enslaved than handed over to the son of the traitor, Carlo Alberto!" On the wall of his palace at Turin was written: "It is all up with us; we have a German King and Queen"—alluding to the Austrian origin of his mother and of his young Queen, Marie Adelaide.

These two—wife and mother—were ruled by clerics and made his life melancholy when he began a course of ecclesiastical reform. One person in every two hundred and fourteen in Sardinia was an ecclesiastic, and the Church had control of all ecclesiastical jurisdiction and could shelter criminals, among other mediæval privileges. To reform these abuses, the King in 1849 approached the Pope with deferential requests, but the Pope absolutely refused to make any changes.

However, the work of reform was firmly pushed on and a law was passed by which the priestly privileges were sensibly cut down, although the King's wife and mother wrung their hands, and the religious press shrieked denunciation. At this time Santa Rosa, the Minister of Commerce and Agriculture, died, and the Church refused him the last sacrament, though he was a blameless and devout member of the Roman Church. This hateful act of intolerance reacted on the clergy, as a matter of course, and gave an impetus to Church reform.

When, in 1855, Victor Emmanuel was so unfortunate as to lose his wife, his mother, and his brother within a month, and the nation as a whole mourned with him, his clerical friends embittered his affliction by insisting with venomous frankness that it was the judgment of Heaven that he had brought upon himself for his religious persecutions.

Strength was Victor Emmanuel's genius: he was not intellectual in any marked degree, but his ministers could work with him and rely upon him. A union between him and Cavour, the two great men of the kingdom, was inevitable. Up to this time Cavour had no general fame except as a journalist, but the King had the insight to recognize his extraordinary powers, and when Santa Rosa died (unshriven) Cavour in his place became Minister of Agriculture and Commerce. "Look out!" said the King to his Prime Minister, d'Azeglio, when this had come to pass, "Cavour will soon be taking all your portfolios. He will never rest till he is Prime Minister himself."

Under the régime of Cavour, railways and telegraph-wires lined the kingdom in all directions; he took off foolish tariffs and concluded commercial treaties with England, France, Belgium, and other Powers. "Milord Cavour" was a nickname showing the dislike aroused by his English predilections, but through him Piedmont repaired the damage of the war of 1848, and grew steadily in prosperity.

Cavour's brilliant intellectual powers seem to have been so limitless that it is rather a relief to think of him personally as only a dumpy little man with an over-big head. Although a born aristocrat, and living in the manner becoming one, he was capable of quite demonstrative behavior. The occasion for this was a dinner given by d'Azeglio. Cavour, seated at table, joked the Premier about his jealousy of Rattazzi; the Premier replied angrily; whereupon the greatest of diplomats arose, seized his plate, lifting it as high as he could, and dashed it to the floor, where it broke into fragments. Then he rushed out of the house, crying:

"He is a beast! He is a beast!"

This quarrel, which sounds like an act from a Nursery Drama, led to a change in the Cabinet, with Cavour left out. But a little later on d'Azeglio resigned and Cavour was Prime Minister.

A marvellous stroke of statesmanship on behalf of his

country was Cavour's intervention in the Crimean War in 1855—three years after Louis Napoleon's coup-d'état. It seemed an act of folly to send fifteen thousand troops from the little Italian State—which had no standing among European Powers—to help England and France. The undertaking seemed to Sardinians an act of insanity; Cavour's colleagues were violently against him. But the King stood by him; so the troops were sent, and the Ministers resigned.

Never was an action more fully justified. At the close of the Crimean War Sardinia had two powerful allies—France and England; and for the first time she was admitted on terms of equality among the "Powers." A significant thing had been said, too, in 1855: "What can I do for Italy?" asked the Emperor Napoleon of Cavour. Cavour was not slow to tell him what could be done; he was convinced that he must look for aid to the vanity and ambition of Napoleon III.

No diplomatic pressure of his, however, availed. During the next two years the attitude of Austria became constantly more unendurable, but still Napoleon would make no move.

It proved to be the most unlikely of events that brought about a consummation of the wishes of Cavour.

On the evening of January 14, 1858, a carriage drove through the Paris streets on its way to the opera. With the appearance of its two occupants all the world is familiar; the wonderful Spanish eyes of the lady, the exquisite lines of her figure—who has not seen them pictured? The smallish man with her had been described by the Crown Prince of Prussia as having "strangely immobile features and almost extinguished eyes." His huge mustache had exaggeratedly long waxed ends, and his chin was covered with an "imperial."

The terrible crash of Orsini's bombs, thrown underneath their carriage, failed to carry out the conspirators' purpose. The Emperor had a slight wound on the nose and the Empress felt a blow on the eye. That was all, except that her silks and laces were spattered with blood from the wounded outside the carriage. They continued their drive and saw the opera to its finish before they were told of the tragedy that had befallen. Eight people had been killed and one hundred and fifty-six wounded by the explosion.

The Empress Eugenie, it is said, showed the greatest composure over the event, but this was not true of her husband. Probably no man of modern times had had so many attempts made on his life as Louis Napoleon, and always, before, he made light of them, but this last one, resulting in such cruel slaughter, completely unnerved him. He now lived in a tremor, dreading the vengeance of still others of the revolutionary ex-friends of his youth, but he dared not relax the despotic grip with which he ruled his land. How could he placate them? He wore a cuirass under his coat; he had wires netted over the chimneys of the Tuileries, so that bombs should not burst on his hearth; a swarm of detectives were around him wherever he went, and always the question asked itself in his mind: What should he do to take off the curse of fear from his life?

Cavour, Victor Emmanuel, the whole of Italy, were filled with rage and disgust at the news of Orsini's attempt. Orsini —an Italian! That must be the end of all their hopes of help from France! But in the summer of 1848 Cavour was summoned to the Emperor at Plombières, and during two days there the agreement was formulated by which France and Italy united against Austria. This was Louis Napoleon's solution of his problem—to help Italy at least sufficiently to annul the hate of every assassin on the peninsula. According to the Prince Regent of Prussia, he chose "la guerre" instead of "le poignard."

No written record was made of the bargain between Napoleon and Cavour; but we know that it gave Savoy and Nice to France, and made one innocent royal victim, the young Princess Clotilde, Victor Emmanuel's daughter, who was there betrothed by proxy to Prince Jerome Napoleon.

It was at Plombières that Napoleon with some naïveté said to Cavour: "Do you know, there are but three *men* in all Europe; one is myself, the second is you, and the third is one whose name I will not mention." Napoleon was not alone in his high estimate of Cavour. In Turin they said: "We have a Ministry, a Parliament, a Constitution; all *that* spells Cavour."

At his reception on New Year's Day, 1859, Napoleon astounded everyone by greeting the Austrian Ambassador with these words: "I regret that our relations with your Government are not so good as they have been hitherto." This ostentatious expression was equal to publication in a journal. Immediate war was looked for by everyone. Piedmont, France, and Austria openly made bellicose preparations.

Although on the 18th of January, 1859, a formal treaty was made, by which France was bound to support Piedmont if attacked by Austria, Napoleon hesitated and tried to back out of his agreement. It will never be known by what tortuous system of diplomacy Cavour compelled Austria herself to declare war, but it was done, April 27th.

Cavour's intrigues during these days were dazzlingly complicated; he had to deal on one hand with his Imperial ally, and on the other with shady revolutionary elements—and to keep his right hand in ignorance of what his left hand did. He summoned Garibaldi to Turin; Garibaldi, in his loose red shirt and sombrero with its plume, with his tumultuous hair and beard, struck dismay to the heart of the servant who opened the door. He refused to admit him, but finally agreed to consult his master. "Let him come in," said Cavour. "It is probably some poor devil who has a petition to make to me." This was the first meeting of the statesman and the warrior. When told of the French alliance, Garibaldi exclaimed: "Mind what you are about! Never forget that the aid of foreign armies must be, in some way or other, dearly paid for." But his adherence was whole-heartedly given to Victor Emmanuel, and at the end of the short campaign Italy rang with his name.

For months past, Austria had been pouring troops into Italy —there seemed no limit to them. Garibaldi, by the end of April, was in command of a band of Cacciatori delli Alpi, a small force, but made up of the iron men of North Italy, worthy of their leader.

On May 2d Victor Emmanuel took the command of his army; it comprised fifty-six thousand infantry in five divisions, one division of cavalry in sixteen squadrons, with twelve field-guns and two batteries of horse artillery. May 12th, the French Emperor rode through the streets of Genoa amid loud acclamations; the city was hung with draperies and garlands in his honor. At Alessandria he rode under an arch on which was inscribed, "To the descendant of the Conqueror of Marengo!" In all he had one hundred and twenty-eight thousand men, including ten thousand cavalry.

It was a short campaign, but the weeks were thick with battles, and the battle-fields with the slain.

The first engagement was at Genestrello, May 20th. The Austrians, driven out, made a stand at Montebello, where, though twenty thousand strong, they were routed by six thousand Sardinians. The armies of the Emperor and King forced the Austrians to cross the Po, and there retire behind the Sesia. On the 30th the Allies crossed the Sesia and drove the foe from the fortified positions of Palestro, Venzaglio, and Casalino.

Next came Magenta—a splendid triumph for MacMahon; the Austrian loss was ten thousand men; that of the French between four thousand and five thousand. Meantime, Garibaldi had led his Cacciatori to the Lombard shores of Lake Maggiore, had beaten the Austrians at Varese, entered Como, routed the enemy again at San Fermo, and was now proceeding to Bergamo and Brescia with the purpose of cutting off the enemy's retreat through the Alps of the Trentino.

On the 8th of June Victor Emmanuel and Napoleon III. made their triumphal entry into Milan—from whence every Austrian had fled. Everyone remembers how MacMahon, now Duke of Magenta, caught up to his saddle-bow a child who was in danger of being crushed by the crowd. The Emperor and the King soon moved on from Milan. By the 23d their head-quarters were fixed at Montechiaro, close to the site of the coming battle of Solferino.

On the day before the battle, the lines of the Allies lay near the Austrian lines, from the shore of the Lake of Garda at San Martino to Cavriana on the extreme right. On the evening of the 23d there was issued a general order regulating the movements of the allied forces: Victor Emmanuel's army was sent to the extreme left, near Lake Garda; Baraguay d'Hilliers was given the centre in front of Solferino, which was the Austrian centre; to his right was MacMahon, next Marshal

Niel, and then Canrobert at the extreme right, while the Emperor's guard were ordered here and there in the changes of the battle.

The enemy, under Field-Marshal Stadion, held the entire line of battle strongly, with one hundred and forty thousand men.

Solferino has been the scene of many combats; it is a natural fighting-ground, and the Austrians had barricaded themselves at all the strong points of vantage.

At five in the morning of the 24th Louis Napoleon sat in his shirt-sleeves, after his early coffee, smoking a cigar, when tidings came to him that the fighting had begun. In a few minutes he was driving at full speed to Castiglione, and on the way he said to an aide: "The fate of Italy is perhaps to be decided to-day." It was he indeed who decided it; whatever else is said of him, it was he who struck a great blow for Italy at Solferino.

It was the great day of Napoleon III.; he has never been considered a notable soldier, but throughout this day, in every command issued, he displayed consummate military ability.

The sun glared in the intense blue above with tropical heat, when, at Castiglione, Napoleon climbed the steeple of St. Peter's Church and beheld the expanse of Lake Garda, growing dim towards the Tyrolean Alps. There was the remnant of an ancient castle—a sturdy tower—guarding the village of Solferino, called the "Spy of Italy." Already a deadly fire from its loopholes poured on Baraguay d'Hilliers's men, who faced it bravely, but were falling in terrible numbers.

He could see the Austrian masses swarming along the heights uniting Cavriana with Solferino. The Piedmontese cannon booming from the left told that Victor Emmanuel was fighting hard, but his forces were hidden by hills. It was at once plain to him, from his church-steeple, that the object of the Austrians was to divert the attack on Solferino—the key of their position—by outflanking the French right, filling up the gap between the Second and Fourth Corps, and thus cutting the Emperor's army in two. Coming down from his height, Napoleon at once sent orders to the cavalry of the Imperial Guard to join MacMahon, to prevent his forces from being divided. Altogether the Emperor's plan seems to have been clear and definite; his design was to carry Solferino at any cost, and then, by a flank movement, to beat the enemy out of his positions at Cavriana. Galloping to the top of Monte Fenil, the Emperor beheld a thick phalanx of bayonets thrust its way suddenly through the trees of the valley; it was a huge body of Austrians sent to cut off the line of the French. There was not a minute to be lost; he sent orders to General Manêque, of the Guard, to advance at once against the Austrian columns. With magnificent rapidity the order was executed, and the Austrians—a great number—were beaten back far from the line of battle.

The Austrian batteries placed on the Mount of Cypresses and on the Cemetery Hill of Solferino were keeping up a deadly fire on the French.

Baraguay d'Hilliers brought Bazaine's brigade into action against the one, and the First Regiment of Zouaves rushed up the other, only to be hurled back by the enemy as they reached the steep slope. A horrible confusion followed these two repulses, the Zouaves and General Negrier's division being fatally mixed and fighting with each other like furies. But General Negrier kept his head and collected his troops, scattered all over the hillocks and valleys. Then, with the Sixty-first Regiment of the line and a battalion of the One Hundredth Regiment, he started resolutely to mount the Cemetery Hill. It was a deadly march; the enemy, holding the advantage, disputed every turn and twist of the ascent. Twice Negrier's troops rushed up along the ridge-like path, but the circular wall of the cemetery, bored with thousands of holes, through which rifles sent a scathing hail, was strong as a fortress to resist them. It was sheer murder to take his men up again; Negrier abandoned the attack.

The enemy's cannon-balls from the three defended heights fell thick and fast on Monte Fenil, where Napoleon and his aides breathlessly watched the progress of the drama.

Many of the Cent-Gardes who formed the Imperial escort were shot down; the Emperor was in the midst of death. The Austrians had been strongly re-enforced and held to the defence of Solferino more obstinately than ever.

But, notwithstanding, the French were gaining ground; the left flank of the Austrians was at last broken by the artillery of the French reserve, and the whole army felt a thrill of encouragement.

A number of French battalions were now massing themselves about the spur of the Tower Hill of Solferino, but it was impossible to proceed to the attack while solid Austrian masses stood ready to pounce upon their flank.

A few fiery charges scattered the enemy in all directions, and a tempest of shouts rang out when Forey gave the order to storm the Tower Hill. The drums beat, the trumpets sounded. "Vive l'Empereur!" echoed from the encircling hills. "Quick" is too slow a word for French soldiers. The Imperial Guard, chasseurs, and battalions of the line rushed up with such fierce velocity that it was no time at all before the heights of Solferino were covered with Napoleon's men. Nothing could stand against such an electric shock—the Tower Hill was carried, and General Lebœuf turned the artillery on the defeated masses of Austrians choking up the road that led to Cavriana.

The convent and adjoining church, strongly barricaded, yielded after repeated attacks, and then Baraguay d'Hilliers and Negrier made a last attempt on the Cemetery Hill. That narrow path that led up to it was strewn with bloody corpses, but neither the dead resting in their graves nor these new dead could be held sacred. A strong artillery fire on the gate and walls stopped the rifles from firing through the holes, and in this pause Colonel Laffaile led the Seventy-eighth Regiment up. They burst in the gate of the cemetery—there were not many there to kill!—they were soon on their way towards the village.

Their way lay through a checker-board of tiny farms and fields, separated by stone walls wreathed with ivy. Little chapels, dedicated to favorite saints, stood in every enclosure. Houses, walls, and chapels had all been turned into barricades by the Austrians. Douay's and Negrier's men had to fight their way to the village through a rain of bullets from unseen enemies. Now they took the narrow path winding up by the Tower Hill into the streets of the village; when nearly at the top the clanking of heavy artillery-wheels told them that the enemy were retreating and carrying off the very guns that had played such havoc on their ranks from the top of Tower Hill. It took but a short time to capture them, and then they were fairly in the village, chasing the last straggling Austrians through the streets.

Solferino was in the hands of the French; but the fate of the battle was not yet decided, for Cavriana was a strong position, and Stadion and his generals had made a careful study of its possibilities.

At two o'clock MacMahon's left wing was completely surrounded by the enemy, but moving forward on the right he boldly turned the Austrian front, and swept everything before him to the village of San Cassiano, adjoining Cavriana. The village was attacked on both sides and carried by Laure's Algerian sharpshooters, but the Austrians still held Monte Fontana, which unites San Cassiano to Cavriana, and repulsed Laure's men with deadly skill.

Re-enforced, they made a splendid dash and took Monte Fontana, but the Prince of Hesse brought up reserves and won it back for the Austrians. Napoleon now ordered Mac-Mahon to push forward his whole corps to support the attack, and as Manêque's brigade and Mellinet's grenadiers had succeeded in routing the enemy from Monte Sacro, they were ordered to advance on Cavriana.

Lebœuf placed the artillery of the Guard at the opening of the valley facing Cavriana, and Laure's Algerian sharpshooters after a prolonged hand-to-hand conflict with the Prince of Hesse's men carried Cavriana at four o'clock. Two hours later Napoleon was resting in the Casa Pastore, where the Austrian Emperor had slept the night before. The sultry glare of the day had culminated in a wild, black storm; the wind was a hurricane, and it was under torrents of rain that the Austrians made their retreat, while the thunder drowned the noise of Marshal Niel's cannon driving them from every stand they made.

Such overwhelming numbers had been brought to bear on the French that day that their defeat would have been almost certain if it had not been for Napoleon's generalship and his modern rifled guns. These were new to the Austrians, who became panic-stricken at their effect.

The Piedmontese troops, under their "Rè Galantuomo," fought as nobly as their brilliant allies that day. The young Emperor Francis Joseph commanded in person at San Martino, but it was Benedek that Victor Emmanuel had to reckon with —the best General of all the Austrian Staff. He beat him out of San Martino, and to the Italians the combat of June 24th is known as the Battle of San Martino to this day.

The scorching sun of the next morning shone upon twenty-two thousand ghastly dead. It has been believed that the horrible sights and scents of this battle-field sickened the Emperor and cut short the campaign, but who can tell? Was it perhaps Eugenie's influence—always used in favor of the Pope? Or was it that he realized that the movement could now only end in the complete liberation of Italy—a consummation that he regarded with horror? All that is known is this: three days after the Austrians had been driven back to their own country, and while all Italy went mad with joy at the victory—while Mrs. Browning was writing her "Emperor Evermore"—a cruel satire on later events—it became known that Napoleon had sent a message to the Austrian Kaiser asking him to suspend hostilities.

The two Emperors met at Villafranca, a small place near Solferino. At the close of their interview Francis Joseph looked humiliated and sombre—Louis Napoleon was smilingly at ease. He, the parvenu, had made terms with a legitimate Emperor, and was pleased with himself. He had arranged that Lombardy was to be united to Piedmont, while Venetia remained Austrian. When Victor Emmanuel was told of these terms he could only say coldly that he must ever remain grateful for what Napoleon *had* done, but he murmured "Poor Italy!"

And Cavour? Cavour was struck to the heart. Had he arranged such a finale as *this* with the upstart Emperor—that he should leave the game when it suited his pleasure, and make terms with the Austrian Emperor all by himself—insolently disregarding Victor Emmanuel? He wept with grief and anger. He left at once for the camp, and there he told the Emperor his opinion of him in stinging words. He begged his King to repudiate the treaty and reject Lombardy, but Victor Emmanuel, although as bitterly disappointed as Cavour, felt that he must be prudent for his people's sake.

Angered at the King's refusal, Cavour resigned his office and retired to his farms at Leri, but after a few months he was back in his old place in the Cabinet. All his hopes and ambitions came back—although physically the shock had broken him—and he labored for Italy till his death in June of 1861. The whole Italian people, from King to peasant, knew that they had lost their best friend. But Cavour's life work was nearly finished. Garibaldi had taken up the work of emancipation where Napoleon had abandoned it, and before he left him forever, to Cavour was given the triumph of hearing his beloved master proclaimed King of Italy.

THE STORMING
OF BURKERSDORF HEIGHTS

WHEN, in 1740, Wilhelm Friedrich of Prussia died, the friends whom his heir had gathered about him at his pleasant country-house at Reinsberg were doomed to see a blight fall on their expectations such as had not been known since Poins and Falstaff congratulated themselves on having an old friend for their King.

When the young Prince came to the throne as Frederick II., thought these trusting people, Prussia, instead of being a mere barracks overrun with soldiers and ruled by a miser, would become the refuge of poets and artists. Its monarch would be a man of peace, caring for nothing beyond the joys of philosophy, poetry, music, and merry feasts—this, of course, providing for an indefinite extension of the enchanted life he and his companions led at Reinsberg.

They had the best of reasons for this belief: the antagonism between the Prince and his father had begun almost as soon as the rapture of having an heir had become an old story to Friedrich Wilhelm. The tiny "Fritz," with a cocked hat and tight little soldier-clothes, drilling and being drilled with a lot of other tiny boys—and frightfully bored with it all the time—was a standing grievance to his rough, boorish father. "Awake him at six in the morning and stand by to see that he does not turn over, but immediately gets up. . . . While his hair is being combed and made into a queue, he is to have his breakfast of tea." This was the beginning of his father's instructions to his tutors when, at seven, he passed out of his governess's hands.

Notwithstanding the fine Spartan rigor of this programme, the boy came up a dainty, delicate little fellow, who turned up his nose at boar-hunting and despised his father's collection of giants, and loved to play the flute and make French verses. Friedrich Wilhelm was anything but a bad monarch; he was moral in a century when nothing of the sort was expected of monarchs; he made the Prussian army the best army in the world; he even had affections; but for a man of these virtues he was the most intolerable parent of whom there is a record.

The brilliant Wilhelmina, Frederick's dearly loved sister, whose young portraits show her as very like her brother, has this characteristic scene in her "Memoirs." Their sister, Princess Louisa, aged fifteen, had just been betrothed to a margrave, and the King asked her—they were at table—how she would regulate her housekeeping when she was married. Louisa, a favorite, had got into the way of telling her father home-truths, which he took very well, as a rule, from her. On this occasion she told him that she would have a good table well served; "better than yours," said Louisa; "and if I have children, I will not maltreat them like you, nor force them to eat what they have an aversion to." "What do you mean by that?" said the King. "What is there wanting at my table?" "There is this wanting," she replied; "that one cannot have enough, and the little there is consists of coarse potherbs that nobody can eat." The King, who was not used to such candor, boiled with rage. "All his anger," says the Princess Wilhelmina, "fell on my brother and me. He first threw a plate at my brother's head, who ducked out of the way, then let fly another at me." After he had made the air blue with wrath, directed at Frederick, "we had to pass him in going out," and "he aimed a great blow at me with his crutch—which, if I had not jerked away from it, would have ended me. He chased me for a while in his wheel-chair, but the people drawing it gave me time to escape into the Queen's chamber."

One always imagines this charming young Princess in the act of dodging some sort of blow from Friedrich Wilhelm, who was nicknamed "Stumpy," privately, by his dutiful son and daughter. The habit of hating his son became an insanity; to kick him and pull his hair, break his flute, and take away his books and his brocaded dressing-gown—that was ordinary usage; it came to the point where he nearly strangled him, and later he condemned him to death for trying to run away to his uncle, George II., in England. When this sentence had been changed to a term of imprisonment, the poor young Prince had a much better time of it; his gaolers were kinder than his father.

By the time he emerged from this captivity he had gained much wisdom—the cold wisdom of selfishness and dissimulation. In after years the father and son became profoundly attached to each other, but Frederick was always obliged to humor and cajole his pig-headed sire, to lie more or less, and generally adopt an insincere tone, in order to avert wrath and suspicion—a very hateful necessity to a natural truth-teller, for Frederick was by nature a great lover of facts. Although his training as a politician and a soldier included a thorough education in guile, the tutors of his childhood were simple, honest people, who gave him a good, truthful start in life.

Friedrich Wilhelm, now that his heir was twenty-one years old, thought it high time to put an end to various vague matrimonial projects and get a wife for him straightway. Frederick, having found that obedience was, on the whole, better than captivity, was submissive and silent—to his father; but his letters to his friends and his sister shrieked with protestations against a marriage in which his tastes and feelings were not so much as thought of. Above all things he wished to be allowed to travel and choose for himself, and he had a morbid horror of a dull and awkward woman. It did not much matter, he thought, what else his wife was if she were clever conversationally, with grace and charm and fine manners. Beauty was desirable, but he could get along without it, if only he could feel proud of his consort's wit and breeding. The bride of his father's choosing was the Princess Elizabeth of Brunswick-Bevern—a bashful and gawky young person, with as little distinction as a dairy-maid. But he subdued his rage and married her, and, indeed, seems always to have treated her with kindly deference, although he made no pretence of affection.

Still carrying out his father's wishes, he served in a brief campaign, and afterwards regularly devoted a portion of his time to military and political business. Friedrich Wilhelm was now pleased with his son to the extent of buying for him a delightful residence—Reinsberg—and giving him a tolerable income, and Frederick revelled in his new freedom by building conservatories, laying out pleasure-gardens, playing his flute to his heart's content, writing poor French verses, and solacing himself for the "coarse potherbs" of his childhood by exquisite dinners. They had the best musicians for their concerts at Reinsberg—the Crown Prince and his friends, with the Crown Princess and her ladies. It was here, in 1736, that Frederick began—by letter—his famous friendship with Voltaire, that survived so many phases of illusion and disillusion.

It must be said of Frederick's friends—who were mostly French—that they were men of highly trained intelligence, but they were not acute enough to know what sort of king their Prince would make.

When his father passed away, Frederick felt as sincere a grief as if there had never been anything but love between them; always afterwards he spoke of him with reverence, and he learned to place a high value on the stern discipline of his early life—which is still to some extent a model for the bringing up of young Hohenzollerns.

It was a handsome young King who came to the throne in 1740. His face was round, his nose a keen aquiline, his mouth small and delicately curved, and all was dominated by those wonderful blue-gray eyes, that, as Mirabeau said, "at the bidding of his heroic soul fascinated you with seduction or with terror." Even in youth the lines of the face showed a sardonic humor. One can well imagine his replying to the optimistic Sulzer, who thought severe punishments a mistake: "Ach, mein lieber Sulzer, you don't know this—race!" In the old-age portraits the face is sharp and hatchet-like, the mouth is shrunken to a mean line, but the great eyes still flash out, commanding and clear.

The reign began with peace and philanthropy: Frederick II. started out by disbanding the giant grenadiers, the absurd monstrosities that his father had begged and bought and kidnapped from everywhere; he started a "knitting-house" for a thousand old women; abolished torture in criminal trials; set up an Academy of Sciences; summoned Voltaire and Maupertuis; made Germany open its eyes at the speech, "In this country every man must get to Heaven in his own way"; and proclaimed a practical freedom of the press—all in his first week.

The fury of activity now took possession of Frederick which lasted all his life. He had the Hohenzollern passion for doing everything himself; the three "secretaries of state" were mere clerks, who spared him only the mechanical part of secretarial duties. His system of economy was rigid. While looking over financial matters one day he found that a certain convent absorbed a considerable fund from the forest-dues, which had been bequeathed by dead dukes "for masses to be said on their behalf." He went to the place and asked the monks, "What good does anybody get out of those masses?" "Your Majesty, the dukes are to be delivered out of Purgatory by them." "Purgatory? And they are not out yet, poor souls, after so many hundred years of praying?" The answer was, "Not yet." "When will they be out, and the thing settled?" There was no answer to this. "Send me a courier whenever they are out!" With this sneer the King left the convent.

Stern business went on all day, and in the evening, music, dancing, theatres, suppers, till all hours; but the King was up again at four in the summer—five in winter. In early youth Frederick had known a period of gross living, from which he suffered so severely that his reaction from it was fiercely austere. After his accession, a young man who had been associated with this "mud-bath," as Carlyle has named it, begged an audience. The King received him, but rebuked him with such withering speech that he straightway went home and killed himself.

Only five months of his reign had passed when the event occurred that put an end to the ideal monarch of Frederick's subjects. Charles VI., Emperor of Germany, was dead. For years he had worked to bind together his scattered and wobbling empire, and by his "Pragmatic Sanction" secure it to his daughter, Maria Theresa, contrary to the rule that only male heirs should succeed, and she was on the day of his death (October 20th) proclaimed empress.

If the young Maria Theresa had been married to the young

Prince Frederick of Prussia, as their reigning parents had at
one time decided, European history would undoubtedly have
been different, though historians may be mistaken in thinking
that much trouble would have been saved the world. In view
of the fact that both these young people were extravagantly
well endowed with the royal gifts of energy and decision,
one must be permitted to wonder whether Frederick, as the
spouse of the admirable Maria Theresa, would have ever become known as "the Great." But at all events it would have
prevented him from rushing in on her domains and seizing
Silesia as soon as she was left with no one but her husband—
a man of the kindly inert sort—to protect her; and we
should have lost the good historical scene of Maria Theresa
appearing before her Hungarian Diet, with the crown on her
beautiful head, thrilling every heart as she lifted her plump
baby, Francis Joseph, and with tears streaming down her face
implored its help against the Prussian robber.

We can still hear the thunderous roar of the loyal reply,
"We will die for our Sovereign, Maria Theresa!"

Nevertheless, by December the Prussian robber was in Silesia with thirty thousand men, engaged in finding out that
he was really made to be a warrior. By May he held every
fortified place in the province; by June Maria Theresa was
forced to cede it to him—since which time it has always been
a loyal part of Prussia. "How glorious is my King, the youngest
of the kings and the grandest!" chanted Voltaire in a letter to
Frederick—who, one is pleased to know, found the praise
rather suffocating.

The genius of Frederick was next put to a considerable
test in the way of match-making—a delicate art, particularly
when practised for the sake of providing the half-barbarous
Empire of Russia with mated rulers.

The Czarina Elizabeth—Great Peter's daughter—wished the
King to find a German bride for her nephew-heir, who was
afterwards Peter III. A true Hohenzollern, Frederick felt
himself quite equal to this task—as to any other. From a
bevy of young princesses he selected the daughter of the
poverty-stricken Prince of Anhalt-Zerbst, because of the un-
mistakable cleverness the girl had shown, though not fifteen.

She was handsome as well, and Elizabeth re-named her "Catharine," changed her religion, and the marriage came off in 1745. Frederick had displayed great acumen, but it would puzzle a fiend to contrive a more diabolical union than that of Peter and Catherine!

Meanwhile, Maria Theresa had been preparing to fight for Silesia again. Without waiting for her, Frederick pounced upon Prague and captured it. After her armies in Silesia and Saxony had been put to flight by her adversary at Hohenfriedberg and Sorr and Hennersdorf and Kesselsdorf, the Empress yielded. On Christmas Day, 1745, when the treaty was signed that gave Silesia again to Prussia—it was known as the Peace of Dresden—Berlin went wild, and for the first time shouts were heard among the revellers, "Vivat Friedrich *der Grosse!*" The Austrians might call him "that ferocious, false, ambitious King of Prussia," but as a matter of fact he was not more false nor ferocious than the other rulers, only infinitely more able. Frederick had made for himself a great name and raised his little kingdom—of only two-and-a-half millions of people—to a noble standing among nations. The eyes of the world were fixed upon the hero to see what he would do next. What he did was to swear that he "would not fight with a cat, again," and to build himself a charming country home—his palaces, and even Reinsberg, were too large. In May, 1747, he had his housewarming at little Sans Souci, where for the next forty years most of his time was spent. There were twenty boxes of German flutes in the King's cabinet at Sans Souci, and infinite boxes of Spanish snuff; and there were three arm-chairs for three favorite dogs, with low stools to make an easy step for them. There was another favorite at Sans Souci who was said to look like an ape, although he was mostly called the "skinny Apollo." How one would like to have seen the King walking the terraces, with "white shoes and stockings and red breeches, with gown and waistcoat of blue linen flowered and lined with yellow"! while men with powdered wigs and highly colored clothes, and women whose heads bore high towers of hair unpleasantly stuffed and decorated with inconsequent dabs of finery followed him, all talking epigrams and doing attitudes—polite people had to hold themselves in curves in the eighteenth century.

These were good years for Prussia: her law-courts were reformed; her commerce flourished, and so did agriculture; potatoes were introduced—they were at first considered poisonous; a huge amount of building was done, and the army was drilled constantly under Frederick's eyes. Each year saw it a better army; its chief must have known that he was preparing for the great struggle of his life, although he took as keen an interest in keeping up the high standard of his new opera-house in Berlin, both as to music and ballet, as he did in the skilfullest manœuvres of his troops.

Maria Theresa had never for a moment given up Silesia in her heart. She was a woman of austere virtues, but these did not stand in the way of schemes which she would have thought too despicable to be used against anyone but the King of Prussia. The Czarina of Russia had been made to hate him by a series of carefully devised plots—she looked on him as her arch-enemy—and within six months after the Peace of Dresden she had signed, with Maria Theresa, a treaty which actually proposed the partitioning of Frederick's kingdom, which was to be divided between Russia, Austria, and Poland, while he was to become a simple Margrave of Brandenburg!

To get the signature of Louis XV. involved harder work still for the virtuous Empress—but she did it. It was to ask it of the Pompadour—in various affectionate letters, beginning "My dear Cousin," or "Madame my dearest Sister." The Pompadour was also shown some stinging verses of Frederick's, with herself as subject, and she (representing France) became the firm ally of Maria Theresa.

Through an Austrian clerk's treachery Frederick became aware of this stupendous conspiracy against him—but not till 1755, when it was well matured. It seemed incredible that he could think of keeping these great countries from gobbling up his little State. He could not have done it, indeed, if it had not been for a certain Englishman. It was an Englishman who saved Frederick and Prussia—the "Great Commoner," Pitt, who, having on hand a French war of his own, raised a Hanoverian army to help himself and Frederick, and granted him a welcome subsidy of six hundred and seventy thousand pounds a year.

His ten years' drilling had given Frederick a fine army of one hundred and thirty thousand men. The infantry were said to excel all others in quickness of manœuvres and skilled shooting, while the cavalry was unsurpassed.

Frederick, without waiting for his foes to declare war and mass their mighty forces, began it by a stealthy, sudden move into Saxony, September, 1756. October 1st, at Lowositz, in Bohemia, he defeated von Browne, and, returning, captured the Saxon force of seventeen thousand and took them bodily—all but the officers—into his own army.

England was delighted with this masterly act of her ally. He was known there as "the Protestant hero," which was not quite true to facts; certainly Frederick protested against the old religion, but he was far from being on with the new one. His saying, "Everyone shall go to Heaven in the way he chooses," had been applauded in England, but they were not familiar with his reply when a squabble as to whether one or another set of hymn-books should be used was referred to him: "Bah! let them sing what tomfoolery they like," said the "Protestant hero." Had France and Austria, however, succeeded in obliterating Prussia, it is likely that Protestantism too would have been done for in Germany.

Frederick having himself begun the Seven Years' War, the confederated German States, with Russia, France, and Sweden, formally bound themselves to "reduce the House of Brandenburg to its former state of mediocrity," France—very rich then—paying enormous subsidies all around. England—with Hanover—alone espoused Prussia's cause. During 1757 four hundred and thirty-seven thousand men were put in the field against Frederick. Only his catlike swiftness saved him from being overwhelmed again and again. In April he made another rush—like an avalanche—on Bohemia, and won another great victory at Prague, but he was terribly beaten by General Daun in June at Kolin. Still, he kept up courage, and played the flute and wrote innumerable French verses of the usual poor quality in odd moments. In November, at Rossbach, he met an army of French and Imperialists over twice as large as his own, and by a swift, unexpected movement broke them, so that they were scattered all over the country. Every German felt proud of this French defeat, whether he were Prussian or not. It was the first time the invincible French had ever been beaten by a wholly German army, with a leader of German blood. The brilliant victory of Leuthen followed Rossbach.

But although the world was ringing with Frederick's name, and he was acknowledged to be one of the greatest generals of history, the resources of his powerful enemies were too many for him. At last it seemed that a ruinous cloud of disaster was closing around him and darkening the memory of his glorious successes.

The defeat of Kunersdorf in 1759 would have completely wiped out his army if the over-cautious Austrian General Daun had followed up his victory. "Is there no cursed bullet that can reach me!" the Prussian monarch was heard to murmur in a stupor of despair after the battle. He carried poison about him, after this, to use when affairs became too bad. A severe blow followed Kunersdorf—George II. died, October, 1760; George III. put an end to Pitt's Ministry—and this was the end of England's support.

The winter of 1761–62 saw Frederick at his lowest ebb. England's money had stopped; his own country, plundered, devastated in every direction, afforded no sufficient revenue. Fully half of the Prussian dominions were occupied by the enemy; men, horses, supplies, and transport could hardly be procured. The Prussian army was reduced to sixty thousand men, and its ranks were made up largely of vagabonds and deserters—the old, splendidly disciplined troops having been practically obliterated.

He played no more on his flute—poor Frederick! At Leipzig an old friend sighed to him, "Ach! how lean your Majesty has grown!" "Lean, ja wohl," he replied; "and what wonder, with three women (Pompadour, Maria Theresa, and Czarina Elizabeth) hanging to my throat all this while!"

The Allies felt that it was only a matter of a short time before they should see their great enemy humbled to the position of Elector of Brandenburg. From this abasement Frederick was suddenly saved in January, 1762. Life held another chance for him. The implacable old Czarina was dead; her heir, Peter III., was not merely the friend, but the enthusiastic adorer of Frederick of Prussia. Although thirty-four years old and the husband of Catherine (the young lady Frederick had taken such pains to select for him so many years ago), Peter had been kept out of public affairs as if he were a child. Neither he nor Catherine was allowed to leave the Palace without permission of the Czarina; they were surrounded with spies, and kept in a gaudy and dirty semi-imprisonment—the traditional style for heirs to the Russian throne. Under this system they became masters of deceit. Catherine, in her cleverly unpleasant "Memoirs," tells how they managed to escape and visit people without being found out; how she, when ill and in bed, had a joyous company with her, who huddled behind a screen when prying ladies-in-waiting entered. But the most painful part is the account of Peter, who seems to have had more versatility in hateful ways than anyone outside of Bedlam. Crazily vivacious over foolish games, brutal when drunk, and silly when sober, one wonders how for so many years Catherine endured him.

There was a saving grace, though, in him: he worshipped the King of Prussia.

Frederick adroitly rose to the occasion: releasing all his Russian prisoners, he sent them, well clad and provisioned, back to their country. February 23d the Czar responded by a public declaration of peace with Prussia and a renunciation of all conquests made during the war. His General, Czernichef, was ordered to put himself and his twenty thousand men at the disposal of the Prussian hero, and on May 5th a treaty of alliance between Prussia and Russia was announced—to the horror and disgust of France and Austria. They had relied on Czernichef, but Czernichef himself was a sincere admirer of his new Commander-in-Chief and delighted in the change. The Russian soldiers all shared this feeling: they called Frederick "Son of the lightning."

The French were being held by the Hanoverian army; Sweden had retired from the war; with Russia on his side,

Frederick felt that he might hold out against Austria till peace was declared by the Powers—peace with no provision made for the partition of his kingdom.

In planning his next campaign—the last of the war—it was evident to Frederick that nothing could be done without recapturing the fortress of Schweidnitz, recently captured by Loudon, the Austrian General. The Austrians held all Silesia, and they must be put out of it, but with Schweidnitz in their hands this was impossible.

Fortunately for Frederick, Daun was appointed commander-in-chief of the Austrians, the General who had been execrated throughout the empire for his failure to follow up Frederick after Kunersdorf. In mid-May Daun took command of the forces in Silesia, and with a force of seventy thousand men made haste to place himself in a strong position among rugged hills to guard Schweidnitz. Schweidnitz, with a garrison of twelve thousand picked men and firm defences, it was impossible to attack while Daun was there. Frederick made repeated efforts to force Daun to give up his hold on the fortress, threatening his left wing, as his right wing seemed impregnably situated; but Daun, although forced to change his position from time to time, kept firmly massed about Schweidnitz. Frederick at last, then, resolved to attempt the impossible, and, his forces now augmented by Czernichef's to eighty-one thousand, determined on storming the Heights of Burkersdorf, where Daun's right wing was firmly intrenched. The last of Frederick's notable battles of the war—a conflict upon which the destinies of Prussia turned—it was planned and executed by him with a consummate brightness and cleverness that more than justifies the Hohenzollern worship of their great ancestor.

Burkersdorf Height, near the village of the same name, which was also occupied by Daun, lies parallel to Kunzendorf Heights, where Frederick's army lay. It is a high hill, very steep, and half-covered with rugged underbrush on the side next to Frederick's position, and Prince de Ligne and General O'Kelly—serving under Daun—had made it bristle with guns. Artillery was Daun's specialty; his guns were thick wherever the ground was not impracticably steep, and palisades—

"the pales strong as masts and room only for a musket-barrel between"—protected the soldiery; they were even "furnished with a lath or cross-strap all along for resting the gun-barrel on and taking aim." In fact, Burkersdorf Height was as good as a fortress. East of it was a small valley where strong intrenchments had been made and batteries placed. Farther east, two other heights had to be captured—they were also well defended—Ludwigsdorf and Leuthmannsdorf.

By the 17th of July Frederick had all his plans matured, and had made his very first move—that is, he had sent Generals Möllendorff and Wied on a march with their men to put the enemy on a false scent—when he received a call from Czernichef at his head-quarters. It was paralyzing news that Czernichef brought: Peter, the providential friend, had been dethroned by the partisans of his clever wife, Catherine.

After a reign of six months the young Czar had completely disgusted his subjects: he had planned ambitious schemes of reform, and at the same time had made despotic encroachments. After delighting the Church with important concessions, he proposed to virtually take away all its lands and houses. He overdid everything, like the madman he was. He offended his army by dressing up his guards in Prussian uniforms and teaching them the Prussian drill, while he wore constantly the dress of a Prussian colonel, and sang the praises of our hero until his people were sick of the name of "my friend, the King of Prussia."

Russian morals in the eighteenth century were like snakes in Ireland—there were none. In this respect Catherine was not superior to her husband, but in mental gifts she was an extraordinary young woman. Her tact, her poise, her intelligence, would have made a noble character in a decent atmosphere. Peter had recognized her powers and relied on them, and she had endured him all these years, thinking she would one day rule Russia as his Empress. But since his accession he had been completely under the dominion of the Countess Woronzow, a vicious creature, who meant to be Catherine's successor. And Catherine, when Peter threatened her and her son Paul with life-long imprisonment, had on her side finally begun a plot, which resulted in her appealing to the Guards, much as Maria Theresa had appealed to her Diet of Hungary. Everyone was tired of Peter, and no voice was raised against his deposition, whereupon Catherine assumed the sovereignty of Russia, to the great relief and satisfaction of all Russians. The brutal assassination of poor Peter by Catherine's friends —not by her orders—followed in a few days.

It was the intention of Catherine, on beginning her reign, to restore Elizabeth's policy in Russian matters and recommence hostilities against Frederick; but on looking over Peter's papers she found that Frederick had discouraged his wild schemes, and that he had begged him to rely on his wife and respect her counsels, and this produced a revulsion of feeling. She resolved that she would not fight him; nor, on the other hand, would she be his ally; the secret message that had come to Czernichef, and which he communicated to Frederick, was that Catherine reigned, and that he, her general, was ordered to return immediately to St. Petersburg.

One can only guess at Frederick's emotions at this news. Life must have seemed a lurid melodrama, presenting one hideous act after another. "This is not living," he said, "this is being killed a thousand times a day!" On the eve of the attack on Burkersdorf his ally had been taken away from him; his own forces were now weaker than those of Daun, and he did not see his way to a victory.

But the genius of Frederick could not allow him to give in to the destinies. His resourcefulness came to his rescue. He simply begged Czernichef to stay with him for three days. Three days must elapse before his official commands came. Frederick, with all the potency of his personal fascination, implored the Russian during that time to keep the matter secret, and, without one hostile act against the enemy, to *seem* to act with him as though their relations were unchanged. Czernichef consented; it was one of the most devoted acts that was ever done by a man for pure friendship; he well knew, and so did Frederick, that he might lose his head or rot in a dungeon for it, but—his own heroism was great enough to make the sacrifice.

The drama accordingly went on: on the evening of the 20th, with the forces of Möllendorff and Wied, who had puzzled the enemy and returned, with Ziethen and Czernichef—this last, of course, only for show—Frederick silently marched into Burkersdorf village and took by storm the old Burkersdorf Castle—an affair of a few hours—while Daun's forces fled in all directions from the village. Then, through the night, trenches were dug and batteries built—forty guns well placed. At sunrise the whole Prussian army could be seen to be in motion by their opponents.

At four o'clock Frederick's famous cannonade began, concentrated upon the principal Height of Burkersdorf. General O'Kelly's men were too high to be reached by the cannon, but it was Frederick's object to keep a furious, confusing noise going on, to help draw attention from Wied and Möllendorff, who were doing the real fighting of the day. Möllendorff was to storm O'Kelly's height, and Wied the Ludwigsdorf Height beyond, but Frederick had arranged a spectacular drama by which the foe was to be deceived as to these intentions.

It was not for nothing that Frederick had personally overlooked his theatres and operas all these years. His knowledge of scenic displays, and their effect on the minds of an audience, stood him in good stead this day. The Prussian guns continued a deafening roar, hour after hour, with many blank charges, and the bewildered commanders of the allied Austrians watched from their elevation the small man on his white horse giving orders right and left. He wore a three-cornered hat with a white feather, a plain blue uniform with red facings, a yellow waistcoat liberally powdered with Spanish snuff, black-velvet breeches, and high, soft boots. They were shabby, old clothes, but the figure had a majesty that everyone recognized. The difficulty among the officers on the heights was to find out what were the orders Frederick was giving so freely. His generals, who were much smarter in their dress than he, dashed off in all directions, and marched their troops briskly about, keeping the whole line of the enemy on the alert.

Daun, ignorant of the St. Petersburg revolution and its consequences, and seeing the Russian masses drawn up threateningly opposite his left wing, which he commanded, dared not concentrate his whole force on Burkersdorf, but from time to time sent bodies of men to support de Ligne and O'Kelly. As no one could tell what spot to support, no line of action could be agreed upon. The Commandant of Schweidnitz, General Guasco, with twelve thousand men, came out of the fortress to attack the Prussian rear, but, fortunately for Frederick, one of his astute superiors sent him back.

Meantime, while this uproar and these puzzling operations were going on, Wied had taken his men out of view of the Austrians by circuitous paths to the gradual eastern ascent of Ludwigsdorf and moved up in three detachments. Battery after battery he dislodged, but when he came in sight of the huge mass of guns and men at the top, it seemed wild foolishness to try to get there. It could never have been done by a straight, headlong rush; they crawled along through thickets and little valleys, creeping spirally higher and higher, dodging the fire from above, till at last a movement through a dense wood brought them to the rear and flank of the foe. Then, with a magnificent charge of bayonets, they sent them flying, and passed on to the easy rout of the troops on Leuthmannsdorf.

On Burkersdorf Height O'Kelly's men were looking for an attack on the steepest side, where they were best fortified, but Möllendorff's troops had gone by a roundabout route to the western slope, where, after some searching, they found a sheep-track winding up the hill-side. Following this, they came to a slope so steep that horses could not draw the guns. And then the men pushed and pulled them along and up, until the Austrians spied them from above, and the cannon-balls came crashing down into them. But under this fire they planted their guns, and did such gallant work with them that they were soon at the top, dashing down the defences. It was a tough struggle; the defences were strong—there were line after line of them—and the Austrians had no idea of yielding. They fought like tigers until the fire from the muskets set the dry branches of their abatis ablaze, and Möllendorff quickly closed in around them and forced them to surrender. Frederick's orchestra still boomed on, and the show of officers on prancing steeds and parading troops kept re-enforcements from coming to assist the men on Burkersdorf.

It was noon when Möllendorff had achieved his task, and Daun ordered the army to fall back. But Frederick kept his cannon going, as if with a desperate intention, till five, to make matters appear more dangerous than they really were to Daun. He was successful; at nightfall Daun led his entire army away, silently and in order, and he never troubled Frederick again.

He left fourteen guns behind him and over one thousand prisoners, and quite two thousand deserted to Frederick in the next few days.

And Czernichef, who had stood by him so nobly? He was full of warmest admiration for Frederick's curious tactics and their success, and the King must have been eternally grateful to him. He marched for home early next morning—and he was neither beheaded nor imprisoned by Catherine when he got there; one is very glad to know that.

Frederick was now free to besiege Schweidnitz; its reconquest gave him back Silesia and left him to long years of peace at Sans Souci. It is fair to conclude that these were happy years, since his happiness lay in incessant work; it needed the most arduous toil to get his country into shape again, but Prussia deserved it.

"To have achieved a Frederick the Second for King over it was Prussia's great merit," says Carlyle.

THE TEXT: HISTORY AND ANALYSIS

THE TEXT: HISTORY AND ANALYSIS

WAR DISPATCHES

GREECE

No. 1. An Impression of the "Concert"

Crane's first report of the Greek-Turkish War was datelined 'On Board French Steamer *Guadiana*' but was almost certainly written after he had arrived in Athens. Of the observed newspaper versions, all printed between May 8 and May 10, 1897, four accounts are undated, one is noted only as April, but one is datelined April 22, another April 26, and a third May 3. It seems clear that these latter newspapers selected a date to suit their concept of what was reasonably current: the May 3 date, fortuitously, was that on which the piece had appeared in England in the *Westminster Gazette*. Even the earliest date, April 22, is far too late for composition on board the steamer, since there is no reason to distrust the dateline *Athens, April 17* prefixed to his unpublished dispatch, in manuscript, reprinted here as No. 2. It is probable that the common master copy from which the newspapers derive had a date in the dateline which was insufficiently current for most of them to observe. It is barely possible that the New York *Sun's* April 22 represents that date, although the case must remain quite uncertain. Indeed, Crane had plenty of time before the April 17 dispatch to write "An Impression of the 'Concert'." J. Cazemajou, *Stephen Crane, Ecrivain Journaliste* (Paris, 1969), page 128, establishes from French shipping records that the *Guadiana* left Marseilles with forty-two passengers at 5 P.M. on April 3 under the command of Captain Merlin. She reached Suda Bay, her first port of call, on April 7 at 12 o'clock noon and pulled out at 3 P.M. after a three-hour stay. Crane could not have boarded the ship, instead, at Constantinople on her return journey, and thus called at Suda Bay on or about April 15. Professor Cazemajou has privately informed the present editor that his further researches establish that the ship left Batum at 5:30 P.M. on April 15 but followed a different itinerary from her outward voyage and positively did not call at Crete before reaching Marseilles on May 3. It follows that Crane wrote the report at his leisure in Athens, perhaps before April 17, perhaps as late as April 22. If the April 22 date is at all accurate, its lateness might be explained if one wishes to conjecture that the letter series was arranged after he had arrived in Greece, not before. Something is to be said for this speculation (see footnote 1).

The publication of this dispatch on May 3, 1897, in the English journal the *Westminster Gazette* as the first of a series entitled "With Greek and Turk" suggests that Crane had the assignment for a series of 'letters' or commentary essays that he was expected to write for the McClure syndicate on a regular basis.[1] It would appear that these were to be different in nature from the dispatches he had agreed to cable Hearst's *New York Journal*; and the hypothesis is reasonable that McClure negotiated for these as an independent contract and then sold them in England to the *Gazette* while distributing them in the United States. That the *Gazette* published each letter earlier than the newspapers would indicate that Crane mailed the pieces in manuscript to Robert McClure in London. The textual evidence of the present letter, like that of the rest, suggests, indeed, that Robert McClure had a typescript and carbon made in London from Crane's papers and that one copy went to the *Gazette* whereas the other was rushed to the New York office of the syndicate by ship. From this copy McClure's in New York then had a typesetting prepared from which proofs were struck for distribution to subscribing newspapers.

One oddity exists, however: only the first, second, and the last of the series printed by the *Gazette* as "With Greek and Turk" (that is, Nos. 1, 4, and 13) were generally syndicated by the McClure firm under its own copyright; the rest seem to have been sold to the *New York Journal*, which in turn sent them (copyrighted by Hearst) to its own string of subscribing newspapers, not all of which were interested. What happened can be subject only to speculation. We cannot know whether the *Journal* objected to the use of Crane's material in this double manner, and felt that it had contracted for his whole output; or whether the *Journal* paid a price for exclusive rights that was satisfactory to McClure; or both. Whatever the reason, Nos. 1 and 13 were distributed more widely than the others (No. 4 less so) and to a different group of newspapers, the *Sun* being the outlet in New York City for Nos. 1 and 13.

On the evidence of the present letter, two lines of text radiate from

---

[1] The *Westminster Gazette*, no. 1303, for April 28, 1897, page 1, announces that Crane will send a 'series of letters describing the Græco-Turkish war'; Crane is stated to have left Athens for the front over a week before and to be now with the Greek army. In the London *Daily Chronicle* for May 3, 1897, the *Gazette* advertised: 'With Greek and Turk. The First of a Series of Letters on the Græco-Turkish War, by Stephen Crane, Author of "The Red Badge of Courage," Will Appear in the Westminster Gazette To-day, May 3rd.'

a common original, which must have been the London-made type-script and its carbon or carbons.[2] On the one side stands the *Gazette* and on the other the American newspaper texts which—whatever their own differences caused by unique error—concur in collective substantive variation against the *Gazette* save for the few examples of a typesetting error made in the common proof-copy which might be corrected by certain newspapers to agree fortuitously with the right *Gazette* form.[3]

Nine examples of No. 1 have been observed. The earliest appearance was that in the *Westminster Gazette* (WG), IX (May 3, 1897), 1–2, entitled 'WITH GREEK AND TURK. | BY STEPHEN CRANE, AUTHOR OF "THE RED BADGE OF COURAGE." | I.—AN IMPRESSION OF THE "CONCERT." ' This had the notice *Copyright U.S.A., 1897*, but no date of filing.

The eight American newspapers are as follows:

(N[1]): New York *Sun*, Sunday, May 9, 1897, page 6, signed, headlined 'HALF A DAY IN SUDA BAY. ‖ *A MERCHANT SHIP'S VISIT TO THE* |

[2] Hypothetically, Robert McClure could have had a typescript made for the *Gazette* and sent the manuscript to the United States, or vice versa. The evidence of verbal or of accidentals variation would not ordinarily indicate which of the three available possibilities was the correct one. However, a straw in the wind that the McClure master proof was set from an English typescript may perhaps be discerned in the sporadic manner in which some newspapers agree with the English forms *afterwards* and *towards*, apparently under the influence of copy. It is also significant, very likely, that the *Gazette* (WG) and most of the newspapers agree in their paragraphing except for the unique *Sun* differences.

[3] Examples of absolute disagreement between the two lines are found in WG *would* but N *could* (6.17), *peaceably* versus *peacefully* (7.19), omission versus *cut* (9.20), and so on, with the censorship of *damned* in the newspapers between 9.25–27 being of especial interest. At 7.18 the proof (and perhaps the typescript) evidently had the error *Russian*, although one newspaper agreed with WG in the correct plural. An interesting error appears at 7.36 in which only three newspapers had the initiative to correct the proof error *complexion* to the WG reading *complexity*. On the evidence of 8.5 and 12.23 the proof had the consistent error (perhaps drawn from the manuscript through the typescript) of *Kaiserine* for *Kaiserin*. The plural *gigs'* instead of the singular (9.31) was also a proof mistake. Some difficulty seems to have obtained in the proof about the steamer's name. The Louisville *Courier-Journal* spelled it *Guardiana* in the heading and also the text at 6.5 but thereafter *Guadiana*. Strangely, the Portland *Oregonian* after starting with *Guadiana* ended at 11.22 and 12.20 with *Guardiana*. One can only conclude that the proof (and possibly the typescript and manuscript) here and there read, incorrectly, *Guardiana* (just possibly a Cora spelling) but most of the journals somehow had been sufficiently acquainted with the name of the Spanish river to spell the ship's name correctly. Nevertheless, the case is an odd one. The proof probably had some form of suggested headlines, for a few words and phrases like *Impression, Concert, Powers, Off Crete*, and *The Peace of Europe* appear in several newspapers, and it is clear that McClure advertised Crane as the author of *The Red Badge of Courage*.

EUROPEAN FLEET. ‖ A Hedge of Battle Ships About Which Crawled | Bottle-Green Scorpion-like Torpedo Boats—|Activity on the Freight and Mail Car-|rying Merchantman—French Seamanship. | *Copyright, 1897, by the S. S. McClure Company.'* Datelined April 22.

(N²): *Detroit Free Press,* May 9, page 17, signed, headlined 'THE FROWNING FLEET OF THE POWERS IN SUDA BAY. ‖ THE SCENE DESCRIBED BY | THE AUTHOR OF "THE RED | BADGE OF COURAGE." ‖ Stephen Crane's Realistic Impres-|sions and Crisp Comments. ‖'. A four-column illustration has the legend 'WARSHIPS OF THE POWERS IN SUDA BAY, CRETE.' Undated.

(N³): *Pittsburgh Leader,* May 9, page 19, headlined 'EUROPE'S MAILED ARM. ‖ A VIEW OF THE FLEET OF THE | POWERS OFF CRETE. ‖ Author of "The Red Badge of Cour-|age" at the Seat of War—Graphic | Picture of the Deadly Squadron | That Is "Concerting" the "Peace of | Europe"—English, Russians, French, | Germans, Italians, Turks, Austrians. ‖ BY STEPHEN CRANE. | (Copyrighted, 1897, S. S. McClure Co.)'. Undated.

(N⁴): Portland *Oregonian,* May 8, page 6, signed, headlined 'AT THE SEAT OF WAR ‖ A VIEW OF THE FLEET OF THE | POWERS OFF CRETE. ‖ A Graphic Picture of the Deadly | Squadron That Is "Concert-ing" | the "Peace of Europe." ‖ (Copyright, 1897, by S. S. McClure Co.)'. Datelined May 3.

(N⁵): Louisville *Courier-Journal,* May 9, page 12, signed, headlined 'STEPHEN CRANE'S PEN PICTURE OF THE POWERS' FLEET OFF CRETE. | [wavy rule] | (Special Correspondence of the Courier-Journal.) | [to the left] The Novelist Describes the Situa-| for the Benefit of Courier-|Journal Readers. ‖ [to the right] The Red Badge of Courage Au-|thor As War Corres-|pondent. ‖'. Datelined April 26.

(N⁶): *Omaha Daily Bee,* May 10, page 2, reprinted in the same type-setting by the *Omaha Weekly Bee,* May 12, page 2, signed, headlined 'FLEET OF THE GREAT POWERS ‖ PRESERVING 'THE PEACE OF EUROPE' ‖ Stephen Crane's Impressions of the | Ironclad Concert Up-holding | Moslem Rule in the Levant. ‖ (Copyright 1897, S. S. McClure Co.)'. The dateline reads April.

(N⁷): *Boston Globe,* May 9, page 33, signed, headlined 'STEPHEN CRANE AT CRETE. ‖ Great Steel Animals Menacing a Sunburned Island | Seemed a Joke—How the Mighty Fleet of the | European Concert and the Turk Appeared to | an American—The Bloodthirsty Tot of a | Middy and the Differing Smiles of the French | and of the Russians. ‖'. Undated.

(N⁸): *St. Paul Pioneer Press,* May 9, page 20, headlined 'THE FLEETS | NOW OFF CRETE | [short decorative rule] | VIEW OF THE SEA FORCES OF THE | TURK'S ALLIES. | [short decorative rule] | The Author of "The Red Badge of | Courage" Visits the Seat of War | and Nar-rates His Observations in | Characteristic Fashion—Fine Pic-|ture of the Deadly Squadrons | That are "Concerting" the "Peace | of Europe" to the End That the | Spirit of Liberty May Be Crushed. ‖ By Stephen Crane. ‖ (Copyright, 1897, S. S. McClure Co.)'. Undated.

Although it seems clear that WG was set in England from the typescript or carbon, and $N in the United States from the twin copy, some odd evidence develops, especially in N[1], the New York *Sun* text. The other newspapers reprinted the basic-proof text with only an occasional cut to fit the material into the available space, N[7] having the deepest cuts of this variety. But the *Sun* rewrite desk, in addition to substantial cuts, made a number of material alterations that quite change the substantive authority of the text. That the *Sun* derives from copy intimately related to that behind the other newspapers is demonstrated by its adherence to the N readings against those substantive variants found in WG. Indeed, WG and N[1] never agree against the N majority in any true substantive reading without the concurrence of at least one other newspaper. On the other hand, the accidentals of N[1] are often in agreement with those of WG against the other N versions in whole or in part.

No hypothesis seems constructable that can explain all the facts in terms of a difference in transmission. N[1] could not have been set from the exact WG copy (that is, either WG proof or the typescript itself behind WG) because of its adherence to the key variants of the N-line as against WG, particularly to the N-line censorship involving the uses of *damned* and the accompanying omission of *bold* at 9.25–27. Hence if some special relationship does exist between WG and N[1], one would need to conjecture that N[1] was set, instead, from the same typescript (or carbon) that was used in New York as the copy for the McClure master proof. Such a typescript would be the mate of the WG copy but—and this is essential—already edited by McClure to remove the objectionable language in 9.25–27.

At first sight this theory would solve the problem, but a string of difficulties follow. That the *Sun* would request the printer's copy and not the usual proof from McClure is fantastic; hence we should need to take it that, although McClure had a printing shop of its own or regular arrangements with a printer, in this case—as with No. 13, or with the sketch "New York's Bicycle Speedway," printed by the *Sun* on July 5, 1896—it hired the *Sun* to set up the copy from which the proofs for mailing would be struck. It would then be necessary to speculate that the *Sun* rewrite man found it easier to rework the typescript than the tightly set proof from his own composition room. This theory would work for the present article, but it stretches plausibility with No. 13 where the *Sun* rewriting consists of only a few verbal substitutions, and it loses all credibility with "New York's Bicycle Speedway," the McClure proof of which is preserved. Secondly, such a theory would require each of the six substantive variants in which WG and $N disagree outside of the 9.25–27 censorship area to be a WG departure from copy, a by no means impossible happening, however. It would then follow that in setting up the type-script the printer of the master proof did not depart from his copy in a single substantive, no matter how indifferent. This is theoretically possible but far from probable as a proposition, and it would need to apply to No. 13 as well, where the evidence is ambiguous.[4]

The evidence of substantive variation, then, does not encourage any theory of different copy for N^1 than for N^{2-8}, and it is to the accidentals that one must turn in search of a different kind of evidence. The first difficulty in assigning the frequently close relationship of the WG and N^1 punctuation to the transmission instead of to similar styling is that it requires the McClure typescript made in London to have altered the light punctuation of Crane's manuscript to a heavy, professional printing-house style, for N^1 to have followed this styling, but for the compositor of the McClure master proof systematically to have modified the rigor of the heavy punctuation back in the direction of Crane's own characteristics.[5] The question of the significance of this punctuation is not an easy one to answer. WG is certainly heavier on the whole than N^1 and may well have increased the number of commas over its copy. On the other hand, two newspapers, N^4 and N^7, had compositors who were themselves rather heavy punctuators and on some occasions seem to have deserted their copy (as indicated by general $N^{1-3,5-6,8}$ agreement) to add commas that fortuitously agree with similarly added WG commas. The question is then to be raised whether in view of this $N^{4,7}$ practice the N^{2-8} news-papers are actually so uniform against the N^1 punctuation system as to allow one to suppose that they all followed one copy whereas WG and N^1 followed another. Indeed, the major difficulty develops that,

---

[4] Certain WG errors may be observed, as certainly in the omission of *cut* (9.20), and probably the reading *could* for $N *would* (6.17). At 7.18 it is possible that the WG compositor or editor corrected a typescript singular *Russian* (as did N^5), and the same agent may have been responsible for *made* instead of $N *make* (9.38), which is very likely what Crane wrote in error. If one chooses to believe that WG *Then* (10.37) is an unauthoritative insertion and not an N proof omission, and (against the evidence) that N *peacefully* is correct and WG *peaceably* (7.19) is a WG change from copy, then the roll is complete and the N proof would have been substantively impeccable. In No. 13 two completely neutral variants—WG *the corner* for $N *a corner* (69.26) and *This* for $N *The* (71.24) would need to be assigned as WG errors, not mistakes in the proof typesetting; the WG capitals in 70.16, so tempting to assign to Crane, would be WG's invention. At 70.7 WG,N^1 *We* for the error *He* in N^{2-4} would need to be taken as a proof error, too faithfully followed by N^{2-4}, instead of a typist's error independently corrected by WG and N^1.

[5] The remark has no evidential value, but nevertheless it would be odd for the McClure New York office conjecturally to tinker with the punctuation throughout the copy while editing the substantives only in the censorship of one passage. Whether two compositors in the *Sun's* composing room would differ so in their treatment of the styling as between Nos. 1 and 13 is not demonstrable.

in fact, the accidentals of N^4, the Portland *Oregonian*, have almost as close a relationship to those of N^1 as do the accidentals of N^1 to WG. If these are also to be explained by some quirk in the textual transmission, and not as fortuitous hits, some larger hypothesis must be constructed that would take in this matter as well as the relationship of WG and N^1. Here probability breaks down.

Indeed, when one comes to examine the nature of the special agreements between N^1 and N^4, one sees that they are mostly in the punctuation and almost exclusively in the addition of commas when the majority of the newspapers wants them. Typical examples are the $N^{1,4}$ commas around the phrase *as small as . . . wall* (5.24–25) which are unique, the comma after *wide* (5.28) in which N^7 joins, the comma after *air* (7.5) in which N^6 joins, and the commas surrounding the phrase *like a Land of Despair* (6.1) in which both N^{6-7} join. That these concurrences are the result of similar styling, generally against the basic copy, may be indicated by the various times that N^1 and N^4 disagree, with or without support from other sources. Examples are the comma after *cape* (5.20) in WG,$N^{4,7}$ against no comma, the comma after *man* (6.13) in WG,N^1 but no comma elsewhere, the comma after *fixed* (6.15) in $N^{1,5,7}$ but none elsewhere, the comma after *it* (6.29) in WG,$N^{2-5,8}$ but none in $N^{1,6-7}$, or the comma after *fine* (6.30) in WG,N^{4-5} against no comma in $N^{1-3,6-8}$. In other accidentals $N^{4,8}$ agree uniquely with WG in *North* (6.14), but N^1 uniquely with WG in *Admiral* (9.16).

When the full collation is surveyed, the occasions in which WG, N^1, and N^4 agree with each other against the rest always represent heavy punctuation, but these special concurrences are matched by the number of times in which one or more newspapers (especially the heavy-punctuating N^7) join them in their styling, as in the added commas around *indeed* (9.6–7) in WG,$N^{1,4,7-8}$ or the added comma after *it* (9.40) in WG,$N^{1-2,4}$. The evidence suggests very strongly, therefore, that just as the appearance of a special relationship between N^4 and N^1 is due to chance, so the appearance of a special relationship between WG and N^1 has insufficient demonstrable evidence (including substantive coincidence) to warrant the complicated hypothesis that would account on transmissional grounds for what appears to be merely a mutual preference for relatively heavy punctuation alien to Crane's own habits. The manner in which N^1 and N^4 may agree with WG against each other seems to cancel out any special transmissional relationship, and the number of times that the heavy N^7 joins N^1 and WG in a threesome also serves to cast doubt on a special transmissional relationship between WG and N^1.

The evidence of the accidentals, thus, proves to be a standoff like those of the substantives, without the necessary demonstrable features separating N^1 from N^{2-8} and linking it with WG. Finally, the evidence of No. 13 may be applied. Like No. 1, this No. 13 was also printed by the *Sun* and distributed to the same group of other newspapers although a few that had accepted No. 1 declined No. 13. For any textual theory of special transmission in No. 1 to be credible, the same would need to apply to No. 13. The section of the textual analysis devoted to No. 13 discusses this matter and reaches the conclusion that despite a few possible special links between WG and the *Sun*, the whole weight of the evidence is unequivocally in favor of N^1 joining the other newspapers as set from the McClure master proof. This fact casts such serious doubt on the speculation that McClure's would have used the *Sun* instead of its own printer, as to destroy the very foundation for any textual hypothesis that requires this unusual procedure.

The present editor, therefore, rejects the possibility that N^1 could have been set from the edited typescript that had been used for the master proof, and adopts the normal working theory that all of the newspapers derive from the McClure proof, which was itself set up from common copy with that behind WG, although several times censored by McClure's.

Even so, the textual situation is not altogether simple. All of the substantives, and a great many—but by no means all—of the accidentals characteristics of the McClure master proof can be reconstructed from the various N printings. On the other hand, since WG radiates independently of this proof from the common typescript copy, it is of technically equal authority with this proof insofar as the proof can be reconstructed with confidence. Any single newspaper is at one farther remove than WG from the ultimate authority of the manuscript as filtered through its typescript form. Nevertheless, whenever the evidence suffices to reconstruct the master proof from the collective evidence of the newspapers,[6] this reconstruction

---

[6] An extreme case would be the lack of a comma after *phenomenon* (5.9) in $N or the concurrence in *could* (6.17). Scarcely less extreme would be the lack of a comma after *Camperdown* (9.18) in $N^{1-6,8}$ versus the N^7 comma, the lack of a comma after *bridge* (11.21) in N except for a comma in N^4, or the lack of a comma after *stern* (10.18) in N except for the comma in $N^{1,6}$. Acquaintance with the characteristics of the several authorities gives an editor reasonable confidence, for example, that the master proof had no comma after *impulses* (11.30), even though one appears in $N^{1,4,7}$. More speculative, perhaps, is the conjecture that $N^{2-3,8}$ would not have adopted a Crane characteristic and omitted the commas in the adjective series *great high sun-burned* (6.20–21) without the support of the master proof, so that the conventional commas of the rest stem from the usual compositorial normalization.

may be said to equal WG in its nearness to the basic typescript and thus to be of equal authority.

Yet some individual document must be selected as copy-text since the reconstructed proof is too incomplete in its details to qualify. With this requirement in view, the *Westminster Gazette* typesetting is chosen since as a unit it is one step closer to ultimate authority than any individual newspaper. (This technical authority cannot obscure, however, the number of times that WG appears to depart from Crane's known accidentals characteristics on occasions when the reconstruction of the master-proof readings offers accidentals that conform to Crane's habits.) On the other hand, WG and N are of equal theoretical authority for the substantives of this text since for substantives the master proof can be reconstructed with absolute accuracy. Crane, in Greece, could in no way have read proof on any version and so have inserted fresh authority after the dispatch of his manuscript; hence substantive variation between WG and N must represent correctness and error, not two degrees of correctness as would have been exemplified by the results of authorial revision. In all cases, then, where the typescript itself is not supposed to be in error, each verbal variant must be right in WG and wrong in N, or vice versa, and a choice between them can be made critically on this basis according to one's concept of Crane's style and one's conjectures about the editorial process behind the WG text and the N master proof. Semibibliographical evidence applies occasionally. That is, given the working hypothesis adopted for the textual transmission, no unique reading in any individual newspaper can possibly be accepted unless by pure chance it happens to correct what is taken to be an error in the typescript faithfully reproduced by the other authorities. Such an extreme case has not been identified in the present text; hence all unique readings have been automatically rejected within the eight observed newspapers that constitute the N-line of the text. However, a unique reading in WG is in a different category since, in a manner of speaking, its text is the equivalent of the sum of all the newspapers. Only a few cases occur of this divergence in verbals between the two radiating authorities, and these must be judged on their merits. The WG omission of *cut* at 9.20 seems to be a real printer's error; the singular *Russian* at 7.18 in $N (-N^5)$ is only a little less certainly an error in the master proof. The presence or absence of *Then* (10.37) is almost a tossup, but the WG reading for *peaceably-peacefully* (7.19) seems to be authorial, on the evidence of *The O'Ruddy* text (see the Textual Note). A few readings reveal themselves as errors in the master proof by the excellent guesses of several newspaper compositors to correct them. In this category come the genitive *gigs'* (9.31) in $N^{2-3,5}$ corrected to the singular *gig's* by $N^{1,4,6-8}$, or *complexion* (7.36) in $N^{2-3,5-6}$ corrected to the WG reading *complexity* by $N^{1,4,7}$. In these cases the WG readings confirm the sporadic unauthoritative but good N guesses (unless WG guessed too). An interesting case that must go back to a difficulty in the basic typescript or manuscript is the syntax that affects the meaning in $N^{2,4,6-7}$ *tableau, the* (6.36) which WG and $N^{1,3,5,8}$ render as *tableau. The* (see the Textual Note).

Although the closeness in transmission of WG to the common typescript copy weighed heavily in the practical requirement that it be selected as the copy-text, whenever enough newspapers agree against WG in an accidentals difference to suggest that the reading of the proof can be recovered, the situation changes in that such separate details of the reconstructed proof can be regarded as of equal authority with the corresponding separate details of WG. In these cases of equal transmissional authority the editor has chosen to depart from the WG copy-text by emendation from N when the variant in N is in a form recognizably more characteristic of the accidentals of Crane's manuscripts, the assumption here being that the proof behind N had followed more faithfully than WG the manuscript-derived reading of the typescript. In this manner the resulting eclectic text by conflation of the two lines of equal authority attempts to recover as nearly as may be the characteristics of the lost typescript and its carbon. Bibliographical reconstruction can go no farther back than this lost typescript, although speculation may suggest that such errors as *Guardiana* (5.1; 6.5; 11.22; 12.20) and *Kaiserine* (8.5; 12.23) may have slipped into the typescript (and thence into the master proof) from the lost manuscript. However, in contrast to readings from the typescript, no reading of the manuscript can be reconstructed bibliographically.

This report was reprinted by Fryckstedt from N^1 and by Stallman from N^5.

No. 2. THE SPIRIT OF THE GREEK PEOPLE

Written in black ink on one side of two leaves of cheap ruled wove paper 315 × 210 mm., the rules 9 mm. apart, this unpublished holograph dispatch is datelined Athens, April 17, and may well represent Crane's first attempt at reporting the Greek-Turkish War. The manuscript is preserved in the Special Collections of the Columbia University Libraries, where it is labeled, perhaps incorrectly, as unfinished. Alterations are made in the same ink, and are recorded in the Historical Collations section of the apparatus. The manuscript is untitled: the present heading was assigned by Stallman, who first reprinted the piece. On the verso of fol. 2, in a strange hand, is written 'Athens' and below it what may be either a large question mark or a figure '2'.

No. 3. STEPHEN CRANE SAYS GREEKS CANNOT BE CURBED

Datelined Athens, April 20, this piece represents the first of the known cables that Crane sent to Hearst's *New York Journal* as distinct from the 'letters' or commentary pieces like No. 1 that he wrote on the war for McClure's syndicate. The *Journal* customarily rewired these cabled reports to the *Chicago Tribune*, to its sister Hearst paper the San Francisco *Examiner*, and occasionally to other newspapers. The textual problem arises whether, ordinarily, Crane's own cable was retransmitted to these other journals as received, or whether the *Journal* first edited it before relaying the story. The present report has only one substantive in which two recipients agree against the *Journal*, and a couple of accidentals. Thus the evidence here is insufficient to decide the case. However, the example of some other reports where evidence is available suggests that ordinarily a copy of the rewrite (although not necessarily in the same state of preparation as that found in the final *Journal* text) would be telegraphed at the earliest opportunity without waiting for the preparation of *Journal* proof. Textual authority is involved in this matter, of course, for substantive and even accidentals variants in which the *Tribune* and *Examiner* or the Philadelphia *Press* agree against the *Journal* could result (a) from errors in the *Journal* typesetting or possibly from the subsequent proofreading or cutting at the *Journal* of the rewrite copy that had been put into type; (b) from an inadvertent and repeated error in the transmission of the original rewrite or its carbon; or (c) in theory (and several times in practice) from wiring of the rewrite copy in early stages of preparation. In the first and third instances authority would reside in the readings in which the subsidiary newspapers agreed, since they would be closer to the authority of the cable as represented by the original rewrite copy than as represented by the copydesk further revision or by compositorial error. In the second, if it could be demonstrated as an actual fact,[7] the *Journal* would be the most authoritative document. The total evidence of these cables and their treatment indicates, as remarked above, that one copy, usually, of the rewrite was wired to different papers in succession and hence that the agreement of other newspapers against the *Journal* will usually signify superior authority when fortuitous mutual sophistication of a real or apparent error is not in question. For example, in the present article the printing in the *Tribune* and *Press* of the awkward word *be* (15.26) omitted in the *Journal* and *Examiner* suggests independent editing of the original rewrite that had contained the word more than it suggests independent insertion. (No evidence is present for the transmission of this dispatch in different stages of preparation.) And since very strong evidence appears in these reports that the accidentals of punctuation and of paragraphing were telegraphed from the rewrite, as well as the substantives, the omission in the three outside newspapers of the comma before *anyhow* (15.25) present in the *Journal* seems to represent the reading of the rewrite copy (which happens to coincide with Crane's own usual practice) altered by the *Journal* compositor. In the cabled dispatches, then, the closest an editor can come to the ultimate authority of the details of Crane's lost manuscript, filtered through the cable transmission, is the reconstruction of the rewrite editor's copy, preferably in its earliest stage.

The following examples of No. 3 have been observed:

(N[1]): *New York Journal*, April 30, 1897, page 1, datelined Athens, April 29, headlined 'STEPHEN CRANE SAYS | GREEKS CANNOT BE CURBED. ‖ Describes for the Journal the Warlike Spirit That | Makes Athenian Shopkeepers Drop Their | Yardsticks for Guns. ‖ STEPHEN CRANE. | [oval portrait drawing] | (Copyright, 1897, by W. R. Hearst.) | By Stephen Crane.'

(N[2]): *Chicago Tribune*, April 30, page 2, headlined 'STEPHEN CRANE ARRIVES IN ATHENS. ‖ Novelist Says the Greeks Fully Realize | the Odds Which Are Arrayed | Against Them. ‖ [SPECIAL CABLE BY STEPHEN CRANE.]'. The note *Copyright, 1897* is added to the dateline.

(N[3]): San Francisco *Examiner*, April 30, page 1, headlined 'STEPHEN CRANE, "EXAMINER-|JOURNAL" CORRESPONDENT. | The distinguished author has been sent to the scene of the Turko-|Grecian war by "The Examiner-Journal," and to-day his first dispatch | is presented. | [portrait drawing] | "To-Day Greece is Armed | To Fight for Her Life." ‖ BY STEPHEN CRANE. | Special Cable to "The Examiner," Copyright, 1897, by W. R. Hearst'.

[7] Since each telegraphed transmission to subsidiary newspapers would be independent, error in transmission would normally create only a unique variant in one newspaper. The identification of a repeated error in transmission, not in copy, as distinct from a *Journal* correction of copy, would be impossible to make.

(N⁴): Philadelphia *Press*, April 30, page 1, signed, headlined 'STEPHEN CRANE IS AT ATHENS. ‖ The Distinguished Novelist Cables to "The Press" His | Impressions of the War Fever at the Greek Capital. ‖ SPECIAL CABLE DESPATCH TO "THE PRESS," BY STEPHEN CRANE, COPY-RIGHT, 1897'.

The copy-text is N¹, representing the printed version closest in point of transmission to the rewrite copy made up from the cable, but emended as advisable from the agreement of two or more of the other newspapers. Reprinted from N¹ by Fryckstedt and by Stallman.

No. 4. GREEK WAR CORRESPONDENTS

This McClure 'letter' was not printed in the *Westminster Gazette* and it was bought in the United States by so few newspapers that its existence was unknown until 1969, when it was found by Professor Bernice Slote in the *Pittsburgh Leader* and reprinted by her in the *Prairie Schooner*, Fall, 1969, pages 293–296. Since then three other newspaper versions have turned up in the Portland *Oregonian*, *St. Paul Pioneer Press*, and *Denver Republican*. The *Leader* is datelined Athens, May 7, which is a made-up date, or a simple error, for Crane was at the battle of Velestino on May 6 and did not return to Athens for some days. The *Oregonian* dateline of Athens, Greece, May 1, seems more trustworthy, in part because it faithfully repeats the naïve formula found in the manuscript of No. 2, and in part because May 1 is a reasonable date for impressions of the Greek capital, like cabled No. 3 datelined April 29.

(N¹): *Pittsburgh Leader*, Sunday, May 16, 1897, page 21, headlined 'THE WAR CORRESPONDENTS. ‖ STEPHEN CRANE TALKS OF AMERI-| CAN AND ENGLISH EXAMPLES. ‖ The Earl of Perth Amboy, N.J., Who | Objects to the Size of the Parthenon, | and the English Representative | Who Understands the Whole East-|ern Question, Simply Because He Is | a British Subject. ‖ BY STEPHEN CRANE. | (Copyright, 1897, S. S. McClure Co.)'.

(N²): Portland *Oregonian*, May 16, page 18, signed, headlined 'FOL-LOWERS OF WAR ‖ INTERNATIONAL COMPLICATIONS | DEVELOP CORRESPONDENTS. ‖ Stephen Crane Writes of Those Who | Are Now at the Seat of | War in Europe. ‖ (Copyright, 1897, by S. S. McClure Co.)'. To its dateline N² adds '(Special Correspondence.)'.

(N³): *St. Paul Pioneer Press*, May 16, page 19, headlined 'GREEK WAR CORRESPONDENCE ‖ BY STEPHEN CRANE. ‖ (Copyright, 1897, S. S. McClure Co.)'. The dateline is simply Athens, Greece, without date.

(N⁴): *Denver Republican*, May 16, page 17, headlined '[within a frame of type-orn.] GREEK WAR CORRESPONDENTS ‖ Athens Is Full of a Busy,

Buzzing Throng of the | Fellows | BY STEPHEN CRANE.' The dateline is Athens, Greece, May 3.

The texts of these four observed versions radiate from the master proof that would have been set up from the typescript presumably made in London from Crane's manuscript. Although they are of equal textual authority, on the whole the accidentals of N^1 are closer to Crane's usual characteristics than those of N^{2-4}, and thus the *Pittsburgh Leader* print has been chosen as copy-text, although emended a few times from N^{2-4} when these latter seem to follow more faithfully what can be conjectured to represent the accidentals, as well as the substantives, of the master proof. Not printed by Fryckstedt or by Stallman.

No. 5. CRANE AT VELESTINO

As Velestino on May 4–6, 1897, was the crucial battle of the war, so Crane's cable received extraordinary attention when it reached the *New York Journal,* not only in the *Journal's* own treatment in its publication on May 11 but also in the syndication. Insufficient evidence has been preserved by which to unravel with absolute precision the extremely complex textual situation, although at the end of this section some general hypotheses will be offered. Moreover, no single fully authoritative text was published; nor can such a text be put together in eclectic form except in part, since the recovery of something approximating the original cable as a whole from the different versions of the editorial rewrite jobs would be highly speculative. Three main forms of the text exist, at least two of which have subversions. These are 5(I), the Greater New York edition of the *New York Journal* (N^{1a}) with a just-possible subversion in N^6, the San Francisco *Examiner*; 5(II), the out-of-town edition of the *New York Journal* (N^{1b}) with a subversion in the *Chicago Tribune* (N^2) and in the Philadelphia *Press* (N^3); and 5(III) the *Kansas City Star* (N^7), a shortened text, with a subversion found in the Portland *Oregonian* (N^8) and the Salt Lake City *Tribune* (N^9), and with variant subversions in the *Omaha World-Herald* (N^{10}) and in the *Beatrice* (Neb.) *Daily Express* (N^{11}) or *Kearney Daily Hub* (N^{12}).

The description of the observed newspaper publications follows:

(N^{1a}): *New York Journal,* May 11, 1897, pages 1–2, with 'EDITION FOR GREATER NEW YORK' above the front-page heading 'NEW YORK JOURNAL | AND ADVERTISER'. The unsigned dispatch is printed in three single columns on page 1 with the runover (without headline) on page 2 beginning with 'smoke. Shots began' (22.11). The headline reads 'CRANE AT VELESTINO, ‖ Pen Picture of | the Great | Battle. ‖ VALOR OF GREEKS. ‖ Repulsed Charge | After Charge | of Turks. ‖ MOSLEMS' BIG LOSS. ‖ Journal Correspon-|dent Saw Victors' | Forced Re-|treat. ‖ By Stephen Crane. | (Copyright, 1897, by W. R. Hearst).' The dateline is Athens, May 10—(By Courier from Volo.). In the upper right corner, above the second and third columns, is a large drawing purporting to represent 'Stephen Crane, the Journal's War Correspondent.', showing a man with a Red Cross armband holding field glasses, in the background horse-drawn artillery against a rocky landscape. Copy at Rutgers University.

(N¹ᵇ): *New York Journal*, May 11, pages 1–2, the untitled edition for out of town. The signed dispatch is printed solid across four columns, the cut as in N¹ᵃ being placed instead above the left part of the wide column. The headline reads 'STEPHEN CRANE AT VELESTINO. ‖ The Journal's Special Cor-|respondent Describes | the Battle. ‖ VALOR OF THE GREEKS. ‖ Pen Picture of the Field of Strife | and the Repulse of Turk-|ish Hordes. ‖ VICTORS HAD TO RETREAT. ‖ By Stephen Crane. | [Copyright, 1897, by W. R. Hearst.]'. The dateline is, By Courier from Volo to Athens, May 10. The one-column runover on page 2 begins with 'supposed them all to be' (26.23–24) and on page 2 is headlined 'STEPHEN CRANE AT VELES-TINO. ‖'. Copy at Library of Congress, date-stamped May 13, 1897.

(N²): *Chicago Tribune*, May 11, page 1, headlined 'STEPHEN CRANE DESCRIBES A BIG BATTLE ‖ Terrific Fighting Between the Greek and Turkish Armies | at Velestino Portrayed in Vivid Narrative. ‖ MOSLEMS ARE EIGHT TIMES BRAVELY REPULSED. ‖ Order to Retreat is Unac-countable and Received with Sullen | Fury by the Officers and Their Troops. ‖ PLAIN OF BATTLE BLACK WITH WOUNDED AND DEAD. ‖ Company of Reserves Coming to the Front Pauses at a Wayside Shrine to | Pray When a Shell Demolishes It. ‖ LIEUTENANT WHILE ROLLING A CIGARET IS SHOT THROUGH THE NECK ‖ (Special Cable by Stephen Crane.)'. The dateline is Volo, via Athens, May 10.—[Copyright, 1897.].

(N³): Philadelphia *Press*, May 11, page 2, headlined 'STEPHEN CRANE IN BATTLE. ‖ The Brilliant Young American Novelist Cables to "The | Press" a Description of the Fight at Velestino | and the Greek Retreat in the Presence | of Victory. ‖ SPECIAL CABLE DESPATCH TO THE "PRESS," COPYRIGHT, 1897.' The dateline is Volo, May 10, and the story is signed at the foot.

(N⁴): *Boston Globe*, May 11, page 7, headlined 'VELESTINO A GRE-CIAN GETTYSBURG. ‖ Stephen Crane Tells of the Fierce Three Days' | Battle with the Moslem in Thessaly. ‖ Though Outnumbered, They Had Whipped the Turks | When Order to Retreat Came. ‖ By Stephen Crane.' The dateline is the same as in N¹ᵇ. At the foot is '(Copyright.)'.

(N⁵): *Buffalo Evening News*, May 11, pages 1, 5, headlined 'RED BADGE OF COURAGE. ‖ Graphic Description of the Battle of Velestino, | Where the Greeks Fought with Des-|perate Valor. ‖ BY STEPHEN CRANE. | (Copyright, 1897, by W. R. Hearst.)'. The dateline is the same as in N¹ᵇ. The runover on page 5 is headlined 'RED BADGE | OF COURAGE. ‖'.

(N⁶): San Francisco *Examiner*, May 11, pages 1–2, headlined 'CRANE AT VELESTINO. ‖ The Famous Novelist Describes the | Great Battle of the War. ‖ FIERCE FIGHTING FOR THREE LONG DAYS. ‖ With Vivid

Words the Author of the "Red Badge | of Courage" Tells of Real Carnage | on a Stricken Field. || [portrait of Crane] | By Stephen Crane. | (Special Cable to "The Examiner," Copyright, 1897, by W. R. Hearst.)'. The runover is headlined 'CRANE AT VELESTINO. ||'; the dateline as in N¹ᵃ.

(N⁷): *Kansas City Star*, May 11, page 1, headlined 'CRANE'S STORY OF A BATTLE || THE AUTHOR OF "THE RED BADGE OF | COURAGE" SEES WAR. || Graphic Description of Two Days of the | Fight—Coolness and Bravery of the | Greeks—Turks Held in Check—Smo-|lenski's Rage Over Retreat Orders. ||'. No signature or copyright appears. Inset in the first column is a portrait of Crane with the legend 'STEPHEN CRANE, NOVELIST AND WAR | CORRESPONDENT.' The dateline is New York, May 11.

(N⁸): Portland *Oregonian*, May 12, pages 1–2, headlined 'THE BATTLE OF VELESTINO. || Stephen Crane's Description of the | Victory Which Preceded Retreat.' The runover on page 2 is headlined 'THE END IS IN SIGHT. ||'. The dateline is the same as N⁷; no copyright or signature appears.

(N⁹): Salt Lake City *Tribune*, May 12, page 2, headlined 'HOW GREEKS FOUGHT || Graphic Story of the Battle | of Velestino. || VICTORY TURNED TO DEFEAT. || Greeks Had Repulsed the Turks Af-|ter Three Days of Hard Fighting | and were Congratulating One An-|other on the Outcome, when They | were Amazed and Outraged at the | Receipt of Orders to Retreat—Inci-|dents of the Fight, Illustrating | Heroism of the Greeks. ||'. The dateline is as in N⁷; no signature or copyright appears.

(N¹⁰): *Omaha World-Herald*, May 12, page 5, headlined 'STEPHEN CRANE AT VELESTINO. || American Author's Account of the | Graeco-Turkish Battle.' The dateline is as in N⁷; no signature or copyright appears. The text in the same setting, including headline, was also printed in the *Omaha Weekly World-Herald*, May 14, page 10.

(N¹¹): *Beatrice Daily Express* (Nebraska), May 12, page 1, headlined 'BATTLE OF VELESTINO. || An Eyewitness's Thrilling Description of | Smolenski's Victory.' The dateline is New York, May 12; no signature or copyright appears.

(N¹²): *Kearney Daily Hub*, May 12, page 1. The same typesetting, including headline, as N¹¹.

All of the 5(i) and 5(ii) versions read *May 10* in the dateline, by courier from Volo. From his own account we know that Crane arrived on the battlefield on May 5, the second day, and from Cora Crane's account (reprinted in the Imogene Carter section) we know that Crane reached Volo by train on Thursday night the 6th after the end of the battle. When the cable was actually written is anybody's guess. Cora's brief dispatch from Volo was datelined May 9, from Athens by courier, and was printed in the *Journal* on May 10. If she sent it by courier from Volo on Friday, May 7, two days would seem to be the time required to reach Athens. Thus if the same interval held for Crane's dispatch, he would have sent it off by hand on Saturday, May 8, to reach Athens on the 10th. A slight piece of evidence suggests that Saturday may have been the date. In the 5(I–II) texts the description of the second day of the battle (Wednesday) recounts that the Turkish soldiers made eight charges *on this day*; but in the shortened versions under 5(III), which seem to represent a form of the text in some respects relatively close to the cable, the reading is *on Saturday*. It is possible that this slip occurred because Crane was writing out his report on Saturday, May 8, the day he would seem to have sent it off. On the other hand, the day may have been confused by the rewrite man in New York who made up the 5(III) form of the dispatch.

The 5(I) form of the text, appearing in the Greater New York, or city, edition of the *Journal* has been observed only in Hearst's San Francisco *Examiner* (N⁶). Thirty-nine substantive variants appear between the two newspapers, some of which provide evidence for evaluating the *Journal* text. Most of these variants are unique with N⁶ and the odds favor them to be N⁶ departures from N¹ᵃ made in the transmission or by the N⁶ compositor, although in the nature of the case some may be true readings from the rewrite copy corrupted by the N¹ᵃ compositor, or perhaps altered in a later version of this copy sent to the N¹ᵃ composing room. When they occur in text where N¹ᵃ itself differs from the other versions, no evidence exists by which the actual N⁶ corruptions can be distinguished from possible true readings.[8] However, when N⁶ varies from N¹ᵃ in areas where one or the other agrees with texts in different traditions, some assumptions can be made. For instance, if N⁶ agrees with only a single other newspaper against N¹ᵃ, the odds favor no connection between the two but instead a fortuitous hit;[9] and, naturally, when N¹ᵃ agrees with the other traditions and N⁶ is completely unique, not much can be said for N⁶ authority.

The authority of the N⁶ variant can usually be established when it concurs with the other two lines of the text against N¹ᵃ. The most obvious case comes at 21.36 where N¹ᵃ reads, uniquely, *Legation* but N⁶ joins N¹ᵇ⁻⁵,⁷ in the obviously correct *Legion*. Logic requires 22.18 to be in the same category, since the N¹ᵃ *line* stands uniquely against N⁶ and N¹ᵇ⁻⁵,⁷⁻⁹ *lines*, and so at 19.22 with unique N¹ᵃ *Greeks'* versus

[8] Fortunately these are confined to two cases, at 21.1 where N⁶ reads *normal* versus N¹ᵃ *the normal* but N¹ᵇ,⁴⁻⁵ *a normal*; and 21.8 where N⁶ reads *a battle* for N¹ᵃ *battle* and N¹ᵇ,⁵,⁷ *battles*.

[9] Examples are 19.29 where N⁶ reads *the Turks for* and N³ *Turks in* versus *Turks* in the rest; 19.39 where N⁵,⁶ read *cloth* versus *a cloth* in the rest; N⁵,⁶ *Turkish* for *the Turkish* (20.10); N⁶,⁹ *in the* for *to the* (22.12); and N³,⁶ *and the men* for *the men* (22.18). The N⁶ agreement with N²,⁸ in *Evzones* versus *Ephzones* (22.32) probably has no significance either.

N^6 and N^{1b-5} *Greek*.[10] An interesting reading occurs at 21.10. Here N^{1a} has the error *the description of which read*, N^6 *the descriptions of which read*, N^7 (in the 5[III] line) *the description of which reads*, whereas N^{1b-5} have *whose descriptions read*. Since N^7 in some part relates to the 5(I) line more closely than it does to 5(II), its evidence might favor N^{1a}; but in fact, the 5(I) copy itself probably had the error *description read*, which was corrected independently in a different way by the N^6 compositor and by either the N(III) rewrite man or the N^7 compositor. In these circumstances the evidence of 5(II), which derives from the same cable independently of 5(I), may tilt the scales slightly toward the harder plural reading and the superior authority of N^6 unless one were to speculate that the cable itself read *description read* (not just the N^{1a} copy), in which case no determination of authority would be possible for the phrase.

Other difficult questions are posed by N^6 variation. One of these concerns the authority of N^{1a} *than thunder or avalanche* against the N^6 reading *than thunder or an avalanche* (20.3–4), which is also the reading of $N^{1b,4-5}$ but with the 5(II) subversion *than an avalanche of thunder* in N^2 and *than the thunder of an avalanche* in N^3. Here N^{7-12} agree with N^{1a}. The evidence suggests that N^{7-12} establish the reading of the 5(I) line and that the N^6 variant is a sophistication without any relation to N^{1b}. That is, the earlier form of the 5(II) text as in N^{2-3} indicates that the $N^{1b,4-5}$ reading was the final version, not the 5(II) original. Hence N^6 is not likely to have any authority, for it could represent the cable reading only if N^{1b} by pure chance reverted to the cable when the final copy for 5(II) was being prepared. But then, N^6 would need to be set from earlier copy than N^{1a}, which is possible; but it is not at all probable on the total evidence that the copy for N^6 was a state of 5(I) earlier than that from which 5(III) derives. The $N^{1b,4-5}$ concurrence with N^6, then, is almost certainly quite fortuitous.

The next example illustrates the complexity of the evidence. At 20.15, N^{1a} reads *Scattered fragments*, and $N^{1b,4-5}$ *and their scattered fragments*. In the earlier line of 5(II) N^2 has *The scattered fragments*, which may seem to be confirmed by the same reading in N^7 despite the N^3 variant *while scattered fragments*. Thus when N^6 joins $N^{2,7}$ in *The scattered fragments* it would seem at first sight almost demon-

---

[10] Of course, the N^{1a} error at 22.18 is demonstrable because N^6 joins there with the 5(II) and 5(III) traditions and the possibility, thus, that N^6 could be a lucky hit has no bearing on the evidence for N^{1a} error. The variant at 19.22, though probable, is less certainly an error since the 5(III) line has been cut here and cannot corroborate 5(II). Thus the hypothesis that N^{1a} is in error rests completely on the N^6 concurrence with the 5(II) line, for otherwise N^{1a} and N^{1b-5} are equal in authority.

strable that this was the reading of the original copy in both lines. But the subversion of 5(III) represented by N^{8-9}, which has a slightly different origin from N^7 and is here joined by the variant and further condensed subversion N^{10}, agrees with N^{1a} in *Scattered fragments* and thus appears to indicate that the N^{1a} reading is not an independent error. The case is almost a standoff. Despite the N^3 reading, which may be the result of editorial tinkering, it would seem that the syntactical difference between the early and late states of 5(II) is an actual one, with the compounding of the clauses in N^{1b} (and the substitution of *their* for *the*) a later revision of the two sentences in the original rewrite copy, in which case the early 5(II) version agreed with 5(I) in the syntax. However, whether the variant *The scattered* in the early state of 5(II) was also the reading of an early state of 5(I) as represented by N^6 is more doubtful, in part because the exact relationship of N^{8-9} to the possible states of N^{1a} is not certain. A similar problem is posed by the final N^6 variant to be considered, and it is particularly unfortunate that a 5(III) cut in the area prevents it from being a witness. Here at 19.17 N^{1a} and N^{1b} agree in the reading *after a three days' successful fight*, but N^{2-3} read *three days of successful fighting* and N^6 *three days' successful fighting*. It is hard to avoid the conclusion that the early copy in 5(II) as represented by N^{2-3} read *fighting*, and that the N^{1b} reading *a three days' successful fight* is a later version in the final copy (on the analogy of *the whole three days' fight* [24.15] [11] found in N^{1b-4}) which by chance agrees with the N^{1a} reading.

If so, the question is raised whether the N^6 *three days' successful fighting* is not also representative of an earlier state of N^{1a}. This is a difficult question to answer since the total evidence is relatively slight. Moreover, evidence is not usually clearcut that would distinguish a variant in N^{1a} as stemming either from the rewrite copy itself or else from compositorial error. That is, at 21.10 it seems fairly reasonable to assume that N^{1a} *description . . . read* is a faithful reproduction of an error in the copy, in which case the N^6 variant has no true authority unless one is willing to hypothesize that the N^{1a} reading was not an error in the original copy but was made when an earlier state was being retranscribed. If so, then the N^6 reading could hypothetically represent the form in the earlier and correct state. On the other hand, whether N^{1a} *Greeks'* (19.22), *Legation* (21.36), and *line* (22.18) were errors introduced in a later state or are N^{1a} compositorial de-

---

[11] How interchangeable *fight* and *fighting* could be may be illustrated by the unauthoritative N^5 variant *fighting* at 24.15 for N^{1b-4} *fight*.

partures from copy that read the same as N^6 is scarcely to be determined. On the whole it would appear that N^6 *an avalanche* (20.4) is an unauthoritative variant. Yet some evidence exists to suggest that in 19.17 *three days' successful fighting* and in 20.15 *The scattered fragments* the N^6 variants may indeed represent the readings of an original state of the rewrite copy for N^{1a} that was subsequently altered before being sent to the *Journal* composing room, in what would almost certainly under the circumstances have been a retranscription of the original copy. If so, perhaps some or all of the N^{1a} errors at 19.22, 21.36, and 22.18 were also introduced in such a copy and are not compositorial variants. The slim evidence will take us no farther. The only comment that remains is that if two states of the 5(I) copy did indeed exist, the differences between them were comparatively slight and in no wise compare with the marked differences between what may reasonably be taken as two demonstrable states of the rewrite copy for 5(II).

The first real problem in the 5(II) line of the text is the fact of its existence. That this version was separately prepared for the out-of-town edition is not subject to question, although the reason is obscure. The word count of the two versions is not so far apart as to encourage a theory that a different rewrite, throughout, was ordered for the purpose of filling the markedly disparate space. Although in column-inches the N^{1b} version takes up much more space than N^{1a}, the difference is almost wholly accounted for by the larger type adopted in N^{1b} for the four-column-wide setting. The two texts are relatively close in their length as measured by net wordage.[12]

Obviously, the out-of-town edition gave the story the bigger spread. Yet it would be dangerous to speculate that the wish for a livelier version than that produced for N^{1a}, the city edition, gave rise to the independent rewrite. Present-day newspapers run off the out-of-town edition earlier than the city edition, and on the evidence of No. 10, it is certain that this practice was followed by the *Journal* in 1897. Thus if anything the N^{1b} text had to be ready earlier than the N^{1a}; yet it is demonstrable that one text does not derive from the other. It is true that the earlier state of the 5(II) rewrite in N^{2-3} is closer in many, although not in all respects, to N^{1a} than is the subsequent state represented by $N^{1b,4-5}$. Yet the evidence suggests that this resemblance does not come about because early 5(II) derives from 5(I), or the reverse, but instead that it develops from the greater closeness

---

[12] N^{1a} runs to 1,707 words, and N^{1b} to 1,743, by actual count.

of the N^{2-3} subversion to the cable, also reproduced faithfully by N^{1a} in these respects. In the absence of any positive evidence for derivation one from the other, the only working hypothesis is that $5(I)$ and $5(II)$ were written up independently, and probably close to simultaneously, from the cable dispatch.[13]

The final version of the $5(II)$ text as found in N^{1b} was put on the wire to the *Boston Globe* (N^4) and the *Buffalo Evening News* (N^5). The N^4 text has nine unique variants and the N^5 text nineteen, all of which one may presume result either from errors in the transmission or in the respective composing rooms.[14] In two additional readings N^{4-5} agree against N^{1b}. The first is an error in N^{4-5}, *sufferers* for correct *the sufferers* of N^{1b} (25.13); the second, N^{4-5} *orders* for the N^{1b} error *order* (27.9), seems to expose an N^{1b} compositorial corruption. At 25.13 it would seem the wired copy had the error but the N^{1b} compositor corrected it. Another copy error may have been transmitted at 23.31, where N^{1b} has the misprint *New Yorks*, which seems to be the reason for N^3 *America* and N^5 *New Yorkers*. Something of a tossup occurs at 27.4, where N^{1b} and N^4 agree in *the left*, correct parallel structure in the phrase *the centre and the left*, against N^5 *left*. The N^5 reading could easily be put down to casual variation were it not that *left* is the reading of N^{2-3} and also of the $5(I)$ line, and indeed of $5(III)$ as illustrated in N^7. That *left* was the reading of the early state of the $5(II)$ copy would seem to be established. However, it may be anybody's guess whether the reworked $5(II)$ copy read *the left*, which was the form transmitted and reproduced in N^4 but casually varied in N^5; or whether both states of the copy read *left* and the pull toward parallel structure influenced both the N^{1b} and N^4 compositors to add the *the*. The present editor guesses that the two readings were characteristic of the two states of the copy, that the *the*

---

[13] The comparatively large number of typos in N^{1b} suggests such haste in setting and printing as led to the omission of proofreading, or at least of careful proofreading. But since the order of printing the two editions is not demonstrable—although it was pretty certainly $5(II)$ and then $5(I)$—this evidence of haste cannot be brought to bear on the general problem of priority in the order of writing up the copy for the two editions, if indeed any significant difference exists. That the $5(I)$ text was wired only to Hearst's San Francisco *Examiner* may just possibly suggest that it was the first available; but other factors might well have entered into the decision that could upset a speculation on this fact.

[14] The N^4 variants may be found at 23.30–31, 24.14, 24.25, 25.11(2), 25.15–16, 26.1, 27.7, and 27.24. The N^5 variants appear at 23.8–9, 23.10, 23.14, 23.31(3), 24.15, 24.19(2), 24.24, 24.27, 24.29, 25.11(2), 25.18, 25.23, 25.36, 26.6, and 26.27. By *unique* is meant unique within the $N^{1b,4-5}$ sequence. Occasional agreement with one other newspaper in the $5(II)$ line is taken to represent fortuitous, not significant, variation, as in the omission at 23.31 of *now* in $N^{3,5}$ or at 25.18 the addition of *the* in *the regulation* in $N^{3,5}$.

was added in the reworking, and that the N^5 reading was the one that departed from copy.[15] Finally, perhaps the most curious feature of the copy behind N^{1b} that was wired to N^4 and N^5 is the eyeskip of seven words in all three newspapers present at 23.14–15, an error that was presumably made in the retyping that produced the final state of the 5(II) rewritten copy.

The relation between the two states of 5(II) remains to be determined. That N^{2-3} represent an early version of the subsequently revised N^{1b} text—probably the original form of the out-of-town edition rewrite copy made up from the cable—is the working hypothesis that best fits the evidence. Of the approximately seventy-three readings in which N^{2-3} agree with each other either exactly or in close paraphrase against the other texts in the 5(II) line about twenty-eight join N^{2-3} against both N^{1a-b} in whole or in part; but the further forty-five agree with N^{1a} against the N^{1b} reading. These readings place N^{2-3} in a closer relation to N^{1a} than is N^{1b} and thus illustrate the intermediate nature of the N^{2-3} text in respect to the cable. A practical example comes at the end of the dispatch. N^{1a} provides a perfectly coherent account. Crane wanted to see the engineer of the last train to reach Velestino and then to return to Volo, *but could not* (23.2). The engineer who had brought the train in is praised in relation to the bravery of the soldiers. In some unstated manner he has suffered a railroad accident as well as the heavy bombardment that is now going on. Then Crane continues, *All the way down on the train a man covered with bloody bandages talked to me in wild Greek.* In the N^{2-3} text a typical Crane understatement *but was in a hurry myself* (27.21–22) replaces the laconic *but could not* (which must be taken as an N^{1a} editorial paraphrase). That Crane never did see the engineer is shown by the next statement, also containing a typical Crane phrase (paraphrased in N^{1a} perhaps because of its colloquial nature), *He was a daisy, anyhow.* Then after remarking on the accident and bombardment, Crane mentions some unidentified man who—presumably still at Velestino—talked to him wildly in Greek.[16] Perhaps in an effort to unite these disparate and seemingly diffuse details, or misled by the

[15] The grounds for this guess are admittedly not much. Almost certainly the cable would not have contained the *the,* since cables saved as much as possible by omitting words that could automatically be inserted at the rewrite desk (although Crane would be likely to violate this rule). Hence the addition, to give superior accuracy of specification, would be a natural part of the N^{1b} reworked copy. The fact that N^5 has twice the number of errors found in N^4, in addition, makes one cautious about selecting an N^5 variant over the N^4 reading.

[16] N^{2-3} read: *A man in a bloody bandage talked to me wildly in Greek. I can't quote him.* The bit, *I can't quote him,* sounds authentic and may have been cut from N^{1a} because of its confession of inadequacy.

curious omission in $N^{2\text{-}3}$ (if present in the cable) of the fact that the conversation was on the train back to Volo,[17] the N^{1b} rewrite man invented a meeting between Crane and the engineer by combining the engineer with the man who was bandaged. Two points become apparent. First, N^{1a} and N^{1b} are not directly connected, since N^{1b} depends upon the omission of the train journey in $N^{2\text{-}3}$. Second, N^{1b} is not the original text since to split the bloodily bandaged engineer who talked to Crane in wild Greek (in N^{1b}) into an engineer whom he did not meet and a separate man who talked to him is not a progression one would wish to argue for, especially in view of the numerous readings in which $N^{2\text{-}3}$ join N^{1a} against N^{1b}. A third may be added. The key phrase *He was a daisy* joins $N^{2\text{-}3}$ and N^{1b} in one tradition against N^{1a} where it is missing. If one is searching for an order, the typical Crane addition of *anyhow* in $N^{2\text{-}3}$, wanting in N^{1b}, should show the reading of the cable.

The apparent paradox illustrated by this example can be resolved if we accept the independent radiation of N^{1a} and of $N^{2\text{-}3}$ from the cable. Under these circumstances it seems most probable that the copy for N^{1a} and what was to become N^{1b} was being worked on almost simultaneously by two rewrite men, one aiming at the Greater New York edition and the other at the out-of-town edition and the two usually subscribing newspapers, the *Chicago Tribune* and Philadelphia *Press*. Whatever the circumstances, it is clear that the $N^{2\text{-}3}$ version was the forerunner of N^{1b}, which was reworked from the copy behind $N^{2\text{-}3}$—perhaps by a still different editor—before being sent to the composing room for the *Journal's* own out-of-town edition.[18]

On May 11 the *Journal* prepared a shortened version for syndication, and on May 12 two other dispatches that were more severely cut. The earliest form of this general 5(III) version is found in N^7, the *Kansas City Star* for May 11, the only newspaper observed, unfortunately, with this specific text. In general the N^7 dispatch resembles N^{1a} more than N^{1b} although it contains a number of readings

[17] The N^{1a} allusion *All the way down on the train* may be an N^{1a} invention to get Crane from Velestino to Volo, mentioned in the last sentence. In "A Fragment of Velestino" Crane devotes some attention to the strategic importance of the railroad. Since the dispatch was datelined Volo, Crane certainly took the train. But the narrative is sketchy.

[18] The relatively few agreements between N^{1a} and $N^{2\text{-}3}$ are enough to establish common cable copy but not enough to suggest a rewriting by one version of the other. The various typographical errors in N^{1b}, indicative of haste and perhaps even of no proofreading, suggest that N^{1b} variation from its copy would be confined to compositorial error and that N^{1b} would not have been altered by the further revisions of a proofreader.

from the 5(II) line. The next day [19] the *Journal* sent out a shorter text, which was substantially the N[7] version with additional cuts. The fact that the two observed newspapers, the Portland *Oregonian* (N[8]) and the Salt Lake City *Tribune* (N[9]) agree in this version save for nonsignificant variation between themselves establishes that it is a separate and authentic form of the text syndicated by the *Journal* and not simply an independent cutting of the N[7] report that had been picked up. Moreover, the N[8-9] unique variant *marching* at 21.6 for N[1-6] *march* shows a close link between the two reprints of the subversion. This joins with a small number of mutual agreements in variation from N[7] in which N[8-9] disregard N[7] errors by returning to N[1a-b] copy,[20] or appear to reflect difficulties in N[1a-b] and perhaps in the cable,[21] to indicate that the copy for N[8-9] derived directly from that behind N[7] without reference to any other source.[22]

[19] In the observed newspapers only the first shortened version represented by N[7] appeared on May 11. All the others, N[8-12], were not published until Wednesday, May 12, by which time the end of the battle on May 6 was almost a week old. This time lag no doubt accounts for the increasing brevity of the *Journal's* syndicated versions.

[20] For example, at 21.15 N[8-9] *close* for N[7] *closely* follows the reading of N[1-6] and thus exposes an error in the N[7] transmission or typesetting.

[21] An illustration occurs at 20.29 where N[8-9] read *in fury* for N[1a,5-6] *infrequently*, N[1b,3-4] *unfrequently*, and the N[2,7] error *frequently*. The N[8-9] variant seems to represent an attempted patching of some slip that may have originated in the cable. Other examples are found at 21.17, 22.12, and 22.30.

[22] A few variants between N[8] and N[9] raise the question whether the copy was indeed identical. Minor matters like the N[8] agreement with N[1a-b] in *Greek* at 18.31 versus N[3,7,9-12] *the Greek* are no doubt indications of unique fortuitous error, especially when in the same textual line N[9] agrees with N[1a-b] *Turks* versus N[7-8,10-12] *the Turks*. Perhaps this hypothesis of chance may also apply to the agreement of N[1a] and N[8] at 22.17 in not paragraphing *There* versus N[9] indentation. (N[10-11] are not witnesses.) It may well be significant that N[8] varies uniquely from the concurrence of N[7,9] much more frequently than N[9] varies from N[7-8], thus indicating a certain freedom in the treatment of the text by N[8]. Two readings need attention, however. The first occurs at 20.5–6 where N[9] omits *It was the most beautiful sound of my experience, barring no symphony. The crash of it was ideal.* Since these sentences appear in N[1a-b] and in N[7-8,10], the omission in N[9] might be put down merely to editorial treatment were it not that N[11-12] also make the same cut. Yet since it is most unlikely that N[11-12] represent a divergent textual tradition, the omission would seem to have been N[9]'s option and not the result of variant copy. A similar conclusion may be reached in respect to the second variant. Here at 20.29–30 a question of modification is involved. N[1a] reads: *When night came shells burst infrequently, lighting the darkness. By the red flashes I saw the wounded taken to Volo.* On the other hand, N[1b] alters the modification as part of a reparagraphing: *When night came shells burst unfrequently, lighting the darkness with red flashes.* [¶] *I saw the wounded taken to Volo.* N[7], which in general derives from N[1a], agrees with N[1a], and this agreement is also found in N[8] and in N[10], the latter concurrence establishing the reading of the copy behind N[8]. But N[9] takes the N[1b] modification by ending the sentence with *flashes*. Fortunately, this can be assigned to

The final observed form of the text, a second subversion of 5(III),
is a more drastically shortened dispatch found on May 12 in the
Omaha World-Herald (N^{10}) and also in the *Beatrice Daily Express*
(N^{11}) and the *Kearney Daily Hub* (N^{12})—these last two in the same
typesetting and therefore presenting only one witness. Except for
three independent cuts the N^{11-12} text is the same as N^{10} and obviously
derives from the same source, apparently by radiation.[23] The origin
of the N^{10-12} subversion cannot be assigned without some difficulties
cropping up in any explanation offered. That its copy was not the
same as the copy behind N^{8-9} but with further cuts may be inferred
from its failure to follow the unique N^{8-9} *in fury* at 20.29 and its return to the $N^{1a,5-6}$ variant *infrequently* ($N^{1b,3-4}$: *unfrequently;* $N^{2,7}$
error: *frequently*). The question then arises whether it radiates independently of N^{8-9} from the copy behind N^7, which would be the next
most natural source of transmission. In favor of this origin is the use
by N^{10-12} of the introductory formula that had been started by N^7 (and
followed by N^{8-9}) to take the place of the 5(I,II) text at 18.27–30.
Also in favor is the N^{10-12} observance (with N^{8-9}) of the cuts at 19.1–5,
19.36–37, and 20.7–8 that N^7 had made in the 5(I,II) text, while cutting further at 19.11–35 than the 19.17–35 N^{7-9} excision. These agreements do not appear to be the result of chance. Further evidence
comes in the agreement of N^{10-12} with four readings that had originated with N^7: 18.32, $N^{7-8,10-12}$ *the Turks* for $N^{1-6,9}$ *Turks;* 19.6, N^{7-12}
the army for N^{1-6} *this army;* 19.39–20.1, N^{7-10} *roof* for $N^{1a,6}$ *tin roof,*
N^{1b-5} *resonant roofing;* and 20.12, N^{7-12} *on Saturday* for N^{1-6} *this day.*
To these may be added 18.31 $N^{3,7,9-12}$ *the Greek* for $N^{1-2,4-6,8}$ *Greek,*
since the N^3 reading would seem to be a chance hit and not a transmissional variant. Even though the context of the two readings at
18.31 and 18.32 makes random variation easy, the variants at 19.6,
19.39–20.1, and 20.12 seem removed from chance.

The chief difficulty with the hypothesis that the copy behind N^7
furnished the basis for the N^{10-12} version as well as the N^{8-9} form is
the odd fact that mixed in with the N^7 readings followed by N^{8-9} are
some readings in which N^{10-12} diverge from the N^7 forms and return
to readings that appear to have their origin in the 5(I) line or that

---

N^9 sophistication, and not to a difference in the N^{8-9} copy, since N^9 retains the
phrase *by the red flashes* from $N^{1a,7}$ and does not follow N^{1b} in *with red flashes.*
In short, the evidence strongly favors common copy from which N^8 and N^9
radiate.

[23] N^{10} unique readings at 20.3 and 20.11–12 are not followed by N^{11-12}, but
N^{11-12} do follow the new N^{10} variant at 20.2–3 *It was like* for N^{1-9} *It was more
impressive than.*

are characteristic of both 5(I) and 5(II). In fact, all may be said to revert to 5(I) since the three readings of this nature that involve 5(II) represent N^{10-12} rejection of substantives unique with N^{7-9} as against common readings of N^{1a} and N^{1b}. These are 19.1, $N^{1-6,10-12}$ *good fighters* versus N^{7-9} *great fighters*; 9.9, $N^{1-6,10-12}$ *beautifully in check* versus N^{7-9} *back*; and 19.11, $N^{1-6,10-12}$ *orders* versus N^{7-9} *order*. However, the more specific evidence involves a return to the 5(I) readings where N^7 (followed by N^{8-9}) had deserted its general 5(I) copy for 5(II) readings. These cases are 19.7–8, $N^{1a,6,10-12}$ *He knew that his army had victory within its grasp* for $N^{1b-5,7-9}$ *He was at that time perfectly confident of success*; 19.9–10, $N^{1a,6,10-12}$ *killing them as fast as they fell upon him* for N^{1b-5} *and inflicting heavy loss* (N^5: *a heavy loss*) and N^{7-9} *and inflicting upon them heavy losses*; and 19.10–11, $N^{1a,6,10-12}$ *In the middle of intoxication* (N^6: *the intoxication*) *of victory came the orders* (N^6: *orders*) *to fall back. Why?* for $N^{1b-5,7-9}$ *Then came the orders to fall back* (N^{2-3}: *orders*; N^{7-9}: *the order*).

A purely mechanical explanation is difficult to contrive. Although 5(I) copy in some form is certainly the major source for N^{10-11}, as it is for N^7, no explanation can hold that N^{10-12} bypass the N^7 copy and return completely to 5(I). The preliminary formula at 18.27–30, the various identical cuts, and at least three important residual readings that started with N^7 (19.6; 19.39–20.1; 20.12) all dictate some influence from the 5(III) tradition of the text. Since N^{10-12} as a whole cannot derive at first hand either from the 5(I) copy or from the copy sent out to N^7 and also used in cut form for N^{8-9}, the question naturally arises whether just as N^{2-3} are conjectured to stem from an earlier state of 5(II) than is represented by $N^{1b,4-5}$, so N^{10-12} may have been made up from an earlier state of 5(III) than is represented by N^{7-9}. Such a hypothesis would neatly explain the N^{7-9} readings still present in N^{10-12} as well as the N^{7-9} readings rejected by N^{10-12} in favor of the common readings of 5(I,II). The serious problem remains, however, of the N^{7-9} readings also rejected by N^{10-12} in which N^{7-9} had gone over to the 5(II) tradition away from its general 5(I) source. If the earliest form of the 5(III) copy had been strictly 5(I), and somehow readings from 5(II) had been conflated in the final copy, then no bar would exist to the hypothesis that N^{10-12} derive from an early version of 5(III). The difficulty, of course, is to account satisfactorily for such conflation.

Moreover, one reading remains in N^{7-12} that derives from 5(II) and represents the only clear case in which N^{10-12} ever follow an N^7 reading that agrees with 5(II) instead of with 5(I): this is 20.12, $N^{1b-5,7-12}$

each for $N^{1a,6}$ *every*.[24] This seems to present a real anomaly, but an explanation may be possible. That is, before the first N^{10-12} long cut at 19.11–35 (which merely extends the N^{7-9} cut at 19.17–35) N^{10-12} may or may not follow readings [25] original with N^{7-9}; but in every case (except for the conjecturally nontransmissional variant at 19.1 discussed in footnote 24 above) N^{10-12} reject the N^{7-9} variants departing from 5(I) that come from some state of the 5(II) copy.[26] The inference is that in the area of 18.27–19.11 N^{10-12} are drawn from some state of the text behind 5(III)—which is to say behind N^7—in which the small original N^7 variants from 5(I) at 18.31, 18.32, and 19.6, and the special cuts were already present but in which readings drawn from the 5(II) line had not yet appeared. On the other hand, after 19.35, or immediately following the brief N^{7-12} cut at 19.36–37, no firm evidence is present for the influence on the N^7 copy of 5(I) to the exclusion of 5(II),[27] and—in contrast to the situation in the area before the cut—the single time (at 20.12) that N^{7-9} follow a 5(II) reading instead of the 5(I) norm, the 5(II) reading is retained in N^{10-12}. The evidence is admittedly slim; but if it is indeed significant, then the conjecture may be made that whereas before the cut N^{10-12} derive from, let us say, an earlier state of 5(III), yet after the cut the copy transcribed to form the N^{10-12} typescript was the copy that lay directly behind N^{7-9}. The basis for this conjecture is as follows.

[24] A less clear case is 19.1 $N^{1b-2,4-5,7-12}$ *and stayers* for $N^{1a,3}$ *stayers* (N^6 error: *slayers*). The difficulty with this as evidence is that it concerns a series of three in which the *and* before the third element *stayers* would be a natural typist's addition, such as is perhaps found in the only original N^{10} reading confirmed by N^{11-12}, the contaminated error *It was like* at 20.2–3 for N^{1-9} *It was more impressive than*. Worthy of note is the fact that the 5(II) series is actually *good fighters and long fighters and stayers* whereas 5(I) is *good fighters, long fighters, stayers*; but N^{7-9} reads *great fighters, long fighters and stayers*. Thus N^{10-12} agree with $N^{1b-2,4-5,7-9}$ in reading *and stayers* but disagree with $N^{1b,3-5}$ and agree with $N^{2,7-9}$ in *long fighters* instead of *and long fighters*, and agree with the common 5(I,II) *good fighters* against N^{7-9} *great fighters*. Under these circumstances little weight can be placed on the N^{10-12} reading *and stayers,* and it must be discarded as evidence.

[25] N^{10} follows two relatively indifferent readings at 18.31 and 18.32 (each of which was also subject to variation in other texts) but also one probably significant reading at 19.6. It returns to two significant 5(I,II) readings at 19.1 and 19.9, and to one possibly indifferent reading at 19.9–10 where N^{7-9} had printed an original variation.

[26] These occur at 19.7–8, 19.9–10, and 19.10–11 and are all significant. It is worth notice that in this area N^{10-12} are as indifferent to the N^{2-3} subversion in 5(II) as they are to the regular N^{1b} line of the text. Indeed, throughout the N^{10-12} text no influence from N^{2-3} independent of N^{1b} can be seen.

[27] This cut from 19.11–35 is fairly close to the N^{7-9} cut of 19.17–35. From the point of view of N^{10-12}, the cut was only from 19.11–16.

Insofar as we can tell from the single piece of evidence, the fact is significant that after the cut N^{10-12} vary only once (and that in a non-transmissional manner) [28] from N^{7-9} whereas before the cut they may vary from readings that originate in 5(III). However, when 5(III) substitutes a 5(II) reading, N^{10-12} always vary by a return to 5(I). After the cut a 5(II) reading also occurs in 5(III) in the area where N^{10-12} are witnesses but they follow it.

A choice of one of two different hypotheses should explain the curious evidence: (1) after the cut the copy for N^{10-12} changed from an early to a late form of the 5(III) copy; or (2) throughout there was only one basic typescript for 5(III) but before the cut some alterations were made by hand in the copy that was wired to N^{7-9} (chiefly changes from the 5[II] version) but these were not made after the cut—at least not systematically—so that the N^{10-12} copy before and after the cut reproduces the basic 5(III) typescript unaltered by hand.

The second of these two possibilities better suits the evidence and is adopted here as the working hypothesis. In relating the N^{10-12} subversion to N^7, the basic 5(III) text that also produced N^{8-9}, two options were always present: either the conflation of 5(II) with 5(I) took place in some late state of the copy behind 5(III), or else the 5(III) copy never varied and it was the copy behind N^{10-12} that conflated the 5(I) variants with the 5(III) version to produce the mixed N^{10-12} text. The evidence was too conflicting for an entirely mechanical theory of transmission to produce both the N^{7-9} and the N^{10-12} forms. This case could not be decided on its own merits, however, without extending the range of the evidence to include an overall view of the characteristics of 5(III) after the N^{10} dispatch stopped, with especial reference to its complete relationship to the 5(II) and 5(I) lines.

The N^{7-9} cut at 19.17–35 does indeed seem to mark a watershed. That is, between 19.7 and 19.17 N^7 follows 5(II) in ten major substantive variants from 5(I) while at the same time agreeing with 5(I) against 5(II) in nine such readings.[29] It is interesting to observe

[28] The restoration of N^{1a} readings prevents any speculation that the N^{10-12} form originated with N^{10}, which had been sent the N^{8-9} copy, and that N^{10} in turn passed on its original variants to N^{11}.

[29] The readings in which N^{7-9} agree substantively with 5(II) are: 19.7–8 *was . . . success*; 19.9–10 *and inflicting . . . loss*; 19.10–11 *Then came . . . back* (*In the middle . . . Why?* transferred in N^{7-9} to follow 19.16); 19.11 *due to reverses*; 19.11 (N^7 joins N^{2-3} in omitting $N^{1b,4-5}$ *else* or N^{1a} *of the sort*); 19.13 (N^7 joins N^{1b-5} in omitting N^{1a} *may have . . . reason*); 19.14 *General Smolenski*; 19.15 (N^7 joins N^{2-3} in *raged* for $N^{1b,4-5}$ *raged and fumed* and N^{1a} *raged . . . general*); 19.15–16 *but orders . . . obeyed*; 19.16 *hence . . . Volo*. The readings in which N^{7-9} join 5(I) against 5(II) are: 18.30–31 *has proved*; 18.31 *when well . . . successfully*; 18.32 *Turks . . . outnumbered*;

that the $5(\text{II})$ readings adopted in N^{7-9} form a continuous cluster between 19.7 and 19.17 in which $5(\text{II})$ seems to be the only copy. Following the end of the cut at 19.35, however, the situation changes drastically. From here $5(\text{I})$ is the almost exclusive copy and to the end of the report only a handful of $5(\text{II})$ agreements appear. Although some of these are very definite concurrences, others may possibly be due to chance or to alterations in $N^{1a,6}$. Among the more certain are 20.12, $N^{1b-5,7-12}$ *each* for $N^{1a,6}$ *every*; 21.7–8, $N^{1b-5,7}$ mention of *books* as the source of incorrectness although in different terms as against no mention in $N^{1a,6}$; 21.31, $N^{1b-5,7}$ *first pair had* for $N^{1a,6}$ *first pair having*; 21.34, $N^{1b-2,4-5,7}$ *wild and furious* (N^2: *wild, furious*; N^7: *wild with rage and furious*) versus $N^{1a,3,6}$ *furious*; 21.38, $N^{1b-5,7}$ *He had* for $N^{1a,6}$ *I noticed*; and probably 21.9, $N^{1b,3-5,7}$ *take* for $N^{1a,2,6}$ *to take*. This is not much of a bag. Finally, a very odd group of three must be added. These comprise 21.6, $N^{1b,4-5,7}$ omit, $N^{1a,2-3,6,8-9}$ *for*; 21.6, $N^{1b-5,7}$ *blue clothed* for $N^{1a,6,8-9}$ *blue-clad*; and 21.6, $N^{1b-5,7}$ *infantry of the Greeks* (N^3: *infantry, Greeks,*) for $N^{1a,6,8-9}$ *Greek infantry*. The highly significant thing here is that in this cluster, N^{8-9}—although otherwise showing every evidence of having stemmed from the copy behind N^{7-9}—desert the N^{7-9} agreement with $5(\text{II})$ to revert to $5(\text{I})$ in exactly the same manner as at 19.7–17 N^{10-12} had followed $5(\text{I})$ when N^{7-9} had changed from $5(\text{I})$ to $5(\text{II})$ text. This situation cannot be accidental and presumably reflects the same causes for N^7 divergence. Under the circumstances it would be most difficult to envisage different states of various typescripts, and thus the conjecture that in 19.7–17 N^7 substituted the $5(\text{II})$ readings by hand would seem to be confirmed by the N^7 departures from what should have been the basic typescript readings exemplified by N^{8-9}. However, the circumstances would differ slightly. Whereas in 19.7–17 it would appear that N^{10-12} were wired from a carbon of the $5(\text{III})$ typescript that had not been annotated as had the original copy wired to N^7 and also to N^{8-9}, at 21.6 the copy of the same typescript wired to N^{8-9} had not been annotated as had the N^7 copy. (N^{10-12} are no longer witnesses at this point, unfortunately.) However, an explanation for this anomaly seems possible. If we except the agreement of N^{8-12} with $N^{1b,5,7}$ in *each* for $N^{1a,6}$ *every* at 20.12, no certain concurrences of N^7 with $5(\text{II})$ occur between the resumption of N^7 text after the 19.17–35 N^{7-9} cut (the watershed) and these odd readings at 21.6 in which annotation apparently begins again in N^7 but not in N^{8-9}. Moreover, this lack of accord in annotation may not be confined merely to this small cluster, for between 21.7 and 21.38 (the remaining area of annotation from

18.32 *This battle has*; 19.1 *long*; 19.1–2 *It must . . . Larissa*; 19.3 *I know . . . rejoiced*; 19.3–4 *this . . . champagne*; 19.6 *no.*

5[II] in the N^7 copy) N^{8-9} cuts prevent these texts from acting as witnesses for the five remaining N^7 agreements with 5(II). The conjecture would seem to be reasonable that in fact the *each-every* variant at 20.12 in N^{7-12} is probably not an annotation but a departure in 5(I) from its copy that had originally read *every*. If so, the editor of the copy wired to N^7 seems to have begun a second stage of annotation, independent of the typescript carbon for N^{8-9}, at 21.7, and if N^{8-9} had printed the same text it is reasonable to suppose that it would have continued to present the 5(I) readings in contrast to N^7, as it did at 21.7.[30]

One possible curiosity involving the readings introduced by annotation into N^7 may be mentioned. Of the ten of these readings at 19.7–17, in six the earlier N^{2-3} subversion of 5(II) agrees with $N^{1,4-5}$, the later text. In the four readings where it disagrees, N^{7-9} follow the N^{2-3} forms: these are the omission at 19.11 of $N^{1a,6}$ *of the sort* or $N^{1b,4-5}$ *else*, and the reading at 19.15 *raged* for *raged and fumed*. To these may perhaps be added, from the five substantive agreements, the accidentals beginning of a new sentence with *But* at 19.15–16 where $N^{1b,4-5}$ had continued the sentence with *but*. These concurrences would tend to encourage a conjecture that the 5(II) document on which the editor drew for his source of annotation was a copy of the N^{2-3} typescript. On the other hand, although perhaps not much weight can be put on N^{2-3} *orders* at 19.11 but $N^{1b,4-5}$ *the orders* and N^{7-9} *the order*, a legitimate difference does appear at 19.14, where N^{2-3} join $N^{1a,6}$ in *Smolenski* but $N^{1b,4-5,7-9}$ read *General Smolenski*. After this section, when annotation resumes at 21.5 or 21.7 the evidence is not helpful. As with the early reading at 19.14, one finds that at 21.6 N^{2-3} join N^{1a} and N^{8-9} in the word *for*, which is omitted by $N^{1b,4-5,7}$. Nowhere else do N^{2-3} as a unit depart from N^{1a}, although each varies separately in a few trifling readings that cannot constitute evidence. Just possibly the N^7 editor used a carbon of the copy for N^{2-3}, the original of which may have undergone slight additional revision before being put on the wire.[31] It is at least a possibility, according to the evidence of 19.11, 19.15, and perhaps of 19.15–16.

[30] Just possibly the N^7 annotation began at 21.5 where $N^{1,6}$ read *such circumstances as these*, $N^{1b,4-5}$ *the circumstances*, N^2 *some circumstances*, and N^7 *such circumstances*. N^3 omits the phrase. Since N^{8-9} are cut here they cannot tell us whether the N^7 omission of *as these* marks the start of the editor's activities. Probably it does.

[31] N^7 joins N^2 alone in a few readings at 21.7, 21.9(?), and 21.35 and in a cut at 19.4–5, this forming part of a larger cut in N^7. To suppose that these are transmissional variants and not fortuitous would require a difference in the basic copy for N^2 and for N^3, a proliferation of draft typescripts one would not wish to suggest. They are not necessarily N^3 errors.

The question of the copy for N^7—as for N^{8-9} and N^{10-12}—is more than an academic matter, since only when the transmission is established can the authority of the readings be determined and the possibility be evaluated whether lost early forms of the copy, perhaps closer to the original cable, could have been their source. In this problem the N^7 text is the key since in one way or another it is to its basic copy that N^{7-12} refer. That N^7 was the earliest wired of the condensed syndicated versions is indicated by the fact that it is the only one to have been printed on May 11, the date of the New York publication. Its readings demonstrate that it was made up from some state of the 5(I) copy, but before it was approved and wired to the *Kansas City Star* the editor substituted some readings at 19.7–17 and 21.7–38 from the 5(II) copy, perhaps from a typescript representing the intermediate N^{2-3} version. With the possible exception of 20.12, *each-every*, confirmable evidence has not been observed to suggest that the 5(I) copy providing the basis for the 5(III) tradition was in an earlier state than that represented in the *Journal's* city edition. A similarly negative result comes in general from the San Francisco *Examiner* (N^6) readings, the one newspaper known to have reprinted the 5(I) text. On the other hand, the lack of confirmation by duplicate appearance in radiating sources, like N^{6-7}, except at 20.15 may not demonstrate the unity of 5(I) and the nonauthority of all divergences, for confirmation would be impossible if, say, N^6 was wired from the finished 5(I) copy but 5(III) had been made up from an earlier state. This situation would produce a series of readings that would appear to originate in the 5(III) copy [32] and thus could be either authoritative early readings subsequently altered in 5(I) or else unauthoritative 5(III) variants developing in its typescript.[33]

Some stylistic variants in N^7 suggest that a certain amount of independent variation was produced in the 5(III) typescript. For example, if at 19.6 N^{7-12} *the army* derives from some earlier source, then one must believe that N^{1a} and N^{1b} in their lines independently altered to the same form *this army*. A perhaps clearer case is found at 19.39–20.1 where Crane is comparing the sound of musketry to *rain on a roof*. That is the reading of N^7. If it were the cable's, then independently in dissatisfaction N^{1a} came up with *tin roof* and N^{1b} with *reso-*

---

[32] Subject, of course, to checks against their being conflations provided by N^{10-12} before 19.11 and by N^{8-9} after 19.35.

[33] Because of the variable N^{8-12} cuts, N^7 is sometimes an independent witness whose testimony is hard to evaluate. The derived texts offer a check on departures from copy by the N^7 compositor (or a Kansas City editor), but when they are wanting the evidence vanishes.

nant roofing. The reverse of this process may seem more probable. Similarly, if *on Saturday* at 20.12 derived from the cable, we should need to take it that N^{1a} and N^{1b} independently hit upon the same reading *this day*. Some N^7 readings that are unique in an area where N^{8-9} or N^{10} could confirm are manifest errors, like *cigar* for *cigarette* at 21.22, and these are certainly to be attributed to the local N^7 editor or compositor. But when N^7's subversions agree with a variant originating in N^7, it is clear that the anomaly stood in the wired copy; in such cases when the 5(I,II) lines agree against 5(III), as in N^{7-9}'s omission of *of howitzers* at 22.6, the total evidence suggests that these are not transmissional variants from some different copy behind 5(III) but instead that they are unauthoritative products of the making up of the 5(III) typescript.

Two interesting cases develop when 5(I,II) are in agreement but the N^7 variant is so unusual as to require special editorial attention. One of these comes at 21.32–33 in the amusing narrative of the officer who told his orderly to bring him another pair of field glasses but was misunderstood and received a bottle of wine. N^7 records that he *shot the messenger, who misunderstood the order and brought a bottle of wine*. Unfortunately at this point N^{8-9} have been cut so that we have no means of knowing whether to attribute this oddity to the 5(III) typescript or to the *Kansas City Star* editor. That N^7 is in error can be demonstrated by the confirmation given the 5(I,II) account by No. 6, "A Fragment of Velestino," where the officer also merely lectures his orderly while holding fast to the bottle of wine. The main point of interest, then, is not whether N^7 is to be taken seriously as representing some lost stage of the text, but instead how such an absurdity could have got into it. The explanation is not far to seek. The normal copy for 5(III)—that is to say, 5(I)—at this point reads *An officer of a battery sent a man to the rear after another pair of field glasses, the first pair having been smashed by a musket ball. The man brought a bottle of wine, having misunderstood the order.* The 5(II) line is variant, . . . *His first pair had been broken by a rifle shot* [N^{2-3}: *musket shot*]. *The man brought a bottle of wine. He had misunderstood.* This happens to be a passage in which the editor of 5(III) was drawing on 5(II) readings to annotate the copy, and for 5(I) *first pair having been smashed* he adopts 5(II) *first pair had been broken*. Then—the key to the N^7 error—he substituted 5(II) *shot* for 5(I) *ball*. We cannot know whether, as seems probable, the hand alteration caused difficulty in the transmission, but it seems obvious that the text arrived in Kansas City without the period after *shot* so that it read something like 'shot the man brought a bottle', which was rationalized to the N^7 reading on the assumption that *shot* was a verb instead of a noun. In this case, then, N^7 can be absolved of willfully inventing the strange episode, *shot the messenger, who misunderstood the order and brought a bottle of wine.*

The absolving of N^7 in this matter is of some importance, because an outright invention here, perverting a normally transmitted text, might have had a bearing on the next case. At 21.4 after Crane's strong denunciation of the German officers who served the Turkish batteries, 5(I,II) conclude, *I consider these German officers hired assassins.* It is bad luck that N^{8-9} have been cut at this episode so that the origin of the unique N^7 continuation cannot be demonstrated: *hired assassins, sent out by the ridiculous popinjay who presides as 'war lord' over the German people.* It is not concrete evidence to remark that this seems to have the true Crane ring. Nevertheless, it so perfectly carries on his notorious anti-German bias and is so characteristic of his occasional intemperance in language that one can easily imagine him cabling to New York these words which no alert newspaper editor would dream of printing. It would not be unusual, therefore, for the passage to have been transcribed in at least one of the copies but subsequently deleted although not before the man responsible for 5(III) had picked it up. Some strength is given to this hypothesis by the fact that at 21.4 this passage immediately precedes the start at 21.5, or at least at 21.7, of the annotation of the basic 5(I) copy by reference to 5(II). The present editor conjectures, therefore, that the N^7 words were part of Crane's cable and are authoritative. Then, that they had never been a part of the 5(I) copy—or had been cut from it if transcribed—but instead that they were a part of the state of the copy of 5(II) that the rewrite man for 5(III) was consulting and had not yet been cut from it. (If so, something of an argument could be made that this was closely related to the intermediate N^{2-3} copy and not to the final copy for N^{1b}.) Finally, that as a part of his conflation of his basic copy with 5(II) already to be seen in this passage and to be continued in the immediately following text, this man picked up the popinjay continuation and added it to his revisions that were to produce the mixed 5(III) line. Such a hypothesis has the virtue of still preserving the copy for 5(I) in only a single identifiable form, not divided into early and late states as was 5(II) in its N^{2-3} and $N^{1b,4-5}$ variants.

Examples that would link N^7 variants with a derivation from an early state of 5(I) are subject to the same explanation, since the pattern establishes that the readings common to N^7 and 5(II) do not originate in some ur-text later revised to become 5(I). For instance, at 21.7–8 in the passage in which Crane discusses the leisurely nature of battles, $N^{1a,6}$ read sparely, *The swiftness of chronological order of battle is not correct.* $N^{1b,4-5}$ are somewhat amplified: *The swiftness in the chronology of battles is not correct in most books.* Although N^{2-3} have slightly different independent arrangements, both contain the phrase *in most books.* N^7 reads, however, in somewhat embroidered manner, *The swiftness of battles as chronicled in the story books evidently is all in the imagination.* At first sight—especially in view of N^7's use of Crane's favorite *evidently*—it is tempting to speculate that this might come from an ur-version of the text, condensed by 5(I) and varied by 5(II). But any such guessing would be idle, for this passage immediately follows on the cluster at 21.5–7 where (on the solid evidence of N^{8-9}, missing for 21.7–8) the 5(III) annotations of 5(I) copy by reference to 5(II) began. The 5(III) editor, therefore, must have taken over the detail about the books from 5(II), not from an early state of 5(I) copy, and elaborated it in his own way. If this is so at 21.7–8, it must also be so in the next sentence at 21.8, where even the typical Crane *evidently* comes from 5(II) although something of the sort seems to have been present in all but the final N^{1a} copy. The 5(I,II) texts agree in the simple infinitive *lunch*[34] and do not support the more elaborate jocularity of *to take a lunch in the club* (21.9). Here, as before—though not in the preceding sentence—5(I) and 5(II) provide some sort of check. Thus if N^7 had represented the ur-reading, both 5(I) and 5(II) would need not only to have cut *at the club* independently but also to have reduced *to take a lunch* to *lunch* (5[II]) or to *to lunch* (5[I]). In No. 6 the phrase is *to lunch*.

Thus evidence that might seem to suggest the derivation of 5(III) from some ur-text of 5(I) dissipates on close examination. Except for some possible last-minute touchings-up before being sent to the composing room, only the single known state of the 5(I) version can be discerned. In this respect, therefore, 5(III) is almost exclusively a derived text without independent authority for a reconstruction of the cable wording. On a few occasions, however, it serves to confirm the N^{1a} readings in cases where N^6 varies,[35] and it may have a limited usefulness in distinguishing N^{2-3} forms from N^{1a}. Its only real contri-

---

[34] Under the influence of preceding *get a shave*, N^2 unsupported by N^3 makes the editorial change *get a lunch*. Report No. 6 has *to lunch in comfort*.

[35] At 18.31 the usefulness of N^7 as a check is partially negated by the concurrence of N^{1a-b} in *well led* against N^6 *called upon*. Thus N^7 *well led* is useful but not essential to identifying here an N^6 editorial or compositorial variant. At 19.10, however, N^7 is more valuable in confirming N^{1a} *intoxication* versus N^6 *the intoxication,* and *the orders* versus $N^{2-3,6}$ *orders* even though the N^{7-9} form is *the order.* No common N^{6-7} variation against N^{1a} appears except for the nonsignificant *and also to* which unsplits the N^{1a} *and to also* (22.12).

bution is the preservation of Crane's outburst against the German emperor, apparently drawn from an uncorrected state of the typescript behind N^{2-3}.

If anything is certain it is that the copy behind N^{2-3} was an early form of the revised copy that was finally approved for $N^{1b,4-5}$. A minimum of forty-two distinct readings exist in which N^{2-3} join $N^{1a,6}$ against $N^{1b,4-5}$, to which may be added five more in which N^3 joins $N^{1a,6}$ when N^2 is wanting. It will be observed that these are almost exclusively very small differences in the forms of single words or phrases, nothing elaborate and nothing of meaningful variation.[36] They are the sort of thing that a rewrite man, typing up the final copy for the city edition N^{1b} might casually alter. Whether it was *Desperate Turkish cavalry* in N^{2-3} or *The desperate Turkish cavalry* (20.12–13), *gaunt hills* in N^{2-3} or *the gaunt hills* (20.27), *watched for a long time* in N^{2-3} or *watched a long time* (21.6), *the battery* in N^{2-3} or *a battery* (22.12)—these are trifling changes. N^{2-3} and N^{1a} specify that the English legionary was wounded *in the head* (21.37), a detail that gets skipped in N^{1b}. Small changes in idiom may be made, as whether it was *no fault* in N^{2-3} of this army, or N^{1b} *not the fault* (19.6); whether the legionary *came from the left* in N^{2-3} or *came in from the left* (21.36); or whether *it seemed* an extraordinary order in N^{2-3} or *seemed to be* (22.25). What were thought to be clarifying details might be added, as *at the same time* in N^{1b} (23.4) wanting in $N^{1a,2-3}$. The N^{1b} editor allowed himself a few elaborations, such as adding *fatalistic* (20.25) to the Turkish *religion*, the detail *and fumed* to N^{2-3} *raged* (19.15), and the substitution of *rifle* for *musket* (21.32). At 20.17, on the evidence of No. 6, he misunderstood or made an inadvertent error in typing, when he produced the reading *no expressions of horror* for *no expression, no horror* in $N^{1a,2-3}$. It would seem reasonably clear that these variations were consciously or unconsciously made, as slight stylistic improvements or as indifferent transmissional changes, when the final typescript copy was being made up for the *Journal* city-edition composing room and for wiring

---

[36] The forty-two occur at 5(1): 19.6 *no*, 19.14 *Smolenski*, 19.15 *raged*, 19.28 *the vastly*, 19.34 *base*, 20.2 *I . . . dreamed*, 20.7 *This is*, 20.13 *The desperate*, 20.17 *no horror*, 20.18 *to be*, 20.19 *of*, 20.19 *this*, 20.23 omit *it continued*, 20.25 omit *fatalistic*, 20.26 *it was*, 20.27 *gaunt*, 20.27 *fighting on*, 20.28 *their*, 21.1 *the*, 21.3 *not*, 21.6 *for*, 21.10 *whirlwind*, 21.32 *musket*, 21.36 *came*, 21.37 *in the head*, 22.1 *the battle*, 22.2 *News*, 22.2 *from the left*, 22.11 *indicated*, 22.12 *the battery*, 22.16 *seemed*, 22.16 *There was*, 22.22,26 *Smolenski*, 22.23 *left*, 22.25 *seemed an*, 22.28 *the*, 22.29 *batteries*, 22.39 *came*, 22.39 *the last*, 22.39 *on*, 23.4 omit *at the same time*. The five readings in which N^2 is wanting or itself varies but N^3 agrees with N^{1a} against N^{1b} are: 19.20 *Greeks*, 19.22 *right*, 19.24 *left*, 19.36 *of*, 22.10 *toward*.

to Chicago, Philadelphia, and Buffalo, and perhaps other unobserved newspapers.

The textual import of this group of forty-seven variants is perfectly clear. In any reconstruction of the form of the cable, the independent agreement of $N^{1a,6}$ with this group of N^{2-3} readings is as solid evidence for the cable readings as is the agreement of $N^{1a,6}$ with N^{1b-5}, or with $N^{1b,4-5}$.

A minumum of twenty-eight distinct readings exist in which N^{2-3} agree against N^{1a} and N^{1b} (in general) and their reprints.[37] The most interesting of these are two passages in which N^{2-3} contain material of some substance wanting in N^{1a-b}. The first is at 22.26 where N^{1a-b} read laconically *They say Smolenski wept*, to which N^2 (and N^3 with minor variation) adds *I did not see him weep, but would have done so had I been he*. The second comes at 20.17–18. N^{1a} reads *no horror to be seen*. To this N^{1b} adds *there were simply the movements of tiny doll tragedy*. N^{2-3} contain this addition although in two variant forms, continue with a new variant bridge,[38] and then join in the further new addition, *The difficulty of the [N^3: a] war correspondent's career is he can never tell where the exciting thing is going to break out*. It is difficult to imagine the rewrite man making up the N^{2-3} draft from the cable and adding these details without any authority. Something of a clue may be provided by variants at 19.26. N^{1a} prints, *How the soldiers talked!* and $N^{1b,4-5}$ *The talk goes among the soldiers that . . . .* The N^{2-3} versions are close to N^{1b}. N^2 reads *and, well, the talk goes among the soldiers* but N^3, *Well, talk goes among the soldiers that . . . .* Again, the colloquial *well* is more likely to come from Crane than from a rewrite man, and gives every indication of having been edited out independently by the editors both of N^{1a} and of N^{1b}, who no doubt also excised the personal comment about the difficulties of a war correspondent's career (half an apology for having missed the first day of the battle), and also the personal remark that Crane would himself have behaved like Smolenski. These are natural excisions, and they seem to have been made.

---

[37] These are: 18.27–28 *In the first place*, 19.3 *it occasioned*, 19.11 omit N^{1a} *of the sort* or N^{1b} *else*, 19.17 *fighting*, 19.17 omit *were*, 19.19 omit *a*, 19.25 *in*, 19.26 *Well*, 19.28 *understand*, 19.29 *have*, 19.30 *want*, 19.39 *resonant* for *a resonant* or *a tin*, 20.2 omit *It was*, 20.18 *The difficulty of a war correspondent's*, 20.28 *positions*, 20.33 *and*, 20.36 *are*, 20.36–37 *are* or *were*, 20.39–21.1 *them*, 22.1 *was*, 22.2 omit *had*, 22.9 *had begun*, 22.14 omit *this* or *it*, 22.26 *I did not . . . been he*, 22.28 *orders*, 23.2–3 *anyhow*, 23.5 *a bloody*, 23.5 *can't*.

[38] N^2 reads, *simply as movements of tiny dolls. The tragedy of it at close quarters must have been tremendous*, whereas N^3 has *simply the movements of tiny dolls in the tragedy. Closer it must have been tremendous*.

It is apparent, therefore, that not all of the unique N^{2-3} variants against N^{1a-b} can be assessed automatically as errors or as the rewrite man's fantasies, and thus that the concurrence of N^{1a} and N^{1b} is not invariably a guarantee of faithfulness to the cable. The Crane locution *In the first place* (see "Stephen Crane's Own Story," No. 17, 89.17) that begins the N^{2-3} dispatch is no doubt another victim of the editorial pencils. Given Crane's fondness for slipping into the present tense, it is also probable that N^{2-3} *understand* for N^{1a-b} *understood* (19.28), *have whipped* for N^{1a} *had whipped* and N^{1b} *whipped* (19.29), *want* for *wanted* (19.30), *are* for *were* (20.36), and N^2 *are* (despite N^3 *were*) for *had* (20.37) are also cable characteristics normalized in the later versions.

We may suppose that when the typescript made up from the cable was first completed, one copy was put on the wire to Chicago and Philadelphia, and another copy was kept, further revised, and eventually sent to the *Journal* compositors for the out-of-town edition, with its carbon, say, wired to Boston, Buffalo, and so on. The exact nature of the copy wired to Chicago and Philadelphia is perhaps subject only to speculation, but the evidence suggests that a clean copy was made from the first draft, and in the process of this transcription some few unauthoritative variants developed, as would be expected. The unique N^{2-3} divergences from joint N^{1a-b}, then, appear to be a mixture of authoritative cable readings independently altered by the editors of N^{1a} and revised N^{1b} and of unauthoritative readings springing from the extra transmissional process to which the physical copy wired to N^{2-3} had been subjected. The distinction between the two is not easy. To the list discussed above that seems authoritative one may readily add the appearance of *anyhow* in N^{2-3} at 23.2–3 to an also characteristic phrase omitted in N^{1a} but printed in N^{1b-5}. At 19.11 it would seem that both N^{1a} and N^{1b} were dissatisfied with the abruptness of the N^{2-3} copy *something* and felt that more was needed but chose different words to add. Variants that appear to have crept into the typing of the wire-copy of N^{2-3} and therefore to be unauthoritative are *positions* for *position* (20.28), *concluded* for *conclude* (22.1),[39] the omission of *had* (22.2),[40] *had begun* for N^{1a} *began* but N^{1b} *was begun* (22.9), or the

[39] This variant is part of a larger one. N^{1a-b} read *Most wounded men conclude,* which in N^3 becomes *Most of the wounded concluded.* The N^2 local editor gilded the lily by giving Crane a first-person reference (for which he was sometimes satirized but in this case did not deserve): *I concluded.*

[40] Perhaps this should be put in the doubtful category, but the chance exists that the *had* before *tried* was omitted in the N^{2-3} typescript because of fancied parallel structure with the following *failed.*

omission of N^{1a} *it* but N^{1b} *this* (22.14).[41] Two similar variants at 20.2 and 20.33 where N^{2-3} print one sentence which N^{1a-b} break into two are slightly doubtful typing changes since the N^{1a-b} changes to form two sentences are conventional enough. (But see 19.17–18 discussed in footnote 42 below.) This group may conclude with N^{2-3} *them* for N^{1a} *these officers* and N^{1b} *they are* (20.39–21.1) and probably *a bloody bandage* for *bloody bandages* (23.5). The rest are distinctly speculative and almost indifferent.[42]

Since both N^2 and N^3 freely edited the copy wired them,[43] sometimes what seems to have been the cable language can be recovered, though speculatively, from only one witness. An example occurs at 22.6, where N^{1a} reads briefly, *and the battery of howitzers opened on them.* In reference to the new troops who had prayed at the shrine while coming up (as we learn only from No. 6), N^{1b} reads, still briefly, *New battalions on the right opened up*, which omits all reference to the howitzers. But that these howitzers were in the cable seems to be established by the variant N^{2-3} texts. N^2 reads, *The Greek battery*

---

[41] Possibly this reading is in the category of 19.11, above, where it is conjectured both N^{1a-b} repaired in a different manner a fancied gap. But here the gap is an actual one, whether in the cable or in the transmission to the N^{2-3} wire-copy. Some word is definitely called for.

[42] For example, the N^{2-3} omission of *a* before N^{1b} *a resonant roofing* is a tossup. If *resonant* were the wording of the cable (which is arguable), perhaps the omission is authoritative. But if the cable read *tin roof* with N^{1a}, then *a* is required provided Crane spent the *Journal's* money on cabling an article here. Whether at 23.5 Crane cabled *can't* or *cannot* is scarcely to be determined. At 18.31–32 where N^{1a} reads simply *cope successfully with Turks, even though outnumbered* and N^{1b} varies with *successfully cope with the overwhelming numbers of Turks*, whether the *the* is an intrusion in the final N^{1b} typescript or an omission in the N^{2-3} is problematical. At 19.17–18 the omission of *were* is consequent upon the formation of one sentence in N^{2-3} for two in N^{1a-b}. Here the only possible clue is to point out that at 20.2 and 20.33 N^{1a-b} have two sentences where N^{2-3} join them into one, and perhaps this may suggest a trick of the typist of the N^{2-3} copy. At 19.25 the example of N^{1a}'s *of this* shows that N^{2-3} *in this* is close to authority in comparison with the revised N^{1b}'s specification *under Smolenski's.* But whether N^{1a} *of* or N^{2-3} *in* is what Crane cabled is a tossup. Finally, at 19.17 N^{1a-b} join in *a three days' successful fight*, which should establish N^{2-3} *three days of successful fighting* as aberrant were it not for the odd hit that N^6 (set from N^{1a} copy) reads *three days' successful fighting*. Even so, one may guess that the same idiomatic considerations that caused N^6 to change its copy also operated on the typist of the N^{2-3} copy.

[43] The *Chicago Tribune's* versions of other dispatches show similar independence, and the Philadelphia *Press* texts of *Journal* dispatches are often divergent from copy. In the present dispatch a further variation is introduced in N^3 by its frequent omission of the articles *the* and *a*, apparently in an attempt to fake the realism of cable style. Not only on the evidence of this dispatch but on that of the others in this volume, it would be fantastic to take it that the wired copy had omitted these articles, especially when the evidence is clear that even punctuation and probably paragraphing were customarily wired.

of Howitzers threw a few shells. New battalions on the right opened up. The N^3 version is more typical because less conventional: *but the Greek battery of howitzers threw them into a fit. New battalions on the right opened up.* Here it would seem that N^{1a} has cut the reference to the new battalions in favor of the howitzers and appropriated for the howitzers the word *opened* which the cable had applied to the new battalions. In contrast N^{1b} removed the howitzers in favor of the battalions. Only N^{2-3} give both. But it would appear that N^2 substituted *a few shells* after *threw* for the slangy N^3 *them into a fit;* the reverse would be more difficult to envisage. The odds may favor, then, the guess that in this passage N^3 reproduces, just about verbatim, the original rewrite made of the cable. Another example may be cited. N^{1a}, as so often, is condensed: *The Greeks fought all the time with the artillery fire on them* (20.22–23), whereas in N^{1b} the sentence is *The artillery fire upon them was almost eternal.* Since this is a revision, necessarily, in N^{1b}, it would seem that the N^3 version comes closer both to the N^{1a} and N^{1b} forms than does N^2. N^3 reads *The artillery fire was upon them eternally* whereas N^2 has *The Turkish artillery fired upon them eternally.*

The evidence in the 5(II) line, then, can be utilized in different ways to reconstruct with fair accuracy the original rewrite for the out-of-town edition made from the cable, with difficulty only when N^2 and N^3 vary between themselves and also from N^{1b}. If only one more newspaper version companion to N^{2-3} would turn up, something like practical certainty might be achieved. For the 5(I) line, in which no more than a single rewrite copy can be detected, variation between N^{1a} and N^6 in cases when both diverge from 5(II) can usually be decided with the assistance of N^7, or—when N^7 has been conflated with 5(II)—by reference to N^{8-9} and to N^{10-12} according to their independent derivation from the 5(I) copy behind N^7. When the 5(I) and 5(II) traditions diverge with no partial bridge between them, the reading of the cable can be the subject only for speculation.

Although as indicated above some success can be had in reconstructing eclectically the cable, occasionally in quite extended passages, no really continuous text for reading purposes can be managed without constantly intervening gaps. The present edition therefore instead of attempting a partial and unsatisfactory synthesis prints both 5(I) and 5 (II), each accompanied by its own apparatus, with no more than simple correction of manifest error. The copy-texts are respectively N^{1a} and N^{1b}. It is obvious that the text for 5 (II) using the N^{1b} copy-text is farthest from the cable of any in this line since it has been subjected to a second stage of rewriting in preparation for the out-of-town *Journal* publication. On the other hand, a text based on the more authoritative N^{2-3} prints would run into trouble when N^2 and N^3 vary not only from N^{1b} but from each other, and no authoritative readings could be selected in such areas. A generally more authoritative text than N^{1b} might have been managed by emending the N^{1b} copy-text whenever N^{2-3} concur; but this would still be an unsatisfactory hybrid production that mixed authority with nonauthority in those readings where N^{2-3} varied and the unauthoritative N^{1b} rewrite text would have been followed. The $5(\text{III})$ line of the text owns such authority as stems from its radiation from the copy behind $N^{1a,6}$ and in that sense $5(\text{III})$ is not a derived text. However, it is not an independent line in relation to the cable, as is true for $5(\text{I})$ and $5(\text{II})$, and therefore has not been reprinted. Its readings, as well as those of the radiating subversions N^{8-9} and N^{10-12} may be consulted in the general Historical Collation to the whole report, in which—keyed to the $5(\text{I})$ text—all substantive variants in $5(\text{II})$ and $5(\text{III})$ are recorded. Throughout this section of the textual analysis, except when specific analysis was being made of the N^{1b} text in its own terms, the page-line references have been to the $5(\text{I})$ text—not that it is the more authoritative (a decision between $5[\text{I}]$ and $5 [\text{II}]$ as a whole is impossible in this respect), but simply that it furnishes the most convenient and stable text to use as a basis for recording the collation of variants. Thus references are as much to the general Historical Collation as they are to $5(\text{I})$ specifically. Printed by Fryckstedt from N^{1b} and by Stallman from N^{1a}.

No. 6. A FRAGMENT OF VELESTINO

The second of the McClure syndicated letters was "A Fragment of Velestino," printed in the *Westminster Gazette* as part II (27.28–33.38) and its continuation (34.1–39.37), and then part III (39.38–44.23), of the series "With Greek and Turk" on June 3, 4, and 8, 1897, all on pages 1–2.[44] The standard heading advertised Crane as author of *The Red Badge of Courage* and noted that each part was 'Copyright U.S.A., 1897.' The series is not datelined, but a footnote was appended to the June 3 part reading: 'Mr. Stephen Crane's letters

---

[44] The title and the text of the *Gazette* report consistently spell the name *Velestimo*, which probably represents the spelling of the manuscript transferred to the typescript. It is *Velestimo* similarly in Cora Crane's inscription of the dictated manuscript No. 14, "A Portrait of Smolenski."

have by some accident been considerably delayed in transmission, but we make no apology for publishing them three weeks after the events to which they relate, since their literary interest, as impressions of the battlefield, are in no way diminished by the lapse of time.—Ed. *W.G.*'

(N[1]): *New York Journal,* Sunday, June 13, 1897, pages 24–25, printed with a two-page spread but with five substantial cuts. On page 24 the headline reads, 'That Was the ROMANCE, | This Is the | REALITY, | The Battle To-day in Greece|— a Fact. | by | STEPHEN CRANE.' The page 25 part of the spread is headlined ' "The Red Badge of Courage" — A Story.' A very large illustration by Dan Smith joins the two pages, consisting of a panorama of the battlefield scene, Crane sitting in observation, with the main legend, in type, 'Mr. Stephen Crane, Novelist and Special War Correspondent for the Journal, on the Battlefield of Velestino in the Thick of the Fight.' Subsidiary legends, in type, indicate the various parts of the illustration by quotations. The first and second, on page 24, read respectively: ' *"On the lonely road from Velestino there appeared the figure of a man. He came slowly, and with a certain patient steadiness. A great piece of white linen was wound around under his jaw, and finally tied at the top of his head in a great knot, like the one grandma ties when she remedies her boy's toothache."* ' and ' *"Continually there was in the air a noise as if some one had thrown an empty beer bottle with marvellous speed at you. This hooting and whistling of some of the shells was like nothing if not like the flight of an empty beer bottle."* ' On page 25 the two legends read: ' *"The trenches on the left of the height became tumultuous with smoke and long, thin rifle flashes. As the dark streams, rivulets, of of the enemy poured along the plain, a large number of batteries opened, and great black shells, whirling and screaming, fled over the heads of the men in the trenches. There was going to be a good, tight little fight."* ' and ' *"The heads of the loose skirmishing columns of the enemy became hidden in rolling masses of smoke. The Turks were shooting low. Few bullets went over the trench. Many fell below it, and a certain number with great regularity went pum-pum-pump into the earthwork."* ' Substantively, these correspond to the *Journal* text except that in the third the word *part* is omitted in the legend after *left.* No copyright notice appears; the piece is signed.

(N[2]): San Francisco *Examiner,* June 27, page 21, headlined 'That Was the ROMANCE: "The Red Badge of Courage." | This Is the REALITY: A Battle of To-Day in Greece. ‖ BY STEPHEN CRANE.' As with N[1], no dateline is present, and the story is signed at the foot.

The difference in date between June 13 for N[1] and June 27 for N[2] combines with the unusual similarity in the headlines and, for the *Examiner,* the unusual textual fidelity to its source, to indicate that the report was mailed, not wired, to the *Examiner* and that the copy was a clipping, not a typescript. Hence N[2] is a fully derived text with no authority whatever. The copy-text is the full version in the *Westminster Gazette,* emended as necessary from the radiating authority N[1] when it would appear that WG has editorially altered the substantives or its compositor (or editor) the accidentals. So far as observed, no other newspapers carried this report. Printed by Fryckstedt from the shorter N[1] version and by Stallman from the *Gazette*.

No. 7. THE BLUE BADGE OF COWARDICE

Crane's cable describing the retreat on Volo by the Greek army was sent from Chalkis to Athens and there cabled to New York on May 11, 1897.

(N[1]): *New York Journal* printed it without variation in both editions on May 12, page 3, datelined Athens, May 11—(By Courier from Chalkis), with the headline 'THE BLUE BADGE | OF COWARDICE. || Stephen Crane Writes of the Thou-|sands Who Suffered Because the | Crown Prince Was a Craven. || The Retreat of Smolenski and the Flight of Women | and Children from Volo — Landed Any-|where Without Food or Shelter. || By Stephen Crane.' No copyright notice was printed.

(N[2]): The text was put on the wire to the *Chicago Tribune* where it was printed on May 12, pages 1, 3, signed, with the headline 'STEPHEN CRANE DESCRIBES FLIGHT OF GREEKS FROM VOLO. ||It Was Not a Panic, but an Emigration—Pitiable Condition of the Homeless, | Starving Refugees—Wrathful, Sullen Retreat of the Army, with Curses | for the Faintheartedness of the Prince Who Will Rule Them. || (Special Cable by Stephen Crane.)'. The dateline is the same as that in N[1] except that '[Copyright, 1897]' has been added. The runover on page 3 is headed 'STEPHEN CRANE AT VOLO || PICTURESQUE DESCRIPTION OF THE | GREEK EVACUATION. || Pitiable Condition of the Refugees, | Who Lack Both Food and Shelter—|Wrathful, Sullen Retreat of the | Army—Curses for the Fainthearted-|ness of Their Commander-in-Chief|—Turks Are Not Harmless, Wooly | Lambs. ||'.

(N[3]): Philadelphia *Press*, May 12, page 2, signed, and headlined 'STEPHEN CRANE SEES VOLO'S FEAR || The Young Novelist Describes Vividly for "The Press" the | Wholesale Evacuation of the Greek Port by the | Fear-Stricken Population at the Approach | of the Moslem Host. || SPECIAL CABLE DESPATCH TO "THE PRESS." COPYRIGHT. 1897.' Dateline is as in N[1].

(N[4]): San Francisco *Examiner*, May 12, pages 1–2, headlined 'HORRORS | OF WAR IN | DEFEAT. || Stephen Crane Depicts | the Scenes at | Volo. || Flight of the Populace | Before the Hated | Turk. ||'. The headline then continues with reference to the special news, prefixed to Crane's dispatch, that the Powers have offered to mediate and Greece has accepted the terms. There follows '|| By Stephen Crane. | (Special cable to "The Examiner." | Copyright, 1897, by W. R. Hearst)'. The runover on page 2 is headed 'HORRORS OF WAR | IN DEFEAT. ||'. The dateline is that of N[1].

(N[5]): *Boston Globe*, May 12, page 7, headlined 'CURSED THE PRINCE. || Greek Retreat from Volo in Rage at | Leader's Incompetence. || Over 8000 Refugees Crowd Into a | Little Village of a Few Houses|—Women and Children in Heaps, | Hungry and Homeless, Exemplify | the Horrors of War. ‖ By Stephen Crane.' Dateline as in N¹; at the end,' '(Copyright.)'.

(N⁶): *Buffalo Evening News*, May 12, pages 1, 7, headlined 'PITIABLE SCENES AT VOLO. ‖ Stephen Crane's Pen Picture of the War Viewed | From the Deserted Homes. ‖ By Stephen Crane. | (Copyright, 1897, by W. R. Hearst.)'; the runover on page 7 is headlined 'GREEK TROOPS | LEAVING CRETE. ‖'. Dateline as in N¹.

(N⁷): *Kansas City Star*, a shortened version, May 12, page 2, headlined 'STEPHEN CRANE'S IMPRESSIONS. ‖ The Young Author on Smolenski's Retreat | and Misery of Fugitives.' The dateline is New York, May 12.

The copy-text is N¹, the *New York Journal,* which has gone through one less stage of transmission, emended occasionally in its accidentals from the general concurrence of the other texts. No evidence suggests that an early version of N¹ was wired to the subscribing newspapers N²⁻⁵ which was then altered in N¹ by proofreading or by further editing: except for questions of usage at 45.24, 47.19, and 47.25, and the correction of a few misprints in N¹, all substantive variants in N²⁻⁷ are unique with the newspaper concerned. Nevertheless, some suspicion may be felt that the *Buffalo Evening News* version (N⁶) could represent the earliest text of the N¹ form, and the present editor is inclined to this position. At 46.15 it is possible the N⁶ copy-reader introduced the personal note in *I witnessed the great evacuation* where the others read *It was the great evacuation.* The N¹ *soldier's equipments* where N²⁻⁷ read *soldiers'* might be rationalized when in N⁶ one sees the singular *equipment,* even though with *soldiers'* (45.4). In line with the N⁶ *I witnessed* is the immediacy of *had a United States vessel been here* where the others read *there* (45.38). It is odd that N⁶ generalizes *the Greek warships lie a few hundred yards away* when the others specify *four hundred yards* (46.20–21). The oddest variant of all, however, comes at 46.34 where for *There is where the hard fighting will be done* N⁶ reads *the 40-yard fighting,* a football metaphor typical of Crane's use of sporting language. Some of the N⁶ readings must be misprints, like *gray* for *gay* (45.16); and N⁶ *accusation* for *situation* (46.19) is certainly a mistake. Others like *cheers* for *cries* (44.28) or *peculiar* for *particular* (45.22) are possibly authoritative, and *this village* for N¹⁻⁴ *the village* and N⁵,⁷ *a village* (47.19) is more than possible. In short, if these readings had been confirmed by a single other newspaper the case would be clinched. As it is, the oddity that only this one newspaper would be wired an early text (unless it was an accident in some manner that is not to be explained)⁴⁵ joins with the latent possibility that they are

⁴⁵ Other news stories like No. 5 were wired to the *Chicago Tribune,* a regular customer, in a hurry and hence sometimes in a text that had not been given the final touches. But the *Buffalo Evening News* not being in this category, some

copyreader's alterations to prevent the emendation of the copy-text as if the hypothesis for N^6 authority were firmly based. Printed by Fryckstedt and by Stallman from N^1.

No. 8. YALE MAN ARRESTED

The brief cable about Montgomery's arrest was datelined Athens, May 13, and was syndicated to appear in the newspapers on May 14.

(N^1): *New York Journal*, May 14, 1897, page 3, headlined 'YALE MAN ARRESTED. ‖ George Montgomery, '92, Corre-|spondent of a London Paper, | Captured by Greeks. ‖ By Stephen Crane. | (Copyright, 1897, by W. R. Hearst.)'.

(N^2): *Chicago Tribune*, May 14, page 3, headlined 'AMERICAN IS AR-RESTED IN GREECE. ‖ Acting as an English Correspondent | and Wearing a Swagger and | a Turkish Fez. ‖ [SPECIAL CABLE BY STEPHEN CRANE.]'. The dateline, as in N^1, is followed by 'Copyright, 1897.]'.

(N^3): Philadelphia *Press*, May 14, page 2, signed, and headlined 'AMERICAN ARRESTED. ‖ Correspondent of a London Paper | Seized by Greeks. | Special Cable Despatch to "The Press," Copy-|right, 1897.' The dateline is like N^1.

(N^4): *Buffalo Evening News*, May 14, page 5, headlined 'AMERICAN ARRESTED. ‖ But He Was the Correspondent | of a London Newspaper | and Wore a Fez. ‖ By Stephen Crane. | (Copyright, 1897, by W. R. Hearst.)'.

The copy-text is N^1, the *New York Journal*, which seems to have sent out its own text to the various newspapers. The N^2 variants look more like N^2 editing, which was always individualistic, than like an early version. Printed by Fryckstedt and by Stallman from N^1.

No. 9. THE DOGS OF WAR

This account of the finding of Crane's pup Velestino is quite certainly a 'letter' and not a cable, on the evidence of its subject matter but chiefly because the May 30 date of printing in the *New York*

---

theory of an accident that provided this copy would need to be contrived. If the wires to Chicago, San Francisco, Philadelphia, and Boston had all gone out from one copy, but the wire to Buffalo was an afterthought and somehow the early copy got substituted, one could understand the anomaly; but such speculative reconstructions are idle without some shred of corroborative evidence. It is a pity, because the Buffalo version in certain readings could well be closer to Crane's cable. (Yet see No. 10 for an instance when the *Buffalo Evening News* was wired a later form of the copy than the other newspapers, so that hypothesis is at least possible.) See also the mixup in No. 47.

Journal for events that must have been concluded no later than the second week of May does not suggest urgency, nor is there a dateline. However, it must have been written and sent out by courier ahead of Crane's return to Athens (despite the ending of the story), for he boarded ship at St. Marina on May 18 and arrived in Athens on May 22. Whether Crane had this sent directly to the *Journal* or through the usual intermediary of McClure's London office (as seems probable) is not to be determined, for this was the second of his 'letters' not printed in the *Westminster Gazette*.

(N¹): *New York Journal*, May 30, 1897, page 18, signed, headlined 'Stephen   THE DOGS OF WAR   Crane | A Fascinating Story of the Battlefield of Greece, | By the Author of | "The Red Badge of Courage." ' The *Journal* gave this anecdote something of a spread, as it was to do for No. 6 on June 13. An illustration of a Greek boy, carrying a rifle, with three puppies on leads, accompanies the headline, and a large cut with the legend 'THE DOG.' occupies the center of the page, flanked to the upper left by a cut of three Greeks, the center figure holding the dog, entitled 'THE DOG AMONG HIS FRIENDS', and to the lower right by the picture of a youth with the legend 'THE BOY WHO LOST THE DOG'. These are stated to be 'From photographs taken by the Journal's kodak in Greece and sent by Stephen Crane.'

(N²): San Francisco *Examiner*, Sunday, June 13, page 4. Its title used a redrawn cut of the Greek boy and three puppies, but none of the other cuts appears. The story is signed at the foot but is without copyright notice.

The appearance in the *Examiner* two weeks after that in the *Journal* suggests that the copy, though without the cuts, was mailed. The reproduction of the N¹ accidentals is in general so exact, and the number of substantive variants so few (only four not connected with altering reference from the *Journal* to the *Examiner*), that radiation from a common typescript (and carbon) original is not to be contemplated seriously. Although the question whether the copy was a *Journal* proof or clipping cannot be settled, the N² variants give no clear sign of stemming from uncorrected proof, although such transmission would not be impossible. The N² text, therefore, is a derived one without independent authority, and N¹ becomes the copy-text. Reprinted by Fryckstedt and by Stallman from N¹.

No. 10. STEPHEN CRANE TELLS OF WAR'S HORRORS

Two dispatches under one headline, one by Julian Ralph and the other by Crane, appeared side by side in the *New York Journal* on

May 23, datelined Athens, May 22 (On Board the St. Marina, Which Left Chalkis, Greece, May 18.). Of the four observed newspapers that carried the *Journal's* dispatch, Hearst's San Francisco *Examiner*, and also the *Buffalo Evening News,* ran the Ralph story, but it did not appear in the *Chicago Tribune* and the Philadelphia *Press*.

(N[1]): *New York Journal,* Sunday, May 23, 1897. The Greater New York edition (N[1a]) ran it on page 35 but the out-of-town edition (N[1b]) on page 37. The headline reads 'STEPHEN CRANE AND JULIAN RALPH TELL OF | WAR'S HORRORS AND TURKEY'S BOLD PLAN. ‖ Dark Side of War, with Its Wounded Soldiers and Panic-Stricken Women | and Children, Portrayed—Sultan Pouring a Vast Army Into Greece, | with the Object of Holding It and Defying the Powers. ‖ [to the left] By Julian Ralph. | (Copyright, 1897, W. R. Hearst.) | [to the right] By Stephen Crane. | (Copyright by W. R. Hearst.)'.

(N[2]): *Chicago Tribune,* May 23, 1897, pages 1–2, headlined ' 'MID DEAD AND DYING ‖ Stephen Crane Tells of Some | of the Horrors of War. ‖ ON AN AMBULANCE SHIP. ‖ His Fellow Passengers 800 Bul-|let Torn Greeks. ‖ CORPSES AMONG THE LIVING ‖ Chorus of Moaning and Wailing from | the Lower Deck. ‖ TAKING REFUGEES FROM ST. ALIDA. ‖ [SPECIAL CABLE BY STEPHEN CRANE.]'. The dateline is Athens, May 22.—[Copyright, 1897.].

(N[3]): Philadelphia *Press,* May 23, p. 2, signed, headlined 'STEPHEN CRANE ON WANING WAR ‖ The Young Novelist Cables "The Press" a Brilliant Story of | the Closing Days of Greece's Struggle | with Turkey. ‖ SPECIAL CABLE DESPATCH TO "THE PRESS," COPYRIGHTED, 1897.' The dateline is the same as N[1].

(N[4]): San Francisco *Examiner,* May 23, page 13, headlined 'VAN-QUISHED GREEK AND VICTORIOUS TURK. | [to the left] Horrors of War on a Transport Ship, | Where Dying Hellenes Pillow Their | Heads on the Dead. ‖ BY STEPHEN CRANE. | Special Cable to "The Examiner," Copyright, 1897, by W. R. Hearst.' The dateline is the same as N[1].

(N[5]): *Buffalo Evening News,* May 23, pages 1, 8, headlined 'DEAD AND DYING. ‖ Picture of a Hospital Boat and | the Closing Scenes of | the War. ‖ By Stephen Crane. | (Copyright, 1897, by W. R. Hearst.)'. The headline for the runover on page 8 reads 'TURKEY FOR WAR. ‖'. The dateline is the same as N[1].

The text of this dispatch has its points of interest. In the *New York Journal* the out-of-town edition N[1b] has three typographical errors corrected by the Greater New York edition N[1a] (which itself made a typo in correcting N[1b]) as well as one substantive reading *them* sophisticated to *him* (54.5) in the N[1a] review (see the Textual Note). Since otherwise the typesetting is identical, it is evident that the N[1b] setting was the original, and that it was proofread and corrected before the N[1a] edition was printed. The text that was wired to N[2-5] is the full version which was cut seriously in N[1], four passages and three additional sentences totalling some 457 words being sacrificed to the *Journal's* space requirements and hence not previously reprinted. Whether the *Journal* itself set these passages and then excised them when making up the page or whether the cuts were marked in the copy sent to the composing room and never set is not demonstrable. Unlike some of the other dispatches, where considerable revision might be made in the *Journal* copy after an early telegraphing of a draft version, in No. 10 only one reading betrays revision in N^1 from the wired copy as evidenced by agreement of the subscribing newspapers against N^1. This occurs at 55.36–37 where N^{2-3} (N^4 is cut here) have one form of modification that has been sophisticated in N^1 (see the Textual Note). However, N^5 agrees with N^1, effectively demonstrating that its copy was wired from some slightly different form from that sent N^{2-3}. If this single change were made in the rewrite sheets before they were sent to the N^1 composing room, and if this same copy or a duplicate were the source of the wire to N^5, then no conjectures are possible. However, if this change had been made in the proof, and a corrected proof wired to Buffalo, then we should have evidence that the full text had originally been set up by N^1 but trimmed to space requirements. No decision is possible, unfortunately, for either theory involves difficulties. Against the possibility that more than one small revision would be made in reviewing this copy must be balanced the difficulty in taking it that this change was made in the course of a proofreading that missed the typos at 54.32, 54.34–35, and 56.40. Textually the matter is not crucial, for the order of the change at 55.36–37 is established anyway; what is of interest is the question of the kind of copy that the *Journal* sent out and particularly whether it ever wired from its proof—a point that cannot be altogether settled. No other N^5 reading seems to represent more than a local compositorial slip.

One distinct anomaly is present in the *Tribune* text, however, where a dateline from Stylidia (*i.e.*, Stylis) on May 19 (a day later than the first dispatch) introduces the change of scene at 54.33. Moreover, the introduction of this dateline is accompanied by the omission of the first two sentences found in all other texts: *This is Wednesday I think. We are at Stylidia.* Again, the inferences that may be drawn are far from certain. It may be that N^{3-4} (N^5 is excluded because of its copy) found the dateline intrusive and suppressed it independently. It may be that it was present only in a slightly earlier form of the copy wired to Chicago, even though it would represent the only difference. The N^2 omission of the two introductory sentences might, of course, reproduce the wired copy, which would mean that the *Journal* rewrite man who removed the dateline supplied them in its place to mark the change of scene. That the informality of the first sentence stemmed from such an editor instead of from Crane may be thought doubtful, however, in which case the two sentences would have been deleted by the N^2 editor, who found the dateline sufficient. The case is most obscure, including the N^2 form *St. Alida* for *Stylidia* throughout and the problem whether this was the cable form reproduced in an early rewrite but subsequently altered in the other copies of the story from which the *Journal* sent its telegrams.

Also in question is the status of the N^2 reading at 54.39–55.1 of *boat, at Bay St. Marina, where the field hospital is located, was requested* for N^{3-5} *boat that carried the wounded was requested.* (N^1 is cut at this point.) Here we seem to be on firmer ground. Up to this sentence no mention has been made of the newspaper boat carrying any wounded, and, in fact, according to the dispatch the boat carried wounded along with the refugees and hospital stores only on its return (56.2–3) and later when it evacuated the hospital at St. Marina (56.25–27). This dispatch is singularly confused about times and places, and it may be that the N^2 editor, looking ahead to 56.25–27 tried to clarify a reference in his text like *that carried the wounded* which had no antecedent. But it is also possible that in reviewing the dispatch in the form sent to Chicago the N^1 copyreader tried to join the two halves of the dispatch and mixed up the Greek steamer from Chalkis to Athens and its eight hundred wounded with the newspaper steamer. This may seem the more probable since, in fact, the Stylis episodes occurred before, not after, the ostensible start of the dispatch on board the steamer from Chalkis, which must have left Chalkis for Athens on May 20 or 21. It would seem, then, that the *Chicago Tribune* did indeed receive an earlier form of this dispatch than the other newspapers and that certain of its readings are closer to the cable than the rewritten version. On the other hand, the unique N^2 variants are not many, and some must be due to the Chicago editing, which was usually omnipresent. Perhaps the only other reading that might have a chance to be the original form obscured by revision in the later versions is *breast* for *bosom* at 54.7.

Since it is the form of the typesetting closest to the copy, without the further stage of transmission by telegram, the *New York Journal* must be selected as the copy-text. However, on the principle that it is the original form of this typesetting before proofreading (which in the nature of the case is liable to introduce unauthoritative changes, as happened in N^{1a} even while correcting mechanical errors), the out-of-town edition N^{1b} has been chosen as the specific copy-text over the later state of the setting represented by the city edition N^{1a}. The substantive form of the syntax at 55.36–37, represented by the N^{2-3} agreement, has been used to emend the copy-text, and a scattering of accidentals from other newspaper agreements has been substituted to restore the copy forms that were modified by the N^1 compositor. In addition one important variant (that at 54.39–55.1) has been drawn from N^2 (as against the N^{3-5} version of cut N^1), taken to represent the earliest version of the dispatch. Although the May 19 dateline at 'Stylidia' seems authentic in N^2, it has been omitted in this reading text. When N^1 is wanting, N^2 becomes the copy-text, with reference made to variant forms in N^{3-5} of the same text. Printed by Fryckstedt and by Stallman, both from N^{1b}.

No. 11. GREEKS WAITING AT THERMOPYLÆ

Crane's Thermopylæ cable was datelined Lamia, May 22, via Athens, May 23, and appeared in the newspapers on May 24, 1897.

(N^1): *New York Journal*, May 24, 1897, page 10 in the Greater New York edition but page 2 in the out-of-town edition. The text of the two is identical. N^1 is headlined 'GREEKS WAITING | AT THERMOPYLÆ || Soldiers Eager for An-|other Chance at | the Turks. || RUMORS OF ARMISTICE. || Wild Turkish Irregulars | May Precipitate a | Battle. || OFFICERS WOULD QUIT. || Men in Charge of the Hellenic | Forces Express Themselves | for Peace. || ONLY EVZONES NOW AT LAMIA. || Main Body of the Army Has Already | Marched Away for the New Posi-|tion—Thermoplyæ Has | Been Widened. || By Stephen Crane. | (Copyright, 1897, by W. R. Hearst)'.

(N^2): *Chicago Tribune*, May 24, page 2, headlined 'GREEK ARMY GATHERING AGAIN AT PASS OF THERMOPYLÆ. || Stephen Crane Says Turkish Regulars Are Great Fighters and They Do Not | Know an Armistice from a Pie or a Truce | from a Trilobite. || [SPECIAL CABLE BY STEPHEN CRANE.]'. The dateline is as in N^1 with the addition of the simple notice, 'Copyright, 1897.'

(N^3): San Francisco *Examiner*, May 24, page 1, headlined 'AT THERMOPYLAE THEY WAIT. || Where Leonidas Held at Bay the Persian Hosts, Stands | the Forlorn Hope of Greece. || There Fifty Thousand of the Flower of the Hellenic Army Will | Resist the Fierce Onslaught of Turks When the Roll | of War-Drums Sounds Again. || BY STEPHEN CRANE. | (Special Cable to "The Examiner," Copyright, 1897, by W. R. Hearst.)'. The dateline is the same as in N^1.

(N^4): Philadelphia *Press*, May 24, page 2, signed at the foot, and headlined 'STEPHEN CRANE AT THERMOPYLAE || The Young American Author Cables "The Press" the Con-|dition of Affairs at the Historic Pass—More Fight-|ing is Anticipated. || SPECIAL CABLE DESPATCH TO "THE PRESS," COPYRIGHT, 1897.' The same dateline as in N^1.

Certain shared readings link the N^1 and N^4 texts against those for N^2 and N^3. The most prominent is the substantive agreement in which $N^{1,4}$ *come . . . recognize* reads *came . . . recognized* in N^{2-3} (57.20). Even more significantly, four times, at 57.3, 57.14, 57.26, and 57.29, $N^{1,4}$ paragraph the text where N^{2-3} run on without indentation.[46] These readings suggest that the copy telegraphed to N^{2-3} was in a different state from that sent to N^4 and used by N^1. The simplest hypothesis would be that N^{2-3} copy was sent off from a carbon of the original rewrite but that N^4 was wired from a copy of the slightly worked-over original. Given the N^1 misprint *triliobite* (58.4) but more particularly the unique N^1 reading *have been marched* for *have marched* (57.9) and possibly the unique N^1 *Leonidas's* for *Leonidas'* (58.23), which might have prevented the N^4 sophistication or mistake *Leonidas fought*, this copy would fit the evidence better than an N^1 proof. The two readings above, and also a few small accidentals variants unique with N^1, would then have occurred in the composing room. However, in any case the *Journal* readings shared by N^4 would represent departure from the form of the rewrite copy made from the cable and hence would lack authority. The copy-text is N^1 since its accidentals have gone through one less stage of transmission, but this has been emended when the concurrence of the other authorities, and especially of N^{2-3}, suggests that the N^1 compositor departed from his copy. Reprinted by Fryckstedt and by Stallman from N^1.

No. 12. MY TALK WITH "SOLDIERS SIX"

This McClure 'letter' first appeared in the *Westminster Gazette* (WG) in two parts on June 14–15, 1897, pages 1–2, comprising the fifth and sixth sections of the series "With Greek and Turk." Its title was "Some Interviews." Part VI begins with 63.10 and its heading repeats that of V. As before, Crane is advertised as the author of *The Red Badge of Courage*, and the notation is made, 'Copyright U.S.A., 1897.' At the very end, under the title NOTES OF THE DAY, the *Gazette* printed the following:

---

[46] In view of the N^{2-4} concurrence in the hyphens in *stout-hearted* (57.10) and *full-blown* (58.28) versus *stout hearted* and *full blown* in N^1, and in the normal comma after *do* at 58.27 versus no comma, there may be no significance to $N^{1,4}$ *let up* at 57.26 but *let-up* in N^{2-3}. On the other hand, the N^{2-4} agreements here may parallel the substantive N^{2-4} agreement at 57.9, for which see below.

Mr. Stephen Crane's interviews with Greek soldiers after the *débâcle*, of which we publish a further installment this morning, are human documents of immense interest. But they represent not the actual facts so much as a frame of mind. The soldier after a defeat invariably blames his superiors. Even in the thick of the fight, when some order is given which he does not understand, or some hardship, as he thinks, inflicted upon himself which his comrades do not share, he is apt to curse aloud at the stupidity and the idiocy of the commanding officer. That aspect of warfare Mr. Crane himself has pictured for us most vividly in his "Red Badge of Courage." So it is natural that the Greek soldier who is conscious of having done his best should turn and upbraid the King and the Crown Prince. It does not follow that either is to blame, and it is certain that if they are in any respect to blame the burden laid upon them is infinitely heavier than they deserve. But the picture is human and true, and carries its own morals for kings and statesmen who, before going to war, fail to sit down and count up the cost. We are glad to think, however, that since Mr. Crane wrote, a more rational state of opinion has asserted itself in Greece.

(N[1]): *New York Journal*, Sunday, June 20, 1897, page 18, signed, with the headline 'MY TALK WITH "SOLDIERS SIX." By Stephen Crane. ‖ The Journal's Special War Correspondent at the Front in the Turko-Greek War. ‖ "One Soldier sat by the roadside nursing a sore foot. I gave him a cigarette and he | smiled. I said to him: "How did you feel in your first fight?" " ' The dateline is Athens, June 1, which may be authentic. A five-column cut is provided with the legend 'John Bass, the Journal's Special War Correspondent, in the First Trench at the Battle of Velestino. | FROM A PHOTOGRAPH TAKEN BY THE CORRESPONDENT OF THE LONDON TIMES.' No copyright notice is printed.

(N[2]): San Francisco *Examiner*, July 4, page 6, signed, and headlined 'MY TALK WITH "SOLDIERS SIX." By Stephen Crane.' The dateline has been moved to Athens, June 10.

The difference in date and the general fidelity of the features of the slightly cut text to those of N[1] suggest, as with other such 'letters,' that N[2] was set from copy mailed from New York. This copy was either a carbon of the original typescript or, perhaps more likely, an early proof. However, N[2] does not agree with WG against N[1] except in a few trifling readings that have no significance, and therefore does not seem to be a witness of any value to N[1] compositorial strayings when N[1] and WG differ. It is, then, a thoroughly derived text of no independent authority.

Both WG and N[1] received a small amount of editing. However, the *Journal* setting seems to be particularly careful in reproducing the accidentals from Crane's manuscript that apparently have filtered through the typescript sent over from London at Robert McClure's instance. Thus although both *Gazette* and *Journal* are technically of equal authority, in this case the *Journal* has been chosen as copy-text although it has been freely emended from WG when advisable to remove errors and conjectured N¹ editorial and compositorial intervention. Reprinted by Fryckstedt from N¹ and by Stallman from WG.

No. 13. THE MAN IN THE WHITE HAT

The last of the 'letters' was printed as part VII of "With Greek and Turk" in the *Westminster Gazette* (WG), June 18, 1897, pages 1–2, entitled "The Man in the White Hat." Its heading was in the standard form, including the copyright notice. McClure syndicated it in the United States in a number of Sunday newspapers on July 11. The delay between the English and American publication was about a fortnight more than for the earlier parts of the series, the reason being unknown unless it had something to do with the failure of the *New York Journal* to take the piece. The textual transmission remains the same; that is, McClure's seems to have sent out proofs from a typesetting made from the carbon, say, of the typescript ordered by Robert McClure in London from Crane's manuscript mailed from Greece. No American newspaper has a dateline.

(N¹): New York *Sun*, July 11, 1897, sec. II, page 2, signed, headlined 'UNDER THE WHITE HAT. ‖ *A REVOLUTIONIST IN ATHENS THAT* | *DIDN'T REVOLT.* ‖ He Was Appropriately Arrayed and He Had | the Voice and the Words, but Somehow | One Servant and One Sentry Stemmed the | Rising Tide of Popular Turbulence.'

(N²): *Philadelphia Inquirer*, July 11, page 28, headlined 'THE | WHITE HAT IN | GREECE ‖ How It Served as the Inspiration | of Revolt in | Modern Athens ‖ By STEPHEN CRANE ‖'.

(N³): *Pittsburgh Leader*, July 11, page 21, headlined 'THE WHITE HAT IN GREECE. | HOW IT SERVED AS THE INSPIRA-|TION OF REVOLT IN ATHENS. ‖ It Has Figured in All Revolutions, | and Now It Shows Itself in Greece. | Worn by the Hero of the Moment, | It Almost Causes an Uprising—The | Contempt of a Royal Palace Guard. | A Trying Political Situation. ‖ BY STEPHEN CRANE. | (Copyright 1897. S. S. McClure Co.)'.

(N⁴): Portland *Oregonian*, July 11, page 19, signed, headlined 'WHITE HAT IN GREECE ‖ HOW IT SERVED AS INSPIRATION | OF REVOLT IN MODERN ATHENS. ‖ Figured in all Revolutions and Now | It Shows Itself in Greece—A | True Story of Human Interest. ‖ (Copyright, 1897, by S. S. McClure Co.)'.

(N⁵): *Denver Republican*, July 11, page 21, headlined 'WHITE HAT IN GREECE ‖ How It Served as the Inspiration of Revolt in Modern | Athens. ‖ BY STEPHEN CRANE. | (Copyright, 1897, by S. S. McClure Co.)'.

All newspapers have a cut, signed R. W. L. (N² has the same, but unsigned), showing the Man in the White Hat addressing a crowd, the palace in the background, all with the same legend, 'The Hero of the Moment and the Revolutionary White Hat.' The similarity of headlines indicates that a suggested headline had been set in the proof sent out by McClure, although N^1 chose to ignore it.

A quite remarkable agreement in accidentals shows that N^{2-5} were set from common copy, the McClure proofs mailed with the cut. On the other hand—although to a much lesser extent than in No. 1—the *Sun* text diverges from the others to agree with WG in one substantive and in nine different accidentals. Of these accidentals the use in both of the English spelling *moulded* for *molded* in N^{2-4} (70.6) and the unique dash after *¹glowed* (70.20) are the most important, although something should be said for the agreement in capitalization with WG against the others in *Royal Guard* (69.21; 70.35) and *Chamber* (69.22) despite N^1 *royal palace* (69.9) *palace* (69.19 *et seq.*) and *Deputy* (69.22) for WG *Royal Palace, Palace,* and *deputy.* If the substantive agreement had been in a misprint against N^{2-5} correct reading, the case would be stronger than it is, for WG and N^1 join in the correct *We* at 70.7 where N^{2-5} follow the error *He.*

However, the evidence that N^1 was set from the same McClure proof as N^{2-4} outweighs these relatively slender likenesses. For instance, although N^1 and WG agree in comma punctuation versus N^{2-5} five times (twice in commas where N^{2-5} have none, and thrice in no punctuation when N^{2-5} have commas), N^1 joins N^{2-5} against WG nine times in printing a comma where WG has no punctuation and ten times in failing to punctuate where WG has commas.[47] Although N^1 and WG agree in the unique dash after *¹glowed* (70.20), N^1 joins N^{2-5} in a comma after *purple* (70.38) where a dash appeared in WG. Moreover, where WG has an exclamation point after *um* (72.8) and *Well* (72.9), N^{1-5} agree solidly in a comma and no punctuation respectively. WG hyphenates *sentry box* (69.20; 70.34; 71.16), *cable car* (70.12), and *café table* (70.27) but N^{1-5} divide without hyphenation. In short, the qualitative agreements of N^1 with WG are matched by disagreements; and quantitatively N^1 agrees with N^{2-4} versus WG by about four to one. Under these circumstances one has no choice but to take it that the more carefully edited WG and N^1 corrected

---

[47] Commas in N^{1-5} where WG wants punctuation occur after *Constitution* (69.8), *palace* (69.9), *crowd* (69.19), *plaza* (69.20), *sentry-box* (70.34), *steps* (70.34), *crowd* (71.7), and *acclamations* (71.10) [N^4 has no comma at 71.10]. No punctuation appears in N^{1-5} where WG has commas after *and* (69.22), *session* (69.23), *corner* (69.26), *appears* (70.17), *speech* (70.30), *thing* (71.9), *and* (71.11), *countrymen* (71.12), *strength* (71.37), *incident* (72.12) [N^4 has a comma at 72.12].

what is after all a fairly obvious error, *He* for *We* (70.7), or if the mistake occurred in proof, that N¹ alone corrected it.

Since the *Westminster Gazette* is one step closer to the typescript than any of the newspapers, which were set from an intermediate proof, it is selected as copy-text but is freely emended where the agreement of the newspapers reconstructs the details of the master proof in such a manner as to create an equal authority with WG and where these N readings appear to be more characteristic of Crane than their WG counterparts.

No. 14. A PORTRAIT OF SMOLENSKI

This unpublished report is preserved in manuscript in the Columbia University Libraries Special Collections. The first leaf is untitled; hence the caption has been added by the present editor. The manuscript consists of five leaves of cheap wove unlined paper, measuring 270 × 214 mm. It is written throughout on the rectos in black ink in Cora Crane's hand with her corrections in the same ink but also a few corrections in Crane's hand. That Crane dictated it to her (as he did No. 15) and that it is entirely his own work is the opinion of the present editor; but the matter is not beyond dispute since Miss Gilkes attributes it to Cora.

The date of composition is uncertain. No indication is given that the war is still not in progress; in fact, the final sentence could have been written only before the ceasefire on May 20. The conjecture may be made that it followed very shortly after the writing of No. 6, "A Fragment of Velestino." It is interesting that in No. 6 at 28.14–16 a sentence reads, *In fact, the mountain side is so steep that the entire town there is displayed as if one looked at a lithograph.* This agrees very well with the first paragraph of No. 14. Obviously this report was never intended to be a cable but perhaps is an abortive 'letter': from 72.22–24 it is evident that Crane envisaged accompanying illustrations to be drawn from lithographs he would have enclosed with his copy.

This report has been printed in Miss Lillian Gilkes' edition of the London newsletters of Cora Crane (1972).

No. 15. THE EASTERN QUESTION

This report is preserved in manuscript in the Columbia University Libraries Special Collections. The first leaf is untitled; hence the

caption must be arbitrarily supplied and the present editor follows
Stallman's choice. The manuscript consists of six leaves of cheap
unruled wove paper, 270 × 214 mm., unwatermarked. The writing is
in black ink on the rectos only. The first page and two-thirds of the
second are in Cora's hand, but then Crane takes over at 76.34 with
And yet it puts to flight, putting a period before Cora's *and* and capitalizing it at the end of the line; his *yet it puts . . .* continues with
the start of the next line. It would seem that he dictated the early part
to Cora and then wrote the rest himself. Revisions in Cora's part are
in his hand.

In the blank space on the first page left for the title is written *not
used,* perhaps in Cora's hand. The word count of 2,000 is circled at
the upper left of this first page. On the verso of each leaf is the word
count for the page, cumulatively added, the last notation being 1,770
on the verso of the fifth leaf. The first page is written on the turned-
around verso of a leaf numbered in Crane's hand 28, with the roman
numeral XI beneath it. The conclusion on page 6 is marked by Crane's
signature and a grid. This page is written on the turned-around verso
of a leaf that had been discarded after a false start. It was originally
numbered 9 in Cora's hand, and she started with 'Another p' but
both have been deleted. To the right of the deleted 9 Crane wrote a 6
and then, below Cora's deleted start, he began a paragraph with 'In
fact he displayed to all these people who understood him that he was
a person with something always up his sleeve.' In this sentence,
which is not marked out, *always* was originally written before *something* but has been deleted and interlined with a caret after. The leaf
had evidently been one of Cora's discards for some unknown work of
her own or of Crane's dictation; but the same page number 6 on recto
and verso in Crane's hand and the fact that his sentence would satisfactorily carry on after the end of page 5 with *. . . the law of pugilism* (79.33) indicates that it is a false start of his own in this same
article. It is worth noting that even as it is, he still made a false start
on the final page 6, beginning with a paragraph *He portrayed* before
deleting it and writing the final paragraph starting *One could hardly
. . .* (79.34). The words in the present text at 78.38–39 placed
between square brackets are part of the final line of page 4, which has
crumbled away leaving only the evidence of the tops of some letters.
However, from a photograph taken by Columbia some years ago when
the leaf was in better preservation than today, it is possible to reconstruct with some confidence the mutilated words except for the final
one, which is completely worn off. The *an* enclosed in pointed brackets
is strictly a guess, and the word could as readily be *all.* No guide is

present except for the context. Reprinted by Stallman from the manuscript.

No. 16. THE TURKISH ARMY

This incomplete article is preserved in the Columbia University
Libraries Special Collections on a single leaf of laid unruled paper
327 × 206 mm., watermarked with a coronet above three concentric
circles within which sits a woman holding a lily in her right hand
and a spear in her left. A shield with a cross emblazoned on it is on
her left. The writing is on the recto only, in black ink. The article
starts in Cora's hand but with the word *Moreover* (81.11) one word
in from the left margin, four lines from the foot, Crane begins in the
same ink. The page ends with the last line complete and in mid-
sentence, indicating that very likely one or more leaves of its continuation have been lost. This is the more certain because of Crane's
word-count figure 450 on the verso. The start in Cora's hand is no
doubt at Crane's dictation. The alterations are in his hand throughout
save for the few that Cora made *currente calamo*. This article was
mentioned and partly quoted from in Lillian Gilkes' *Cora Crane* but is
reprinted here for the first time.

FLORIDA

No. 17. STEPHEN CRANE'S OWN STORY

The news story of the sinking of the *Commodore* and of Crane's sur-
vival was printed in the newspapers on January 3, 1897, with a
Jacksonville, Florida, January 2 dateline. The release was a long one
and probably served to take a considerable edge off Crane's own
delayed account, which seems to have been syndicated by Bacheller,
at least in part, and appeared in a relatively few newspapers on
January 7, with a Jacksonville, January 6, dateline. So far as has been
observed only four papers ran the full (or the relatively full) text, one
ran a considerably cut version, and several contented themselves with
a few excerpts pieced out with a running summary of the omitted
portions.

(N[1]): *New York Press*, January 7, 1897, pages 1–2, signed, headlined 'STEPHEN CRANE'S OWN STORY ‖ He Tells How the Commodore Was Wrecked | and How He Escaped. ‖ FEAR-CRAZED NEGRO NEARLY SWAMPS BOAT ‖ Young Writer Compelled to Work in Stifling Atmosphere | of the Fire Room. ‖ BRAVERY OF CAPTAIN MURPHY AND HIGGINS ‖ Tried to Tow Their Companions Who Were on the Raft—|Last Dash for the Shore Through the Surf. ‖ Copyright, 1897, by The Press Company, Limited.' This is the full version save for a cut at 87.13–38, the text of which has not previously been recovered from the other newspapers. The *Press* devoted six of the seven columns of its front page to the story, including a two-column cut of Crane with the caption 'STEPHEN CRANE, ‖ Whose Story of the Sinking of | the Filibuster Commodore Is | Printed in To-day's Press.'

(N[2]): Philadelphia *Press*, January 7, pages 1, 3, signed, headlined 'STEPHEN CRANE | TELLS THE TALE ‖ The Novelist Telegraphs "The | Press" a Graphic Recital of | the Commodore's Loss. ‖ HOW HE ESCAPED FROM THE SEA. ‖ The Auspicious Start, the Over-|whelming Leak, the Deser-|tion of the Vessel. ‖ AFLOAT ON TOSSING WAVES. ‖ In a Little Dingy Four Men Saw the | Sea Burial of the Filibuster. | Seven of the Men Who | Took to the Rafts | Perished. ‖ Telegraphed to "The Press" by Stephen Crane, | Copyright, 1897.' On the first page appeared a two-column cut of Crane, the same as in N[1] but redrawn, headed 'STEPHEN CRANE.' and below it 'The brilliant young novelist who telegraphed to "The Press" the thrilling | story of the sinking of the filibuster, The Commodore.' The runover on page 3 is headlined 'STEPHEN CRANE | TELLS THE TALE. ‖'. The text is complete.

(N[3]): *Chicago Record*, January 7, pages 1–2, signed, headlined 'OUT OF THE SEA. ‖ Novelist Crane Tells of His Ship-|wreck and Narrow Escape | from Death. ‖ Thrilling Recital of the Fatal Expedi-|tion of a Cuban Fili-|buster. ‖ Loss of the Little Steamer Commodore | in a Heavy Sea Off the | Florida Coast. ‖ Desperate Efforts Made to Save the | Sinking Ship and Launching | of Lifeboats. ‖ Fatal Plunge of the First Mate and Sad Death | of "Billy" Higgins, the | Ship's Oiler. ‖ Copyright, 1897, by the Bacheller Syndicate. | Special to the Chicago Record.' The full text is printed and a drawing of Crane is inset.

(N[4]): New Orleans *Times-Democrat*, January 7, page 1, headlined 'CRANE TELLS THE STORY' ‖ Wreck of the Filibuster | Commodore. ‖ Graphic Description of the Sink-|ing of the Vessel. ‖ Account of the Voyage and Fatal End-|ing of the Expedition. ‖ Some Humorous Incidents Con-|nected with the Short Cruise. ‖ Stephen Crane, the Novelist, Tells of His | First Filibustering Venture. ‖ Special to The Times-Democrat.' The text is complete. A staff artist has drawn cuts of a portrait of Crane and an alleged picture of the *Commodore*. The story is signed and carries the notice '(Copyright, 1897, by the Bacheller Syndicate.)'.

(N[5]): *Chicago Tribune*, January 7, page 1, headlined 'AS TOLD BY CRANE. ‖ Experiences of the Novelist | on the Commodore. ‖ AT MERCY OF WAVES ‖ Story of the Wreck of the Cuban | Filibuster. ‖ CAST AWAY ON THE WATERS ‖ Boats Manned After Vain Efforts to | Save the Ship. ‖ PERILOUS VOYAGE TO THE SHORE. ‖'. The dateline is New York, Jan.

6.—[Special.]. The introductory paragraph (for which see the Historical Collation) speaks of Crane writing his story for the *New York Press*. The report is very considerably cut, with a few summary links.

(N[6]): *Boston Record*, January 8, page 3, headlined 'STEPHEN CRANE'S STORY OF HIS SHIP-|WRECK.' The dateline is Key West, Fla., Jan. 7. A drawing of Crane is inset in the first column. Only a few excerpts are given, with summaries. Because of the date, there is a chance that this text could derive from an N[1] clipping despite some independence shown in the accidentals, but the evidence of its retention of *very* at 91.22 (for which see below) may seem to indicate that it was indeed printed from wired copy.

(N[7]) *New Bedford Mercury*, January 9 (?). This text is known from a clipping in a Crane scrapbook in the Barrett Collection at the University of Virginia. The name of the newspaper and the date is given in Cora's hand. The New Bedford Public Library, however, disclaims all knowledge of this article in its file of the *Mercury*. This clipping derives from N[6] but is more deeply cut and is without dateline. Since it copies N[6], it can have no independent authority.

(N[8]): *St. Paul Pioneer Press*, January 9, pages 1, 4, headlined 'AS TOLD BY CRANE. ‖ Experiences of the Young Novelist | on the Commodore.' This has the dateline Chicago, January 8, and is a reprint of the story from the *Chicago Tribune* (N[5]), with no independent authority.

(N[9]): London *Morning Leader*, January 20, page 8, headlined 'STEPHEN CRANE'S ESCAPE. ‖ THE STORY OF HIS ADVENTURE | RELATED BY HIMSELF. ‖ [*Exclusive to "The Leader."*]'. This prints only a few excerpts, with a certain amount of summary. No dateline is present. The text is derived.

(N[10]): London *Daily Mail*, January 21, heading the Daily Magazine section, page 7, and printing a picture of Crane. The headline is 'S. S. COMMODORE, | FILIBUSTER. | Her Loss Described by Mr. Stephen | Crane.' This gives a series of excerpts, acknowledging the *Chicago Record* as its source, and has a portrait redrawn from the *Record*. The text is derived and without authority, therefore.

One of the several problems associated with this report is the circumstances of its sale, which seem to have a bearing on its textual transmission. The *New York Press* copyrighted it in its own name and appears to have had some control over its distribution so far as can be told from the limited evidence. That is, the *Chicago Tribune* version acknowledges the *Press* as its source and gives a New York dateline, something that it did not do for the Greek and the Cuban dispatches that it took from the *New York Journal* and, on an occasion or two, from the New York *World*. Its text, moreover, is in the N[1] line. On the other hand, the Philadelphia *Press* and *Chicago Record* join in a text in another tradition. The statement of the Philadelphia *Press* that Crane had telegraphed the report direct to it may be discounted, and it would seem that this N[2] version originates from the same source as does N[3], the *Chicago Record*, which prints the Bacheller

Syndicate copyright. The *Chicago Tribune* short version (N⁵) presents a separate problem in that no others have been discovered to serve as a basis for generalization, except that N^5 is in the N^1 line. The N^9 or London *Leader* text must be derived, according to its date, but its exact source is in doubt. Although what slight evidence there is suggests that it is in the tradition of N^1 (in punctuation within its short space it reproduces N^1 dashes found in no other text) but its paragraphing several times joins with the $N^{2\text{-}3}$ line against N^1. N^9 prints text from 87.13–18 that was part of the N^1 cut, and so cannot derive from the specific *New York Press* account that is known. However, since derivation from a nonmetropolitan source is unlikely, the possibility exists that some unobserved edition of the *New York Press*, without the cut, was the N^9 copy. If this is so, N^9 could be used as something of an authority for the few lines it prints of the N^1 cut. Actually, only one reading is involved: N^9 prints *and had turned* at 87.14–15 where $N^{2\text{-}3}$ read *and turned* and N^4 *this turned*. The one or two N^9 variants elsewhere from the observed N^1 text do not seem likely to represent different readings in this conjectured *Press* edition.

The available evidence, then, suggests that both Bacheller and the *New York Press* syndicated the story; and indeed this overlap might account for the fact that the report was sold to two Chicago newspapers, each newspaper printing the text in a different tradition. The rest of the background is pure guesswork. It would be a natural assumption that Crane in fact telegraphed the report to Bacheller. The conditions under which Bacheller then seems to have made a deal with the *New York Press* can scarcely be reconstructed, especially as Crane was supposed to be reporting the Cuban situation for the *New York Journal*.

The question of the two textual traditions and their origin is also obscure since it is bound up with this double syndication. Evidence exists in N^1 of some amount of editing, as in the double omission of *very* (91.22; 94.8), which Crane's editors disliked, and probably the substitution of *gag* for *guy* (92.14). The extent of this editing is difficult to evaluate, partly because it does not always distinguish itself readily from typist or compositorial sophistication, and partly because the numerous cuts in N⁵, the longest of the witnesses to the N^1 line of the text, prevent the establishment of many of the variants as actually in the basic copy and not originating in the N^1 composing room. Thus one cannot be sure whether N^1 *were* for $N^{2\text{-}3}$ *was* (86.11), *woke* for *awoke* (88.17), *almost went* for *went almost* (89.3), as examples, were actually representative of the N^1 copy and therefore evidence for transmission. However, the agreement of N⁵ with N^1

he cried for *cried* (89.10), *up* for *up to* (89.27), *man* for *person* (90.9–10), and in the omission of *then* (89.14), indicates clearly enough that where evidence exists N^1 itself and the N^1 line are the same. Because of the small amount of text available, it is impossible to use the evidence of $N^{5-6,9}$ to check N^1 with any thoroughness. Indeed, with two exceptions, when these texts differ from N^1 they also differ from N^{2-3} and thus expose the unauthoritative nature of their variation. One exception is the N^6 retention of *very* at 91.22, evidence that this reading, at least, may be assigned to N^1 editing at a stage subsequent to the wiring (or mailing, to Boston) of the story from the *Press* ($N^{5,9}$ are cut here). The second is somewhat doubtful but on the whole the reading of N^1 is confirmed as that in its copy and no error. The chief engineer at 92.39–93.2 obeyed the captain in N^1 as docilely *as a scholar in riding school*, whereas N^2 and N^6 agree in reading *in a riding school* (N^3 has a different version). Since N^4 here agrees with N^1 although in major part in another line of the text, the $N^{2,6}$ phrase is more likely to be independent sophistication than authoritative.

However, insufficient as the amount of text is for satisfactory analysis, enough is present to indicate that in some respects the N^1 punctuation formed part of the story wired by the *Press* to Chicago. For example, N^5 agrees with N^1 against N^{2-3} in the absence of commas after *duty* (89.4) and *language* (89.12); also in commas versus N^{2-3} lack of punctuation after *Afterward* (91.15), *aft* (91.15), and *wind* (92.8). More important, at 89.12 and 90.9–10 N^5 joins N^1 in starting a new sentence where N^{2-3} merely began a new clause. There is general but not entirely consistent paragraphing agreement between N^1 and N^5 or N^6.

The evidence of the substantives and of the accidentals combines to indicate with sufficient weight that N^1, and its subsidiary versions, stems from a different state of the text than do N^{2-3}. That is, one copy did not serve as the basis for N^1 and for N^{2-3}; instead, each line goes back to some form of different copy. The nature of this double form of the copy is, of course, crucial for the editorial reconstruction of the text.

Two main hypotheses suggest themselves. In the first, Bacheller would have typed up the story from Crane's telegram and furnished the *Press* with its carbon. The *Press* edited this copy, put it on the wire, and then sent it to its own printers. This hypothesis has in its favor at least two clearcut common errors in the two lines: *the group of the sand* in N^1 at 87.3, but *the grove of the sand* in N^2 (N^3 wisely omits the phrase), where N^4, no doubt correctly, emended to *the grip of*. In the second, at 87.11, all three texts read *When the Commodore came to enormous rollers,* which must surely be an error for *the enormous rollers,* also corrected by N⁴. On the other hand, even editing would not, seemingly, account for the run of N¹ variants, and it is clear that most of them were not unique with N¹ but were shared by others in its textual tradition, insofar as the evidence goes. Not all of the remaining variants could have followed from the editing since seven of them are positive errors. These are N¹ *munition* for *munitions* (85.11), *ship* for *ships* (86.34), *up* for *up to* (89.27), *over to* for *over* (91.31), *he* for *we* (94.22), and the omission of *out* (88.28). Some of these may be N¹ compositorial errors, as at 88.28 and 94.22, but three can be shown to have originated in N¹ copy. At 85.11 the unique N⁴ sophistication *ammunition* suggests that its copy read *munition* with N¹, and the N¹ reading at 86.34 is shared by N⁴ and that at 89.27 by N⁴⁻⁵. This evidence is backed by the testimony of the accidentals. It is clear that the N¹ and the N²⁻³ lines differed occasionally in their punctuation in a manner that can refer back only to their respective copy. Editing is unlikely to account for all such variants; and it is even less likely to be wholly responsible for what can be described as a completely different system of paragraphing indention between the two lines.

The hypothesis, then, that appears to fit the evidence in a more satisfactory manner is that Bacheller made its own typescript from the telegram and then turned the telegram itself over to the *New York Press,* or else that Crane sent the same telegrams to the *Press* and to Bacheller—a strong possibility. The different accidentals system was largely imposed upon the N¹ and the N²⁻³ lines in the process of working up their own typescripts from the telegram, and certain omissions and errors seem to have been made in this process, just as one or two errors are found in N²⁻³ that are not present in N¹, most notably *roars* for N¹ *waves* and N⁴ *roarers* (92.9). An apparent error of *man* for *mate* appears in N²⁻³ (87.27) in the passage cut in N¹. The common errors of both lines at 87.3 and 87.11 (correct only in N⁴) must be referred back to the telegram itself, as may certain of the errors in either line that could readily be altered by the other, such as that in N²⁻³ at 92.9 and in N¹ at 92.28.

The evidence of the full version in the New Orleans *Times-Democrat* (N⁴) is difficult to assess without another example. Its Bacheller copyright notice indicates that it belongs generally in the N²⁻³ line as against the N¹ tradition, and its readings confirm this assignment. When in the substantives N²⁻³ disagree with N¹, in all but two cases (86.34; 89.27) N⁴ concurs with N²⁻³. These two seem to represent original errors in the basic telegram, the first of which could have been corrected by N^{2-3} independently if it were not in their copy but the second not quite so readily perhaps. When N^{2-3} disagree with each other, N^4 has no preference but may follow one or the other indifferently, although on the balance it prefers N^2. Of the four full versions, N^4 has more unique readings than any other. Various of these are clearly errors like *deck* for *duty* (89.4) or the absurd *officer* for *oar* (91.27). A number appear to represent editorial reworking or misunderstanding, like *up on his beaten face* for *upon his weather-beaten face* (88.35) or the recasting of the cook's asseveration into a question at 91.1.

Several important readings are correct only in N^4. Prominent among these are *the grip of* (87.3), *the enormous* (87.11), *mate* (87.27), and *²was* (88.14). These are not beyond the powers of an editor, and perhaps an editor might be credited with *roarers* at 92.9 which corrects N^{2-3} *roars* and the N^1 sophistication *waves*. If it was an editor who corrected 87.39, he was alert, for N^4 uniquely sees the difficulty in the common reading *the Commodore was* (87.39) and reads *the Commodore's wake was*. A chance exists, of course, that these were in fact the readings of its copy, and it is true that there are possible hints that somehow its copy did occasionally differ from the regular tradition in small respects. For instance, it may be that for N^{1-2} the stevedores *processioned* both N^{3-4} independently sophisticated to *proceeded* (85.3), or that both N^2 and N^4 separately hit upon the word *dozing* for $N^{1,3}$ *drowsing* (89.8), or that both preferred the old weak ending *gotten* for N^3 *got* (87.14) and *forgotten* for $N^{1,3}$ *forgot* (92.17). On the other hand, the cluster of readings in which $N^{2,4}$ agree in 87.13–15 is odd, for in addition to *gotten* both concur in *many of the ship's* for *the ship's* of $N^{1,3}$ (87.13), although N^4 continues with unique *crew* for N^{1-3} *company*, and also in the *breeze that was* for $N^{1,3}$ the *breakers that were* (87.15). The case at 91.28–29 is odd. Here $N^{2,4}$ agree in constructing a sentence with a dependent clause with *when* for the independent clause starting with *then* of $N^{1,3}$; but then N^2 (but not N^4) deserts the construction and prints *and* in line 91.29, with $N^{1,3}$, which makes a syntactical hash. Some difference in the copy seems indicated here. Yet these are the only examples and they do not suggest significant or far-reaching differences. What they do, however, is to make one pause over some unique N^4 readings that might otherwise have been brushed off as editorial revisions. It may be that free rewriting created N^4 *When the Commodore came to the enormous rollers that flee over the bar a certain light-hearted song sprang from the throats of many of the ship's crew*, which reads in N^1 *light-heartedness departed from the ship's company* and in N^{2-3}

light-heartedness departed from the throats of the ship's company [N²: *many of the ship's*; N³: *light-hearted mess*] (87.12–13). If so, the same difficulty with light-heartedness departing from throats that presumably led N¹ to omit the phrase may have caused N⁴ to alter the context to agree with *throats*, especially since the next sentence calls for no song and carries on the sense of the N¹⁻³ text: the *Commodore* then began to turn handsprings and soon the crew agreed that *life on the rolling wave was not the finest thing in the world.* If this is a fair sample of N⁴ rewriting, then it would be dangerous to take seriously any of its unique variants that alter the sense, although one may regret abandoning the unusual change from N¹⁻³ *to make sure that we did not take on board at some place along the river men for the Cuban army* (86.27–29) made by N⁴ in *take on board at that place any journeymen for the Cuban army.*

Although occasionally the punctuation and more rarely the paragraphing agreements between N⁴ and N¹ against N²⁻³ are somewhat puzzling, the weight of the evidence places N⁴—although rather a maverick—in the N²⁻³ line. Its textual variants must apparently be put down to free editorial alteration plus, perhaps, some corruption in the transmission of the Bacheller text. This point raises the problem of how Bacheller got the text to his subscribers. Since the news story of the rescue appeared on January 3, datelined January 2, there would seem to have been insufficient time for Crane to write this lengthy article and telegraph it to Bacheller, and then for Bacheller to put it into type and distribute it by mail. It is a practical certainty that Bacheller sent out telegrams to his subscribers, in which case some of the textual variation is more explicable than if the newspapers had typeset from common proof. With this hypothesis agrees the fact that though the main headline in N²,⁴ seems to indicate that Bacheller sent out a suggested heading, and though he seems also to have suggested that a portrait of Crane should accompany the story, he did not dispatch a cut for this purpose. The portraits are all of different workmanship and represent two different poses.

The acceptance of the working hypothesis that the *New York Press* line and the Bacheller line differed in their basic copy means that the N¹ tradition and the N²⁻⁴ tradition are theoretically of equal authority since each radiates independently from the original telegram, which is as close to the lost manuscript as textual reconstruction can go. This being so, agreement of N¹⁻⁴ in accidentals and in substantives constitutes absolute authority as very likely reproducing the telegram in all such readings. The problem comes in the divergences of the two lines. Here one is at a disadvantage since no full-length independent witness in the same line has been turned up to confirm the N^1 readings as being identical with its printer's copy, the typescript copy that was wired to the other newspapers but printed only in part in the observed examples. The copy behind N^1, thus, cannot be reconstructed as a whole so fully as can that behind N^{2-4}.

With all its faults, however, it is appropriate to select N^1 as the copy-text, since according to the working hypothesis that governs the editorial method it is one step closer to the telegram than N^{2-4} which have gone through the extra transmissional stage of wired copy. However, the uncertain status of N^1 without a confirming complete text in the same tradition makes emendation possible from N^{2-4} on a freer basis than might otherwise be acceptable. Neither N^2, N^3, nor N^4 alone is trustworthy in its evidence, but when the three concur it is a certainty that the Bacheller copy is being repeated faithfully. In substantives the present editor feels that on the whole the N^{2-4} variants are more trustworthy than the N^1 readings. This may result in part from the more carefully typed copy that evidently was made by Bacheller but also in part from the conclusion one may draw that Bacheller was not concerned to edit the copy to the degree that may be observed in the N^1 text. Almost invariably, therefore, the N^{2-4} substantive variants have been adopted as emendations to the copy-text. The accidentals present a more difficult problem. In theory N^1, as the copy-text, has the superior authority; but as has been remarked above the N^1 text does not necessarily repeat its copy and one has no check at all on its fidelity except when N^5 (and even N^6 and N^9 despite their more doubtful status) is present. Moreover, when N^{2-4} agree, they remove in theory the extra stage of their telegraphic transmission and acquire an authority that is equal to the N^1 tradition when witnesses are present and indeed might theoretically be superior as a whole to N^1 (which is only an isolated example of the N^1 line in considerable part) since for long stretches no means are present to determine N^1's fidelity to its copy. Thus the editor has adopted the following method for dealing with the accidentals. Since N^1 as the copy-text is slightly closer to the telegram, its authority is respected almost invariably when N^{2-4} disagree. However, when N^1 is the only witness to its line, the agreement of N^{2-4} promotes these documents to equal authority with N^1. Sometimes, however, $N^{1,5}$, say, will agree against N^{2-4}. Under these circumstances any lingering doubt about the faithfulness of N^1 to its copy is removed and the differences can be traced with some confidence back to the two typescripts that were made from the telegram, although involved in this matter of their respective styling is the obscure question of how much of the accidentals of punctuation, paragraphing, and word-division was in fact telegraphed. In all cases of disagreement, when both lines are theoretically equal in authority, no systematic choice of one line over the other can logically be made. That is, no reason obtains always to prefer one over the other without critical discrimination except as an irreproachable means of avoiding the necessity of editorial decision and thus of obtaining at least a formal consistency. The present editor in such two-text situations has always elected to choose between the two authorities on the basis of Crane's usual characteristics as revealed in his manuscripts. This procedure has in it the seeds of a closer approximation to the conjectured features of the manuscript behind the telegram than would result from a rigid adherence to either tradition in cases of doubt; and it has the virtue of treating these accidentals on the same critical plane as the choice of substantives between the two equal lines. This being a special case, however, and the examples not numerous, the rejected N^{2-4} punctuation variants are listed with an N^1 *stet* as part of the record of emendations so that the evidence will not be suppressed.

This report was reprinted by Fryckstedt from N^1.

No. 18. THE FILIBUSTERING INDUSTRY

Discovered by Professor Bernice Slote only in 1969, in her searching of the *Pittsburgh Leader*, this new addition to the Crane canon was then reprinted from the *Leader*, May 2, 1897, in the *Prairie Schooner*, Fall, 1969, pages 287–292, along with No. 4, another discovery. Since then two other versions have been uncovered and by their help a more satisfactory text is now possible than from any single witness. The common proofs from which these newspapers set the article contained various substantive errors which were corrected, although unauthoritatively, by the individual newspapers.

No copyright notice is present in the three observed versions; yet these are newspapers that often took material from the Bacheller syndicate (although they also took No. 4 from McClure), and it is a reasonable guess that Bacheller distributed the article just as this syndicate had some rights in No. 17 and its distribution. The dates in the dateline are obviously manufactured: the *Denver Republican* assigns it to April 27, the *Pittsburgh Leader* to April 28, and the *St. Paul Pioneer Press* to May 1. One would suppose that some earlier date was present in the Bacheller proofs which each newspaper altered in its own way to make more current. A reference to the *Commodore* disaster establishes that this article was written after No. 17 and thus between early January 1897 and early April. That the syndicate would have held it after receipt is difficult to credit. Hence it is possible that Crane wrote it on shipboard after March 20 when he sailed for England, or finished it on the voyage to Greece, after April 1. If mailed from England, Bacheller would have received it in more than enough time to set it into type and distribute it for May 2 publication. If it was sent from Greece after April 5, the delay would be somewhat more explicable, perhaps.

(N¹): *St. Paul Pioneer Press*, May 3, 1897, page 3, headlined 'THE FILIBUSTERING INDUSTRY. ‖ By Stephen Crane. ‖'.

(N²): *Denver Republican*, May 2, page 21, signed, headlined 'THE FILIBUSTERING INDUSTRY ‖ Stephen Crane Describes Its Rise and | Suppression. ‖ TOO MUCH PUBLICITY KILLED IT ‖ The Filibusters Told the Newspaper | Men How They Did It and Thus | All Their Plans Were Laid Bare |—How Florida Public Sentiment | Baffled the Government for a | Time—Filibusters and Revenue | Officers. ‖'.

(N³): *Pittsburgh Leader*, May 2, page 24, headlined 'FILIBUSTERING ‖ THE CENTER OF THE INDUSTRY | FOUND IN JACKSONVILLE, FLA. ‖ Stephen Crane Gives an Idea of How | It is Carried on and the Difficulties | the Friends of Cuba, Engaged in | It, Have Had to Encounter—Pink-|erton Detectives Not Held in Rev-|erence in That Pro Cuba City ‖ BY STEPHEN CRANE.'

CUBA

No. 19. THE TERRIBLE CAPTAIN OF THE CAPTURED PANAMA

This telegram datelined Key West, Florida, April 27, represents the first known dispatch sent by Crane to the New York *World* as its correspondent in the Spanish-American War.

(N¹): New York *World*, April 28, 1898, page 3, signed, headlined 'THE TERRIBLE CAPTAIN | OF THE CAPTURED PANAMA. | (*Copyright, 1898, by the Press Publishing Company, New York World.*) | (*From a Special Correspondent of The World.*)'.

(N²): Philadelphia *Press*, April 28, page 3, signed, headlined 'STEPHEN CRANE'S PICTURE | OF THE SPANISH DOWNFALL ‖ Scenes Distressing to Castilian Pride on Board the Cap-|tured Liner Panama at Key West—The Strutting | Captain Humiliated by Palmetto Logs. ‖ COPYRIGHT, 1898, PRESS PUBLISHING COMPANY, NEW YORK "WORLD."' The dateline is the same as N¹ except for the omission of *Fla.*

The N² text is occasionally corrupt, as when N¹ *a sleepy, pale, dead-gone crowd* (103.28–29) becomes *asleep—a pale, dead-gone crowd*. Smoothing, or a misunderstanding, seems to be exhibited in N² *lined like a map* for N¹ *lined like an ape's* (104.29). Nevertheless, N² corrects the egregious N¹ (compositorial?) error *four-armed* (103.22). The chief problem rests in a few readings that are of a piece in which N² gives the information, wanting in N¹, that the *Panama* was brought into harbor *to-day* (103.18), with a consequential change of tense of N¹ *lay* to *has lain* (103.21) and of N¹ *had come* to *has come* (103.19). As a matter of fact, the *Panama* was captured on April 25, the day that Congress declared war, and was brought into Key West by the lighthouse tender *Mangrove* on April 26 (which would be the day before the *to-day* of the dateline), and this event had been duly reported in the newspapers on April 27. It would seem, then, that in the matter of *to-day* the *Press* was carelessly reprinting the words of the Crane telegram sent it by the *World* which had been deleted by a more alert *World* copyreader. It would then follow that the tense changes were made, also unauthoritatively, by this N¹ copyreader and should be restored to the text in order to reproduce what Crane sent. Other N² variants might prove to be authoritative also if another witness could be found to confirm them. On the other hand, it is unlikely that these would have originated in an earlier form of the dispatch put on the wire to Philadelphia before final rewriting to send to the N¹ composing room. The case of the reference to *to-day* seems to be a special one, and ordinarily the *Press* seems to have received a later state of dispatches than other newspapers like the *Chicago Tribune*, as in Nos. 20–21, although apparently not so in No. 27. Reprinted by Fryckstedt from N¹.

No. 20. SAMPSON INSPECTS HARBOR AT MARIEL

Crane's second dispatch, datelined On Board United States Flagship, *New York*. Havana, April 29, via Key West, April 30, achieved somewhat wider circulation since it was concerned with a naval engagement, even though a trifling one.

(N¹): New York *World*, Sunday, May 1, 1898, page 3, signed, headlined 'SAMPSON INSPECTS | HARBOR AT MARIEL. | [short decorative rule] | Port Protected Only by Old Batteries an Excellent | Point for the Landing of an American | Army of Invasion. || FLAGSHIP FAILS TO DRAW THE FIRE | OF THE BATTERIES ABOUT HAVANA. || A Cavalry Troop Fires on the New York Close in Shore | and Capt. Chadwick Himself Trains the Gun | Which Puts the Troop to Flight. ‖ (*Copyright, 1898, by the Press Publishing Company, New York World.*) | (*Special Cable Despatch from a Staff Correspondent.*)'.

(N²): Philadelphia *Press*, May 1, page 2, signed, headlined 'STEPHEN CRANE'S | STORY OF A SKIRMISH. ‖ The Noted American Author Vividly Describes | the Act of the New York in Firing Upon | the Guns Near Cabanas. ‖ CAVALRY TROOP FIRED ON THE SHIPS. ‖ A Shell in Their Midst Scattered Them in all Directions to | Drink Cognac and Boast of a Victory by a Little | Band of Fifty Over a Great | Battleship. ‖ COPYRIGHT, 1898, PRESS PUBLISHING COMPANY, NEW YORK "WORLD." ' The dateline reads, With the Blockading Squadron. Havana, April 29, via Key West, April 30.

(N³): *Chicago Tribune*, May 1, page 2, headlined 'CRANE SEES CA-BANAS SHELLED ‖ Captain Chadwick of the Flagship Him-|self Mans a Gun and Proves His | Good Marksmanship. ‖ [SPECIAL CABLE BY STEPHEN CRANE.]'. A simple notice of copyright is run after the dateline, which agrees with N¹.

(N⁴): *Omaha Daily Bee*, May 1, pages 1–2, signed, headlined 'GUNS SPEAK AGAIN ‖ Admiral Sampson Gives Spaniards Another | Smell of Powder. ‖ NEW YORK OPENS ON A CUBAN FORTRESS ‖ Only a Few Shells Necessary to Accomplish | Its Purpose. ‖'. The headline then continues with the description of a new story attached to the Crane piece sent from Atlanta, Georgia. A copyright notice appears and to the standard dateline is appended, '(New York World Cablegram—Special Telegram.)'.

The concurrence from time to time of N²⁻⁴ in punctuation and in paragraph indention against N¹ indicates that N¹ copy was sent to the composing room while its carbon, presumably, was being wired. However, two states of this copy seem to reveal themselves. It is odd indeed that N³⁻⁴ agree against N¹⁻² in having misprints *port* for *point* (105.29), *shuffle* for *snuffle* (106.24), and *armed* for *aimed* (106.35), and also in *round* for *around* (107.6) and in calling ships *it* instead of *she*. They also agree in a comma after *big* versus no comma (105.31), a period for an exclamation point after *battery* (106.26), in the division *after port* and *after starboard* (106.31,35), in *today* and *tonight* versus hyphenations (107.8,26) and in a period for an exclamation after *cognac* (107.9). Although some of these accidentals agreements may be fortuitous, in general it is likely that they join the substantive misprints to indicate some real similarity in the copy as against the state of the N¹⁻² copy.

Such a distinction would not be unexpected in view of the evidence in some other dispatches (from the *Journal* as well as from the *World*) that the *Chicago Tribune* was likely to be rushed a dispatch in a somewhat earlier state of preparation than found in the New York source, and sometimes in the Philadelphia text also. The only question, indeed, might be the latent possibility that Chicago, not New

York, had rewired the dispatch to Omaha (the *Tribune* style called for *it* for ships), in which case N^4 would not be an independent witness unless it had been sent the identical telegram as received by Chicago.[48] Very oddly, however, N^3 agrees with N^1, and N^4 with N^2, in a series of variant paragraphing indentions at 105.21,24; 106.15,17,20,34,39; 107.1. Some of these $N^{2,4}$ agreements—breaking the connection between N^3 and N^4—could have resulted from independent rearrangement into longer units of unusually short $N^{1,3}$ paragraphs; but the number is too large and some of the circumstances are too unusual for all of these to be fortuitous. How to reconcile this evidence with the substantive and with the other accidentals agreements that appear to join N^{1-2} and N^{3-4} is completely obscure, for these concurrences are quite antithetical to this paragraphing evidence for a relationship between $N^{1,3}$ and between $N^{2,4}$.

At any rate, whatever the exact circumstances, it seems clear that N^{2-4} radiate independently from some form or forms of the N^1 typescript and not from the N^1 typesetting. Under these circumstances each is of equal authority, and concurrence in N^{2-4} against the N^1 copy-text is definite grounds for emendation of what would have been variation in the N^1 copy introduced in the *World* composing room. That N^{3-4} represent an earlier state of the N^1 copy is still probable in spite of the odd discrepancies in the evidence. Reprinted by Fryckstedt and by Stallman from N^1.

No. 21. INACTION DETERIORATES THE KEY WEST FLEET

Datelined On Board the *World's* Despatch Boat *Triton*, off Havana, May 4—Key West, May 5, this short telegram appeared in the newspapers on May 6.

(N^1): New York *World*, May 6, 1898, page 3, signed, headlined 'INACTION DETERIORATES | THE KEY WEST FLEET. ‖ Torpedo-Boats, with Their Frail | Construction, Especially Lia-|ble to Accident. | (Copyright, 1898, by the Press Publishing Company, | New York World.) | (Special Cable Despatch to The World.)'.

(N^2): Philadelphia *Press*, May 6, page 2, signed, headlined 'CHAFE OVER IDLENESS. ‖ Stephen Crane Writes of the Rest-|lessness Felt in the

[48] No such evidence of a possible rewiring from Chicago to Omaha is present in the other dispatches printed by the *Tribune* and the *Bee*. In No. 22, not reprinted by the *Tribune*, the verbal agreements against the *World* are similarly found in the *Bee* and in the Philadelphia *Press*. On the whole it would seem probable that the *Bee* is actually an independent authority, radiating from an early state of the copy for N^1.

Squadron. | Special Despatch to "The Press." ' The dateline repeats the information in N[1], although rearranged. No copyright notice is present.

(N[3]): *Chicago Tribune*, May 6, page 2, headlined 'MEN ARE ANXIOUS TO FIGHT. || Longer the Delay the Greater Grows the | Danger They Must Face in | Battle. || [SPECIAL CABLE BY STEPHEN CRANE.]'. The standard Press Publishing Co. copyright follows the dateline, which is substantially in the N[1] form.

(N[4]): *Omaha Daily Bee*, May 6, page 1, headlined 'MEN ON WAR SHIPS ARE UNEASY. || They Want to Fight Rather Than to | Lie Still. | (Copyright, 1898, by Press Publishing Co.)'. The dateline is substantially like that of N[1] and to it is added '(New York World Cablegram—Special Telegram.)'. Reprinted in the same setting in the *Evening Bee*, May 6, page 7.

The N[1] copy-text is emended in an accidentals reading or two where the agreement of two or more other newspapers suggests departure from the wired typescript copy by the N[1] compositor. Two shared substantive variants by N[3-4] seem to mark a slightly earlier state of this original typescript and have been adopted as probably nearer to the cable than the copyreader's second thoughts. Printed by Fryckstedt from N[1].

No. 22. STEPHEN CRANE'S PEN PICTURE OF C. H. THRALL

From a Key West telegram datelined May 7, this interview was printed in newspapers on Sunday, May 8, the date that the *World* printed, on the same page as Crane's story, Thrall's own narrative, "Thrilling Adventures of World Scout in Cuba," which may be consulted in Stallman, pages 124–129.

(N[1]): New York *World*, May 8, 1898, page 19, signed, headlined 'STEPHEN CRANE'S PEN | PICTURE OF C. H. THRALL. || (*Copyright, 1898, by the Press Publishing Company, New York World.*) | (*Special Cable Despatch to the World.*)'.

(N[2]): Philadelphia *Press*, May 8, page 2, signed, headlined 'THE AMERICAN BLOCKADE | AS VIEWED FROM HAVANA || Stephen Crane Writes of the Adventures of | a Daring Correspondent Who Visited | Cuba's Capital Since the Blockade | Was Begun. || COPYRIGHT, 1898, PRESS PUBLISHING COMPANY, NEW YORK "WORLD." ' The dateline is like N[1].

(N[3]): *Omaha Daily Bee*, May 8, page 1, signed 'STEVE CRANE.', headlined 'CONDITION OF THINGS IN HAVANA. || Spaniards Have Food Enough to Last | Two Months. | (Copyright, 1898, by Press Publishing Co.)'. To the standard dateline is added '(New York World Cablegram—Special Telegram.)'.

Perhaps because of its own Thrall story on the same page, the *World* cut a passage of eighty-six words (109.24–32) which is found in N²⁻³ and reprinted here for the first time. Some substantive and accidentals agreements of N²⁻³ against N¹ indicate, as with other dispatches, that the copy sent to the *World* composing room had been slightly revised from that wired to subscribing newspapers. Such authenticated variants from N²⁻³ have been used to emend the N¹ copy-text. For the omitted passage N³ seems on the whole to be the more faithful witness and becomes the copy-text; but it is unfortunate that a third authority in their tradition has not been found, since both N² and N³ in other dispatches have a history of editorial tinkering, and hence the variants between the two in this passage have had to be adjudicated on what appear to be their merits, not on bibliographical evidence. Reprinted from N¹ by Fryckstedt and by Stallman.

No. 23. WITH THE BLOCKADE ON CUBAN COAST

The dateline is On Board *World* Tug *Three Friends*, off the Coast of Cuba, May 6, via Tampa, May 8. Printed on May 9.

(N¹): New York *World*, May 9, 1898, page 7, signed, headlined 'WITH THE BLOCKADE | ON CUBAN COAST. | [short decorative rule] | The Reality Altogether Un-|like the Popular Con-|ception of It. ‖ MORE PEACEFUL THAN PEACE. ‖ Not, as the Landlubber Imagines, a | Close Assembling of Ships in | Front of Havana. ‖ (From a Staff Correspondent of The World.)'. No copyright notice appears.

(N²): Philadelphia *Press*, May 9, page 3, signed, headlined 'AT THE GATES | OF HAVANA. ‖ Stephen Crane Writes for | "The Press" Incidents of a | Day on the Blockade. ‖ HUNTING FOR A SPANISH GUNBOAT ‖ Majestic Pace of the Flagship | and the Hustling News-|paper Boats. ‖ EVERYBODY ANXIOUS FOR FIGHT ‖ Shore Batteries Withhold Their Fire | Even When American Vessels Pre-|sent an Easy Mark—Wonder-|ing About the Course of | Events in Havana. ‖ Copyright, 1898, Press Publishing Company, | New York World.' The dateline is the same as N¹.

The copy-text is N¹. Reprinted from N¹ by Fryckstedt and by Stallman.

No. 24. SAYINGS OF THE TURRET JACKS IN OUR BLOCKADING FLEETS

The only observed example of this piece was printed in the New York *World* (N¹), Sunday, May 15, 1898, page 33, headlined 'SAYINGS OF THE TURRET JACKS | IN OUR BLOCKADING FLEETS. | [short decorative rule] | BY STEPHEN CRANE.' No dateline or copyright notice is present. This would seem to be from a manuscript mailed, not cabled, to the *World*. Reprinted by Fryckstedt from N[1].

No. 25. HAYTI AND SAN DOMINGO FAVOR THE UNITED STATES

Datelined Porto Plata, San Domingo, May 15, this report was printed in the New York *World*, May 24, 1898, page 7, signed, headlined 'HAYTI AND SAN DOMINGO | FAVOR THE UNITED STATES, | [short decorative rule] | Englishmen and the Natives Generally Espouse Our | Cause—Frenchmen and Germans | Sympathize with Spain. ‖ (Special Correspondence to The World.)'. The rubric *Special Correspondence* and the discrepancy between dateline and publication indicate that this was printed from a manuscript mailed, not cabled, to New York. No other newspaper publication has been observed. Reprinted by Fryckstedt and by Stallman from N[1].

No. 26. NARROW ESCAPE OF THE THREE FRIENDS

On Sunday, May 29, 1898, page 23, the New York *World* (N[1]) printed this report, signed, and headlined '[within a frame of type-orn.] NARROW ESCAPE OF | THE THREE FRIENDS. | A Story of the Week by Stephen Crane.' The dateline 'Key West, May 20' is a false one since according to No. 27 that was the day Crane left on a cruise on the *Three Friends* that did not bring him back to Key West until May 26 when he filed No. 27, although May 25 for a return is, of course, possible. The encounter of the *Three Friends* with the *Machias* must have happened on this trip. Very likely Crane wrote the story at sea and filed or mailed it on his return, the *World* holding it for a Sunday feature. No other newspaper seems to have published it. Reprinted from N[1] by Fryckstedt and by Stallman.

No. 27. HOW SAMPSON CLOSED HIS TRAP

This previously unrecorded dispatch is datelined Key West, May 26, and narrates events between Friday, May 20, when the *Three Friends* left Key West, and Wednesday, May 25, off the Santa Maria Keys on the Cuban coast. As early as May 20 newspapers had rumored the presence of Cervera in Santiago and increasingly positive but unofficial confirmations continued until Schley made it official on May 29 when he arrived at daybreak off the harbor. The *World's* headlines, which do not reflect Crane's telegram, were written in view of the newspaper stories on May 26 which reported with some positiveness that the Spanish fleet had arrived at Santiago on May 19 and was now trapped by Sampson and Schley.

(N[1]): New York *World*, May 27, 1898, page 3, signed, headlined 'HOW SAMPSON | CLOSED HIS TRAP. | [short decorative rule] | Big Fleet Got Behind Cervera | and Prevented Any Possi-|ble Escape. ‖ SCHLEY PUR- SUED ENEMY. ‖ Then the Admiral's Ships Closed | All Passages Leading to the | East of Santiago. ‖ WORLD'S TUG TRAILED FLEET. ‖ Corres- pondents Hoped to See a Bat-|tle, but Instead Saw Only Some | Fine Manoeuvring. ‖ Copyright, 1898, by the Press Publishing Company, | New York World.) | (Special from a Staff Correspondent.)'.

(N[2]): Philadelphia *Press*, May 27, page 2, signed, headlined 'SAMP- SON'S FLEET ON THE ALERT. ‖ How the Warships Sped Away from Before Havana to | Head Off Cervera Described by Stephen Crane, | the Noted Author. ‖ COPYRIGHT, 1898, PRESS PUBLISHING COMPANY, NEW YORK WORLD.' The dateline is like N[1].

(N[3]): *Chicago Tribune*, a day later, on May 28, page 13, headlined 'IN THE WAKE OF | SAMPSON OFF THE | CUBAN COAST. ‖ Stephen Crane Tells of a Hasty De-|parture from Havana and the | Taking of a Position on Guard | Near Santa Maria Keys. ‖ [SPECIAL CABLE BY STEPHEN CRANE TO | THE NEW YORK WORLD AND CHICAGO TRIBUNE.]'. The dateline is like N[1].

Both N[2] and N[3] are cut although in different places. Unfortunately these rather deep excisions prevent both newspapers from acting as checks on the N[1] readings throughout; and when only N[2] or N[3] is present, variants between it and N[1] are difficult to evaluate. Except for the common error *greatly* for N[1] *gently* (122.21), the two do not cover enough similar text for us to be certain that, as usual, they were sent a joint version that was in a somewhat earlier state of prepara- tion than that finally printed by N[1]. However N[2] *fine-bred* at 123.3 for N[1] *fine lined* looks enough like an N[1] copyreader's objection to Crane's sporting language applied to a cruiser to seem acceptable as an original reading. Similarly, N[2] *sunk* for *sank* (122.32) and N[2] *Rhine* for N[1] *Rhenish* (122.39) may well be N[1] revised readings al- though not so certainly so as to justify emendation of the N[1] copy-text.

Why the *Chicago Tribune* waited a day, in a most unusual fashion, before printing this dispatch is not to be determined although perhaps it had something to do with the growing belief that the contents would be of lesser interest if Cervera were indeed bottled firmly within Santiago. Not before reprinted.

No. 28. CHASED BY A BIG "SPANISH MAN-O'-WAR"

The events narrated in this report occurred between May 29 and June 2 when the tug *Somers N. Smith* returned to Key West. The report is without dateline or copyright notice and would have been mailed to the *World* and used at its leisure.

(N¹): New York *World*, July 3, 1898, Sunday Supplement, page 4, signed, headlined 'CHASED BY A BIG "SPANISH MAN-O'-WAR." | STEPHEN CRANE'S | Thrilling Story of a Hair-Raising Experience on an | Unarmed New York World Despatch | Boat Off Cuba.'

No other publication has been observed. Reprinted from N¹ by Fryckstedt and by Stallman.

No. 29. IN THE FIRST LAND FIGHT FOUR OF OUR MEN ARE KILLED

Printed in the New York *World* on Monday, June 13, with the dateline On Board The World Despatch-Boat Triton, Off Guantanamo, via Port Antonio, Jamaica, June 12, this is only in part a Crane dispatch since it was put together and cabled by Ernest McCready from notes dictated by Crane. The full account of how McCready lured Crane away from the fighting in order to get him to write a dispatch and then had to compromise on taking dictation is told in a lengthy letter from McCready to B. J. R. Stolper, dated January 22, 1934, in the Columbia University Libraries, supplemented by the reminiscences of Ralph Paine (*Roads of Adventure*, Cambridge, Mass., 1922, pages 243–247). The story is digested by R. W. Stallman in *Stephen Crane: A Biography*, pages 365–367, 606; the editor is indebted to Professor Stallman for photographs of the McCready letter that authenticate the dispatch. The dispatch was not signed, no doubt, as Professor Stallman remarks, because McCready considered it to be a joint effort. The facts about Dr. Gibbs in the differing final paragraph of both *World* versions certainly came from the newspaper files, not from the cable.

The publication of this dispatch was slightly complex. The earlier version (N¹ᵇ) was presumably printed in the out-of-town edition of the *World* as indicated by a number of typos. Curiously enough, a major cut includes the suggestion that the bodies of the dead Marines had been mutilated by the Spaniards, the part of the story that was to create so much discussion that eventually only an official denial quieted the outrage. In this edition the brief story starts in the lower part of the righthand page 1, two columns wide, with a runover on page 2. The headline reads: 'Four of Our Men Killed, | Including Surgeon John | Blair Gibbs. ‖ OUR MEN BATTLED | FOR THIRTEEN HOURS ‖ Spanish in Force Crept Upon | the Outposts at Guanta-| namo—Their Loss Heavy. ‖ (Copyright, 1898, by the Press Publishing Company, New York World.) | (Special Cable Despatch to The World.)'.

The fuller version (N¹ᵃ), the text of which is reprinted here, was given the place of honor in the upper left of page 1 of the city edition, with a headline that spread across the whole of the page: 'IN THE FIRST LAND FIGHT 4 OF OUR MEN ARE KILLED. ‖ Among Them Was Assistant Surgeon John Blair Gibbs, of New York—|Marines Battled Fiercely at Guantanamo Harbor for Thirteen Hours—|The Spanish, in Force, Attacked and Drove in Outposts—The | Americans Repulsed a Midnight Charge with Great Valor. ‖'. In a rule-box to the right under the first line of the headline is 'OUR DEAD IN FIRST | FIGHT ON CUBA'S SOIL. | Assistant Surgeon JOHN BLAIR GIBBS, of | New York. | Sergt. CHARLES H. SMITH, of Smallwood. | Private WILLIAM DUNPHY, of Gloucester. | Private JAMES McCOLGAN, of Stoneham, | Mass.' The copyright notice and dateline are identical, being in the same typesetting as N¹ᵇ, and the whole of the dispatch is in the same typesetting except for the lines reset in N¹ᵃ to correct typos. No. 30, which follows, carries Crane's denial of the allegation that the bodies had been mutilated. Not previously reprinted.

No. 30. ONLY MUTILATED BY BULLETS

On Thursday, June 16, 1898, page 5, the *Boston Globe* (N¹) carried the signed story headlined 'ONLY MUTILATED BY BULLETS. ‖ Report That Officers and Men Who | Looked at Bodies of Dead Marines | Were Misled by Fearful Wounds. | (By Stephen Crane.)'. At the end was the rubric '(Copyright, 1898, New York World.)'. The dateline was Camp McCalla, Guantanamo Bay, June 14, 6 P.M., via Kingston'.

(N²): The next day the Philadelphia *Press*, June 17, page 2, printed the same report, signed at the end, datelined United States Camp McCalla, Guantanamo Bay, June 14, via Kingston, Jamaica, June 16, and headlined 'DENIES MUTILATION OF BODIES ‖ Novelist Stephen Crane Asserts That a Surgeon's Investi-|gation Proves

That the Awful Wounds Were Made | by Mauser Bullets. ‖ COPY-
RIGHT, 1898, PRESS PUBLISHING COMPANY, NEW YORK
WORLD.' The date of June 16 from Kingston is probably the *Press's*
own invention to make its delay in publication more plausible.

A search of both of the editions of the New York *World* has failed
to turn up evidence that the *World* itself printed this dispatch. Nevertheless, even though the *Chicago Tribune*, which usually published
Crane's reports in the *World*, also omitted it, the appearance of the
article in the *Boston Globe* and the Philadelphia *Press* authenticates
the article as having been put on the wire by the *World*. One can only
speculate why the *World* did not publish Crane's cable. The answer
may lie in the fact that only one day earlier, on page 1 of the June 15
issue, the *World* with its usual sensationalism had featured the mutilation story under the bold four-column headline 'MUTILATION OF
OUR MARINES | TOO HORRIBLE FOR DESCRIPTION ‖ Universal
Sentiments of Horror Expressed at | Dastardly Work of the Spanish
Butchers at Guantanamo. ‖'. The covering stories, complete with
interviews of public figures, featured in a box a quotation from Admiral Sampson's official report that confirmed the barbaric mutilation.
Under these circumstances the *World* may well have preferred not to
kill the story too abruptly, or to trust to the word of Crane alone, and
thus proposed to await the official statement before committing itself.

Although doubt has been cast on the authorship, the report is
signed in the two observed newspapers and seems quite definitely to
have originated as a signed dispatch with the *World*. Crane had been
at Guantanamo with the marines (see Nos. 29, 31, 32) and, in fact,
left the camp at daybreak on June 13 for the Cuzco engagement. The
dispatch could have been written on the 12th or 13th and sent off on
the 14th when the dispatch boat returned after his departure. The
incident reported had occurred on the night of June 8, the bodies
being discovered on Thursday June 9. The original incident had been
reported in the full text of No. 29 although not in the shorter version.
Reprinted by Fryckstedt from N².

NO. 31. CRANE TELLS THE STORY OF THE DISEMBARKMENT

Crane's account of the landing of the American troops was printed
immediately below the end of No. 33 both in the *World* and the *Boston Globe*, although written earlier as attested by its dateline and the
events described. The difficulty of sending dispatches by newspaper
boat to Jamaica or other points for cabling to New York held up eye-

witness reports for several days, but the extreme discrepancy here suggests that this story was mailed in manuscript with No. 33.

(N[1]): New York *World*, July 7, 1898, page 8, signed, headlined 'CRANE TELLS THE STORY | OF THE DISEMBARKMENT. ||'. The dateline is Daquiri, June 22, 5.10 P.M. The general copyright notice above No. 33 was intended to cover this story as well, since it was included under the four-column headline for No. 33.

(N[2]): *Boston Globe*, July 7, page 2 of a five o'clock extra edition. The dispatch with its dateline as in N[1] follows the end of No. 33 without separate headline.

The copy-text is N[1]. No differences occur in N[2] that do not appear to be compositorial. Reprinted from N[1] by Fryckstedt and by Stallman.

No. 32. THE RED BADGE OF COURAGE WAS HIS WIG-WAG FLAG

The New York *World* (N[1]) printed this story, datelined Guantanamo Camp. June 22, on July 1, 1898, page 3, signed, headlined 'THE RED BADGE OF | COURAGE WAS HIS | WIG-WAG FLAG. | [short decorative rule] | Sergeant of Marines Signalling the Dolphin the Cen-|tral Figure in Stephen Crane's Story of the | First Fight at Guantanamo Bay. || (Special from a Staff Correspondent.)'. The length of the piece and the lapse of time between dateline and publication suggest that it was mailed in manuscript to the *World*, a conjecture strengthened by the absence of any reference to cable in the newspaper deck. So far as observed, the *World* was the only newspaper that published the report. Reprinted by Fryckstedt and by Stallman from N[1].

No. 33. STEPHEN CRANE AT THE FRONT FOR THE WORLD

Datelined Siboney, June 24, this report did not appear until July 7, when the *World* gave it a four-column spread and the Boston *Globe* issued a five-o'clock extra.

(N[1]): New York *World*, July 7, page 8, signed, headlined 'STEPHEN CRANE AT THE FRONT FOR THE WORLD. | [short decorative rule] | The Author of "The Red Badge of Courage," the Most Notable War Story | of Recent Years, Written Before He Ever Saw an Actual Engage-|ment, Was in the Thick of Battle with the Rough Riders. || HE TELLS THE REAL STORY OF | THEIR GLORIOUS BAPTISM OF FIRE. || Heedless of Danger That Surrounded Them, Noisily, Carelessly They Went to Death | with Superb Courage—The Heroism of Marshall, the Correspondent, and | Other Thrilling Episodes Brought Intimately Before the Reader. || (*Special*

Correspondence of The World.—Copyright, 1898, by the Press Publishing Company, New York World.)'.

(N²): *Boston Globe*, July 7, page 2, headlined 'GLOBE EXTRA! ‖ 5 O'Clock. ‖‖ CRANE IN WAR. ‖ Young Novelist Writes | About Reality. ‖ Rough Riders Went to Their | Death Gaily. ‖ Noisily, Carelessly, They Marched, | While All Around Them in the | Dense Undergrowth the Guerillas | Gave the Cooing Sound of the | Wood Dove, Which Sent Terror | Into the Hearts of Those Who | Knew Its Meaning. ‖'. The dateline was 'New York, July 7.—The World to-day prints the following dispatch by Stephen Crane:', followed by the N¹ dateline.

The similarity of headlines, the closeness of the texts, and the manner in which the two newspapers ran the two reports No. 31 and No. 33 in conjunction suggest that proofs of N¹ were sent by train to the *Globe* for both stories, a conjecture assisted by the N² extra, and the introduction not previously utilized for telegraphed dispatches. If so, N² is a derived text except for possible preservation of early N¹ readings altered before printing, but—if present—these cannot be distinguished from N² compositorial slips. On the other hand, the rubric 'Special Correspondence' that prefixes the N¹ report, and the difference in time between dateline and publication, suggest that the *World* text was set from manuscript and not from a cable or telegram. Reprinted by Fryckstedt and by Stallman from N¹.

No. 34. ROOSEVELT'S ROUGH RIDERS' LOSS DUE TO A GALLANT BLUNDER

Crane's brief cable about the Rough Riders' skirmish was datelined Playa del Este, June 25, and published on June 26.

(N¹): New York *World*, Sunday, June 26, 1898, page 2, signed, headlined 'ROOSEVELT'S ROUGH RIDERS' LOSS | DUE TO A GALLANT BLUNDER. ‖ (Copyright, 1898, by the Press Publishing Company, New York World.) | (Special Cable Despatch to The World.)'.

(N²): Philadelphia *Press*, June 26, page 3 in one edition and page 4 in another, signed, headlined 'STEPHEN CRANE CALLS IT A BLUNDER. ‖ The Noted Writer Asserts That Roosevelt's Men Were | Caught Unawares by the Enemy in Ambush—Ameri-|cans Made a Brilliant Fight. ‖ COPYRIGHT, 1898, PRESS PUBLISHING COMPANY, NEW YORK WORLD.' The dateline is the same as N¹. In the two editions the typesetting is identical and no variations appear in the text.

The copy-text is N¹, but at 146.16 N² seems to preserve a reading conjecturally present in the cable and later revised by the N¹ copyreader: the N¹ *Spanish* is not found in Crane except as an adjective and N² *Spaniards* is his habitual form. This has been substituted as an emendation. In the light of this reading *could not be* (146.13–14) from N^2 is also taken over into the copy-text to replace N^1 *couldn't have been*, which looks like a sophistication. Reprinted from N^1 by Fryckstedt and by Stallman.

No. 35. HUNGER HAS MADE CUBANS FATALISTS

The dateline Siboney, June 27, but publication on July 12, indicates that this report was not cabled but, instead, mailed in manuscript, a suggestion confirmed by the use of the term *Special Correspondence* that was never applied to cables.

(N^1): New York *World*, July 12, 1898, page 4, signed, headlined 'HUN-GER HAS MADE | CUBANS FATALISTS | [short decorative rule] | No Cheering When Shafter's | Forces Landed at | Daiquiri. ‖ THEY ARE GOOD SCOUTS, BUT— ‖ American Troops Do Not Look | With Favor on Them and They | Do not Understand Us. ‖ ROUGH RIDERS SURPRISED THEM ‖ Steady Advance in Face of Deadly | Fire Filled Them with Won-|der and Admiration. ‖ (Special Correspondence of The World.)'.

(N^2): Philadelphia *Press*, July 12, page 3, signed, headlined 'HOW THE ARMY PREPARED | TO CAPTURE SANTIAGO. ‖ Stephen Crane De-scribes for "The Press" | Scenes and Incidents Before the Recent | Attack —Difference Between Ameri-|can and Cuban Styles, | in Fighting. ‖ SPE-CIAL CORRESPONDENCE OF "THE PRESS." '. The dateline is the same as N^1.

(N^3): *Boston Globe*, July 12, page 3, headlined 'JOURNEY TO HILLS. ‖ Stephen Crane Describes Trip | With Scovel. ‖ With Cuban Escort They Went Almost | As Far as Santiago. ‖ Insurgent Has Turned Into Abso-|lutely Emotionless Character Ex-|cept When Maddened by Battle|—Little Intercourse Between | Him and American Soldier. ‖ (By Stephen Crane.)'. At the foot of the report is '(Copyright, 1898, New York World.)'. The date-line is the same as N^1.

The text of this report exhibits a few problems. That N^{2-3} radiate from common copy is demonstrated by their agreement against N^1 in several substantives as well as by their concurrence in various acci-dentals where N^1 differs. The variant accidentals may perhaps be im-puted to the N^1 compositor or proofreader so that the N^{2-3} agreement should be meaningful as the reproduction of their copy. The difficulty comes in assessing the relationship of the N^1 copy to that for N^{2-3}. One may suspect, although not demonstrate, that with a report of so little urgency copy was mailed, not telegraphed, to Philadelphia and to Boston, in which case a typescript with carbons would need to be made up from Crane's manuscript. If this is so, then the N^1 copy could have been this typescript, or just possibly—if copies were short —Crane's own manuscript could have been sent to the N^1 composing room. Which procedure was adopted would, of course, influence one's view of the authority of the substantive as well as accidentals variants where N^{2-3} disagree with N^1.

These variants in some part at least differ in their nature from the substantives in earlier reports where two or more out-of-town newspapers agree against the New York text. In those cases many of the variants were assignable as the readings of an earlier state of the typescript made up from the cable and thus closer to its authority than the revision that was performed for the New York text in this typescript after it had been telegraphed out of town but before it was set. A few of the variants would also be compositorial slips in the New York text. Whatever the cause, the authority of the original typescript could be recovered by agreement of two or more out-of-town newspapers that revealed the readings telegraphed to them. Since each telegram was an independent operation, the chances for agreement by two or more such newspapers in a transmissional error were minimal.

However, these conditions do not hold in the present report, which does not seem to have been telegraphed. Moreover, the variant substantives are, at least in some part, of a different kind from those previously encountered in that several are clearcut errors. No doubt can exist that N^{2-3} *On time* is an error for N^1 *In time* (150.9), and N^2 *on a party* and the N^3 attempted improvement *in a party* are errors for N^1 *on a path* (150.10). What may have been another mistake in the typescript that was mailed out occurs shortly before at 150.7 where N^2 seems to reproduce the typescript *sky* whereas N^3 improves to *the sky* and N^1 reads *a sky*. This is a curious little cluster of errors and it serves to cast serious doubt on the related *lined* in N^{2-3} for N^1 *limned* (150.6) which might otherwise have seemed an indifferent reading. Another variant, N^{2-3} *question*, is literally accurate, at 149.35–36, but N^1 *questions* is isolated and might as readily be an N^1 compositorial slip. Another little cluster occurs between 151.35–37, where N^{2-3} join in *mango tree* for N^1 *laden mango tree*, and in the repeated *impassable mountains* for N^1 *impossible mountains*. With the possible exception of *questions* at 149.35–36, it would seem that these variants are of a piece and must stand or fall together. The first group has no ambiguity: the N^1 readings are correct and the N^{2-3} are errors. Since *limned-lined* must be associated with two obvious mistakes, we can see that a reading of some subtlety was subject to variation where correction was scarcely called for in the manner of *party* to *path*. This is a useful hint when one comes to the second group. That it was subject to the same conditions that produced the first may perhaps be illustrated by the reading *laden mango tree*. Here a reference is being made back to 151.17–21: *the escort sighted a tree laden with mangoes. . . . That escort broke formation and scattered, flitting noiselessly and grabbing.* Under these circumstances it would seem most probable that *laden* was actually in Crane's manuscript, not in the mind of a copyreader, and that somehow N^1 reproduces the right reading and N^{2-3} the mistaken omission. If this is so, then the slightly strained *impossible mountains* in N^1 must also be correct, and *impassable* a sophistication even though a hyperbolic one.

It is possible that the typescript that must have been made from Crane's manuscript created these errors but that the N^1 copyreader recollated the typescript (necessary for the restoration of *laden* and perhaps for *limned*) before sending the *World's* copy to the compositors. On the other hand, it is much simpler if we were to take it that N^1 got these readings right because it was set from the manuscript itself and not from a faulty copy. Alternatively, it could have been set from an accurate typescript whereas another typescript and carbons needed to be made for mailing to a number of newspapers that might be interested, such as the *Chicago Tribune* which did not use the piece. The evidence is insufficient for a firm decision except on the single point that in a manner somewhat like the two suggested the copy for N^1 was more accurate than the basic copy for N^{2-3}.

If this hypothesis is true for the substantives, then the matter of the accidentals must be examined. Here we are on very uncertain ground because the N^1 compositor could vary these from his copy with a freedom not to be permitted with the substantives. Hence the working hypothesis that assigns superior authority to the N^1 substantives need apply with much less force to the cases when in accidentals N^{2-3} agree against N^1. One might argue that at 146.22–147.1 the N^1 dashes after *nurses* and *war* are more likely to represent 'improvements' than the substitution of commas for the clarifying structural dashes. Also that the short incomplete sentence at 148.39–40, *Even if we have to make some of the volunteers wait a little.* in N^{2-3}, is more characteristic of Crane than the N^1 hitching to the preceding sentence. Hence even with the working hypothesis adopted for this text it is still possible for N^{2-3} in conjunction to reproduce typescript accidentals that could reflect Crane's manuscript more faithfully than the N^1 compositor even if he were setting from manuscript. Thus although a strictly conservative methodology would ignore this evidence in N^{2-3} agreement and faithfully reprint the N^1 text, the present editor takes it that in fact the odds somewhat favor the authority of these joint N^{2-3} accidentals over the N^1 corresponding readings, and a few of the most characteristic have been used to emend the N¹ copy-text. Reprinted from N¹ by Fryckstedt and Stallman.

No. 36. PANDO HURRYING TO SANTIAGO

The only observed publication of this cable, datelined June 30 from Playa del Este appeared in the New York *World* (N¹), July 1, 1898, page 2, signed, headlined 'PANDO HURRYING TO SANTIAGO; | CUBANS SAY THEY WILL STOP HIM | (Copyright, 1898, by the Press Publishing Company, New York World.) | (Special Cable Despatch to the World.) | (From One of The World's Staff of War Correspondents at the Front.)'. Reprinted by Fryckstedt from N¹.

No. 37. ARTILLERY DUEL WAS FIERCELY FOUGHT ON BOTH SIDES

Again, the only observed publication of this brief cable, datelined Playa del Este, July 1, was that in the New York *World* (N¹), July 3, 1898, page 2, signed, headlined 'ARTILLERY DUEL WAS FIERCELY | FOUGHT ON BOTH SIDES. ‖ (Copyright, 1898, by the Press Publishing Company, New York World.) | (Special Cable Despatch from one of The World's Staff Correspondents at | the Front.)'. Reprinted from N¹ by Fryckstedt and by Stallman.

No. 38. NIGHT ATTACKS ON THE MARINES AND A BRAVE RESCUE

This brief report must have been mailed since although it is datelined July 4 from Guantanamo it was not published in the New York *World* (N¹) until July 16, 1898, page 2, where it is signed and headlined 'NIGHT ATTACKS ON THE MARINES | AND A BRAVE RESCUE. ‖ (From a Special Correspondent of The World.)'. No other newspaper seems to have published it. Reprinted by Fryckstedt and by Stallman from N¹.

No. 39. STEPHEN CRANE'S VIVID STORY OF THE BATTLE OF SAN JUAN

What is perhaps Crane's most famous report was datelined In Front of Santiago, July 4, via Old Point Comfort, Va., July 13. Whenever it was actually written, it was filed on the day that Crane arrived in the

United States, invalided from Cuba. Since it was published on July 14, he probably sent it in a telegram from Old Point Comfort.

(N^{1a-b}): New York *World*, July 14, 1898, page 3, signed. The *World's* city edition (N^{1a}) and out-of-town edition (N^{1b}) treated the story somewhat differently in text and in subheadings but the typesetting itself is identical except for the cutting, and the headline is the same for both editions, 'STEPHEN CRANE'S VIVID STORY | OF THE BATTLE OF SAN JUAN. | [short decorative rule] | Victory Gained Not by the | Officers, but by the Auda-|cious Bravery of the Men. ‖ "GRAND POPULAR MOVEMENT." ‖ With or Without Orders, They | Marched Doggedly Forward | in the Face of Death. ‖ DESPERATE VALOR AT EL CANEY. ‖ Cuban Soldiers Demoralized, Lazy, | Worthless and Heartily Despised | by the American Troops. ‖ (Copyright, 1898, by the Press Publishing Company, | New York World.) | (Special from a World Staff Correspondent.)'. The city edition (N^{1a}), which was the later of the two, introduced four very large two-column subheadings within frames of wavy rules to supplement or to substitute for conventional subheadings in the earlier N^{1b}. To make room for these it cut four passages from N^{1b} at 160.9–30, 161.11–17, 162.13–17, and 164.22–28.

(N^2): *Chicago Tribune*, July 14, page 3, headlined 'HOW SAN JUAN | WAS TAKEN. ‖ Stephen Crane's Graphic Story | of American Valor Be-|fore Santiago. ‖ THEORIES OF WAR DEFIED ‖ Boys in Blue Win a Battle Against | Every Known Rule of | Strategy. ‖ FIGHTING WITHOUT ORDERS. ‖ [BY STEPHEN CRANE.]'. The dateline is the same as in N^1. The text of N^2 makes ten cuts several of which contain within larger excisions the N^{1a} cuts; on the other hand, N^2 prints 164.22–28 which had been cut in N^{1a}. It joins N^{1a-b} in a cut at 164.10–14 of material found only in N^3, but in view of the general run of N^2 cuts this isolated example would seem to be a chance hit. In short, no special relationship can be traced in N^2 either to N^{1a} or to N^{1b} as distinctive texts, and given the evidence of N^3 it is practically certain that the texts wired to N^2 and to N^3 were identical although subjected to varying treatment in Chicago and in Boston.

(N^3): *Boston Globe*, July 14, page 4, headlined 'HOW IT WAS DONE. ‖ Stephen Crane Describes the | Battle of San Juan. ‖ Success Due to Gallantry of the | American Private. ‖ Intrenched Hills Taken by a Front | Attack Without the Aid of the | Artillery—Such a Thing Thought | to be Impossible—How Spanish | Guerrillas Fired on Our Wounded|—American Officers and Soldiers | Hold the Cubans in Supreme | Contempt. ‖ (By Stephen Crane.)'. The dateline is as in N^1. At the foot of the report is printed '(Copyright, 1898, New York World.)'. This N^3 version prints all the text in N^{1b} cut in N^{1a}. In addition, at 160.1–8, 164.10–14, and 166.5–12 it contains a total of 217 words of text found neither in N^{1a-b} nor in N^2, which must have been independently cut in New York and Chicago.

(HW): *Harper's Weekly*, XLII (July 23, 1898), 722, headed 'IN FRONT OF SANTIAGO. | FROM STEPHEN CRANE'S ACCOUNT OF THE BATTLE IN THE | NEW YORK "WORLD," JULY 14. | *July 4*.' This is a severely cut reprint of the N^{1a} text and, being wholly derived, is without authority.

Since N^1 is one step closer to Crane's original, it is selected as the copy-text in the city-edition form, N^{1a}, for convenience of notation,

The four passages omitted in N^{1a} are supplied with the N^{1b} out-of-town edition as copy-text. At 160.1–8, 164.10–14, and 166.5–12 N^3 furnishes the copy-text for the only observed occurrence of these passages, cut from N^{1-2} no doubt because of their harsh and personal animus and reprinted for the first time in the present edition. The deep N^2 cuts prevent any assumptions being made about N^1 authority from N^{2-3} agreement in variant readings since none appear save for an accidental or two. However, since N^3 in the absence of N^2 has a secondary authority, one substantive and a handful of accidentals emendations have been taken from it and used to emend the N^1 copy-text. The result is intended to come as close as possible to the full form of the report as sent by Crane from Old Point Comfort. Reprinted from N^{1b} by Fryckstedt and by Stallman.

No. 40. SPANISH DESERTERS AMONG THE REFUGEES AT EL CANEY

This cable, datelined El Caney, July 5, via Port Antonio, July 7, was printed in the New York *World* (N^1), July 8, 1898, page 4, signed, headlined 'SPANISH DESERTERS AMONG | THE REFUGEES AT EL CANEY. ‖ (Copyright, 1898, by the Press Publishing Company, New York World.) | (Special Cable from a World Staff Correspondent.)'. No other newspaper version has been observed. Reprinted from N^1 by Fryckstedt and by Stallman.

No. 41. CAPTURED MAUSERS FOR VOLUNTEERS

Crane's dispatch datelined July 7 from General Shafter's headquarters was not published until July 17 and hence was written, not cabled.

(N^1): New York *World*, July 17, 1898, page 17, signed, headlined 'CAPTURED MAUSERS | FOR VOLUNTEERS. | [short decorative rule] | Better Rifles than the Old | Springfields Now | Carried. ‖ BLACK POWDER CRIMINAL. ‖ Use of It Makes Troops a Fine | Target for the Enemy Using Smokeless. ‖ LESSON OF SANTIAGO FIGHT. ‖ (Special from a Staff Correspondent of The World.)'.

(N^2): Philadelphia *Press*, July 17, page 3, signed, headlined 'HARD TO FIGHT | AN UNSEEN FOE ‖ Stephen Crane on Disadvan-|tages of Springfields Com-|pared with Mauser Rifles. ‖ Special Correspondence of "The Press."' The dateline is the same as in N^1.

Interestingly, this N^2 version contains two paragraphs (169.37–170.10) that were not present in N^1 and thus are reprinted here for the first time. The individual verbal variants in N² are difficult to assess in the absence of a third witness and in view of the *Press's* occasional unauthoritative divergences in other dispatches. However, the editor has allowed himself the luxury of a few emendations of accidentals and of one substantive emendation, thought to be characteristic of Crane, conjecturally altered in the N¹ composing room or by the N¹ copyreader after copy had been sent to Philadelphia. Reprinted by Fryckstedt and by Stallman from N¹.

No. 42. REGULARS GET NO GLORY

This last report that Crane wrote for the New York *World* is datelined Siboney, July 9, but must have been mailed since it did not appear until July 20 in the *World* although on July 19 in other newspapers.

(N¹): New York *World*, July 20, 1898, page 6, signed, headlined 'REGULARS GET NO GLORY. ‖ People Are Interested Only in the | Fighting of Volunteers—Tommy | Atkins's Counterpart. | (Special Correspondence of The World.)'.

(N²): Philadelphia *Press*, July 19, page 2, signed, headlined 'STEPHEN CRANE SKETCHES | THE COMMON SOLDIER. ‖ Word Picture of the Faithful Fighter in the | Ranks, Who Criticises Campaign Plans, | But Obeys Orders and Dies, | When Need Be. ‖ SPECIAL CABLE DESPATCH TO "THE PRESS," COPYRIGHT, 1898.' The false statement that this is a cable is explained by the dateline Siboney, July 18, an attempt to smarten up a report that must have seemed of lesser interest otherwise.

(N³): *Boston Globe*, July 19, page 6, headlined 'PRIVATE NOLAN. ‖ Stephen Crane Says a Word | For the Regular. ‖ "The Best Man Standing on Two Feet | On God's Green Earth." ‖ "Nolan, no Longer Sweating, Swear-|ing, Over-Loaded, Hungry, | Thirsty, Sleepless, but Merely a | Corpse, Attired in About 40 | Cents' Worth of Clothes"—|"Here's Three Volleys and Taps | to Him." ‖ (By Stephen Crane.)'. The dateline is the same as in N¹.

The textual situation seems to be identical with No. 35, which appears to have had the same transmission. That is, the variants in which N²⁻³ agree against N¹ are either suspect or plain errors of the kind that would develop if the copy transmitted to Philadelphia and to Boston instead of radiating directly from the same copy used by the N¹ compositor had in fact been a slightly defective copy of it, either a copy of the typescript made from Crane's manuscript, or a copy of the manuscript itself in case it was the manuscript that was used as N¹ printer's copy. There is little chance that the joint N²⁻³ variants represent early authority. The corruption is most readily seen in the N²⁻³ sophistication *Saratoga* for *Santiago* (171.34), which completely mistakes Crane's sense. He is far from implying that the proud young volunteer is disporting himself at Saratoga although his picture in the paper has him in Cuba; instead, this volunteer, who is pictured on horseback, is actually sweating it out as a dismounted cavalryman in Cuba since his horse has not yet been transported from Tampa. Under these special conditions the three joint N^{2-3} substantive variants have been rejected, and a survey produces no joint N^{2-3} accidentals variants that are so characteristic as to justify emendation of the N^1 copy-text although in the nature of the case they may exist unsuspected.[49] Reprinted by William Gibson (*The Red Badge of Courage and Selected Prose* [New York, 1956]) and by Fryckstedt and Stallman from N^1.

No. 43. A SOLDIER'S BURIAL THAT MADE A NATIVE HOLIDAY

Crane's first report for the *New York Journal*, on Puerto Rico, was datelined from Ponce on August 5, but since it was not published until August 15 he must have sent the manuscript to New York.

(N^1): *New York Journal*, August 15, 1898, page 2, out-of-town edition headlined 'A SOLDIER'S BURIAL THAT | MADE A NATIVE HOLIDAY. | [portrait of Crane with the legend 'Stephen Crane, Journal War Correspondent.'] ‖ Stephen Crane Describes a Strange Funeral Pro-|cession from a Newly Captured | Porto Rican City. ‖ By Stephen Crane. | "Like a Soldier."' The Greater New York edition omits 'By Stephen Crane' but is signed at the foot. The rubric 'Special Correspondence of the Journal' appears in the dateline.

(N^2): San Francisco *Examiner*, August 15, page 1, headlined 'A GRAVE | BENEATH | THE PALMS ‖ Burial of an Ameri-|can Soldier at | Ponce. ‖ An Incident of the War | in a West India | Island. ‖ FAREWELL TO A HERO. ‖ Babel of Sounds From Chat-|tering Natives Punctuate | the Chaplain's Prayer. ‖ HUMOR GRINS AT PATHOS. ‖ Lights and Shadows at the | Funeral of One of the Na-|tion's Dead Braves. ‖ BY STEPHEN CRANE. ‖ Special Correspondence | of "The Examiner." ‖ "Like a Soldier."' The dateline is the same as in N^1.

(N^3): *Kansas City Star*, August 22, page 5, headlined 'DEATH DID NOT QUIET THEM. ‖ The Funeral of an American in Ponce Made | the Natives Gay. | Stephen Crane in the New York Journal.' The dateline reads simply Ponce, Porto Rico, without date.

Since it seems probable that the story was wired to San Francisco, Hearst's second newspaper, the *Examiner* account radiates no doubt

[49] Possible variants of this nature are N^{2-3} *wounded,"* or for N^1 *wounded."* Or (171.23); *information* with a comma for N^1 no comma (172.32); *gallantly* with a comma for N^1 semicolon (173.8); *and if* for N^1 *and, if* (173.8); and a paragraph indention at *Here's* (173.30).

from the same copy as N¹ and hence is authoritative although one step further than N¹ from Crane's original. However, in the absence of an authoritative third witness the substantive variants in N² cannot be evaluated. No reading seems to require emendation of the N¹ copy-text and thus alteration from N² has been confined to a few accidentals which may represent N¹ compositorial departure from copy. On the other hand, the publication of the story one week later by N³ suggests that copy was mailed to Kansas City from New York, and the readings indicate that this was a clipping of N¹. Thus N³ seems to be a completely derived and unauthoritative text. The significance of "*Like a Soldier*" that follows the deck in both N¹ and N² is obscure. It may perhaps represent Crane's original title sent with the story and mistaken for part of the text. Reprinted from N¹ by Fryckstedt and by Stallman.

No. 44. GRAND RAPIDS AND PONCE

Although the opening of this report would seem to place it before No. 43, its dateline with the rubric 'Special Correspondence of the Journal' is Ponce, August 7, two days later, and it appeared in the *Journal* on August 17, following No. 43 on August 15. But, of course, its beginning is really retrospective and its description of Ponce as a city is without reference to date.

(N¹): *New York Journal*, August 17, 1898, page 4, the title 'GRAND RAPIDS AND | PONCE' is part of a drawn decorative heading, followed, in type, by 'The Strange Contrast of | Men and Manners That | Prevails To-day in the | Porto Rican City. ‖ BY STEPHEN CRANE, | JOURNAL WAR CORRESPONDENT.' Four humorous illustrations have drawn legends, 'HE BURST INTO HORSE | LAUGHTER', 'Romantic—but | patrolled by | Wisconsin', 'The Car collides', and 'The Porto | Rican | "glad hand." '

(N²): *Kansas City Star*, August 21, page 5, headlined 'THE WONDERS OF PONCE. ‖ And How They Appeared to an Aston-|ished American. | Stephen Crane in the New York Journal.' The dateline is the same as in N¹. The four *Journal* illustrations are redrawn and given type legends. Two differences appear: in the first illustration N¹ 'HORSE' Becomes N² 'HOARSE' and in the second (the fourth in N²) 'Wisconsin' becomes N² 'MICHIGAN', both changes that reproduce the forms in the text. To these may be added a third. In the same illustration the hand-drawn legend reads 'Romantic—but | patrolled by | Wisconsin', which is reproduced in the N² type legend as 'ROMANTIC—BUT—PA-|TROLLED BY MICHIGAN'. The origin of the wrong dash after 'BUT' appears to be an extra long horizontal stroke to form the 't' in N¹ that was misunderstood.

Since the copying of the illustrations prevents any theory that the text was wired from New York to Kansas City, the only real question is whether a clipping of N¹ served as copy for N² or perhaps a proof that could have been in an earlier textual state than the printed N¹ version. The fact that the illustrations are redrawn suggests that the *Journal* did not send them out as cuts with the copy, and the lack of any other printings of this article also suggests that the *Journal* was not attempting to syndicate the story with accompanying illustrations. Indeed, on the additional evidence of Nos. 45 and 46 it is possible that the *Journal* did not send out copy at all and that the *Star* reprinted it when the *Journal* was received in due course. It is odd that the *Examiner* showed no interest in this series, and perhaps it was not sent there either. The probability that N² was set up from an actual copy of the *Journal* is supported by the difference in the date of the two publications and also by the extraordinarily close agreement of the two texts in accidentals as well as in substantives, the accidentals especially being what one expects in a derived text and not such as radiate from common copy. Hence no alterations from N² can be accepted in the N¹ copy-text save for the single correction of an N¹ misprint.

Two curious textual problems exist. In the N¹ illustrations the drawn caption for the first reads *He Burst into Horse Laughter*, with an appropriate picture of a laughing horse. However, the text reads *hoarse laughter* (176.21). Here it would seem that the illustrator's punning sense overcame him so that he distorted the text, for *hoarse laughter* seems to be correct on the evidence of No. 52, *it has caused a certain number of men in the regular army of the United States to laugh hoarsely and bitterly* (195.2–4). On the other hand, no such easy answer is possible for the second. The drawn legend for the second illustration reads *Romantic—but Patrolled by Wisconsin*. This refers, but with an essential difference, to the concluding sentence, *And so the city lies in the sun, dirty, romantic and patrolled by Michigan*. According to R. A. Alger, *The Spanish-American War* (1901), the Second and the Third Wisconsin Volunteer Infantry under the command of Major-General James H. Wilson, were stationed at temporary headquarters in Ponce before moving to San Juan. No mention is made of Michigan regiments in what purports to be a complete list of the occupation forces in Puerto Rico. The final sentence quoted goes back to 177.6–12: *They were all burning in the sunshine and dimmed by the white dust of a tropic city. They were all guarded by the American soldier, a calm, bronze and blue man with a bayonet. And herein lay the supreme interest, the interest of the juxtaposition of Michigan and Porto Rico—Grand Rapids serenely sitting in judgment upon the affairs of Ponce.* It is just barely possible that the reference to Michigan here is not to the patrolling soldiers but to the general ambience of the mid-West culture brought into juxtaposition with the Spanish, and Grand Rapids is intended to stand for the mid-West in general, not to the specific origin of the soldiers. But such an interpretation lacks the proper background in the story since the only previous reference to Americans in the city except for the soldiers (and the correspondents) is *American buggies*. It would seem, then, that *Grand Rapids serenely sitting in judgment upon the affairs of Ponce* must refer to the occupying troops. If Michigan is simply a generic reference to the whole mid-West, then in the last sentence to be *patrolled by Michigan* applies as well to mid-West soldiers as to Michigan regiments. But given the summary reference of the last sentence, to be patrolled by Wisconsin would produce a clash, even though it was literally accurate according to the regiments garrisoned in Ponce.

One would think nothing of the anomaly, and take it that Crane had simply mistaken the regiments, if it were not for the legend to the illustration, *Patrolled by Wisconsin*. The evidence of the caption suggests that the illustrator read over the manuscript itself, and made notes, before it was set into type, or at the very least saw an early proof. And it would seem that in the form in which the illustrator saw the text, the reading was *patrolled by Wisconsin*. That the final text read *Michigan* would seem to have been the responsibility of the copy-reader, or perhaps the proofreader, who was troubled by the apparent clash of references and thus smoothed out the somewhat rough-edged shift from the general (Wisconsin has no city like Grand Rapids with its peculiar associations) to the specific. Under these circumstances, and on the evidence of the caption, it would seem to represent a re-covery of Crane's original reading to make this emendation from the illustration.

This article was for a long time unrecorded and was turned up and printed from N² by Matthew J. Bruccoli in the *Stephen Crane News-letter*, IV (Fall, 1969), 1–3. Not reprinted in Fryckstedt or in Stallman.

No. 45. THE PORTO RICAN "STRADDLE"

The difference between the dateline from Juana Diaz, August 10, and the publication on August 18, together with the rubric 'Special Corre-spondence of the Journal' which appears in the dateline, indicates that this report was sent on in manuscript, not by cable.

(N^1): *New York Journal*, August 18, 1898, page 3, signed, with a decorative heading 'THE PORTO RICAN | "STRADDLE" | BY | STEPHEN CRANE' also containing a picture of Crane within a circle. The type headline that follows reads 'The Embarrassing Situation in Which | the Porto Rican Finds Himself | Just at the Present Time. ||'. Four illustrations appear with the type legends, ' "A long, low, rakish plug, | with a maximum speed | of seven knots." ', ' "When he is one the | Porto Rican is forever | nodding and smiling." ', ' "They Were a Sulky, | Shifty, Bad | Lot." ', and ' "It was the first Ameri-|can scout." '

(N^2): *Kansas City Star*, August 28, page 5, headlined 'IT WAS HARD TO CHOOSE. || But the Porto Rican Soldiers Finally Joined | the American Side. | Stephen Crane in the New York Journal.' The date was removed from the dateline, leaving only Juana Diaz, Porto Rico. The same four illustrations, but redrawn, appear with the same captions except that the second reads, in error, *When he is one of the Porto Ricans* etc.

The delay in the Kansas City publication, the redrawn illustrations, the absence of publication in any other newspapers, the closeness of the N^2 text to that in N^1, and the history of this particular series all join in evidence to indicate that N^2 is a completely derived text, reprinted from a copy of the *Journal* when it reached Kansas City. The two minor corrections to the N^1 copy-text drawn from N^2 have no authority, therefore. Reprinted from N^1 by Fryckstedt and by Stallman.

No. 46. HAVANA'S HATE DYING, SAYS STEPHEN CRANE

On the conclusion of the Puerto Rican campaign and the signing of a ceasefire on August 12, 1898, Crane was able to make his way to Cuba and slipped into Havana, illegally, by late August. The present report, datelined Havana, August 25, is the first of a series that he wrote on conditions in the defeated country. Within the dateline appears the rubric 'Special Correspondence of the Journal'.

(N^1): *New York Journal*, September 3, 1898, page 5, headlined 'HAVANA'S HATE DYING, | SAYS STEPHEN CRANE. || Thanks to the Local Editors, the | City No Longer Scowls on | All Things American. || (Copyright, 1898, by W. R. Hearst.) | By STEPHEN CRANE.' Four illustrations signed 'R.' appear with the legends, 'Found the Correspondent Drinking | with the Soldiers.', 'They Used to Scorn Americans in | Havana.', 'The Merchants Heartily Welcome | the Americans.', and 'Correspondents Must Then Take to | the Treetops.' For the manuscript articles like this the inference would be that the *Journal* would set from a typescript made from the manuscript or, if it were clean enough, from the manuscript direct.

(N^2): *Kansas City Star*, Sunday, September 11, page 5, headlined 'THE SPIRIT IN HAVANA. || It is Gradually Changing in Favor of the | Americans. | Stephen Crane in the New York Journal.' The dateline reads simply, Havana. The first and fourth of the *Journal* illustrations are used, redrawn. In the captions *Found* is omitted from the first, and in the last *May* replaces *Must Then*. This is a much shortened derived text set up from N¹ and without authority.

Reprinted from N¹ by Fryckstedt and by Stallman.

No. 47. STEPHEN CRANE SEES FREE CUBA

This is the first of three cables (assuming that No. 48 is also a cable) Crane sent from Havana before resuming for good his written articles by mail. The dateline is Havana, August 26, via Key West August 27.

(N¹): *New York Journal*, Sunday, August 28, 1898, page 43, headlined 'STEPHEN CRANE | SEES FREE CUBA. || Says the Desire | for Annexa-tion | Is Growing. || Food Plenty in Ha-|vana, Starving | in Matansas. || (Copyright, 1898, by W. R. Hearst.) | Special Cable Dispatch. | By Stephen Crane.' A picture of Crane, within an oval, accompanies the lower headline.

(N²): *Chicago Tribune*, August 28, page 4, somewhat abbreviated, headlined 'THEY FAVOR | ANNEXATION. || Residents of Havana Willing | to See Union with This | Country. || FEAR OF THE CUBANS. || Much Is Expected from the Gov-|ernment of the Amer-|icans. || STARVATION AT MATANZAS. || [SPECIAL CABLE BY STEPHEN CRANE TO | THE NEW YORK JOURNAL AND THE CHI-|CAGO TRIBUNE.]'. The dateline is the same as in N¹.

(N³): San Francisco *Examiner*, August 28, page 17, headlined 'HA-VANESE FOR | ANNEXATION. || The Conquered Spaniards on | the Island Dred Their | Cuban Foes. || BY STEPHEN CRANE. | [Special Cable to "The Examiner." | Copyright, 1898, by W. R. Hearst.]'. The dateline is simply Havana, August 27.

The textual situation for this cable dispatch is very odd. Both N² and N³ join in four substantive readings against N¹, in two instances of paragraphing, and in an important semisubstantive. These agree-ments go well beyond the fortuitous hits of independent editing and demonstrate that the copy wired to both newspapers was in a differ-ent state from that used for the N¹ text. This is by no means an un-usual situation since other dispatches have shown that copy in an earlier stage of preparation might be wired and then somewhat re-worked before the New York typesetting. The problem with the pres-ent dispatch is that the nature of the readings indicates that here the reverse is true; that is, the readings of N²⁻³ do not appear to be earlier but instead representative of a later state of the copy than those of N¹. This hypothesis cannot properly be demonstrated, but the direc-tion of the changes seems reasonably clear. In three of these readings N²⁻³ supply the normal article expected before nouns but one that would ordinarily be omitted in cables (184.28,31; 185.2). The fourth reading makes little sense in N¹ and evidently has been mixed up in the transmission: *Every day the Spaniards fear anything like an onslaught from the Cuban troops, hungry for many things of which they have been long deprived* (184.29–31). By omitting the anomalous *anything like* N²⁻³ straighten out the sense. What the cable actually read can be only speculative, but it is possible to guess that *anything like* belongs before *annexation* of the preceding sentence, which then would read: *The feeling* [or *Feeling*] *here grows stronger for anything like annexation*. Finally, the N¹ sentence is rather incoherent: *The armored cars still run on all trains, each car containing about thirty soldiers, their rifles in miserable condition, and the soldiers look as bad as reconcentrados* (185.32–34). Whether right or not, the N²⁻³ revision at least makes sense: *about thirty soldiers. Their rifles are in miserable condition, and the soldiers look as bad as reconcentrados.* At (185.36) the N²⁻³ removal of the N¹ comma after *Betancourt* helps to make better sense although it is evident that the sentence is still seriously corrupt.

The paradox, then, prevails that a rough text was printed in New York and a smoother and worked-over text was wired to Chicago and San Francisco. What happened is anyone's guess. Possibly the copy was switched in error so that the rough sheets were sent to the N¹ composing room instead of the reworked text. Possibly the early form was set in type for the out-of-town edition with the intention of making necessary changes in the later Greater New York edition which for some reason or other were not made. (The two editions have been compared and are identical.) It would be comforting to know the reasons, but the textual facts as they stand are sufficient for editorial decision. This must follow a similarly paradoxical line. In other dispatches the earlier readings of the preliminary state of a dispatch have ordinarily been preferred as closer to the cable text and therefore not subject to the sophistication of the rewrite desk. On the other hand, in the present dispatch it is not a question of substituted words thought to be more suitable by the copyreader, but chiefly the supplying of useful articles always omitted from cables on the expectation that they would be added to make a reading text when the cable was prepared for publication. And at 184.29 and to a lesser extent at 185.33, but more importantly at 185.36, the N¹ text is manifestly corrupt and in need of some sort of straightening out. Under these conditions there is little point in being the slave of methodical precedents when the conditions differ. Hence the present editor has chosen to emend the N¹ copy-text by the normal attentions paid to the cable as exhibited in the agreements of the N²⁻³ versions. Reprinted from N¹ by Fryckstedt and by Stallman.

No. 48. STEPHEN CRANE FEARS NO BLANCO

Although the dateline does not mention Key West, as in the cabled dispatches No. 47 and No. 49, the subject matter and the notation Havana, August 28, and publication in the *New York Journal* (N[1]), August 30, 1898, page 5, suggest a telegraphed dispatch. The *Journal's* headline reads 'STEPHEN CRANE | FEARS NO BLANCO ‖ The Young Author Says Havana | Sentiment is Turning in Favor | of Americans. ‖ AMERICAN TROOPS EAGERLY AWAITED. ‖ Wildest Rumors Set Afloat by Spanish Newspapers. | Captain Stewart M, Brice Interviewed, | but Didn't Know It. ‖'. No other appearance has been observed. Reprinted from N[1] by Fryckstedt and by Stallman.

No. 49. STEPHEN CRANE'S VIEWS OF HAVANA

The dateline of this telegram is Havana, September 4, via Key West, September 6. After this dispatch Crane was to send only manuscript articles to the *Journal*.

(N[1]): *New York Journal*, September 7, 1898, page 7, headlined 'STEPHEN CRANE'S | VIEWS OF HAVANA. ‖ He Says Blanco Played an | $800,000 Joke on Span-|ish Patriots. ‖ OUR SOLDIERS THERE. ‖ Constitution of the United States | Printed in Spanish and Sold | on the Streets. ‖ By Stephen Crane. | (Copyright, 1898, by W. R. Hearst.)'.

(N[2]): *Chicago Tribune*, September 7, page 1, headlined 'NO WARSHIP, | NO CASH. ‖ General Blanco Refuses to | Return the $800,000 | Subscribed for a | War Vessel. ‖ PATRIOTS ARE SORRY. ‖ They Conclude That Spanish | Naval Equipment Is an | Unusually Poor In-|vestment. ‖ PLENTY OF FOOD IN HAVANA. ‖ [SPECIAL CABLE BY STEPHEN CRANE TO | THE NEW YORK JOURNAL AND THE CHI-|CAGO TRIBUNE.]'. The dispatch is updated by the dateline, Havana, September 6.

Since no third witness is present to confirm any of the N[2] variants, no way exists to distinguish Chicago editorial and compositorial alterations from possible differences from N[1] in the copy wired. Thus the substantive readings of the N[1] copy-text are all accepted, by default. Reprinted from N[1] by Fryckstedt and by Stallman.

No. 50. THE GROCER BLOCKADE

This signed report without dateline was printed in the *New York Journal* (N[1]), September 23, 1898, page 6, headlined '[to the left]

THE GROCER BLOCKADE. [to the right] STEPHEN CRANE IN-VESTI-|GATES HAVANA'S FALL.' No other newspaper printings have been observed. Reprinted by Fryckstedt and by Stallman from N¹.

No. 51. AMERICANS AND BEGGARS IN CUBA

The manuscript of this untitled and unfinished report is preserved in the Columbia University Libraries Special Collections. It consists of three leaves of unwatermarked ruled hotel stationery of the Grand Hotel "Pasaje," (275 × 212 mm.), the versos of which Crane used for his inscription in pencil. Previously reprinted by Stallman, whose title is adopted here.

No. 52. MEMOIRS OF A PRIVATE

Without dateline this signed report appeared in the *New York Journal* (N¹), Sunday, September 25, 1898, page 26, headlined '[to the left] MEMOIRS OF A PRIVATE. [to the right] DICTATED TO AND TAKEN DOWN | BY STEPHEN CRANE.' The statement of dictation is, of course, only part of the story's fictitious setting. No other appearances have been observed. Reprinted from N¹ by Fryckstedt and by Stallman.

No. 53. THE PRIVATE'S STORY

This report associates itself with No. 50 as one told by a soldier in the regular army but in fact it describes Crane's own homecoming. It was printed without dateline in the *New York Journal* (N¹), September 26, 1898, page 6, headlined '[to the left] THE PRIVATE'S STORY. [to the right] STEPHEN CRANE RETELLS | IT FOR THE JOUR-NAL.' No other appearances have been observed. Reprinted from N¹ by Fryckstedt and by Stallman.

No. 54. STEPHEN CRANE MAKES OBSERVATIONS IN CUBA'S CAPITAL

Signed, and datelined Havana, September 20, this report was not printed in the *New York Journal* (N¹) until October 2, 1898, page 26, where it was headlined '[to the left] STEPHEN CRANE [to the right] MAKES OBSERVATIONS | IN CUBA'S CAPITAL.' So far as is known, no other newspaper used it. Reprinted from N¹ by Fryckstedt and by Stallman.

No. 55. HOW THEY LEAVE CUBA

Signed and without dateline this article appeared in the *New York Journal* (N¹), October 6, 1898, page 6, headlined '[to the left] HOW THEY LEAVE CUBA. [to the right] STEPHEN CRANE DE-|SCRIBES A SAD SIGHT.' Not observed elsewhere. Reprinted from N¹ by Fryckstedt and by Stallman.

No. 56. STEPHEN CRANE IN HAVANA

Datelined October 3, and signed, this report was published by the *New York Journal* on Sunday, October 9, 1898, page 27, headlined '[to the left] STEPHEN CRANE IN HAVANA. [to the right] HE SEES THE COMIC | SIDE OF THINGS.' Not observed elsewhere. Reprinted by Fryckstedt and by Stallman from N¹.

No. 57. HOW THEY COURT IN CUBA

This report is signed and datelined Havana, Oct. 17.

(N¹): *New York Journal*, October 25, 1898, page 6, headlined '[to the left] HOW THEY COURT IN CUBA. [to the right] STEPHEN CRANE DESCRIBES THE | SLOW PROCESS.'

(N²): San Francisco *Examiner,* November 13, page 4, headlined 'COURTING IN CUBA ‖ It Is Full of Circumlocution and Bulwarks and | Clever Football Interference. ‖'. The article is signed and without dateline.

The length of time between the two publications is sufficient evidence that the story was not wired to San Francisco. On the other hand, the fact that N² prints two passages totaling 115 words (204.23–29; 205.1–4) not present in N¹ and not previously recorded is sufficient indication that N² was not set from a clipping of N¹. The choice comes down to a proof of the full version intended for N¹ but cut when the time came to fit the report into the newspaper page, or else the carbon of the typescript made up from Crane's manuscript. One would like to know which, since in the first instance the text would be derived with little or no authority but in the second it would have equal standing with N¹. In addition, it would be interesting to know what the usual procedure was in handling Crane's reports, even though the *Examiner* had exhibited no interest in the preceding series and was to show none in the remainder. Under these circumstances it is a pity that no firm evidence in favor of one or other alternative can be detected. All that can be said is that the *Examiner's* accidentals are remarkably close to those of N¹ and it is unusual to find the identical paragraphing and so little signs of *Examiner* editing. On the whole the most reasonable guess is that a proof was mailed to San Francisco, but at best this is only a guess. The N² substantive variants cannot be identified as early proof readings but instead resemble compositorial or perhaps editorial choices. The copy-text for the report is N¹, but the N² added passages are clearly Crane's and have been inserted. Reprinted from N¹ by Fryckstedt and by Stallman.

No. 58. STEPHEN CRANE ON HAVANA

For the first time this report is copyrighted by Crane himself, but otherwise the format and the position of the article in the *Journal* resemble the preceding ones. So far as observed it was not used by any other newspaper than the *New York Journal* (N¹), which printed it on November 6, 1898, page 26. The article is signed and is datelined Havana, October 28, which is about a week later than the actual date (see below). The headline reads '[to the left] STEPHEN CRANE ON HAVANA. [to the right] WHY CUBA IS BY NO MEANS | A KLONDIKE. ‖ (Copyright by Stephen Crane, 1898.)'. Reprinted from N¹ by Fryckstedt and by Stallman.

This report marks the start of Crane's revolt at being exploited by the *Journal*. The facts are clarified by the typed transcript in the Syracuse University Library of a letter dated Havana, October 21:

My dear Reynolds: I wish you would take the enclosed article to Chamberlain and say that although I am short in my accounts to the Journal, I positively cannot afford to write for twenty dollars a column now since my expenses are cut off. It would be likely to cost five thousand dollars to me in work of a finer kind. Ask them to hike my price to at least 40. If they wont, ask them if they will allow you to syndicate it. I want anyhow soon to arrange a little Syndicate for Cuban letters, one a week. If you are allowed to syndicate try these people at $10 per head for Sunday 30.

> N.Y. Journal
> Phila Press
> Boston Herald
> Chicago Tribune

St. Louis Globe-Democrat
St. Paul Pioneer Press
Buffalo Express.
Then let me know instantly. Will send you another next week. When in *Christ's* name do I get any money.

Crane

What the agent Paul Reynolds did is unknown. Yet it would seem that Reynolds in some way altered the previous arrangements with the *Journal* and it may be that the copyright taken out in Crane's name was an establishment of his right to syndicate the columns, with the *Journal's* permission, even though he never succeeded in establishing any other source of publication. At any rate, as it turned out Crane's days in Havana were numbered even if other newspapers had been interested, which apparently they were not.

No. 59. "YOU MUST!"—"WE CAN'T!"

Datelined Havana, November 4 (although more correctly it would have been October 24), this signed article was printed in the *New York Journal* (N¹), November 8, 1898, page 6, headlined '[to the left] "YOU MUST!"—"WE CAN'T!" [to the right] STEPHEN CRANE ON THE | CUBAN SITUATION. ‖ (Copyright, 1898, by Stephen Crane.)'. No other observed newspaper published it. Reprinted from N¹ by Fryckstedt and by Stallman.

This report must have reached Reynolds on the same day as the manuscript for No. 58, on the evidence of another typed transcript of a Crane ALS in the Syracuse University Library. This is dated Havana, October 24, and its opening sentence refers to No. 58:

My dear Reynolds: I missed the mail-boat with the article on Cuban affairs etc which will reach you at the same time—in which I presented my request to you to go to the Journal people. If they say: "We prefer Crane to work out his debt on the same terms as the original agreement," you reply that the agreement is *not* the same; that they originally paid my expenses but that for many weeks they have not, leaving me in fact fastened here in Cuba with a big hotel bill. I am determined to make a clear slate with them—clean out all indebtedness; but at $20 a column, it is simply *awful*. [¶] If they prove obdurate in the matter of price, ask them how far they consider me bound to them—whether they consider me previleged to syndicate my stuff, giving them the N.Y. rights[.] [¶] Where in hell did you raise the $219.00? Not for The Price of the Harness? That sounds very much like a McClure price. [¶] I may stay here all winter if we can get that syndicate going.

Yours grimly
Crane

No. 60. MR. CRANE, OF HAVANA

The *New York Journal* (N¹) printed this report, datelined Havana, November 4, on November 9, 1898, page 6, headlined '[to the left] MR. CRANE, OF HAVANA. [to the right] We're First in War | But Not in Peace. ‖ (Copyright by Stephen Crane, 1898.)'. It has not been observed elsewhere. Reprinted by Fryckstedt and by Stallman from N¹.

This article is evidently the one referred to in an undated letter (probably between October 25–28, which should have been the report's dateline), from the Syracuse transcripts:

My dear Reynolds: I am resolved now to keep a steady eye on the Journal and send all my stuff through you. This is No. 3; if you syndicate it you will have to send it out for a Wednesday. Better give it to the Journal. It's their style but make them pay more than $20 per column. [¶] McClure would give $30 for his syndicate. [¶] You have not yet receipted for that superb masterpiece The Clan of No-Name. [¶] If I dont receive a rather fat sum from you before the last of the month, I am *ruined*. [¶] In God's name hustle. Cable me anyhow on the 31st—unless of course you send money beforehand.

Crane

No. 61. SPANIARDS TWO

Datelined Havana, November 5 (though correctly it should have been November 1), this report appeared in the *New York Journal* (N¹) on November 11, 1898, page 6, headlined 'SPANIARDS TWO. ‖ By Stephen Crane.' The copyright notice was omitted. Not observed in any other newspaper. Reprinted from N¹ by Fryckstedt and by Stallman.

It is probably this article that was enclosed in the letter from Havana dated November 1, in the Syracuse University transcript:

My dear Reynolds: I herein send another syndicate (or Journal) article. I am afraid these Journal people have ruined me in England. I feel very savage but am bound to make good. I hope you got them to hike the price, damn them. [¶] Convey to Stokes the pleasing information that I have completed about 15000 words of Cuban stories and that he shall have the book for spring, and govern your placing of these articles accordingly. They have come within an ace of ruining my affairs in England; indeed I am not sure they have not done so. [¶] The English rts on the marines go to Blackwoods. [¶] I am working like a dog. When—oh when,—am I to have some money? If you could only witness my poverty!

Crane

No. 62. IN HAVANA AS IT IS TO-DAY

Signed and without dateline this report appeared in the *New York Journal* (N[1]), Sunday, November 12, 1898, page 6, headlined '[to the left] IN HAVANA AS IT IS TO-DAY. [to the right] STEPHEN CRANE WRITES OF | OUR NEW ACQUISITION. ‖ (Copyright by Stephen Crane, 1898.)'. Crane's portrait in a decorated oval frame is inserted at the head of the last column. No other newspaper seems to have printed this article. Reprinted from N[1] by Fryckstedt and by Stallman.

No. 63. OUR SAD NEED OF DIPLOMATS

Signed and datelined Havana, November 9, this last report from Cuba appeared in the *New York Journal* (N[1]), November 17, 1898, page 6, headlined '[to the left] OUR SAD NEED OF DIPLOMATS. [to the right] STEPHEN CRANE LEARNS | IT AT HAVANA. ‖'. No copyright notice is present. Not in the Greater New York edition (N[1a]), but present in the out-of-town edition (N[1b]), is a single line of type beginning a new paragraph and reading *It is said that during the blockade the* (224.10.1). This would appear to represent a continuation of the discussion of the reversals in attitude of citizens of Havana that was cut in proof but the first line of the paragraph left in error, although the mistake was corrected in the other edition. No other variants appear. On this evidence it is possible that in various of the preceding reports in the series that the *Journal* ran on its editorial page, page 6, unknown cuts were made in the originals to fit the articles into a relatively limited space. Reprinted from N[1] by Fryckstedt and by Stallman.

No. 64. MR. STEPHEN CRANE ON THE NEW AMERICA

Crane returned to England in January, 1899. The present interview was printed in the English journal *The Outlook* on February 4, 1899, pages 12–13, headed 'MR. STEPHEN CRANE ON THE | NEW AMERICA.' No other publication is known. Reprinted by Fryckstedt and by Stallman from *The Outlook*.

No. 65. HOW AMERICANS MAKE WAR

This new Crane item, not previously recorded, originated as a letter to the editor of the London *Daily Chronicle* (N[1]), July 25, 1899, page 9. It is signed and dated July 20. The heading given it is 'HOW AMERICANS MAKE WAR. | Some Criticisms and a Conclusion. ‖'. This letter was picked up by the San Francisco *Examiner* (N[2]) and printed on August 28, 1899, page 6, as if it were a news story, shorn of its salutation and signature, but with the subscription 'Stephen Crane in London "Chronicle." ' The headline was 'STEPHEN CRANE | ON GENERAL OTIS ‖'. Although it is possible that Crane might have sent a clipping to the *New York Journal* which did not use it but relayed it to its sister Hearst paper in San Francisco, no N[2] variant suggests an authoritative source and the text seems to be completely derived. The copy-text for this previously unpublished piece, then, is the London *Chronicle*.

ENGLAND

No. 66. THE LITTLE STILETTOS OF THE MODERN NAVY

This signed article first appeared in the *New York Journal* (N[1]), April 24, 1898, page 21, where it was given a full-page spread and an illustrative heading drawn by G. A. Coffin in which the title is part of the picture of a destroyer sinking a warship, 'THE LITTLE STILETTOS OF THE MODERN NAVY | WHICH STAB IN THE DARK | BY | STEPHEN CRANE | WHO WROTE THE | GREATEST BATTLE STORY | OF THE AGE'. This illustrative heading is captioned ' "*Rushing This Way and That, Circling, Dodging, Turning, They Are Like Demons. Hi! Then, for a Grand, Bold, Silent Rush and the Assassin-like Stab*"——'. Above the first two columns is placed this headline, 'THE ASSASSINS IN MODERN BATTLES. ‖ The Torpedo Boat Destroyers That "Perform | in the Darkness An Act Which is More | Peculiarly Murderous Than Most | Things in War." ‖'. To the left of the first column is the drawing of a watch face with the hands at 11:08 and beneath it the caption '60 SECONDS IN WHICH TO | SINK OR BE SUNK. ‖ THE LITTLE CROSS BY THE DIAL | MARKS THE TIME IN WHICH A DE-|STROYER MUST WIN OR LOSE.' Finally, spread across the remaining six columns is this headline, beneath the illustration's caption, reading 'HOW THE DEADLY MODERN TORPEDO DESTROYERS WORK—ELABORATED FROM PHOTOGRAPHS TAKEN AT THE | TRIAL PRACTICE OF

THE YARROW BOATS WITNESSED BY STEPHEN CRANE FOR THE JOURNAL.'

(N²): *Denver Republican*, May 1, page 30, headlined 'TORPEDO BOATS | AND DESTROYERS ‖ Stephen Crane on "Naval | Stilettos That Stab in | the Dark." ‖ Work Which Is "More Peculiarly | Murderous Than Most Things | in War." ‖ "Hi! Then, for a Grand, Bold, Si-|lent Rush and the Assas-|sin-Like Stab." ‖'. This is a derived text, of no authority, set from a clipping of the *New York Journal*, which it credits as its source.

(E1): Cora collected this article in *Last Words* (Digby, Long & Co., 1902), pages 181–189, where it is headed 'THE ASSASSIN IN MODERN BATTLES. | The Torpedo Boat Destroyers that "Perform | in the Darkness. An Act which is more | Peculiarly Murderous than most Things in | War." '

(TMs): In the Barrett Collection at the University of Virginia is preserved a typescript (TMs) of seven leaves of unwatermarked ruled wove paper 265 × 215 mm., the rules 9 mm. apart. This is headed 'THE AS-SASSINS IN MODERN BATTLES. | The Torpedo Boat Destroyers That "Perform in the Darkness | An Act Which Is More Peculiarly Murderous Than Most Things In War." Alterations are made in this typescript in black ink and in pencil. In Cora Crane's hand in the upper left corner of page 1 is written '2150 Words', and she has added the signature 'By Stephen Crane.' (underlined) beneath the main title. She also underlined the two titles, in the second adding 's' to 'Thing' and the final period and quotes after 'War', and a double underline beneath the whole. Below the word count on this page she wrote, in pencil, 'For book'. To the right of the main title is written in blue crayon the large circled figure '12'. Cumulative word counts in Cora's hand appear on the verso of each leaf (the counts are reversed in error on the versos of leaves 4 and 5), starting with 280 on fol. 1ᵛ and ending with 230 added to 1,920 for a total of 2,150 on fol. 7ᵛ. On fol. 3ᵛ appears the false start of typing on the recto: *and cruisers were the final thing in naval construction. He scoff | intelligently,* which was abandoned on discovery of the wordskip. Page 4 is typed on the verso of the original page 1, which has the title and subtitle correctly typed but was apparently discarded when more space was wanted under the main title for the signature to be added later. The typing was reviewed and corrected first in ink and then at a later time in pencil. The majority of the corrections complete words at the end of a line left a letter or two short because of the lack of a margin release on the Crane typewriter, the instrument used for this typescript. A number of others delete the start of such words at the end of a line when it was seen that they could not be finished and thus were typed at the beginning of the next line. Some letters are strengthened or corrected and a misspelling or two is mended, although one is created when at 236.2 correctly typed *Chili* is altered to *Chilli*. Only a few readings are changed. A desirable comma is added after *Europe* (236.26); *Chili* following *China* (236.5) after being altered to *Chilli* in ink is then deleted in pencil when it was seen to clash with the statement at the start of the sentence. At 236.18 *shell* is altered to *shelled*; at 237.2 a blank space had evidently been left in the typing and *1897* was filled in in ink; at 237.5–6 *in U.S.* was interlined after *commissioners*; at 238.20 *four* was interlined after *twenty*; and at 238.24 *with* was interlined above what seems to be deleted typed *for*.

The Barrett typescript is part of a series that derives from the publisher Coates to whom, through Paul Reynolds, Cora sent copies of the stories and articles in *Last Words* when negotiations were in process for Coates to publish the collection in the United States. Some of these typescripts, like "The Great Boer Trek" (see No. 71), were made from the original manuscript or typescript in Cora's possession, but others, like "An Episode of War" (see TALES OF WAR, *Works*, Vol. VI), merely retyped a clipping of the already published magazine text in order to provide sufficient copies for distribution to English and American publishers. Despite one or two anomalies "The Little Stilettos" falls in the latter category. The copying of the *New York Journal* headlines (which could not have been in the original) as the title and subtitle of the typescript is the strongest piece of evidence so that there is no need to appeal to the identity of paragraphing, the very close similarity of accidentals, and even to Cora's fewer errors in spelling as evidence. Tiny suggestions of the printed copy come through as in the ink addition of a comma after *Europe* (236.26) missing in N^1 and originally wanting in TMs. The anomalies mentioned consist in what seems to have been an attempt made before typing to remove references suitable for 1898 but not 1900 and later to alter American references to make them suitable for English readers as well. In the first group comes the change from the present to the past in the references to the four destroyers being built for Japan (238.13–14), in which N^1 *now* was omitted and *are* typed as *were*, as well as the change in N^1 *are now shelling dervishes* (236.17–18) to *shell dervishes* later corrected in ink to *shelled*. In the second comes the omission of *our* in N^1 *our fire commissioners* (237.5–6) and the addition after *commissioners* of ink *in U.S.* Presumably Cora made notes for these changes in the copy she had of N^1 and so followed them in her typing. It is unlikely that the TMs readings reflect her reference to an original that had been editorially altered in these respects in N^1: the changes (if they had been changes in N^1) are by no means required for an American audience and the reversal in the time scheme would be very odd. If a hint is necessary, however, it can come in the treatment of *our fire commissioners*, which in the original typescript read, *that part of the London County Council which corresponds to fire commissioners*. The whole point of the reference is to the American term. It would be possible to conceive that Crane wrote the sentence as found in TMs and that N^1 clarified by adding *our*; but it would be pushing the evidence too hard to take it that Cora found the same difficulty (when actually little or none existed) and independently felt it necessary to add in ink *in U.S.* The greater probability is that her notes deleted *our* as an American reference, and then on reviewing her typescript she saw that she had created a difficulty and so mended it with *in U.S.* The only real oddity comes at 238.14 when in the process of altering the present to the past in the building of four destroyers for Japan she added (*1898*) after *Japan* at the end of the sentence. This might be construed as the reproduction of a note to himself Crane had written in his manuscript (although it would be an oddity in view of his use of the present tense and of *now*—since these can scarcely be assigned as N¹ editorial changes) but the simpler explanation that fits with the body of the other evidence is that it was a note by Cora in the N¹ copy that she did not assimilate.

The text in *Last Words* (E1) was demonstrably set from the ribbon copy of the Barrett TMs carbon. Again there is the similarity of readings; but here some mechanical evidence may be found of a more precise sort than that between N¹ and TMs. For instance, the curious period in the title after *Darkness* is explicable when one sees that TMs ends a line with this word and begins the next line with *At* capitalized (as in N¹). Again, the ink addition *in U.S.* becomes in E1 *in United States* without the necessary article. That the ink correction in the ribbon copy and carbon had not always been identical is shown by the Barrett TMs addition in ink of *four* after *twenty* (238.20) but the E1 retention of *twenty knots* as in the original.

It follows that both TMs and E1 are completely derived texts without authority and the only text that has a direct link with Crane's lost manuscript is N¹, which becomes the copy-text. A few necessary emendations are drawn from TMs but under the circumstances it must be recognized that they have no authority and cannot refer back to a purer text than N¹.

Preserved in the Columbia University Libraries Special Collections are six small scraps of paper containing holograph notes Crane made in preparation for this article, probably on the spot. They read as follows:

[leaf 1]

20 yrs about ‖ Russia, Germany, France, Spain, Italy, Holland, Austria, Japan, China, Ecuador, Chili, Brazil, Argentine, Costa Rico, ‖ Most modern destroy 1 – 220 – B 26 ½ – 6500 H.P. 31 K speed Triple exp engines W.T. Boilers For Jap 4 boats 2 or 3 tor tu 18 torpedoes ª ‖ armed 1 12 pd, 3-5 – 6 pd

[leaf 2]

Germany & France Brassey's Annual more torpedoe boats ‖ Eng more ᵇ destroyes ‖ M torpodoe boat now bui 1 152 – b 15¼ H.P. 2000 Speed fully loaded 24 K ‖ single screw. ‖ Carrying 45 tons load 3 hours run.

[leaf 3]

Have built some boats with quadruple exp. ‖ Small [c] boats draw only 4 or 5 ft water ||| Dont throw big bow wave anymore ||| Worst thing for invisibility would be flame at stack = bad firing. ‖

[leaf 4]

Bow tubes antiquated ||| 2 swivels [d] firing on either beams. ‖ Crew 40 men [e] Officers 3 & [f] 4 officers ‖ Color olive buff slate (best) ‖ English boats always black

[leaf 5]

Large destroyers carry 80 to 100 tons coal — keep sea for about 1 wk at 9 + 10 knots ||| No sense in any attack save against vessels. Only thing possible is attack on dock-gates.

[leaf 6]

Great Yarrow forte small fast boats up to 240.[g] ||| Germanys buys only to copy |||

   [a] torpedoes] *this whole notation starting with* '2 or 3' *was crowded in later*
   [b] more] 'more destroyes' *written below deleted* 'about'
   [c] Small] 'S' *over* 'F'
   [d] 2 swivels] '2' *over* '1'; 'swivels' *followed by deleted* 'astern one am'
   [e] 40 men] *written below deleted* '2 engin. 2 Deck', *leaving* 'Officers' *undeleted in error*
   [f] 3 &] *added below line*
   [g] 240] *written over* '254'

No. 67. SOME CURIOUS LESSONS FROM THE TRANSVAAL

This is the first of the brief series of articles that Crane wrote on the Boer War for the *New York Journal*. It is signed and being without dateline was almost certainly mailed across the Atlantic.

   (N[1]): *New York Journal,* Sunday, January 7, 1900, page 27, signed and headlined '𝕾𝖔𝖒𝖊 𝕮𝖚𝖗𝖎𝖔𝖚𝖘 𝕷𝖊𝖘𝖘𝖔𝖓𝖘 𝖋𝖗𝖔𝖒 𝖙𝖍𝖊 𝕿𝖗𝖆𝖓𝖘𝖇𝖆𝖆𝖑 [leaf orn.] 𝕭𝖞 𝕾𝖙𝖊𝖕𝖍𝖊𝖓 𝕮𝖗𝖆𝖓𝖊 | (Copyright, 1900, by the New York Journal and Advertiser.)'. The first column is headed by the quotation, within an ornamental border, ' *"The bewildering thing* | *to the British mind has* | *been the mauling received* | *at the hands of bewhisk-|ered farmers by many regi-|ments whose records so* | *blazed with glory that* | *they were popularly ac-|counted invincible."* ' A photograph of Crane was inset between the third and fourth columns.
   (N[2]): San Francisco *Examiner,* January 7, page 24, headlined '𝖂𝖍𝖊𝖗𝖊𝖎𝖓 𝖙𝖍𝖊 𝕿𝖗𝖆𝖓𝖘𝖇𝖆𝖆𝖑 𝕴𝖘 𝕹𝖔𝖜 𝕬𝖋𝖋𝖔𝖗𝖉𝖎𝖓𝖌 𝕷𝖊𝖘𝖘𝖔𝖓𝖘 𝖙𝖔 𝖙𝖍𝖊 𝖂𝖔𝖗𝖑𝖉.' Within a decorative border, at the right, is '𝕭𝖞 | 𝕾𝖙𝖊𝖕𝖍𝖊𝖓 | 𝕮𝖗𝖆𝖓𝖊'. At the foot is 'Copyright, 1900, by W. R. Hearst.'

It is probable the *Examiner* was wired the article on receipt in New York, but so far as can be told the N² substantive variants are all unauthoritative. Reprinted from N¹ by Fryckstedt and by Stallman.

No. 68. STEPHEN CRANE SAYS: WATSON'S CRITICISMS OF ENGLAND'S WAR ARE NOT UNPATRIOTIC

The *New York Journal* (N¹) printed this signed article on February 14, 1900, page 8, headlined '[to the left] STEPHEN CRANE SAYS: [to the right] WATSON'S CRITICISMS OF ENGLAND'S | WAR ARE NOT UNPATRIOTIC. ‖ (Copyright, 1900, by the New York Journal and Advertiser.)'. Inset in the first column is the photograph of Crane used in No. 67. No other observed newspaper used the piece. Reprinted from N¹ by Fryckstedt.

No. 69. STEPHEN CRANE SAYS: THE BRITISH SOLDIERS ARE NOT FAMILIAR WITH THE "BUSINESS END" OF MODERN RIFLES

In the Columbia University Libraries Special Collections is preserved the holograph manuscript of this article, written in black ink on one side of three sheets of paper, 206 × 127 mm., the first sheet watermarked with a crown above the words *Victoria Exhibition Note 1899*, the second sheet being the verso of a piece of stationery from the Hotel St. Petersbourg, Paris. The manuscript is untitled but is signed at the end. On the verso of the second leaf is the word count of the recto, 310 circled, which is then added to the 250 words of the first leaf for a total of 560. On the verso of the third leaf is the total 648 words formed by adding 88 to 560, and beneath this the phrase '650 words'. In the upper left corner of this verso is 'published by' and, in a different ink, below, 'Journal | in N.Y.' The word counts are in Cora's hand.

(N¹): *New York Journal*, February 14, 1900, page 8, signed, headlined '[to the left] STEPHEN CRANE SAYS: [to the right] The British Soldiers Are Not Familiar with | the "Business End" of Modern Rifles. ‖'. No dateline or copyright notice appears.

(N²): San Francisco *Examiner*, February 14, page 3, datelined New York, February 13, headlined 'TOMMY ATKINS IGNORANT | OF MODERN RIFLE'S POWER ‖ By Stephen Crane. | (Special by leased wire, the longest in the world.)'.

That the manuscript is found among other of Crane's effects preserved by Cora indicates that a typescript was prepared at Brede for mailing to the *Journal*. This typescript was presumably the copy wired to N^2 from New York. The N^1 text is remarkably in agreement with the manuscript. Indeed only two verbal divergences are found. The first—*went* for *came* (246.14)—is shown to be an editorial change in N^1 since N^2 agrees with MS *came*. The second, the omission at 246.11 of the short sentence *Everybody thought he did*, was a typescript alteration since here N^{1-2} are in agreement. The authority of this omission is difficult to assess. It may have been in the nature of an eyeskip, or Crane could have excised it in the typescript before mailing. All one can say is that the piece is better off without it. The Columbia MS shows that the article had originally ended with Crane's signature after the sentence ending *steady valor of British troops."* (247.10) and that the present conclusion was an afterthought.

The present edition takes MS as the copy-text, of course, since it has prime authority for the accidentals. Variant accidentals agreed in by N^{1-2} indicate that the typescript did not always follow the MS faithfully in punctuation and in word-division. The N^2 substantive variants must all be errors. Reprinted from N^1 by Fryckstedt.

No. 70. MANUSCRIPT FRAGMENT

In a collection of seventeen leaves catalogued as "Miscellaneous Fragments" the Columbia University Libraries Special Collections preserves this brief start of a report that was soon abandoned. The trigger was a brief item in the London *Times* of November 21, 1899, datelined New York, November 19, which after commenting on the overoptimistic reports of General Otis's attempts to pacify the Philippines, concludes: "What Americans desire to be told is whether the Philippine territory is to be not only overrun but permanently occupied and administered. English criticism has taught us much on that point. Whether General Otis and his commanding officer in Washington have profited by this criticism as others have done, and whether these great personages have really learned the lessons of lasting conquest is what this country wishes to know, but does not yet know." It was the reference to the beneficial effects of English criticism that stung Crane into starting this abortive reply.

No. 71. THE GREAT BOER TREK

The date of composition of this essay is not known but on April 19, 1900, Paul Reynolds wrote Crane that he had sold it to the *Cosmo-*

politan for $100 and had so cabled him. Reynolds continues: "I cabled you because I did not know whether or not you had tried to sell the article over there and I did not want to run the risk of having it published in England before it was published over here. The Cosmopolitan say they will use it at an early date. You asked me to get you $50.00; I have got you $100.00. I doubted whether I could sell the article; there has been so much written on the Boer War and it was declined by several magazines before the Cosmopolitan took it" (TLS Columbia University). The essay is largely drawn from George M. Theal, *History of the Boers in South Africa* (1887), or just possibly from his redaction *South Africa* in The Story of the Nations series published by Unwin, perhaps the 1894 edition, with slight reference to one or more other authorities. Thus it bears all the marks both in origin and in style of the research work of Kate Lyon (Frederic), who in the early months of 1900 was working up material for Crane's *Great Battles of the World.* January or February, close in time to Crane's *Journal* articles, would be a safe guess.

Little else is known of its history. On April 25, 1900, Reynolds wrote to Cora: "I sent all the money I had to Mr. Crane two or three weeks ago. I cabled him that I had sold 'The Great Boer Trek' for $100; I have not got the money for that as yet, but I have written to the Cosmopolitan asking them to send me the money" (TLS, Columbia University). The piece came out in the *Cosmopolitan*, XXIX (June, 1900), 153–158, headed 'THE GREAT BOER TREK. | BY STEPHEN CRANE.' On June 18, 1900, Reynolds wrote to Cora: "I have received the money for 'The Great Boer Trek.' After taking out my commission and some charges for a cablegram, etc. it leaves $87.35. [¶] My lawyer informs me that the law requires me to pay the money to the executor of Mr. Crane's estate, and as soon as I receive a proper certificate showing the executor's appointment and qualification I shall be glad to send him the money. [¶] You will understand that I should be very glad to pay you the money, but my lawyer tells me that I must follow the legal course or else be held responsible for not doing so" (TLS Columbia University). On July 5, 1900, Reynolds wrote to Cora at Port Jervis, N.Y.: " 'The Great Boer Trek' has already been printed in the Cosmopolitan so that I cannot send you proofs" (TLS, Columbia University). A note that he has paid Judge Crane for "The Great Boer Trek" is included in a letter to Cora of May 14, 1901 (the printed 1900 date on the letterhead has not been altered), from Reynolds informing her of the advance from Coates for *Last Words* (TLS, Columbia University). Before this, however, Reynolds makes a significant reference. On October 23, 1900, he wrote Cora a long letter about the possible sale of *Last Words* to Stokes, objecting to the heterogeneous nature of the volume and urging her to put into it at least four or five good stories that would convince Stokes that the volume would sell. He lists the titles of seventeen sketches in his possession, all of which are titles that were to appear in *Last Words* and thus represent either typescripts or clippings, or references, that Cora had previously sent him for the book. He prefaces this list with the following statement: "You asked me to send a copy of the 'Great Boer Trek' so I send it herewith. With regard to the stories you wished me to get, which have appeared in the New York Press, and Tribune, can't you give me some date when they appeared? I asked the Press to send me the stories, and they say they cannot put their hands upon them, but if I will give them the date they will be glad to hunt them up" (TLS, Columbia University).

In the Barrett Collection of the University of Virginia Library is preserved the black carbon of a typescript of thirteen numbered pages, with a two-leaf supplement hand-numbered 14 and 15 containing the Retief "Proclamation." The leaves are of wove unwatermarked paper, 330 × 200 mm., which have been folded for mailing, including the "Proclamation" in the same folds. The typing was done on the Crane typewriter and almost certainly by Cora Crane, who has gone through the copy adding omitted letters at the ends of lines and correcting obvious typing errors. At a later time she also reviewed the copy and brought it into general conformity with the substantives of the *Cosmopolitan* (Co) version. It is Cora, too, who wrote in the upper left corner 'by | Stephen Crane' and who signed the essay 'Stephen Crane' at the end on page 13. This typescript is part of a series in the Barrett Collection of the typescripts received by Coates for *Last Words* when the firm was contemplating its American publication, but subsequently returned to Reynolds. It was, then, made up by Cora specifically with book publication in view, and it must represent the typescript that she returned to Reynolds subsequent to her receipt from him of the copy he mailed her on October 23, 1900.

A puzzle is hereby created. That "The Great Boer Trek" was not mentioned in Reynolds' list of seventeen items is not strange, perhaps, since he must have abstracted it from the file of these stories and so no longer listed it for Cora as a story in his possession. The question is, why did Cora want a copy returned and what was the nature of the copy that Reynolds sent her. Reynolds had sold the article to the *Cosmopolitan*. Thus if he were originally sent the manuscript he would have had in his keeping the carbon of the typescript he had had made up for sale. On the other hand, if he had been sent a typescript, he would have had only a clipping from the *Cosmopolitan* in his file, assuming that he had not requested the return of the printer's copy, as indeed he would have no reason to do. The copy that he returned to Cora, then, might have been either the carbon of the original typescript or a clipping of the *Cosmopolitan*.

In turn, if the Cranes had sent Reynolds the manuscript, Cora at this time would have had no copy in her possession and would need one if she were contemplating adding "The Great Boer Trek" to the English edition—which in fact she never did even though it is clear that her initial intention was to have it included in the American publication. Yet all the evidence we have suggests that in 1900, and also in 1899, once Cora became Crane's typist, all material was typed and not sent out in manuscript form. Thus the odds favor her having sent Reynolds a typescript in the first place so that he would have in his files only the *Cosmopolitan* clipping, unless he had received a carbon along with the ribbon copy. On the whole we may conjecture that what Cora wanted was the *Cosmopolitan* text in order to correct the copy she was preparing, belatedly, for *Last Words*. As with Stokes publishing *Wounds in the Rain* and preferring what he assumed was the more correct printed copy to typescripts, one reason why Cora seems so often to have typed up clippings as copy for *Last Words* may not have been solely her lack of manuscripts or typed carbons but, perhaps, in addition, her assumption that the printed copy would be more correct than manuscripts or carbons of typescripts in her possession. We have no means of knowing whether she ever offered "The Great Boer Trek" to the English publishers of *Last Words* and it was declined. Like *Great Battles of the World*, which had no interest for the English magazine market and was commissioned exclusively for the United States, a mere compilation of common historical sources on South Africa could scarcely have sold in England, and perhaps was never offered there. It may be, therefore, that Cora was thinking exclusively of the American edition of *Last Words* (unless she was desperate to fill out the volume) and hence did not require an extra typescript copy for Digby, Long & Co., the publishers. Finally, the paper of the Barrett typescript differs from that of the other typescripts prepared for Stokes and then transferred to Coates.

It is more than possible, therefore, that what Cora wanted from Reynolds was a copy of the *Cosmopolitan* text so that she could revise the carbon of the original typescript in her possession by collation—as indeed she did—and then she sent back to Reynolds this corrected typescript to be included with the other *Last Words* material. This might seem to be an abnormal procedure if she had intended "The

Great Boer Trek" from the start to be part of *Last Words*, but if she had not done so and only in October thought of the possibility of piecing out the American edition by this article, it would be a natural enough procedure for her to want to see the *Cosmopolitan* version. What at first sight is odd is only that she was not content to let Reynolds include the clipping. But she played both ends against the middle by having the clipping sent her, bringing her typescript into conformity with it, and then retaining (for possible English book use, if desirable?) what she regarded as the more correct form.

In a sense this argument smacks of special pleading, and it is true that Cora might well have retained her collated typescript and returned the clipping to Reynolds. Here a small piece of evidence may be useful. If, as the above argument goes, the Barrett typescript is indeed the carbon of the original used to set up the *Cosmopolitan* version, it is perhaps significant that the Retief "Proclamation," although typed on the same paper as the original, was not paged with the original and the pagination in the Barrett copy is continued by hand. This seems to point to an initial half-intention to have the "Proclamation" available in typed form but not to include it in magazine publication, where clearly it would be out of place. That it is added to the Barrett carbon, itself in carbon, points to Cora's hope that it could be used to add length to the book. We may only speculate, but it may have occurred to her that awkward as the appendage was, a book publisher might not fancy it if evidence were present that it had not been earlier published with the article. This would explain its inclusion in hand-numbered and in carbon form and it would help to explain why Cora sent the corrected typescript and not the *Cosmopolitan* clipping plus the typed "Proclamation" back to Reynolds. If, instead, she had prepared the Barrett typescript for publication only when she received whatever copy it was that Reynolds sent her in October, it would be odd that within the short time before she must have returned it to him she also secured a *Cosmopolitan* clipping with which to collate it if he had sent a typescript. If he had sent a clipping, it is peculiar that she prepared a typescript from some other copy and then corrected it by the *Cosmopolitan* but did not page the Retief. Given the odds that Reynolds returned her a clipping, and that this was used to correct an already prepared typescript, it should follow on the evidence of the paper and of the "Proclamation" treatment that the preserved typescript-carbon was the original that she had preserved. If so, the Barrett TMs is at only one remove from the manuscript and is thus of relatively high authority.

On the evidence of Reynolds' letter to Cora of July 5, 1900, reminding her that he could not send her proofs since the article was already in print, it is clear that Crane or Cora had not read proof for the *Cosmopolitan* text; and indeed the speed with which the magazine put the piece into print after purchase combined with Crane's serious illness in May to preclude much possibility that the *Cosmopolitan* sent proofs or received them back corrected. One may take it, therefore, that the Co text represents an edited version referring to no other authority than its typescript copy, which probably was identical with the Barrett carbon. If this is so, the Barrett carbon is the sole authority in every respect since Co would derive from its duplicate. If the hypothesis not be accepted that the Barrett carbon was the original made directly from the manuscript, but instead represents a fresh copy made either from the manuscript or from a typed copy in Cora's possession, it would still be free in its uncorrected state from *Cosmopolitan* editing. Moreover, even if it is a copy of a copy, it would be at the same remove as the printed text and therefore equal in authority. Thus since it has not been subjected to housestyling, and at the worst is no more distant from the lost manuscript than the *Cosmopolitan*, it must be selected as the copy-text.

The status of this typescript's substantives is complicated by Cora's alterations. Some of these must represent her own independent editing, like her deletion of *high-handed* at 252.35 in a passage not present in Co. It is also possible that some few of her own changes fortuitously agree with the *Cosmopolitan* text although not deriving from it, in case her independent editorial review of the typescript (as distinct from her correction) differed in point of time from her later attempt to incorporate the *Cosmopolitan* substantives. On the other hand, the vast majority of her alterations refer directly to her endeavor to revise the essay by changing its wording here and there to agree with the *Cosmopolitan* version. That these alterations must represent, in general, the Co editing and do not revert through Co to a purer text is effectively demonstrated by the fact that most of them depart from the reading of the source. An illustration will suffice. For instance, at 255.19–20 TMs originally read, copying Theal, *Potgieter with eleven others went to explore the country* but Cora, following Co, altered *eleven others* to *a party*.

It seems clear, then, that whereas a very few of Cora's alterations could theoretically represent her early collation of TMs back against its copy, the vast majority are unauthoritative. Under these circumstances, the substantives of the copy-text TMs(u)—that is, the original or uncorrected state of the Barrett typescript—have been preferred in all but one or two cases of necessary editing to the handwritten alterations in the TMs(c) or corrected state that can represent only a departure from authority. Because of its editing, the *Cosmopolitan* text is of little or no authority for substantives or for accidentals as compared with TMs. "The Great Boer Trek," thus, is presented here not only with the addition of original passages not previously known because of Co cuts but also with a general texture of words and accidentals of considerably greater authority than in the *Cosmopolitan* version.

The copy-text is TMs(u). The apparatus records all variants from this copy-text made by Cora in the typescript TMs(c). TMs without indication of (u) or (c) means that the typescript has not been altered so that the reading referred to is invariant. The alterations made in ink in TMs(c) are alone recorded and no record is made of the false starts and skips that were repaired in the course of the typing itself. These were mechanical and have no textual significance. Moreover, the various mechanical corrections of typescript faults that Cora made in ink, such as the completion of words in the right margin, have not been recorded. Instead, the collations list only those changes that appear to be made in revision of the original typescript TMs(u), not in its simple correction. The Retief "Proclamation" constitutes a minor problem. The essay itself ends thirteen lines down on page 13 with Cora's inscription of Stephen's signature. The "Proclamation" begins a new leaf and, moreover, one that was perhaps not of the original typing since it and its successor are numbered by hand. Yet the paper is the same and there is every indication that Cora wished to associate the "Proclamation" with the essay in its book form. Whether she was reflecting Crane's wishes in this matter cannot be determined, and it is possible, of course, that she merely typed up some of the notes that had been provided Crane and used them to increase the word count. However, for whatever interest it may possess, the "Proclamation" is herewith printed as in the typescript. Reprinted from Co by Fryckstedt.

No. 72. THE TALK OF LONDON

Although not strictly speaking a war report, the present article does treat of England in wartime and the effect of the Boer War on Europe, and hence it has an appropriateness, in its larger view, as the conclusion of the series of reports of war.

(N¹): *New York Journal,* Sunday, March 11, 1900, page 27, headlined '𝕿𝖍𝖊 𝕿𝖆𝖑𝖐 𝖔𝖋 𝕷𝖔𝖓𝖉𝖔𝖓 [row of three leaves] 𝕭𝖞 𝕾𝖙𝖊𝖕𝖍𝖊𝖓 𝕮𝖗𝖆𝖓𝖊 | [within a decorative frame] *A gathering war cloud* | *and a rumpus in Parlia-|ment.'* Inserted at the foot of the last column is the photograph of Crane, titled 'Stephen Crane'.

(N²): San Francisco *Examiner,* March 11, page 27, headlined '𝕿𝖍𝖊 𝕿𝖆𝖑𝖐 𝖔𝖋 𝕷𝖔𝖓𝖉𝖔𝖓. [row of three leaves] 𝕭𝖞 𝕾𝖙𝖊𝖕𝖍𝖊𝖓 𝕮𝖗𝖆𝖓𝖊.', also with a photograph insert.

The copy was no doubt mailed to New York and then wired to San Francisco so that the *Examiner* is something of an independent witness in cases where N¹ printing departures could have occurred. However, only one or two small corections of N¹ slips seem required. Reprinted from N¹ by Fryckstedt.

IMOGENE CARTER

Crane's coy remark that he was himself Imogene Carter [50] by its terms of reference applied only to the series of London columns to which Cora (in some part assisted by Stephen) engaged herself following the return to England from Greece. On the other hand, on the external evidence of his inscription of part of the Pharsala manuscript, No. 3, and the internal evidence of style, it seems probable that to some extent he had a hand in Cora's dispatches, whether by dictation or by touching up. Certainly Crane-like parts are also mixed with untypical style, but whether in these Crane was attempting to write like a woman or whether they were truly Cora's is impossible to determine. At any rate, the possibility that these dispatches may contain some bits of Crane justify their inclusion in the present volume, just as they were included in the Crane scrapbook preserved in the Barrett Collection of the University of Virginia Library.

No. I. WAR SEEN THROUGH A WOMAN'S EYES

The most elaborate dispatch is datelined Athens, April 26, although it did not appear in the *New York Journal* until May 14, 1897, page 8, two weeks after No. 2 which is datelined Athens, April 29. The dis-

---

[50] *Letters,* p. 145.

patch was signed 'Imogene Carter' and was headlined 'War Seen Through | a Woman's Eyes. ||'. Reprinted by Stallman.

NO. 2. WOMAN CORRESPONDENT AT THE FRONT

On April 30, 1897, page 1, the *New York Journal* printed 'Woman Corre-|spondent at | the Front. || GOES FOR THE JOURNAL. || Imo-gene Carter Braves | Perils of the Field of War. || ONLY WOMAN ON THE SCENE. || Not Daunted by the Stories | of Turks Firing on | Nurses. || By Imogene Carter.' The dateline was Athens, April 29. Reprinted by Stallman.

NO. 3. IMOGENE CARTER'S ADVENTURE AT PHARSALA

In the Columbia University Libraries Special Collections are preserved two manuscripts of this untitled and unfinished article. The first con-sists of two leaves of wove unwatermarked unruled paper 270 × 215 mm., written on one side of the paper in black ink in Stephen Crane's hand, with alterations in his own hand. The second leaf, which is torn and jagged at the foot, holds only nine lines of text and ends possibly in mid-sentence although a closing period may be all that is wanting. The leaf is numbered '2' within a semicircle at top center.

The second section consists of nine leaves of cheap ruled wove paper 224 × 150 mm., paged, written on one side of the paper by Cora Crane. Comparison of Crane's part with Cora's reveals that he was apparently starting to rewrite her narrative in a form more suit-able for publication. It would seem, then, that the second section is entirely her own work and was in no part dictated to her by Crane. It would also seem that, at least at the beginning, he was proposing a thorough rewriting job with publication in view. Presumably when she failed to complete her report, Crane lost interest.

Both manuscripts are edited here in a reading text as if for publica-tion instead of being presented in a diplomatic reprint. The transcrip-tion of Cora's section is complicated by her habit here of using rather indiscriminately a mark like a hyphen, but normally in a lower posi-tion on the line, for a period or a comma, although a handful of legitimate periods and commas are present. Also, she did not usually capitalize a new sentence. In the apparatus all of these short dashes are noted when commas are substituted, and all supplied capital letters are recorded. However, since little or no ambiguity results, the dashes intended for periods are transcribed as periods without record. Cora also used the ampersand instead of *and* more frequently than not; these have been silently expanded. Much of this manuscript was printed by Lillian B. Gilkes in her biography *Cora Crane* (1960), pages 94–95. Although the present editor has made a fresh transcript of the rest from the Columbia University papers, he is much indebted to Miss Gilkes for permission to utilize her private transcript of the first leaf (269.28–270.7: ending with *from whence Turkish*) which is at present missing in the Cora Crane Collection. The leaf had been detached from the rest of the manuscript and filed elsewhere before Miss Gilkes' identification of it as the start of the complete text. Miss Gilkes notes that in making this copy of the page she did not attempt to follow Cora's accidentals with absolute fidelity; thus this part of the text may diverge on a few occasions from the mislaid manuscript in punctuation and possibly in spelling.

No. 4. IMOGENE CARTER'S PEN PICTURE OF THE FIGHTING AT VELESTINO

The last known Imogene Carter dispatch was a cable, datelined Athens, May 9, whereas the others must have been mailed reports.

(N¹): *New York Journal*, May 10, 1897, page 3, printed as one of a series of dispatches under a general headline but with the individual heading 'Imogene Carter's Pen Picture | of the Fighting at | Velestino. ‖ WITH THE HOWITZERS. ‖ Last of the Writers to Go; Shells | Screamed About Her as She | Left the Field. ‖ HER BRAVERY AMAZES SOLDIERS. ‖ Journal's Woman War Correspondent | Has a Narrow Escape from the | Missiles of Death—Train Shelled | on the Way to Volo. ‖ By Imogene Carter. | (Copyright, 1897, by W. R. Hearst.)'.
(N²): San Francisco *Examiner*, May 10, 1897, page 3, headlined 'IMOGENE CARTER TELLS OF VELESTINO. ‖ Another of "The Examiner's" Feminine War Correspondents at the Scene of Hostilities Describes | the Fight That Lost the Thessalian Seaport City of Volo. ‖ BY IMOGENE CARTER. (Special cable to "The Examiner," copyright, 1897, by W. R. Hearst.)'. The dateline is the same as in N¹. The dispatch is printed throughout in capitals like a telegram.

It would seem that the *Examiner* was wired a copy of the cable before it had been completely revised in New York, if the assumption is valid that *squeak* in N² is the original and *escape* an N¹ editorial 'improvement' at 272.9. Presumably the omission of *the* before *Turks* at 272.15 was a compositorial oversight in N¹ although the possibility cannot be overlooked that it was an N² change of the N¹ copy that was still too much in cable form. Reprinted from N^1 by Stallman.

No. 5. MANUSCRIPT NOTES

In the Columbia University Library Special Collections are preserved four sheets of cheap wove grid paper 142 × 100 mm., without watermark, containing hastily written notes in Cora's hand. In the lower part of the third leaf the writing is in black ink, but elsewhere the writing is in pencil. However, at 273.3 the single later correction in the manuscript is made in black ink in the pencil part when *from* is deleted and *to* placed after it. On the verso of the third leaf is written a series of additions that may or may not refer to word counts. First 245+ is given, with 235 below it for a total of 480, to which is added 265 for a final total of 745. Miss Lillian Gilkes quotes from these notes in her *Cora Crane*, page 93, and has very kindly assisted the present editor with his transcript of the difficult writing. The notes are here printed diplomatically, without alteration.

GREAT BATTLES OF THE WORLD

EXTERNAL evidence about the genesis and development of the series of eight articles that were collected under the title *Great Battles of the World* has been preserved only spottily. A reference that is more allusive than precise suggests that Crane and the McClure Syndicate in early 1897 had discussed a series of articles on Civil War battles, but if so the project ended by Crane writing the short stories collected as *The Little Regiment*. Indeed, no connection between the two series can be established, for the idea for *Great Battles* does not seem to have originated with Crane—who at first resisted the proposal—but instead with *Lippincott's Magazine*.

In what seems to be the earliest preserved reference, on April 20, 1899, Pinker wrote Cora: "I am sorry Mr. Crane will not do the battle articles. I think Lippincott would take six, if he would do them; and their representative, to whom I quoted Mr. Crane's objection, says that they would not want elaborate studies of the battles, as it would not be possible in the space contemplated. Perhaps Mr. Crane will think the matter over and write to me again" (TLS, Columbia University). In late June the matter was no further advanced, according to a letter of June 22 to Pinker from Harrison S. Morris, *Lippincott's* editor: "You have my thanks for your kind letter of the 12th. and I trust you will continue to urge Mr. Crane to do the articles on the Great Battles. I do not believe he appreciates how this would sell here [in the United States], both in magazine and book form. His name is identified in the American world with war and everybody would want to read and keep such a book" (TLS, Dartmouth College).

Pinker's enthusiasm for the project (which he foresaw would bring in money that Crane badly needed) seems to have won out over Crane's reluctance, which had apparently been based on his recognition that he knew little of the details of the battles and was scarcely competent to write on them as an expert. By July 3, 1899, Pinker was able to give *Lippincott's* a favorable response, as we know from a letter of July 14 from Morris:

My Dear Sir:—

Your kind letter of July 3rd. regarding the six papers on Great Battles of the World, by Mr. Stephen Crane, is at hand, and we are pleased to learn that Mr. Crane now looks with favor on the plan. We shall cheerfully supply the books needed, through our London agent, Mr. Joseph Garmeson, 36, Southampton St. Covent Garden, with whom please communicate at once.

It will be quite agreeable to us if Mr. Crane will choose the battles to be treated and we hope he can give us one of the articles in as brief a time as possible. At all events, we should like to have the assurance that they shall be speedily forthcoming, that we may announce them for next year.

The price named by you: $1000. for the six articles, covering English and American magazine rights, is correct. We shall, of course, also wish to arrange for the book rights of these articles and as soon as the first one comes in, thus showing us the general style and treatment, we can then judge better what can be done. There should be no difficulty in a mutual agreement for these rights which will be thoroughly satisfactory.

Trusting all this may prove agreeable to Mr. Crane, and that we may have a speedy fulfillment of our idea, which should be kept confidential, I beg to remain,

> Truly Yours,
> Harrison S. Morris
> Editor. [TLS, Dartmouth]

Despite Morris's hopes for an early start, Crane delayed while he attempted to put together *Wounds in the Rain*. He wrote to Pinker, on August 4, "I shall develope Lippincott's plan as soon as I finish the war-stories" (*Letters*, p. 223). What this meant can be seen in an exasperated letter conjecturally dated October 24 from Pinker to Crane about the demands for money that were being made upon him, in which he urges, "Why do you not do the battle articles for Lippincotts?" (*Letters*, p. 236). This provoked Cora's reply, conjecturally dated October 26: "You will have the first of the articles for Lippincotts by Nov. 10th. You must understand the great time it takes to get detail for these things" (*Letters*, p. 238), and another, conjecturally dated about October 30,[51] "One of Lippincott's articles is almost finished, also, but Mr. Crane finds difficulty in getting at it. However you will get it soon" (*Letters*, p. 234). Crane himself, on November 4, writes cheerfully to Pinker, "I have collected about a

---

[51] Stallman conjecturally dated this letter as October 9, but Professor J. C. Levenson believes that October 30 is perhaps more accurate (TALES OF WHILOMVILLE, *Works*, VII, lv). Just possibly this letter precedes Cora's of October 26, in which case it would have been written on October 23 and perhaps crossed Pinker's of October 24. In his footnote 173 to the October 26 letter Stallman is in error in associating the reference to *the first of the articles* with the chronologically earlier, "The Battle of Bunker Hill." The first, "New Orleans," had yet to be written. This mistaken identification is also continued in footnote 203 where it is "New Orleans" that is also in question, not "Bunker Hill."

ton of information on the Battle of New Orleans and the article is now a mere matter of putting together these voluminous notes in their most dramatic form and this I shall manage within a few days" (*Letters*, p. 240). In a letter of December 12 Cora informs Pinker: "Mr. Crane will be in town and come to see you toward the week's end. He will bring you the first article for Lippincott" (*Letters*, p. 248). Thus it would seem that the first of the articles, "The Brief Campaign Against New Orleans," was delivered about mid-December, 1899.

The publication schedule in *Lippincott's* for the series is as follows:

> The Brief Campaign Against New Orleans, March, 1900
> The Storming of Badajoz, April, 1900
> The Siege of Plevna, May, 1900
> The Battle of Bunker Hill, June, 1900
> Vittoria, July, 1900
> A Swede's Campaign in Germany—Leipzig, August, 1900
> A Swede's Campaign in Germany—Lützen, September, 1900
> The Battle of Solferino, October, 1900
> The Storming of Burkersdorf Heights, November, 1900

Once the ice was broken with "New Orleans" Crane moved more rapidly. In a letter conjecturally dated December 18, 1899,[52] along with a request for money Cora writes to Pinker, "The Battle of '*Badajos*' the second one for Lippincott, you shall have by Friday morning" (*Letters*, p. 230). This promise was more or less kept, although with the usual delay, for on January 5 Pinker wrote to Crane: "I received the Badajoz article this morning, and now enclose the type-written copy for correction. Can I have it back by Monday morning, so that I can deliver it to Lippincotts?" (ALS, Columbia). Cora answered in a letter conjecturally dated January 6: "Your letter with copy of 'Badajos' received. . . . Mr. Crane will send corrected copy by tonight's post. . . . This Lippincott article is worth £35—is it not? & there will be another before weeks out" (*Letters*, p. 258). The manuscript of "The Storming of Badajoz" is preserved inscribed by Edith Richie. It is odd that it should have been sent to Pinker to have a typescript made, but on the evidence of these letters this was apparently the procedure. On January 10, 1900, Cora was concerned about the payment for the two completed articles and wrote Pinker: "About the Lippincott articles. They were to pay £200 for 18000 words, in six (6) articles. They seem now to be paying at the rate of

---

[52] The Stallman conjectural date of September 4 is clearly impossible. I am indebted to Professor J. C. Levenson for the opinion that December 18 is acceptable.

£30—each. That will make them pay £50 for the sixth article. Is this right? The £54 credited against 'Battle of Bajados' I suppose means for New Orleans as well" (*Letters*, p. 263).

On January 9 Pinker, in an almost ritual gesture, reminded Cora that "the quickest way to get return would be to complete the Battle articles, and I hope that this is what Mr. Crane is doing" (*Letters*, p. 261). "The Siege of Plevna" was finished shortly, for on January 27 Pinker paid Crane £27 received from Lippincott (ALS, Columbia).

Lippincott had originally intended to collect the articles in book form, and they now moved to secure an agreement. Pinker wrote Crane on February 2, 1900, that "Mr. Lippincott has been in to see me, to ask if you would do two additional Battle stories, making eight in all, so that they will make a more presentable volume. [¶] He tells me that one or two of the articles have been a trifle under the stipulated length, and I promised to ask you to be a little more liberal in the number of words. [¶] Will you please let me know your views as to terms for this book, as Lippincotts would like to arrange for it" (TLS, Columbia). On February 13 Pinker returned to the matter of the book, explaining that Stokes (through its London representative Dominick) would not object to Lippincott's publication of the articles in book form (Stokes held the contract for the next novel, or book) and again asking for a figure to be set on the American book rights (TLS, Columbia). Cora answered the next day asking Pinker to try for £100 (*Letters*, p. 265), and to get it as soon as possible. On February 27 Pinker wrote that the cheque had not been received, "as the London office have to communicate with the other side before accepting the terms" (TLS, Columbia).

However, Lippincott seems to have been unwilling to pay the £100 for the book rights before delivery of the final article. In a letter from Brede on a Tuesday, probably February 20 as Professor Levenson suggests to me, Cora had written, "We hope to hear that Lippincotts cheque and one from Stokes will come soon" (*Letters*, p. 241, to be redated from November 7?, 1899). But shortly news of Lippincott's provisions reached the Cranes, and in a Thursday letter from Brede, probably on March 8, Crane responded that he was sending "Vittoria." He continued: "I rec'd your letter this morning re Lippincott's provisional acceptance. I can send the articles at the rate of one per week. This makes the fifth" (*Letters*, p. 264, misdated February 8, 1900). On the following Saturday (perhaps March 10) Crane again wrote Pinker: "The next battle for Lippincotts is 'Lützen.' It should reach you within ten days. This article will be the one for which £50 is to be paid. [¶] Please stretch yourself on Monday. There will be £30 due from Stokes on the Romance, £30 from Lippincott on Vittoria which with Lippincotts £100 makes £160. I would like to have £100 on Monday" (*Letters*, p. 265, misdated February 10). On March 24, "Lützen (£50) is finished today but the typing will require tomorrow. It will reach you by special stamps" (*Letters*, p. 266). On a Thursday, conjecturally March 29 just before she left to meet Helen Crane in Paris, Cora wrote to Pinker, "I enclose you a bit more of the Battle article. The rest goes to you tomorrow as well as another chapter of Romance" (*Letters*, p. 257, to be redated from conjectured January 4). Finally in a letter conjecturally dated March 31, Crane sends to Pinker "the remainder of the 'A Swede's Campaign in Germany' article" (*Letters*, p. 266). The April 2 hemorrhage put a stop thereafter to Crane's writing.

In her desperate need for money, Cora was not above exaggeration about the completion of the articles so that the £100 would be paid, and she made every effort to secure an advance. In a conjecturally dated April 6 letter to Pinker telling him of Crane's illness, she writes: "I have a battle article—'Solferino'—I will have it up to you in a few days time, it's partly typed. I enclose a note to Lippincott, but it will be quicker to post it direct, asking them to send you a cheque or to deposit it at Brown & Shipley to my credit to meet the cheque given to Doctor Maclagen of 9 Cadogan Place. I don't think they will hesitate as it was a matter of saving Stephen Crane's life" (*Letters*, p. 267). The actual state of "The Battle of Solferino" is better described in an undated letter (probably about April 7–8) from Kate Lyon to Cora, written on her receipt of the news of Crane's illness. As postscripts at the head of the letter are two notes: the one to the left reads, "If it's a question of Stephen's *immediate* comfort, couldn't you raise money from someone?"; that to the right, "(10 P.M. I've just come in and found your letter.)". The letter itself is as follows:

My dearest girl,
    What is the matter with Stephen? I could not tell from your letter. I need not say how sorry I am, you blessed and dearest and best two, that any trouble should come to you. But whatever it is, the dear boy will be sure to throw it off at once, I am sure—— I would have the thing—Solferino —further on, but that I had to spend one day going to my mother and had to go to see Plant.—Now I'll heave away like mad at it. Please tell me, right off, like a dear, if Stephen is not well enough to *go over* what I write? Do you mean me to work it up in a *finished* state for the magazine? and should the length be 6000, or 7000 words? Please tell me anything definite you can about it. I'll do the very best I POSSIBLY can. About another battle, Stephen's line seems to have been decisive conflicts that yet have not been hackneyed like Waterloo. Sedan of course has been written all to pieces. I'll think of lots tomorrow when I get back among the books, and write you.

Keep a brave heart dear girl. God is sure to be good to you, you have been so good to others. What wouldn't I give to be able to help you now. Please write me about the Solferino, and I'll get it to you just as soon as I can, in a shape that won't positively disgrace Stephen. My warmest and gratefulest love to you and Stephen. He's sure to be all right in less than no time. Kate. [ALS, Columbia]

Kate Lyon's function and share in the *Great Battles* will be considered later. From a letter to Crane of March 30 and 31, it is clear that she had been working up the material for him from the very first article. However, "The Battle of Solferino" and "The Storming of Burkersdorf Heights" may be taken as completely Kate Lyon's work, although Crane may at least have read over the articles before they were submitted. If he did so, however, it is unlikely that he made many substantial changes. Moreover, the choice of Burkersdorf as the final battle seems to have been Kate Lyon's own decision.

Cora's quest for money continued. On April 7 she wrote Pinker that she had written to Lippincott (*Letters*, p. 268); on April 11: "My niece is typing the battle article [Solferino] which you shall have this week. I hope my husband will be able to dictate the remainder of the last one [Burkersdorf] from notes soon so that I can get the £100 from Lippincott." She then defends her action in writing to Lippincott to try to secure an advance but apologizes for going over Pinker's head (*Letters*, pp. 270–271). On Monday, April 16, she addresses Pinker: "Mr. Crane says that Lippincotts owe £110—so he makes it. I am sending you a typed copy corrected of last battle article on Tuesday P.M. or Wednesday. Mr. Crane asks if it is possible, if you will send £100—of the Lippincott money" (*Letters*, p. 272). The next day, April 17: "I send you the battle article for Lippincott. Please ask them to send Mr. Crane the Feb. number of magazine [53] also to send *proofs. Always* to send proofs! Please say the mistake in the New Orleans battle could have been mended by the turn of a pen if the proof had been sent. Please let me know just how we stand now with Lippincott. Today the doctor said that Mr. Crane would be better for work in two or three weeks time, that it would divert his mind so the other and last battle article can be finished then" (*Letters*, p. 273). Pinker acknowledged, conjecturally on April 20: "Thank you for your letter enclosing the Battle article. There is one more to come to complete the series.[54] I have asked Lippincotts to be sure & send proofs,

[53] This is a mistake, for "The Brief Campaign Against New Orleans" did not appear until the March issue.

[54] One of the mysteries of the series is the fact that the two lengthy parts of "A Swede's Campaign in Germany" were apparently paid for as one although published in two different issues of *Lippincott's*. Thus "Burkersdorf" was actually

and for a copy of the February number" (*Letters*, pp. 273–274). A postscript from Cora to Pinker on April 24 reads, "*Please* let me know by return just how we stand with Lippincott, & how much they have to pay on delivery of the next battle" (*Letters*, p. 277).

The last article was delivered on May 2, according to a Pinker letter that starts: "Thank you very much for the article, safely received this morning. I have obtained the balance from Lippincotts and have paid into your account today £75" (TLS, Columbia).

The sale of the English book rights was for a long time tedious and frustrating. As early as February 14, 1900, Cora in a postscript had asked Pinker about such a sale (*Letters*, p. 265), but the next reference is in a letter from Pinker to Plant, on June 15, as part of an accounting: "I am also negotiating for the English book rights in the Battles studies contributed to Lippincotts" (TLS, Columbia). Much of the Pinker correspondence about the attempted sale must have been lost, but a few letters are preserved. On August 21, 1900, John Murray wrote Pinker:

> I am much obliged by your letter concerning Mr Stephen Cranes Great Battles. Before coming to a decision, I am compelled to ask one or two questions. [¶] Can you give me a list of the battles? I have seen none of them, and to find a book with this title, starting off with 'Bunkers Hill' is rather staggering to any rudimentary student of History. [¶] I have always some feeling about taking one book of an author, whose other works have as a rule appeared with a different firm. Have not Messrs Methuen published most of Mr Cranes books over here, & if so ought they not to have the first refusal? [ALS, University of Virginia]

Murray declined the book on September 1:

> I have gone to very great trouble to come to a right conclusion with regard to Stephen Crane's 'Great Battles.' The work, despite the excellencies it is bound to have, considering who its author is, is inferior to Stephen Crane's other works; & therefore, although, without doubt, it will sell enough to pay its expenses & have a profit, I feel that I cannot publish it. It would be against our principles to publish the inferior work of any man, merely because thanks to his name & reputation, it would pay. I hope you realise my reasons. [¶] I am, under any circumstances, very much obliged to you for having given us the opportunity of considering this MS, which with the

---

the ninth, according to one accounting, although technically only the eighth in the series. No protest about this inequity seems to have been made. Internal evidence suggests that Crane submitted "A Swede's Campaign" as one continuous article and it was the *Lippincott's* editor who, after cutting, printed it in two parts, assigning the names of the two battles. All references that are preserved from Crane call it simply "Lützen." As for the length, some of the battles like "New Orleans" and "Badajoz" were so much below the contracted number of words that *Lippincott's* may well have felt they were simply recovering their money's worth in the longer two-part Gustavus Adolphus article.

dummy-copy [55] I now return, and, with renewed thanks. [ALS, University of Virginia]

On November 6 Methuen returned the book to Pinker with the letter: "Herewith I return the collection of stories by the late Stephen Crane entitled 'GREAT BATTLES OF THE WORLD', as I regret to say that our reader's report upon it is not sufficiently favourable to warrant our undertaking its publication. [¶] Thanking you for allowing us to consider this work" (TLS, University of Virginia).

After Cora's break with Pinker, her new agent G. H. Perris continued the quest for a publisher. He wrote on January 31, 1901: "Upon your positive refusal to sell the copyright of The Great Battles —it being impossible to persuade Messrs. Nisbet & Co—we have asked for the copy back and are now going to offer it to Messrs. Chapman & Hall. The episode was a very disappointing one but the editor of Messrs. Nisbet & Co was not to be moved from his position that the book was not, as compared with Mr. Crane's best work, at all a good one" (TLS, Columbia). The Chapman and Hall submission was successful, and the book collection was published in England, deposit being made in the British Museum on July 31, 1901.

The first American edition may be described as follows:

[within black single rules] [red] GREAT BATTLES | OF THE WORLD | [black rule] | [red] BY STEPHEN CRANE | [black] *AUTHOR OF "THE RED | BADGE OF COURAGE," ETC.* | ILLUSTRATED BY | JOHN SLOAN ‖ [red orn.] [black] ‖ PHILADELPHIA | J. B. LIPPINCOTT | COMPANY MDCCCCI

Collation: [1]⁸ 2–17⁸ 18⁴, pp. [1–4] 5–7 [8] 9 [10] 11–278 [279–280] (misnumbering 5–7 as 3–5); front. + illustrations facing pp. 58, 70, 108, 162, 220, 230, 272; leaf 7 $11/16$ × 5″, laid unwatermarked text and endpapers, vertical chainlines 22 mm. apart, top edge gilt, other edges trimmed.

Contents: p. 1: half-title, 'GREAT BATTLES | OF THE WORLD'; p. 2: blank; p. 3: title; p. 4: 'COPYRIGHT, 1900 | BY | J. B. LIPPINCOTT COMPANY | *Electrotyped and Printed by* | *J. B. Lippincott Company, Philadelphia, U.S.A.*'; p. 5: 'NOTE' subscribed 'HARRISON S. MORRIS.'; p. 7: 'CONTENTS'; p. 8: blank; p. 9: 'ILLUSTRATIONS'; p. 10: blank; pp. 11–278, text; pp. 279–280: blank.

The Battle of Bunker Hill, p. 11	The Storming of Burkersdorf
Vittoria, p. 31	Heights, p. 79
The Siege of Plevna, p. 63	A Swede's Campaign in

---

[55] This detail explains Murray's surprise at a book starting off with "The Battle of Bunker Hill" but his lack of information about the titles of the other battles. The Lippincott edition, which rearranged the articles from the magazine order, was of course the dummy copy. What the 'MS' was (except clippings of the magazine articles) cannot be determined.

Binding: Red (13.deep Red) smooth linen cloth. *Front*: '[within single dots and dashes rules] Great Battles | of the World | [dots and dashes rule] | [crossed swords and ribbon between two vertical dots and dashes rules] | [dots and dashes rule] | Stephen Crane'. *Spine*: '[dots and dashes rule] | Great | Battles | of the | World | [dashes rule] | Crane | Lippincott | [dots and dashes rule]'. *Back*: blank. All lettering in gilt except blades of swords and ribbon in silver.

Variant: Blue (173. m.gB) smooth linen cloth, wove endpapers, half-title blank, pages bulk 30 mm. as opposed to 26 mm. for the red-bound copy.

Publication: Announced in the *Publishers' Weekly*, December 8, 1900, price $1.50. Copyright applied for and deposit made October 24, 1900, but publication delayed to allow the final installment to be published in the November *Lippincott's Magazine*. Williams and Starrett state that a copy with the notation *second printing* has been observed and that an unknown number of later printings were made, recognizable by the correct spelling of 'forlorn' in the fifth line of page 212 instead of the misprint 'folorn'.

Copies: University of Virginia–Barrett, copy 1 (551389); copy 2 (551391), signed in pencil by the artist John Sloan and dated November, 1900; copy 3 (551390), blue cloth.

The first English edition may be described as follows:

[red] G²REAT BATTLES | [black] of the World. By | Stephen Crane, Author | of "The Red Badge of | Courage," etc. Illus-|trated by John Sloan | [red] London: Chapman & Hall Limited, | [black] Henrietta Street, Covent Garden, W.C. | 1901

Collation: [A]⁶ B–I⁸ K–S⁸ [T]², pp. [i–xii], 1–271 [272], ²1–4; front. + illustrations facing pp. 33, 50, 85, 177, 196, 214, 253; leaf 7½ × 5", wove paper; laid endpapers unwatermarked, horizontal chainlines 27 mm. apart; top edge trimmed, other edges untrimmed.

Contents: pp. i–ii: blank; p. iii: half-title, 'GREAT BATTLES | OF THE WORLD'; p. iv: blank; p. v: title; p. vi: blank; p. vii: 'NOTE', subscribed 'HARRISON S. MORRIS.'; p. ix: 'CONTENTS'; p. x: blank; p. xi: 'ILLUSTRATIONS'; p. xii: blank; pp. 1–272, text; on p. 272: colophon, 'Printed by R. & R. CLARK, LIMITED, Edinburgh'; pp. ²1–4, publisher's advertisements starting 'NEW BOOK BY EFFIE JOHNSON' and ending 'Ella Fuller Maitland's Works'.

The Storming of Badajoz, p. 177   The Battle of Bunker Hill, p. 253
The Brief Campaign Against
    New Orleans, p. 196
The Battle of Solferino, p. 214

Binding: Red (43.m.r.Br) smooth linen cloth; in gilt; *Front*: 'G²REAT
BATTLES | of the World. By | Stephen Crane, Illus-|trated by John
Sloan'; *Spine*: 'GREAT | BATTLES | OF THE | WORLD | STEPHEN
| CRANE | CHAPMAN | AND HALL'; *Back*: blank.
Publication: Announced in the *Publishers' Circular*, June 15, 1901, price
6 shillings. British Museum (9004.c.22) deposit stamp July 31, 1901.
A later binding is reported in red pictorial cloth, decorated in blue and
black, and lettered as in the original except that a Victoria Cross appears on the spine under 'CRANE'; all edges gilt.
Copy: University of Virginia–Barrett (551395).

A Colonial Edition was manufactured by George Bell and Sons. The
title-page is in the same setting as in the Chapman and Hall edition except
for the imprint, '[red] London: George Bell & Sons, and | [black] Bombay,
1901'.

Pages i–ii: blank; p. iii: half-title, '𝕭𝖊𝖑𝖑'𝖘 𝕵𝖓𝖉𝖎𝖆𝖓 𝖆𝖓𝖉 𝕮𝖔𝖑𝖔𝖓𝖎𝖆𝖑
𝕷𝖎𝖇𝖗𝖆𝖗𝖞 || GREAT BATTLES | OF THE WORLD'; p. iv: blank; p. v: title;
p. vi: '*This Edition is issued for circulation in India and the Colonies
only.*' Pagination now follows the first English edition; however
sig. T² is wanting, and in its place appear 16 pp. of catalogue for Bell's
Indian and Colonial Library, June, 1901. The binding is in red (12.s.Red)
rib-cloth. *Front*: '[within blind single-rules] [blind] GREAT BATTLES OF
THE WORLD'; *Spine*: in gilt, '[blind orn.] | GREAT | BATTLES | OF
THE | WORLD || STEPHEN | CRANE | [blind orn.] | [blind device] |
GEORGE BELL & SONS'; *Back*: blind Bell device. University of Virginia–Barrett (551396).
The cheap Colonial Edition was issued in buff paper wrappers; *Front*:
'Bell's Indian & Colonial Library || GREAT BATTLES OF | THE WORLD
| BY | STEPHEN CRANE | AUTHOR OF "THE RED BADGE OF COUR-
AGE," "THE MONSTER," ETC. | Illustrated by JOHN SLOAN | [Bell's
device] | LONDON | GEORGE BELL AND SONS | AND BOMBAY 1901';
Spine: 'GREAT BATTLES | OF THE WORLD | STEPHEN CRANE | No.
390 | [orn.] | LONDON | G. BELL & SONS'; *Back*: advertisements for Bell's
Colonial Editions. Lacks signature T² and is without bound-in catalogue,
but inner covers both front and back and wove endpapers carry advertise-
ments. University of Virginia–Barrett (713027).

The NOTE by the *Lippincott's* editor Harrison S. Morris, which appears in both American and English editions, reads:

These vigorous pictures were among the very last work done by the
lamented pen which gave us "The Red Badge of Courage."
We were aroused by that startling drumbeat to the advent of a new
literary talent. The commonplace was shattered by a fresh and original
force, and every one heard and applauded. Then came the varied fiction,

always characteristic and convincing, and then, at the end, this return to the martial strain.

It was agreed that the battles should be the choice of the author, and he chose them for their picturesque and theatric qualities, not alone for their decisiveness. What he could best assimilate from history was its grandeur and passion and the fire of action. These he loved, and hence the group of glorious battles which forms this volume.

The talent of Stephen Crane was mellowing under the tutelage of experience. He lost none of his dash and audacity even in the sedater avenues of history. He was a strong and native growth of our wonderful soil, and the fruits of him will last while courage and genius are revered.

HARRISON S. MORRIS.

The first English edition is a close reprint, although with the order of the battles changed, of the original Lippincott edition. A few simple corrections appear which are without authority, and a few corruptions.

As will be illustrated in the separate parts of the Textual Introduction, the copy for the Lippincott collection was not a set of the clippings of the magazine articles but instead a set of the uncorrected proofs of these articles. As a result the book text preserves not only a few errors but also original authoritative readings that had been subject to editorial alteration in the final magazine version. Passages excised from the magazine articles are also preserved in the book. In this textual situation the Greg theory of copy-text applies with precision. Except for "The Storming of Badajoz," for which a manuscript is preserved, the copy-text of each article is the *Lippincott's Magazine* version (L), which is the nearest of all preserved documents to the lost typescripts made from the manuscripts. However, when the Lippincott book edition (A1) appears to print substantives that are not the A1 editor's or compositor's changes but instead represent the readings of the original magazine proof set from Crane's copy and later altered by the magazine editor, these substantives are taken over into the critically edited text. The result is the recovery, insofar as possible, of the magazine proofs which in some respects are closer to Crane's copy than the printed magazine version.

The question of Crane's actual part in the writing of these articles remains to be surveyed, though briefly. The preserved correspondence as quoted earlier in this section suggests that the idea for the series originated with Lippincott and for some time was rejected by Crane for reasons that can be interpreted as doubts about his ability to assemble and master the detail at first thought necessary. Lippincott's assurances that a simple and popular series was desired, not an act of creative scholarship, appear to have set these doubts at rest, and it is possible to conjecture that at this time or shortly thereafter [56] Crane or Cora conceived the idea of utilizing the services of Kate Lyon (Frederic) as researcher. Some indication exists that early in the series Crane took the assignment seriously even though he was relying on Kate Lyon for the excerpts from histories that served as the basis for his own writing. It is true that, throughout, the necessary fiction was preserved that the articles were exclusively his own work. Cora loyally maintained this fiction even after his April hemorrhage, as when on April 11 she wrote Pinker that she hoped Crane would be able to dictate the remainder of the last one from notes. This was at a time when Kate Lyon's letter of about April 7–8 suggests that she was to take over the preparation completely and the subject for the eighth article was perhaps not even settled. Yet it is not fiction when Crane wrote Pinker on November 4, 1899, that he had "collected about a ton of information on the Battle of New Orleans and the article is now a mere matter of putting together these voluminous notes in their most dramatic form" (*Letters*, p. 240). Kate Lyon's function, especially in the early articles, seems to have been chiefly to write out lengthy quotations, but one may conjecture that as the series progressed (as suggested by her letter about "Solferino") she found herself in the position more and more of mapping out the structure and even of writing what might be called an early draft of the articles for Crane's revision. The false starts and changes in the preserved manuscript of "The Storming of Badajoz" in Edith Richie's hand attest to the fact that Crane dictated this article from Kate Lyon's notes, although some part may just possibly have been written out direct from these notes or drafts. The Columbia University Libraries Special Collections preserve a sentence from "Bunker Hill" and a few holograph bridge passages for "Vittoria" that introduce lengthy verbatim quotations and indicate that Kate Lyon had not so joined them. Her April 7–8 letter asks if Crane "is not well enough to *go over* what I write" and continues with the query that shows she would need to alter for the last two articles what she had been doing for him previously: "Do you mean me to work it up in a *finished* state for the magazine? and should the length be 6000, or 7000 words?"

A lengthy letter started on March 30, 1900, and continued on March 31, reveals something of her operations and the extent to which Crane relied on her. The immediate subject was the date of the Battle

---

[56] The request for books that Lippincott is to supply may just possibly suggest that at the very start Crane proposed to do his own reading.

of New Orleans (December 8 for January 8) which had evidently aroused critical comment when the error appeared in the magazine's March issue:

30th March

My dear Stephen,

As soon as I can get down to the British Museum I'll look up the New Orleans battle again. Of course all the historians vary about all the things in a war, and I try to piece up a scheme that seems to be the one acknowledged by the most and best authorities. But *can* I have written anything else than January 8th of 1815 for the date of the principal battle! If so, it must have been wild inadvertancy, because that date is printed in my memory, because I wrote it so many times. Certainly it *must* have been the printer who made the statement that it came off on Dec. 8th. I suppose they don't send proofs. I'll see if there's anything anywhere to support Mr Hinds' theory that his ancestor deserves the credit of the December attack. I read of Andrew's starting from New Orleans to conduct it. Still, there's a lot more confusion about N.O. than anything else I've found; and as for the dates, several historians have mixed them up; that's why I felt sure of them.

They had much better historians for the seventeenth century. But I have just found out a grave mistake I've made apropos of Gustavus Adolphus which I hope it is not too late to rectify. After sending the MS. on to you, I was going over, at home, a small book I have from the Hampstead Library, where the dates are given G.A. 1594–1633—and Wallenstein's death Feb. '34. I had no other works to compare it with and make sure, but thought I was safe in sending on the statement that it was only a few months after Lützen that Wallenstein was assassinated, whereas it was a year and 3 months—although I had put down '32 as the date for Lützen, the books so often differ that one feels there's no absolute certainty. However, I have looked it up and there's no possible probable shadow of doubt about 1632. I do hope, if you *have* [not elimin *deleted*] added it to the other, that it can be scratched out before they can get it set up.

I'm awfully, pedantically careful about keeping dates straight—according to the best authority available—but I came an awful cropper with Wallenstein. If I'd had the other books I should have looked them all over and made sure.

March 31st

I've just been looking over my rough notes of N.O., and find the dates are given there repeatedly without any error: surely those date things must be typographical mistakes.

I find this:

"The result of Dec. 23rd was the saving of Louisiana. Being attacked with such impetuosity, the enemy did not proceed to attack, but proceeded to gather his forces together and prepare for a greater conflict."

The date of the treaty of Ghent was Dec. 24th 1814, so I can't imagine what Mr Hinds means by saying that "the printer"—who made the battle Dec. 8th 1815— "confused the date of the treaty with the date of the battle." In the sense that the engagement of Dec. 23rd was the only one which took place between Americans and Britons while they were in a state of war—the treaty being signed the next day—I suppose it *was* [in a sense *deleted*] the real battle of N. Orleans, but without my MS., or *your* printed story, it's impossible for me to have any idea of the way it all reads, or what the criticism means.

I find Colonel Hinds, of the Mississippi Dragoons, (I only named the picturesque [Frenc *deleted*] Creole names, I believe.) [among *deleted*] first in the list of Jackson's troops. When it's possible I'll go through with the engineer's book at the B.M. and see if he speaks of Hinds' attack on his own hook. None of the other authorities speak of it, but maybe there are local records, and it may be true as truth; histories lie so. Years after Bunker Hill they tried to sift the exact truth out of the soldiers, but Frothingham says they all swore to different things.

I enclose the letters: I've copied Mr Hinds' paragraph.

There's such a delightful portrait of old General Picton ["Vittoria"] in the National Portrait Gallery—it must be one of the best portraits extant. He grins and swears at one right out of the canvas, with his big round black eyes.

Yours always
Kate.

Written as a postscript at the head of the first page is the following: "I'll do Solferino with a good backward look at the wretchedness of Italy under Austrians and 'young Italy', Mazzini, Garabaldi, Cavour. And join Napoleon. Always yours Kate". After this is deleted "My notes on N.O." (ALS, Columbia University).

Only a few points need emphasis from this letter. The quotation that Kate Lyon gives from her notes about December 23 does not appear in the printed version, and helps to suggest, what the style itself indicates, that Crane himself did a great deal of work on the New Orleans piece, as the manuscript shows he did on "Badajoz." The error about Wallenstein's death in "A Swede's Campaign in Germany" did not reach print; it is of interest chiefly as showing that Kate Lyon, whether or not she had drafted this article (as it seems she did), sent on further information at a later time for incorporation. The postscript about "Solferino" indicates how carefully Kate Lyon prepared the structure of the articles. As already indicated, it is unlikely that any serious work from Crane is to be found in the two final ones, and the blandness of Kate's style in these does not seem to differ materially from that of the articles immediately preceding. Of course, much of the writing, in any case, was a mere paraphrase from the historical sources; nonetheless, it is probable that Crane revised and rewrote Kate Lyon's drafts to a greater extent than critics have credited, except for the last two when he was incapacitated.

THE BRIEF CAMPAIGN AGAINST NEW ORLEANS

"The Brief Campaign Against New Orleans December 14, 1814–January 8, 1815" was the first printed, as it was the first written, of the series of eight articles entitled "Great Battles of the World." Its initial appearance was in *Lippincott's Magazine*, LXV (March, 1900), 405–411. There its heading, which was to become standard, reads: 'THE BRIEF CAMPAIGN AGAINST NEW ORLEANS | DECEMBER 14, 1814–JANUARY 8, 1815 | BY STEPHEN CRANE | *Author of "The Red Badge of Courage*," *etc.* | FIRST IN A SERIES OF "GREAT BATTLES OF THE WORLD" '. In the Lippincott collection *Great Battles* it was seventh, occupying pages 223–240; in the Chapman and Hall English edition it was sixth, pages 196–213. Curiously, the *Lippincott's Magazine* styling differs from that given the remaining seven. The most obvious feature is the use of arabic numbers for all figures such as the number of troops, and the like, combined with simple numbers for dates like *December 23*, whereas in all the other articles the *Magazine* styles numbers in words and uses forms like *December 23d*. Although examples are scanty, the capitalization system seems to differ for titles or ranks, as in the use of lower case for *the British general* (284.3) as against *the French General* in "Badajoz" (288.21), the next article to be published, or *the two French Marshals* (286.31). The relatively light punctuation system in "New Orleans" differs markedly from the heavy parenthetical style of succeeding articles and approaches close to Crane's own extreme spareness. Several of Crane's characteristic punctuation habits are preserved, including the omission of a comma before *and* in a series of three or more units, as in *built of earth, logs and fence-rails* (282.14–15), whereas later in the series the comma invariably is present. No sign appears of the colon replacing a semicolon, these colons being uncharacteristic of Crane though common in the later articles. The hyphenated form *breast-work* (283.19; 284.25) matches the form in the Richie manuscript of "Badajoz" but not the invariable *breastwork* found later, and it is significant that the Crane form *Afterward* (278.17) is found for the only time in the series instead of *afterwards*. First, it seems evident that the printer's copy originated with Crane and, second, that the treatment of the copy by the magazine was unique for this one article. Although chance may have dictated typesetting here by a compositor who did not thereafter work on the series, it is more probable that beginning with "The Storming of Badajoz" the Lippincott editor restyled the printer's copy to the magazine's taste.

The A1 book compositor used the *Lippincott's Magazine* (L) printed text (possibly in proof form) as his copy. The accidentals are too close to those of L for any other hypothesis to be entertained. With one exception (the date at 285.16, the correction for which must have been sent in) the handful of substantive variants seems to have no authority. The A1 plurals *marshals* (279.32) and *troops* (284.37) correct fairly obvious L errors; *simultaneously* for *simultaneous* at 282.27 is a sophistication, not the correction of an error; and the addition of *already* at 284.6 is an innocuous enough variant. At 282.15 the omission of *In some places* (and the joining of two sentences) is demonstrably an A1 editorial alteration, on the evidence of one of Kate's main sources, A. Lacarriere Latour, *Historical Memoir of the War in West Florida and Louisiana, 1814–15* (Philadelphia, 1816), page 146: "all this was done at various intervals by a different corps . . . this circumstance, added to the cold and incessant rain, rendered it impossible to observe any regularity as to the thickness and height of the parapet, which in some places was as much as twenty feet thick at the top, though hardly five feet high, whilst in other places the enemy's balls went through it at the base."

The reading in A1 that has the greatest claim to being an uncorrected L proof error concerns the time at which the *Carolina* was ordered to drop down the river and open fire on the British. In L it is, correctly, 7.30 *in the evening* (279.22), but in A1 the reading is 7.50. All authorities, including Jackson's letter of December 27, 1814, to the Secretary of War, give the time as 7.30 or *about* 7.30; no known reference mentions 7.50.[57] If this article were alone, it would be a

---

[57] Jackson's letter may be consulted in J. Russell, Jr., *The History of the War Between the United States and Great Britain* (Hartford, Conn., 1815), pp. 285–287. George Robert Gleig, *A Narrative of the Campaigns of the British Army at Washington and New Orleans* (London, 1821), pp. 283–284: "In this manner the day passed without farther alarm; and darkness having set in, the fires were made to blaze with increased splendour, our evening meal was eat, and we prepared to sleep. But about half-past seven o'clock, the attention of several individuals was drawn to a large vessel, which seemed to be stealing up the river till she came opposite to our camp, when her anchor was dropped and her sails leisurely furled. At first we were doubtful whether she might not be one of our own cruisers which had passed the port unobserved and had arrived to render her assistance in our future operations. To satisfy this doubt, she was repeatedly hailed, but returned no answer; when an alarm spreading through the bivouac all thought of sleep was laid aside. Several musket shots were now fired at her with the design of exacting a reply, of which no notice was taken; till at length having fastened all her sails and swung her broad-side towards us, we could distinctly hear some one cry out in a commanding voice, 'Give them this for the honour of America'. The words were instantly followed by the flashes of her guns, and a deadly shower of grape swept down numbers in the camp." This is a known source for the article. Rossieter Johnson, *A History of the War of 1812–15* (New York, 1882), p. 337, also gives the time for the battle as half-past seven.

tossup whether 7.50 was the A1 compositor's error or the misreading of a typescript by the L compositor. The example of similar errors in the other articles, however, suggests the slight possibility that A1 derived its reading from an uncorrected state of the L proof. If so, it would appear to be the only such change in the article.

No information is available whether Crane read proof generally for these articles. The time would usually have been too short between sale and American publication to permit proof to have been sent across the Atlantic. Cora's April 17, 1900, letter to Pinker stating that the error of the date would never have occurred in "New Orleans" if proof had been sent is sufficient to settle the case for this article, and it is probably safe to take it that he saw no proof for any other of the series. As a consequence, the texts of *Great Battles* had no new authority enter during the transmissional process, and variation between the authorities of magazine and book must be subject only to mechanical explanation and to editorial attention. The editorial tinkering that unquestionably went on in connection with the preparation of the magazine texts for print included at the same time, however, some attention to detail, such as the correction of the proof misreading 7.50, if that is indeed the correct explanation for this particular variant. Other articles show similar attention, but the case here is a doubtful one.

In *The O'Ruddy* manuscript owned by Mr. and Mrs. Donald Klopfer of New York City, fol. 97ᵛ, the first leaf of Chapter xxiv, is written on the verso of what appears to be a trial start for some paragraph in this article: 'The majestic name of the Mississippi lent to New Orleans'. Nothing more is to be found of the manuscript or its beginnings.

THE STORMING OF BADAJOZ

"The Storming of Badajoz"[58] was printed in *Lippincott's Magazine*, LXV (April, 1900), 579–585. In Lippincott's American book collection it was placed sixth, pages 205–222; in the English edition it was fifth, pages 177–195.

A manuscript in the hand of Edith Richie is preserved in the Barrett Collection of the University of Virginia Library, consisting of six

[58] The spelling *Badajoz* is adopted in this text from the E1 'correction' of MS,A1 *Badajos*. One of Kate's main sources, Maj. Gen. Sir W. F. P. Napier, *History of the War in the Peninsula . . . 1807–14* (Philadelphia, 1842), has *Badajos;* but another source, W. H. Maxwell, *The Victories of Wellington and the British Armies* (London, 1868), spells it *Badajoz*, as do such other historians known to Kate Lyon as Walter Henry, *Events of Military Life* (London, 1843).

leaves, written on rectos only, of cheap ruled wove paper 10¼ × 8¼″, the rules 10 mm. apart. As usual, the word count for each page is written on the verso, with the cumulative total, which on folio 6ᵛ is 3,245. The first and third pages are written in the tiny script Edith Richie had used to start the manuscript of "The Kicking Twelfth," and this script continues on the first line of folio 2. Then, in normal size, a strange hand takes over and inscribes 288.25–34 (*The infantry began . . . French infantry*); but in mid-sentence Edith Richie returns and carries on the larger script, only to revert to the smaller on folio 3. Thereafter she writes in normal size again until the end. Most of the alterations, which suggest strongly that the manuscript was taken down from dictation, are in Edith Richie's hand, but a few special revisions are made by Cora. According to Edith Richie's letter accompanying the gift of her manuscript of "The Kicking Twelfth," she was accustomed to making a typescript immediately after she had written down a piece from Crane's dictation, and she remarked that he rarely altered anything he had dictated since he seemed to have it all in his mind before he started.[59] However, the letters of Pinker to Crane on January 5, 1900, and of Cora to Pinker on January 6, make it clear that for some unexplained reason this "Badajoz" manuscript was sent to Pinker for typing, that the typescript was returned to Crane for correction, and finally that the corrected typescript was mailed to Pinker.

This exchange seems to have provided the opportunity for at least some of the twenty-seven substantive differences between the manuscript and the magazine text. Prominent among these are two in particular that seem to be authoritative since they are concerned with questions of fact that had already caused difficulty in the manuscript. As early as 287.36 Crane had dictated that *Wellington's troops encamped to the south of the town*, but Cora deleted *south* and substituted *east*. Then at 290.13–15 the manuscript originally read *close to the southern part of the town while his batteries played continually on the front of Fort San Roque and the two eastern bastions, Trinidad and Santa Maria*. Cora altered *southern part* to *eastern part* and *eastern bastions* to *southern bastions*; but in the magazine the correct *northern bastions* is printed and at 290.22 manuscript *southern* is omitted in the magazine before *defences*. Several other changes can be identified as made in the typescript since in L they return variant manuscript readings to the wording of the source. For example, at

<hr />

[59] This letter is preserved in the Berg Collection of the New York Public Library. It is quoted in TALES OF WAR, *Works*, VI, clxxi.

287.14–15 MS reads to *intercept the most probable interference by Soult and Marmont* but L has *to prevent a most probable interference.* The word *intercept* is nowhere found, but W. H. Maxwell has *to prevent any junction between Soult and Marmont* (page 249).[60] At 294.1–3 MS had read *these soldiers . . . turned into the most abandoned, drunken wretches.* The L reading *became the most* comes from Maxwell, page 258, *splendid troops of yesterday had become a fierce and sanguinary rabble.* The third example is less exact than the two just cited, but again the L reading seems to derive from the source. In MS at 291.34–35, describing Ridge's rally of the troops, the wording is *His ladder was imitated by other ladders and the troops scrambled with revived courage after this new and intrepid leader,* whereas the L reading is *His ladder was followed by other ladders.* Maxwell reads (p. 255), *At last one ladder was planted,—a few daring spirits gained the ramparts,—crowds followed them*; but Napier is more precise, Ridge called *on his men to follow, and, seizing a ladder . . . a second ladder was soon placed beside the first* (Book XVI, ch. v, p. 215). W. R. Clinton, *The War in the Peninsula* (London, 1878), page 227: *Ridge sprang forward with a ladder . . . his men followed: a second ladder was planted.* It may be that the strained use of *imitated* provoked an L editorial change to *followed,* but on the analogy of the two more certain examples, it seems possible that the word was altered in the typescript by the same sort of reference back to source that seems to have prompted the other corrections.

At the opposite pole, by some curious evidence in A1, certain variants can be demonstrated to be L editorial or compositorial changes. Eight times, A1—which otherwise follows the L substantives—reverts to the readings of MS against the L variation. The most prominent example is MS,A1 *shattered* but L *rent* (292.21). Interestingly, the rest are very small changes: L *doing* for MS,A1 *doings* (287.4), *into the gate* for *in through the gate* (289.39), *ten* for *10* (291.17), *tempestuously* for *so tempestuously* (291.20), *itself* for *themselves* (292.37), *of the wall* for *of a wall* (293.28), and *the shocking* for *this shocking* (294.14). This series goes well beyond the range of chance hits and must, in some manner, represent A1's return to the typescript forms. If so, something of L's corruption of its copy is revealed by evidence that is not conjectural.

The question of A1 printer's copy is raised by this MS,A1 concurrence in the noted readings. On the whole the heavy punctuation

---

[60] So also Walter Henry, *Events of Military Life,* p. 60: "which the covering army under Sir Thomas Graham and Sir Rowland Hill were determined to prevent."

of L is repeated in A1 with such remarkable fidelity—only a handful of punctuation marks differ—as to put the matter beyond doubt that L was the physical printer's copy.[61] Moreover, ordinarily when L departs substantively from MS, A1 agrees with L even in such cases as seem to represent L editorial interference as in the correction at 287.37 of Crane's characteristic split infinitive, these changes often going beyond what we can reasonably presume was corrected in the typescript. Confirmation that L was the printer's copy may also be found in the cumulative evidence of the other seven articles that points in only one direction.

This being so, an explanation must be found for the eight readings in which A1, not by chance, reverts to the MS wording. Since A1 was not set from a copy of the typescript, it follows that the L copy could not have been a clipping of the final printed magazine version. Instead, as also occurred in the immediately preceding article in the American book sequence—"A Swede's Campaign in Germany"—the copy sent to the A1 printer was proofsheets of L in an earlier state than the 'corrected' typesetting that had printed the magazine. It would seem that whatever changes the editor of L marked in his set of the proofsheets for revises had not been transferred to the duplicate galleys subsequently used by the editor of A1, and thus all of the changed readings ordered by the L editor in this round of the proof were unknown to the editor preparing copy for A1.[62] As a consequence, the A1 readings that agree with MS against L must represent the wording or forms of the manuscript transmitted first to the typescript and then to the original state of the L typesetting from which

[61] The heavy L punctuation is the formal kind favored by editors and printing shops. It would be incredible to take it that this was the special reproduction of MS by the typescript and was thence independently transferred with almost absolute faithfulness to L and to A1—on the assumption that A1 was set from a copy of the typescript and not from L. The very few cases of MS,A1 agreement in accidentals against L appear to be fortuitous. For example, at 293.6 L introduces dialogue by a dash and comma where a period occurs in MS,A1. At 294.8 MS,A1 start a quotation with lower-case *shameless* whereas L prints a capital. However, the quote is not a full sentence, and was therefore subject to A1 styling. Such agreements as MS,A1 *castle* versus L *Castle* mean nothing since A1 customarily reduces L's capitals for titles and in this instance could even have got its hint from the initial appearance in L without a capital at 290.39. Indeed, the one time that A1 varies by capitalizing a word, at 293.32, it agrees with L against MS and hence almost certainly drew its capital from L despite its own previous styling to the contrary. Whether L,A1 *2d* versus MS *2nd* is evidence for A1 derivation from L is hard to say.

[62] That is, assuming in the present article—as he had to do in the special case of "A Swede's Campaign" with its numerous L cuts marked in the typescript—he did not consult the edited typescripts used by the magazine compositor to see if he should take typescript readings altered in the copy by the L editor.

the proofs were pulled. Correspondingly, those readings in which L and A1 agree against MS may be distinguished as (a) alterations made in the typescript by the L editor or the L compositor, or (b) the changes that Crane had marked in the typescript upon its return to Pinker. (The possibility that Cora or Crane ever saw the proof can be dismissed, on the evidence of the time factor and on Cora's letter about the mistake in the "New Orleans" article.) This hypothesis agrees with evidence in "A Swede's Campaign" or in "The Battle of Bunker Hill," and suggests the reason why all but one of the MS,A1 agreements are such trivia. Very pleasantly, it also accounts for the one time that A1 used an arabic number—the 10 at 291.17—where L, as it customarily did, had altered in the copy the typescript arabic figures to their verbal equivalents.[63] It would seem clear that this single 10 having escaped the L copyreading of the typescript was set into type in the proof as an arabic figure and thence reproduced by A1 although caught and changed in other proof by the L editor.

The bibliographical theory that accounts for the MS,A1 agreements against L establishes the eight L variants as unauthoritative and provides useful information for evaluating L variation from A1 in other articles, particularly in "A Swede's Campaign in Germany." Moreover, L,A1 agreement against MS in all other readings establishes, also, the state of the edited typescript (barring L compositorial variants) that produced the proof used as copy for A1 and removes the possibility that any other than the identified eight changes could have resulted from a further stage of proofreading. This being so, only critical analysis can attempt to distinguish the readings in which the typescript copy when sent to the printer differed from the Richie manuscript. These readings would be in three classes: (a) errors in transcription made by the typist and not corrected, or (later) compositorial departures from copy in L; (b) Crane revisions made by hand in the typescript; (c) the L editor's alterations.

The first group (a) cannot be identified with any confidence in the complete absence of evidence. If one were to guess, one could take it that the L reading *blazed* for MS *blared* (289.24) could have arisen more easily from the typist's misreading than from editorial or compositorial sophistication,[64] but speculation of this sort is idle. In fact,

---

[63] The evidence of arabic figures in the Richie manuscript is supported by the unusually faithful L typesetting of "The Brief Campaign Against New Orleans" (which L had not restyled as it did later articles starting with "Badajoz") where for the only time in the series numbers are given in arabic.

[64] This is to assume that the unusual *blared* is correct in MS as written, with *fire* in the sense of *firing* and *blared* as the sound of the firing, not the light caused by the musketry discharge. See the Textual Note for confirmation.

some variants assigned to (c) may actually belong in (a), although they cannot be so distinguished.[65]

As indicated above, a small number of L variants can be identified as changes made in early January at Brede in the typescript Pinker had sent from London. About the real authority of these changes, as representing Crane's own ideas, the present editor has some nagging doubts. That the changes made in the geographical details at 287.36, 290.13, and 290.15 were necessary corrections is beyond question. What is troublesome is that it was Cora who in the review of the manuscript seems to have checked the maps and started the process of change. It may well be that she altered the directions only after consultation with Crane, and it may well be that when the typescript was returned for correction she continued her checking and also secured Crane's approval for the further change at 290.22 that differentiates L from MS. Less confidence can be felt in Crane's approval of the other change she made in the manuscript at 288.16, although it has been accepted in the present edition in default of negative evidence. On the other hand, what are almost certainly two changes made at Brede in the typescript at 287.14 and 294.2, with a third more doubtful one at 291.35, seem to associate themselves with a further round of checking which, on the evidence of the MS changes at 287.36, 290.13, and 290.15, would have been performed by Cora, and here not necessarily under Crane's direction. That is, it is unlikely (given the customs of the day, and the unique preservation of this manuscript) that Pinker returned the manuscript with the typescript. Thus if Cora had occasion to doubt the accuracy of any word, she would have the choice of changing it on her own responsibility, or of checking it against Kate Lyon's notes, principally quotations from various sources. Such a checking of the typescript back against the notes seems to be the only explanation for the perhaps desirable change of *prevent a* for *intercept the* at 287.14 and the almost inexplicable change of neutral *turned into* to *became* at 294.2. The probable alteration of *imitated* (a strained word) to *followed* at 291.35 could also have been the result of this procedure. These have been reluctantly accepted in the present text since they seem to have come from Brede and we have no evidence to prove that Cora did not ask Crane's agreement to her alterations.

The main difficulty they pose is that they are so little distinctive

---

[65] Even so, the textual situation remains the same if MS, as in the present edition, is given prime authority for almost all readings. That is, whether L variants from MS originated in (a) or in (c) is of minor consequence so long as they can be identified as in these two unauthoritative groups and not in (b).

as authorial revisions as to have been assignable to the L editor if evidence about the sources had not been available. It follows that since we have no inkling of the nature of Kate Lyon's notes, or of Cora's further corrections, other equally bland alterations may also have been made in the typescript at Brede and not by the unauthoritative L editor, in which case a major question is raised about their acceptability. To this there is no definitive answer except that the three major sources, Maxwell, Henry, and Napier, would not have provided the L variants and thus some presumptive evidence may perhaps exist that their origin differed. In any event, the case is shaky enough for accepting these changes as truly authoritative, even in the unlikely event that they could be proved to have come from Cora, so that an editor is relatively safe in preferring the manuscript wording. Thus such misunderstandings as the substitution of *arms* for *supplies* at 286.15 or of *eyes* for *eye* at 289.7 may be credited with some safety to the L editor. It is practically certain that in his review of the syntax and usage it was he who unsplit Crane's infinitive at 287.37 and probable that he unsnarled the dubious modification of *as the Duke of Wellington* (286.4–5), substituted *one another's* for *each other's* (292.19), corrected the grammar at 292.29 with the coincidental substitution of *it* for repetitive *the breach*, and perhaps made the necessary change in tense at 292.20. Almost certainly it was he who altered the characteristic *made plain* to the neutral *exposed* (292.16).

Given the working hypothesis for the textual transmission, the unique A1 variants from MS,L agreement present no difficulty. With a precision impossible in the other articles where the manuscripts are wanting, these can be identified positively as A1 editorial alterations or A1 printer's errors. They are all stylistic, like *fox* for *fox's* (288.4), *out of* for *out at* (292.1), *all found to be too short* for *found to be all too short* (293.25). *Port* for *Fort* (291.2) is a printer's error; and *farther* for *further* (287.34) may no doubt be credited to the compositor as well.

The Richie manuscript becomes the copy-text as the document closest to Crane's accidentals. A1 is a derived text and has no authority except for the eight readings in which it confirms the manuscript and its typescript. The eclectic text that results is intended to reproduce the substantives of the manuscript combined with the few Crane substantive revisions in the typescript. The accidentals of the manuscript are the most authoritative preserved [66] but these have

[66] Comparison of both the "Badajoz" and "Kicking Twelfth" Richie manuscripts against Crane's own holograph texts indicates that in most respects the Richie

been corrected as necessary and in some minor respects modified by reference to L in order to associate "Badajoz" in certain styling formalities with the rest of the series.

THE SIEGE OF PLEVNA

"The Siege of Plevna" was published in *Lippincott's Magazine*, LXV (May, 1900), 759–765. It was placed third in the American book collection, pages 63–78, and second in the English edition, pages 33–49.

The *Lippincott's* text, styled in the manner first adopted in "Badajoz," was reprinted in A1 with a small number of changes. Two of these A1 readings are manifest errors. The first occurs at 297.12 and at 298.21 where the Grand Duke is stated in L to have been eighty miles away from Plevna when he ordered the assault, whereas in A1 he is thirty miles. In the second, at 301.9, the L text has the Russians with eighty thousand infantry, but in A1 the figure is thirty thousand. One of Kate Lyon's sources, F. V. Greene, *The Russian Army and Its Campaign in Turkey* (London, 1880), page 143, reads that the Grand Duke was at Tirnova, eighty miles away, when he ordered Krüdener to attack the Turks. Greene gives the number of the Russian infantrymen as 74,000, but another source, W. V. Herbert, *The Defence of Plevna, 1877* (London, 1895), gives the figure as 83,000. The printer's-copy typescript would almost certainly have had arabic numerals for these words, and it is quite possible that a dirty or under-inked 8 could have been misread as a 3 and set thus in the proof: for a similar error see "Great Boer Trek," 250.30. (Less probably the manuscript 8 might have been three times mistaken by the typist as a 3.) The repetition of this mistaken digit in two different contexts, whatever the exact cause of the mistake, lies beyond the powers of chance. It would seem, then, that A1 was set from the proofs of L that had the error, but that the L editor caught the mistake in working over the final proof against the typescript. Another reading in A1 seems to establish setting from L proofsheets. In L, Skobeleff's Cross of St. George was *twisted around his shoulder* (301.4–5) whereas in A1 the reading is *around over his shoulder*. The deletion of *over* from the L proof by the editor seems to be established by the ac-

---

accidentals are very close indeed to what Crane would have written himself. In particular, it seems probable that he included the punctuation in his dictation.

counts in two sources. Archibald Forbes, *Czar and Sultan* (Bristol, 1894), on page 190 quotes the reporter MacGahan, "I met General Skobeleff . . . his Cross of St. George twisted around over his shoulder"; E. Ollier in *Cassell's Illustrated History of the Russo-Turkish War* (London, 1896–97), 1, 416, also quotes MacGahan, "his Cross of St. George twisted round on his shoulder." Evidently *over* stood in the original typesetting and was transmitted from there to A1 although subsequently removed, for some unknown reason, by the L editor.

Some of the A1 variants, then, will have a superior authority to the edited L form. On the other hand, not all differences can be so identified by means of the sources, and there are signs that A1 itself was not without editorial attention that unauthoritatively altered the L text. Not much doubt can exist that A1 *As to* at 295.29 was editorially substituted for L *In regard to* in order to eliminate the awkward echo of the main clause, *one has only to regard the siege.* The A1 deletion of Crane's favorite *very* at 300.16 aligns itself with editors' dislike of this word elsewhere in Crane; probably A1 *concentrated their fire* at 298.3 for L *concentrated themselves* is another A1 improvement, for it would be difficult to imagine the L editor making the reverse change in proof.

The copy-text must be *Lippincott's Magazine* since it alone derives from the copy furnished by Crane. This is emended from A1 when reason exists to take it that the A1 variant represents an early proof reading in L (errors like the *3* for *8* apart), which would carry more authority than the L editor's attentions. On the other hand, not all A1 variants can be accepted since some of these appear to represent the unauthoritative changes of the book editor. Names of persons and places have occasionally been corrected or emended in the present text to correspond to their forms in the sources chiefly laid under contribution.

The formula in L for the title heading changes in this article to a new typography that remains constant for the rest of the series. The general effect is to give greater importance to the title and to Crane's name.

THE BATTLE OF BUNKER HILL

Lippincott's Magazine printed "The Battle of Bunker Hill" in LXV (June, 1900), 924–932, with a map of the Charlestown peninsula placed above the title, the only time an article was so illustrated. In the United States the Lippincott book edition gave this battle the place of honor, as the first, pages 11–30; the English edition buried it as the last, pages 253–272.

For the length of the article somewhat more variation from L than usual is found in A1, reference to the main source substantiating a number of these changes in A1 as drawn from the L proof before the subsequent editorial corrections. For example, at 308.36–37 L reads *Putnam heard them* [the Connecticut troops], *as they neared the Mystic, shouting,* whereas A1 has *Putnam met them.* That A1 is correct can be demonstrated from Richard Frothingham, *History of the Siege of Boston* (2nd edition, Boston, 1851), page 204: "Simon Noyes, 1825, says he [Putnam] rode up to the company he was in, and said: 'Draw off your troops here,' pointing to the rail fence, 'and man the rail fence, for the enemy's flanking of us fast.'" The L reading is a clear case of editorial misunderstanding and consequent sophistication. As another instance, at 310.29 L reads that the reenforcements from Cambridge *would come no farther than Bunker Hill, in spite of Israel Putnam's threats and entreaties. There they staggered about under hay-cocks and apple-trees* but A1 correctly reads *straggled about* on the evidence of Frothingham, page 391, "When we arrived [at Bunker Hill] there was not a company with us in any kind of order, although, when we first set out, perhaps three regiments were by our side, and near us; but here they were scattered, some behind rocks and hay-cocks, and thirty men, perhaps, behind an apple tree." A few other examples are provided in the Textual Notes, although the source in at least one case justifies L against A1 editorial interference: Frothingham (p. 161) reads *court-martials* with L at 312.19 versus A1's *courts-martial.*

It is worth notice that A1 gives the text of the final paragraph (312.21–29) that had been cut in L either because of its moralizing of the battle or else to make room on the last page for the 24-line poem "Victi Salutamus" by Alice van Vliet.

In a group of "Miscellaneous Fragments" consisting of seventeen leaves of manuscript preserved in the Special Collections of the Columbia University Libraries, one leaf in Crane's holograph appears with material from this article. The text with a circled 2 as its page number begins almost halfway down on the page of cheap unwatermarked ruled wove paper and continues only for the sentence represented by 306.30–34. The manuscript reads exactly as in L except that it lacks all punctuation save for the final period. Two alterations were made during the course of writing: after *always* (306.31–32) is a deleted *m* and after *itself* (306.32) is deleted *because.* Whether this was simply a trial, or else an insert to be placed in Kate Lyon's text, is unknown.

The copy-text is *Lippincott's Magazine*, but this is emended from A1 when the evidence of the sources suggests that A1 preserves the original reading from the L proof that served as printer's copy for the book.

"VITTORIA"

" 'Vittoria' " first appeared in *Lippincott's Magazine*, LXVI (July, 1900), 140–150. It was the second in the Lippincott *Great Battles*, pages 31–62, and the first in the English edition, pages 1–31. In both book versions the quotation marks about the title—presumably intended to call attention to the meaning 'Victory'—are omitted. Although the modern spelling is *Vitoria*, the form in *Great Battles* was acceptable and usual in Crane's sources.

On the evidence of a holograph leaf preserved in a group of seventeen "Miscellaneous Fragments" in the Special Collections of the Columbia University Libraries, Crane had his quotations assembled, lettered a, b, c, and so on, and introduced them by his own bridge passages. This leaf contains the introductions at 315.38–316.2 and 316.19 to the quotations that followed. The second has a trial 'And I now' deleted after the deletion of 'I' and the inscription of another 'I' following 'now' but then deleted.

The A1 text restores ten passages, some quite brief like 313.13–15 and others long like 317.1–33, that had been cut from the magazine text. As the original typescript had probably been marked for these cuts, the A1 editor would have had no difficulty in identifying them. In this connection the A1 editor also brought back original text that had been altered to adjust to the cuts by the excision from L of a summary sentence at 318.12 and of a bridge passage at 322.22. That the A1 printer's copy was basically L, despite all these restorations of typescript material, and not the typescript itself, is sufficiently shown by the close equation of the A1 punctuation with the heavy printing-house style of L, as well as the agreement of A1 with such features of L styling as the transfer of what were probably arabic numbers in the typescript to their verbal equivalents. The parallel may also be drawn with "A Swede's Campaign in Germany" for a perhaps clearer example, over much more text, of the same situation where no question can hold about the nature of the printer's copy underlying A1.

As would be expected, the A1 editor corrected the L errors that he observed. In this group may be placed A1 *movement* for L *moment* (316.8), and the necessary insertion of *back* (325.27). Some indication exists that he compared the typescript quotations with the L copy and repaired printer's errors. For instance, in Wellington's charge to his army, L read at 315.15 *and his horse appointments* but A1 correctly reproduces Maxwell, II, 334, *and his horse and horse appointments*. As also would be expected, the A1 editor took it upon himself to 'improve' the text from time to time. Examples appear to be the continuation of parallel structure in *to unite* instead of L's more typical *unite* (318.35). At 324.40 the suspect usage of *This hill had been made the scene* is smoothed to *had been the scene*; the awkward-sounding *artillery rounds of ammunition* at 326.38–39 is normalized to *rounds of artillery ammunition*; and one can conjecture that the A1 editor preferred the more elegant *induce his men to give up* to the blunt L *make his men give up* (327.10), the change also avoiding a repetition of *make*. At 324.34 he seems to have objected to *hissing furrows* and transferred the *hissing* to the *cannon-balls*. It may also be supposed that purism dictated the A1 change of reference at 322.23 from *their* to *its* (see the Textual Notes).

However, some of the A1 variants are difficult to explain as unauthoritative editorial changes. Prominent in this group comes the addition in A1 of Crane's almost monotonously characteristic adjective *great* in an awkward context, *the great guerilla warfare with which Wellington enveloped his forces* (318.19–20), wanting in L. A few lines later A1 adds a word, *really*, in the description of Marshal Soult as *a really fine and capable commander* (318.23–24). This last resembles Crane's frequent use of *very* which was occasionally excised by editors. Neither of these two additions seems possible as A1 editorial invention. Similar is the A1 addition, where L is wanting, of *exalted* in the phrase *an exalted spirit of enthusiasm* at 319.17–18 (see *exaltation* in the description of Cadogan's death at 323.11–12). Some stylistic variants in A1 do not seem to be necessarily editorial. A1 *which was to be always kept in advance* (319.1) resembles a split infinitive in comparison to L *kept always*. The A1 placement of *heroically* in *and Reille had held his ground near the Zadora heroically* (326.22–23) seems awkwardly tacked on in comparison with L *Reille heroically had held his ground* (unless the A1 editor objected to the alliteration). At 325.37 there would seem to be small reason for A1 to add to the repetition of *French* in 325.31–35 by a substitution of *French* for L *enemy*.

These A1 variants that seem to go contrary to normal editorial intervention may be explained by the same hypothesis that in "Badajoz,"

"Plevna," and "Bunker Hill" accounted for the return of A1 to manuscript or to typescript authority in cases of L variation: the use in
" 'Vittoria' " of early *Lippincott's* proofsheets as A1 printer's copy.
The A1 variants, then, that do not seem to be errors [67] and that appear to represent the text in an earlier state of L which would be
closer to the lost typescript, may be used as emendations of the L
copy-text. In this the editorial procedure approximates that in "A
Swede's Campaign in Germany," in which heavy restoration of the
original typescript text from L cuts is encountered, and where the
same problems as in " 'Vittoria' " arise in respect to the readings of
the A1 printer's copy.

A SWEDE'S CAMPAIGN IN GERMANY

I. LEIPZIG

"A Swede's Campaign in Germany" was published in two parts as the
sixth of the series in two different numbers of *Lippincott's Magazine.*
The first, "Leipzig," appeared in LXVI (August, 1900), 299–311. In
Lippincott's *Great Battles* it was fifth in order, on pages 114–164, and
in the English edition it was fourth, on pages 85–135. For the first
time a new styling element is introduced by the opening of spaces to
mark occasional periods in the narrative, these occurring before lines
337.18, 338.39, 342.32, 345.8, 347.24, 348.15, 349.29, and 351.14.
Since these spaces are also present in the remaining articles, it would
seem that they were editorial and bear no relation to markings in the
typescript. Hence they have been consistently omitted in the present
edition.

Like " 'Vittoria' " the text in A1 was considerably expanded from
the magazine, thirteen cuts being restored in the book ranging from
eight words at 336.1–2 to the entire long opening 329.1–335.10. The
general principle of the L cuts seems to have been simply to reduce
the extreme length by omitting background material like 343.23–
344.15 in favor of narrative action. However, certain of the cuts are
too short to be concerned with the total word count, and some of the
excisions were aimed at removing moralizing comments on the ac-

[67] These readings would include a mixture of authoritative proof readings
later altered by the L editor and of printer's errors that were corrected in L. An
example of the latter may be A1 *communication* for L *communications* (319.6–7),
which could be either a printer's mistake in A1 or else an error in the L proof
faithfully reproduced in A1 though later corrected in L. See also A1 *Murillo* for
correct L *Morillo* (322.1).

tion, as in 336.1–2 and possibly 346.11–13; or in reducing criticism of the characters, as with Gustavus at 342.4–7 or 342.30–31; or as in 343.17–18 and possibly 336.31–32 in toning down the anti-Catholic bias, a motive that helps to explain other cuts of comments that might seem antireligious despite the constant praise of Gustavus' piety.

Editorial attention in A1 was not confined to the simple restoration of L omissions, however, for L changes in reference as a consequence of the cuts are also restored to what we may assume were the type-script readings, as at 335.15, 335.18, and 341.26. More important, in both parts of this double article the A1 editor, in a manner not previously noticed, has worked over the place names in an attempt to restore correct forms from the corruption passed on to L from the typescript; and, as in " 'Vittoria'," he may have scanned the quotations in L by comparison with the typescript. Finally there remain a number of substantive variants that require explanation. Some of these resemble the A1 unauthoritative alterations of L copy for stylistic improvement observed in the treatment of other articles. For example, at 336.23 and 336.26 subjects are supplied for the clause after the conjunction in a compound sentence although Crane frequently relied on the initial subject to carry over to the second clause in a double predicate. A typical Crane use of the present tense is put back into context by change to the preterite at 340.27. The direction of these changes does not seem to be in question. On the other hand, various A1 alterations of L readings operate in the contrary direction. For example, at 337.12 A1 introduces a split infinitive, in the Crane manner, for L *openly to ally*; at 336.35 the clear L reference *Gustavus* is replaced by what is in context an ambiguous *he*; at 352.12–13 Crane's favorite collective plural *enemy* appears in A1's *turned the fire of their own guns on the enemy* where L had read *his own guns*. Seemingly these are all the reverse of A1's trend to stylistic polishing; and to the examples cited can be added such further illustrations as the rather awkward insertion in A1 of Crane's frequent adjective *great* in *great talents of Gustavus* (343.4) when the next sentence begins, *To be sure, there was great dissatisfaction*. L reads simply *talents*. Again, at 337.19 A1's substitution of *was free to* for L *could* in the sentence *By his treaty with Denmark he was free to retreat through her territory* would raise no eyebrows if it did not repetitiously echo the preceding sentence, *Gustavus now felt comparatively free to leave Sweden and invade Germany*, an awkwardness that L avoids. At 344.17 no particular need appears to insert the adverb *personally*; and certainly at 345.21 it would be a strange editorial fancy for A1 to pluck *Croatian* out of the blue to add to L's sentence ending *would make Tilly behave more like a person of humanity than a savage* when no other mention of Croatians is made in this article before the battle of Lützen in the next half.

If one reverses the direction of these changes, they look suspiciously like L editorial revisions of the typescript. The L editor could readily wish to avoid gratuitous offense even to remote Croatia when he had elsewhere in this article been concerned about other national sensibilities, including religious feelings. Faced at 337.19 with the repetition in two successive sentences of *was free to* it would be quite natural to remove the inelegance by substituting *could* for the second; and so with the excision of the repetitious *great* at 343.4. The editorial itch to straighten out Crane's split infinitives as at 337.12 has already been illustrated in "Badajoz" (287.37).

In short, these changes seem almost inexplicable as A1 editorial revisions, but they look remarkably like editing in L, in which case A1 must somehow preserve the typescript readings. Here two possibilities suggest themselves. It seems clear that the identification and restoration in A1 of such small L omissions as a phrase or two at 336.1–2, 336.31–32, 343.17–18, and 343.18 could have been managed either by the A1 editor's reference to markings in the typescript or by a collation of L against the typescript in search of cuts; but one may not suppose that so deep a cut as the first one, at least, running from 329.1 to 335.10 was made in the proof. Hence it seems a tenable working hypothesis that the typescript exhibited various editorial markings, made for the L typesetting, to which the editor of A1 could refer. On the other hand, to carry the simple process of restoring cuts over to the deliberate restoration of other editorially altered typescript readings would require the A1 editor to disagree a number of times with the L editor's critical judgment. This may remain a faint possibility to account for such A1 readings as the addition of *brute* at 335.36 or of *personally* at 344.17 or of *Croatian* at 345.21, for the emphasis italics of *your* at 342.16, or the substitution of *blot out* for L *cancel* at 335.12. But it would be difficult to argue that an A1 editor who here, as elsewhere, felt free to modify the text in search of improvement would deliberately restore a split infinitive and two ugly repetitions. Some conscious editorial action cannot be barred, but it will not satisfactorily account for all of the readings. Instead, we seem to have, in addition, some mechanical process intervening that had nothing to do with editorial choice in any positive manner.

In "The Storming of Badajoz" the eight relatively minor readings in which A1 returned to MS where L had varied seemed also to have been produced by some mechanical process, since conscious editorial choice was ruled out for at least six or seven by reason of their nature. There the hypothesis advanced was the relatively simple one that the A1 editor had been working over the L text not in the form of a clipping but in the form of proofsheets, and not necessarily in connection with any comparison or even consultation of the typescript. The proofsheets, however, were not the last revises but some semifinal state and hence they contained typescript readings that in the subsequent review were altered to forms found in the printed magazine text. The return to these earlier readings, therefore, was divorced from any conscious intention of the editor and instead resulted mechanically from the state of the copy sent to the printer. This would also seem to have been the situation with "Leipzig" (and with "Lützen"), but with one difference. Since the typescript of "Badajoz" contained no marked cuts, and presumably no great number of editorially altered readings, and since the A1 editor was not concerned to check its place names or quotations, no need existed to read over the typescript to write or cut out omitted passages for insertion in the proof printer's copy. The evidence, indeed, suggests that the A1 editor, instead, merely read over the proof that he proposed to send to the printer and made such independent alterations as occurred to him.

On the other hand, in "Leipzig" and in "Lützen" the editor would have been forced to consult the typescript to remove the editorial bridgework and other changes consequent upon the cuts. It is possible that in the process his eye might fall on a few readings editorially marked for the L typesetting with which he disagreed and that he restored them in his printer's copy to their typescript form. This hypothesis is quite speculative, however, and is by no means required to explain any of the A1 variants; the case is undemonstrable. What is more certain is that a number of the A1 variant readings from L seem to have been produced mechanically, as in "Badajoz." To these variants must be added the conscious restoration of cuts and their context, and then the A1 editor's own improvements. Thus the A1 variants are likely to fall into four categories: (a) restoration of authoritative typescript readings by the marking of the printer's copy; (b) mechanical restoration of authoritative typescript readings from the proofsheets that had subsequently been altered in L; (c) revisions marked in the copy by the A1 editor on his own account; (d) A1 printer's errors.

Two points will be obvious. First, the one demonstrable distinction that can be made between (a) and (b) concerns the restoration of cuts and their context. These offer no editorial problem. A very small group of readings can be identified as in (b) also when A1 restores the reading of the source against the L departure, these outside of quotations. Second, it will be clear that whether other variant readings come in class (a) or in class (b) is ordinarily a matter only for conjecture, since evidence is wanting that may serve to distinguish cuts and source readings. That is, one may conjecture with some confidence that the split infinitive and the two repetitions already noted represent in A1 the typescript readings in the unaltered proof. On the other hand, whether *Croatian* at 345.21 or *personally* at 344.17 was editorially excised in the typescript or later in the L proof is not demonstrable, although certainly the odds would favor the proof-stage as the time at which most if not all of the small L revisions were made. To these points may be added a third. The identification of the readings in (a) rests at least in part on evidence that may properly be called bibliographical, and so with a few readings to be identified by their sources; but the distinction between (b) and (c) or (d) [68] is almost exclusively a critical affair although decisions may be limited, or guided, by the basic bibliographical hypothesis that some of the A1 variants reproduce the typescript by their derivation from an early stage of L proof. In general, readings in A1 that do not seem susceptible of explanation as L editorial cuts or alterations are, statistically, perhaps more likely to be typescript wording from the early proof-sheets than A1 sophistications or errors.

Lippincott's Magazine must be chosen as the copy-text, of course, since in the transmission it is closest to the lost typescript. Where passages in A1 are wanting in L, the copy-text shifts to A1. Emendation of the L copy-text is further admitted by the restoration, either by addition or by substitution, of those readings from A1 conjectured to represent the words of the typescript whether altered in the typescript or in the L proof. The aim of the eclectic text is to reproduce as nearly as may be the form and content of the lost typescript insofar as the preserved documents permit.

A SWEDE'S CAMPAIGN IN GERMANY

II. LÜTZEN

"Lützen," the second part of the double article, appeared in *Lippincott's Magazine*, LXVI (September, 1900), 462–475. Editorial white

---

[68] And also the distinction between (c) and (d). No (d) error can be isolated with any confidence except perhaps the spelling change at 345.5 and, just possibly, on the evidence of the source, the change from *on* to *in* at 352.19 (see the Textual Note).

spaces occur before lines 354.31, 357.1, 358.35, 360.38, 362.32, 365.15, 367.15, and 368.22. In the Lippincott book *Great Battles*, it occupied pages 164–204, and in the English edition pages 136–176. The Kate Lyon letter to Crane of March 30–31, 1900, shows that her part of the research and write-up had been completed by that date. (The error she writes of did not appear in L and so, if Crane utilized that part of her draft, he was able to delete it.) Although L, A1, and E1 read *Lutzen*, which is the form in one of the important sources, Edward Cust, *Lives of the Warriors of the Thirty Years' War* (London, 1865), in her letter Kate Lyon writes *Lützen*, and this is the generally accepted form in the sources she used.

The textual situation repeats that of "Leipzig." *Lippincott's* made nine cuts restored by A1. Those most clearly designed to shorten the article by omission of background material are the description of Wallenstein (363.29–364.10) and just possibly the account of his conditions (363.9–13), as well as the lengthy summary conclusion (371.1–372.8). One group seems designed to remove too straightforward anti-Catholic descriptions, as at 359.5–7 but particularly at 359.32–360.14. Another seems to excise references to the money that Gustavus exacted in his campaign (354.39–355.4; 360.16–23; 360.30–37). The brief cut at 357.20–23 seems inexplicable except perhaps as a means to hurry along the narrative. Two bridges that the L editor had contrived as a consequence of cuts are removed in A1 in favor of what would be the original typescript readings in the full text (357.24; 360.15). It would seem, also, that L editorial interventions in the original continuous narrative joining "Lützen" to "Leipzig" had been made as a result of the preparation of "Lützen" for separate publication. This explanation covers what are taken to be A1 restorations of the typescript at 353.1, 353.7, 353.16, and 354.11.

As in "Leipzig," the A1 editor concerned himself to correct mistakes in the place names (356.37; 358.17–18; 362.20). His editorial tinkerings on his own responsibility, insofar as they can be conjecturally identified, somewhat exceed in number those that can be distinguished in "Leipzig," but the difference may be illusory. Only a few readings can be identified by their sources as A1 reproductions of the typescript where L proof had been changed.

As in "Leipzig" *Lippincott's* is selected as the copy-text, supplemented by A1 as copy-text for the addition of the L cuts to restore the full text. The several readily identifiable readings of the typescript taken in A1 to reproduce the unaltered proof are used as emendations from the authority of A1. Finally, the readings in A1 conjectured to be unauthoritative editorial revisions are rejected in favor of the copy-text wording. The eclectic text that results attempts to reproduce within the limits of the evidence of the preserved documents the substantives of the lost typescript.

THE BATTLE OF SOLFERINO

"The Battle of Solferino" came out in *Lippincott's Magazine*, LXVI (October, 1900), 613–627. Editorial spaces appear before lines 374.27, 378.25, 381.39, 384.12, 386.7, and 390.10. It was the eighth and last of the series in the American collection, pages 241–278, and seventh in the English, pages 214–252. The dates of its preparation and composition are fixed with some precision by Kate Lyon's two letters of March 30 and April 7–8, and by Cora's April 11 letter to Pinker with its white lie. With Crane suffering from what was to be his fatal illness, there is no chance that he could have done anything but look it over—if that—and hence the article must be assigned completely, or practically so, to Kate Lyon, with whatever typing errors Helen Crane may have introduced and whatever changes Cora may have seen fit to make.

The *Lippincott's* version must be the copy-text. The status of the A1 variants is obscure. Certain of them are fairly clearcut errors, such as *drum* for L *drums* (388.11), *utterance* for *utterances* (375.16), and *Venice* for *Venice and* (373.20). Two readings appear to be A1 editorial improvements: *master* for *the master* (377.4) and *called* for *call* (378.24), to which probably one may add *notwithstanding this* for *notwithstanding* (388.1) The rest are so indifferent as to be unassignable.

THE STORMING OF BURKERSDORF HEIGHTS

"The Storming of Burkersdorf Heights" appeared in *Lippincott's Magazine*, LXVI (November, 1900), 781–794, where it is noticed as 'Last of the Series.' Editorial spaces were used before lines 393.8, 394.17, 395.22, 396.31, 397.29, 399.3, 401.23, 403.4, 405.7, and 408.13. In the Lippincott's *Great Battles* it was placed fourth, pages 80–113; in the English edition it was second, pages 50–84.

The choice of the battle, as well as the composition, seems to have been Kate Lyon's entirely, on the evidence of her letter to Cora of April 7–8. As with "Solferino" it is not likely that Crane's health permitted him to do more than read over the article, but we cannot be sure he did not request some changes or that Cora did not exercise her judgment here and there. Slightly more evidence than in "Solferino" may exist that A1 was set from uncorrected L proofs, but the case is far from decisive. Although the possibility of A1 compositorial error cannot be overlooked, at least a chance exists that the grammatical error *meine* in A1 for correct L *mein* (395.30) reflects uncorrected proof and at 396.34–35 *wabbling* may be an A1 compositorial error or the faithful reproduction of an L typo or misreading. If the evidence of the possible source is valid, the L proof may have read *recapturing* with A1 at 403.6 changed by L later to *capturing* (see the Textual Note) although it must be admitted the reason for such a proof change is obscure. At 406.6–7 the A1 *their opponents* for L *its opponents* could be more explicable as the original, refined by L proof correction, than the reverse. On the other hand, at 404.20 the unsplitting in A1 of L's split infinitive is clearly editorial, and A1 *enabled* for *free* in the L sentence *Frederick was now free to besiege Schweidnitz* (408.13) sounds editorial, particularly in view of the "Leipzig" editorial change of *could* for proof *free to* at 337.19. At 403.14 A1's substitution of *army* for L *force* seems designed to avoid the repetition of *forces* only six words earlier in the sentence, *Daun took command of the forces in Silesia, and with a force of seventy thousand men* . . . . At 398.27 the A1 phrase *boxes of German flutes* for L *boxes with* is probably an attempt at normalization, although at least an outside chance exists that the L *with* is an attempt to avoid the incongruity of boxes of flutes and boxes of snuff in the same sentence.

Any possible authoritative A1 readings conjecturally derived from printer's copy of early L proof are mixed, then, with a number of A1 sophistications; and emendation of the L copy-text is to be engaged in with caution.

F. B.

Appendixes

TEXTUAL NOTES

WAR DISPATCHES

No. 1. an impression of the "concert"

6.36 tableau. The] That WG on the one side joined by $N^{1,3,5,8}$ on the other end the sentence with 'tableau' and start a new sentence with 'The' indicates this to be the reading of the typescript. If correction, or sophistication, is to be conjectured, it must come from $N^{2,4,6-7}$ which read *tableau, the* (N^2 without the comma). Although their version cannot be authoritative, the question remains whether it is not correct and the typescript in error. At first sight it would seem as if they might be correct. That is, the sliding aside of the hills and the widening of the waterway correspond to the movement of the stage-flats being withdrawn until, at the last, the full open stage for the tableau corresponds to the discovery of the inner bay. Not only may this seem to be a logical interpretation, but it is aided, perhaps, by the awkwardness of 'and impressively' unless this phrase refers to the widening of the waterway and, 'like the scenes . . . tableau,' is parenthetical. These are powerful considerations, and indeed they would need to be so to encourage the four observed newspapers to alter the text independently according to their understanding of the intention. It may be they were right. On the other hand, a typist's error here while not impossible, may seem a bit odd, and it may be that the very force of the evidence led to a misunderstanding of Crane's intention. It is perhaps dangerous to rely too heavily on Crane's observance of grammatical concord, but one must suggest that the plural 'scenes', within the presumed parenthesis, must refer to the hills and their withdrawal, and cannot grammatically apply as it should to the waterway. Second, the concept itself is only superficially logical. It is not at all certain that the inner bay as such is to be compared directly to the final tableau—as it must if the scenes are part of a parenthesis, for the final tableau in a theater would show the warships in the bay as the grand finale, but at this point they are not visible until after the inner bay is completely revealed. It follows that the typescript reading can be defended. The single theatrical reference applies to the withdrawal of the hills, compared directly to the sliding back of the flats in preparation for a stage tableau. Although, obviously, the tableau is to be the warships in the bay, the direct reference is not made to them as this tableau, and the tableau reference applies only to the reason for the impressive withdrawal of the stage-flat hills one by one. If this is so, the typescript is right, and Crane has erred only in an awkwardness in his placement of 'and impressively', which in his intention would be in apposition to 'Gradually'. The intended syntax, then, appears to be *Gradually, and impressively, the hills slid aside like the scenes in a melodrama before the final tableau. The water-way widened to an inner bay. Then finally*, etc.

7.18 Russians] The singular 'Russian' in all newspapers except N[5] demonstrates the reading of the typescript, the example of which was powerful enough to cause the N[1] compositor to continue the list all in the singular (see Historical Collation). Whether 'Russian' was an error in the typescript and was corrected by WG, like N[5], or an error in the master proof cannot be determined.

7.19 peaceably] Whether WG 'peaceably' is an English sophistication, or $N 'peacefully' an American one, is not to be demonstrated. On the other hand, just the distinction in this article between 'peaceably' at 7.19 and 'peacefully' at 8.21 is found in THE O'RUDDY (*Works*, IV) with 'peaceable-looking' (235.1–2), 'peaceably' (70.17), although 'peaceful' at 238.36. These examples should indicate that Crane was using 'peaceably' in the present essay accurately and that the WG reading may therefore be taken as correct.

No. 3. STEPHEN CRANE SAYS GREEKS CANNOT BE CURBED

15.26 be a great deal happen] That the omission of 'be' from N[1,3] was an editorial or compositorial intervention seems clear. What is less clear is whether the rewrite editor faithfully reproduced the words of the cable here or whether he wrote 'happen' for 'happening'. However, the case seems too uncertain to warrant other emendation of the N[1] copy-text than the restoration of the omitted 'be', although 'happening' may well be the true lost reading.

No. 5(1). CRANE AT VELESTINO

21.22 legs] All texts read 'lips', which makes little sense. That 'lips' was an error in the transmission of the cable, or in the original copy, may be indicated by reference to No. 6, "A Fragment of Velestino." At 30.39–31.3 Crane writes, 'The officer said something rather good perhaps, and the others all laughed appreciatively but carelessly, their legs wide apart, their caps set rakishly, like a lot of peacefully garrisoned hussars after evening parade.' Again, at 31.13–14, 'In the meantime let him gossip, with his legs wide apart, and pass around the cigarettes.' As in the present text, the careless attitude of the officers is typified by their stance with 'legs wide apart'.

No. 10. STEPHEN CRANE TELLS OF WAR'S HORRORS

54.5 them] As set originally in N[1b], 'Near the hatch where I can see them' continues the description of the soldiers in the hold found only in N[2-5].

Crane then continues with the identification of the man shot in the mouth as among the soldiers whom he can see in the light from the hatch. The N^{1a} reading 'him' obviously comes from a proofreader and is without authority or correctness. Without 53.28–54.4 as in N^{1b} the sophistication would have seemed almost required.

55.2 Stylidia] This seems to be a Crane error. The correct form is 'Stylis'.

55.36–37 particularly. Uprooted] As demonstrated by its appearance in N^{2-3}, this is the version in the rewrite typescript wired earlier than the finally revised form and therefore nearer to Crane's cable. The change in the modification represented by N^1 (and later sent to N^5) with its omitted 'they' represents an 'improvement' almost certainly without reference to the cable.

No. 12. MY TALK WITH "SOLDIERS SIX"

59.5–9 Here are . . . heeded.] The N^1 opening in its informality appears to resemble Crane's reports more than the stiff WG version. The present editor takes it, then, that WG rewrote the first few sentences that in N^1 preface the interviews proper. On the other hand, although the transition in N^1 from the introduction to the interviews is smooth enough, the WG continuation 'Here are some interviews . . . particularly heeded' sounds like Crane, particularly in its emphasis upon the care and conscience with which he has treated the words of the common soldiers. The present editor conjectures that these were present in the typescript but were cut by N^1 since they delayed—from a newspaper view—the immediate getting down to business.

59.32 No.] This reading in WG is typical of the laconic responses found in these interviews. On the other hand, the specific answer in N^1, 'All but two', might seem unlikely to be an editorial invention, although it may well be just that. If Crane wrote the N^1 version, the apparent lack of continuity between the generally affirmative response that all but two *were* good officers, and the next question, 'Why?', is marked, and the continuation of the discussion is entirely negative in its comprehensiveness. Thus WG might have been led to edit an anomaly in the text. This may be easier to credit than the editorial invention of 'All but two', with its jagged edge; but one could suggest that the jagged edge is suspicious and not characteristic of Crane. One may speculate, then, that the N^1 editor, who knew that the sympathies of his readers were strongly on the side of the Greeks, did not want to print Crane's report of the soldier's blanket condemnation of his officers and so relieved it, even at the expense of introducing a gap in logical continuity. See 59.37 below.

59.37 "Well, . . . regiments."] The divergences in the two texts here must come from editorial rewriting in one or the other. This is the one question in the whole piece in which the interviewer, in the N^1 version, argues with the soldier in an attempt to make him change his point of view, which the soldier obligingly does. In the WG text some of the argument is present, but the soldier refuses to be convinced. This response agrees with the soldier's blanket condemnation of his officers above at 59.32, where it was conjectured that the N^1 editor had softened the Crane report as reproduced in WG. If so, then the rewriting of the present exchange, and the soldier's admission, which puts the officers in a more favorable light, is a further part of the editorial intervention, and for the same motives as dictated the interference at 59.32.

63.13–14 simply packed already] This typical Crane expression, edited out in N^1, encourages one to conjecture that the N^1 variants immediately preceding, and no doubt immediately succeeding, are also editorial. Otherwise, there is no evidence one way or the other.

No. 22. STEPHEN CRANE'S PEN-PICTURE OF C. H. THRALL

108.30 think] The idea of eyes that 'do not seem to think' is very odd, especially in context, and N^3 'wink' seems to give a more correct reading. On the other hand, N^2 omits the phrase, so that no other witness is present; and the easiest explanation for the omission is that the N^2 editor was puzzled by the phrase with 'think'. If so, given the nature of the copy from which N^{1-3} independently radiate, it would seem most probable that 'think' was what was cabled (or at least what was received in the cable). Hence, the reading 'wink' would appear to be an enlightened guess on the part of the N^3 editor but without authority even though it may be right. That is, 'wink' is very attractive for its sense, and Crane may have intended it; but on the evidence 'think' was what was received by the *World*.

109.27 commanding at Havana] General Pando seems to have been military commander of Havana; hence General Arolas' command would have been the Havana garrison, or regular army, and so he would not have been commanding 'all Havana', as N^3 has it, for N^2 'at Havana'.

No. 24 SAYINGS OF THE TURRET JACKS IN OUR BLOCKADING FLEETS

113.6 gallows] Nautical dictionaries do not mention a boat with this name, although a supporting structure on the deck may be called a 'gallows'. The *O.E.D.* references to a small boat called a 'galley' that may be rowed seems to confine the word only to a special customs boat on the Thames, or else to sixteenth-century usage. It is possible that Crane is here attempting to reproduce some nautical slang, or perhaps a dialect pronunciation of the sailor. But the word intended is not to be determined and may have been a real confusion on his part.

No. 29. IN THE FIRST LAND FIGHT FOUR OF OUR MEN ARE KILLED

129.6 500 yards] This is the reading of the original typesetting in N^{1b}, altered to '550 yards' when the line was reset in N^{1a} to correct the typo 'arotary' in N[1b]. No evidence is present in N[1a] that the original cable was resurveyed to correct N[1b]. The odds would seem to favor the conjecture, therefore, that the round number '500' was in the original and that '550' was an error in the resetting.

No. 35. HUNGER HAS MADE CUBANS FATALISTS

148.12 visions] N[2] 'vision' seems to be an error resulting from a mistaken connection between the word and 'he will see' at the start of the clause. It would seem that Crane is referring not to the soldierly qualities that have ever come into the Cuban's field of sight but instead into his envisagings, or imaginings. N[3] confirms the plural.

No. 39. STEPHEN CRANE'S VIVID STORY OF THE BATTLE OF SAN JUAN

158.16 formulated] That Crane wrote 'fulminated' as in N[1] is demonstrated by the concurrence of N[2]. Hence N[3] 'formulated' has no authority but is a necessary correction. Some very strained case might be made for 'fulminated' in the sense listed by O.E.D. 2, 'to issue as a thunderbolt', or O.E.D. 5, 'to flash forth like lightning', or even 6, 'to explode with a loud report, detonate, go off.' But the only figurative use recorded is that of censoring or condemning, and it would seem plain that Crane simply mistook the word's meaning and that something like 'formulated' was in his mind.

No. 47. STEPHEN CRANE SEES FREE CUBA

185.36 Betancourt$_\wedge$] The N[1] comma after 'Betancourt' places the large force of insurgents in apposition to the garrison of Matanzas, and thus would have the verb 'are encamped' apply to both. But the garrison of Matanzas would not be stationed twelve miles away. It seems probable that the cable was confused here, or the rewrite man misunderstood. It would seem that two facts are being stated: (1) a garrison of 6,000 is in Matanzas; and (2) a large force of insurgents is encamped within twelve miles of the town. Perhaps the trouble lies in the participle 'amounting' and it should be *amounts*. At any rate, the absence of a comma after 'Betancourt' in N[2-3] confirms the reading of the copy and tends to establish the N[1] comma as the typesetter's or proofreader's.

No. 52. MEMOIRS OF A PRIVATE

195.26 feckless] N[1]'s 'fetless' is not a misprint, since Crane used it again in "The Second Generation," TALES OF WAR, *Works*, VI, 268.21. It is not, however, a word blessed by the O.E.D., and in "The Second Generation" one text tried 'footlessly' and another 'bootlessly' in a vain attempt to make sense of the anomaly. In No. 52 Fryckstedt's emendation 'feckless' seems to be what Crane intended, and is gratefully adopted in the present text.

Doubtless it is of no importance that the *O.E.D.* lists a very early spelling 'fectless'; Crane's ear here was evidently not impeccable.

No. 71. THE GREAT BOER TREK

252.19 colony. In 1834ʌ] TMs, followed by Co, mistook the modification. It was not that £3,000,000 was invested in 1834, but instead it was D'Urban's May Proclamation of Emancipation that took place in 1834. The abolition of slavery in the Empire went into effect in August, 1833 (W. M. Macmillan, *Bantu, Boer, and Briton* [Oxford: Clarendon Press, 1963], pp. 103, 136). See the wrong modification also at 252.21.

253.35 Under] The appearance in TMs of 'Dec. 1834' within parentheses before 'Under' seems to reproduce a note in MS that in TMs and in Co was wrongly transferred to the text. For a similar example, see No. 66, 238.14.

256.37 Moselekatse] TMs and Co read 'Mosega', but this was a place, not a person. According to Theal (p. 202) it was Moselekatse with 12,000 warriors who 'was found on the Marikwa, about fifty miles north of Mosega'.

GREAT BATTLES

THE BRIEF CAMPAIGN AGAINST NEW ORLEANS

284.6 begun] With the possible exception of the time '7.30' or '7.50' at 279.22, no very clear case of the preservation in A1 of early L proof variants exists. The A1 reading 'already begun' may represent such a case, but in context a stronger reason would seem to exist for it to be added by A1 editorial attention (which demonstrably changed a reading at 282.15) than to be removed by the L editor from proof.

THE STORMING OF BADAJOZ

286.11 Congress] The reading of MS is 'disgruntled congress', altered in L to read 'disgruntled part of Congress'. The qualification looks as if it were due to editorial caution modifying Crane's typical flat statement.

286.15 supplies] The L change of MS 'supplies' to 'arms' seems editorial, dictated by the wish to remove the repetition of 'supplies' from the first clause in the sentence. The editor may also have thought 'provisions and supplies' tautological. Yet here, as in " 'Vittoria' " at 313.25, 'supplies' seems to mean chiefly 'arms' so that 'provisions and supplies' seems to be accurate and the MS not in error.

289.24 blared] L, followed by A1, can scarcely be blamed for sophisticating this MS reading to 'blazed', if it had not already been done in the typescript. But for the authority here of MS, see "New Orleans" 280.17–19, describing the first attack of Jackson's men on the British, at night: 'But they had not been long in this awkward position when there was a yell and a blare of flame in the darkness. Some of Jackson's troops had come.'

291.32 Lieutenant Ridge] There is some confusion concerning this officer's rank. One thing is certain—he was not a Lieutenant at the time of his death: H. R. Clinton in *The Peninsular War and Wellington's Campaigns in France and Belgium* (London, 1878), p. 200, "The 5th regiment (Northumberland Fusiliers) was immediately led forward by the dauntless Major Ridge." Napier in his *History of the War in the Peninsula*, III, 215 refers to Henry Ridge as "the heroic Colonel Ridge." A later history of the war, Charles Osman's *A History of the Peninsular War* (Oxford: Clarendon Press, 1914), V, 252, states that "the third man to gain the summit was Colonel Ridge of the 5th Fusiliers"; however in the index to this work he is listed as "Ridge, Henry, Lieut-Colonel, killed at the storming of Badajoz." It would seem that Lieutenant-Colonel is what is required here, and that a slip occurred either in Kate Lyon's notes or in their transmission to the manuscript.

292.16 made plain] This is a typical Crane phrase that was likely to be subject to editorial objection. The L substitute 'exposed' is taken to be editorial, although there is a slight chance that Cora might have made the change in the typescript.

THE SIEGE OF PLEVNA

295.7 seventeen hundred] F. V. Greene, *The Russian Army and Its Campaign in Turkey in 1877–78* (London, n.d.), p. 235, places the population at 6,000–7,000, but another major source, William V. Herbert, *The Defence of Plevna* (London, 1894), p. 133, gives 17,000, a figure also found in Thile von Trothe, ed. Arthur Wagner (Kansas City, Mo., 1896), p. 38. It seems probable that the 17,000 figure was misread as 1700 in Kate Lyon's notes, thus prompting Crane's remark that it was 'a mere village'.

297.18 Schakofskoy] Herbert spells this name 'Schachowskoy' and Greene 'Shakofskoi'. Kate Lyon may have got the spelling 'Schakofskoy' from E. Ollier, *Cassell's Illustrated History* (London, 1896–97).

THE BATTLE OF BUNKER HILL

304.39–305.2 Prescott . . . lanterns,] The authority of the A1 reading over L is indicated by Frothingham's account, p. 122: "Colonel Prescott was at its head, arrayed in a simple and appropriate uniform, with a blue coat and a three-cornered hat. Two sergeants, carrying dark lanterns, were a few paces in front of him, and the intrenching tools followed in the rear."

307.38 president] A1 'president' as against L 'the President' agrees with Frothingham, p. 172, "On the 16th of June he officiated as president of the Provincial Congress."

308.17 breast-work] The single appearance in L at 311.3–4 of the hyphenated form (against the unhyphenated at 308.17, 309.2, 309.12, 311.16) seems to represent a characteristic of the copy that had escaped the L styling. The hyphenated word is found in the Richie manuscript of "Badajoz" and is also present in "New Orleans," a text that L seems to have reproduced from copy with greater faithfulness than the other articles.

309.7 them] In this case Frothingham, p. 134, upholds L 'them' versus the A1 omission: "He then made, a little distance in front of this, another parallel line of fence, and filled the space between them with the new cut grass lying in the fields."

"VITTORIA"

319.20 rose] The A1 variant 'arose' for L 'rose' occurs within two L lines of a probable L editorial omission of 'exalted' (319.17), and the form agrees with Crane's ordinary usage. However, both texts agree at 324.12 in the same phrase, 'Picton rose in his stirrups'. With this parallel it may seem safer to take it that A1 'arose' is a compositorial variant instead of an L proof reading later altered by the editor.

320.10 three hundred] The reading 'three thousand' of all texts is an error, for all the sources agree in three hundred. Walter Henry, *Events of a Military Life* (London, 1843), p. 145, reads "in the crushing of a French column and the death of three hundred men", but William T. Dobson, *A Narrative on the Peninsular Campaign* (London, 1889), pp. 225–226, an abridgement of Napier, is most explicit: the mines at Burgos exploded "when a column of infantry was defiling under the castle . . . in an instant destroyed more than 300 men." One may note the same error in a digit, although a subtracted zero, in the 'seventeen hundred', "Plevna," 295.7.

322.22 spectacle] The A1 omission of L 'on the morning of June 21st' seems to remove an L editorial bridge to take the place of the mention of June 21 at 322.17 in a passage cut by L. The E1 version of this revised sentence is much superior in its modification of the sentence elements but is, of course, unauthoritative.

322.23 their] The phrase in L reads, 'occupied by the French army with the rich uniforms of their officers', but in A1 it is 'its officers'. Crane was mixed in his use of the plural for *enemy* or *army*. The "Badajoz" manuscript reads 'hard-bitten army, certain of its leaders' at 288.6. At 288.26–27 'The cavalry divided itself', but in the next sentence when individuals seem to be in question it is 'they answered' even though the noun referent is still the same 'cavalry'. Greater looseness comes at 289.12–14: 'the army of the allies was entirely without food, but they stuck doggedly to their trenches'. Again the shift seems to come when the army is no longer a unit but a number of individual men. At 289.34–35 *infantry*, which has been singular, becomes a group and 'The infantry with their bayonets followed closely.' At 292.36–37 MS reads 'Column after column hurled themselves', but the L editor seems to have altered this plural to 'itself'. In a similar manner, it is conjectured, the L editor in "Burkersdorf" changed the lost typescript 'their' to 'its' in the sentence that reads in L, 'At sunrise the whole Prussian army could be seen to be in motion by its opponents' (406.5–7). Given the reasons why Crane dropped into *their*, the context in " 'Vittoria' " suggests that 'their officers' was the typescript reading faithfully reproduced in L but altered by the A1 editor to 'its', as the L editor had altered 'their' to 'its' in "Burkersdorf."

323.24 had crossed Tres] The A1 variant 'crossed at Tres' may seem to have been dictated by 323.38; that is, 'at' may have been borrowed to make the two phrases uniform and 'had' is omitted in order to avoid repetition. If this is true, L remains authoritative and the A1 change should be rejected as an editorial tinkering.

324.32–34 cannon-balls . . . long, hissing furrows] Unfortunately the source does not provide the detail about the hissing, which seems to be Crane's invention. Sir George B. L'Estrange, *Recollections* (London, [1874]), p. 87, reads: "A field of corn, standing four or five feet high, and just ready for the sickle, was between us and the wood, and as we advanced through it, besides the bullets from the wood, an occasional cannon-ball bowled along through it, its course being easily seen by the lowering of the ears of corn, as if reaped." From this description it seems reasonably clear that the 'hissing' derives from the sound of the ears as they lowered themselves at the passage of the cannon-ball. Hence the transfer of the adjective in A1 to the cannon-ball itself is unwarranted and a mistaken editorial intervention.

A SWEDE'S CAMPAIGN IN GERMANY
I. LEIPZIG

343.4 authority] That L 'ability' is a proof-alteration of typescript and A1 'authority' seems to be shown by Frederic Schiller, *The History of the Thirty Years' War in Germany*, trans. James M. Duncan (London, 1828) I, 159: "It was therefore a master-stroke of politics, at the moment when a victorious monarch, absolute master of his military operations, advanced to combat an emperor, to deprive the Imperial armies of the only general whose experience and authority could balance the grand talents of Gustavus Adolphus."

351.31 the rear] L 'their rear' may be a proof-alteration and A1 'the rear' the typescript reading, if Kate Lyon used B. Chapman, *The History of Gustavus Adolphus and the Thirty Years' War* (London, 1856), p. 261: "the whole Saxon army . . . took to flight in companies . . . carrying with them the elector, who all the while had kept in the rear of the battle, and who did not stop until he had reached Eilenburg."

352.19–20 on the field] A1's 'in the field' appears to be a departure from authority, on the evidence of Edward Cust, *Lives of the Warriors of the*

Thirty Years' War, Part I (London, 1865), p. 173: "7000 of the enemy lay dead on the field."

A SWEDE'S CAMPAIGN IN GERMANY
II. LÜTZEN

361.17 the son] The L reading 'a son' seems to be unauthoritative, on the basis of Cust, p. 239: "This renowned and extraordinary man was the son of a Moravian Baron."

363.17 moneys] The A1 reading, not L 'money', seems authoritative: Cust, p. 262: "He insisted that all means and monies for carrying on the war should be solely at his command."

369.12–15 whole Yellow Regiment . . . they had fought] In this case editorial tinkering by A1 is exposed in the omission of 'whole' and the substitution of 'he' for 'they'. L agrees with Schiller, III, 114: "The entire yellow regiment . . . lay dead upon the field of battle in the same order which they had so valiantly preserved before they fell."

THE BATTLE OF SOLFERINO

374.25 1806] Although all texts agree in '1806', Giuseppe Mazzini was actually born on June 22, 1805.

376.25 Leri] Since at 391.6 A1 follows L in 'Lèri', its correction of L 'Lèri' at 376.25 is probably accidental. Kate Lyon may have drawn the odd accent from J. A. R. Marriott, *The Makers of Modern Italy* (London, 1889), although in Marriott it is even more in error as 'Léri'. The correct form without accent appears in another of the ascertainable sources, Countess Evelyn Martinengo Cesaresco, *Cavour* (London, 1898), p. 14, and also in Charles de Mazade, *The Life of Count Cavour* (London, 1877), p. 12.

THE STORMING OF BURKERSDORF HEIGHTS

403.6 recapturing] The A1 reading, as against L 'capturing', may be an A1 editorial improvement, but it does agree with Lord Dover, *The Life of Frederic the Second* (London, 1832), II, 111: "The plan of the King of Prussia for the ensuing campaign was to . . . retake Schweidnitz" ('retake' is also used for Schweidnitz on II, 255). Thomas Campbell, *Frederick the Great* (London, 1842–43), III, 371, writes of "The recovery of Dresden and that of Schweidnitz."

403.32 *et seq.* Height] The singular or plural can be used correctly. For example, Thomas Carlyle, *History of Frederick II of Prussia, Called Frederick the Great* (New York, 1866), VI, 224, quoting Templehoff states: "Burkersdorf Height (or Heights, for there are two, divided by the Brook

Weitritz; but we shall neglect the eastern or lower, which is ruled by the other, and stands or falls along with it), Burkersdorf Height is the principal."

403.33–34 Kunzendorf Heights] L and A1 in reading 'Kunensdorf' are closer to 'Kunzendorf' in Kate Lyon's source (Carlyle's *Frederick the Great*) than is the E1 variant 'Kunersdorf' which is found at 403.13 although in another context. E1 confused the matter by attempting to correct A1 'Kunensdorf' with 'Kunersdorf', which lies in Brandenburg whereas Burkersdorf (and Kunzendorf) is in Silesia. The emendation is required, thus, although the typescript may well have read 'Kunensdorf', in error, with L.

EDITORIAL EMENDATIONS IN THE COPY-TEXT

[NOTE: Every editorial change from the copy-texts—whether manuscript, typescript, newspaper, or magazine versions, as chosen—is recorded for the substantives, and every change in the accidentals as well save for such silent typographical alterations as are remarked in "The Text of the Virginia Edition," prefixed to Volume I of this collected edition, with slight modification as indicated in the headnotes to the present apparatus. Only the direct source of the emendation, with its antecedents, is noticed; the Historical Collation may be consulted for the complete history, within the texts collated, of any substantive readings that qualify for inclusion in that listing. However, when as in syndicated newspaper versions a number of texts have equal claim to authority, all are noted in the Emendations listing. Moreover, all documents are listed with their readings when a Virginia edition (V) emendation supersedes documentary authority. An alteration assigned to V is made for the first time in the present edition if *by the first time* is understood *the first time in respect to the texts chosen for collation.* Asterisked readings are discussed in the Textual Notes. The note *et seq.* signifies that all following occurrences are identical in that particular text, and thus the same emendation has been made without further notice. The wavy dash ($\sim$) represents the same word that appears before the bracket and is used exclusively in recording punctuation or other accidentals variants. An inferior caret ($_\wedge$) indicates the absence of a punctuation mark. The dollar sign ($\$$) is taken over from a convention of bibliographical description to signify *all* editions so identified. That is, if N represents newspaper versions in general, and N^{1-6} the six collated newspapers, then $\$N$ would be a shorthand symbol for all of these six texts and would be used even if one text owing to a more extensive cut than simple omission (always recorded in the Historical Collation) did not contain the reading in question. Occasionally a text subsumed under the $\$$ notation may be excluded from agreement by the use of the minus sign. Thus such a notation as $\$N(-N^4)$ would mean that all of the N texts agree with the noted reading to the left of the bracket except for N^4 which, by its absence from the $\$N$ list of agreements, must therefore agree with the reading to the right of the bracket unless otherwise specified. A lengthier way of expressing the same situation would be $N^{1-3,5-6}$. A plus sign may be used as a shorthand indication of the concurrence of all collated editions following the cited edition. For instance, if E1, listed after A1, agrees in a reading with A1, the note may read A1+ instead of A1,E1. Rarely, in dealing with accidentals when only general concurrence of the following editions is in question and exactness of detail would serve no useful purpose, the $\pm$ symbol may be used. Thus if an emendation line read 'said:] $N±; ~, WG' one should understand that the majority of the N texts have a colon instead of the WG comma, but some might have a period or some even a comma. The exact readings of these variant N texts would not, however, affect the conclusion that the basic proof from which the N texts radiate had the colon. If it seemed important to indicate that certain of these variant texts had such and such punctuation, then the listing would do so as most convenient.]

WAR DISPATCHES

No. 1. AN IMPRESSION OF THE "CONCERT"

[The copy-text is WG: *Westminster Gazette*, IX (May 3, 1897), 1–2. Other texts collated are N^1: New York *Sun*, May 9, 1897, p. 6; N^2: *Detroit Free Press*, May 9, p. 17; N^3: *Pittsburgh Leader*, May 9, p. 19; N^4: Portland *Oregonian*, May 8, p. 6; N^5: Louisville *Courier-Journal*, May 9, p. 19; N^6: *Omaha Daily Bee*, May 10, p. 2; N^7: *Boston Globe*, May 9, p. 33; N^8: St. Paul *Pioneer Press*, May 9, p. 20.]

5.1 *Guadiana*—]N^8; ~. WG; ~ , April 22.— N^1; ~ : N^2; ~ . $N^{3,7}$; ~ , May 3.— N^4; Guardiana, April 26.— N^5; Guadiaa, April, 1897.— N^6

5.5 north$_\wedge$] $N^{2,5-7}$; ~ , WG,$N^{1,3-4,8}$

5.9 phenomenon$_\wedge$] $N; ~ , WG

5.11 Pirée] V; Piree WG,$N(-N^1)$; Piræus N^1

5.12 Powers$_\wedge$] $N(-N^{1,4,8}$); ~ , WG,$N^{1,4,8}$

5.16 *et seq.* color] $N; colour WG

5.20 cape$_\wedge$] $N(-N^{4,7-8}$); ~ , WG,$N^{4,7-8}$

5.21 traveler] $N(-N^{1,3}$); traveller WG,N^1; travelers N^3

5.22 cock-sure] $N^{2,5-7}$; cocksure WG,N^1; ~ - | ~ $N^{4,8}$; ~ $_\wedge$ ~ N^3

5.24 *et seq.* torpedo boat] $N(-N^{4-5}$); ~ - ~ WG,N^{4-5}

6.5 toward] $N(-N^{3-4,8}$); towards WG,$N^{3-4,8}$

6.6 excited$_\wedge$] $N(-N^{1,4}$); ~ , WG,$N^{1,4}$

6.13 man$_\wedge$] $N(-N^1$); ~ , WG,N^1

6.13 nor] $N(-N^{1,4}$); or WG,$N^{1,4}$

6.17 could] $N; would WG

6.19 hillsides] $N; ~ - ~ WG

6.20 great$_\wedge$ high$_\wedge$] $N^{2-3,8}$; ~ , ~ , WG,$N^{1,4-7}$

6.27 *et seq.* -colored] $N; -coloured WG

6.28 afterward] $N^{1,5-6}$; afterwards WG,$N^{2-4,7-8}$

6.30 water-way] $N^{2-3,5}$; waterway WG,$N^{4,6-8}$; ~ - | ~ N^1

6.30 fine$_\wedge$] $N(-N^{4-5}$); ~ , WG, N^{4-5}

*6.36 tableau. The] *stet* WG, $N^{1,3,5,8}$

7.1 warships] $N^{1-4,8}$; ~ - ~ WG; ~ $_\wedge$ ~ N^{5-6}; ~ - | ~ N^7

7.12 papers$_\wedge$] $N^{2-6,8}$; ~ , WG,$N^{1,7}$

7.14 hedge$_\wedge$] $N(-N^{1,4}$); ~ , WG,$N^{1,4}$

*7.18 Russians] *stet* WG

7.19 Turks$_\wedge$] $N(-N^1$); ~ , WG,N^1

*7.19 peaceably] *stet* WG

7.21 *et seq.* flagship] $N^{1,4,7-8}$; ~ - ~ WG,$N^{2,5}$; ~ $_\wedge$ ~ $N^{3,6}±$

7.23 traveler] $N(-N^1$); traveller WG,N^1

7.28 dock$_\wedge$] $N(-N^7$); ~ , WG, N^7

7.38 monster,] $N; ~ ; WG

7.38–39 *Camperdown*$_\wedge$ . . . *Revenge*$_\wedge$] $N(-N^{1,5,8}$); ~ , . . . ~ , WG,$N^{1,5,8}$

8.2 *et seq.* battleships] $N^{3,6-8}$; ~ -

$\sim$ WG,N$^{2,4-5}$; $\sim_\wedge \sim$ N$^1\pm$

8.4 *et seq.* harbor] $N; harbour WG

8.8 *Guadiana*$_\wedge$] $N($-$N^{1,5}); $\sim$, WG,N^{1,5}

8.11 harbor$_\wedge$] $N($-$N^{1,4,7}); $\sim$, WG,N^{1,4,7}

8.13 uproar$_\wedge$] $N($-$N^{1,7}); $\sim$, WG,N^{1,7}

8.19 officer$_\wedge$] N$^{2-5}$ (N^2: officers); $\sim$, WG,N$^{1,6-8}$

8.19 *Guadiana*$_\wedge$] N$^{2-5}$; $\sim$, WG, N$^{6-8}$; $\sim$. N^1

8.20 bulwark$_\wedge$] $N; $\sim$, WG

8.23 launch$_\wedge$] $N($-$N^6); $\sim$, WG, N^6

8.25 Frenchmen$_\wedge$ and] $N($-$N^{1,4,6}); $\sim$, $\sim$ WG,N^{1,4,6}

8.26 laughed$_\wedge$ . . . nodded$_\wedge$ . . . chattered$_\wedge$] $N(N^2: chatted); $\sim$, . . . $\sim$, . . . $\sim$, WG

8.27 wit. Whereupon] $N; wit, whereupon WG

8.36 them$_\wedge$] $N($-$N^1); $\sim$, WG, N^1

9.2 language$_\wedge$] N$^{2-4,8}$; $\sim$, WG, N$^{1,5-7}$

9.6–7 Once$_\wedge$ indeed$_\wedge$] N$^{2-3,5-6}$; $\sim$, $\sim$, WG,N$^{1,4,7-8}$

9.7 ship$_\wedge$] $N($-$N^{1,7}); $\sim$, WG,N^{1,7}

9.16 admiral] $N($-$N^1); Admiral WG,N^1

9.18 *Camperdown*$_\wedge$] $N($-$N^7); $\sim$, WG,N^7

9.20 cut] $N; *omit* WG

9.31 forever] $N; for ever WG

9.34–35 boat-hook] N$^{2-3,5,8}$; boathook WG,N^1; $\sim_\wedge\sim$ N$^{4,6-7}$

9.36 fifes$_\wedge$] N$^{3,5-6,8}$; $\sim$, WG,N^{1,4}

9.40 it$_\wedge$] N$^{3,5-6,8}$; $\sim$, WG,N$^{1-2,4}$

10.6 skillful] $N($-$N^{1,8}); skilful WG,N^{1,8}

10.9 shore,] $N($-$N^{1,6}) (N^3: short); $\sim_\wedge$ WG,N^{1,6}

10.10 gunwales$_\wedge$] $N($-$N^1); $\sim$, WG,N^1

10.11 skirts$_\wedge$] $N($-$N^{1,4}); $\sim$, WG,N^{1,4} (N^{3,4}: shirts)

10.15 fro$_\wedge$] $N($-$N^1); $\sim$, WG,N^1

10.18 stern$_\wedge$] $N($-$N^{1,6}); $\sim$, WG,N^{1,6}

10.20 torpedo$_\wedge$ destroyer] $N($-$N^4); $\sim$-$\sim$ WG,N^4

10.27 barge] $N; $\sim$, WG

10.36 them$_\wedge$] $N($-$N^{1,3}); $\sim$, WG,N^{1,3}

10.37 At] $N; Then at WG

11.7 flashes$_\wedge$] $N($-$N^1); $\sim$, WG, N^1

11.11 woman$_\wedge$] $N($-$N^1); $\sim$, WG,N^1

11.14–15 despatch$_\wedge$ boat] $N($-$N^4); $\sim$-$\sim$ WG,N^4

11.21 bridge$_\wedge$] $N($-$N^{4,5}); $\sim$, WG,N^{4,5}

11.27 downstairs$_\wedge$] $N($-$N^{1,7}); $\sim$, WG,N^{1,7}

11.30 impulses$_\wedge$] $N($-$N^{1,4,7}) (N^5: impulse); $\sim$, WG,N^{1,4,7}

11.31 assault$_\wedge$] $N($-$N^7); $\sim$, WG,N^7

11.35 ^{1}buns$_\wedge$] $N($-$N^{1,7}); $\sim$, WG,N^{1,7}

11.37 made$_\wedge$] $N($-$N^{5,7}); $\sim$, WG,N^{5,7}

11.40 gold$_\wedge$] $N($-$N^{1,5,7}); $\sim$, WG,N^{1,5,7}

12.14 officers$_\wedge$] $N($-$N^{1,5,7}); $\sim$, WG,N^{1,5,7}

12.25 afterward] N$^{1,5-6}$; afterwards WG,N$^{2-4,7-8}$

12.26 hills$_\wedge$] $N; $\sim$, WG

12.27 deck$_\wedge$] N$^{2-3,6,8}$; $\sim$, WG, N^{1,4,7}

No. 2. THE SPIRIT OF THE GREEK PEOPLE

[Copy-text is MS: Columbia University Libraries, datelined Apr. 17 [1897].]

13.17 war.] V; war$_\wedge$ MS

13.26 don't] V; dont MS

No. 3. STEPHEN CRANE SAYS GREEKS CANNOT BE CURBED

[The copy-text is N[1]: *New York Journal*, Apr. 30, 1897, p. 1. The other texts collated are N[2]: *Chicago Tribune*, Apr. 30, p. 2; N[3]: San Francisco *Examiner*, Apr. 30, p. 1; N[4]: Philadelphia *Press*, Apr. 30, p. 1.]

14.21 Janina] N[2,4]; Yanina N[1]; Yanin N[3]
14.29 palace$_\wedge$] N[3-4]; ~ , N[1-2]

15.25 fight$_\wedge$] N[2-4]; ~ , N[1]
*15.26 be] N[2,4]; *omit* N[1,3]

No. 4. GREEK WAR CORRESPONDENTS

[The copy-text is N[1]: *Pittsburgh Leader*, May 16, 1897, p. 21. The other texts collated are N[2]: Portland *Oregonian*, May 16, p. 18; N[3]: St. Paul *Pioneer Press*, May 16, p. 19; N[4]: *Denver Republican*, May 16, p. 17.]

15.27.2 GREEK WAR CORRE-SPONDENTS] N[4]; THE WAR CORRESPONDENTS N[1]; FOLLOWERS OF WAR N[2]; GREEK WAR CORRESPONDENCE N[3]
15.28 Athens, Greece, May 1.—] N[2]; Athens, May 7, 1897. N[1]; Athens, Greece— N[3]; Athens, Greece, May 3.— N[4]
16.13 Perth] N[2-4]; Pearth N[1]
16.16 Society] N[2]; society N[1,3-4]
16.17 *et seq.* Eastern] N[2-4]; eastern N[1]
16.17 absurd$_\wedge$] N[3-4]; ~ , N[1-2]

16.26 can't] N[2-4]; cannot N[1]
16.33 fact] N[2-4]; as a fact N[1]
17.5,7 East] N[2-4]; east N[1]
17.9 inured] N[2,4]; immured N[1,3]
17.18 here$_\wedge$] N[3-4]; ~ , N[1-2]
18.6 newspapers$_\wedge$] N[2-4]; ~ , N[1]
18.12–13 who$_\wedge$ . . . kind$_\wedge$] N[2-4]; ~ , . . . ~ , N[1]
18.16 insurgents$_\wedge$] N[2-4]; ~ , N[1]
18.17 there$_\wedge$] N[2-3]; ~ , N[1,4]
18.18 band] N[2-4]; bands N[1]
18.21 But, of course,] N[2,3]; ~ $_\wedge$ ~ ~ $_\wedge$ N[1,4]

No. 5. (I). CRANE AT VELESTINO

[The copy-text is N[1a]: *New York Journal* (Greater New York edition), May 11, pp. 1–2. The other text collated is N[6]: San Francisco *Examiner*, May 11, pp. 1–2.]

18.32 This (*no* ¶)] N[6]; ¶ N[1a]
19.3 ¶ I] N[6]; *no* ¶ N[1a]
19.4 It (*no* ¶)] N[6]; ¶ N[1a]
19.21 Anyhow (*no* ¶)] N[6]; ¶ N[1a]
19.22 Greek] N[6]; Greeks' N[1a]
19.38 tremendous.] N[6]; ~ $_\wedge$ N[1a]
20.23 them$_\wedge$] N[6]; ~ , N[1a]
20.24 numbers$_\wedge$] N[6]; ~ , N[1a]
20.34 awoke$_\wedge$] N[6]; ~ , N[1a]

21.10 descriptions] N[6]; description N[1a]
21.10 While (*no* ¶)] N[6] (The while); ¶ N[1a]
21.14 ¶ The] N[6]; *no* ¶ N[1a]
21.16 I (*no* ¶)] N[6]; ¶ N[1a]
*21.22 legs] V; lips N[1a,6]
21.36 Legion] N[6]; Legation N[1a]
22.6 I (*no* ¶)] N[6]; ¶ N[1a]

22.18 lines] N⁶; line N¹ᵃ
22.18 proudly,] V; ~ ; N¹ᵃ; ~ ∧ N⁶
22.19 time,] N⁶; ~ ∧ N¹ᵃ
22.22 Smolenski] N⁶; Smolinski N¹ᵃ

22.23 Karadjah] *i.e.*, Kardetsa
22.34 An (*no* ¶)] N⁶; ¶ N¹ᵃ
23.5 Greek] N⁶; greek N¹ᵃ

No. 5(II). STEPHEN CRANE AT VELESTINO

[The copy-text is N¹ᵇ: *New York Journal* (out-of-town edition), May 11, 1897, pp. 1–2. Other texts collated are N²: *Chicago Tribune*, May 11, p. 1; N³: Philadelphia *Press*, May 11, p. 2; N⁴: *Boston Globe*, May 11, p. 7; N⁵: *Buffalo Evening News*, May 11, pp. 1,5.]

23.9 greatest] N²+; greates N¹ᵇ
23.13 Turks.] N²+; ~ ∧ N¹ᵇ
23.14–15 generally . . . occasioned] N²⁻³(N³: It occasioned); *omit* N¹ᵇ,⁴⁻⁵
23.26 and∧ later∧] N²⁻⁵; ~ , ~ , N¹ᵇ
23.31 New York] V; New Yorks N¹ᵇ; America N³; New Yorkers N⁵
24.31 this] N²+; tis N¹ᵇ
24.36 expressions] N²+(N²⁻³: expression); erpressions N¹ᵇ
25.7 well] N²+; wll N¹ᵇ
25.8 the gaunt] N⁴⁻⁵; th gaunt N¹ᵇ

25.14 resumed.] N²+; ~ ∧ N¹ᵇ
25.20 batteries.] N²+; ~ ∧ N¹ᵇ
25.22 soldier.] N²+; ~ ∧ N¹ᵇ
25.23 all.] N²+; ~ ∧ N¹ᵇ
25.39 again.] N²+; ~ ∧ N¹ᵇ
26.2 legs] V; lips N¹ᵇ+
26.3 neck.] N²+; ~ ∧ N¹ᵇ
26.11 glasses.] N²+; ~ ∧ N¹ᵇ
26.12 shot.] N²+; ~ ∧ N¹ᵇ
26.12 wine.] N²+; ~ ∧ N¹ᵇ
26.21 ¹over.] N²+; ~ ∧ N¹ᵇ
26.30 gray] N²+; grey N¹ᵇ
27.9 orders] N²+; order N¹ᵇ
27.11 got] N²+; gol N¹ᵇ

No. 6. A FRAGMENT OF VELESTINO

[The copy-text is WG: *Westminster Gazette*, June 3, 4, 8, 1897, pp. 1–2. The other texts collated are N¹: *New York Journal*, June 13, pp. 24–25; N²: San Francisco *Examiner*, June 27, p. 21. The latter is a derived text without authority.]

28.4 reddishy] N¹; reddish WG
28.17 splendor] N¹; splendour WG
28.21 glaring∧] N¹; ~ , WG
28.23 there∧] N¹; ~ , WG
28.24 *et seq.* Velestino] N¹; Velestimo WG (*except* Valestimo at 30.12)
28.30 harbor] N¹; harbour WG
28.33 around] N¹; *omit* WG
29.12 emphasized] N¹; emphasised WG

29.26 ¹This was the product.] N¹; *omit* WG
29.37 levee] N¹; levy WG
29.37 hot] N¹; lonely WG
30.5 *et seq.* toward] N¹; towards WG (*except* at 30.14)
30.10 connection] N¹⁻²; connexion WG
30.30 it] N¹; *omit* WG
31.12 due] N¹; due to WG
31.17 plain] N¹; obvious WG

31.24 outstretching] N[1]; outreaching WG
31.31 large] N[1]; *omit* WG
32.1 here] N[1]; *omit* WG
32.1–2 —could it ever return.]
N[1]; *omit* WG
32.7 chance-comer] N[1] (~ ∧ ~);
spectator WG
32.10 ever] N[1]; *omit* WG
32.29 -colored] V; -coloured WG
33.25 backward] V; backwards
WG
34.13 labor] V; labour WG
34.18 [1]It could . . . thing.] N[1];
omit WG
34.23 hunk] V; hunch WG;
bunch N[1]
35.2–4 This . . . others] N[1];
Shells WG
35.3 beer-bottle] V; ~ ∧ ~ N[1]
35.4 of an] N[1]; of WG
35.6 in] N[1]; on WG
35.13 backward] N[1]; backwards
WG
35.19 crackety-] N[1]; ~ ∧ WG
35.24 targets] N[1]; marks WG
35.27 back] N[1]; *omit* WG
35.34 battles] N[1]; battle WG

36.21–22 As file . . . prayed.]
N[1]; *omit* WG
37.15 rumor] V; rumour WG
38.36 splendors] N[1]; splendours
WG
38.39 ridge] N[1]; ridges WG
39.3 in] N[1]; on WG
40.2 number] N[1]; numbers WG
40.6; 44.18 color] N[1]; colour WG
40.12 And] N[1]; and WG
40.23 opened] N[1]; open WG
40.38–41.1 muscular, as a] N[1];
muscular—a WG
42.9 then] N[1]; *omit* WG
42.11 English:] N[1]; ~ , WG
42.15 him:] N[1]; ~ , WG
42.15 here;] V; ~ : WG; ~ ! N[1]
42.18 said:] N[1]; ~ , WG
42.20 apologize] N[1]; apologise
WG
42.21 re-fire] N[1]; refire WG
42.32–33 one of eight attacks
that the] N[1]; the most ferocious attack the WG
43.21 in] N[1]; on WG
43.25 charging] N[1]; *omit* WG
44.5 dusk] N[1]; dark WG

No. 7. THE BLUE BADGE OF COWARDICE

[The copy-text is N[1]: *New York Journal*, May 12, 1897, p. 3. Other full
texts collated are N[2]: *Chicago Tribune*, May 12, pp. 1,3; N[3]: Philadelphia
Press, May 12, p. 2; N[4]: San Francisco *Examiner*, May 12, pp. 1–2; N[5]:
Boston Globe, May 12, p. 7; N[6]: *Buffalo Evening News*, May 12, pp. 1,7. A
shorter text was also collated, N[7]: *Kansas City Star*, May 12, p. 2.]

45.4 soldiers'] $N(−N[1]); sol-
dier's N[1]
45.12 warships] N[2,4-5,7]; ~ ∧ ~
N[1,3,6]
45.15 summer] N[2,4-6]; Summer
N[1,3]
45.27 idiot∧] N[2,4-6]; ~ , N[1,3]
45.30 battleship] $N(−N[1,4]);
~ ∧ ~ N[1]; ~ - ~ N[4]
45.33 northern] $N(−N[1]);
Northern N[1]
45.36 warships] N[2-5]; ~ ∧ ~ N[1,6]
46.11 harbor] $N(−N[1]); horbor
N[1]

46.20 warships] N[2-5]; ~ ∧ ~ N[1];
~ - | ~ N[6]
46.24,30 Halmyros] N[3]; Salmyros
N[1-2,5]; Almyros N[4,6]
46.28 Turks] $N(−N[1]); Turgs N[1]
47.7 Oreos] V; Areos $N(−N[3]);
Arcos N[3]
47.29 Oreos] N[2]; Areos N[1,4-7];
Arcos N[3]
47.29 Halmyros] N[2-3]; Helmyros
N[1]; Almyros N[4-7]
48.14,15 panic] $N(−N[1]); paic
N[1]

No. 9. THE DOGS OF WAR

[The copy-text is N[1]: *New York Journal*, May 30, 1897, p. 18. The other text collated is N[2]: San Francisco *Examiner*, June 18, p. 4.]

52.1 him.] N[2]; $\sim_\wedge$ N[1]
52.8 you] N[2]; yon N[1]
52.9 "Well——"] N[2]; " $\sim$ "——
      N[1]

52.18 was$_\wedge$ altogether$_\wedge$] N[2]; $\sim$,
       $\sim$, N[1]

No. 10. STEPHEN CRANE TELLS OF WAR'S HORRORS

[The copy-text is N[1b]: *New York Journal* (out-of-town edition), May 23, 1897, p. 37. Other texts collated are N[1a]: *New York Journal* (Greater New York edition), p. 35; N[2]: *Chicago Tribune*, May 23, pp. 1–2; N[3]: Philadelphia *Press*, May 23, p. 2; N[4]: San Francisco *Examiner*, May 23, p. 14; N[5]: *Buffalo Evening News*, May 23, pp. 1,8. N[2] is the copy-text for passages not present in N[1]. N[1] without specification stands for N[1a-b].]

53.28–54.4 Above . . . to me.] N[2-5]; *omit* N[1]
54.2 leg$_\wedge$] N[3-5]; $\sim$, N[2]
*54.5 them] *stet* N[1b-5]
54.15 traveled] N[2-3,5]; travelled N[1]
54.19 shouting$_\wedge$] N[2,4]; $\sim$, N[1,3,5]
54.20 "Hurrah, hurrah] N[2,4]; "Hurrah! Hurrah N[1]; "hurrah, hurrah N[3]; "Hurrah! hurrah N[5]
54.23–29 I . . . it.] N[2-5]; *omit* N[1]
54.32 where] N[1a,2-5]; ere N[1b]
54.34–35 Smolenski's] N[1a,3-5]; Smolenki's N[1b]; Smolentz's N[2]
54.38–55.6 What . . . quay.] N[2-5]; *omit* N[1]
54.39 The *Journal's*] N[5]; Our N[2]; The N[3]; "The Examiner's" N[4]
*55.2,4,17–18,24 Stylidia] N[3-5]; St. Alida N[2]
55.5 While (*no* ¶)] N[3-5]; ¶ N[2]
55.12 Smolenski's] N[3-5]; Smolenksi's N[1]; Smolentz's N[2]
55.14 children$_\wedge$] N[2-5]; $\sim$, N[1]
55.16 fugitives$_\wedge$] N[3-5]; $\sim$, N[1-2]

55.17–35 As we . . . matter.] N[2-5]±; *omit* N[1]
55.23 Thermopylae] N[3,5]; Thermopylæ N[2]
55.26 safety,] N[3-5]; $\sim$ $_\wedge$ N[2]
55.27 Thermopylae] N[3-5]; the Thermopylæ N[2]
*55.36–37 particularly. Uprooted] N[2-3]; $\sim$, uprooted N[1,5]
55.37 [2]they] N[2-3]; *omit* N[1,5]
55.39–56.1 Among . . . loudly.] N[2-3,5]; *omit* N[1]
56.2 Our (*no* ¶)] N[2,4-5]; ¶ N[1,3]
56.14 anchor$_\wedge$] N[3-5]; $\sim$, N[1-2]
56.16 Incidentally,] N[2-4]; $\sim$ $_\wedge$ N[1,5]
56.18–19 Stylidia (N[2]: St. Alida) . . . midnight.] N[2-3,5]±; *omit* N[1,4]
56.33–34 to go] N[2-5]; to | to go N[1]
56.35 soldier.] N[2-5]; $\sim$ $_\wedge$ N[1]
56.37–38 We . . . Chalkis.] N[2-5]; *omit* N[1]
56.37 We (*no* ¶)] N[3-5]; ¶ N[2]
56.40 heroic] N[1a,2-5]; eroic N[1b]

No. 11. GREEKS WAITING AT THERMOPYLÆ

[The copy-text is N[1]: *New York Journal*, May 24, 1897, p. 10. Other texts collated are N[2]: *Chicago Tribune*, May 24, p. 2; N[3]: San Francisco *Examiner*, May 24, p. 1; N[4]: Philadelphia *Press*, May 24, p. 2.]

57.3   They (*no* ¶)] N[2-3]; ¶ N[1,4]
57.9   [1]have] N[2-4]; have been N[1]
57.10   stout-hearted] N[2-4]; ~ ∧ | ~ N[1]
57.14   I have (*no* ¶)] N[2-3]; ¶ N[1,4]
57.20   came . . . recognized] N[2-3]; come . . . recognize N[1,4]
57.26   There (*no* ¶)] N[2-3]; ¶ N[1,4]

57.26   let-up] N[2-3]; ~ ∧ ~ N[1,4]
57.29   I (*no* ¶)] N[2-3]; ¶ N[1,4]
58.4   trilobite] N[2-4]; triliobite N[1]
58.23   Leonidas'] N[2-3]; Leonidas's N[1]; Leonidas N[4]
58.27   do,] N[2-4]; ~ ∧ N[1]
58.28   full-blown] N[2-4]; ~ ∧ ~ N[1]

No. 12. MY TALK WITH "SOLDIERS SIX"

[The copy-text is N[1]: *New York Journal*, June 20, 1897, p. 18. The other texts collated are WG: *Westminster Gazette*, June 14, p. 2; June 15, pp. 1–2; N[2]: San Francisco *Examiner*, July 4, p. 6. The latter is a derived text without authority.]

*59.5–9   Here are . . . heeded.] WG; *omit* N[1]
59.14   *et seq.* Domokos] V; Domoko N[1],WG (–N[1] *at* 68.28,29)
*59.32   No.] WG; All but two. N[1]
59.35   But in] WG; In N[1]
59.35   they] WG; the officers N[1]
59.36   easy.] WG; ~ ? N[1]
59.36   And then . . . killed.] WG; *omit* N[1]
*59.37   "Well, . . . regiments."] WG; "No. It is very hard." N[1]
60.12   Greeks.] WG; ~ ! N[1]
60.20   there was] WG; I met N[1]
61.32   Larissa] WG; Larisa N[1]
61.32   Velestino] V; Velestine N[1]; Velestimo WG
61.33   are] WG; were N[1]
61.33   Lamia."] WG; ~ . ∧ N[1]
62.2   [2]flanked] WG; flnaked N[1]
62.8   Civil War] WG; civil war N[1]
62.23   in] WG; on N[1]
63.11   crowded∧] WG; ~ , N[1]
63.11   turns,] WG; turns to dis-

charge their human freight N[1]
63.12   carriages] WG; carriages wait N[1]
63.12   eight] WG; 8 N[1]
63.13   crowd . . . turns] WG; *omit* N[1]
*63.13–14   simply packed already] WG; already packed N[1]
63.15   were∧ . . . part∧] WG; ~ , . . . ~ , N[1]
63.16   quietly] WG; grimly N[1]
63.16   already] WG; almost N[1]
63.17   suffering—] WG; ~ , N[1]
63.22   white-clothed] WG; ~ ∧ ~ N[1]
63.22   swift-fingered] WG; ~ ∧ ~ N[1]
63.25   anyhow] WG; *omit* N[1]
63.37   an] WG; out a N[1]
64.16   euzonoi] WG; euzoni N[1]
64.17–18   —here] WG; where N[1]
64.20   place∧] WG; ~ , N[1]
64.22   cigarette] WG; cigareete N[1]
64.23   indeed∧] WG; ~ , N[1]

64.23   crime—] WG; ~ , N¹
64.37   "What] WG; ' ~ N¹
65.1   cannon] WG; cannons N¹
65.2   anyone] WG; ~ ₐ ~ N¹
65.18   mountains] WG; mountain N¹
65.24   gates] WG; gate N¹
65.28   He] WG; e N¹
66.2   well led] WG; led well N¹
66.8   were₄] WG; ~ , N¹
66.20,28   café] WG; cafe N¹
67.2   you;] WG; ~ — N¹
67.5   coffee-house] WG; cafe N¹
67.7   The (no ¶)] WG; ¶ N¹
67.9   type] WG; type that N¹
67.14   type₄] WG; ~ , N¹
67.15   -dumpties] N²; -dumptys N¹; -dumphties WG
67.16   -faced₄] WG; - ~ , N¹

67.16   gentle] WG; gently N¹
67.17   him₄] WG; ~ , N¹
67.17   trench, and stick₄] WG; ~ , ~ ~ , N¹
67.20   euzone] WG; Evzone N¹
67.21   wear the] WG; wear a N¹
67.22   close] WG; omit N¹
67.24   , when observing his wound,] WG; omit N¹
67.34   is] WG; omit N¹
67.36   À] WG; A N¹
68.8   Powers] WG; powers N¹
68.21   severe."] WG; ~ .' N¹
68.25   who] WG; whom N¹
68.26   Prince."] WG; ~ .' N¹
68.27   not he] WG; he not N¹
68.29–30   It is in] WG; In N¹
68.31   that] WG; omit N¹
68.33   experience."] WG; ~ .' N¹

No. 13. THE MAN IN THE WHITE HAT

[The copy-text is WG: *Westminster Gazette*, June 18, 1897, pp. 1–2. Other texts collated are N¹: New York *Sun*, July 11, sec. II, p. 2; N²: *Philadelphia Inquirer*, July 11, p. 28; N³: *Pittsburgh Leader*, July 11, p. 21; N⁴: Portland *Oregonian*, July 11, p. 19; N⁵: *Denver Republican*, July 11, p. 21.]

69.8   Constitution,] $N; ~₄ WG
69.9   royal palace,] $N; Royal Palace ₄ WG
69.16   forever] $N; for ever WG
69.19 *et seq.*   palace] $N; Palace WG
69.22–23   and₄ . . . session₄] $N; ~ , . . . ~ , WG
69.26   corner₄] $N; ~ , WG
70.6   molded] N²⁻⁵; moulded WG,N¹
70.17   appears₄] $N; ~ , WG
70.19   this hat] N¹⁻³,⁵; this head-gear WG; that hat N⁴
70.20   glowed,] N²,⁴⁻⁵; ~ — WG,N¹; ~ ₄ N³
70.28   pedestal. Suddenly] $N; ~ ; suddenly WG

70.30   speech₄] $N; ~ , WG
70.34   steps,] $N; ~ ₄ WG
70.35   Guard] N¹; guard WG,N²⁻⁵
70.37   palace₄] N²⁻⁵; ~ , WG,N¹
70.37   mountain₄] N²⁻⁵; ~ , WG, N¹
70.38   purple,] $N; ~ — WG
71.9   thing₄] $N; ~ , WG
71.11–12   and₄ . . . country-men₄] $N; ~ , . . . ~ , WG
71.24   The] $N; This WG
71.37   strength₄] $N; ~ , WG
72.8   um,] $N; ~ ! WG
72.9   Well——" He] N¹,⁴; ~ !"—he WG; ~ —." He N²,⁵; ~ —". He N³
72.12   incident₄] N¹⁻³,⁵; ~ , WG, N⁴

No. 14. A PORTRAIT OF SMOLENSKI

[The copy-text is MS: the untitled manuscript in Cora Crane's hand in the Special Collections of the Columbia University Libraries.]

72.30 No. 1] V; ~ ∧ ~ (possibly ~ ∧ ~ .) MS
72.31 extraordinary] V; exterordinary MS
73.9 Janina] V; Joanina MS
73.11 et seq. Velestino] V; Velestimo MS
73.11 notable] noteable MS
73.17 Smolenski's] V; Smolenskis' MS
73.20 monstrous] V; monsterous MS
73.21 don't] V; dont MS
73.24 assault] V; assult MS
73.32 size,] V; ~ . MS
73.33,35 altogether] V; altogeather MS
74.5 Athens] V; athens MS
74.6 swordsmanship] V; swordmenship MS
74.7 cavalry] V; cavelery MS
74.13 retrieved] V; retreived MS
74.14 military] V; millitary MS

74.15 them,] V; ~ ∧ MS
74.16 days'] V; days MS
74.16 safety] V; safty MS
74.24 it's] V; its MS
74.27 distinctly] V; distimctly MS
74.29 appearance] V; appearence MS
74.30 height] V; hight MS
74.33 duellist] V; duelest MS
74.34 quick,] V; ~ ∧ MS
74.35 bold,] V; ~ ∧ MS
74.38 there] the word is possibly 'then'
75.2 supreme] V; surpreme MS
75.6–7 made. He] V; made he MS
75.7 enormously] V; ennormously MS
75.9 beginning] V; begining MS
75.13 whose] V; whos MS
75.13 division] V; devision MS

No. 15. THE EASTERN QUESTION

[The copy-text is MS: the untitled manuscript in both Cora Crane's and Stephen Crane's hands in the Special Collections of Columbia University Libraries.]

[Cora's hand]
75.19 Britain] V; Britian MS
75.27 benefits] V; benifits MS
76.3 question.] V; ~ ∧ MS
76.3 profession] V; proffession MS
76.4 mystify] V; mystyfy MS
76.17 statesmanship] V; statesmenship MS
76.18 competent] V; compitent MS
76.19 Anybody] V; Any | body MS

76.19 between] V; betwen MS
76.22 Christian] V; christian MS
76.23 diplomacy] V; deplomacy MS
76.30 perceive] V; percive MS
76.31 manoeuverings] V; manoevurings MS
76.31 Sultan's] V; Sultans MS
76.34 [Stephen's hand begins at 'And yet']
76.37; 77.7 ambassadors] V; embassadors MS

77.26   kept] V; keep MS
77.35   maneuvres] V; man-|uvres
         MS
78.3–4   relinquishing] V; re-
         linguishing MS
78.12   *Camperdown*] V; Camper-
         down MS
78.17   Mediterranean] V; Medit-
         teranean MS

78.22   Mohamedans] V; Mo-
         hameddans MS
78.22   massacred] V; masacred
         MS
79.4   necessity] V; neccesity MS
79.31; 80.2   its] V; it's MS
80.1   salaaming] V; salamming
         MS

No. 16. THE TURKISH ARMY

[The copy-text is MS: the untitled manuscript in both Cora Crane's and Stephen Crane's hands in the Special Collections of Columbia University Libraries.]

[Cora's *hand*]
80.5   formidable] V; formidiable
         MS
80.11   wouldn't] V; wouldnt MS
80.16   Moslem] V; Moselem MS
80.17   military] V; milatery MS
80.23   army] V; Army MS
80.23–24 disreputable] V; dis-

         reptuable MS
80.25   Minister] V; minister MS
80.31   now] V; not MS
81.10   army] V; *possibly* Army
         MS
81.11   [Stephen's *hand begins at*
         'Moreover']

No. 17. STEPHEN CRANE'S OWN STORY

[The copy-text is N[1]: *New York Press*, Jan. 7, 1897, pp. 1–2. Other full texts collated are N[2]: Philadelphia *Press*, Jan. 7, pp. 1,3; N[3]: *Chicago Record*, Jan. 7, pp. 1–2; N[4]: New Orleans *Times-Democrat*, Jan. 7, p. 1; shorter texts collated are N[5]: *Chicago Tribune*, Jan. 7, p. 1; N[6]: Boston *Record*, Jan. 8, p. 3; N[7]: New Bedford *Mercury*, Jan. 9; N[8]: St. Paul Pioneer Press*, Jan. 9, pp. 1,4; N[9]: London *Morning Leader*, Jan. 20, p. 8; N[10]: London *Daily Mail*, Jan. 21, Daily Magazine section, p. 7. N[7-10] are derived texts, the readings of which are noted only in the Historical Collation. N[2] is the copy-text for passages not present in N[1].]

85.7   daylight$_\wedge$] *stet* N[1,5]; $\sim$, N[2-4]
85.11   munitions] N[2-3]; munition
         N[1]; ammunition N[4]
85.24   good-bys] V; goodbys N[1];
         good-byes N[2-3]; good byes N[4]
85.30   ¶ Then at] N[2-3,5] (N[5]: ¶
         At); *no* ¶ N[1,4]
85.31   good-bys] N[3,5]; good-|bys
         N[1]; good-byes N[2]; good byes N[4]
86.3   Somehow$_\wedge$] N[2-4]; $\sim$, N[1]
86.9   engines$_\wedge$] *stet* N[1,5]; $\sim$, N[2-4]

86.11   was] N[2-4]; were N[1]
86.15   ¶ But] N[2-3]; *no* ¶ N[1,4]
86.15   Jacksonville$_\wedge$] N[2-4]; $\sim$, N[1]
86.17   mud,] N[2-4]; $\sim$ $_\wedge$ N[1]
86.22   But (*no* ¶)] N[2-4] (N[3]:
         but); ¶ N[1]
86.24   triangle$_\wedge$] N[2-3]; $\sim$, N[1,4]
86.25   mud$_\wedge$] N[2-4]; $\sim$, N[1]
86.31   Southern] N[4]; southern
         N[1-3]
86.32   *Boutwell*$_\wedge$] N[2-4]; $\sim$, N[1]

86.33   pearl$_\Lambda$] N$^{2-3}$; $\sim$, N^{1,4}
86.33   Cheers (*no* ¶)] N$^{2-3}$; ¶ N^{1,4}
86.34   ships] N$^{2-3}$; ship N^{1,4}
86.37   ¶ At] N$^{2-3}$; *no* ¶ N^{1,4}
87.2   time$_\Lambda$ . . . reversed$_\Lambda$] N$^{2-3}$; $\sim$, . . . $\sim$, N^{1,4}
87.3   the grip of] N^4; the group of N^1; the grove of N^2; *omit* N^3
87.3–4   the *Commodore*] N$^{2-4}$; *omit* N^1
87.8   And (*no* ¶)] N$^{2-3}$; ¶ N^{1,4}
87.8   him$_\Lambda$] N$^{2-3}$; $\sim$, N^{1,4}
87.10   words] N$^{3-4}$; word N$^{1-2}$
87.11 ^{2}the] N^4; *omit* N$^{1-3}$
87.12   flee] *stet* N$^{1,3-4}$; flew N^2
87.12   bar,] N$^{2-3}$; $\sim$ $_\Lambda$ N^{1,4}
87.12–13   the throats of] N$^{2-4}$; *omit* N^1
87.13–38   The *Commodore* . . . streak.] N$^{2-4}$; *omit* N^1
87.18   On (*no* ¶)] N$^{3-4}$; ¶ N^2
87.21   In (*no* ¶)] N$^{3-4}$; ¶ N^2
87.21   pilot house] N$^{3-4}$; pilothouse N^2
87.27   mate] N^4; man N$^{2-3}$
87.30   he. But] N$^{3-4}$; $\sim$, but N^2
87.31   presently$_\Lambda$] N$^{3-4}$; $\sim$, N^2
87.33   A (*no* ¶)] N$^{3-4}$; ¶ N^2
87.36   airship] N$^{3-4}$; air | ship N^2
87.39   waters$_\Lambda$] N$^{2-3}$; $\sim$, N^{1,4}
87.39   *Commodore's* wake] N^4; Commodore N$^{1-3}$
88.1   phosphorescence] N$^{2-4}$; phosphoresence N^1
88.5   ¶ Being] N$^{2-4}$; *no* ¶ N^1
88.7   consequently] N$^{2-4}$; in consequence N^1
88.7   sleep,] N$^{2-4}$; $\sim$ $_\Lambda$ N^1
88.9   one's $_\Lambda$ self] N$^{2-3}$; one's-|self N^1; oneself N^4
88.13   ship] N$^{2-3}$; vessel N^1
88.14 ^{2}was] N^4; is N$^{1-3}$
88.16   that] N$^{2-4}$; *omit* N^1
88.17   awoke] N$^{2-4}$; woke N^1
88.18   galley,] N$^{2-4}$; $\sim$ $_\Lambda$ N^1
88.18   , feeling moved,] N$^{2-4}$ (N^4: $_\Lambda$ $\sim$ $\sim$ $_\Lambda$); *omit* N^1
88.18   he] N$^{3-4}$; *omit* N$^{1-2}$
88.19   sentiments.] N$^{2-4}$; $\sim$: N^1
88.19   said,] N$^{2-4}$; $\sim$ $_\Lambda$ N^1

88.20   ship$_\Lambda$] N$^{2-4}$; $\sim$, N^1
88.26   cook, "sometimes] N$^{2-3}$; $\sim$. "Sometimes N^1; $\sim$; "$\sim$ N^4
88.28   me$_\Lambda$ somehow$_\Lambda$] N$^{2-4}$; $\sim$, $\sim$, N^1
88.28   out$_\Lambda$] N$^{2-4}$ (N^2: $\sim$,); *omit* N^1
88.32   seaman$_\Lambda$ named Tom] N$^{2-4}$ (N^4: $\sim$, $\sim$ $\sim$); seaman, Tom N^1
88.35   weather-beaten] N$^{2-3}$; weatherbeaten N^1; beaten N^4
88.38   said:] N$^{2-4}$; $\sim$ $_\Lambda$ N^1
89.1   expeditions,] N$^{2-4}$; $\sim$ $_\Lambda$ N^1
89.3   went almost] N$^{2-4}$; almost went N^1
89.4   duty$_\Lambda$] *stet* N^{1,5}; $\sim$, N$^{2-3}$; deck, N^4
89.5–6   up the stairs] N$^{3-5}$; up the sairs N^1; upstairs N^2
89.8   I (*no* ¶)] N$^{2-4}$; ¶ N^{1,5}
89.10   pilot house] N^{2,4}; pilothouse N^1; $\sim$ - $\sim$ N^3; $\sim$ - | $\sim$ N^5
89.10   cried] N$^{2-4}$; he cried N^{1,5}
89.11   work?] N$^{2-3,5}$; $\sim$. N^{1,4}
89.12   language$_\Lambda$] *stet* N^{1,5}; $\sim$, N$^{2-4}$
89.12   started. Come] *stet* N$^{1,4-5}$; $\sim$; come N$^{2-3}$
89.14   then] N$^{2-4}$; *omit* N^{1,5}
89.15   fire-room] N$^{2-3,5}$; fireroom N^{1,4}
89.22   and$_\Lambda$] N$^{2-4}$; $\sim$, N^1
89.27   up to] N$^{2-3}$; up N$^{1,4-5}$
89.28   the water] N$^{2-4}$; water N^1
89.33   comprehend,] N$^{2-4}$; $\sim$ $_\Lambda$ N^1
90.2–3   fire-room] N$^{2-3}$; fireroom N^{1,4}
90.5   fire-room] N^3; fireroom N^{1,4}; $\sim$ $_\Lambda$ | $\sim$ N^2; $\sim$ - | $\sim$ N^5
90.6   forward$_\Lambda$] N$^{2-3}$; $\sim$, N^{1,4}
90.9–10   person] N$^{2-4}$; man N^{1,5}
90.10   . And] *stet* N^{1,5}; , and N$^{2-4}$
90.15   my] N$^{2-4}$; *omit* N^1
90.16   deed,] N$^{2-4}$; $\sim$ $_\Lambda$ N^1
90.17   This (*no* ¶)] N$^{2-4}$; ¶ N^1
90.18   valise$_\Lambda$] *stet* N^{1,4}; $\sim$, N$^{2-3}$
90.22   "What (*no* ¶)] N$^{2-4}$; ¶ N^1
90.28   ship$_\Lambda$] N$^{2-4}$; $\sim$, N^1

90.29   Higgins] (*no* ¶)] N[2-4]; ¶ N[1]
90.31   which$_\wedge$ . . . swear$_\wedge$] N[2-4];
   ~ , . . . ~ , N[1]
90.34   corduroy] N[2-4]; Corduroy
   N[1]
90.35   leaward] *stet* N[1]; leeward
   N[2-4]
90.37   We (*no* ¶)] N[2-5]; ¶ N[1]
91.1   "Well (*no* ¶)] N[2-4]; ¶ N[1]
91.4   death$_\wedge$] N[2-5]; ~ , N[1]
91.13   hammer-like] N[2-4]; ham-
   merlike N[1,5]
91.15   Afterward$_\wedge$] N[2-4]; ~ , N[1,5-6]
91.15   aft$_\wedge$] N[2-4]; ~ , N[1,5-6]
91.15   standing$_\wedge$] N[2-4,6]; ~ , N[1]
91.22   I (*no* ¶)] N[2-4]; ¶ N[1,6]
91.22   very] N[2-4,6]; *omit* N[1]
91.25   ¶ I] N[2-3,6]; *no* ¶ N[1,4-5]
91.31   over] N[2-4]; over to N[1]
91.36   off$_\wedge$] N[2-4]; ~ , N[1]; ~ ! N[5]
91.36   The (*no* ¶)] N[2-3,5]; ¶ N[1,4]
92.4   As (*no* ¶)] N[2-4]; ¶ N[1,5]
92.4,19   leaward] V; leeward N[1-4]
92.8   wind$_\wedge$] N[2-3]; ~ , N[1,5]; ~ . N[4]
92.9   roarers] N[4]; waves N[1,5];
   roars N[2-3]
92.14   laughed$_\wedge$] *stet* N[1,4]; ~ ,
   N[2-3]
92.14   said:] N[3]; ~ $_\wedge$ N[1]; ~ , N[2,4]
92.14   guy] N[2-4]; gag N[1]

92.17   I (*no* ¶)] N[2-3]; ¶ N[1,4]
92.17   forgotten] N[2,4]; forgot N[1,3]
92.25   rafts$_\wedge$] N[2-6]; ~ , N[1]
92.26   The (*no* ¶)] N[2-4,6]; ¶ N[1,5]
92.26   said:] N[2-3,6]; ~ , N[1,4]; ~ $_\wedge$
   N[5]
92.28   ¶ "Jump] N[2-3,6]; *no* ¶ N[1,4-5]
92.28   in,"] N[2-6]; ~ !" N[1]
92.28   here] N[2-4]; there N[1,5-6]
92.38   The (*no* ¶)] N[2-5]; ¶ N[1,6]
93.1   raft,] N[2-4,6]; ~ $_\wedge$ N[1]
93.13   silence$_\wedge$] *stet* N[1,4]; ~ , N[2-3]
93.24   But (*no* ¶)] N[2-6] (N[2,4]:
   but); ¶ N[1]
93.27   backward,] N[2-4,6]; ~ $_\wedge$ N[1]
93.28-29   line$_\wedge$ . . . [2]hand$_\wedge$] *stet*
   N[1,4]; ~ , . . . ~ , N[2-3,6]
93.30   [1]wild,] N[2,4-5]; ~ — N[1]; ~;
   N[3]
93.35   The (*no* ¶)] N[2-4]; ¶ N[1,6]
93.36   ¶ We] N[2-3,5]; *no* ¶ N[1,4,6]
93.39   She (*no* ¶)] N[2-5]; ¶ N[1,6]
94.4   words,] N[2-4,6]; ~ — N[1]
94.7   The (*no* ¶)] N[2-3]; ¶ N[1,4]
94.8   very] N[2-4]; *omit* N[1]
94.15   quarterdeck] N[2-3]; ~ $_\wedge$ ~
   N[1]; ~ - | ~ N[4]
94.19   to me seem] N[3-4]; seem to
   me N[1-2]
94.22   we] N[2-4]; he N[1]

No. 18. THE FILIBUSTERING INDUSTRY

[The copy-text is N[1]: *St. Paul Pioneer Press*, May 3, 1897, p. 3. Other texts collated are N[2]: *Denver Republican*, May 2, p. 21; N[3]: *Pittsburgh Leader*, May 2, p. 24.]

94.24   Fla.] V; Fla., May 1. N[1];
   Fla., April 27.— (Special Correspondence.) N[2]; Fla., April
   28, 1897. N[3]
94.31   midnight,] N[2-3]; ~ $_\wedge$ N[1]
95.11   talk] N[2-3]; a talk N[1]
95.18   administration,] N[2-3]; ~ $_\wedge$
   N[1]
95.28-29   seven hundred dollars]
   N[3]; $700 N[1-2]
95.32   place$_\wedge$] N[2-3]; ~ , N[1]

95.37   I am] N[2-3]; I'm N[1]
96.16   citizens$_\wedge$] N[2-3]; ~ , N[1]
96.17   shadows,] N[2-3]; ~ $_\wedge$ N[1]
96.24   marshals,] N[2-3]; ~ $_\wedge$ N[1]
96.25   Americo-] N[2-3]; American-
   N[1]
96.35   the *Dauntless*] V; "The
   Dauntless" N[1]; The Dauntless
   N[2-3]
96.36 *et seq.*   *Three Friends* . . .
   Commodore] V; "Three

Friends" . . . "Commodore" N[1]; Three Friends . . . Commodore N[2-3]

96.37   fact,] N[2-3]; $\sim_\wedge$ N[1]

96.37   is] V; are N[1-3]

97.1   the *Dauntless*] V; the "Dauntless" N[1]; the Dauntless N[2-3]

97.2   North] N[2]; north N[1,3]

97.2   *et seq.* sea-going] N[2-3]; seagoing N[1]

97.4   *Sea King*] V; "Sea King" N[1]; Sea King N[2-3]

97.20   to] N[3]; to be N[1-2]

97.21   reasons] N[2]; reason N[1,3]

97.23–24   oppressed] N[2-3]; attended N[1]

97.24   many] N[2-3]; *omit* N[1]

97.26   those] N[2-3]; these N[1]

97.34   busily] N[2-3]; buisily N[1]

98.1   *Boutwell*] V; "Boutwell" N[1]; Boutwell N[2-3]

98.5   Cuba$_\wedge$] N[2-3]; $\sim$, N[1]

98.9   his] N[2-3]; *omit* N[1]

98.12   course,] N[2-3]; $\sim_\wedge$ N[1]

98.18   sake,] N[2-3]; $\sim_\wedge$ N[1]

98.22   crime,] N[2-3]; $\sim_\wedge$ N[1]

98.39   employer$_\wedge$] N[2-3]; $\sim$, N[1]

99.5–6   of the . . . Some] N[2-3]; *omit* N[1]

99.5   process$_\wedge$] N[3]; $\sim$, N[2]

99.9   And] N[2-3]; And they have N[1]

99.13   Cubans,] N[2-3]; $\sim_\wedge$ N[1]

99.24   telegraph] N[3]; Telegraph N[1]

99.30   unconsciously] N[2-3]; unconseriously N[1]

No. 19. THE TERRIBLE CAPTAIN OF THE CAPTURED PANAMA

[The copy-text is N[1]: New York *World*, Apr. 28, 1898, p. 3. The other text collated is N[2]: Philadelphia *Press*, Apr. 28, p. 3.]

103.6   cables] N[2]; cabes N[1]

103.8   newspapers$_\wedge$] N[2]; $\sim$, N[1]

103.11   York$_\wedge$] N[2]; $\sim$, N[1]

103.14   things$_\wedge$] N[2]; $\sim$, N[1]

103.18   to-day,] N[2]; *omit* N[1]

103.19   has] N[2]; had N[1]

103.21   has lain] N[2]; lay N[1]

103.21   bay$_\wedge$] N[2]; $\sim$, N[1]

103.22   four $_\wedge$ armed] N[2]; $\sim$ - $\sim$ N[1]

104.14   ¶ The] N[2]; *no* ¶ N[1]

104.16   It (*no* ¶)] N[2]; ¶ N[1]

104.19   man$_\wedge$] N[2]; $\sim$, N[1]

104.21   hurt$_\wedge$] N[2]; $\sim$, N[1]

104.28   gangway] N[2]; gang N[1]

104.35   meantime] N[2]; mean time N[1]

104.37–38   logs. And] N[2]; logs, and N[1]

105.6   again$_\wedge$] N[2]; $\sim$, N[1]

105.7   happened.] N[2]; $\sim$; N[1]

105.9   But] N[2]; Put N[1]

No. 20. SAMPSON INSPECTS HARBOR AT MARIEL

[The copy-text is N[1]: New York *World*, May 1, 1898, p. 3. Other texts collated are N[2]: Philadelphia *Press*, May 1, p. 2; N[3]: *Chicago Tribune*, May 1, p. 2; N[4]: *Omaha Daily Bee*, May 1, pp. 1–2.]

105.11   via$_\wedge$] N[2-4]; $\sim$. N[1]

105.11   The (*no* ¶)] N[2-4]; ¶ N[1]

105.15   speaking$_\wedge$ off Havana$_\wedge$] N[2-4]; $\sim$, . . . $\sim$, N[1]

105.18   The (*no* ¶)] N[2-4]; ¶ Th N[1]

105.20; 107.25   torpedo $_\wedge$ boats] N[2-4]; $\sim$ - $\sim$ N[1]

105.22   dispatch] N[2-4]; despatch N[1]

105.29   entrance$_\wedge$] N[2,4]; $\sim$, N[1,3]

105.30 right$_\wedge$] N$^{2-4}$; $\sim$, N^1
105.30 stands] N$^{3-4}$; stand N$^{1-2}$
105.31 There (*no* ¶)] N$^{2-4}$; ¶ N^1
105.31 smooth $_\wedge$ bore] N^4; $\sim$ -
    $\sim$ N^1; smoothbore N^2; $\sim$ - |
    $\sim$ N^3
106.3 north.] N$^{2-4}$; $\sim$ $_\wedge$ N^1
106.13 smooth $_\wedge$ bores] N$^{2-4}$;
    $\sim$ - | $\sim$ N^1
106.21 steerage$_\wedge$] N^{2,4}; $\sim$, N^{1,3}
106.22 deck] N$^{2-4}$; gun deck N^1
106.22 "Man (*no* ¶)] N$^{2-4}$; ¶ N^1
106.22 battery."] N$^{2-4}$; $\sim$!" N^1
106.23 $_\wedge$The] N$^{2-4}$; " $\sim$ N^1
106.24 terrible$_\wedge$] N^{2,4}; $\sim$, N^{1,3}

106.31,33 after $_\wedge$ port] N$^{3-4}$;
    afterport N^1; $\sim$ - $\sim$ N^2
106.31,35 four] N$^{2-4}$; 4 N^1
106.32 yards,] N$^{2-4}$; $\sim$ $_\wedge$ N^1
106.34 Captain] N$^{2-4}$; Capt. N^1
106.35 after $_\wedge$ starboard] N$^{3-4}$;
    $\sim$ - | $\sim$ N^1; $\sim$ - $\sim$ N^2
107.6 Meanwhile$_\wedge$] N$^{2-4}$; $\sim$, N^1
107.8 today] N$^{3-4}$; $\sim$ - $\sim$ N$^{1-2}$
107.11 flagship.] N^{2,4}; $\sim$! N^{1,3}
107.15 However (*no* ¶)] N$^{2-4}$; ¶
    N^1
107.16 eyesight$_\wedge$] N^{2,4}; $\sim$, N^{1,3}
107.26 tonight] N$^{3-4}$; $\sim$ - $\sim$
    N$^{1-2}$

No. 21. INACTION DETERIORATES THE KEY WEST FLEET

[The copy-text is N^1: New York *World*, May 6, 1898, p. 3. Other texts collated are N^2: Philadelphia *Press*, May 6, p. 2; N^3: *Chicago Tribune*, May 6, p. 2; N^4: *Omaha Daily Bee*, May 6, p. 1.]

108.1 and] N$^{2-4}$; nd N^1
108.4 delay] N$^{3-4}$; the delay N$^{1-2}$
108.7 torpedo boats N$^{2-4}$; $\sim$ - $\sim$
    N^1

108.10 about] N$^{3-4}$; at all times
    N$^{1-2}$
108.15 long$_\wedge$] N^{2,4}; $\sim$, N^{1,3}

No. 22. STEPHEN CRANE'S PEN PICTURE OF C. H. THRALL

[The copy-text is N^1: New York *World*, May 8, 1898, p. 19. Other texts collated are N^2: Philadelphia *Press*, May 8, p. 2; N^3: *Omaha Daily Bee*, May 8, p. 1. The copy-text for 109.24–32 is N^3.]

108.29 open,] N$^{2-3}$; $\sim$ $_\wedge$ N^1
*108.30 think] *stet* N^1
109.3 ¶ As] N$^{2-3}$; *no* ¶ N^1
109.4 Ask (*no* ¶)] N$^{2-3}$; ¶ N^1
109.8 crying:] N$^{2-3}$ (N^3: $\sim$,);
    omit N^1
109.8 "Oh (*no* ¶)] N$^{2-3}$; ¶ N^1
109.10 calmed,] N$^{2-3}$; $\sim$ $_\wedge$ N^1
109.14 per] N$^{2-3}$; a N^1
109.16 They (*no* ¶)] N$^{2-3}$; ¶ N^1
109.16 left$_\wedge$] N$^{2-3}$; $\sim$, N^1
109.18 out] N$^{2-3}$; *omit* N^1

109.19 squadron] N$^{2-3}$; suadron
    N^1
109.22 chieftain] N$^{2-3}$; chieftan
    N^1
109.23 knows$_\wedge$] N$^{2-3}$; $\sim$, N^1
109.24–32 As to . . . knows.]
    N$^{2-3}$; *omit* N^1
*109.27 at] N^2; all N^3
109.28 reconcentrados] N^2; re-
    concentradoes N^3
109.35 day$_\wedge$] N$^{2-3}$; $\sim$, N^1
110.2 The (*no* ¶)] N$^{2-3}$; ¶ N^1

No. 23. WITH THE BLOCKADE ON CUBAN COAST

[The copy-text is N¹: New York *World*, May 9, 1898, p. 7. The other text collated is N²: Philadelphia *Press*, May 9, p. 3.]

110.17	harbor] N²; Harbor N¹	112.7	jacks∧] N²; ~ , N¹
110.23	horizon∧] N²; ~ , N¹	112.7	quarterdeck] N²; ~ - ~ N¹
110.24 *et seq.*	torpedo boat] N²; ~ - ~ N¹	112.10	upholding] N²; up holding N¹
110.24–25	vacillating∧] N²; vac-cillating, N¹	112.32–33	and∧ as usual∧] N²; ~ , ~ ~ , N¹
111.14	tubs] N²; tubes N¹	112.34	quarterdeck] N²; ~ | ~ N¹
111.18	gun-deck] N²; gundeck N¹	112.35	band∧] N²; ~ , N¹
111.26,34	inshore] N²; in shore N¹		

No. 24. SAYINGS OF THE TURRET JACKS IN OUR BLOCKADING FLEETS

[The copy-text is N¹: New York *World*, May 15, 1898, p. 33.]

113.1	"We've] V; ∧ ~ N¹	114.22	on] V; *omit* N¹
*113.6	gallows] *stet* N¹		

No. 25. HAYTI AND SAN DOMINGO FAVOR THE UNITED STATES

[The copy-text is N¹: New York *World*, May 24, 1898, p. 7.]

117.11	correspondent] V; core-spondent N¹	117.16	the] V; *omit* N¹

No. 26. NARROW ESCAPE OF THE THREE FRIENDS

[The copy-text is N¹: New York *World*, May 29, 1899, p. 25.]

119.19 death,] V; ~ ∧ N¹

No. 27. HOW SAMPSON CLOSED HIS TRAP

[The copy-text is N¹: New York *World*, May 27, 1898, p. 3. The other texts collated are N²: Philadelphia *Press*, May 27, p. 2; N³: *Chicago Tribune*, May 28, p. 13.]

121.2	dogging] V; dodging N¹⁻²	121.31	Channel] N²⁻³; channel N¹
121.2 *et seq.*	battleship] N²; ~ - ~ N¹	122.8	Havana∧] N²⁻³; ~ , N¹

122.15   A (*no* ¶)] N³; ¶ N¹⁻²
122.18   ¶ Our] N³; *no* ¶ N¹⁻²
122.37   Old] V; old N¹⁻²
122.37   Channel] N²; channel N¹
123.1   this] N²; the N¹
123.3   fine-bred] N²; fine lined N¹
123.7   torpedo ∧ boats] N²; ~ - ~ N¹

123.11   down∧] N²; ~ , N¹
124.15   Maria] V; Marie N¹˒³
124.16,25 Nicholas] N³; Nicolas N¹
124.19   southern] N³; Southern N¹
124.21,25 Channel] N³; channel N¹

No. 28. CHASED BY A BIG "SPANISH MAN-O'-WAR"

[The copy-text is N¹: New York *World*, July 3, 1898, supplement p. 4.]

125.4,13   Apollinaris] V; apol-linaris N¹

127.30; 128.2   despatch-boat] V; ~ ∧ ~ N¹

No. 29. IN THE FIRST LAND FIGHT FOUR OF OUR MEN ARE KILLED

[The copy-text is N¹ᵃ: New York *World* (city edition), June 13, 1898, p. 1. The other text collated is N¹ᵇ: New York *World* (out-of-town edition), June 13, pp. 1–2.]

129.5   Both were] N¹ᵇ; Each was N¹ᵃ
*129.6   500] N¹ᵇ; 550 N¹ᵃ

129.9   mutilated] V; mulitated N¹ᵃ
129.31   José] V; Jose N¹ᵃ

No. 30. ONLY MUTILATED BY BULLETS

[The copy-text is N¹: *Boston Globe*, June 16, 1898, p. 5. The other text collated is N²: Philadelphia *Press*, June 17, p. 2.]

131.3   Captain] N²; Capt N¹
131.6   Mauser] N²; mauser N¹
131.6   bullets∧] N²; ~ , N¹
131.9   fifteen] N²; 15 N¹
131.11   *et seq.* Lieutenant] N²; Lieut N¹
131.12 *et seq.*   Sergeant] N²; Sergt N¹

131.13   The (*no* ¶)] N²; ¶ N¹
131.13   twelve] N²; 12 N¹
131.14   ten] N²; 10 N¹
131.18   There (*no* ¶)] N²; ¶ N¹
131.18   was∧ . . . distinctly∧] N²; ~ , . . . ~ , N¹

No. 31. CRANE TELLS THE STORY OF THE DISEMBARKMENT

[The copy-text is N¹: New York *World*, July 7, 1898, p. 8. The other text collated is N²: *Boston Globe*, July 7, p. 2.]

132.1   white-duck] N²; ~ ∧ ~ N¹
132.34   pantomime] N²; panto-mine N¹

132.37 *et seq.*   General] V; Gen. N¹⁻²
133.16   bathtubs] N²; bath∧ tubs N¹

No. 32. THE RED BADGE OF COURAGE WAS HIS WIG-WAG FLAG

[The copy-text is N¹: New York *World*, July 1, 1898, p. 3.]

134.15 *et seq.* Captain] V; Capt.
  N¹
134.28 Colonel] V; Col. N¹
135.16 soldiers] V; sildiers N¹
135.27 symbol] V; sympol N¹

136.37 *et seq.* Lieutenant] V;
  Lieut. N¹
137.33 been] V; ben N¹
139.6 of the] V; o fthe N¹
140.23,25 Sergeant] V; Sergt.
  N¹

No. 33. STEPHEN CRANE AT THE FRONT FOR THE WORLD

[The copy-text is N¹: New York *World*, July 7, 1898, p. 8. The other text collated is N²: *Boston Globe*, July 7, p. 2.]

145.37 meantime] N²; ~ ∧ ~ N¹

No. 34. ROOSEVELT'S ROUGH RIDERS' LOSS DUE TO A GALLANT BLUNDER

[The copy-text is N¹: New York *World*, June 26, 1898, p. 2. The other text collated is N²: Philadelphia *Press*, June 26, p. 3.]

146.3 Lieutenant-Colonel] V;
  Lieut.-Col. N¹; Lieutenant Colonel N²
146.13–14 could not be] N²;

couldn't have been N¹
146.16 Spaniards] N²; Spanish
  N¹

No. 35. HUNGER HAS MADE CUBANS FATALISTS

[The copy-text is N¹: New York *World*, July 12, 1898, p. 4. The other texts collated are N²: Philadelphia *Press*, July 12, p. 3; N³: *Boston Globe*, July 12, p. 3.]

146.22–147.1 nurses, . . . war,]
  N²⁻³; ~ — . . . ~ — N¹
147.9 Santiago] N²⁻³; Sanitago
  N¹
147.11 bulletin ∧ board] N²⁻³;
  ~ - ~ N¹
147.34 districts∧] N²⁻³; ~ , N¹
*148.12 visions] *stet* N¹
148.29 fact,] N²⁻³; ~ ∧ N¹
148.32 ¶ Thus] N²⁻³; *no* ¶ N¹
148.34 And (*no* ¶)] N²⁻³; ¶ N¹
148.39 somewhat. Even] N²⁻³;
  ~ , even N¹

149.3 Colonel] N²; Col. N¹; Col∧
  N³
149.20 near] N²; nea N¹
149.32 coolly] N³; cooly N¹,²
149.35 our] N²,³; out N¹
150.1 Guatemalan] V; Guatamalan $N
150.4 marvelous] N²⁻³; marvellous N¹
150.5 firelight] N²⁻³; fire light N¹
151.40 away,] N²⁻³; ~ ∧ N¹
152.3 one half-hour] N²; ~ ∧ ~ ∧
  ~ N¹; ~ - | ~ ∧ ~ N³

No. 36. PANDO HURRYING TO SANTIAGO

[The copy-text is N¹: New York *World*, July 1, 1898, p. 2.]

152.18 *et seq.* General] V; Gen. N¹

No. 37. ARTILLERY DUEL WAS FIERCELY FOUGHT ON BOTH SIDES

[The copy-text is N¹: New York *World*, July 3, 1898, p. 2.]

153.7   shrapnel] V; sharpnel N¹

No. 38. NIGHT ATTACKS ON THE MARINES AND A BRAVE RESCUE

[The copy-text is N¹: New York *World*, July 16, 1898, p. 2.]

154.8 *et seq.* Lieutenant] V; Lieut. N¹

No. 39. STEPHEN CRANE'S VIVID STORY OF THE BATTLE OF SAN JUAN

[The copy-text is N¹ᵃ: New York *World* (city edition), July 14, 1898, p. 3. The other texts collated are N¹ᵇ: New York *World* (out-of-town edition), July 14, p. 3; N²: *Chicago Tribune*, July 14, p. 3; N³: *Boston Globe*, July 14, p. 4; HW: *Harper's Weekly*, July 23, p. 722, which is a derived text from N¹ and without authority.]

155.20   learn₎] N³; ~ , N¹

156.3   slow₎] N³; ~ , N¹

156.9   Paso] HW; Pasco N¹,³

156.16   and₎ . . . over₎] N³; ~ , . . . ~ , N¹

156.22   see] N³; seen N¹

156.28   meantime] N³; mean time N¹

157.3   Javanese₎] N³; ~ , N¹

157.7,14,19   blockhouse] N³; ~ - ~ N¹

157.34   but—— !] N³; ~ !—— N¹

*158.16   formulated] N³; fulminated N¹⁻²

158.20   yelled:] N²⁻³; ~ , N¹

158.31; 159.27   attachés] HW; attaches $N

159.13   many₎ others] N²⁻³; ~ , ~ N¹

160.1–8   After . . . bursting.] N³; *omit* N¹⁻²

160.1,5   guerillas] V; guerrillas N³

160.9–30   As . . . day.] N¹ᵇ,³; *omit* N¹ᵃ,²

160.32;161.1   Borrowe] N³; Burrowe N¹

160.37   has] N³; have N¹

161.2   crowd₎ . . . us₎] N³; ~ , . . . ~ , N¹

161.11–17   Somebody . . . high.] N¹ᵇ,³; *omit* N¹ᵃ,²

161.11   time₎] N³; ~ , N¹ᵇ

161.25   gray₎] N³; ~ , N¹

161.26   according] N³; acording N¹

161.30   intrenchments] V; entrenchments N¹,³

162.13–17   News . . . so on.]

N^{1b,3}; *omit* N^{1a}; The siege . . .
so on. *omit* N²
164.10–14 If he . . . regiments.]
N³; *omit* N¹⁻²
164.22–28 After . . . drug.]
N^{1b-3}; *omit* N^{1a}
165.20 d——] N³; —— N¹; *omit*
N²

165.30 bushwhacked] N²⁻³; bush-
wacked N¹
166.5–12 In the . . . wounded.]
N³; *omit* N¹⁻²
166.5 fifty-two] V; 52 N³
166.11 guerillas] V; guerrillas N³

No. 41. CAPTURED MAUSERS FOR VOLUNTEERS

[The copy-text is N¹: New York *World*, July 17, 1898, p. 17. The other text collated is N²: Philadelphia *Press*, July 17, p. 3.]

169.1 time_] N²; ~ , N¹
169.29 was] N²; were N¹
169.37–170.10 The experiences
. . . Spaniards.] N²; *omit* N¹
170.5 five hundred . . . a thou-

sand] V; 500 . . . 1000 N²
170.12 -Jorgensens_] N²; ~ , N¹
170.16 condition_] N²; ~ , N¹
170.18 -Jorgensen_] N²; ~ , N¹

No. 42. REGULARS GET NO GLORY

[The copy-text is N¹: New York *World*, July 20, 1898, p. 6. The other texts collated are N²: Philadelphia *Press*, July 19, p. 2; N³: *Boston Globe*, July 19, p. 6.]

171.30 them] N²⁻³; then N¹

173.30 forty] V; 40 $N

No. 43. A SOLDIER'S BURIAL THAT MADE A NATIVE HOLIDAY

[The copy-text is N¹: *New York Journal*, Aug. 15, 1898, p. 2. The other texts collated are N²: San Francisco *Examiner*, Aug. 15, p. 1; N³: *Kansas City Star*, Aug. 22, p. 5. N³ is derived from N¹ and without independent authority.]

174.11 women_] N²; ~ , N¹
175.6 raucous] N²; rancous N¹
175.12 -bronze,] N³; ~ . N¹; ~ —
N²
175.14 important] N²; importat
N¹

175.26 life——"] V; ~ " ——
N^{1,3}; ~ ." N²
175.30 cemetery wall_] N²; ~ ~ ,
N¹
175.39 clambake_] N²; ~ , N¹

No. 44. GRAND RAPIDS AND PONCE

[The copy-text is N¹: *New York Journal*, Aug. 17, 1898, p. 4. The other text collated is N²: *Kansas City Star*, Aug. 21, p. 5. The latter is a derived text without authority.]

176.22   Daiquiri] V; Baiquiri N$^{1-2}$ 178.25   Wisconsin] V; Michigan
177.36   is] N^2; it N^1 N$^{1-2}$

No. 45. THE PORTO RICAN "STRADDLE"

[The copy-text is N^1: *New York Journal*, Aug. 18, 1898, p. 3. The other text collated is N^2: *Kansas City Star*, Aug. 28, p. 5. The latter is a derived text without authority.]

181.13   Porto Ricans] N^2; ~ - ~   181.35   "Well] N^2; $_\wedge$ ~ N^1
         N^1 181.35   won't] N^2; wont N^1

No. 46. HAVANA'S HATE DYING, SAYS STEPHEN CRANE

[The copy-text is N^1: *New York Journal*, Sept. 3, 1898, p. 5. The other text collated is N^2: *Kansas City Star*, Sept. 11, p. 5. The latter is a derived text without authority.]

182.25   as of] V; of N$^{1-2}$ 184.2   Pasaje] V; Pasage N^1
183.13   Inglaterra] V; Ingleterra   184.5   luxuries$_\wedge$] V; ~ , N^1
         N$^{1-2}$

No. 47. STEPHEN CRANE SEES FREE CUBA

[The copy-text is N^1: *New York Journal*, Aug. 28, 1898, p. 43. The other texts collated are N^2: *Chicago Tribune*, Aug. 28, p. 4; N^3: San Francisco *Examiner*, Aug. 28, p. 17.]

184.28   The feeling] N$^{2-3}$; Feeling   can N^1
         N^1 185.3   ¶ Reports] N$^{2-3}$; *no* ¶ N^1
184.29   fear] N$^{2-3}$; fear anything   185.9   said:] N$^{2-3}$; ~ , N^1
         like N^1 185.33   soldiers. Their rifles are]
184.31   The Spaniards (*no* ¶)]   N$^{2-3}$; soldiers, their rifles N^1
         N$^{2-3}$; ¶ Spaniards N^1 *185.36 Betancourt$_\wedge$] N$^{2-3}$; ~ , N^1
185.2   the American] N$^{2-3}$; Ameri-

No. 48. STEPHEN CRANE FEARS NO BLANCO

[The copy-text is N^1: *New York Journal*, Aug. 31, 1898, p. 5.]

187.29   interests."] V; ~ . $_\wedge$ N^1 187.36   American$_\wedge$] V; ~ , N^1
187.30 $_\wedge$For] V; "~ N^1 188.2   it."] V; ~ . $_\wedge$ N^1

No. 49. STEPHEN CRANE'S VIEWS OF HAVANA

[The copy-text is N^1: *New York Journal*, Sept. 7, 1898, p. 7. The other text collated is N^2: *Chicago Tribune*, Sept. 7, p. 1.]

189.22 *et seq.* warship] N^2; war 190.13 from the] N^2; fro mthe N^1
ship N^1

No. 50. THE GROCER BLOCKADE

[The copy-text is N^1: *New York Journal*, Sept. 23, 1898, p. 6.]

191.20; 193.8 warships] V; war
ships N^1

No. 51. AMERICANS AND BEGGARS IN CUBA

[The copy-text is MS: the untitled manuscript in the Special Collections of Columbia University Libraries.]

193.23 absurd] V; adsurd MS 194.20 besiege] V; beseige MS
194.10 soon] V; soons MS

No. 52. MEMOIRS OF A PRIVATE

[The copy-text is N^1: *New York Journal*, Sept. 25, 1898, p. 26.]

194.28 a club] V; club N^1 195.18 won't] V; wont N^1
195.11 culprit.] V; $\sim$ $_\wedge$ N^1 *195.26 feckless] V; fetless N^1
195.11–12 search-lights] V; $\sim$ $_\wedge$ | 195.29 criminals] V; crim$_\wedge$ | inals
$\sim$ N^1 N^1

No. 53. THE PRIVATE'S STORY

[The copy-text is N^1: *New York Journal*, Sept. 6, 1898, p. 6.]

197.7 Chamberlain's] V; Cham-
berlin's N^1

No. 55. HOW THEY LEAVE CUBA

[The copy-text is N^1: *New York Journal*, Oct. 6, 1898, p. 6.]

200.28 love.] V; $\sim$, N^1 201.5 attitude] V; att tude N^1
200.35 for] V; or N^1

No. 56. STEPHEN CRANE IN HAVANA

[The copy-text is N¹: *New York Journal*, Oct. 9, 1898, p. 27.]

202.36   annoyance] V; annoynce
N¹

No. 57. HOW THEY COURT IN CUBA

[The copy-text is N¹: *New York Journal*, Oct. 25, 1898, p. 6. The other text collated is N²: San Francisco *Examiner*, Nov. 13, p. 4.]

204.23–29   A leathery . . . igno-   205.1–4   The moon . . . acci-
   rance.] N²; *omit* N¹   dent.] N²; *omit* N¹

No. 58. STEPHEN CRANE ON HAVANA

[The copy-text is N¹: *New York Journal*, Nov. 6, 1898, p. 26.]

206.17   ringer";] V; ~ ;" N¹   207.31   ingenuous] V; ingenious
207.1   small] V; smal N¹   N¹
                                           209.6   on;] V; ~ : N¹ (*uncertain*)

No. 59. "YOU MUST!"—"WE CAN'T!"

[The copy-text is N¹: *New York Journal*, Nov. 8, 1898, p. 6.]

209.18   warships] V; war ships N¹   210.32–33   manigua] V; manugue
209.28   Inglaterra] V; Ingleterra   N¹
   N¹   212.12   won't] V; wont N¹

No. 60. MR. CRANE, OF HAVANA

[The copy-text is N¹: *New York Journal*, Nov. 9, 1898, p. 6.]

214.2   Havana] V; Ha‸|vana N¹   215.1   probably] V; probab y N¹
214.24   just!" And] V; just! "And
   N¹

No. 63. OUR SAD NEED OF DIPLOMATS

[The copy-text is N¹ᵃ: *New York Journal* (Greater New York edition), Nov. 17, 1898, p. 6. The other text collated is N¹ᵇ: *New York Journal* (out-of-town edition), Nov. 17, 1898, p. 6.]

222.34–36   "It . . . me."] V; ‸ ~   223.21,22   warships] V; war ships
   . . . ~ . ‸ N¹   N¹
223.5 *et seq.*   won't] V; wont N¹

No. 64. MR. STEPHEN CRANE ON THE NEW AMERICA

[The copy-text is *The Outlook*, Feb. 4, 1899, pp. 12–13.]

228.6–7   whosoever] V; whomso-   228.21   humor] V; humour O
ever O

No. 66. THE LITTLE STILETTOS OF THE MODERN NAVY WHICH STAB IN THE
DARK

[The copy-text is N^1: *New York Journal*, Apr. 24, 1898, p. 21. The other
texts collated are N^2: *Denver Republican*, May 1, 1898, p. 30 (*derived from
N^1*); TMs: UVa.–Barrett typescript; E1: *Last Words*, Digby, Long & Co.,
London, 1902. Both TMs and E1 are derived texts with no independent
authority. TMs is divided into TMs(u), the original type, and TMs(c), the
ink revisions or corrections made by Cora.]

236.5   China,] TMs(c),E1; China, N^{1-2},TMs(u)
Chili, N^{1-2},TMs(u)   240.2   battened] N^2,TMs(c),E1;
236.26   Europe,] TMs(c),E1; ~ ∧   battered N^1,TMs(u)

No. 67. SOME CURIOUS LESSONS FROM THE TRANSVAAL

[The copy-text is N^1: *New York Journal*, Jan. 7, 1900, p. 27. The other text
collated is N^2: San Francisco *Examiner*, Jan. 7, p. 24.]

241.18   won't] N^2; wont N^1 242.8   decision∧ . . . parties∧]
241.33   world."] N^2; ~ . ∧ N^1 N^2; ~ , . . . ~ , N^1

No. 69. STEPHEN CRANE SAYS: THE BRITISH SOLDIERS ARE NOT FAMILIAR
WITH THE "BUSINESS END" OF MODERN RIFLES

[The copy-text is MS: the untitled manuscript in the Special Collections of
Columbia University Libraries. The other texts collated are N^1: *New York
Journal*, Feb. 14, 1900, p. 8; N^2: San Francisco *Examiner*, Feb. 14, p. 3.]

245.19.2   STEPHEN . . . RIFLES]   246.21   *et seq.*   familiar] N^{1-2}; fa-
N^1; *omit* MS; TOMMY ATKINS   milar MS
IGNORANT OF MODERN RI-   246.34   don't] N^{1-2}; dont MS
FLE'S POWER N^2 247.5   field-hospital] V; ~ ∧ ~
246.11   He said] N^{1-2}; Everybody   MS,N^{1-2}
thought he did. He said MS   247.9   shown] N^{1-2}; shone MS
246.16–17   acquaintances] N^{1-2};   247.12   cinematograph] N^{1-2};
acquintances MS   cineomatagraph MS
246.20   ceiling] N^{1-2}; cieling MS

No. 70. MANUSCRIPT FRAGMENT

[The copy-text is MS: the untitled manuscript in the Special Collections of Columbia University Libraries.]

247.15 Philippines] V; Phillipines MS

247.19 receive] V; recieve MS

No. 71. THE GREAT BOER TREK

[The copy-text is TMs(u): the uncorrected UVa.–Barrett typescript. The other texts collated are TMs(c): the corrected typescript; Co: *Cosmopolitan*, June, 1900, pp. 153–158. TMs(u) errors in spelling or punctuation which have been ink-corrected are not listed in the emends but will be found in the Alterations in the Typescript.]

247.22 *et seq.* government] Co; goverment TMs

248.3 *et seq.* between] Co; betwen TMs

248.5 fervors] Co; fervours TMs

248.9 seemed to be] V; seem to be TMs(u); seemed to have been TMs(c),Co

248.10 other's] Co; others TMs

248.12 privilege] Co; privilige TMs

248.24–25 fieldcornets] V; field cornets TMs,Co

248.32 bargain-] Co; bargin- TMs

248.37 any more] Co; anymore TMs

248.39 Spaniards] Co; Spainards TMs

249.1 natives] Co; natived TMs

249.2 French,] Co; ~ ∧ TMs

249.3 seventeenth century] Co; 17th-century TMs

249.9 Colony] Co; Coloney TMs

249.10 "bastards,"] Co; " ~ ", TMs

249.18 ridiculous] Co; rediculous TMs

249.18 described] Co; discribed TMs

249.21 rooms."] Co; ~ ". TMs

249.24 ten thousand] Co; 10000 TMs

249.25 colony,] Co; ~ ∧ | TMs

249.26 Government] V; goverment TMs; government Co

249.39 fifty-eight] Co; 58 TMs

250.1 in] TMs(c),Co; *omit* TMs(u)

250.9 fifty] Co; 50 TMs

250.10 Jan. But] V; ~ , But TMs; ~ , but Co

250.14–15 ten thousand pounds] Co; £10000 TMs

250.15 Governor] Co; govenor TMs

250.18 thirty-nine] Co; 39 TMs

250.19 *et seq.* received] Co; recieved TMs

250.31 heemraden." In] V; ~ ". I TMs; heemraden, and in Co

251.3 divided] Co; devided TMs

251.16 Natives] Co; Native TMs

251.16 them∧ [the Boers];] Co; ~ , (~ ~ ;) TMs

251.19 commando] Co; cammando TMs

251.21 their] V; his TMs,Co

251.22 After,] Co; ~ ∧ TMs

251.25 *et seq.* receive] Co; recieve TMs

251.25 goods,] Co; ~ ∧ TMs

251.36 passed] Co; passes TMs

251.36 July, 1828,] Co; ~ ∧ ~ ∧ TMs

252.1 Good,"] Co; ~ ʌ" TMs
252.2 Governor] Co; governor TMs
252.3 et seq. its] Co; it's TMs
252.3 Napier] V; Napeer TMs
252.4 Governor] V; governor TMs
252.13 1806,] V; ~ ʌ | TMs
252.14 five hundred] V; 500 TMs
252.16 favor] Co; favour TMs
252.16–17 (many . . . strongly)] Co; , ~ . . . ~ , TMs(u); (~ . . . ~ ,) TMs(c)
252.18 three million pounds] Co; £3000000 TMs
*252.19 colony. In 1834ʌ] V; colony, in 1834. TMs; colonyʌ in 1834. Co
252.21 throughout] TMs(c),Co; through TMs(u)
252.21 Empireʌ] V; ~ , TMs,Co
252.21 August,] Co; ~ ʌ TMs
252.21 was] Co; omit TMs
252.22 1st] V; 1st- TMs(u); on the 1st of TMs(c),Co
252.30,40 Order in Council] V (Orders at 252.39); order in council TMs (orders at 252.39)
252.32 etc.] V; etc. TMs
252.33 Order] V; order TMs
252.33 definite] V; difinite TMs
252.34 labor] V; labour TMs
252.35,39 Governor] V; governor TMs
252.38 of] V; od TMs
252.38 two thousand] V; 2000 TMs
253.6 each] Co; e;ch TMs
253.8 one hundred] Co; 100 TMs
253.8 Londonʌ] Co; ~ , TMs
253.10 purchased] Co; purchassed TMs
253.13 Council] Co; council TMs
253.17 colony] Co; coloney TMs
253.17–18 forty-five] Co; 45 TMs
253.20 Government] V; goverment TMs; government Co
253.21 five hundred] Co; 500 TMs
253.26 thirty] Co; 30 TMs
253.27 of Triechard's party]

TMs(c)(Triechards),Co; omit TMs(u)
253.28 savages] TMs(c),Co; savages of Triechard's party TMs(u)
253.28 Delagoa] Co; Delago TMs
253.30–31 twenty-six] Co; 26 TMs
253.32 height] V; hight TMs,Co
253.32 another] Co; anothet TMs
253.33–34 twelve and twenty thousand] Co; 12000 and 20000 TMs
*253.35 Under] V; (Dec. 1834) Under TMs; December, 1834, under Co
253.36 Kaffirland] Co; Kafirland TMs
254.3 Secretary of State . . . Colonies] Co; secretary of state . . . colonies TMs
254.4 April,] Co; ~ ʌ TMs
254.28 themselves] Co; them | selves TMs
254.29 Britain] Co; Brittain TMs
254.33–34 Boer looks] Co; Boers look TMs
254.35 him] Co; them TMs
254.36 unintelligible,] Co; ~ ʌ TMs
254.36 industry,] Co; ~ ; TMs
255.1–2 five thousand to ten thousand] Co; 5000 to 10000 TMs
255.5 Quathlamba] V; Quathtamba TMs,Co
255.5 Mountains] Co; mountains TMs
255.10 Moselekatse] V; Moselekatze TMs,Co
255.14 Potgieter,] Co; ~ ʌ | TMs
255.16 Moselekatse] V; Moseleketse TMs(u); Moseleketge TMs(c); Moselekatze Co
255.20 eleven others] V; 11 others TMs(u); a party TMs(c), Co
255.27 Matabele] Co; Matable TMs
255.29 fifty] Co; 50 TMs
255.30 entrance,] Co; ~ ʌ TMs

255.37 one hundred and fifty-five] Co; 155 TMs

255.37 one thousand one hundred] Co; 1100 TMs

256.1 food, while] TMs(c), Co; ~ . While TMs(u)

256.1 forty-six] Co; 46 TMs

256.8 et seq. Moselekatse] V; Moselekatze TMs,Co

256.8–9 One hundred and seven] Co; 107 TMs

256.9 forty] Co; 40 TMs

256.11 Matabele] TMs(c),Co; Matable TMs(u)

256.12–13 four hundred] Co; 400 TMs

256.13 seven thousand] Co; 7000 TMs

256.15 Vet (they . . . Winburg) which] Co [Winburg),]; Vet. They . . . Winburg. which TMs(u); Vet, (They . . . Winburg) which TMs(c)

256.18 6th,] Co; 6th- TMs

256.19 constitution,] Co; ~ ∧ TMs

256.20 nine] Co; 9 TMs

256.20 supreme] Co; surpreme TMs

256.23 landdrost] V; lauddrost TMs; landrost Co

256.24 Retief] TMs(c),Co; Mr. Retief TMs(u)

256.30–31 Uys, . . . leaders,] Co; ~ ∧ . . . ~ ∧ TMs

256.31 impressed] Co; inpressed TMs

256.32 Retief] Co; Riteif TMs

256.36 one hundred and thirty-five] Co; 135 TMs

256.37 Pieter] Co; pieter TMs

*256.37 Moselekatse] V; Mosega TMs,Co

256.37–38 twelve thousand] Co; 12000 TMs

256.39 nine days'] Co; 9 days TMs

257.1 one thousand] Co; 1000 TMs

257.4 forfeited] Co; fortified

TMs(u); forfieted TMs(c)

257.5 of] od TMs

257.6 Bechuanaland] Co; Betshuanaland TMs

257.16 allowed] Co; alowed TMs

257.17–18 et seq. Umkungunhlovu] V (after Theal); Umkunguhloon TMs,Co

257.25 seven hundred] Co; 700 TMs

257.26 Sikonyela,] V; Sikouyela ∧ TMs; Sikouyela, Co

257.26 Mantatee] V; mantater TMs; Mantater Co

257.27 Sikonyela] V; Sikouyela TMs,Co

257.30 February,] Co; Feb. TMs

257.31 seventy] Co; 70 TMs

257.31 thirty] Co; 30 TMs

257.34 et seq. Umzimvubu] V (after Theal); Umzimvooboo TMs,Co

258.3–4 Blaauwkrans] V; Blaanwkrauz TMs,Co

258.10–11 eight hundred] Co; 800 TMs

258.18 preferred] Co; prefered TMs

258.19 November, 1838,] Co; Nov.∧ 1838∧ TMs

258.20 Pretorius] Co; Pretorias TMs

258.21 Commandant-General] Co; ~ ∧ ~ TMs

258.21–22 four hundred and sixty-four] Co; 464 TMs

258.25 fifty-seven] Co; 57 TMs

258.30 defeat] V (after Fryckstedt); omit TMs,Co

258.36–37 ten thousand or twelve thousand] Co; 10000 or 12000 TMs

258.37 December 16th,] V; Dec. 16th- TMs; December 16, Co

259.2 three thousand] Co; 3000 TMs

259.3 crimson] Co; crimsom TMs

259.4 has] Co; had TMs

259.8 et seq. Panda] V (after Fryckstedt); Pauda TMs,Co

259.11   January, 1840,] Co; Jan.
    1840., TMs
259.12   four thousand] Co; 4000
    TMs
259.12–13   February 10th,] Co;
    Feb. 10th- TMs
259.14–15   conquerors] Co; con-
    quorors TMs
259.22   Umfolosi] V; Imfolosi
    TMs,Co
259.23   Rivers] Co; rivers TMs
259.24   national] Co; National
    TMs
259.24   "a] TMs(c),Co; "A
    TMs(u)
259.24–25   twenty-one] Co; 21
    TMs

259.25   'hurrah'] V; "~" TMs;
    ∧ ~ ∧ Co
259.27–28   'Thanks . . . vic-
    tory!' "] Co; "~ . . . ~ !" TMs
259.31   nomadic] Co; namadic
    TMs
259.34   Napier,] Co; ~ ∧ TMs
260.1   12th,] V; 12th∧ TMs; 12,
    Co
260.5   (1)] V; (1.) TMs
260.10   (2)] V; (2.) TMs
260.10   the severe] TMs(c); se-
    vere TMs(u)
260.17   odium] V; odeum TMs
260.20   favor] V; favour TMs
260.20   foresee] V; forsee TMs
261.7   in peace] V; inpeace TMs

No. 72. THE TALK OF LONDON

[The copy-text is N[1]: *New York Journal*, Mar. 11, 1900, p. 27. The other
text collated is N[2]: San Francisco *Examiner*, Mar. 11, p. 27.]

262.24   Algeria,] N[2]; ~ ∧ N[1]   263.16   Ireland∧] N[2]; ~ , N[1]

No. 3. IMOGENE CARTER'S ADVENTURE AT PHARSALA

[The copy-text is MS: the untitled manuscript in both Cora Crane's and
Stephen Crane's hands in the Special Collections of Columbia University
Libraries.]

[Crane's *hand*]

269.5–6,22   Pharsala] V; Phersala
    MS
269.8   evidently] V; ev-|-dently
    MS
269.20   me.] V; ~ ∧ MS
269.21   ¹coffee-house] V; ~ ∧ ~
    MS
269.21   principal] V; principle
    MS
269.23   wouldn't] V; wouldnt MS
269.27   dingy] V; dingey MS
[269.28   Cora's *hand begins* '¶ At']
270.8   cognac] V; coniag MS
270.9   A] V; a MS
270.10–11   furniture. It] V; ~ , it
    MS

270.11   lighted] V; light MS
270.18   returned] V; return MS
270.19   Pharsala] V; Phasala MS
270.20   the coffee-house∧] V;
    coffee house- MS
270.22   the pool] V; pool MS
270.22   He] V; he MS
270.22   patroled] V; paroled MS
270.23   Every] V; evy MS
270.24   the door,] V; door∧ MS
270.24   He] V; he MS
270.24–25   the door] V; door MS
270.25   piling] V; pilling MS
270.25   Several] V; several MS
270.27   receive] V; recieve MS

270.29   Finally] V; finally MS
270.29   When] V; when MS
270.30   came,] V; ~ – MS
270.31   the door,] V; door – MS
270.31   caught] V; cought MS
270.33   rifle,] V; ~ – MS
270.34   It] V; it MS
270.35   awakened] V; awaken MS
270.37   porch,] V; poarch – MS
270.38   mutter. Finally] V; ~ , finally MS
270.39   "The Gendarmes] V; "the Gendarms MS
271.1   opened] V; open MS
271.1   At] V; at MS
271.3   a quarter] V; quater MS
271.3   up,] V; ~ – MS
271.4   the floor] V; floor MS
271.4   embarrassing] V; embarressing MS
271.8–9 respectful] V; resptful MS
271.9   As] V; as MS
271.9   woman, they] V; ~ – They MS
271.10   astonishment,] V; ~ – MS
271.11   -quarters the] V; -quaters. The MS
271.11   sleeps] V; sleep MS
271.13   the village,] V; village_∧ MS

271.14–15 the balcony] V; balcony MS
271.15   superb] V; suppurb MS
271.15–16 Caesar] V; Ceasar MS
271.16   C.—] V; ~ _∧ – MS
271.16   me,] V; ~ – MS
271.17   On] V; on MS
271.18   Velestino] V; Velestimo MS
271.20   fifty,] V; ~ – MS
271.21   Occasionally] V; occasiony MS
271.21   cavalryman] V; cavelryman MS (*possibly* caveleryman)
271.23   approached] V; approachd MS
271.23   Infantry] V; infanty MS
271.23   soldiers] V; soldirs MS
271.24   going_∧] V; ~ – MS
271.24   road,] V; ~ _∧ MS
271.25   On] V; on MS
271.28   Just] V; just MS
271.29   queerly] V; querly MS
271.29   storks'] V; storks MS
271.30   noises_∧] V; ~ – MS
271.33   road_∧] V; ~ – MS
271.34   quarters] V; quaters MS
271.34   Prince,] V; ~ . MS
271.36   benefit] V; benifit MS
271.36   tourists] V; tourist MS

NO. 4. IMOGENE CARTER'S PEN PICTURE OF THE FIGHTING AT VELESTINO

[The copy-text is N[1]: *New York Journal*, May 10, 1897, p. 3. The other text collated is N[2]: San Francisco *Examiner*, May 10, p. 3.]

272.9   squeak] N[2]; escape N[1]   272.15   the Turks] N[2]; Turks N[1]

GREAT BATTLES OF THE WORLD

THE BRIEF CAMPAIGN AGAINST NEW ORLEANS

[The copy-text is L: *Lippincott's Magazine*, LXV (Mar., 1900), pp. 405–411. The other texts collated are A1: *Great Battles of the World*, J. B. Lippincott, Philadelphia, 1901; E1: *Great Battles of the World*, Chapman & Hall, London, 1901. E1 is a derived text without authority.]

278.7   battle—] A1; ~ ,— L
279.21 *et seq.*   *Carolina*] E1; Carolina L,A1
279.32   marshals] A1; marshall L
280.13   ²a] A1; *omit* L
281.5 *et seq.*   *Louisiana*] E1; Louisiana L,A1
283.24   thousands.] A1; ~ ∧ | L
*284.6   begun] *stet* L
284.37   troops] A1; troop L
285.3–4   four . . . sixty-four] A1; 4,264 L

285.5   three . . . thirty-three] A1; 333 L
285.6   four . . . thirteen] A1; 4 . . . 13 L
285.7   eight thousand] A1; 8,000 L
285.7   nine hundred] A1; 900 L
285.8   fourteen hundred] A1; 1400 L
285.8   five hundred] A1; 500 L
285.16   January] A1; December L

THE STORMING OF BADAJOZ

[The copy-text is MS: manuscript in the Barrett Collection, University of Virginia, inscribed by Edith Richie with the exception of 288.25–34 'The . . . infantry' which is in a strange hand. The other texts collated are L: *Lippincott's Magazine*, LXV (Apr., 1900), pp. 579–585; A1: *Great Battles of the World*, J. B. Lippincott, Philadelphia, 1901; E1: *Great Battles of the World*, Chapman & Hall, London, 1901. E1 is a derived text without authority. Only the earliest source for an emendation is given here; full details are in the Historical Collation.]

286.0 *et seq.*   Badajoz] E1; Badajos MS,L,A1
286.3   Rodrigo] E1; Rodrigues MS,L,A1
286.7; 287.5   Parliament] L; parliament MS
*286.11   Congress] L; congress MS
*286.15   supplies] *stet* MS
286.22–23   one hundred thousand] L; 100,000 MS
287.12,15   Elvas] V; Eloas MS+
287.13   two-thirds] L; ~ ∧ ~ MS
287.14   prevent a] L; intercept the MS
287.15   advanced,] L; ~ ∧ MS
287.16   made] L; performed MS
287.28   five thousand] L; 5,000 MS
287.30–31   three hundred feet] L; 300 ft. MS
287.32–33   bomb-proof] L; ~ ∧ ~ MS
288.2   two hundred yards] L; 200 yds. MS

288.11–12   one hundred and sixty yards] L; 160 yds∧ MS
288.15–16   yards . . . feet] L; yds∧ . . . ft. MS
288.16   four thousand feet] L; 4,000 ft∧ MS
288.25   The infantry] L; The Infantry MS
288.26   cavalry] L; Cavalry MS
288.29   Portuguese] L; Portugese MS
288.32   commander,] L; Commander∧ MS
288.36–37   three hundred] L; 300 MS
289.1   besiegers] L; beseigers MS
289.19,33   Picurina] V; Picerina MS+
289.20 *et seq.*   five hundred] L; 500 MS
289.21 *et seq.*   fifty] L; 50 MS
289.22   nine] L; 9 MS
*289.24   blared] *stet* MS
289.25   palisades] L; palissades MS

289.31 *King Lear*] E1; King Lear MS,L; "King Lear" A1

289.35–36 Fifty-second] L; 52nd MS

289.36 Second Battalion] L; 2nd batallion MS

290.5 eighty-six] L; 86 MS

290.8 general] A1,E1; General MS,L

290.9 Picurina] V; Picarina MS; Picerina L+

290.10 one] L; on MS

290.15 northern] L; eastern MS (*interlined below deleted* southern)

290.20 Forty-eight] L; ∼ ∧ ∼ MS

290.22 defences] L; southern defences MS

290.39–291.1 eighteen . . . feet] L; 18 to 24 ft∧ MS

291.3 Vincente,] L; ∼ ∧ MS

291.4 *et seq.* Fourth] L; 4th MS

291.11 castle] L; Castle MS

291.17 ten] L; 10 MS

291.18 Forty-eighth] L; 48th MS

291.18 *et seq.* First] L; 1st MS

291.19 *et seq.* Battalion] L; batallion MS

291.19 Regiment] V; regiment MS+

291.25 bayoneted] L; bayonetted MS

291.26 besieged] L; besieged and also the besieged MS

*291.32 Lieutenant] *stet* MS+

291.35 followed] L; imitated MS

292.9 bags full] L; bag's-full MS

292.15 enemy,] L; ∼ ∧ MS

*292.16 made plain] *stet* MS

292.18–19 besieged and besiegers] L; beseiged and beseigers MS

292.20 amounted] L; amount MS

292.26–27 one hundred fusiliers] L; 100 fusileers MS

292.30 sword-blades] L; ∼ ∧ ∼ MS

292.37 *et seq.* Forty-third] L; 43rd MS

292.38–39 Infantry),] L; ∼) ∧ MS

293.9 one hundred] L; 100 MS

293.11 inside,] V; ∼ ∧ MS+

293.21 Pardaleras] L; Pardeleras MS

293.26 thirty feet] L; 30 ft∧ MS

293.31 bastions. General] L; ∼ (∼ MS

294.2 became] L; turned into MS

THE SIEGE OF PLEVNA

[The copy-text is L: *Lippincott's Magazine*, LXV (May, 1900), pp. 759–765. The other texts collated are A1: *Great Battles of the World*, J. B. Lippincott, Philadelphia, 1901; E1: *Great Battles of the World*, Chapman & Hall, London, 1901. E1 is a derived text without authority.]

295.7 mere village of] A1; village of a mere L

*295.7 seventeen hundred] *stet* L+

295.8 Widdin] V; Widen L; Widin A1,E1

295.16 *et seq.* Krüdener] V; Krudener L+

295.17 Nikopolis] A1; Nicopolis L

296.38 re-enforced] A1; reinforced L

297.11 telegraphed] A1; telegraphed him L

*297.18 *et seq.* Schakofskoy] V; Schahofskoy L+

298.17 generals] A1; Generals L

299.11,14 Zotoff] V; Totoff L+

300.11 men. The . . . anticipating] A1; men, but the victory was fruitless. Anticipating L

300.14 success] A1; victory L

300.16 Schnidnikoff] V; Schmidnikoff L+

301.5 over] A1; *omit* L

301.32 2polite] A1; a polite L

THE BATTLE OF BUNKER HILL

[The copy-text is L: *Lippincott's Magazine*, LXV (June, 1900), pp. 924–932. The other texts collated are A1: *Great Battles of the World*, J. B. Lippincott, Philadelphia, 1901; E1: *Great Battles of the World*, Chapman & Hall, London, 1901. E1 is a derived text without authority.]

303.17–18   when on . . . news]
A1; when he was told this
news on his arrival in May L
303.29 *et seq.   Cerberus*] E1; Cerberus L,A1
*304.39–305.2   Prescott . . . lanterns,] A1; With two sergeants
carrying dark lanterns, Prescott walked at their head L
305.29 *et seq.   Lively*] E1; Lively
L,A1
305.29–30   *Somerset . . . Glasgow . . . Falcon . . . Symmetry*] E1; Somerset . . . Glasgow . . . Falcon . . . Symmetry L,A1
306.15   him:] V; ~, — L, A1;
~ₐ — E1
306.22   generals] A1; Generals L
306.28–29   insolently] A1; impudently L
306.29   one;] A1; ~ : L
306.32   its] A1; it L

306.37–38   Brigadier-General]
A1; ~ ₐ ~ L
307.5   Chester] A1; Chester's L
307.22–24   pageant— . . .
train—] V; ~ , — . . . ~ ,
— L+
307.30–31   however— . . .
Yankees—] V; ~ , — . . . ~ ,
— L+
*307.38   president] A1; the President L
*308.17; 309.2; 309.12; 311.16
breast-work] V; breastwork L+
308.36   met] A1; heard L
308.37   shouting:] V; ~ , —L,A1;
~ ₐ —E1
*309.7   them] *stet* L
310.29   straggled] A1; staggered
L
311.10   bravely:] E1; ~ , — L,A1
312.21–29   The most . . . forever."] A1; *omit* L

"VITTORIA"

[The copy-text is L: *Lippincott's Magazine*, LXVI (July, 1900), pp. 140–150. The other texts collated are A1: *Great Battles of the World*, J. B. Lippincott, Philadelphia, 1901; E1: *Great Battles of the World*, Chapman & Hall, London, 1901. A1 is the copy-text for passages not present in L. E1 is derived and without authority.]

313.2   Badajoz] E1; Badajos L,A1
313.13–15   But . . . changed.]
A1; *omit* L
313.27–314.5   The winter . . .
efficiency.] A1; *omit* L
315.15   and horse] A1; *omit* L
315.38   general] A1; General L
316.8   movement] A1; moment L
316.24   ²the] A1; *omit* L
317.1–33   The incident . . . British.] A1; *omit* L

317.7   ₐvamos,ₐ] E1; "*vamos*," A1
317.16–18   Portugal— . . . government—] V; ~ , — . . . ~ ,
— A1; ~ , . . . ~ ; E1
318.4–12   He was . . . nothing.]
A1; Wellington's army now
numbered seventy thousand
men, of whom forty thousand
were British. L
318.13   ¶ There] A1; *no* ¶ L
318.19   great] A1; *omit* L

318.23   really] A1; *omit* L
318.24–28   The weak . . . chief.] A1; *omit* L
318.35 *et seq.*   Esla] V; Elsa L+
319.17   an exalted] A1; a L
*319.20   rose] *stet* L
*320.10   hundred] V; thousand L+
320.10–11   soldiers, the last to leave,] A1; soldiers L
322.15 *et seq.*   Arinez] V; Ariniz L+
322.17–21   The early . . . conflict."] A1; *omit* L
*322.22   spectacle] A1; spectacle on the morning of June 21st L
*322.23   their] *stet* L
322.28–38   In his . . . front."] A1; *omit* L

323.1,4   Morillo] V; Murillo L+
*323.24   had crossed Tres] *stet* L
323.38   Light Division] E1; light division L,A1
324.13   -camp:] E1; ~ , — L,A1
324.22–28   Maxwell . . . battle."] A1; *omit* L
*324.32–34   cannon-balls . . . furrows] *stet* L
325.4   hill] A1; Hill L
325.27   back] A1; *omit* L
327.36–328.3   Alison . . . overthrow."] A1; *omit* L
328.11   -field!] A1; ~ . L
328.19   general] A1; General L

A SWEDE'S CAMPAIGN IN GERMANY
I. LEIPZIG

[The copy-text is L: *Lippincott's Magazine*, LXVI (Aug., 1900), pp. 299–311. The other texts collated are A1: *Great Battles of the World*, J. B. Lippincott, Philadelphia, 1901; E1: *Great Battles of the World*, Chapman & Hall, London, 1901. A1 is the copy-text for passages not present in L. E1 is a derived text without authority.]

329.1–335.10   At . . . Europe.] A1; *omit* L
332.34 *et seq. to* 335.10   King] V; king A1,E1
334.11–12   her— . . . honorable—] V; ~ , — . . . ~ , — A1,E1
334.23 *et seq.*   Elector] V; elector A1,E1
335.10   The (*no* ¶)] A1; ¶ L
335.12   blot out] A1; cancel L
335.12   now] A1; *omit* L
335.15   Gustavus] A1; Gustavus Adolphus, King of Sweden, L
335.18   Gustavus] A1; Gustavus Adolphus L
335.26   generals] A1; Generals L
335.30   Lübeck] V; Lubeck L+
335.30   Ratzeberg] V; Ratzeburg L+
335.36   brute] A1; *omit* L

336.1–2   , and which . . . whatever.] A1; *omit* L
336.10   Gustavus's] A1; Gustavus' L
336.31–32   and a foe . . . Germany] A1; *omit* L
336.35   he] A1; Gustavus L
337.2 *et seq.*   de] A1; De L
337.12   to openly] A1; openly to L
337.19   was free to] A1; could L
338.12–19   There . . . me."] A1; *omit* L
339.12–14   A painting . . . Gardie.] A1; *omit* L
339.16–17   Wallenstein— . . . Friedland—] V; ~ , — . . . ~ , — L+
339.19   now being] A1; being now L
340.25   Leipzig] E1; Leipsic L,A1

340.35–341.24 In July . . .
Ruthven.] A1; *omit* L
340.37 Marquis] V; marquis
A1,E1
340.39 King] V; king A1,E1
341.13 reads:] V; ~ , — A1,E1
341.23 King's] V; king's A1,E1
341.26 the King] A1(king);
Gustavus L
342.4–7 The truth . . . him.]
A1; *omit* L
342.16 *your*] A1; your L
342.30–31 He once . . . yours."]
A1; *omit* L
*343.4 authority] A1; ability L
343.4 great] A1; *omit* L
343.17–18 , who . . . cardinal]
A1; *omit* L
343.18 , among other arguments,] A1; *omit* L
343.18 Cardinal] V; cardinal
A1,E1
343.23–344.15 Ferdinand . . .
Catholic.] A1; *omit* L
343.37–38 Emperor] V; emperor
A1,E1
344.17 personally] A1; *omit* L
344.26–345.2 This horrible . . .
chaste.] A1; *omit* L

345.3 Field . . . but he] A1;
This old man L
345.12,22–23 Frankfort-on-the-
Oder] E1; ~ ∧ ~ ∧ ~ ∧ ~ L,A1
345.21 Croation] A1; *omit* L
346.1 Landsberg-on-the-Warth]
E1; ~ ∧ ~ ∧ ~ ∧ ~ L,A1
346.11–13 It is . . . force.] A1;
omit L
346.12 Elector] V; elector A1,E1
348.21 idea—] V; ~ ; L; ~ , —
A1,E1
349.14,30 Torgau] A1; Jorgau L
349.36 queen] A1; Queen L
350.6–7 Havelberg] A1; Havelburg L
351.9 manner] A1; matter L
351.20 horse—] A1; ~ , — L
351.20 -bitten"—] V; ~ ," — L+
351.28 Fürstenberg] V; Furstenburg L; Furstenberg A1,E1
*351.31 the rear] A1; their rear L
351.34–35 Saxons— . . .
much—] V; ~ , — . . . ~ ,
— L+
352.4 "They (*no* ¶)] A1; ¶ L
352.13 their] A1; his L
*352.19 on] *stet* L

A SWEDE'S CAMPAIGN IN GERMANY
II. LÜTZEN

[The copy-text is L: *Lippincott's Magazine*, LXVI (Sept., 1900), pp. 462–
475. The other texts collated are A1: *Great Battles of the World*, J. B.
Lippincott, Philadelphia, 1901; E1: *Great Battles of the World*, Chapman &
Hall, London, 1901. A1 is the copy-text for passages not present in L. E1
is a derived text without authority.]

353.0 *et seq.* Lützen] V; Lutzen
L+
353.1 Tilly's] A1; General Tilly's
L
353.1 fortunes] A1; fortune L
353.7 Gustavus] A1; Gustavus
Adolphus, King of Sweden L
353.11 or] A1; nor L
353.16 he] A1; Gustavus L
354.11 Leipzig] A1; the battle of
Leipzig L

354.13–14 Königshofen] V;
Konigshofen L+
354.37 now] A1; *omit* L
354.39–355.4 The Count . . .
service.] A1; *omit* L
355.17 More (*no* ¶)] A1; ¶ L
355.36 queen] A1; Queen L
356.11–12 a space of rest] A1;
omit L
356.14 splendors] A1; splendor
L

356.22   ambassador] A1;
    Ambassador L
356.37   Kreutznach] A1; Krentz-
    nach L
357.20–23   But he . . . enter-
    prise!"] A1; omit L
357.20   Horn:] V; ~ , — A1;
    ~ ∧ — E1
357.24   He] A1; But he L
358.17–18 et seq.   Ingolstadt] A1;
    Ingoldstadt L
358.30   , indeed,] A1; omit L
359.5–7   So . . . League.] A1;
    omit L
359.15   another horse] A1;
    another L
359.32–360.14   But the . . . for
    this.] A1; omit L
360.6,13,17,33   King] V; king
    A1,E1
360.15   He] A1; At Munich he L
360.16–23   There were . . .
    statues."] A1; omit L
360.30–37   The guns . . . army.]
    A1; omit L

*361.17   the son] A1; a son L
361.28   von] A1; Von L
362.20   Glogau] A1; Slogan L
363.9–13   Neither . . . approval.]
    A1; omit L
363.9–10,10–11; 364.4   Emperor]
    V; emperor A1,E1
*363.17   moneys] A1; money L
363.29–364.10   The gorgeous
    . . . consequences.] A1; omit
    L
364.22   to Wallenstein. But the
    latter] A1; But Wallenstein L
364.37   Turning (no ¶)] A1; ¶ L
365.12; 366.16   Naumburg] A1;
    Naumberg L
366.19   touched] A1; affected L
368.18   say:] A1; ~ , — L
*369.12–14   whole . . . they]
    stet L
369.37   movement] A1; move-
    ments L
370.29   great] A1; Great L
371.1–372.8   Nothing . . . well-
    disciplined."] A1; omit L

THE BATTLE OF SOLFERINO

[The copy-text is L: *Lippincott's Magazine*, LXVI (Oct., 1900), pp. 613–
627. The other texts collated are A1: *Great Battles of the World*, J. B.
Lippincott, Philadelphia, 1901; E1: *Great Battles of the World*, Chapman &
Hall, London, 1901. E1 is a derived text without authority.]

*374.25   1806] stet L+
375.37   di] V; de L+
376.2   than] A1; that L
*376.25   Leri] A1; Lèri L
381.29   Rattazzi] V; Ratazzi L+
390.6–7   with—] E1; ~ , — L,A1

390.20   victory—] V; ~ , — L; ~ ,
    A1,E1
390.21   events—] A1; ~ , — L
391.6   Leri] V; Lèri L+
391.8–9   back— . . . him—] A1;
    ~ , — . . . ~ , — L

THE STORMING OF BURKERSDORF HEIGHTS

[The copy-text is L: *Lippincott's Magazine*, LXVI (Nov., 1900), pp. 781–
794. The other texts collated are A1: *Great Battles of the World*, J. B.
Lippincott, Philadelphia, 1901; E1: *Great Battles of the World*, Chapman &
Hall, London, 1901. E1 is a derived text without authority.]

392.20–21   boys— . . . time—]
    V; ~ , — . . . ~ , — L+

393.10   "Memoirs."] V; "~ : " L,
    A1; *Memoirs.* E1

393.29   crutch—] V; ~ , — L+
394.32   bashful and] A1; bashful, L
395.39–396.1   Maupertuis] V; Maupertius L+
396.2   way";] E1; ~ ," L; ~ ; " A1
397.38   -Zerbst] V; -Herbst L+
398.12–13   Prussia— . . . Dresden—] V; ~ , — . . . ~ , — L+
398.27   of German] A1; with German L
398.35   yellow"!] V; ~ !" L+
399.8   army;] A1; ~ : L
399.18–19   plots— . . . -enemy—] V; ~ , — . . . ~ , — L+
401.20   Kunersdorf—] V; ~ , — L+
*403.6   recapturing] A1; capturing L

403.27–28   war— . . . turned—] V; ~ , — . . . ~ , — L+
*403.32   et seq. Burkersdorf Height] stet L+ (Height of Burkersdorf at 406.9)
* 403.33–34   Kunzendorf Heights] V; Kunensdorf Height L; Kunensdorf Heights A1; Kunersdorf Heights E1
404.2   soldiery;] A1; ~ : L
404.7–8   captured— . . . defended—] V; ~ , — . . . ~ , — L+
404.11 et seq.   Möllendorff] V; Möllendorf L+
405.39–406.3   Czernichef— . . . show— . . . Castle— . . . hours—] V; ~ , — . . . ~ , — . . . ~ , — . . . ~ , — L+
406.6   their] A1; its L

WORD-DIVISION

1. *End-of-the-Line Hyphenation in the Virginia Edition*

[NOTE: No hyphenation of a possible compound at the end of a line in the Virginia text is present in the copy-texts except for the following readings, which are hyphenated within the line in the copy-texts. Except for these readings, all end-of-the-line hyphenation in the Virginia text may be ignored except for hyphenated compounds in which both elements are capitalized.]

9.9	speaking-|tube		279.6	cock-|sure
9.14	fiery-|hearted		279.14	well-|regulated
9.34	boat-|hook		287.32	bomb-|proof
10.21	bottle-|green		289.35	Fifty-|second
15.2	To-|day		296.10	sweet-|tempered
16.28	iron-|clad		299.33	great-|coats
34.37	blood-|red		300.7	re-|enforcements
35.19	-crack-|crackle		300.8	hand-|to-
37.27	gun-|barrels		300.21	pell-|mell
54.38	terror-|stricken		308.34	field-|pieces
59.8	view-|point		309.7	new-|mown
63.18	trousers-|leg		311.3	breast-|work
67.15	brown-|faced		311.26	-to-|hand
90.2	fire-|room		321.22	sixty-|five
103.28	dead-|gone		323.5	Seventy-|first
107.3	eight-|inch		323.33	over-|confidence
109.7	white-|faced		324.7	-de-|camp
122.27	wig-|wagging		324.32	cannon-|balls
135.24	business-|like		328.26	make-|trouble
157.9	summer-|resort		332.6	twenty-|fourth
176.14	twisty-|wise		345.35	ill-|gotten
195.11	search-|lights		355.5	Frankfort-|on-
212.15	well-|informed		356.3	thirty-|seventh
228.18	heaven-|sent		357.28	seventy-|two
230.33	bush-|whacked		361.3	horror-|stricken
231.33	high-|minded		365.27	willow-|trees
238.17	-horse-|power		374.1	counter-|irritant
246.17	fire-|arms		379.15	twenty-|five
246.39; 247.3	field-|hospital		379.28	market-|place
253.16	forty-|five		384.35	field-|guns
253.30	twenty-|six		387.23	Sixty-|first
259.24	twenty-|one		390.10	twenty-|two

2. End-of-line Hyphenations in the Copy-Texts

[NOTE: The following compounds, or possible compounds, are hyphenated at the end of the line in the copy-texts. The form in which they have been transcribed in the Virginia text, listed below, represents the practices of the respective copy-texts so far as can be determined, and in cases of doubt the form is that generally found in Crane manuscripts.]

6.21	sun-burned	238.3	twelve-pounder
6.34	blood-red	238.4	six-pounder
12.28	good-natured	239.4	bottle-green
14.18	side-walk	239.5	stoke-room
17.34	simple-minded	249.10	well-treated
21.6	blue-clad	252.35	high-handed
25.2	bookkeepers	256.9	half-breeds
35.37	absent-mindedly	263.18	tomtoms
36.12	blanket-rolls	269.17	coffee-house
45.17	overlooking	269.21	²coffee-house
46.10	hill-tops	271.11	Head-quarters
48.17	outpost	280.29	overwhelming
57.21	first-class	281.3	-in-law
69.20; 71.16	sentry-box	283.30	bottle-green
85.31	good-bys	284.22	full-tilt
87.12	light-heartedness	284.32	breast-work
93.23	tugboat	301.14	good-nature
106.12	flagship	302.7	sugar-loving
123.30	blood-red	304.21	warm-hearted
129.32	helter-skelter	304.38	homespun
132.17	blue-jackets	304.39	old-fashioned
134.11	searchlight	307.1	southwestern
140.30	panic-stricken	309.15	twelve-pound
147.29	hard-tack	312.19	court-martials
152.8	headlong	333.39	staircases
157.19	blockhouse	337.29	forty-three
157.36	two-thirds	343.29	twenty-one
165.28	rummiest-looking	346.4	-in-law
165.32	bad-eyed	354.2	lawgiver
168.10	headquarters	358.36	bedside
174.14	high-pitched	372.7	well-disciplined
176.20	quarterdeck	374.15	crazy-quilt
197.31	five-dollar-	386.11	shirt-sleeves
210.33	sweetheart	387.28	ridge-like
214.10	steamship	393.31	wheel-chair
214.18	stretched-out	393.35	nicknamed
220.37	war-worn	395.25	blue-gray
223.4	-and-so	398.19	two-and-
225.30	one-fifth	402.11	semi-imprisonment
226.38	spent-shell	403.11	-in-chief
230.25	machine-guns	403.24	eighty-one
236.17	gunboats	404.3	cross-strap

3. *Special Cases*

[NOTE: In the following list the compound is hyphenated at the end of the line in the copy-texts and in the Virginia edition.]

6.29   steel-colored (i.e., steel-colored)

28.27   sun-shine (i.e., sunshine)

71.24   wind-shaken (i.e.,
wind-shaken)

133.38   blue-jackets (i.e.,
blue-jackets)

169.7   Seventy-first (i.e.,
Seventy-first)

202.22   side-walks (i.e., sidewalks)

225.4   knot-holes (i.e., knotholes)

236.20   sea-combat (i.e., sea-combat)

296.11   sheep-skin (i.e., sheepskin)

324.27   sun-shine (i.e., sunshine)

350.32   light-hearted (i.e.,
light-hearted)

HISTORICAL COLLATION

[NOTE: Substantive variants from the Virginia text are listed here, together with their appearances in the collated texts. Collated texts not noted for any reading agree with the Virginia-edition reading to the left of the bracket. Variations in paragraphing, for substantive texts only, are listed, but no record is made when such variations have been accepted as emendations and the facts have been noted in the list of Editorial Emendations in the Copy-Text. Paragraphing variation in derived texts is not recorded even when a basically derived text may have substantive authority. Finally, owing to the special nature of the transmission, paragraphing variants in cabled dispatches have not been listed. Typographical errors not forming acceptable words have not been recorded in editions after the first. Variants in datelines are not noted since these are provided in the textual history. In the notation a plus sign indicates concurrence of all collated editions following the one cited. For this and for other conventions of shorthand notation, see the general headnote to the list of Editorial Emendations.]

WAR DISPATCHES

No. 1. AN IMPRESSION OF THE "CONCERT"

[The copy-text is WG: *Westminster Gazette*, May 3, 1897, pp. 1–2. Other texts collated are N^1: New York *Sun*, May 9, 1897, p. 6; N^2: *Detroit Free Press*, May 9, p. 17; N^3: *Pittsburgh Leader*, May 9, p. 19; N^4: Portland *Oregonian*, May 8, p. 6; N^5: Louisville *Courier-Journal*, May 9, p. 19; N^6: *Omaha Daily Bee*, May 10, p. 2; N^7: *Boston Globe*, May 9, p. 33; N^8: *St. Paul Pioneer Press*, May 9, p. 20.]

5.2   intention] expectation N^1

5.7   headland] headline N^6

5.10   everyone] every one $N^{1,5}$

5.11   Pirée] Piree WG,$N(−N^1)$; Piræus N^1

5.12   *et seq.* Powers] powers N $(−N^{5,7})±$

5.18–19   faint . . . exalted] *omit* N^2

5.18   turned] *omit* N^8

5.21   traveler] travelers N^3

5.23   their] the N^8

5.27   was] *omit* $N^{1,4}$

6.1   Land of Despair] land of despair $N^{1-2,4,6-8}$; "Land of Despair" N^3; land of Despair N^5

6.5   *Guadiana*] Guardiana N^5

6.5   toward] towards WG,$N^{3-4,8}$; toward us N^2

6.5–6   faint indication . . . cleft] faint little cleft among the hills N^1

6.5   indication] indentation N^5; indications N^8

6.10 one's] one's own N[5]
6.13 nor] or WG,N[1,4]
6.14 North] north $N(−N[4])
6.17 could] would WG
6.17 Surely] *omit* N[1]
6.23 Meanwhile] *omit* N[1]
6.25–26 objected . . . ship.] objected to the roll and heave of the ship without pause from Marseilles. N[1]
6.27 -colored] *omit* N[1]
6.28 afterward] afterwards WG, N[2-4,7-8]
6.33 the Turkish flag] Turkish N[1]
6.35 and] *omit* N[1]
6.36 tableau. The] tableau, the N[4,6-7]; tableau_∧ the N[2]
6.38 like] *omit* N[1]
6.40 the top-gear] a top-gear N[3]; top-gear N[4]
7.3 *et seq.* Concert] concert $N (−N[2,5])±
7.3–4 —the Concert, mind you,] *omit* N[1]
7.5 the air] air N[2]
7.5 This] The N[4]
7.14 ram-bows] rainbows N[7]
7.15 outline] outlines N[6]
7.18 Russians] Russian $N(−N[5])
7.18–19 Germans . . . Austrians] German, French, Italian, Turk, and Austrian N[1]
7.19 peaceably] peacefully $N
7.20–21 in twelve ways] *omit* N[1]
7.22 eyes, while the] eyes. The N[1]
7.25,37 she] it N[6]
7.32 of a kind] *omit* N[1]
7.36 complexity] complexion $N (−N[1,4,7])
7.36 (twice); 8.2,19,20,24 her] its N[6]
8.4–5 ships, while the] ships; the N[1]
8.5 *Kaiserin*] Kaiser|in N[3]; Kaiserine N[5-6]
8.6 On the other hand,] *omit* N[1]
8.12 the small] small N[3]
8.17 heaven-born] *omit* N[1]
8.19 officer] officers N[2]
8.19–20 to signal . . . him] *omit* N[1]

8.21 she] it N[6]
8.21–22 It was . . . see] *omit* N[1]
8.22 come] came N[1]
8.23 turn] turned N[1]
8.23 on] under N[1]
8.24 bat] bumped N[1]; but N[3]
8.24 into her] into it N[6]
8.24 and scrape] scraping N[1]
8.26 chattered] chatted N[2]
8.29 Indeed,] *omit* N[1]
8.30 bright] a bright N[2]
8.30 And] But N[1]
8.31 these] the N[1]
8.35–38 Whenever . . . sublime.] *omit* N[7]
8.36 Frenchmen] Frenchman N[2]
8.39 didn't] did not N[4]
9.1 crowded] crowded about N[1]
9.4 but—my] but on my N[8]
9.4 Napoleonic] napoleonic N[2,4,7]
9.6 amusements] amusement N[6]
9.10 -sized] -size N[8]
9.14 of course] sure N[1]
9.15–16 Of course] *omit* N[1]
9.16 his admiral] *omit* N[2]
9.18–19 immediately. Against] immediately against N[2]
9.20–21 They . . . circumstances.] *omit* N[1]
9.20 cut] *omit* WG
9.23 and perhaps almost] and, and perhaps, almost N[5]; and—perhaps—almost—N[2-4,7]; and, perhaps, almost N[1]
9.23 but] *omit* N[2]
9.24 of the wild] the dreams of wild N[1]
9.25 damned] little $N
9.26 God] god $N(−N[1])
9.26 Battle] battle $N(−N[5]); all battle N[5]
9.26 that] who N[1]
9.27 ¹damned] little $N
9.27 bold] *omit* $N
9.27 ²damned] *omit* $N
9.31 gig's] gigs' N[2-3,5,8]
9.33 gorgeous] fine N[1]
9.33 native's] natives N[1]
9.35–10.12 It . . . boat.] *omit* N[7]

9.35–36 these . . . heard] *omit* N²
9.36 sacred] *omit* N²
9.37 cannot] can not N³⁻⁵
9.38 made] make $N
10.3 West] west $N(−N¹,⁸)
10.4 out] *omit* N²
10.7 Westerner] westerner $N (−N¹,⁴,⁸)
10.9 shore] short N³
10.10 The] Then N⁸
10.11 skirts] shirts N³,⁴
10.11–12 none who wears] none who wore N⁸
10.12 skirts] shirts N³
10.12 could] can N¹
10.18 band on] band of N⁶
10.21 from the sea] from sea N³
10.23 anchorage] anchor N⁸
10.24 ¶ Then] *no* ¶ N⁸
10.26 listlessly] *omit* N¹
10.26–31 French . . . Dublin.] *omit* N⁷
10.31 All the same] *omit* N¹
10.32 These] Those N¹
10.35 circumstance] circumstances N⁶
10.37 trys] attempts N¹; trays N³
10.37 At] Then at WG
10.38 was slipping] slipped N²
10.39 over-side] over the side N⁴
10.40 thing—] thing∧ N³,⁶
11.1 a festival] festival N³
11.1 on] *omit* N³
11.2 at it] of it N³⁻⁴
11.2–3 an audience] spectators N¹
11.4 lined] *omit* N¹
11.6 In . . . hills,] *omit* N⁷
11.6 meantime] mean time N¹
11.6 hills] hill N¹
11.7 burn] burst N¹
11.11–12 a Cunarder] an Atlantic liner N²; a Cunader N³,⁸; an ocean liner N⁷
11.15 arrived] arriving N³

11.19–20 There . . . her.] *omit* N¹
11.19–20 Revenue Marine] revenue marine $N(−N¹,³,⁵); revenue navy N³
11.22; 12.20 *Guadiana*] Guardiana N⁴
11.24 Turks] Turk N²,⁴
11.28 quite] quiet and N⁶; quiet, N⁷
11.29 that] because N¹
11.29–30 governed . . . time,] *omit* N⁸
11.30 impulses] impulse N⁵
11.30–32 making . . . gaily.] *omit* N¹
11.38 could think] thinks N⁴
12.3 colleges] college N⁸
12.3 us, perhaps,] us∧ perhaps∧ N²,⁴; us∧ perhaps, N⁶
12.4 idea] ideas N²
12.4 this] the N¹
12.4 hang-dog] hand-dog N⁶
12.5 has] had N²
12.19 these] the N⁷
12.20 hove] weighed N¹
12.20 Suda] Duda N³
12.23 *Kaiserin*] Kaiser N³; Kaiserine N⁶; Kaiser In N⁸
12.23–24 distinct] indistinct N⁴
12.25 afterward] afterwards WG, N²⁻⁴,⁷⁻⁸
12.26–29 The mother . . . better.] *omit* N⁵
12.27 had come] came N¹
12.28 passengers] passenger N⁴

Subheadings

(N⁶)

6.11.1 Calm as a Graveyard.
7.33.1 Exhibit of Ironclads.
8.28.1 Exchanging Smiles.
10.12.1 Scorpions of the Sea.
11.21.1 The Turk Was There.

No. 2. THE SPIRIT OF THE GREEK PEOPLE

[The copy-text is MS: Columbia University Libraries, datelined Apr. 17 [1897].]

Alterations in the Manuscript

12.31   good] *interlined aboved de-leted* 'well'
13.3   by] *preceded by deleted* 'that'
13.7   government that] *interlined with a caret above deleted* 'man which'
13.9   arming] *interlined above de-leted* 'army'
13.13   improbable] *preceded by de-leted* 'highly'
13.15   with it] *interlined with a caret*
13.15   accord] *preceded by deleted* 'own'
13.19   has been] *interlined with a caret above deleted* 'is'
13.19   interesting.] *original period deleted and* 'at these times' *added but then deleted and pe-riod after* 'interesting' *restored*
13.21   have been] *interlined with a caret above deleted* 'are'
13.22   great] *preceded by a deleted downstroke*
13.25–26   Conservative] 'C' *over* 'c'
13.29   comes] 's' *added after origi-nal deleted* 's'

13.29   kept] 'pt' *interlined above deleted* 'ep'
13.30   Turks] 's' *added later*
13.32–33   the dignity] 'the' *inter-lined above possible* 'adm'
13.33   on] *interlined above deleted* 'here'
13.36   Well, but] *upstroke of* 'b' *starts over an original comma, probably without intent to de-lete it*
13.36   him.] *interlined above de-leted* 'them'
13.37   fight] *interlined with a caret*
13.39   Cretans] 'r' *over possible* 'e'
14.2   shells] *second* 's' *added later*
14.4   ships] *preceded by deleted* 'rigging'
14.7   seems.] *period altered from question mark*
14.9   spectacle] *second* 'c' *altered from beginning of an* 'l' *up-stroke*
14.10   Europe."] *period and quotes added before following* 'and Greece' *altered to* 'And Greece' *but then deleted*
14.17   like] *followed by deleted* 'the'

No. 3. STEPHEN CRANE SAYS GREEKS CANNOT BE CURBED

[The copy-text is N[1]: *New York Journal,* Apr. 30, 1897, p. 1. The other texts collated are N[2]: *Chicago Tribune,* Apr. 30, p. 2; N[3]: San Francisco *Examiner,* Apr. 30, p. 1; N[4]: Philadelphia *Press,* Apr. 30, p. 1. Since this is a telegraphed dispatch, no paragraphing is listed.]

14.21   Janina] Yanina N[1]; Yanin N[3]
14.21–22   the southwestern . . . Turkey] *omit* N[3]
14.22   the hard] hard N[4]
14.24   requires] required N[2]
14.24   a longer] longer N[3]
14.25   the] *omit* N[3]
14.30–15.3   Practically . . . life.] *omit* N[2]

14.30   and] to N[3]; *omit* N[4]
14.31   other] *omit* N[3]
15.2   classes] the city N[3]
15.9   been] *omit* N[4]
15.18–19   king's . . . parliament's] King's . . . Parliament's N[2-3]
15.18   war, not] war, N[3]
15.23   calmly] briefly N[3]
15.26   be] *omit* N[1,3]

No. 4. GREEK WAR CORRESPONDENTS

[The copy-text is N[1]: *Pittsburgh Leader*, May 16, 1897, p. 21. The other texts collated are N[2]: Portland *Oregonian*, May 16, p. 18; N[3]: *St. Paul Pioneer Press*, May 16, p. 19; N[4]: *Denver Republican*, May 16, p. 17.]

15.30 one hundred and thirty-one] 131 N[2,4]
16.4 natural] *omit* N[2]
16.9 were] are N[4]
16.15 that it] and it N[4]
16.26 can't] cannot N[1]
16.31 ingenuous] ingenious N[2-3]
16.33 fact] as a fact N[1]
16.34 see] *omit* N[4]
16.35 [1]Eastern] Western N[2-3]
17.2 aught] ought N[2]
17.5 peoples] people N[2-3]
17.5 here] there N[4]
17.9 inured] immured N[1,3]

17.11 situation to which] situation on which N[4]
17.11 official had] consul had N[4]
17.18 the first] first N[4]
18.18 band] bands N[1]
18.19 provinces] province N[4]

Subheadings

(N[4])

16.12.1 From Perth Amboy.
17.3.1 An English Instance.
17.36.1 Some Genuine Men.

No. 5 (I). CRANE AT VELESTINO

[The copy-text is N[1a]: *New York Journal* (Greater New York edition), May 11, 1897, pp. 1–2. The other text collated is N[6]: San Francisco *Examiner*, May 11, pp. 1–2. Since this is a telegraphed dispatch, no paragraphing is listed.]

18.31 well led] called upon N[6]
19.1 stayers] slayers N[6]
19.3 Greece] Greeks N[6]
19.3 the] *omit* N[6]
19.5 retreated] retired N[6]
19.10 intoxication] the intoxication N[6]
19.11 the orders] orders N[6]
19.17 a three . . . fight] three days' successful fighting N[6]
19.21 could] *omit* N[6]
19.22 Greek] Greeks' N[1a]
19.27 the few] a few N[6]
19.29 Turks] the Turks N[6]
19.29 three] for three N[6]
19.32 Pharsala] Pharsalos N[6]
19.39 a cloth] cloth N[6]
20.4 avalanche] an avalanche N[6]
20.10 the Turkish] Turkish N[6]
20.15 Scattered] The scattered N[6]
20.26 Sometimes] Some | times N[6]

20.27 among . . . fighting] *omit* N[6]
20.28 position] own N[6]
21.1 the normal] normal N[6]
21.8 chronological] the chronological N[6]
21.8 battle] a battle N[6]
21.8 A] Often a N[6]
21.9 often] *omit* N[6]
21.10 descriptions] description N[1a]
21.10 While] The while N[6]
21.11 changed] change N[6]
21.12 the rocky] a rocky N[6]
21.16 the trench] a trench N[6]
21.22 legs] lips N[1a,6]
21.36 Legion] Legation N[1a]
22.3 flank] Greek flank N[6]
22.4 all to be] to be all N[6]
22.6 the battery] a battery N[6]
22.10 slowly] *omit* N[6]
22.12 to also] also to N[6]

22.12   to the] in the N[6]
22.18   lines] line N[1a]
22.18   the officers] Officers N[6]
22.18   the men] and the men N[6]
22.23   Karadjah] Kraadjah N[6]
22.23   Pharsala] Pharsalos N[6]
22.32   Ephzones] Evzones N[6]

Subheadings

(N[1a])

19.21.1   (point. |) Troops Were Confident.

20.8.1   Many Turks Slain.
21.5.1   War Is Not Swift.
22.1.1   Futile Attempt to Turn Flank.
22.30.1   Made an Orderly Retreat.

(N[6])

19.37.1   The Sound of Battle.
21.5.1   War Takes a Long Time.
21.35.1   Scenes and Incidents.

No. 5 (II). STEPHEN CRANE AT VELESTINO

[The copy-text is N[1b]: *New York Journal* (out-of-town edition), May 11, 1897, pp. 1–2. Other texts collated are N[2]: *Chicago Tribune*, May 11, p. 1; N[3]: Philadelphia *Press*, May 11, p. 2; N[4]: *Boston Globe*, May 11, p. 7; N[5]: *Buffalo Evening News*, May 11, pp. 1,5. Since this is a telegraphed dispatch, no paragraphing is listed.]

23.8   By . . . Athens] Volo, via Athens N[2]; Volo N[3]
23.8   Velestino] In the first place Velestino N[2-3]
23.8–9   will surely] is sure to be N[3]; will N[5]
23.9   as] for N[2]
23.9–10   The Greek reverse began] The Greeks began reverses N[3]
23.10   reverse] reserve N[5]
23.11   that] *omit* N[3]
23.11   Greek] the Greek N[3]
23.11–12   could . . . led] when well led, could N[2]
23.12   with the] with N[2-3]
23.13   and] *omit* N[2]
23.14   and stayers] stayers N[3]
23.14   been] caused N[5]
23.14–15   generally . . . occasioned] *omit* N[1b,4-5]
23.15   and it] It N[3]
23.16   upon] on N[4]
23.16–17   It . . . happy.] *omit* N[2]
23.18   it was] through N[2]
23.18   not the] no N[2-3]
23.22   heavy] a heavy N[3]
23.22   the orders] orders N[2-3]

23.23   else] *omit* N[2-3]
23.24   General] *omit* N[2-3] (N[4-5]: Gen.)
23.24 *et seq.*   Smolenski] Smolentz N[2]
23.24–25   sacrificed Volo] was a sacrifice N[2]
23.25   and fumed] *omit* N[2-3]
23.25   but] But N[3]
23.26   the Turks] Turks N[3]
23.27   a three . . . fight] three days of successful fighting N[2-3]
23.28   The] *omit* N[3]
23.28   were] *omit* N[2-3]
23.28   their] the N[2]; *omit* N[3]
23.28–29   Then . . . retreat.] *omit* N[3]
23.29   Prince ordered the] Prince's order of N[2]
23.29–24.3   I think . . . Prince.] *omit* N[2]
23.30   the far left] far to the left N[3]
23.30   near Pharsala] *omit* N[3]
23.30–31   but . . . point.] *omit* N[4]
23.31   now] *omit* N[3,5]
23.31   New York] New Yorks N[1b]; America N[3]; New Yorkers N[5]

23.31   knows] know N[5]
23.32–24.1   at Velestino] *omit* N[3]
24.2–3   which . . . Prince] *omit* N[3]
24.3   downcast] have cast down N[2]
24.3–4   under Smolenski's] in this N[2-3]
24.4   The talk] and, well, the talk N[2]; Well, talk N[3]
24.4–8   that nobody . . . again.] "Nobody . . . again." N[2]
24.6   understood] understand N[2-3]
24.6   that . . . vastly] the vastly N[2-3]
24.7   Turks] the Turks N[2]
24.7   but] but then N[3]
24.7   whipped this] have whipped a N[2-3]
24.8   three] in three N[3]
24.8   they wanted] want N[2-3]
24.9   the orders] orders N[3]
24.10   days'] days of N[2]
24.11   than I did] *omit* N[3]
24.11   I did] I, as N[2]
24.13   practically uncovered] would practically uncover N[2]
24.14   of supplies] *omit* N[2-3]
24.14   came] I came N[2-3]; came on N[4]
24.15   three] of the three N[3]
24.15   fight] fighting N[5]
24.16   on] *omit* N[2]; of N[3]
24.18   tremendous. In] tremendousₐ in N[2]
24.18–19   it sounded] *omit* N[2]
24.19   the tearing of] the noise of tearing N[2]; tearing N[3]
24.19   a cloth] cloth N[5]
24.19   Nearer] Near N[5]
24.20   a resonant] resonant N[2-3]
24.20   by] at hand N[2]; *omit* N[3]
24.20   it was] was N[2]
24.20   long] a long N[2]; like N[3]
24.21–22   had . . . dreamed] I had never dreamed it N[2-3]
24.22   It was] *omit* N[2-3]
24.23   thunder or an avalanche] an avalanche of thunder N[2]; the thunder of an avalanche N[3]
24.24   human] the human N[5]

24.25   no] *omit* N[4]
24.27   is] *omit* N[5]
24.27   from] *omit* N[2-3]
24.27–30   The other . . . hands.] *omit* N[2]
24.29   great,] as great as N[3]
24.29–30   the Greeks fierce . . . hands.] Greeks. N[3]
24.29   the Turkish] Turkish N[5]
24.32   Desperate] The desperate N[2-3]
24.32   a steep] the steep N[3]
24.32–33   The insane] and the insane N[3]
24.32–33   The insane . . . squadrons] —an insane and almost wicked act. Whole squadrons N[2]
24.34   and their scattered] The scattered N[2]; while scattered N[3]
24.36–37   no . . . horror] no expression, no horror N[2-3]
24.37   [1]were] *omit* N[2-3]
24.37–38   there . . . tragedy.] — simply as movements of tiny dolls. The tragedy of it at close quarters must have been tremendous. The difficulty of a war correspondent's career is he can never tell where the exciting thing is going to break out, and N[2]; simply the movements of tiny dolls in the tragedy. Closer it must have been tremendous. The difficulty [*etc. as in* N[2]] break out. N[3]
24.39   by] of N[2-3]
24.39   on] *omit* N[2-3]
25.1   The Greek] Greek N[3]
25.3–4   The artillery . . . eternal] The Turkish artillery fired upon them eternally N[2]; The artillery fire was upon them eternally N[3]
25.4   it continued] *omit* N[2-3]
25.6   fatalistic] *omit* N[2-3]
25.8   they were] it was N[2-3]
25.8   the gaunt] gaunt N[2-3]

25.9 they were] *omit* N²⁻³

25.10 the position] their positions N²⁻³

25.10–11 burst_∧ unfrequently,] burst_∧ unfrequently_∧ N⁴; burst, unfrequently_∧ N⁵

25.11 unfrequently] frequently N²; infrequently N⁵

25.11 darkness] dark N⁴

25.11 red] *omit* N⁴

25.11 flashes] flames N⁵

25.13 the sufferers . . . silent.] They were mostly silent. N²; Mostly the soldiers were silent. N³

25.13 the sufferers] sufferers N⁴⁻⁵

25.14 In] and in N²

25.14 the musketry] a musketry N²; musketry N³

25.14 It] and N²⁻³

25.15 The batteries] Batteries N³

25.15–16 ²The . . . resumed.] *omit* N⁴

25.15 The whole] and the whole N²⁻³

25.16 were] are N²⁻³

25.16–17 to . . . ¹Greeks] to the Greeks' N³

25.17 Greeks had] Greek guns are N²; Greeks' were N³

25.17–18 The Turkish] while the Turkish N³

25.18 regulation] the regulation N³,⁵

25.19 I] and I N²

25.19 the German] German N³

25.20 the Turkish] Turkish N³

25.20 I think] and think N³

25.20 they are] them N²⁻³

25.21 a normal] the normal N²⁻³

25.21 a man] man N²⁻³

25.22 As a consequence] *omit* N²⁻³

25.22 he ultimately] ultimately he N³

25.23 and] *omit* N²⁻³

25.23 I] *omit* N³

25.23 these] the N⁵

25.24 hired] as hired N³

25.24 strong feelings] a strong feeling N²

25.24–25 under the circumstances] *omit* N³

25.24 under the] under some N²

25.25 a long] for a long N²⁻³

25.25 of the] *omit* N³

25.26 a small] the small N²

25.27 The swiftness . . . battles] The chronology of the swiftest battles N²; The swiftness, chronological, of battles N³

25.29 lunch] get a lunch N²

25.29 take] to take N²

25.30 whirlwinds] a whirlwind N²; the whirlwind N³

25.30 attack] attacks N⁵

25.31 the rocky] rocky N³

25.32 The fighting] Fighting N³

25.32–33 only . . . then. The] The only detail visible to me was the N²; only the forms of N³

25.33 The men in the trenches] men in trenches N³

25.33 were] *omit* N²⁻³

25.34 the dirt] dirt N³

25.34 carefully. The] carefully as the N²; carefully, being seen. The N³

25.35 close] up close N³

25.35 and the] The N²

25.35 Every ridge was] from every ridge N³

25.36 the trench] his trench N²; the trenches N⁵

25.37 twisted his] twisted the N³

25.37–38 the empty] empty N³

25.38 behind] behind him N³

26.1 trench] trenches N⁴

26.2 legs] lips N¹ᵇ⁻⁵

26.2 and in a] in a N²; and in N³

26.4 kneeled] and kneeled N²

26.4 the battle] battle N³

26.4 Men] The men N²

26.6 Reserves] A company of reserves N²

26.6 There] *omit* N²; where N³

26.6–7 the men] men N⁵

26.8 and demolished] demolished N³

26.8 The men] and the men N[3]
26.10 An] The N[2]
26.10 a battery] the battery N[2]
26.11 His] the N[3]
26.11 rifle] musket N[2-3]
26.12 had] *omit* N[3]
26.13 Meanwhile] and meanwhile N[2]
26.14 twelve hundred] 1,200 N[4-5]
26.14 away] distant N[3]
26.14 wild and] wild, N[2]; *omit* N[3]
26.15 [1]of] *omit* N[2]
26.17 in] *omit* N[2-3]
26.18 wounded] wounded in the head N[2-3]
26.18 His head was] *omit* N[2]; and it had been N[3]
26.18 bandaged with] bandaged in N[2]
26.20 his sleeve] the sleeve N[3]
26.20 said] said that N[3]
26.21 [1]over] over, and most of the soldiers wounded N[2]
26.21 Most wounded conclude] I concluded N[2]; Most of the wounded concluded N[3]
26.21 a battle] the battle N[2-3]
26.21 is] was N[2-3]
26.21–22 I heard] The news N[2]; News N[3]
26.22 from the left] from left was N[2]
26.22 that] impressed us that N[3]
26.22 had] *omit* N[2-3]
26.26 New] The Greek battery of Howitzers threw a few shells. New N[2]; but the Greek battery of howitzers threw them into a fit. New N[3]
26.26 opened] opened up N[2-3]
26.26 and I] I N[2]
26.27 attack] *omit* N[5]
26.27–28 in the . . . The] In . . . Volo, the N[3]
26.28 Volo] Vola N[2]
26.28 was] had N[2-3]
26.30 across] across to N[2]; across toward N[3]
26.30 were] *omit* N[2-3]
26.31 also] and also N[3]

26.32 a battery] the battery N[2-3]
26.33 and] to N[3]
26.34 this] *omit* N[2-3]
26.34 in a] There was a N[2]
26.34 ferocious] furious N[3]
26.35 The] and the N[2]
26.35 to be] *omit* N[2-3]
26.35 After] There was N[2-3]
26.36 banging] banging and N[3]
26.37 defeat there was] their defeat caused N[2]
26.38 and . . . all] Satisfaction was over all and N[2]; *omit* N[3]
26.38 The] *omit* N[2-3]
26.39 the men] and the men N[3]
27.3 General] *omit* N[2-3] (N[4-5]: Gen.)
27.4 the left] left N[2-3,5]
27.4 Kardetsa] Karditza N[2]; Karde Tsa N[3]
27.5 Pharsala] Pharsalos N[3]
27.5 We] and we N[2]
27.6 to be] *omit* N[2-3]
27.7 order] one N[4]
27.7 wept.] I did not see him weep, but would have done so had I been he. N[2-3] (N[3]; didn't . . . I would *etc.*)
27.8–9 It . . . thing. The] The curious thing was the N[2]; a curious thing. The N[3]
27.9 our orders] our order N[1b]; the orders N[2-3]
27.10 They] and N[3]
27.10 their] *omit* N[2-3]
27.10–11 for Turks] *omit* N[3]
27.11 Your] and your N[2]
27.13 Ephzones] Evzones N[2,4-5] (N[5]: evzones)
27.13 two thousand] 2000 N[3-5]
27.16 soldiers] soldier N[3]
27.18 distinctly] distinctively N[2]
27.19 troops] troops marched N[2]
27.19 in usual time] *omit* N[3]
27.19 in] in their N[2]
27.19 kept] and kept N[2]
27.20 along. It was] *omit* N[2-3]
27.20 over] on N[2-3]
27.20 for] in N[3]
27.22 somewhat of] *omit* N[2-3]

27.22 Still . . . daisy.] He was a daisy, anyhow. N²⁻³
27.23 The] A N²; *omit* N³
27.23 of a] of N²⁻³
27.23 accident] accidents N²
27.24 at the same time] *omit* N²⁻³
27.24 a bad] bad N³
27.24–25 and . . . bandages] A man in a bloody bandage N²⁻³
27.24 and the] and this N⁴
27.25 in wild] wildly in N²
27.25 cannot] can't N²⁻³

Subheadings

(N¹ᵇ)

23.27.1 Greeks Confident They Could Have Held Valestino.
24.17.1 The Roar and Sound of the Great Battle.
25.13.1 The Battle Resumed in the Morning.
26.16.1 Manoeuvering of the Hostile Forces.

(N²)

24.17.1 Roll of Musketry Tremendous.

25.1.1 (them. |) With Patience of Bookkeepers.
25.23.1 (all. |) German Officers Hired Assassins.
26.5.1 Pause to Cross Themselves.
26.24.1 New Battalions Open Up.
27.7.1 Retreat Wrathful and Sullen.

(N³)

23.23.1 Volo Is Sacrificed.
24.16.1 (day. |) Crane's First Big Battle.
25.1.1 (them. |) Greeks Fight with Patience.
25.32.1 (hills. |) Fighting from the Trenches.
26.39.1 Alas! The Order to Retreat.

(N⁵)

23.23.1 Defeat after Three Days' Fighting.
25.39.1 Wept over the Body.
26.24.1 The Battle on the Right Flank.
27.7.1 The Turks and Retreat.

No. 5. CRANE AT VELESTINO

General Historical Collation

[The copy-text is N¹ᵃ: *New York Journal* (Greater New York edition), May 11, 1897, pp. 1–2. Other texts collated are N¹ᵇ: *New York Journal* (out-of-town edition), May 11, pp. 1–2; N²: *Chicago Tribune*, May 11, p. 1; N³: Philadelphia *Press*, May 11, p. 2; N⁴: *Boston Globe*, May 11, p. 7; N⁵: *Buffalo Evening News*, May 11, pp. 1,5; N⁶: San Francisco *Examiner*, May 11, pp. 1–2; N⁷: *Kansas City Star*, May 11, p. 1; N⁸: Portland *Oregonian*, May 12, p. 2; N⁹: Salt Lake City *Tribune*, May 12, p. 2; N¹⁰: *Omaha World-Herald*, May 12, p. 5; N¹¹: *Beatrice Daily Express*, May 12, p. 1; N¹²: *Kearney Daily Hub*, May 12, p. 1. N¹¹⁻¹² are in the same typesetting and hence constitute only one text.]

18.27–30 When . . . conclusion, but] The Journal publishes a cable dispatch [N⁸: cablegram] from Stephen Crane, who saw the battle of Velestino, where General [N⁹: Gen.] Smolenski hurled back Edhem Pasha. Mr. Crane says: N⁷⁻¹²
18.27–28 When this war is done] *omit* N¹ᵇ,⁴⁻⁵; In the first place N²⁻³
18.28 Velestino will be famed]

Velestino will surely be famous N[1b-2,4-5] (N[5]: *omit* surely); Velestino is sure to be famous N[3]

18.28 as its greatest battle] as one of the greatest battles of this war N[1b-5] (N[2]: for one)

18.29 The Greeks . . . Larissa] The Greek reverse began at Larissa N[1b-2,4-5] (N[5]: reserve); The Greeks began reverses at Larissa N[3]

18.30 the swiftest possible conclusion, but] a quick conclusion, but N[1b-5] (N[3]: But)

18.30–31 has proved] proved N[1b-5]

18.31 that] *omit* N[3]

18.31 Greek] the Greek N[3,7,9-12]

18.31 when well . . . successfully] could, when well led, successfully cope N[1b,3-5]; when well led, could successfully cope N[2]; when called upon can cope successfully N[6]

18.32 Turks] the overwhelming numbers of Turks N[1b,4-5]; overwhelming numbers of Turks N[2-3]; the Turks N[7-8,10-12]

18.32 even though outnumbered] *omit* N[1b-5]

18.32 This battle has] It N[1b-5]

19.1 good] great N[7-9]

19.1 long] and long N[1b,3-5]

19.1 stayers] and stayers N[1b-2,4-5,7-12]; slayers N[6]

19.1–5 It must . . . happy.] *omit* N[7-12]

19.1–2 It must . . . Larissa.] It must have been generally surprising after Larissa N[2-3]; *omit* N[1b,4-5]

19.3 I know all Greece rejoiced] It must have been general rejoicing throughout Greece N[1b,4-5] (N[5]: have caused); and it occasioned general rejoicing throughout Greece N[2-3] (N[3]: [*omit* and] It)

19.3 Greece] Greeks N[6]

19.3–4 this battle's . . . champagne] its effect upon the Greek soldiers was great N[1b-5] (N[4]: effect on)

19.3–4 the Greek] Greek N[6]

19.4–5 It made . . . happy.] *omit* N[2]

19.5 retreated] retired N[6]

19.5–6 it was] through N[2]

19.6 no] not the N[1b,4-5]

19.6 this] the N[7-12]

19.7–8 knew . . . grasp] was at that time perfectly confident of success N[1b-5,7-9]

19.9 beautifully in check] back N[7-9]

19.9–10 killing . . . upon him] and inflicting heavy loss N[1b-5] (N[3]: a heavy); and inflicting upon them heavy losses N[7-9]

19.10–11 In . . . back. Why?] Then came the orders to fall back N[1b-5,7-9] (N[2-3]: came orders; N[7-9]: came the order)

19.10 intoxication] the intoxication N[6]

19.11 the orders] orders N[6]

19.11–35 Reverses . . . myself. But] *omit* N[10-12]

19.11 Reverses] due to reverses N[1b-5,7-9]

19.11 of the sort] else N[1b,4-5]; *omit* N[2-3,7-9]

19.12–13 may have . . . reason] *omit* N[1b-5,7-9]

19.14 Smolenski] General Smolenski N[1b,4-5,7-9] (N[4-5,9]: Gen.); Smolentz N[2]

19.14 that] *omit* N[7-9]

19.14 sacrificed Volo] was a sacrifice N[2]; would be at the sacrifice of Volo. N[7-8]; would mean the sacrifice of Volo N[9]

19.15 raged . . . general.] raged and fumed, N[1b,4-5]; raged. N[2-3,7-9]

19.15–16 But . . . orders] but orders must be obeyed N[1b-5,7-9] (N[3,7-9]: But)

19.16 and the Turks occupied Velestino] hence the occupation by the Turks of Velestino, and, later, the fall of Volo N^{1b-5} (N^3: by Turks); hence the occupation by the Turks, first, of Velestino, and later of Volo N^{7-9} (N^{7-8} *add*: In the middle of intoxication of victory came the orders to fall back. Why? *see* 19.10–11)

19.17 And] *omit* N^{1b-5}

19.17–35 And this . . . myself. But] *omit* N^{7-9}

19.17 a three . . . fight] three days of successful fighting N^{2-3}; three days' successful fighting N^6

19.17–18 The troops were jubilant] the troops jubilant N^2; troops jubilant N^3

19.18 the commander] their commander $N^{1b,4-5}$; commander N^3

19.18–19 —and . . . retreat] *omit* N^3

19.18 and] *omit* $N^{1b-2,4-5}$

19.18–19 Prince ordered a] Prince's order of N^2; Prince ordered the $N^{1b,4-5}$

19.19–24 My notion . . . left.] *omit* N^2

19.19 My notion is that] I think $N^{1b,3-5}$

19.20 the far left] far to the left N^3

19.20 Greeks.] Greeks, near Pharsala $N^{1b,4-5}$

19.20–21 Probably . . . point.] *omit* N^4

19.20 Probably] but probably $N^{1b,3,5}$

19.20 by] *omit* $N^{1b,3,5}$

19.20 now] *omit* $N^{3,5}$

19.20 New York] New Yorks N^{1b}; New Yorkers N^5; America N^3

19.21 knows] know N^5

19.21 could] *omit* N^6

19.22 Greek] Greeks' N^{1a}

19.22 right] right at Velestino $N^{1b,4-5}$

19.22–23 who saw the worst of it] *omit* $N^{1b,3-5}$

19.24 left.] left, which was under the immediate command of the Prince $N^{1b,4-5}$

19.25 of retreat] to retreat N^{1b-5}

19.25 have crushed] downcast $N^{1b,3-5}$; have cast down N^2

19.25 of this] under Smolenski's $N^{1b,4-5}$; in this N^{2-3}

19.26 How the soldiers talked!] The talk goes among the soldiers that $N^{1b,4-5}$; and, well, the talk goes among the soldiers N^2; Well, talk goes among the soldiers that N^3

19.26–30 ∧Nobody . . . again.∧] "Nobody . . . again." N^2

19.26 Nobody] that nobody $N^{1b,3-5}$

19.26 wanted] wants N^{1b-5}

19.27 the few] a few N^6

19.27 have fallen] fall N^{1b-5}

19.28 understood] understand N^{2-3}

19.28 the vastly] that there was a vastly $N^{1b,4-5}$

19.28 the Turks] Turks $N^{1b,3-5}$

19.28 but] but then N^3

19.29 had] *omit* $N^{1b,4-5}$; have N^{2-3}

19.29 whipped the] whipped this $N^{1b,4-5}$; whipped a N^{2-3}

19.29 Turks] the Turks N^6

19.29 three] for three N^6; in three N^3

19.30 wanted] they wanted $N^{1b,4-5}$; want N^{2-3}

19.30 again.] again. This was the situation when the orders came. N^{1b-5} (N^3: when orders)

19.31 Some . . . battle] Of the first two days' combat some other correspondents saw more N^{1b-5} (N^2: days of)

19.31–32 than I did] *omit* N^3

19.31–32 I did] I, as N^2

19.32 Pharsala] Pharsalos N^6

19.33 that] *omit* N^{1b-5}

19.34 practically uncovered] would practically uncover N^2

19.34 base] base of supplies $N^{1b,4-5}$

19.35 did not spare myself] came immediately, but too late to see the whole three days' fight

N^{1b-5} (N^{2-3}: I came; N^4: came on; N^3: of the three; N^5: fighting)

19.35 But] omit N^{1b-5}

19.35 only] omit $N^{1b-5,8}$

19.36 of] on $N^{1b,4-5}$; omit N^2

19.36–37 I had . . . battle.] omit N^{7-12}

19.36 seen] been in N^{1b-5}

19.37 my] the N^{1b-5}

19.38 musketry] musketry fire N^{1b-5}

19.38 tremendous. From a] tremendous. In the $N^{1b,3-5}$; tremendous in the N^2

19.38–20.1 From . . . crash.] omit N^{11-12}

19.38–39 it was] it sounded $N^{1b,3-5}$; omit N^2

19.39 tearing] the tearing of $N^{1b,4-5}$; the noise of tearing N^2

19.39 a cloth] cloth N^{5-6}

19.39 nearer] Near N^5

19.39–20.1 a tin roof] a resonant roofing $N^{1b,4-5}$; resonant roofing N^{2-3}; a roof N^{7-10}

20.1 up] by $N^{1b,4-5}$; at hand N^2; omit N^3

20.1 it was] was N^2

20.1 a long] long $N^{1b,4-5}$; like N^3

20.2 beautiful as . . . dreamed] beautiful as had never been dreamed $N^{1b,4-5}$; beautiful as I had never dreamed it N^{2-3}; as beautiful as any I had ever dreamed of N^8

20.2–3 It was . . . ¹than] It was like N^{10-12}

20.2 It was] omit N^{2-3}

20.3 Niagara] the Niagara N^{10}

20.3–4 thunder or avalanche] an avalanche of thunder N^2; the thunder of an avalanche N^3

20.4 avalanche] an avalanche N^{1b-6}

20.4 human] the human N^5

20.5–6 It was . . . ideal.] omit $N^{9,11-12}$

20.6 no] omit N^4

20.7–8 This is . . . there.] omit N^{7-12}

20.7 This is] This is from $N^{1b,4}$; This from N^5

20.7–11 Another might . . . hands.] omit N^2

20.7 Another] The other $N^{1b,3-5}$

20.9 the Turks] Turks $N^{1b,3-5}$

20.9 enormous. The] great, the $N^{1b,4-5}$; as great as the N^3

20.9–10 the Greeks] Greeks N^3

20.10–11 was so . . . hands] omit N^3

20.10 was so] omit $N^{1b,4-5}$

20.10 that] omit $N^{1b,4-5}$

20.10 the Turkish] Turkish N^{5-6}

20.11 shielded] often shielding $N^{1b,4-5}$

20.11–12 Eight . . . made] The Turks made eight charges N^{1b-5}; Eight charges the Turkish soldiers made N^8; Eight charges by the Turks were made N^{10}

20.12 on this day] this day N^{1b-5}; on Saturday N^{7-12}

20.12 and they were] and were N^{1b-5}

20.12 every] each $N^{1b-5,7-12}$

20.13 The desperate] Desperate $N^{1b,4-5}$

20.13 their enemy on] omit N^{1b-5}

20.13 a steep] the steep N^3

20.14 The insane, wicked squadrons] The insane and almost wicked squadrons $N^{1b,3-5}$ (N^3: and the insane); —an insane and almost wicked act. Whole squadrons N^2

20.14 insane, wicked] omit N^9

20.15 Scattered] and their scattered $N^{1b,4-5}$; The scattered $N^{2,6-7}$; while scattered N^3

20.16–23.7 From a distance . . . here.] omit N^{11-12}

20.17 There was] omit N^{1b-5}

20.17 no expression] omit N^7

20.17 no expression, no horror] no expressions of horror $N^{1b,4-5}$

20.18 to be] were to be $N^{1b,4-5}$

20.18 seen.] seen; there were simply the movements of tiny doll tragedy. $N^{1b,4-5}$; —simply as movements of tiny dolls. The tragedy of it at close quarters must have been tremendous. The difficulty of the war correspondent's career is he can never tell where the exciting thing is going to break out, and N^2; simply the movements of tiny dolls in the tragedy. Closer it must have been tremendous. The difficulty of a war correspondent's career is, he can never tell where the exciting thing is going to break out. N^3

20.19 the assaults] these assaults N^{1b-5}

20.19 of] by $N^{1b,4-5}$

20.19 this] on this $N^{1b,4-5}$

20.19 to] for N^{1b-5}

20.20–26 The Greek . . . well.] omit N^9

20.20 The Greek] Greek N^3

20.20 with the] with N^{10}

20.20 steadiness] patience N^{1b-5}

20.21 complaining] complained N^{10}

20.21–22 magnificent] fine N^{1b-5}

20.22–23 The Greeks . . . on them] The artillery fire upon them was almost eternal $N^{1b,4-5}$; The Turkish artillery fired upon them eternally N^2; The artillery fire was upon them eternally N^3

20.23 on them] upon them N^8

20.23 even in a musketry lull] it continued even when the musketry lulled, $N^{1b,4-5}$; even when the musketry lulled, N^{2-3}

20.25 religion] fatalistic religion $N^{1b,4-5}$

20.25–26 never daunted] perfectly undaunted N^{1b-5}

20.26 Sometimes] Some | times N^6

20.26 it was] they were $N^{1b,4-5}$

20.27 among . . . fighting] omit N^6

20.27 gaunt] the gaunt $N^{1b,4-5}$

20.27 fighting on] they were fighting on $N^{1b,4-5}$

20.27 green plains] the fine green plain N^{1b-5}

20.28 their position.] the position. $N^{1b,4-5}$; their positions. $N^{2-3,9}$; their own. N^6

20.29 burst infrequently,] $\sim _\wedge \sim _\wedge$ N^4; $\sim$, $\sim _\wedge$ N^5

20.29 infrequently] unfrequently $N^{1b,3-4}$; frequently $N^{2,7}$; in fury N^{8-9}

20.30 darkness] dark N^4

20.30 darkness. By . . . flashes I saw] darkness with red flashes. I saw N^{1b-5} (N^4: omit red; N^5: red flames); darkness by red flashes. I saw N^9

20.31 among them] omit N^{1b-5}

20.31–32 They . . . silent] the sufferers being mostly silent $N^{1b,4-5}$ (N^{4-5}: sufferers); mostly the soldiers were silent N^3

20.33–23.7 In the gray . . . here.] omit N^{10}

20.33 In] and in N^2

20.33 the musketry] a musketry N^2; musketry N^3

20.33 began again] was resumed N^{1b-5}

20.33 It] and N^{2-3}

20.34 batteries] The batteries $N^{1b-2,4-5}$; Batteries N^3

20.34–35 and soon . . . resumed] omit N^4

20.34–35 and soon the whole play] The whole affair $N^{1b,5}$; and the whole affair N^{2-3}

20.34 soon] omit N^{7-9}

20.36 were] are N^{2-3}

20.36 to those . . . Greeks] to the Greeks' N^3

20.36–37 who had] The Greeks had $N^{1b,4-5}$; The Greek guns are N^2; The Greeks' were N^3

20.37–21.5 The Turkish . . . as these.] omit N^{8-9}

20.37–39 The Turkish . . . fire]

The Turkish guns were regulation field pieces. I learned to curse the German officers who directed the fire of the Turkish batteries $N^{1b-2,4-5}$ (N^2: and I; N^5: the regulation); while the Turkish were the regulation field pieces. I learned to curse German officers who directed the fire of Turkish batteries, N^3; while the Turkish guns were of the regulation field pattern, served by German officers N^7

20.39–21.1 I think . . . are] and think N^3

20.39–21.3 I think . . . at all.] *omit* N^7

20.39–21.1 these officers are] they are $N^{1b,4-5}$; them N^{2-3}

21.1 the normal] a normal $N^{1b,4-5}$; normal N^6

21.1 results] outgrowth N^{1b-5}

21.2 a man] man N^{2-3}

21.2 first of all be] be first of all N^{1b-5}

21.2–3 ultimately he] As a consequence, he ultimately $N^{1b,4-5}$; He ultimately N^2

21.3 not] and not $N^{1b,4-5}$

21.3 I] *omit* N^3

21.3 these] the N^5

21.4 hired assassins] as hired assasins N^3; hired assassins, sent out by the ridiculous little popinjay who presides as 'war lord' over the German people. N^7

21.4 strong feelings] a strong feeling N^2

21.4–5 under . . . these] *omit* N^3

21.5 such . . . these] the circumstances $N^{1b,4-5}$; some circumstances N^2; such circumstances N^7

21.6 for] *omit* $N^{1b,4-5,7}$

21.6 blue-clad] blue clothed $N^{1b-5,7}$

21.6 Greek infantry] infantry of the Greeks $N^{1b-2,4-5,7}$; infantry, Greeks, N^3

21.6 march] marching N^{8-9}

21.7 into] in N^9

21.7 a small] the small $N^{2,7}$

21.7–10 War . . . whirlwind.] *omit* N^{8-9}

21.7–8 The swiftness . . . correct.] The swiftness in the chronology of battles is not correct in most books. $N^{1b,4-5}$; The chronology of the swiftest battles is not correct in most books. N^2; The swiftness, chronological, of battles is not correct in most books. N^3; The swiftness of battles as chronicled in the story books evidently is all in the imagination. N^7

21.8 chronological] the chronological N^6

21.8 battle] a battle N^6

21.8 A man] Evidently one N^{1b-5}; Often a man N^6; The writer N^7

21.9 to lunch] lunch $N^{1b,3-5}$; get a lunch N^2; to take a lunch in the club N^7

21.9 to take] take $N^{1b,3-5,7}$

21.9 often] *omit* N^6

21.10 the descriptions of which] the description of which $N^{1a,7}$; whose descriptions N^{1b-5}

21.10 read] reads N^7

21.10 a whirlwind] whirlwinds $N^{1b,4-5}$; the whirlwind N^3

21.10–11 While I watched] *omit* N^{1b-5}; The while I watched N^6

21.11 changed] change N^6

21.11 attack] attacks N^5

21.12 the rocky] rocky N^3; a rocky N^6

21.12 hill] hills N^{1b-5}

21.12–13 Then . . . view.] The fighting was then obscure to the view, only a detail being observable now and then. $N^{1b,4-5}$; The fighting was then obscure to view. The only detail visible to me was N^2; Fighting was then obscure to view only the forms of N^3

21.14 The Greeks . . . snugly]
The men in the trenches were
snugly $N^{1b,4-5}$; the men in the
trenches, snugly N^2; men in
trenches snugly N^3

21.14 the dirt] dirt N^3

21.15 firing] and firing N^{1b-5}

21.15 carefully, while the] carefully. The $N^{1b,4-5}$; carefully as
the N^2; carefully, being seen.
The N^3

21.15 close] closely N^7; up close
N^3

21.15 before them.] and the roar
was great. $N^{1b,3-5}$; The roar
was great. N^2

21.16 Every . . . smoke.] from
every ridge fringed with
smoke. N^3

21.16 I saw soldiers] Occasionally
a soldier N^{1b-5}; I saw the soldiers N^6

21.16 the trench] his trench N^2;
the trenches $N^{5,7-9}$; a trench
N^6

21.17 ease off and take a] eased
off, took a N^{1b-5}; eased of an
attack, N^7

21.17 their canteens] his canteen
N^{1b-5}; the canteens N^7

21.17–18 twist their . . . belts]
twisted his . . . belt $N^{1b-2,4-5}$;
twisted the . . . -belt N^3

21.18 the empty] empty N^3

21.18–19 behind . . . say] behind, said $N^{1b-2,4-5}$; behind
him, said N^3

21.19 comrade] comrade over his
shoulder N^{1b-5}

21.19 Then they] and N^{1b-5}; They
then N^8

21.21 I noticed] *omit* N^{1b-5}

21.21 up] *omit* N^8

21.21 in the rear] back N^{1b-5}

21.21 a trench] the trench $N^{1b-3,5}$;
the trenches N^4

21.22 cigarette] cigar N^7

21.22 legs] lips $N

21.22 In this] and in a $N^{1b,4-5}$; in
a N^2; and in N^3

21.23 a shot . . . neck] was shot
through the neck N^{1b-5}

21.23 the trench] a trench N^8

21.24 and knelt weeping] kneeled
$N^{1b,3-5}$; and kneeled N^2

21.24 the battle] the battle, and
wept. $N^{1b,4-5}$; battle and wept.
N^3

21.24–25 The men] Men $N^{1b,3-5}$

21.26 The reserves] Reserves
$N^{1b,3-5}$; A company of reserves
N^2; The reserve N^7

21.26 The men] There the men
$N^{1b,4}$; where the men N^3; There
men N^5

21.28 and demolished] demolished
N^3

21.28 The men] and the men N^3

21.29 to the] at the N^{1b-5}

21.30–22.1 An officer . . . ^{2}over.]
omit N^{8-9}

21.30 An] The N^2

21.30 a battery] the battery N^2;
an active battery N^7

21.31 the first pair having] His
first pair had $N^{1b-2,4-5}$; the first
pair had $N^{3,7}$

21.31 smashed] broken $N^{1b-5,7}$

21.32 musket ball] rifle shot
$N^{1b,4-5}$; musket shot N^{2-3}

21.32–33 The man . . . misunderstood.] and shot the messenger, who misunderstood the
order and brought a bottle of
wine. N^7

21.32–33 having misunderstood]
He had misunderstood $N^{1b-2,4-5}$;
He misunderstood N^3

21.33 Meanwhile] and meanwhile
N^2

21.34 1,200] twelve hundred N^{1b-3}

21.34 off] away $N^{1b-2,4-5}$; distant
$N^{3,7}$

21.34 was furious] was wild and
furious $N^{1b,4-5}$; was wild, furious N^2; wild with rage and
furious N^7

21.34 the man's] his man's N^7

21.35 but he] *omit* N^7

21.35 ^{1}of] *omit* $N^{2,7}$

21.36 Legion] Legation N[1a]

21.36 came] came in N[1b,4-5]

21.37 in the head] *omit* N[1b,4-5]

21.37 He was] His head was N[1b,4-5]; *omit* N[2]; and it had been N[3]; which was N[7]

21.37 bandaged with] bandaged in N[2]

21.38 I noticed] He had N[1b-5,7]

21.39 his sleeve] the sleeve N[3]; the sleeve of his coat N[7]

21.39 said] said that N[3]

22.1 [1]over] over, and most of the soldiers wounded N[2]

22.1 Most . . . men conclude] I concluded N[2]; Most of the wounded concluded N[3]

22.1 men] *omit* N[1b,4-5]

22.1 the battle] a battle N[1b,4-5]

22.1 is] was N[2-3]

22.2 News came] I heard N[1b,4-5]; The news N[2]; News N[3]; News then came N[8]

22.2 from the left] from left was N[2]; *omit* N[8]

22.2 that the] impressed us that the N[3]

22.2 had] *omit* N[2-3]

22.3 flank] Greek flank N[6]

22.3–4 I saw . . . fray.] *omit* N[7-9]

22.4 all to be] to be all N[6]

22.4 thick of the fray] thickest of the fight N[1b-5]

22.6 and the battery . . . them.] New battalions on the right opened, N[1b,4-5]; The Greek battery of Howitzers threw a few shells. New battalions on the right opened up. N[2]; but the Greek battery of howitzers threw them into a fit. New battalions on the right opened up N[3]

22.6 the battery] a battery N[6]

22.6 of howitzers] *omit* N[7-9]

22.6 I saw] and I saw N[1b,3-5]

22.7 troops] other troops N[1b-5]

22.7 attack] *omit* N[5]

22.7–9 in the direction of Volo.

[¶] The] In the direction of Volo, the N[3]

22.8 Volo] Vola N[2]

22.9 fight] fighting N[8]

22.9 began] was begun N[1b,4-5]; had begun N[2-3]

22.10 slowly moved] moved slowly N[1b-5]; moved N[6]

22.10 toward the] across the plain. The N[1b,4-5]; across to the N[2]; across toward the N[3]; forward toward the N[7-9]

22.11 indicated] were indicated N[1b,4-5]

22.12 hill and to also] hill, also to N[1b-2,4-5]; hill and also N[3]; hill and also to N[6-7] (N[7]: hills)

22.12 the battery] a battery N[1b,4-5]

22.12 to the] in the N[6,9]

22.13 and drive] to drive N[3]

22.14 it] this N[1b,4-5]; *omit* N[2-3]

22.14 in a] There was a N[2]

22.14–15 ferocious] furious N[3]

22.15 [1]fight] fight in the woods N[1b-5]

22.15 The] and the N[2]

22.15 where the fight occurred] *omit* N[1b-5]

22.16 seemed] seemed to be N[1b,4-5]

22.16 There was] After N[1b,4-5]

22.16–17 and then] *omit* N[1b-2,4-5]; and N[3]

22.17 defeated] *omit* N[1b-5]

22.17 There was] After this attack and defeat there was N[1b,3-5]; after this attack, and their defeat caused N[2]

22.18 all] *omit* N[1b-5]

22.18 lines, the officers] line, the officers N[1a]; lines and satisfaction over all. The officers N[1b,4-5]; lines. Satisfaction was over all and officers N[2]; lines. Officers N[3,6]

22.18 the men] and the men N[3,6]

22.19 mind you] *omit* N[9]

22.21 order] orders N[1b-5]

22.22–24 Smolenski . . . retired.] *omit* N[9]

22.22,26 Smolenski] General Smolenski N[1b,4-5] (N[4-5]: Gen.); Smolentz N[2]

22.23 left] the left N[1b,4]

22.23 Karadjah] Kardetsa N[1b,4-5]; Karditza N[2]; Karde Tsa N[3]; Kraadjah N[6]

22.23 Pharsala] Pharsalos N[3,6]

22.24 We] and we N[2]

22.25 seemed an] seemed to be an N[1b,4-5]

22.25 order] one N[4]

22.26 Smolenski wept.] Smolentz wept. I did not see him weep, but would have done so had I been he. N[2]; Smolenski wept. I didn't see him weep, but I would have done so had I been he. N[3]

22.27 down] down then N[1b-5]

22.27–28 retreat. A . . . that the] retreat. It was a curious thing. The N[1b,4-5]; retreat. The curious thing was the N[2]; retreat, a curious thing. The N[3]

22.28 the order] our order N[1b]; the orders N[2-3]; our orders N[4-5]

22.29 They] and N[3]

22.29 batteries] their batteries N[1b,4-5]

22.29–30 for the Turks] for Turks N[1b-2,4-5]; omit N[3,7]

22.30 Your . . . way.] omit N[7-9]

22.30 Your] and your N[2]

22.32 Ephzones] Evzones N[2,4,6,8]; evzones N[5,9]; Euzones N[7]

22.32 2,000] two thousand N[1b-2]

22.33 and] omit N[1b-5]

22.33 in the] in N[7]

22.33 brightened] lighted N[1b-5]

22.34–23.7 An order . . . here.] omit N[7-9]

22.35 soldiers] soldier N[3]

22.37 distinctly] distinctively N[2]

22.37–38 moved . . . and] omit N[3]

22.37 moved] omit N[1b,4-5]; marched N[2]

22.37 at the] in N[1b,4-5]; in their N[2]

22.38 and kept] kept N[1b,3-5]

22.39 came] came along N[1b,4-5]

22.39 the last] It was the last N[1b,4-5]

22.39 on] over N[1b,4-5]

22.39 for] in N[3]

23.1 time] while N[1b-5]

23.1 received] got N[1b-5]

23.2 but could not] but was in somewhat of a hurry myself N[1b-5] (N[2-3]: omit somewhat of)

23.2–3 There are . . . army.] Still I saw him. He was a daisy. N[1b,4-5]; He was a daisy, anyhow. N[2-3]

23.3 A] The N[1b,4-5]; omit N[3]

23.3 a railroad accident] railroad accidents N[2]; railroad accident N[3]

23.4 bombardment is] a bombardment at the same time is N[1b,4-5]

23.4 a bad disease] bad disease N[3]

23.4–5 All the way . . . bandages] and the engineer in bloody bandages N[1b,4-5] (N[4]: this engineer in); A man in a bloody bandage N[2-3]

23.5 in wild] wildly in N[2]

23.5 Greek.] Greek. I cannot quote him N[1b-5] (N[2-3]: I can't)

Subheadings

(N[7])

19.11.1 (Why? |) The Beauties of a Battle.

20.28.1 Night and the Second Day.

21.16.1 (smoke. |) Incidents of the Battle.

22.3.1 (failed. |) Hot Fighting— Then Retreat.

(N[9]: *utilizes and capitalizes the text as subheadings*)

20.14 (were |) Practically Annihilated.

21.23 (shot |) Went through His Neck.

No. 6. a fragment of velestino

[The copy-text is WG; *Westminster Gazette*, June 3, 4, 8, 1897, pp. 1–2. The other texts collated are N¹: *New York Journal*, June 13, pp. 24–25; N²: San Francisco *Examiner*, June 27, p. 21.]

28.4 reddishy] reddish WG
28.18 evening] the evening N²
28.21 The (*no* ¶)] ¶ N¹⁻²
28.24 *et seq.* Velestino] Velestimo WG (*except* Valestimo *at* 30.12)
28.26–27 the infantry] infantry N¹⁻²
28.33 around] *omit* WG
28.39 Under (*no* ¶)] ¶ N¹⁻²
29.4 this] the N¹⁻²
29.11 old] *omit* N¹⁻²
29.26 ¹This was the product.] *omit* WG
29.28–29 distant] distinct N¹⁻²
29.31 a new] new N²
29.37 levee] levy WG
29.37 hot] lonely WG
29.37 was] were N²
30.5 *et seq.* toward] towards WG (*except at* 30.14)
30.6 that] which N¹⁻²
30.12–21 The part . . . nuisance.] *omit* N¹⁻²
30.30 it] *omit* WG
30.30–31 knivesₐ . . . difficulty,] ~ , . . . ~ ₐ N¹⁻²
30.39 The] One N¹⁻²
31.1 the others] they N¹⁻²
31.12 due] due to WG
31.14 not have] have not N¹⁻²
31.17 plain] obvious WG
31.24 outstretching] outreaching WG
31.31 large] *omit* WG
31.37 cobbles] cobble N¹⁻²
31.39 streets] street N¹⁻²
32.1 here] *omit* WG
32.1–2 —could it ever return] *omit* WG
32.7 chance-comer] spectator WG
32.7 then] *omit* N¹⁻²

32.10 ever] *omit* WG
32.11–34.15 There was . . . worse.] *omit* N¹⁻²
33.25; 35.13 backward] backwards WG
34.18 ¹It could . . . thing.] *omit* WG
34.23 hunk] hunch WG; bunch N¹⁻²
34.28 As (*no* ¶)] ¶ N¹⁻²
34.28 most] the most N¹⁻²
34.32–39 The crest . . . near it.] *omit* N¹⁻²
34.39 Continually (*no* ¶)] ¶ N¹⁻²
35.2–4 This . . . others] Shells WG
35.4 of an] of WG
35.6 in] on WG
35.8 obvious] convincing N¹⁻²
35.14 pattering] patter N¹⁻²
35.24 targets] marks WG
35.27 back] *omit* WG
35.34 battles] battle WG
35.35 fast] first N¹; *omit* N²
36.16 winter] *omit* N¹⁻²
36.21–22 As file . . . prayed.] *omit* WG
36.23 hooting] hootling N¹⁻²
36.31–38.29 Naturally . . . occurs.] *omit* N¹⁻²
38.39 ridge] ridges WG
39.3 in] on WG
39.6 half] half of N¹
39.7 shiny] shining N¹⁻²
39.9–37 To the rear . . . way.] *omit* N¹⁻²
40.2 number] numbers WG
40.4 old] *omit* N¹⁻²
40.6 any expression] and expressions N¹; and expression N²
40.11 its mystery] its majesty N¹⁻²
40.16 was] were N²

40.18   ²enemy] army N¹⁻²
40.19   the black] a black N¹⁻²
40.23   opened] open WG
40.30   The (no ¶)] ¶ N¹⁻²
40.38–41.1   muscular, as a] muscular—a WG
41.6   emotion—once he] emotion. [¶] Then he N¹⁻²
41.8   there] then N¹⁻²
41.14   at sea during a storm] during a storm at sea N¹⁻²
41.18   This] The N¹⁻²
41.20–31   All . . . men.] omit N¹⁻²
42.2   of the] of N²
42.5   this] his N¹⁻²
42.9   The (no ¶)] ¶ N¹⁻²

42.9   then] omit WG
42.19   am] am a N¹
42.32   It (no ¶)] ¶ N¹⁻²
42.32–33   one of . . . that the] the most ferocious attack the WG
42.38–43.20   A lot . . . phantoms.] omit N¹⁻²
43.21   in] on WG
43.25   charging] omit WG
43.28–32   Meanwhile . . . directions.] omit N¹⁻²
43.36   subalterns] subaltern N²
44.5   dusk] dark WG
44.7–8   woolly grey] gray woolly N¹⁻²
44.14   -cloaked] -coated N¹⁻²

No. 7. THE BLUE BADGE OF COWARDICE

[The copy-text is N¹: *New York Journal*, May 12, 1897, p. 3. Other full texts collated are N²: *Chicago Tribune*, May 12, pp. 1,3; N³: Philadelphia *Press*, May 12, p. 2; N⁴: San Francisco *Examiner*, May 12, pp. 1–2; N⁵: *Boston Globe*, May 12, p. 7; N⁶: *Buffalo Evening News*, May 12, pp. 1,7. A shorter text was also collated, N⁷: *Kansas City Star*, May 12, p. 2. Since this is a telegraphed dispatch, no paragraphing is listed.]

44.24   Athens . . . Chalkis).—] New York, May 12.—In a cable message to the Journal, Stephen Crane says of the retreat from Velestino: N⁷
44.26   the enemy] an enemy N⁴
44.28   was] were N⁴⁻⁵
44.28   cries] cheers N⁶
44.29   up] omit N⁵
44.29   *et seq.*   Smolenski's] Smolentz's N²
45.2–3   the officers] officers N⁴
45.4   soldiers'] soldier's N¹
45.4   equipments] equipment N⁶
45.5   the army] they N⁵
45.7   they] omit N⁴
45.7   fall] befall N²
45.10   ships] the ships N⁴
45.13–46.3   The foreign . . . flight.] omit N⁷
45.14   Turk] Turks N⁶
45.15   in time] in the time N²
45.16   for] of N²

45.16   gay] gray N⁶
45.19   transport] transmit N²
45.22   particular] peculiar N⁶
45.24   of] of a N²ˑ⁴
45.26   the lack] lack N⁴
45.26   aid] air N³
45.28   accursed] omit N³
45.34–35   certain harbor] conclusive safety N²
45.37   United States] U S N⁵
45.38   there] here N⁶
46.1–2   the foreigners] foreigners N⁴
46.4   The] After describing the exodus of the Greeks from Volo, Mr. Crane says: "The N⁷
46.5   Epirus] Espirus N²
46.6–7   do not] don't N⁵
46.7   as] are N⁷
46.7   haste] hate N⁵
46.9–47.11   Your . . . sides.] omit N⁷
46.9–10   the Turks] Turks N⁴

46.10–12 decks . . . were] deck . . . was N³
46.13 the little] little N⁴
46.15 It . . . great] I witnessed the N⁶
46.19 situation] accusation N⁶
46.20 the Greek] Greek N⁴
46.20 four] a few N⁶
46.21 the Greeks] that the Greeks N³
46.24,30 Halmyros] Salmyros N¹⁻²,⁵; Almyros N⁴,⁶
46.27 *et seq.* Domokos] Domoko N⁵
46.28 Prince] price N⁵
46.30 a] *omit* N⁴
46.32 further] farther N⁶
46.34 is . . . hard] the 40-yard N⁶
46.35 the report] report N⁴
46.39 the transports] transports N⁴
47.1 positively] *omit* N⁶
47.7 Oreos] Areos N¹⁻²,⁵⁻⁶; Arcos N³
47.9 on the fields] in the fields N⁴
47.9–10 great bonfires] a great bonfire N⁴
47.11 the babies] babies N⁴
47.12 we] one N⁴
47.19 the village] a village N⁵,⁷; this village N⁶
47.22 own] *omit* N⁴
47.23 such] *omit* N⁵
47.24 likely] be likely to N³
47.25 of] *omit* N²; of the N⁴,⁶⁻⁷
47.26–27 Warships . . . foreign] *omit* N⁷
47.29 Oreos] Areos N¹,⁴⁻⁷; Arcos N³
47.29 Halmyros] Helmyros N¹; Almyros N⁴⁻⁷
47.30 will] and will N²
47.32 will] may N⁴
47.34–48.15 Rumor . . . emigration.] *omit* N⁷
47.35 for] of N⁶
47.35 the people] people N⁴
47.36 food] food shortly N²
47.38 not] *omit* N³

48.1 troops] the troops N⁶
48.3 if] if the N⁴
48.8 our country] our own country N⁵
48.12 Every] and every N⁵
48.14 that the] a N⁴

Subheadings

(N¹)

45.18.1 Ships Thronged with Fugitives.
46.3.1 The Turk Not Lamblike.
46.37.1 Swarming on the Ships.
47.33.1 The Army Out of Provisions.

(N²)

46.3.1 Not Mild Wooly Lambs.
46.22.1 Same Old Order.
47.3.1 Go Hungry.
47.20.1 Skies Do Not Open These Days.
47.36.1 Future of Greece.

(N³)

45.14.1 The Scene at Volo.
46.8.1 Saw the Turks Coming.
46.30.1 Prince Will Not Retreat.
47.16.1 Terrible Suffering of the People.
48.1.1 (back. |) Greeks Want to Fight.

(N⁴)

45.8.1 Turks Move Slowly.
45.29.1 Ships Loaded with Refugees.
46.8.1 Sudden Evacuation of Volo.
46.37.1 Will Stand at Domokos.
47.21.1 (food. |) Pitiable Plight of Fugitives.
47.36.1 Tired of Falling Back.

(N⁶)

45.14.1 The Town of Volo.
46.30.1 The Prince and the Battle.
47.20.1 There Is No Food.
47.36.1 The Future of Greece.

No. 8. YALE MAN ARRESTED

[The copy-text is N¹: *New York Journal,* May 14, 1897, p. 3. Other texts collated are: N²: *Chicago Tribune,* May 14, p. 3; N³: Philadelphia *Press,* May 14, p. 2; N⁴: *Buffalo Evening News,* May 14, p. 5. Since this is a telegraphed dispatch, no paragraphing is listed.]

48.16   an American] *omit* N³
48.16   American∧] ∼ , N²
48.17   the Greek] a Greek N²
48.18   the company of] company with N²
48.19   for] on the charge of N²
48.21–23 Bindter . . . war.] Bindter, the correspondent of

an Austrian newspaper, was also arrested. N²
48.27   When . . . Athens the] They . . . Athens. The N²
48.29   spies. The people] spies, and N²
48.30   The . . . released] *omit* N²
48.30   is] is a N²

No. 9. THE DOGS OF WAR

[The copy-text is N¹: *New York Journal,* May 30, 1897, p. 18. The other text collated is N²: San Francisco *Examiner,* June 18, p. 4.]

49.8   in blue overcoats] *omit* N²
50.3   spraddled] straddled N²
50.5   little] a little N²
50.8,11   *The Journal*] "The Examiner" N²

50.21–22   the *New York Journal*] "The Examiner" N²
51.9   great] large N²
52.7   *New York Journal*] San Francisco 'Examiner,' N²

No. 10. STEPHEN CRANE TELLS OF WAR'S HORRORS

[The copy-text is N¹ᵇ: *New York Journal* (out-of-town edition), May 23, 1897, p. 37. Other texts collated are: N¹ᵃ: *New York Journal* (Greater New York edition), p. 35; N²: *Chicago Tribune,* May 23, pp. 1–2; N³: Philadelphia *Press,* May 23, p. 2; N⁴: San Francisco *Examiner,* May 23, p. 14; N⁵: *Buffalo Evening News,* May 23, pp. 1,8. N² is the copy-text for passages not present in N¹. N¹ without specification stands for N¹ᵃ⁻ᵇ. Since this is a telegraphed dispatch, no paragraphing is listed.]

53.21   nice] *omit* N⁵
53.24   the men] men N⁴
53.25   an] as N³; a N⁵
53.28–54.4   Above . . . to me.] *omit* N¹
53.29   and groans] *omit* N³
53.30   the trenches] their trenches N³
54.2   endured] endure N⁴

54.5   them] him N¹ᵃ
54.7   bosom] breast N²
54.7   a dead] the dead N³
54.7–12   He had . . . other.] *omit* N⁴
54.15   the Chalkis] Chalkis N⁴
54.15–17   Already . . . in it.] *omit* N⁴
54.18   we] he N⁴

54.18   Piraeus] the Piraeus N[4]
54.19   extra] extras N[2,4]
54.23–29   I . . . it.] *omit* N[1]
54.23   watch] watching N[4]
54.24   the Turks] Turks N[4]
54.33   This is . . . Stylidia.] St. Alida, May 19.—N[2]
54.34   upon] on N[5]
54.34–35 *et seq.*   Smolenski's] Smolentz's N[2]
54.35   Thermopylae] Thermonvlae N[1a]
54.36   the Turks] Turks N[4]
54.37   Halmyros] Palmyros N[2]; Almyros N[5]
54.38–55.6   What . . . quay.] *omit* N[1]
54.39   *The Journal's*] Our N[2]; The N[3]; "The Examiner's" N[4]
54.39–55.1   boat, at Bay . . . located,] boat that carried the wounded N[3-5]
55.2,4,17–18,24   Stylidia] St. Alida N[2]
55.6   where . . . quay] *omit* N[4]
55.9   in] *omit* N[4]
55.10   All the] All N[4]
55.13   twenty] twenty-four N[4]
55.15   -war's] -war N[3,5]; -wars' N[2]
55.17–35   As we . . . matter.] *omit* N[1]
55.18–23   The beautiful . . . safe.] *omit* N[4]
55.19   lemons] lemon N[3]
55.20   as] *omit* N[3]
55.21   their city] the city N[3]
55.25   Its . . . soldiers.] *omit* N[4]
55.26   183] one hundred and eighty-three N[4]
55.27   the warships] warships N[4]
55.27   Thermopylae] the Thermopylæ N[2]
55.28   the small] small N[4]
55.29–31   There . . . again.] *omit* N[4]
55.29   wind] wind blowing N[5]
55.30   warships] warship N[5]
55.33–56.1   There . . . loudly.] *omit* N[4]
55.36   old] *omit* N[5]

55.36–37   particularly. Uprooted] particularly, uprooted N[1,5]
55.37   they had] where they had N[2]
55.37   [2]they] *omit* N[1,5]
55.39–56.1   Among . . . loudly] *omit* N[1]
56.2   an emigrant] the emigrant N[4]
56.3   the sick] sick N[4]
56.3   The *Journal* steamer] The steamer N[2-3]; "The Examiner's" steamer N[4]
56.4   Marina] Martini N[4]
56.4   the hospital] hospital N[4]
56.15   with] *omit* N[2]
56.18–19   Stylidia . . . midnight.] *omit* N[1,4]
56.18   utterly] seemed N[3]
56.20   Belline] Relline N[5]
56.30   idly] incidentally N[3]; *omit* N[4]
56.31   said, and he] said. He N[4]
56.33   too] was too N[2]
56.33–34   to go] to | to go N[1]
56.35   sent] went N[2]
56.36   was] and was N[4]
56.36   the leg] his leg N[4]
56.37–38   We . . . Chalkis.] *omit* N[1]
56.38   and then . . . Chalkis] *omit* N[4]
56.39   war] the war N[4]
56.39   glory and] glory in N[3]

Subheadings

(N[1])

54.12.1   Wounded Taken to Athens.
54.32.1   Retreat toward Thermopylae.
55.16.1   Suffering of Women and Children.

(N[2])

53.27.1   Marvelous Endurance.
54.12.1   Taking Them to Athens.

54.22.1 Where Words Are Inadequate.
54.32.1 Panic at St. Alida.
55.13.1 (march. |) Flee from the Turks.
56.4.1 Returning for Bread.
56.29.1 Act of Mercy.

(N³)

54.17.1 Endless Procession of Stretchers.

55.23.1 A City of the Dead.
56.4.1 Vain Search for Bread.

(N⁵)

54.3.1 (thought. |) Scenes of Death.
54.22.1 Officers Turned Away.
54.37.1 All Terror-Stricken.
55.16.1 Taking of Stylidia.
55.35.1 Refugees Were Dazed.
56.17.1 Hospital at St. Marina.

No. 11. GREEKS WAITING AT THERMOPYLAE

[The copy-text is N¹: *New York Journal*, May 24, 1897, p. 10. Other texts collated are N²: *Chicago Tribune*, May 24, p. 2; N³: San Francisco *Examiner*, May 24, p. 1; N⁴: Philadelphia *Press*, May 24, p. 2. Since this is a telegraphed dispatch, no paragraphing is listed.]

57.6 the] a N³
57.7 officers] the officers N³
57.9 ¹have] have been N¹
57.13 the new] a new N³
57.15 ¹They] These soldiers N²
57.15 always] *omit* N²
57.20 came . . . recognized] come . . . recognize N¹,⁴
57.22 in the] within N³
57.23 the town] town N³
57.26 a] *omit* N³
58.1 irregulars] regulars N²
58.4 the] *omit* N³
58.6 the most] most N³
58.6 cruelty] cruelties N⁴
58.10 Greek] the Greek N³
58.19 significant] suggestive N⁴
58.19–20 Whatever . . . stop.] *omit* N³
58.21 admits] admit N³⁻⁴
58.23 Leonidas'] Leonidas's N¹;

Leonidas N⁴
58.24 fight] battle N³; fought N⁴
58.26 the supreme] supreme N³
58.27–29 I would . . . change.] *omit* N³

Subheadings

(N¹)

57.11.1 Only Evzones Left Behind.
57.25.1 (of it. |) Preparations for Resistance.
58.5.1 Tales of Cruelties Plentiful.
58.20.1 New Thermopylae Strong.

(N⁴)

57.16.1 Greeks Expect More Fighting.
58.12.1 Officers Are Tired.

No. 12. MY TALK WITH "SOLDIERS SIX"

[The copy-text is N¹: *New York Journal*, June 20, 1897, p. 18. The other texts collated are WG: *Westminster Gazette*, June 14, p. 2; June 15, pp. 1–2; N²: San Francisco *Examiner*, July 4, p. 6. The latter is a derived text **without authority.**]

58.30   June 1] June 10 N²
58.30–59.5   Since . . . opinion.]
Many newspapers, particularly
in America, have celebrated in
type their correspondents' interviews with the King of
Greece as with the Crown
Prince, and with others who
have had only a little more to
do with the war. WG
59.5–9   Here are . . . heeded.]
omit N¹⁻²
59.14 *et seq.*   Domokos] Domoko
N¹⁻²,WG (−N¹ *at* 68.28,29)
59.17,18   Afterward] Afterwards
WG (*l.c. at* 59.18)
59.32   No.] All but two. N¹⁻²
59.35   But] *omit* N¹⁻²
59.35   they] the officers N¹⁻²
59.36   easy.] easy? N¹⁻²
59.36   And then . . . killed.] *omit*
N¹⁻²
59.37   "Well, . . . regiments."]
"No. It is very hard." N¹⁻²
60.3   Prince] Prince's WG
60.4   not he] he not WG
60.5   all] *omit* WG
60.20   there was] I met N¹⁻²
60.25   euzonoi] euzone WG
60.28   I (*no* ¶)] ¶ WG
60.29   ¶ "Which] *no* ¶ WG
60.38 *et seq.*   Velestino] Velestimo
WG
61.16   leader.] leader's? WG
61.32   Larissa] Larisa N¹
61.32   Velestino] Velestine N¹;
Velestimo WG
61.33   are] were N¹⁻²
62.3   very] *omit* WG
62.7   thought] thoughts WG
62.23   in] on N¹⁻²
62.28   the] *omit* WG
62.29   a] the WG
63.6   they] they also WG
63.11   turns,] turns to discharge
their human freight N¹⁻²
63.12   carriages] carriages wait
N¹⁻²
63.13   crowd . . . turns] *omit*
N¹⁻²

63.13–14   simply packed already]
already packed N¹⁻²
63.16   quietly] grimly N¹⁻²
63.16   already] almost N¹⁻²
63.18–19   trousers-leg] trouser leg
WG
63.25   anyhow] *omit* N¹⁻²
63.27–36   Sometimes . . . near
him.] *omit* N²
63.30   surgeons] surgeon WG
63.32   is fed] *omit* WG
63.37   an] out a N¹⁻²
63.38   thronged] thronging WG
64.2   lay] lie WG,N²
64.4   On] *omit* WG
64.16   euzonoi] euzoni N¹⁻²
64.17   had] has WG
64.17–18   —here] where N¹⁻²
64.19   When the] When a N²
64.20   to him] *omit* WG
64.26–33   "Does . . . back."] *omit*
N²
65.1   cannon] cannons N¹⁻²
65.18   mountains] mountain N¹⁻²
65.24   toward] towards WG
65.24   gates] gate N¹⁻²
65.26   tossed] threw WG
65.28   in] on WG
65.34   Who] Whom WG,N²
65.36   not he] he not WG
66.2   well led] led well N¹⁻²
66.11   down] *omit* WG
66.17   that] *omit* WG
66.25   inside], inside, other WG
66.37   furnaces] furnace N²
67.5   coffee-house] cafe N¹⁻²
67.6   ordinary] ordinarily N²
67.9   type] type that N¹⁻²
67.16   gentle] gently N¹⁻²
67.21   wear the] wear a N¹⁻²
67.22   close] *omit* N¹⁻²
67.23   a] an N²
67.24   when observing his wound]
omit N¹⁻²
67.34   is] *omit* N¹⁻²
67.36–37   afterward] afterwards
WG
68.12   is beaten] beaten WG
68.17   further] farther WG
68.19   to war] *omit* WG

68.25   who] whom N¹⁻²
68.27   not he] he not N¹⁻²
68.29–30   It is in] In N¹⁻²

68.31   that] *omit* N¹⁻²
68.31   when he was not beaten]
        omit WG

No. 13. THE MAN IN THE WHITE HAT

[The copy-text is WG: *Westminster Gazette*, June 18, 1897, pp. 1–2. Other texts collated are N¹: New York *Sun*, July 11, sec. II, p. 2; N²: *Philadelphia Inquirer*, July 11, p. 28; N³: *Pittsburgh Leader*, July 11, p. 21; N⁴: Portland *Oregonian*, July 11, p. 19; N⁵: *Denver Republican*, July 11, p. 21.]

69.12   reared] showed N¹
69.16   forever] for ever WG
69.16   tooling] toiling N³⁻⁴
69.16–17   other way] other N⁴
69.19   face] front N²
69.20 *et seq.*   euzone] evzone N¹
69.21   framed] inclosed N²
69.25–26   came racing around] came round N³
69.26   the corner] a corner $N
70.3   calmly] quietly N³
70.6   scheme] color N²
70.7   We] He N²⁻⁵
70.7   lay] laid N²
70.16   Two- . . . Radicals] two miles beyond the extreme edge of the radicals $N
70.16   Where] When N¹
70.19   this hat] this head-|gear

WG; that hat N⁴
70.25   that fronted] *omit* N¹
70.32   quietly] quiet N¹
71.3   shamed] ashamed N⁴
71.4   he would speak to the King] *omit* N³
71.9   were there] there were N³
71.11   his table] the table N²
71.12   began] he began N¹
71.14   throng] crowd N³
71.17   or] nor N¹
71.20   thoughtfully] *omit* N¹
71.24   The] This WG
71.31   stooped] stopped N¹
71.35.1   *omit space* N¹
72.3   peaceful] *omit* N¹
72.8   at last] *omit* N¹
72.10   to the crowd] *omit* N³

No. 14. A PORTRAIT OF SMOLENSKI

Alterations in the Manuscript

72.18   but] *interlined above deleted* 'But'; *preceding period deleted*
72.19   a great] *originally* 'them. A great' *but deleted and* 'a' *inserted*
72.22   feat] 'a' *over start of* 't'
72.24   Perhaps] 'P' *over* 'p'
72.24   breadth] 'a' *over* 'd'
72.25   It] 'I' *over* 'i'
72.28   Judging] 'J' *over* 'T'
72.28   an] *interlined above deleted* 'the'

73.6   Greek] *final* 's' *deleted*
73.10   Perhaps] ¶ *sign precedes*
73.13,24   cavalry] *interlined by* Stephen Crane *above deleted* 'cavelery' *after he had first attempted to mend the misspelling*
73.14   equestrian] *interlined by* Stephen Crane *above deleted* 'esquerium' (?)
73.14   heroic] 'c' *over possible* 'e'
73.17   outstretched] 'a' *deleted after final* 'e'
73.19   Greek] *final* 's' *deleted*
73.19   artists] *interlined*

73.20 monstrous] MS 'monsterous' *made by altering 'r' to 'er'*

73.22 As] ¶ *sign precedes*

73.23 ¹the] *interlined with a caret preceding* 'most'

73.26 soldiers] *second* 's' *written over illegible letter, possibly an original deleted* 's'

73.36 it.] *following upstroke deleted*

74.1 are said] 'are' *interlined by* Stephen Crane *with a caret*

74.6 It] ¶ *sign precedes*

74.7 aim] *first minim of* 'm' *altered from a doubtful* 'r'

74.7 artillery] 'e' *inserted*

74.8 nothing] 't' *mended*

74.9 futilely] *interlined by* Stephen

Crane *above deleted* 'futilly'

74.13 retrieved] MS 'retreived' *with* 'i' *over* 'a'

74.14 at Velestino.] *interlined with a caret drawn over a period*

74.17 Crown] 'C' *over* 'c'

74.18 Smolenski] 'i' *over doubtful* 'u', *perhaps* 'ie'

74.23 Smolenski's] 'm' *over* 'o'

74.25 of] *interlined above deleted* 'to'

74.25 make] *interlined by* Stephen Crane *above deleted* 'be'

74.32 Frenchmen] 'F' *over* 'f'

74.38 there] *the word is possibly* 'then'

75.13 superb] *altered by* Stephen Crane *from* 'surpurb'

No. 15. THE EASTERN QUESTION

Alterations in the Manuscript

[Cora's *hand; later alterations in* Stephen's *hand*]

75.16 one] *interlined with a caret above deleted* 'a'

75.19 Britain] MS 'Britian' *interlined above deleted* 'Britten' *in which the* 'en' *has been written over what may be* 'ian'

75.22 existence] *second* 'e' *over* 'a'

75.26 wish] *preceded by deleted* 'wh'

75.29 puzzle] 'zz' *altered from* 'ss'

75.30 on] *interlined with a caret above deleted* 'for'

75.31 still] *interlined with a caret*

76.1 achieved] *first* 'e' *inserted*

76.2 political] *interlined above deleted* 'economical'

76.3 He] 'H' *over* 'h'

76.3 profession] *second* 'f' *deleted*

76.4 mystify] MS 'mystyfy' *in which second* 'y' *over possible* 'er'

76.7 advantageous] *preceded by deleted* 'com'

76.9 or] *preceded by deleted* 'and'

76.9 on his] 'h' *mended: any resemblance to* 'this' *is accidental*

76.10 upon] 'u' *over one or two illegible letters*

76.12 altogether] 'a' *following first* 'e' *deleted*

76.13 understood] *preceded by deleted* 'thought'

76.14 it must] *preceded by deleted* 'this'

76.16 calamity] 'mi' *written over* 'mt'

76.19 Anybody] 'A' *over* 'a'

76.19 negotiations] *interlined above deleted* 'negociations'

76.21 national] *preceded by deleted* 'dip'

76.21 should] 'sh' *over* 'ca' *preceded by* 'can' *deleted and interlined* 'coul' *deleted*

76.23 diplomacy] 'l' *over* 'o' *or* 'a'

76.25 invariably] 'a' *interlined with a caret*

76.26 History] 'or' *over* 'ro'

76.27 purely] *interlined with a caret*

76.28 proof] *second* 'o' *over start of* 'f'

76.29 name] *preceded by deleted* 't'

76.30 Anyone] *preceded by deleted* 'The'

76.30 the Orient] *interlined above deleted* 'Constantinople'

76.31 manoeuverings] MS 'ma-noeuvurings' 'e' *inserted between* 'o' *and* 'v'

76.32 crisis] *second* 'i' *over* 'e'

76.34 bazaar] *final* 'a' *over* 'r'; *preceded by deleted* 'bas' *with* 'z' *over* 's'

[Stephen's *hand begins at* 76.34 'And']

76.34 And] 'A' *over* 'a' *and preceding period inserted*

76.35 to] *interlined*

76.36 one] *interlined with a caret*

77.2 Turk] *final* 's' *deleted*

77.2 appoints] 's' *added later*

77.3 a] *preceded by deleted* 'the'

77.4–6 At . . . regime.] *added later*

77.7 his] *preceded by deleted* 'he shall'

77.9 Tewfik] 'e' *over* 'i'

77.10 ¹you] 'y' *over* 'o' *and start of letter with a tall ascender*

77.11 ¹He] *preceded by deleted* 'He You'

77.13 is] *interlined above deleted* 'has'

77.13 that] *interlined with a caret*

77.14 you wonder] *interlined with a caret*

77.15 learn] *interlined above deleted* 'see'

77.16 rascal] 'ra' *over* 'm'

77.17 repay] 're' *squeezed in*

77.27; 78.17 Mediterranean] *first* 'a' *over* 'e'

77.28 five] *interlined above deleted* 'three'

77.32 would] 'w' *over* 'c'

77.34 But] *interlined above deleted* 'Then'

77.35 maneuvres] MS 'man-|uvres'

with 'uvres' *preceded by deleted* 'ov'

78.2 Powers] 'P' *over* 'p'

78.2 having] 'in' *over* 'e'

78.3 find] 'finding' *interlined above deleted* 'find' *and then* 'ing' *deleted*

78.7 that] *interlined above deleted* 'who'

78.8 defend] *followed by deleted* 'this'

78.15 as he] *interlined with a caret*

78.15 attempts] 's' *interlined above deleted* 'ing'

78.19 Since] *preceded by deleted* 'When th'

78.20 took] *preceded by deleted* 'ha'

78.20 cause] *interlined above deleted* 'reason'

78.21 occupy] *interlined above deleted* 'blockade'

78.23–24 Is it . . . prevent?] *interlined above deleted* 'This remains a proposition yet to be proven because the Cretans have never had that particular and supreme reputation for massacre which is the heritage of the Turk. If they have never yet have massacred anybody it is legal to exempt them [them *interlined with a caret*], partially at least, from this charge.'

78.24 If] *preceded by* 'Furthermore' *interlined with a caret and deleted*

78.24 Crete] 'r' *over* 'e'

78.26 massacre?] *question mark over period*

78.26 to] *preceded by deleted* 'the'

78.30 it] *interlined with a caret*

78.30 further] *interlined with a caret*

78.30 even] *interlined with a caret*

79.1 a] *interlined with a caret*

79.1 in common.] *interlined above deleted* 'to do.'

79.4　And] 'A' *over* 'a' *and preceding period inserted*

79.4　the necessity] 'the' *altered from* 'this'; 'neccesity' *preceded by deleted* 'expedient'

79.4　for the] 'the' *interlined above deleted* 'an'

79.4　exists] *final* 's' *over* 'ed'

79.5　raise] *final* 'd' *deleted*

79.5　semblances] *final* 's' *added; preceded by deleted* 'a'

79.6　squadrons] *followed by deleted period*

79.6　²the] 'e' *over* 'i'

79.11　in] *preceded by deleted* 'of'

79.13　perplexed] *first* 'p' *over illegible letter probably* 'a'

79.18　who] *interlined with a caret*

79.18　never] *interlined with a caret*

79.19　clearly] *preceded by* **deleted** 'th'

79.19　seated] 'ed' *over* 'ing'; *followed by deleted* 'up'

79.20　coolly] *second* 'l' *over what is doubtfully the start of a* 'y'

79.21　smile] *interlined above deleted* 'success'

79.23　greater] *interlined above deleted* 'large aspect'

No. 16. THE TURKISH ARMY

Alterations in the Manuscript

[Cora's *hand*]

80.5　formidable] 'i' *over* 'a'; *probably an* 'i' *is intended after* 'd'

80.8　skilful] *originally* 'skillful' *but the* 'l' *before* 'f' *deleted*

80.8　diplomacy] *followed by deleted* 'he is now'

80.9　known] 'k' *over doubtful* 'c'

80.10　is] *interlined with a caret*

80.10　doubtful] 'ful' *interlined with a caret above deleted* 'fl'

80.11　wouldn't] 'nt' *over doubtful* 'n'

80.12　meant] 'e' *inserted*

80.17　stirred] *interlined above deleted* 'stired'

79.25　gentleman] 'a' *over doubtful* 'e'

79.26　diplomats] *followed by deleted* 'of Europe'

79.26　have] *interlined above deleted* 'had'

79.29　chose] *altered from* 'choose'

79.29　that] *second* 't' *over upstroke*

79.29　together] *interlined*

79.31　if its] 'if' *interlined with a caret before deleted* 'his' *and then deleted, and interlined more clearly before* 'it's'

79.31　and if] 'if' *added later*

79.34　One] *above is the deleted false start* 'He portrayed'

79.34　observe] *preceded by deleted* 'think'

79.36　too] *second* 'o' *added later*

79.36　Nor] 'N' *over* 'n' *and preceding period altered from a comma*

79.37　broken] *preceded by deleted doubtful* 's'

79.38　be] *preceded by deleted* 'have made an'

80.3　rose] *initial* 'a' *deleted*

80.17　spirit] *altered from* 'sperit' *or* 'sprit'

80.18　fired] *preceded by deleted* 'd'; *followed by deleted* 'a' *and then deleted* 'new' *mended to* 'anew'

80.23　army] 'y' *mended*

80.24　assembled] 'd' *mended*

80.25　Greek] *interlined above deleted* 'Turkish' *in* Cora's *hand*

80.26　newspapers] *interlined above deleted* 'world'

80.31　statements] *preceded by deleted* 'facts'

81.1　²the] 't' *over* 'i' *followed by possible* 't' *or* 's'

81.2　this] 's' *mended*

81.5 shells] *preceded by deleted*
  'artillery'
81.6 explode] 'de' *over doubtful*
  're'
81.8 As] 'A' *over* 'a'
81.10 exist] *final* 's' deleted
81.11 legend] *preceded by deleted*
  'ledg'

[*Stephen's hand begins at* 81.11

'Moreover']

81.12 Turkish] 'u' *over* 'r'
81.13 an American] *preceded by*
  deleted 'looked as if the the
  man had wrapped himself'
  and, on line below, deleted
  'were not soldierly, not even
  peasant-like;'

No. 17. STEPHEN CRANE'S OWN STORY

[The copy-text is N¹: *New York Press*, Jan. 7, 1897, pp. 1–2. Other full texts collated are N²: Philadelphia *Press*, Jan. 7, pp. 1,3; N³: *Chicago Record*, Jan. 7, pp. 1–2; N⁴: New Orleans *Times-Democrat*, Jan. 7, p. 1; shorter texts collated are N⁵: *Chicago Tribune*, Jan. 7, p. 1; N⁶: Boston *Record*, Jan. 8, p. 3; N⁷: *New Bedford Mercury*, Jan. 9; N⁸: *St. Paul Pioneer Press*, Jan. 9, pp. 1,4; N⁹: London *Morning Leader*, Jan. 20, p. 8; N¹⁰: London *Daily Mail*, Jan. 21, Daily Magazine section, p. 7. N² is the copy-text for passages not present in N¹. Variant paragraphing is not listed since this is a telegraphed text.]

85.1 It] New York, Jan. 6—[Special.]—Stephen Crane, the novelist, who had an exciting experience as one of those on board the filibuster Commodore, which foundered at sea, writes the story of the wreck and his narrow escape to the New York Press. He is now in Jacksonville, Fla., recovering from the effects of the hardships he suffered. He writes: "It N⁵; Chicago, Jan. 8.— Stephen Crane, the novelist, who had an exciting experience as one of those on board the filibuster Commodore, which foundered at sea, writes the story of the wreck and his narrow escape to the New York Press, says a New York special to the Tribune. He is now in Jacksonville, Fla., recovering from the effects of the hardships he suffered. He writes: "It N⁸

85.1–91.3 It . . . Now the whistle] Stephen Crane has finally

embraced his opportunity and given us a personal experience of shipwreck as it came near to him on the Commodore. It is tremendously vivid, and illustrates the young fellow's strength as a writer as well as his own conduct demonstrated the good stuff there was in him. Says he:— [¶] The whistle N⁶⁻⁷ (N⁷: *no* —)

85.1–87.10 It . . . shore.] It was on New Year's Day that the SS. Commodore, with her hatches yawning, took in load after load of ammunition and rifles alongside the quay at Jacksonville, U.S.A. She was to play the part of a Cuban filibuster, and on board of her was Stephen Crane, the American novelist. As she put her head to sea she was cheered away on her voyage—it was the last she was ever to take. As Stephen Crane says: N⁹

85.1–88.30 It . . . that."] Not long ago the cable brought us news of the loss of the Commodore, while endeavouring to convey arms and ammunition to the men struggling for Cuban independence. On board were several newspaper correspondents, including Mr. Stephen Crane, the author of "The Red Badge of Courage," which attracted no small amount of attention in this country last year, while in America it was the book of the year. The "Chicago Record" containing Mr. Crane's account of his adventure on the filibustering steamer is just to hand. It seems that the Commodore was unlucky from the very start. She sailed on New Year's Eve, but no sooner had she left her moorings than a thick fog settled down on the river. Twice she ran aground, and when, after considerable delay, she got clear, she put to sea in the teeth of a terrible gale. But Mr. Crane must tell his experiences in his own words:— N[10]

85.2   Year's. The] ~ , the N[3,5,8]
85.3   negro] colored N[2]
85.3   processioned] proceeded N[3-4]
85.10–18 Everything . . . her.] omit N[5,8]
85.11 munitions] munition N[1]; ammunition N[4]
85.12 proceeding] proceedings N[2]
85.13 up] omit N[3]
85.15 to Cuba] omit N[4]
85.17 United States interests] the United States' interest N[4]
85.17 Johns] John's N[2-4]
85.18 sign] signs N[3]
85.20–30 Many . . . Then] omit N[5,8]
85.20 the men] them N[2]
85.26 custom] customs N[4]
85.26 house. The] house, and the N[3]
85.28 Johns] John's N[2,4]

85.30 dock] docks N[3]
85.30 amid] aimed N[2]
85.31 she . . . her] it . . . its N[5,8]
86.1–4 In . . . wails.] omit N[5,8]
86.3   to] at N[3]
86.3   impressed] impress N[4]
86.7   so] now N[2]
86.8   heard] heaved N[4]
86.9   thump, thump, thump] thump, thump N[3]; thump N[5,8]
86.11–89.4 But . . . In the meantime] summary in N[5,8]
86.11 was] were N[1]
86.11 hifalutin] hifalution N[3]
86.11 emotions] emotion N[3]
86.13 cook's] cook N[3]
86.23 Boutwell] Boutweel N[3]
86.26 again we] we again N[4]
86.27 along] again N[3]
86.28 some . . . men] that place any journey-|men N[4]
86.30 Day] day N[3-4]
86.34 Commodore] commodore N[3]
86.34 ships] ship N[1,4]
87.3   the grip of] the group of N[1]; the grove of N[2]; omit N[3]
87.3–4 the Commodore] omit N[1]
87.8   then] omit N[3]
87.8   whistle] whistles N[3]
87.9   Kilgore] Kilgeth N[3]
87.10 this was] these were N[3]
87.10 words] word N[1-2]
87.11 the enormous] enormous N[1-3]
87.12 flee] flew N[2]
87.12–13 a certain . . . Commodore] she N[9]
87.12 light-heartedness] light-hearted mess N[3]; light-hearted song N[4]
87.12 departed] sprang N[4]
87.12–13 the throats of] omit N[1]
87.13 the ship's] many of the ship's N[2,4]
87.13 company] crew N[4]
87.13–38 The . . . streak.] omit N[1]
87.14 gotten] got N[3,9]

87.14–15　and turned] this turned N[4]; and had turned N[9]

87.15　breeze that was] breakers that were N[3,9]

87.16　southeast there] southeast. There N[4]

87.17　a] omit N[4]

87.17　on] in N[3]

87.17　not] omit N[4]

87.18–93.18　On . . . silence.] summary in N[9]

87.18　amidships] amidship N[3]

87.21　of] in N[3]

87.22　postures] similar postures N[3]

87.22–23　of complete . . . stomachs] omit N[3]

87.23　to . . . stomachs] omit N[4]

87.27　mate] man N[2-3]

87.28　dashed] washed N[4]

87.31　American] among the N[4]

87.34　Day] day N[3]

87.38　coast] past N[4]

87.39　Commodore's wake] Commodore N[1-3]

88.2–3　flashing] flasking N[3]

88.4　rhythmical] rhythmatical N[3]

88.4　and mighty] omit N[4]

88.5　inexperienced] experienced N[3]

88.6　considerable . . . excitement] a mental strain N[4]

88.7　consequently] in consequence N[1]

88.7　he] omit N[4]

88.7　I] omit N[3]

88.8　myself] omit N[3]

88.9　one's self] oneself N[4]

88.9–10　Every . . . lurched‸] The ship lurched. N[4]

88.10–13　and it . . . ship.] but was not. N[4]

88.11　nor] or N[3]

88.12　accursed] abused N[3]

88.13　ship] vessel N[1]

88.14　a bench] the bench N[2]

88.14　²was] is N[1-3]

88.14–15　of a portly and] portly and has a N[2]

88.15　and by] but by N[4]

88.16　this] his N[4]

88.16　that] omit N[1]

88.17　awoke] woke N[1]

88.18　and] omit N[2]

88.18　feeling moved, he] omit N[1]; feeling moved, N[2]

88.18–19　himself of] off N[2]; omit N[4]

88.20　observations] observation N[2]

88.21　going] omit N[2]

88.22　in the neck] omit N[4]

88.24　Are] Is N[2]

88.25　going . . . out,] a N[2]

88.26　damned] d—— N[2]; omit N[3]; D—D N[4]

88.27　and they . . . right,] omit N[2]

88.27　they] omit N[4]

88.27　and it] but it N[4]

88.28　out] omit N[1]

88.31　Finding . . . sleep, I] "Finding . . . sleep," he says, "I N[10]

88.31　back] omit N[10]

88.32　named] omit N[1]

88.32　from Charleston] omit N[10]

88.34　those] the N[4]

88.34　forward] forword N[2]

88.35　from] of N[4]

88.35　upon] up on N[4]

88.35　weather-] omit N[4]

88.38　through] done N[10]

88.38　I've] I have N[2]

89.1　good] great N[2]

89.2　I will] I'll N[2]

89.3　in] on N[4]

89.3　in the corner . . . house] omit N[2]

89.3　went almost] almost went N[1]

89.4　came] come N[2]

89.4　duty] deck N[4]

89.5–6　up the stairs] upstairs N[2]

89.6　cried] cried out N[10]

89.6　to the captain] omit N[5,8,10]

89.6　that] omit N[5,8]

89.8　drowsing] dozing N[2,4]

89.9　of the little . . . back] omit N[8]

89.10　cried] he cried N[1,5,8]

89.14　then] omit N[1,5,8]

89.14   Go] Go and N[10]
89.15   bail] bale N[3,10]
89.16–91.2   The engine . . . do.”]
    summary in N[10]
89.16–18   by . . . place, it] *omit*
    N[5,8]
89.16   represented] presented N[4]
89.17   taken . . . kitchen] resem-
    bling the middle N[4]
89.18   insufferably] insufficiently
    N[2]
89.19–25   There . . . Higgins. He]
    Here a young oiler, Billy Hig-
    gins, N[5,8]
89.20   swirling and] *omit* N[4]
89.21   among] amongst N[2]
89.21   machinery] the machinery
    N[4]
89.21   and clattered] clattered N[4]
89.25   sloshing] slopping N[4]
89.25   this inferno] this infernal
    place N[4]; *omit* N[5,8]
89.26   a chain of men] the chain-
    men N[4]; the chain of men N[5,8]
89.26   extended] wended N[4]
89.27   up to] up N[1,4-5]
89.27–90.4   Afterward . . .
    bucket.] *omit* N[5,8]
89.28   point] place N[4]
89.28   the water] water N[1]
89.34   and sudden ruin] rush N[4]
89.37   and me] and I N[3]; *omit* N[4]
89.38   the direction] the directions
    N[3]; direction N[4]
90.1   Presently] and presently N[2]
90.1–2   and there] There N[2]
90.5   hard] the hard N[5,8]
90.6   again. Going forward] *omit*
    N[5,8]
90.6–7   as I went] *omit* N[5,8]
90.7   lowering] manning N[4]
90.9–10   person] man N[1,5,8]
90.10   the hell] the h—— N[2]; *omit*
    N[3]; h—l N[4]
90.12–25   Returning . . . It was]
    omit N[5,8]
90.14   him in] him N[3]
90.15   my] *omit* N[1]
90.17   so] as N[3]
90.22–23   blank, blank, blank]

omit N[2]; —— —— —— N[3]
90.24   he's] he is N[2,4]
90.25   that] *omit* N[5,8]
90.26   top of the deckhouse] deck
    N[4]
90.26–29   The deckhouse . . .
    sea.] *omit* N[5,8]
90.27   with] at N[4]
90.28   there] *omit* N[4]
90.31–32   which . . . car] *omit*
    N[5,8]
90.32   She] It N[5,8]
90.33–34   We . . . boat.] *omit*
    N[5,8]
90.35   her] it N[5,8]
90.36   the deck] deck N[4]
90.38–91.2   and in . . . do.”] *omit*
    N[5,8]
91.1   my God] *omit* N[3]
91.1   that's] who knows N[4]
91.2   do] do now N[2]
91.3   Now] *omit* N[2,5-7]
91.4   there ever] ever there N[10]
91.5   in the voice of] *omit* N[4]
91.5–9   ¹It . . . end.] *omit* N[5,8]
91.7   a wind] the wind N[10]
91.8   white] while N[4]
91.9   to . . .probably] too proba-
    bly N[4]
91.9   man's] a man's N[7]
91.10–92.10   It . . . Commodore.]
    omit N[7]
91.10   now that] then N[6]
91.11–14   To . . . water.] *omit* N[6]
91.11   To] At N[4]
91.11   who] we N[2]
91.12   lifeboat he] lifeboat. He N[2]
91.12   terms] the terms N[4]
91.13   ²and] *omit* N[3]
91.15   Afterward] Afterwards N[10]
91.15–17   standing . . . hand and]
    omit N[5,8]
91.17–20   gave . . . idea, and]
    omit N[5,8]
91.19   was about] *omit* N[4]
91.22   I . . . then] and then turned
    N[5,8]
91.22   very] *omit* N[1]
91.23   around] about N[10]
91.24   bed] *omit* N[6]

91.25 with . . . water] *omit* N[5,8]
91.26–35 and they . . . sir."] *omit* N[5,8]
91.26 they] then he N[4]
91.27 fend] send N[6]
91.27 oar] officer N[4]
91.28–92.10 They . . . *Commodore.*] *omit* N[6]
91.28 handed] hauled N[3,10]
91.28 then] when N[2,4]
91.29 boat] bow N[2]
91.29 and] *omit* N[4]
91.31 in] *omit* N[4]
91.31 over] over to N[1]
91.33–92.10 The captain . . . *Commodore.*] *summary in* N[10]
91.34 Graines] Grains N[4]
91.36 then] there N[2]; *omit* N[5,8]
91.37 rail] railing N[4]
91.38 a voice] *omit* N[4-5,8]
91.38 you.] you? N[4]
92.8 wind and as] wind. As N[4]
92.9 roarers] waves N[1,5,8]; roars N[2-3]
92.9 upon] on N[5,8]
92.12 clear] *omit* N[5,8]
92.12–16 as our . . . later] *omit* N[5,8]
92.12 rose] rode N[6-7]
92.13–20 She . . . ship.] *omit* N[6-7]
92.14 guy] gag N[1]; joke N[10]
92.15 on . . . fellows] *omit* N[10]
92.15 didn't] did not N[2]
92.16 later still] still later N[4]
92.17–20 I had . . . ship.] *omit* N[5,8]
92.17 ¹had] *omit* N[10]
92.17 forgotten] forgot N[1,3,10]
92.18 much] *omit* N[4]
92.20–21 to the ship] *omit* N[5,8]
92.22–23 and we . . . us] *omit* N[5,8]
92.23 gunwale] gunwales N[2]
92.23 swamp] sink N[10]
92.24 first] *omit* N[4]
92.25 alongside] *omit* N[5,8]
92.26 them] *omit* N[5,8]
92.28 here] there N[1,5-8,10]
92.30–35 This . . . fortitude.] *omit* N[5,8]

92.30 morning] the morning N[6-7]
92.32 on] in N[4]
92.32 stern] stem N[7]
92.34–35 Here . . . fortitude.] *omit* N[6-7]
92.36 I remember] *omit* N[5,8]; I remembered N[7]
92.36 clambered] clamored N[3]; climbed N[6-7]
92.36–37 and stood . . . waves] *omit* N[5,8]
92.38–93.27 "Jump," . . . line.] *summary in* N[10]
92.38 Jump] Jump in N[4]
92.38 cried] cries N[2]
92.39–93.2 and the . . . school] *omit* N[5,8]
93.2 docilely] docile N[6-7]
93.2 scholar . . . school] schoolboy N[3]
93.2 in] in a N[2,6-7]
93.4–9 He . . . time.] *omit* N[5,8]
93.4–18 He . . . silence.] *omit* N[6-7]
93.7 leaped] leaped in N[4]
93.7 death] his death N[2,4]
93.10 And] *omit* N[5,8]
93.11–12 and . . . us] *omit* N[5,8]
93.12 strode,] stood_∧ N[4]
93.13–16 One . . . downward.] *omit* N[5,8]
93.17–18 Still . . . silence.] *omit* N[5,8]
93.18 this] *omit* N[2]
93.20 Of . . . perfectly] We N[5,8]
93.21–23 our . . . circumstances] *omit* N[5,8]
93.22 water's] waters N[6]
93.24 these] those N[2]
93.24–35 and would . . . line.] *omit* N[5,8]
93.25 but] by N[4]
93.26 I was . . . rafts.] *omit* N[9]
93.26 I] It N[3]
93.28 this negro] him N[2]; the Negro N[7,9]; negro stoker N[10]
93.28 first] *omit* N[10]
93.31 this] the N[9]; his N[10]
93.32 to be turned] turned N[6-7,10]
93.33–35 His . . . us.] *omit* N[7]

93.35   of the line] the line N[10]
93.37–38   and   all . . .   ³silence,]
    omit N[5,8]
94.1   afar] *omit* N[5,8]; far N[10]
94.1   dove] dived N[10]
94.2   swallowed] swallowed up N[4]
94.2   this] the N[4]
94.2   this frightful maw of] *omit*
    N[5,8]
94.2   And] *omit* N[4]
94.2–6   And . . . pin.] *omit* N[5,8]
94.4   far] *omit* N[4]
94.5–23   The . . . dead.] *omit*
    N[6-7,9]; *summary in* N[10]
94.7–23   The   history . . . dead.]
    summary in N[5,8]
94.8   very] *omit* N[1]
94.13   toward] towards N[2]
94.16   Daytona] Dayton N[4]
94.17   had] *omit* N[2]
94.19   to me seem] seem to me N[1-2]
94.22   we] he N[1]
94.22   sand] the sand N[4]

Subheadings

(N[1])

85.18.1   Exchanging Farewells.
86.4.1   Felt Like Filibusters.
86.22.1   (necessary. |) Help from
    the Boutwell.
86.33.1   (gold. |) Aground Once
    More.
87.13.1   (company. |) Sleep Impos-
    sible.
88.13.1   The Cook Is Hopeful.
88.30.1   One Man Has Enough.
89.13.1   Helps in the Fireroom.
89.30.1   No Panic on Board.
90.4.1   Lowering Boats.
90.17.1   (him. |) Human Hog Ap-
    pears.
91.2.1   A Whistle of Despair.
91.22.1   (dingy. |) In the Ten-Foot
    Dingy.
91.39.1   Higgins Last to Leave
    Ship.
92.17.1   (us. |) Helping Their
    Mates.

93.2.1   The Mate's Mad Plunge.
93.18.1   Tried to Tow the Rafts.
93.35.1   (us. |) The Commodore
    Sinks.

(N[2])

85.18.1   Farewells Are Said.
87.38.1   Over the Flaming Waves.
88.25.1   A Prophecy of Salvation.
89.2.1   First Tidings of Ill.
90.11.1   First Boat Lowered.
91.9.1   The First Mate Raged.
92.15.1   Men on the Commodore.
92.35.1   Jumped into the Sea.
93.12.1   (us. |) Three Men Re-
    mained.
93.27.1   (line. |) Tried to Reach
    the Boat.
94.4.1   Long Struggle for Shore.

(N[3])

85.29.1   Felt Some Like Filibusters.
86.14.1   Were Stuck in the Mud.
87.10.1   Began   to   Turn   Hand-
    spring.
87.29.1   Where Florida Seems Nar-
    row.
88.13.1   Expected   Something   to
    Happen.
89.2.1   Ordered to the Lower Re-
    gions.
89.15.1   Seemed Like an Inferno.
90.6.1   (again. |) Talk of Lowering
    Boats.
91.2.1   Voice of Despair and Death.
92.15.1   The   Third   Boat   Had
    Foundered.
92.37.1   Fatal Plunge of the First
    Mate.
93.17.1   (raised. |) Turned into a
    Demon.

(N[4]: *utilizes and capitalizes the text
as subheadings*)

86.5   To Feel Like Filibusters.
87.11–12   That Flee over the Bar
88.26–27   I Have These D—d Feel-
    ings

89.36　There Was Never a Panic
91.9　A Song of Man's End.
92.29　Most Harrowing Hesitation.
93.33　The Face of a Lost Man

(N⁵)

86.1.1　(cheered. |) Felt Like Filibusters.
88.30.1　First Word of Coming Disaster.
89.15.1　Mystic　and　Grewsome Shadows.
90.11.1　To the Lifeboats.
91.14.1　"Shove Off."
92.4.1　(ship. |) Waiting for the End.
92.17.1　(us. |) Third Boat Founders.

93.11.1　(raft |) Left to Their Fate.
93.24.1　(it, |) Down Goes the Commodore.

(N⁹: *utilizes and capitalizes the text as subheadings*)

87.18　Finest Thing in the World."
93.25–26　Something Critical Came to Pass.

(N¹⁰: *utilizes and capitalizes the text as subheadings*)

89.6–7　There　Was　Something Wrong
91.15　When I Went Aft,
92.28　Cried the Captain,
93.37–38　No Shrieks, No Groans,

No. 18. THE FILIBUSTERING INDUSTRY

[The copy-text is N¹: *St. Paul Pioneer Press*, May 3, 1897, p. 3. Other texts collated are N²: *Denver Republican*, May 2, p. 21; N³: *Pittsburgh Leader*, May 2, p. 24.]

95.11　talk] a talk N¹
95.37　I am] I'm N¹
96.7　then] *omit* N³
96.12　²you] *omit* N³
96.24　a view] in view N²⁻³
96.25　Americo-] American- N¹
96.37　reputation] reputations N³
96.37　is] are N¹⁻³
97.20　to] to be N¹⁻²
97.21　reasons] reason N¹,³
97.23–24　oppressed] attended N¹
97.24　many] *omit* N¹
97.26　those] these N¹
97.38–39　got . . . *Commodore*] *omit* N³
98.2　bid] bade N³
98.2　genial] cordial N³

98.3–5　and gave . . . heard] *omit* N³
98.9　his] *omit* N¹
99.5–6　of the . . . Some] *omit* N¹
99.9　And] And they have N¹
99.12　insurgent] insurgents' N²
99.21　its] his N³
99.23–25　not . . . of it] *omit* N²
99.30　national] natural N²⁻³

Subheadings

(N²)

95.12.1　The Pinkerton Detectives.
96.14.1　Had Government Assistance.
97.8.1　Crews Eager to Enlist.
98.10.1　Some Tales Untold.

No. 19. THE TERRIBLE CAPTAIN OF THE CAPTURED PANAMA

[The copy-text is N¹: New York *World*, Apr. 28, 1898, p. 3. The other text collated is N²: Philadelphia *Press*, Apr. 28, p. 3. Since this is a cabled dispatch, no paragraphing is listed.]

103.1   unmitigated] *omit* N²
103.6   lone] long N²
103.11   Spanish] *omit* N²
103.18   to-day,] *omit* N¹
103.19   has] had N¹
103.21   has lain] lay N¹
103.22   four ₐ armed] four-armed N¹
103.23   very] a very N²
103.23   a most] most N²
103.25   and proved] who prove N²
103.27   their] the N²
103.28   a sleepy, pale] asleep—a pale N²
103.30   approaching] the approaching N²
103.30   everything] and everything N²
104.16   seems] seems that N²

104.23   *The World's*] a N²
104.28   gangway] gang N¹
104.29   lined like an ape's] like a map N²
104.35   meantime] mean time N¹
105.8   in] in the N²

Subheadings

(N²)

103.16.1 Change in Spaniards' Spirits.
104.7.1   Captain Wants to Go Ashore.
104.36.1 Palmetto Logs Betrayed.

No. 20. SAMPSON INSPECTS HARBOR AT MARIEL

[The copy-text is N¹: New York *World*, May 1, 1898, p. 3. Other texts collated are N²: Philadelphia *Press*, May 1, p. 2; N³: *Chicago Tribune*, May 1, p. 2; N⁴: *Omaha Daily Bee*, May 1, pp. 1–2. Since this is a cabled dispatch, no paragraphing is listed.]

105.12 *et seq.* her] its N³⁻⁴
105.18   Spaniards] Spanish N⁴
105.22   newspaper] newspapers N²
105.27   bay] Bay N³
105.28   An] *omit* N⁴
105.29   point] port N³⁻⁴
105.30   stands] stand N¹⁻²
106.3   very] *omit* N³
106.3   is] are N³
106.5–6 up . . . hardly] *these two lines are transposed in* N⁴
106.11   raised] arose N²; rose N⁴
106.13–14 bores, the] bores of the N⁴
106.14   very] *omit* N³
106.17   On] One N⁴
106.18   white-clad] white | cloud N⁴
106.19 *et seq.* She] It N³⁻⁴
106.22   the deck] the gun deck N¹; deck N²

106.24   snuffle] shuffle N³⁻⁴
106.25   an ovation] applause N³
106.27   decks] deck N⁴
106.32   into] in N²
106.35   aimed] armed N³⁻⁴
106.35   gun] guns N⁴
106.39   continued] continued on N³
107.3   after] fat N²
107.3   those] these N²
107.6   around] round N³⁻⁴
107.8   Yes] Oh N²
107.9   More cognac!] [More cognac.] N³
107.12   states] *omit* N³; states that N⁴
107.13   a man] saw a man N³
107.14   was] *omit* N³
107.18   decks] hecks N⁴
107.19   an] *omit* N⁴
107.22   part] port N²

Subheadings

(N²)

105.9.3   With the Blockading
Squadron.
105.26.1   The Only Defenses.
106.15.1   (flagship. |) Man the
Port Guns.
106.30.1   Fired Six Shells.
107.5.1   Spanish Version.

(N³)

106.9.1   Looks for Bigger Game.
106.33.1   Captain Chadwick Mans
a Gun.

(N⁴)

106.9.1   Unworthy of Attention.
107.5.1   Spanish Boasts.

No. 21. INACTION DETERIORATES THE KEY WEST FLEET

[The copy-text is N¹: New York *World*, May 6, 1898, p. 3. Other texts collated are N²: Philadelphia *Press*, May 6, p. 2; N³: *Chicago Tribune*, May 6, p. 2; N⁴: *Omaha Daily Bee*, May 6, p. 1. Since this is a cabled dispatch, no paragraphing is listed.]

107.30   -minute] minutes' N²
108.3   the ships] ships N⁴
108.4   delay] the delay N¹⁻²
108.4   one] *omit* N⁴
108.5   our] the N⁴
108.6   just as . . . unnecessary.]
certain. N⁴
108.9   service, and in] services. In
N⁴
108.10   about] at all times N¹⁻²
108.12   regular] *omit* N³
108.12   this] the N²,⁴
108.13   100] 100 degrees N⁴

No. 22. STEPHEN CRANE'S PEN PICTURE OF C. H. THRALL

[The copy-text is N¹: New York *World*, May 8, 1898, p. 19. The other texts collated are N²: Philadelphia *Press*, May 8, p. 2; N³: *Omaha Daily Bee*, May 8, p. 1. The copy-text for 109.24–32 is N³. Since this is a cabled dispatch, no paragraphing is listed.]

108.17–19   Charles . . . Cuba.]
omit N²⁻³
108.20   Thrall] the correspondent
Thrall N²
108.25   good] *omit* N³
108.30   and do not seem to think]
omit N²
108.30   think] wink N³
109.3   deeds] deed N²
109.8   streets] street N²
109.8   crying:] *omit* N¹
109.12   upon] up on N³
109.14   per] a N¹
109.15   ensued] resulted N²
109.16   that] *omit* N³
109.17   content] contented N²
109.18   out] *omit* N¹
109.24–32   As to . . . knows.]
omit N¹
109.27   at] all N³
109.28   in] *omit* N²
109.32   knows] knew N²
109.33   being] brings N³
109.38   Major, W. D. Smith,]
(Major W. D. Smith), N³

Subheadings

(N²)

109.17.1   (content. |) Blanco's
Many Proclamations.

No. 23. WITH THE BLOCKADE ON CUBAN COAST

[The copy-text is N¹: New York *World*, May 9, 1898, p. 7. The other text collated is N²: Philadelphia *Press*, May 9, p. 3. Since this is a cabled dispatch, no paragraphing is listed.]

110.12 ¹on] off N²
110.12 after] aft N²
110.19 the blockade] blockade N²
111.7 gotten] got N²
111.10 every] each N²
111.12 watches] watch N²
111.14 tubs] tubes N¹
111.18 the jack] jack N²
111.27 keen∧] keel, N²

111.32–33 the position of] *omit* N²
112.14 ²the flagship] *omit* N²
112.16 enigmatical] enigmatic N²

Subheadings

(N²)
112.13.1 (*Indiana.* |) Hoping for the Guns to Roar.

No. 24. SAYINGS OF THE TURRET JACKS IN OUR BLOCKADING FLEETS

[The copy-text is N¹: New York *World*, May 15, 1898, p. 33.]

114.22 on] *omit* N¹

No. 25. HAYTI AND SAN DOMINGO FAVOR THE UNITED STATES

[The copy-text is N¹: New York *World*, May 24, 1898, p. 7.]

117.16 the] *omit* N¹

Subheadings

116.9.1 Englishmen Our Friends.

116.29.1 Some Who Fear Us.
117.13.1 World Boat Cheered at Porto Plata.

No. 27. HOW SAMPSON CLOSED HIS TRAP

[The copy-text is N¹: New York *World*, May 27, 1898, p. 3. The other texts collated are N²: Philadelphia *Press*, May 27, p. 2; N³: *Chicago Tribune*, May 28, p. 13. Since this is a cabled dispatch, no paragraphing is listed.]

121.1–27 *The World . . . more.*] *omit* N³
121.1 *The World*] A Newspaper N²
121.2 dogging] dodging N¹⁻²
121.21 can't] can N²
121.28 So he] Cervera N³
122.2 here] *omit* N³
122.4 of] at N³

122.5 of] on N²
122.6 steamed] steam N²
122.6–7 defenses] defense N²
122.7 very] *omit* N³
122.14 a] the N²
122.21 gently] greatly N²⁻³
122.22–25 Meanwhile . . . happen.] *omit* N³

122.28   Then] *omit* N[2]
122.28   Monday] on Monday N[3]
122.29   her] its N[3]
122.31–123.37   Heroically . . . so.]
    omit N[3]
122.31   on] in N[2]
122.32   sank] sunk N[2]
122.37   Old] old N[1-2]
122.39   Rhenish] Rhine N[2]
123.1   this] the N[1]
123.3   fine-bred] fine lined N[1]
123.35–124.25   The   whole . . .
    Channel.] *omit* N[2]
123.39   again] *omit* N[3]
124.1   formed] found N[3]
124.5   ever] over N[3]

124.6   stayed] staid N[3]
124.12   then] *omit* N[3]
124.15   Maria] Marie N[1,3]
124.16,21   Old] old N[3]
124.16,25   Nicholas] Nicolas N[1]
124.20   eastward] eastern N[3]

Subheadings

(N[2])

121.27.1   Havana's Defenses Grow
    Better.
122.25.1   New York Heads for the
    Sea.
123.21.1   Signals from Every War-
    ship.

No. 29. IN THE FIRST LAND FIGHT FOUR OF OUR MEN ARE KILLED

[The copy-text is N[1a]: New York *World* (city edition), June 13, 1898, p. 1. The other text collated is N[1b]: New York *World* (out-of-town edition), June 13, pp. 1–2. All variants in N[1b] are recorded here. Since this is a cabled dispatch, no paragraphing is listed.]

128.14   Mass.] *omit* N[1b]
128.19   morning.] ∼ ∧ N[1b]
128.26   guard,] ∼ ∧ N[1b]
128.28   company] Company N[1b]
128.29   the camp] th camp N[1b]
128.29   fighting] fightng N[1b]
129.5   Both were] Each was N[1a]
129.6   500] 550 N[1a]
129.6   a rotary] arotary N[1b]
129.7–130.13   Their . . . gueril-
    las.] *omit* N[1b]
130.18–37   Dr. John . . . Associa-

tion.] Assistant Surgeon Gibbs, who was killed, was a son of Major Gibbs of the regular army, who fell in the Custer massacre. He used to practice his profession in New York City, but entered the army at the outbreak of the war at Richmond, Va. He was one of the most popular officers of the force. N[1b]

No. 30. ONLY MUTILATED BY BULLETS

[The copy-text is N[1]: *Boston Globe*, June 16, 1898, p. 5. The other text collated is N[2]: Philadelphia *Press*, June 17, p. 2. Since this is a cabled dispatch, no paragraphing is listed.]

131.6   effect] effects N[2]
131.18   [1]and] *omit* N[2]

131.20   in safety] safely N[2]

No. 31. CRANE TELLS THE STORY OF THE DISEMBARKMENT

[The copy-text is N¹: New York *World*, July 7, 1898, p. 8. The other text collated is N²: *Boston Globe*, July 7, p. 2.]

131.21 Daiquiri] Baiquiri N²
132.4 The (*no* ¶)] ¶ N²
132.10 raising] rising N²
132.14 a hundred] 100 N²
132.28 To (*no* ¶)] ¶ N²
133.5 General (*no* ¶)] ¶ N²
133.8 Baldwin] *omit* N²
133.12 In (*no* ¶)] ¶ N²
133.22 Then] *omit* N²
133.27–28 companies] companions N²

133.36 Wild (*no* ¶)] ¶ N²
133.37 lines (*no* ¶)] ¶ N²
134.11 Night (*no* ¶)] ¶ N²

Subheadings

(N¹)

132.12.1 Difficult Work.
132.36.1 Anxious Cubans.
133.26.1 An Exciting Night.

No. 33. STEPHEN CRANE AT THE FRONT FOR THE WORLD

[The copy-text is N¹: New York *World*, July 7, 1898, p. 8. The other text collated is N²: *Boston Globe*, July 7, p. 2.]

142.4.1 *omit*] NEW YORK, July 7— The World today prints the following dispatch by Stephen Crane: N²
142.9 from] from from N²
142.11 But (*no* ¶)] ¶ N²
143.14 The (*no* ¶)] ¶ N²
143.16 wound] went N²
144.6 ²Mauser (*no* ¶)] ¶ N²
144.27 aplenty] plenty N²
144.31 Mauser] *omit* N²

Subheadings

(N¹)

142.20.1 Through the Thickets
143.8.1 Superb Courage.
143.28.1 Silence—Action!
144.13.1 Green Heroes.
145.2.1 Marshall's Courage.
145.25.1 New York to the Fore!

No. 34. ROOSEVELT'S ROUGH RIDERS' LOSS DUE TO A GALLANT BLUNDER

[The copy-text is N¹: New York *World*, June 26, 1898, p. 2. The other text collated is N²: Philadelphia *Press*, June 26, p. 3. Since this is a cabled dispatch, no paragraphing is listed.]

146.13–14 could not be] couldn't have been N¹
146.16 Spaniards] Spanish N¹

No. 35. HUNGER HAS MADE CUBANS FATALISTS

[The copy-text is N¹: New York *World*, July 12, 1898, p. 4. The other texts collated are N²: Philadelphia *Press*, July 12, p. 3; N³: *Boston Globe*, July 12, p. 3.]

147.8 Regular Cavalry] Regiments Cavalry N²; regiment, cavalry, N³
147.10 ¶ No] *no* ¶ N²
147.12 crowds] crowd N³
147.15 soldier] soldiers N²
147.18 our] the N³
147.19 soldiers] soldier N³
147.29 But (*no* ¶)] ¶ N³
147.32 ¶ Everybody] *no* ¶ N³
147.32 the kind] kind N²
147.36 The (*no* ¶)] ¶ N³
147.38 mannered] *omit* N²
148.1 ¶ But] *no* ¶ N²
148.1 specious] spacious N³
148.3 The (*no* ¶)] ¶ N²
148.8 know] known N³
148.10 ¶ When] *no* ¶ N²
148.12 visions] vision N²
148.12 The (*no* ¶)] ¶ N²
148.13–14 warfare] war N²
148.14 going, going] going, N²
148.17 ¶ The] *no* ¶ N²
148.28 minutes'] minutes N²
148.28 firing] fighting N³
148.31 term] terms N²
148.32 five] the five N³
149.6 Springfields] Springfield N²
149.7–20 The tall . . . green.] *omit* N³
149.7 their bare] the bare N²
149.8 ¶ We] *no* ¶ N²
149.9,16 The (*no* ¶)] ¶ N²
149.19 ¶ At] *no* ¶ N²
149.20 A (*no* ¶)] ¶ N³
149.22–23 down and down] down, down N³
149.28 aswing] swinging N²
149.28 One (*no* ¶)] ¶ N²
149.30 "Where (*no* ¶)] ¶ N³
149.32 "I (*no* ¶)] ¶ N²
149.35 To (*no* ¶)] ¶ N²
149.35 our] out N¹

149.35–36 questions] question N²⁻³
149.36 "In (*no* ¶)] ¶ N²
149.36 street] *omit* N³
150.6 limned] lined N²⁻³
150.7 a sky] sky N²; the sky N³
150.9 In] On N²⁻³
150.10 on a path] on a party N²; in a party N³
150.23 slunk] slung N²
150.26 hillside] hillsides N²
150.32 ²men] *omit* N²
150.32 The (*no* ¶)] ¶ N³
150.34 ¶ To] *no* ¶ N³
150.34 make . . . short] shorten a long story N³
150.34 were] was N²
150.35 badgering] bad going N²
150.36 those] these N²
151.1 ¶ We] *no* ¶ N³
151.3 Then (*no* ¶)] ¶ N³
151.6–28 I had . . . beef.] *omit* N³
151.23 to] of N²
151.23 a-plenty] a plenty N²
151.26 genially] generally N²
151.28 It (*no* ¶)] ¶ N³
151.34 ¶ We] *no* ¶ N³
151.34 fifteen] *omit* N²
151.35 laden] *omit* N²⁻³
151.36,37 impossible] impassable N²⁻³
151.38 Whereupon (*no* ¶)] ¶ N³
151.40 ¶ We] *no* ¶ N³
151.40 padded] paddled N²
152.2 the black] with the black N²
152.4 of an ordinary host] *omit* N²
152.5 thirty-one] 81 N³
152.9–10 "Run! . . . Run!"] "Run! run! run!" N²⁻³
152.11 ¶ "I] *no* ¶ N²⁻³
152.13 ¶ "Run! . . . Run!"] *no* ¶ "Run! Run! Run!" N²

152.14 ¶ "If] *no* ¶ N²
152.16 "Ah] "Run N³

Subheadings

(N¹)

147.21.1 Cubans Are Fatalists.
148.28.1 Regulars Not Appreciated.
149.18.1 Good Place for a Sani-
tarium.
150.33.1 Looked Down into Santiago.
151.21.1 Mango-Fed Cubans Revolt.
151.39.1 World's Boat Disappears.

(N²)
147.21.1 Cubans Give No Thanks.

148.12.1 (his visions. |) Rough
Riders a Revelation.
148.40.1 Exploring Santiago Hills.
150.7.1 Cuban Entrenchments.
150.33.1 A Long Climb to See
Santiago.
151.26.1 One Pound of Beef for
Thirty Men.

(N³)

147.14.1 Emotionless Cuban.
148.16.1 Scene of Fight of June
24.
150.2.1 Posts Built with Machete.
151.3.1 (machetes. |) Looked on
Santiago.
151.38.1 (coast. |) Three Friends
Steam Away.

No. 39. STEPHEN CRANE'S VIVID STORY OF THE BATTLE OF SAN JUAN

[The copy-text is N¹ᵃ: New York *World* (city edition), July 14, 1898, p. 3.
The other texts collated are N¹ᵇ: New York *World* (out-of-town edition),
July 14, p. 3; N²: *Chicago Tribune*, July 14, p. 3; N³: *Boston Globe*, July 14,
p. 4; HW: *Harper's Weekly*, July 23, p. 722, which is a derived text from
N¹ and without authority. Since this is a cabled dispatch, no paragraphing
is listed.]

155.1 Inkerman]   Inkermann
N²,HW
155.2 a fog] the fog N³
155.4–10 No . . . had.] *omit* HW
155.20–157.39 As near . . .
hurt.] *omit* N²
155.36 o'clock] *omit* N³
156.4 blocked] blockaded N³
156.8,36 Grimes's] Grimes' N³
156.9 Paso] Pasco N¹,³
156.21 spaces] space N³
156.22 see] seen N¹
156.24–35 The . . . previously.]
omit HW
156.26 their ordeal] ordeals N³
156.27 it] them N³
156.28 meantime] mean time N¹
156.30 crinkled] or crinkled N³
156.36 At] *omit* N³
157.7 sort of] sort of a HW

157.9–13 There . . . cane.] *omit*
HW
157.26 o'clock] *omit* N³
157.30–32 There . . . miles.]
omit HW
157.33 smokeless] smokeless powder N³
157.33–39 There . . . hurt.] *omit*
HW
157.38–39 the timbers] timbers N³
158.5–8 Why . . . it.] *omit* HW
158.7 being] *omit* N³
158.10 were never] never were N³
158.15 woods] words N²
158.16 formulated]   fulminated
N¹⁻²,HW
158.20 By God] *omit* N²; By G—d
N³
158.23 coursed] now coursed N³
158.28 couldn't] could not N³

158.31,32 very] *omit* N²
158.34 much agitated] *omit* HW
158.34–35 absolute slaughter] *omit* HW
158.36 little] *omit* HW
158.36 shoulders. He . . . who] shoulders, and HW
159.7 shoulders] shoulder HW
159.10 slow∧] slow, N³
159.11 the insensible] insensible N³
159.18–20 Their . . . approach.] *omit* N²
159.20 guerillas] the guerrilas HW
159.21–23 had come . . . road and] *omit* N²
159.23 either] the other N³
159.26–162.2 Red Cross . . . meadow.] *omit* N²
159.27–160.30 The move . . . day.] *omit* HW
160.1–8 After . . . bursting.] *omit* N¹
160.9–30 As . . . day.] *omit* N¹ᵃ
160.32; 161.1 Borrowe] Burrowe N¹
160.35 give] gave N³
160.36 to] in N³
160.37–161.3 In the . . . insistence.] *omit* HW
160.37 has] have N¹
161.1 high] far N³
161.11–17 Somebody . . . high.] *omit* N¹ᵃ,HW
161.27 From . . . smoke and] *omit* N³
161.30–162.6 Back . . . Assembly.] *omit* HW
161.30 thousand] 1000 N³
161.32 were other] were many N³
161.36 the houses of] *omit* N³
162.2–12 The army . . . are."] N² *places after* lurking guerillas. | *line* 162.25
162.9 hungry] *omit* N³
162.12 hell!] well, N³; *omit* N² (l. 162.25+)
162.13–17 News . . . so on.] *omit* N¹ᵃ

162.13–166.12 News . . . wounded.] *omit* HW
162.14–17 The siege . . . so on.] *omit* N²
162.17 And so on.] Aid soon. N³
162.25–32 A mile . . . cans.] *omit* N²
162.31 Other regiments] Others N³
163.1 very] *omit* N²
163.2–5 again. The . . . fire.] *omit* N²
163.6 in] *omit* N²
163.6–9 Lawton's . . . line.] *omit* N²
163.9 on] of N³
163.10 now] *omit* N²
163.17 could not] couldn't N³
163.31 can] could N³
164.3 obligation] obligations N²
164.9 before . . . undertone] *omit* N²
164.10–14 If he . . . regiments.] *omit* N¹⁻²
164.20 very] *omit* N²
164.22–28 After . . . drug.] *omit* N¹ᵃ
164.24 eat, eat] eat N²
164.26 Dr.] *omit* N³
164.35 bestarred] be-starved N³
164.38 the 2d of July] July 2 N³
164.38 the 1st] July 1 N³
165.4 the 2d] July 2 N³
165.14 those] these N³
165.15 fires] fire N³
165.20 d——] —— N¹; *omit* N²
165.22 very] *omit* N²
165.30 us] *omit* N²
165.31 doddering] *omit* N²; tottering N³
166.1 refugee] refugees N³
166.2 prisoner] prisoners N³
166.2–3 guerilla] guerrillas N³
166.3 insurgent] insurgents N³
166.4 —all of them] *omit* N³
166.5–12 In the . . . wounded.] *omit* N¹⁻²

Subheadings

(N[1a])

155.25.1   Misinformed as to Spanish Strength
156.17.1   Short Lull in the Battle.
157.13.1   Grimes Smashed Them.
159.39.1   Borrowe's Dynamite
Gun.
162.26.1   Camping on the Ground
They Won.
164.9.1   Demoralized by Aid.

[*In addition to the above, N[1a] has
four two-column subheadings
placed indiscriminately in mid-
sentence. Line numbering is that
of the last word in the first of the
two columns before the subhead-
ing.*]
156.26.1   (had |) Laughed at Dan-
ger.
157.34.1   (use |) A Misfit Balloon.
158.30.1   A Haze of Bullets.
162.36.1   (at |) Shots in the
Night.

(N[1b])

155.25.1   Misinformed as to Spanish Strength
156.17.1   Short Lull in the Battle.
157.13.1   Grimes Smashed Them.
157.39.1   A Misplaced Balloon.

158.30.1   Foreign Attaches Said
"Impossible"
159.39.1   Profound Patience of the
Wounded.
160.30.1   Borrowe's Dynamite
Gun.
162.12.1   Lawton's Heavy Losses.
162.26.1   Camping on the Ground
They Won.
163.10.1   Cubans Held in Contempt.
164.9.1   Demoralized by Aid.
164.37.1   The Battle of July 2.

(N[2])

158.14.1   Sight to Thrill the Blood.
159.2.1   Wounded by Hundreds.
159.25.1   Army Takes Its Glory
Calmly.
163.18.1   No Cubans Assisting.
164.5.1   Speaks Only to Beg.
164.34.1   at all. |) Situation Needs
a Gomez.

(N[3])

156.15.1   joined there. |) Artillery-
men Excited.
157.39.1   "There Go Our Boys."
159.9.1   Those Spanish Guerrillas.
161.5.1   Sat on the Conquered
Crest.
162.39.1   Contempt for the Cubans.
165.24.1   Hard Lot of Prisoners.

No. 40. SPANISH DESERTERS AMONG THE REFUGEES AT EL CANEY

[The copy-text is N[1]: New York *World*, July 8, 1898, p. 4.]

Subheadings

(N[1])

167.8.1   Women Meet Insurgent
Kindred.

168.3.1   Amazed at Kind Treatment.

No. 41. CAPTURED MAUSERS FOR VOLUNTEERS

[The copy-text is N¹: New York *World*, July 17, 1898, p. 17. The other text collated is N²: Philadelphia *Press*, July 17, p. 3.]

169.1 certainly it] it maybe it N²
169.2 very] *omit* N²
169.5 ¶ We] *no* ¶ N²
169.11 they have] it has N²
169.12 they could] the soldiers could N²
169.29 was] were N¹
169.29 always] *omit* N²
169.31 exactly] *omit* N²
169.37–170.10 The experiences . . . Spaniards.] *omit* N¹
170.15 ten or maybe fifteen thou-

sand] 10,000 or maybe 15,000 N²
170.19 respects it is] particulars N²
170.27 If (*no* ¶)] ¶ N²

Subheadings

(N²)

169.19.1 Fighting with Specters.
170.10.1 Mausers for Our Men.

No. 42. REGULARS GET NO GLORY

[The copy-text is N¹: New York *World*, July 20, 1898, p. 6. The other texts collated are N²: Philadelphia *Press*, July 19, p. 2; N³: *Boston Globe*, July 19, p. 6.]

170.31 July 9] July 18 N²
171.2 The (*no* ¶)] ¶ N³
171.4 is, rather,] ~ ∧ ~ ∧ N³
171.5 Now (*no* ¶)] ¶ N³
171.8 United States] U.S. N³
171.13 The (*no* ¶)] ¶ N³
171.13 doesn't] does not N²⁻³
171.15 ¶ The] *no* ¶ N³
171.16 Sturtevant] Stutevant N²
171.16 goodness] goodness' N²⁻³
171.17 chappy] chapple N³
171.18 Whereas (*no* ¶)] ¶ N³
171.19 -sized] -size N³
171.20 in celebration] on the celebration N³
171.23 If (*no* ¶)] ¶ N³
171.24 through] though N²
171.30 them] then N¹
171.34 Santiago] Saratoga N²⁻³
171.38 the muddy] muddy N³
171.40 One (*no* ¶)] ¶ N³
172.1 time] the time N²
172.7 barracks] the barracks N³

172.8 rights] right N²
172.11 End (*no* ¶)] ¶ N³
172.16 He knows (*no* ¶)] ¶ N³
172.19–20 does not] doesn't N³
172.22 In (*no* ¶)] ¶ N³
172.23 of] *omit* N²
172.24 that] *omit* N³
172.25–26 regular. ¶ After] regulars after N³
172.26 regular's] regulars N²; regulars' N³
172.28–29 such and such] *omit* N³
172.33 "This (*no* ¶)] ¶ N³
172.36 *et seq.* Orders] orders N²⁻³
172.38–39 he simply . . . anywhere] *omit* N³
172.39 It (*no* ¶)] ¶ N³
173.4 -sized] size N³
173.6 so] as N³
173.9–10 It is . . . public.] *omit* N²
173.9,13 It (*no* ¶)] ¶ N³

173.21   the others] others N³
173.22   finally] *omit* N²⁻³
173.30   Here's (*no* ¶)] ¶ N²⁻³
173.31   maybe] may be N²
173.32   fairer, squarer] fair, square
        N³
173.32   paper] papers N³

Subheadings

(N²)

171.20.1   Private of No Conse-
          quence.
173.2.1   Society Man Also a
          Fighter.

No. 43. A SOLDIER'S BURIAL THAT MADE A NATIVE HOLIDAY

[The copy-text is N¹: *New York Journal*, Aug. 15, 1898, p. 2. The other texts collated are N²: San Francisco *Examiner*, Aug. 15, p. 1; N³: *Kansas City Star*, Aug. 22, p. 5. N³ is derived from N¹ and without independent authority.]

174.3   the men] men N²
174.13   a crowd] the crowd N²
174.14   arose a] rose N²
174.15   necks, pointed, dodged]
        necks and dodged N²
174.18   wearing] with N²
174.22   the coffin] a coffin N²
174.27   ¶ The] *no* ¶ N²
174.27   followed] and followed N²
174.28   Ponce (*no* ¶)] ¶ N²
175.5   ¶ A] *no* ¶ N²
175.9–10   the indifferent] indiffer-
          ent N²
175.11   the chatter] chatter N²
175.16–17   surmounted] sur-
          rounded N²
175.20–21   in order] *omit* N²
175.27   the ejaculations] ejacula-
        tions N²
175.28   came over] came from over
        N³

175.28   many] so many N²
175.29   toward] forward toward N³
175.29   a bit] the bit N²
175.32   imperturbably] impertura-
        bly N²
175.36   then] *omit* N²
175.38   ¶ A] *no* ¶ N²
176.1   the call] a call N²
176.4   sad, sad] sad N³
176.6   heavenly] heavy N²

Subheadings

(N¹)

174.26.1   The Voyage of the
          Hearse.
175.25.1   The Humors of a Fu-
          neral.

No. 44. GRAND RAPIDS AND PONCE

[The copy-text is N¹: *New York Journal*, Aug. 17, 1898, p. 4. The other text collated is N²: *Kansas City Star*, Aug. 21, p. 5. The latter is a derived text without authority.]

176.9   *Journal*] *omit* N²
176.22   Daiquiri] Baiquiri N¹⁻²
177.26–28   When . . . death.]
          omit N²

177.36   is] it N¹
178.25   Wisconsin] Michigan N¹⁻²

No. 45. THE PORTO RICAN "STRADDLE"

[The copy-text is N[1]: *New York Journal*, Aug. 18, p. 3. The other text collated is N[2]: *Kansas City Star*, Aug. 28, p. 5. Since this latter is a derived text, its paragraphing variants have not been recorded.]

178.29–32 One . . . manners.] *omit* N[2]

179.3 one of the *Journal's* correspondents] a correspondent N[2]

179.15–16 in the little . . . church] *omit* N[2]

179.21 answers] answer N[2]

179.26 slowed] clowed N[2]

179.31–34] We crossed . . . York.] *omit* N[2]

179.39–40 Chickens . . . road.] *omit* N[2]

180.19 He is . . . night.] *omit* N[2]

181.1–2 "Look . . . him."] *omit* N[2]

No. 46. HAVANA'S HATE DYING, SAYS STEPHEN CRANE

[The copy-text is N[1]: *New York Journal*, Sept. 3, 1898, p. 5. The other text collated is N[2]: *Kansas City Star*, Sept. 11, p. 5. Since the latter is a derived text, its variant paragraphing has not been recorded.]

182.17–21 The people . . . Americans.] *omit* N[2]

182.25 as of] of N[1-2]

182.29–30 who . . . fronts."] *omit* N[2]

183.1–3 and one . . . looks] *omit* N[2]

183.6 out] *omit* N[2]

183.14–184.7 It becomes . . . blockade.] *omit* N[2]

No. 47. STEPHEN CRANE SEES FREE CUBA

[The copy-text is N[1]: *New York Journal*, Aug. 28, 1898, p. 43. The other texts collated are N[2]: *Chicago Tribune*, Aug. 28, p. 4; N[3]: San Francisco *Examiner*, Aug. 28, p. 17. Since this is a cabled dispatch, no paragraphing is listed.]

184.28 The feeling] Feeling N[1]

184.29 fear] fear anything like N[1]

184.31 The Spaniards] Spaniards N[1]

185.1 hearty] a hearty N[2]; *omit* N[3]

185.2 the American] American N[1]

185.3–4 prevented] to prevent N[3]

185.6–8 These . . . pleasure.] *omit* N[2]

185.8 pleasure] with pleasure N[3]

185.11 had] have N[3]

185.15 protect] protects N[2]

185.15–21 Even . . . quantity.] *omit* N[2]

185.16 conqueror] a conqueror N[3]

185.19 the stevedores] stevedores N[3]

185.21 quality, never quantity] the quality, never in the quantity N[3]

185.23 lie] die N[3]

185.24 feel] say N[2]

185.24 the Red] that Red N[3]

185.28–29 The Spanish . . . fly-
    ing.] *omit* N²
185.32 The armored] Armored N³
185.33 are] *omit* N¹
185.34 reconcentrados] the recon-
    centrados N³

Subheadings

(N²)

185.13.1 Want American Protec-
    tion.

No. 48. STEPHEN CRANE FEARS NO BLANCO

[The copy-text is N¹: *New York Journal*, Aug. 31, 1898, p. 5.]

Subheadings

(N¹)

186.22.1 An Imaginary Interview.
187.17.1 Little Hope for Span-
    iards.

187.35.1 Waiting for American
    Troops.
188.29.1 How Crane Avoids
    Blanco.

No. 49. STEPHEN CRANE'S VIEWS OF HAVANA

[The copy-text is N¹: *New York Journal*, Sept. 7, 1898, p. 7. The other text collated is N²: *Chicago Tribune*, Sept. 7, p. 1. Since this is a cabled dispatch, no paragraphing is listed.]

189.23 had] *omit* N²
189.29 *et seq.* deal] good deal N²
190.6–7 but the victims . . .
    grin] *omit* N²
190.17 very] *omit* N²
190.34 past] passed N²
190.36 even more still] more
    N²
191.2 any such] such a N²

191.15–16 But . . . weapon.]
    omit N²

Subheadings

(N²)

190.12.1 American Troop in Ha-
    vana.
190.38.1 Idleness of the Army.

No. 51. AMERICANS AND BEGGARS IN CUBA

[The copy-text is MS: the untitled manuscript in the Special Collections of Columbia University Libraries.]

Alterations in the Manuscript

193.22 are] *written over* 'is'
193.23 Probably] *preceded by de-
    leted* 'It w'
194.4 hideous] *preceded by de-
    leted* 'a gr'
194.6 passers-by] *followed by de-
    leted period*
194.17 him] *preceded by deleted*
    'them'

194.18 the] *written over* 'a'
194.18 beggars] *final* 's' *added*
194.18 approach] *final* 'es' *deleted*
194.21 because] *followed by de-
    leted* 'you'
194.23 beggars] *preceded by de-
    leted* 'Cuba'
194.23 It] *followed by deleted* 'm'

No. 52. MEMOIRS OF A PRIVATE

[The copy-text is N¹: *New York Journal*, Sept. 25, 1898, p. 26.]

194.28   a club] club N¹   195.26   feckless] fetless N¹

No. 55. HOW THEY LEAVE CUBA

[The copy-text is N¹: *New York Journal*, Oct. 6, 1898, p. 6.]

200.35   for] or N¹

No. 57. HOW THEY COURT IN CUBA

[The copy-text is N¹: *New York Journal*, Oct. 25, 1898, p. 6. The other text collated is N²: San Francisco *Examiner*, Nov. 13, p. 4.]

203.13–14   young women] women N²
203.18   was] were N²
203.27   ²in] at N²
204.9   had] has N²
204.23–29   A leathery . . . ignorance.] *omit* N¹

205.1–4   The moon . . . accident.] *omit* N¹
205.15   dared] dare N²
205.32–38   After . . . moon.] *omit* N²

No. 58. STEPHEN CRANE ON HAVANA

[The copy-text is N¹: *New York Journal*, Nov. 6, 1898, p. 26.]

207.31   ingenuous] ingenious N¹

No. 63. OUR SAD NEED OF DIPLOMATS

[The copy-text is N¹ᵃ: *New York Journal* (Greater New York edition), Nov. 17, 1898, p. 6. The other text collated is N¹ᵇ: *New York Journal* (out-of-town edition), Nov. 17, 1898, p. 6.]

224.10–11   stomach. ¶ An] stomach. [¶] It is said that during   the blockade the | ¶ An N¹ᵇ

No. 64. MR. STEPHEN CRANE ON THE NEW AMERICA

[The copy-text is *The Outlook*, Feb. 4, 1899, pp. 12–13.]

228.6–7   whosoever] whomsoever O

No. 65. HOW AMERICANS MAKE WAR

[The copy-text is N^1: *London Daily Chronicle*, July 25, 1899, p. 9. The other text collated is N^2: San Francisco *Examiner*, Aug. 28, 1899, p. 6. Since the latter is a derived text, its variant paragraphing has not been recorded.]

229.1   the journals] journals N^2
229.3   an expression] a matter N^2
229.5   ¹our] our own N^2
230.24 play] plan N^2

230.31 in the] in N^2
230.34 with a] with N^2
231.31 this] it N^2

No. 66. THE LITTLE STILETTOS OF THE MODERN NAVY WHICH STAB IN THE DARK

[The copy-text is N^1: *New York Journal*, Apr. 24, 1898, p. 21. The other texts collated are N^2: *Denver Republican*, May 1, 1898, p. 30 (*derived from* N^1); TMs: UVa.–Barrett typescript; E1: *Last Words*, Digby, Long & Co., London, 1902. TMs is divided into TMs(u), the original type, and TMs(c), the ink revisions or corrections made by Cora.]

235.1   In] Stephen Crane in the New York Journal: In N^2
235.13 mists] mist E1
235.22 or out] *omit* TMs,E1
235.23 ordinary] ordinarly N^2
236.2   Chili] Chilli TMs(c)
236.5   China,] China, Chili, N^{1-2}, TMs(u)
236.10 battle . . . Armstrong,] *omit* N^2
236.17–18 are now shelling] shell TMs(u); shelled TMs(c); shelled the E1
236.20 sea-] *omit* N^2
236.35 an innovation] innovation TMs,E1
237.4   brigade] fire brigade E1
237.5   to] with N^2
237.5   our] *omit* TMs,E1
237.5–6 commissioners] commissioners in U.S. TMs(c); commissioners in United States E1
237.15–17 Then . . . boats.] *omit* N^2
237.24 process] course E1
237.33 26½] 26¼ N^2
237.36 a hundred] 100 N^2,E1

238.6   buff] bluff N^2
238.13 The four] Four TMs(c),E1
238.13 now] *omit* TMs,E1
238.14 are] were TMs,E1
238.14 Japan.] Japan.   (1898) TMs; Japan (1898). E1
238.17 from her] from N^2
238.18 all] *omit* TMs,E1
238.20 24] twenty TMs(u),E1; twenty-four TMs(c)
238.32 larger] large TMs(u)
238.37 up] *omit* TMs,E1
238.39 tubes] boats N^2
239.1   greater] great TMs,E1
239.2   on swivels] on the swivels N^2
239.24 harbor] harbour TMs(c)
240.1   bucking] balking N^2
240.2   battened] battered N^1,TMs(u)

Subheadings

(N^2)

236.3.1   The Torpedo Mania.
236.33.1 England's Torpedo Boat Destroyers.

237.24.1 The Destroyers Are Graceful.

238.14.1 What Torpedo Boats Are Like.

239.6.1 The Terror of Battleships.

239.30.1 Demons of the Deep.

No. 67. SOME CURIOUS LESSONS FROM THE TRANSVAAL

[The copy-text is N¹: *New York Journal*, Jan. 7, 1900, p. 27. The other text collated is N²: San Francisco *Examiner*, Jan. 7, p. 24.]

240.24   an] any N²
241.13   It (*no* ¶)] ¶ N²
241.23   ¶ He] *no* ¶ N²
241.39   proudest] proud N²

242.2   fight] do N²
242.20   traditions] the traditions N²
243.14   enemy's] enemies' N²

No. 69. STEPHEN CRANE SAYS: THE BRITISH ARE NOT FAMILIAR WITH THE "BUSINESS END" OF MODERN RIFLES

[The copy-text is MS: the untitled manuscript in the Special Collections of the Columbia University Libraries. The other texts collated are N¹: *New York Journal*, Feb. 14, 1900, p. 8; N²: San Francisco *Examiner*, Feb. 14, p. 3.]

245.27   knew] know N²
245.29   kinds] kings N²
246.2   Here (*no* ¶)] ¶ N²
246.11   He said] Everybody thought he did. He said MS
246.13   ¶ But] *no* ¶ N²
246.14   came] went N¹
246.26   pot] shoot N²
246.33–34 first of all] *omit* N²
246.38   knowledge] a knowledge N²

Alterations in the Manuscript

245.24   people] *preceded by deleted* 'nation'
245.26   relations] *interlined above deleted* 'people'
245.27   knew] *interlined*
246.1   write] *preceded by deleted* 'right'
246.2   this soldier] *interlined with a caret above deleted* 'he'
246.29   knowledge.] *preceded by deleted* 'game'

246.30   north-west] *preceded by deleted* 'I'
246.31   gold-mounted,] *preceded by deleted* 'dia'; *followed by a deleted hyphen before the comma added*
246.35   badly] *preceded by deleted* 'bady'
246.35   scorched] 't' *after* 'r' *deleted*
246.39–247.1; 247.3–4,5 field-hospital] *interlined above deleted* 'dressing station'; *comma doubtful in* l. 247.5
247.1   merely] *interlined with a caret*
247.5   under] *followed by a deleted possible hyphen*
247.7   latest] *interlined above deleted* 'last'
247.9   valor] *preceded by deleted* 'volor'
247.10   Yes; . . . would] *below this line appears the deleted signature* 'Stephen Crane'

No. 70. MANUSCRIPT FRAGMENT

[The copy-text is MS: the untitled manuscript in the Special Collections of Columbia University Libraries.]

247.15   operating] 'operated'   *altered to* 'operating'

No. 71. THE GREAT BOER TREK

[The copy-text is TMs(u): the uncorrected UVa.–Barrett typescript. The other texts collated are TMs(c): the corrected typescript; Co: *Cosmopolitan*, June, 1900, pp. 153–158. Typed-out alterations are not recorded, but substantive alterations made by Cora are.]

248.9   seemed to be] seem to be TMs(u); seemed to have been TMs(c),Co
248.10   other's] others TMs
248.25   fierce] *omit* TMs(c),Co
248.31   matters] all matters Co
248.32–33   the Dutch . . . same.] their religious ideals bear the strongest resemblance one to the other. TMs(c),Co
249.21–22   The sting . . . fact that the] The TMs(c),Co
249.31   intolerable] *omit* TMs(c), Co
250.1   in] *omit* TMs(u)
250.4   were] was Co
250.5   Frederik] Frederick Co
250.9   fifty] fifty men TMs(c),Co
250.12–13   shot down . . . by.] shot and killed. TMs(c),Co
250.21   only do so] do so only Co
250.26   hung] hanged Co
250.30   ¶ In] *no* ¶ Co
250.30   1828] 1823 Co
250.31   landdrosts] landrosts TMs(c),Co
250.31   In] I TMs
250.31   In their place] and in the place of them Co
250.34   —what must have seemed a last touch of insolence—] *omit* TMs(c),Co

250.36–37   —otherwise . . . returned] *omit* Co
250.37   Shortly] Soon Co
250.37   this] *omit* Co
250.39   were] was TMs(c),Co
251.16   Natives] Native TMs
251.19   Boers were] Boer was TMs(c),Co
251.20   their] his TMs(c),Co
251.21   their] his TMs,Co
251.26   or] nor Co
251.33   apprentices] apprenticed Co
251.36   passed] passes TMs
252.3   its] it's TMs
252.3–15   Sir George . . . imported.] *omit* Co
252.19   colony. In] ~ , in TMs; ~ ᴧ in Co
252.21   throughout] through TMs(u)
252.21   Empireᴧ] ~ , TMs,Co
252.21   was] *omit* TMs
252.22   1st] 1st- TMs(u); on the 1st of TMs(c),Co
252.23–40   These slaves . . . council.] *omit* Co
252.35   high-handed] *omit* TMs(c)
253.8   cross to] *omit* Co
253.26   northward; all] ~ . All TMs(c),Co
253.27   of Triechard's party] *omit* TMs(u)

253.28 savages] savages of Triechard's party TMs(u)
253.28 Delagoa] Delago TMs
253.35 Under] (Dec. 1834) Under
TMs; December, 1834, under
Co
253.36 Kaffirland] Kafirland TMs
254.9 fanatical] *omit* TMs(c),Co
254.10 races] races as TMs(c),Co
254.10 themselves] the Boer farmers TMs(c),Co
254.12 houses] homes Co
254.14 Purchasers] Purchases of
the vacated property TMs(c),
Co
254.19 further] farther Co
254.33–34 Boer looks] Boers look
TMs
254.35 him] them TMs
255.5 Quathlamba] Quathtamba
TMs,Co
255.6–7 the disorganized] small
disorganized Co
255.7–9 known as . . . State]
omit Co
255.9 were] resided Co
255.10;256.8,39 Moselekatse] Moselekatze TMs,Co
255.13; 256.3 under the] under
TMs(c),Co
255.16 Moselekatse] Moseleketse
TMs(u); Moseleketge TMs(c);
Moselekatze Co
255.19 Moselekatse] Moselekatge
TMs(c); Moselekatze Co
255.20 eleven others] 11 others
TMs(u); a party TMs(c),Co
255.27 Matabele] Matable TMs
256.11 Matabele] Matable
TMs(u)
256.23 landdrost] lauddrost TMs;
landrost Co
256.24 Retief] Mr. Retief TMs(u)
256.26 take an oath to] *omit* Co
256.32 Retief] Riteif TMs
256.37 Moselekatse] Mosega TMs,Co
256.39 nine days'] 9 days TMs
257.4 forfeited] fortified TMs(u);
forfieted TMs(c)

257.6 Bechuanaland] Betshuanaland TMs
257.7 desert] Desert Co
257.17–18 *et seq.* Umkungunh-
lovu] Umkunguhloon TMs,Co
257.25 stolen] recently stolen
TMs(c),Co
257.26,27 Sikonyela] Sikouyela
TMs,Co
257.26 Mantatee] mantater TMs;
Mantater Co
257.34 *et seq.* Umzimvubu] Umzimvooboo TMs,Co
258.3–4 Blaauwkrans] Blaanwkrauz TMs,Co
258.8 Weenen] Weemen Co
258.12 an] *omit* Co
258.20 Pretorius] Pretorias TMs
258.26 singing] the singing
TMs(c),Co
258.30 defeat] *omit* TMs,Co
258.37 December] on December
TMs(c),Co
258.37 16th] 16 Co
259.4 has] had TMs
259.6 fled and . . . fire] set the
place on fire and fled Co
259.7 further] farther Co
259.8 *et seq.* Panda] Pauda TMs,
Co
259.22 Umfolosi] Imfolosi TMs,Co
259.39 recent] *omit* Co
260.1 12th] 12 Co
260.2 wagons.] wagons, crossing
the Vaal. TMs(c),Co
260.3–261.18 Pieter . . . Retief.]
omit Co
260.10 the severe] severe TMs(u)

Alterations in the Typescript

248.9 seemed] 'ed' *added*
248.9 be] TMs 'have been' *interlined above deleted* 'be'
248.15 Netherlands] 'i' *after first*
'e' *struck out*
248.25 fierce] *deleted before* 'Kaffirs'
248.29 extreme] 'me' *over* 'em' *of
original* 'extreem'

248.32–33   the Dutch . . . same.] *deleted and* 'their religious ideals bear the strongest resemblance one to the other.' *interlined*

249.7   habit] *a second* 'b' *struck out*

249.13–14   platforms] 't' *over* 'r'

249.21–22   The sting . . . that the] *deleted and* 'The' *added in margin before* 'Colonial'

249.31   intolerable] *deleted preceding* 'grievance'

250.1   in 1812] 'in' *interlined*

250.9   fifty] *followed by interlined* 'men'

250.12–13   shot down . . . by.] 'down' *and* 'while . . . by.' *deleted and comma after* 'killed' *made into a period*

250.31   landdrosts] *second* 'd' *struck out*

250.34   —what must have seemed a last touch of insolence] *deleted*

250.39   there were] 're' *of* 'there' *over* 'ir' *with* 'was' *interlined above deleted* 'were'

251.19   Boers were] *final* 's' *and* 'were' *deleted and* 'was' *interlined above* 'were'

251.20   their] *deleted and* 'his' *interlined*

252.8   colony] 'e' *before* 'y' *struck out*

252.16–17   (many . . . strongly)] *parentheses inserted, the first over a comma, but the second after a comma*

252.21   throughout] 'out' *interlined with caret*

252.22   1st] TMs '1st-' *deleted and* 'on the 1ˢᵗ of' *interlined*

252.35   high-handed] *deleted preceding* 'governor'

253.26   northward; all] *altered to* 'northward. All'

253.27   of Triechard's party] *interlined with a caret after* 'those'

253.28   savages] *following* 'of Triechard's party' *deleted*

254.9   fanatical] *deleted*

254.10   races] *following* 'as' *interlined with a caret*

254.10   themselves.] *deleted and* 'the Boer farmers.' *interlined*

254.14   Purchasers] *second* 'r' *struck out; following is* 'of vacated property' *interlined with a caret*

254.27   instance] *following comma struck out*

255.16   Moselekatse] TMs 'Moseleketse' *with* 'g' *over second* 's'

255.19   Moselekatse] *with* 'g' *over second* 's'

255.20   eleven others] TMs '11 others' *deleted and* 'a party' *interlined*

255.33   "roers"] *first quotes added*

256.1   food, while] *altered from* 'food. While'

256.3   the] *deleted preceding* 'Commandant'

256.11   Matabele] *first* 'e' *interlined with a caret*

256.15   Vet (they . . . Winburg) which] *a period following* 'Vet' *altered to a comma and parenthesis inserted before* 'They' *and after* 'Winburg' *over a period*

256.24   Retief] *preceded by deleted* 'Mr.'

257.4   forfeited] TMs 'fortified' *deleted and* 'forfieted' *interlined*

257.25   stolen] *preceded by deleted* 'recently'

258.9   emigrants] 'i' *changed from* 'e'

258.20   Pretorius] *a second final* 's' *struck through*

258.24   wherever] 'ver' *over* 'on', *and then deleted and interlined later*

258.26   singing] *preceded by* 'the' *interlined with a caret*

258.31   revenge.] *period altered from a comma*

258.37 December] TMs 'Dec.' *preceded by interlined* 'on'
259.24 "a salute] 'A' *reduced by a slant stroke*
259.35 "all] *quotes added*
260.2 wagons.] *period altered to* comma *and* 'crossing the Vaal' *added*
260.3–4 Pieter . . . emigration.] *added by* Cora
260.10 severe] *a preceding* 'the' *interlined with a caret*

No. 72. THE TALK OF LONDON

[The copy text is N[1]: *New York Journal*, Mar. 11, 1900, p. 27. The other text collated is N[2]: San Francisco *Examiner*, Mar. 11, p. 27.]

262.5 ¶ The] *no* ¶ N[2]
262.18 ¶ Italy] *no* ¶ N[2]
262.23 Russia's (*no* ¶)] ¶ N[2]
262.37 "So (*no* ¶)] ¶ N[2]
263.12 expression. When] ~ , as when N[2]
263.21 Mr. A. J. (*no* ¶)] ¶ N[2]
263.25 The (*no* ¶)] ¶ N[2]
263.26 again. And] *omit* N[2]
263.32–34 It was . . . noisy.] *omit* N[2]

No. 3. IMOGENE CARTER'S ADVENTURE AT PHARSALA

[The copy-text is MS: the untitled manuscript in both Cora Crane's and Stephen Crane's hands in the Special Collections of Columbia University Libraries.]

269.5–6,22 Pharsala] Phersala MS
269.21 principal] principle MS
270.11 lighted] light MS
270.18 returned] return MS
270.19 Pharsala] Phasala MS
270.22 the pool] pool MS
270.22 patrolled] paroled MS
270.24,24–25,31 the door] door MS
270.35 awakened] awaken MS
271.3 a] *omit* MS
271.4 the floor] floor MS
271.11 sleeps] sleep MS
271.13 the village] village MS
271.14–15 the balcony] balcony MS
271.18 Velestino] Velestimo MS
271.29 storks'] storks MS
271.36 tourists] tourist MS

Alterations in the Manuscript

[Crane's *hand*]

269.1 now] *above this but seemingly not connected with it is a deleted word ending* 'ard', *the first letter of which is perhaps* 'c'
269.2 exuberantly] 'x' *over start of some other letter*
269.3 war] *interlined with a caret*
269.4 no] *preceded by deleted* 'ral'
269.7 barred] *preceded by deleted* 'perhaps'
269.9 passed] *preceded by deleted* 'past'
269.10 an] *interlined with a caret*
269.10 whisper] *interlined above deleted* 'tones'
269.11 one] *preceded by deleted* 'a famous'
269.12 a term] *preceded by deleted* 'the' *with an interlined* 'the' *also deleted*
269.13 [1]to] *interlined above deleted* 'an'
269.24 [2]they] *interlined with a caret*

269.27   walls] *preceded by deleted* 'h'

[*Cora's hand begins at* 269.28 'At']

270.10   all] *interlined with a caret*
270.14   pool] *interlined above deleted* 'billiard'
270.18   diligence] *preceded by deleted* 'sleep in the' *and inserted* 'the'
270.18   by which she] *interlined above deleted* 'and'
270.18   returned] *followed by deleted* 'by it'
270.21   Greek] *interlined with a caret*
270.24   He] MS 'he' *over* 'so'
270.29   secured] 'se' *over* 'lo'
270.31   caught me] 'm' *over* 'h'

270.32   a] *over* 'm'
270.33   hand,] *followed by deleted* 'trying to te'
271.2   called] 'c' *over* 'd'
271.3   quarter] 'g' *over* 'h'
271.8   and] *preceded by deleted* 'not one'
271.17   which] *interlined above deleted* 'with'
271.18   troops] *preceded by deleted* 'soldiers'
271.23   Infantry] MS 'infanty' *interlined above deleted doubtful* 'infany'
271.29   constructed] *preceded by deleted* 'constr'
271.32   coming] *preceded by deleted* 'Turk'
271.33   rough] *preceded by deleted* 'road'

No. 4. IMOGENE CARTER'S PEN PICTURE OF THE FIGHTING AT VELESTINO

[The copy-text is N[1]: *New York Journal*, May 10, 1897, p. 3. The other text collated is N[2]: San Francisco *Examiner*, May 10, p. 3. Since this is a telegraphed dispatch, no paragraphing is listed.]

272.9   squeak] escape N[1]   272.15   the Turks] Turks N[1]

GREAT BATTLES OF THE WORLD

THE BRIEF CAMPAIGN AGAINST NEW ORLEANS

[The copy-text is L: *Lippincott's Magazine*, LXV (Mar., 1900), pp. 405–411. The other texts collated are A1: *Great Battles of the World*, J. B. Lippincott, Philadelphia, 1901; E1: *Great Battles of the World*, Chapman & Hall, London, 1901. E1 is a derived text without authority.]

278.17   Afterward] Afterwards A1, E1
279.8; 280.1   23] 23d A1
279.14,16   eternal] Eternal A1,E1
279.22   7.30] 7.50 A1,E1
279.32   marshals] marshall L
280.13   ²a] *omit* L
280.15   force] forces A1,E1
280.28   north] North A1,E1

281.1   24] 24th A1
282.15   -rails. In . . . it was twenty] -rails in some places twenty A1,E1
282.27   simultaneous] simultaneously A1,E1
284.6   begun] already begun A1,E1
284.37   troops] troop L
285.16   January] December L

THE STORMING OF BADAJOZ

[The copy-text is MS: manuscript in the Barrett Collection, University of Virginia, inscribed by Edith Richie with the exception of 288.25–34 'The . . . infantry' which is in a strange hand. The other texts collated are L: *Lippincott's Magazine*, LXV (Apr., 1900), pp. 579–585; A1: *Great Battles of the World*, J. B. Lippincott, Philadelphia, 1901; E1: *Great Battles of the World*, Chapman & Hall, London, 1901. E1 is a derived text without authority.]

286.0 *et seq.* Badajoz] Badajos MS,L,A1
286.3 Rodrigo] Rodrigues MS,L, A1
286.4–5 who . . . ¹Wellington.] who, as the Duke of Wellington, influenced England after Waterloo. L+
286.11 Congress] part of Congress L+
286.12 forever] for ever E1
286.15 supplies] arms L+
287.4 doings] doing L
287.12,15 Elvas] Eloas MS+
287.14 prevent a] intercept the MS
287.16 made] performed MS
287.24 16th] 16 E1
287.34 further] farther A1,E1
287.37 to first] first to L+
288.4 fox's] fox A1,E1
288.12 Picurina] Picerina L+
289.7 eye] eyes L+
289.19 on] of L+
289.19,33 Picurina] Picerina MS+
289.24 blared] blazed L+
289.39 in through] into L
290.4 Gaspar] Gasper A1,E1
290.9 Picurina] Picarina MS; Picerina L+
290.10 one] on MS
290.15 northern] eastern MS
290.22 defences] southern defences MS
290.22 *et seq.* 2nd] 2d L,A1
291.2 Fort] Port A1,E1
291.20 and so] and L
291.26 besieged] besieged and also the besieged MS

291.28–29 toward] towards L+
291.35 followed] imitated MS
291.39–292.1 out at] out of A1,E1
292.2 ¹and] but L+
292.9 bags full] bag's-full MS
292.16 made plain] exposed L+
292.19 each other's] one another's L+
292.20 amounted] amount MS
292.21 shattered] rent L
292.29 the breach were] it was L+
292.35–36 hopeless quality] hopelessness L+
292.37 themselves] itself L
293.21 Pardaleras] Pardeleras MS
293.25 found . . . too] all found to be too A1,E1
293.28 a wall] the wall L
294.2 became] turned into MS
294.4 everyone] every one E1
294.14 this] the L

Alterations in the Manuscript

[*Unless otherwise specified, the alterations are in* Edith Richie's hand.]

286.3 was] *interlined with a caret above deleted* 'is'
287.8 siege] *altered from* 'seige'
287.15 Soult] *final* 'e' *deleted*
287.36 east] *written by* Cora *below deleted* 'south'
288.2 in width] *preceded by deleted* 'from which'
288.7 desire] *final* 's' *deleted*
288.9 nearest to] 'to' *over a period*

288.12   Fort] *preceded by deleted* 'the b'
288.12   sound] *preceded by deleted* 'muffled'
288.16   with a] 'a' *interlined with a caret above deleted* 'the' *in* Cora's *hand*

[*strange hand*]

288.26   allies] 'es' *over* 'y'

[Edith Richie's *hand*]

289.2   condition] *preceded by deleted* 'was'
289.4   gate] 'g' *over* 'G'
289.36   Foot] 'F' *over* 'f; followed by deleted* 'fell almost on the'
290.9   Picurina] MS 'Picarina' *with first* 'a' *altered from* 'e' *or* 'a' *although* 'e' *over* 'u' *is also a possibility*
290.13   eastern] *interlined by* Cora *below deleted* 'southern'
290.15   northern] MS *reads* 'east-

ern' *interlined by* Cora *below deleted* 'southern'
290.20   army] *preceded by deleted* 'force'
290.26–27   dam of the inunda-tion.] *interlined below deleted* 'bridge'
290.28   dam] *followed by deleted* 'inundation'
291.22   placed] *interlined above deleted* 'put up'
292.10   Light] 'L' *doubtfully over* 'l'
293.10   actually] *preceded by deleted* 'had'
293.11   bastion] *preceded by deleted* 'batter' and the start of a* 'y', *the* 'tt' *being uncrossed*
293.21   Pardaleras] MS *reads* 'Par-deleras' *which seems to have been the original reading, but then the first* 'e' *was altered to an* 'a' *but then an* 'e' *circled was interlined*
293.36   next morning] *interlined with a caret*

THE SIEGE OF PLEVNA

[The copy-text is L: *Lippincott's Magazine*, LXV (May, 1900), pp. 759–765. The other texts collated are A1: *Great Battles of the World*, J. B. Lippin-cott, Philadelphia, 1901; E1: *Great Battles of the World*, Chapman & Hall, London, 1901. E1 is a derived text without authority.]

295.7   mere village of] village of a mere L
295.8   Widdin] Widen L; Widin A1,E1
295.16 *et seq.*   Krüdener] Krudener L+
295.17   Nikopolis] Nicopolis L
295.29   In regard to] As to A1,E1
297.11   telegraphed] telegraphed him L
297.12; 298.21   eighty] thirty A1, E1
297.18 *et seq.*   Schakofskoy] Scha-hofskoy L+
298.3   themselves] their fire A1,E1

298.8   irregulars] irregular A1,E1
299.3   31st] 31 E1
299.11,14   Zotoff] Totoff L+
299.12   for] *omit* A1,E1
300.4   two-thirty to three] half-past two o'clock to three o'clock E1
300.11   men. The . . . anticipat-ing] men, but the victory was fruitless. Anticipating L
300.14   success] victory L
300.16   Schnidnikoff] Schmidni-koff L+
300.16   very] *omit* A1,E1
300.39   12th] 12 E1
301.5   over] *omit* L

301.9   eighty] thirty A1,E1
301.18   also] *omit* A1,E1
301.32   ²polite] a polite L

301.34   19th] 19 E1
302.9   11th] 11 E1

THE BATTLE OF BUNKER HILL

[The copy-text is L: *Lippincott's Magazine*, LXV (June, 1900), pp. 924–932. The other texts collated are A1: *Great Battles of the World*, J. B. Lippincott, Philadelphia, 1901; E1: *Great Battles of the World*, Chapman & Hall, London, 1901. E1 is a derived text without authority.]

303.17–18   when on . . . news] when he was told this news on his arrival in May L
304.3   12th] 12 E1
304.6   8th] 8 E1
304.18   13th] 13 E1
304.39–305.2   Prescott . . . lanterns,] With two sergeants carrying dark lanterns, Prescott walked at their head L
305.21   ¶ They] *no* ¶ E1
306.3   the trellises] trellises A1,E1
306.28–29   insolently] impudently L

306.32   its] it L
307.5   Chester] Chester's L
307.38   president] the President L
308.10   come] came A1,E1
308.36   met] heard L
309.7   them] *omit* A1,E1
310.28   of] if A1
310.29   straggled] staggered L
312.11   France] in France A1,E1
312.19   court-martials] courts-martial A1,E1
312.21–29   The most . . . forever."] *omit* L
312.29   forever] for ever E1

"VITTORIA"

[The copy-text is L: *Lippincott's Magazine*, LXVI (July, 1900), pp. 140–150. The other texts collated are A1: *Great Battles of the World*, J. B. Lippincott, Philadelphia, 1901; E1: *Great Battles of the World*, Chapman & Hall, London, 1901. A1 is the copy-text for passages not present in L. E1 is a derived text without authority.]

313.0   "Vittoria"] ∧ ~ ∧ A1,E1
313.2   Badajoz] Badajos L,A1
313.13–15   But . . . changed.] *omit* L
313.27–314.5   The winter . . . efficiency.] *omit* L
315.15   and horse] *omit* L
316.8   movement] moment L
316.24   ²the] *omit* L
317.1–33   The incident . . . British.] *omit* L
318.4–12   He was . . . nothing.] *omit* L
318.12   nothing.] nothing. [¶] Wellington's army now numbered seventy thousand men, of whom forty thousand were British. L
318.19   great] *omit* L
318.23   really] *omit* L
318.24–28   The weak . . . chief.] *omit* L
318.35 *et seq.*   Esla] Elsa L+
318.35   unite] to unite A1,E1
319.1   kept always] always kept A1,E1
319.6–7   communications] communication A1,E1
319.17   22d] 22 E1
319.17   an exalted] a L

319.20   rose] arose A1,E1
319.22   16th] 16 E1
319.34   25th] 25 E1
320.1   31st] 31 E1
320.10   hundred] thousand L+
320.10–11   the last to leave] *omit* L
322.1   Morillo] Murillo A1,E1
322.15 *et seq.*   Arinez] Ariniz L+
322.16 *et seq.*   pass] Pass E1
322.17–21   The early . . . conflict."] *omit* L
322.17   21st] 21 E1
322.22–23   The valley . . . officers.] The valley, occupied by the French army, with the rich uniforms of its officers, was a superb spectacle. E1
322.22   spectacle] spectacle on the morning of June 21st L
322.23   their] its A1,E1
322.28–38   In his . . . front."] *omit* L

323.1,4   Morillo] Murillo L+
323.24   had crossed Tres] crossed at Tres A1,E1
324.22–28   Maxwell . . . battle."] *omit* L
324.32–34   cannon-balls . . . long, hissing furrows] hissing cannon-balls . . . long furrows A1,E1
324.40   made] *omit* A1,E1
325.27   back] *omit* L
325.37   enemy] French A1,E1
326.22   heroically] A1,E1 *place after 'Zadora'*
326.38–39   artillery . . . ammunition] rounds of artillery ammunition A1,E1
327.5   one-half] a-half E1
327.10   make his men give] induce his men to give A1,E1
327.14   29th] 29 E1
327.36–328.3   Alison . . . overthrow."] *omit* L

A SWEDE'S CAMPAIGN IN GERMANY

I. LEIPZIG

[The copy-text is L: *Lippincott's Magazine*, LXVI (Aug., 1900), pp. 299–311. The other texts collated are A1: *Great Battles of the World*, J. B. Lippincott, Philadelphia, 1901; E1: *Great Battles of the World*, Chapman & Hall, London, 1901. A1 is the copy-text for passages not present in L. E1 is a derived text without authority.]

329.1–335.10   At . . . Europe.] *omit* L
335.12   blot out] cancel L
335.12   now] *omit* L
335.15   Gustavus] Gustavus Adolphus, King of Sweden, L
335.18   Gustavus] Gustavus Adolphus L
335.28–29   Magdeburg] Madgeburg A1
335.30   Lübeck] Lubeck L+
335.30   Ratzeberg] Ratzeburg L+
335.31   Camin] Cammin A1
335.36   brute] *omit* L
336.1–2   and which . . . whatever] *omit* L

336.13   Lübeck] Lubeck A1,E1
336.23   but] but England A1,E1
336.26   but] but he A1,E1
336.31–32   and a foe . . . Germany] *omit* L
336.35   he] Gustavus L
337.12   to openly] openly to L
337.19   was free to] could L
338.12–19   There . . . me."] *omit* L
339.12–14   A painting . . . Gardie.] *omit* L
339.19   now being] being now L
340.25   Leipzig] Leipsic L,A1

340.27 seems] seemed A1,E1
340.35–341.24 In July . . . Ruthven.] *omit* L
341.26 the King] Gustavus L
342.3 did] did do A1,E1
342.4–7 The truth . . . him.] *omit*
L
342.16 *your*] your L
342.30–31 He once . . . yours."]
omit L
343.4 authority] ability L
343.4 great] *omit* L
343.17–18 who . . . Cardinal]
omit L
343.18 among other arguments]
omit L
343.23–344.15 Ferdinand . . .
Catholic.] *omit* L
344.17 personally] *omit* L

344.26–345.2 This horrible . . .
chaste.] *omit* L
345.3 Field . . . but he] This old
man L
345.5 Mansfeld] Mansfield A1,E1
345.21 Croation] *omit* L
346.11–13 It is . . . force.] *omit*
L
346.36 20th] 20 A1,E1
347.15 23d] 23 E
349.13 ¹the] *omit* A1,E1
349.14,30 Torgau] Jorgau L
350.6–7 Havelberg] Havelburg L
351.9 manner] matter L
351.28 Fürstenberg] Furstenburg
L; Furstenberg A1,E1
351.31 the rear] their rear L
352.13 their] his L
352.19 on] in A1,E1

A SWEDE'S CAMPAIGN IN GERMANY

II. LÜTZEN

[The copy-text is L: *Lippincott's Magazine*, LXVI (Sept., 1900), pp. 462–475. The other texts collated are A1: *Great Battles of the World*, J. B. Lippincott, Philadelphia, 1901; E1: *Great Battles of the World*, Chapman & Hall, London, 1901. A1 is the copy-text for passages not present in L. E1 is a derived text without authority.]

353.0 *et seq.* Lützen] Lutzen L+
353.1 Tilly's] General Tilly's L
353.1 fortunes] fortune L
353.7 Gustavus] Gustavus Adolphus, King of Sweden L
353.11 or] nor L
353.16 he] Gustavus L
354.11 Leipzig] the battle of Leipzig L
354.13–14 Königshofen]
Konigshofen L+
354.37 now] *omit* L
354.39–355.4 The Count . . .
service.] *omit* L
355.29 on to] on A1,E1
356.3 13th] 13 E1
356.11–12 a space of rest] *omit* L
356.12 10th] 10 L
356.14 splendors] splendor L

356.37 Kreutznach] Krentznach L
357.20–23 But he . . . enterprise!"] *omit* L
357.24 He] But he L
358.17–18 *et seq.* Ingolstadt] In-
goldstadt L
358.30 indeed] *omit* L
359.5–7 So . . . League.] *omit* L
359.15 another horse] another L
359.18 ²that] which A1,E1
359.32–360.14 But the . . . for
this.] *omit* L
360.15 He] At Munich he L
360.16–23 There were . . . statues."] *omit* L
360.30–37 The guns . . . army.]
omit L
361.17 the son] a son L
361.36 long] *omit* A1,E1

362.20 Glogau] Slogan L
362.22 million] millions E1
362.29 hand] hands E1
362.33 to again] again to A1,E1
363.8   powers] power A1,E1
363.9–13 Neither . . . approval.]
  omit L
363.17 moneys] money L
363.25 and in] In A1,E1
363.29–364.10 The gorgeous . . .
  consequences.] *omit* L
364.22 to Wallenstein. But the
  latter] But Wallenstein L

364.32 3d] 3 E1
365.12; 366.16 Naumburg] Naum-
  berg L
365.24 6th] 6 E1
365.35 no] neither A1,E1
366.19 touched] affected L
369.12 whole] *omit* A1,E1
369.14 they] he A1,E1
369.16 had also] also had A1,E1
369.37 movement] movements L
370.26 get] *omit* A1,E1
371.1–372.8 Nothing . . . well-
  disciplined."] *omit* L

THE BATTLE OF SOLFERINO

[The copy-text is L: *Lippincott's Magazine*, LXVI (Oct., 1900), pp. 613–627.
The other texts collated are A1: *Great Battles of the World*, J. B. Lippin-
cott, Philadelphia, 1901; E1: *Great Battles of the World*, Chapman & Hall,
London, 1901. E1 is a derived text without authority.]

373.8   ¶ The] *no* ¶ A1,E1
373.20 Venice and] Venice, A1,E1
373.29 awaken] wake A1,E1
374.7   ¶ But] *no* ¶ A1,E1
375.8   "materialism and Machiavellism."] ₄materialism and
  Machiavellism.₄ E1
375.16 utterances] utterance A1,
  E1
375.33 *et seq.* everyone] every one
  E1
375.37 di] de L+
376.25 Leri] Lèri L
377.4   the master] master A1,E1
378.3   flee] fly A1,E1
378.14 23d] 23rd E1
378.24 call] called A1,E1
379.6   April,] April of A1,E1

379.35;391.14 forever] for ever
  E1
380.9   were] are A1,E1
381.29 Rattazzi] Ratazzi L+
384.11 27th] 27 E1
384.33 2d] 2 E1
384.36 12th] 12 E1
385.7   20th] 20 E1
385.27 The (*no* ¶)] ¶ A1,E1
385.28,34 23d] 23rd E1
386.2   guard] guards E1
388.1   notwithstanding] notwithstanding this A1,E1
388.11 drums] drum A1,E1
388.23 That] The A1,E1
390.8   24th] 24 E1
390.10 the] *omit* A1,E1
391.6   Leri] Lèri L+

THE STORMING OF BURKERSDORF HEIGHTS

[The copy-text is L: *Lippincott's Magazine*, LXVI (Nov., 1900), pp. 781–
794. The other texts collated are A1: *Great Battles of the World*, J. B.
Lippincott, Philadelphia, 1901; E1: *Great Battles of the World*, Chapman &
Hall, London, 1901. E1 is a derived text without authority.]

394.32 bashful and] bashful, L
395.30 mein] meine A1,E1

395.39–396.1 Maupertuis] Maupertius L+

396.34–35   wobbling] wabbling A1,E1

396.38   20th] 20 E1

397.38   -Zerbst] -Herbst L+

398.17   nor] and A1,E1

398.27   of] with L

399.16 *et seq.*   anyone] any one E1

400.9   Saxony, September] Saxony in September E1

400.9   1st] 1 E1

400.17 *et seq.*   Everyone] Every one E1

401.20   October] in October E1

402.27   23d] 23 E1

402.31   5th] 5 E1

403.6   recapturing] capturing L

403.14   a force] an army A1,E1

403.33   Kunzendorf] Kunensdorf L,A1; Kunersdorf E1

403.34   Heights] Height L

403.39   impracticably] impractically A1,E1

404.11 *et seq.*   Möllendorff] Möllendorf L+

404.20   to virtually] virtually to A1,E1

406.6   their] its L

406.12   draw] to draw E1

406.17   ¶ It] *no* ¶ A1,E1

406.20   The (*no* ¶)] ¶ A1,E1

408.13   free] enabled A1,E1

408.18   ¶ "To] *no* ¶ A1,E1